ENEMIES

FOREIGN AND

DOMESTIC

MATTHEW BRACKEN

Steelcutter Publishing

Orange Park, Florida

10th Edition 2013

This is a work of fiction. The events and characters
described herein are products of the author's imagination.
Any similarities to actual persons are entirely coincidental.

Copyright © 2003 Matthew Bracken
All Rights Reserved.

ISBN 0-9728310-1-0

Library of Congress Control Number
2003098331

Printed in the United States of America

www.EnemiesForeignAndDomestic.com

For Ellie with all my love and admiration,
without whom this book could not have been written,
and for Brendan and Lauren, who lovingly endure me.

Acknowledgments

Many thanks to Henry Battleborn, Joe Brower, Charles Byrd, Robert Capko, Peter Diggins, Tom Eaker, Elizabeth Elliott, Jerry Fitzgerald, H. J. Halterman, Jeff Head, Rob Henry, Arthur Hines, Jim Kononoff, Caylen Perry, Matt Riley, Timothy Russell, Jeffrey L. Smith, Oleg Volk, Clare Strange for the cover, and Doc Zox for the cover art.

In a hundred ways, Enemies Foreign And Domestic was improved by these friends. Any errors or omissions are entirely my own.

And a late salute to John D. MacDonald, without whom there never would have been a Travis McGee.

Also by author Matt Bracken:

Domestic Enemies: The Reconquista
A novel about the deconstruction of the American national identity and the loss of the Southwest. (2006)

Foreign Enemies And Traitors
A novel about defending the Constitution during a dirty civil war and the Greater Depression. (2009)

Castigo Cay
The first in the Dan Kilmer series, about a former Marine Corps sniper trying to live free in an unfree world. (2011)

The first hundred pages of each novel may be read at
www.EnemiesForeignAndDomestic.com

Author's Note

Some of the technical details concerning ballistics and explosives have been altered or left intentionally vague in order to render them unusable by misguided readers of this work. The principles and effects described are completely accurate notwithstanding those self-imposed constraints.

The privacy issues raised, such as the use of digital face-scanning cameras, wireless communications interception, and the use of data-mining for behavior predicting programs are all very real. As useful as these methods may be in our ongoing war against fanatical Muslim terrorist groups, one cannot but be alarmed that these tools and many others, so reminiscent of George Orwell's 1984, will eventually be used against all Americans.

The issue of the steadily increasing militarization of law enforcement, and in particular federal law enforcement, I will leave for the reader to judge.

www.EnemiesForeignAndDomestic.com

"Before a standing army can rule, the people must be disarmed; as they are in almost every kingdom of Europe. The supreme power in America cannot enforce unjust laws by the sword; because the whole body of the people are armed, and constitute a force superior to any bands of regular troops that can be, on any pretense, raised in the United States."

Noah Webster, 1787
"An Examination into the Leading Principles of the Federal Constitution"

Prologue

The home team was set to receive the kickoff of their season opener. The 80,000 football fans packing the stadium were on their feet looking down at the two teams lined up on the sunlit green field. It was a mild September Sunday in the Maryland suburbs of the nation's capital, and every seat was taken by loyal fans wearing maroon and gold, fans who were fervently wishing to see their team improve last season's dismal record and make a run for the playoffs. The crowd noise reached a sustained roar as they watched the kicker trot toward the teed-up football, they saw the two teams rush at each other, and they followed the flight of the ball high into the air.

In the midst of this jubilant celebration, in the center of the western end zone upper deck, a forty-year-old architect from Annapolis was struck by something on the left temple. He immediately collapsed forward, spurting blood over his friends and several other fans as he fell across the seats below. His shocking injury occurred while the football was still arcing through the air and down the field, so at first the louder screaming of the fans surrounding his crumpled, bleeding body went unnoticed by the rest of the crowd around them.

Every two seconds a similar scene was repeated with horrifying variations across the western upper deck stands, as one fan after another was dealt a sudden bloody wound to the face, head, neck, shoulder, arm or chest. A few victims were killed outright, and some were only slightly grazed, but many received searingly painful wounds that caused them to shriek and scream, flinging blood in all directions. Every two seconds another tableau of unexpected violent trauma was created, sending out radiating bands of alarm as the shouted word spread from mouth to ear among the trapped thousands: *snipers!* The waves of horror emanating from each new victim spread, merged and multiplied until the entire upper deck section became engulfed in seething animal panic.

A minute after the first victim was struck, with the kickoff returned to the twenty-yard line and the home team huddled to pick their first play, the continuing frenzied crowd activity in the western upper deck stands was noticed by several cameramen around the stadium. The perplexed stadium video director selected a close-up scene of some of the excited fans and switched that camera onto the stadium's two Jumbotron screens. They immediately showed a house-sized image of a woman, her mouth open in an unheard scream, vainly using her hands to try to halt the flow of blood from a man's face.

The rest of the 80,000 fans saw the ghastly open wound and his blood-covered wife on the fifty-foot-tall video screens, and the panic began to spread from one end of the stadium to the other. Police radios crackled with reports of death and injury, police marksmen dashed out and scanned the stadium's upper tiers and light towers through their binoculars and rifle scopes. The sudden appearance of black-clad police marksmen with their rifles shouldered was noticed by mystified fans throughout the stadium, adding depth to the rippling fear.

Complete pandemonium erupted through the western upper deck as the realization spread like a wind-whipped forest fire that an unseen sniper had them all in his deadly crosshair gaze. Six thousand adrenaline glands pumped out their ultimate fight-or-flight hormone. Unthinking mob psychology seized the crowd, and nearly all of the fans who were penned up in the killing zone stampeded down the steps and over the chairs. This fear-driven horde charged straight over the smaller and slower fans in their desperation to reach the perceived safety of one of the four exit tunnels.

It had taken well over an hour before the game for six thousand cheerful individuals to fill all of the seats on the steeply sloping upper deck. Many of the fans routinely grew dizzy and flirted dangerously with vertigo while climbing the concrete stairs, which were as high and as steeply pitched as the roof of a cathedral. Now, gripped by primal terror and racing down to the exits, the thousands of fans attempted to do the impossible, they all attempted to escape the unrelenting rain of bullets in less than a single minute.

Police, paramedics, security personnel and the just plain curious were beginning to rush from the stadium's inside concourse through the tunnels to the stands when they ran headlong into the leading elements of the outpouring human tide. This slowed them enough to precipitate immediate jams at each of the four exits. But the terror of the fleeing mobs in the stands above the exit tunnels did not abate as the bullets continued to fall, and the crush began in earnest.

A hundred tightly pressed bodies, propelled by fear and assisted by gravity, pushed hard against each unlucky person already wedged against the safety railing at the bottom of the upper deck. The rails bent outward as the human avalanche gathered momentum, and then they buckled and victims began to tumble over. The falling victims were still holding tightly onto those above, pulling them over as well, and the solid cascade began. Dozens and then hundreds of linked victims fell past the VIP sky boxes, thudding down onto the unfortunate fans packed into the lower stands ninety feet below.

He was jolted back from a peaceful place by blows to his head. He heard a gruff voice say "wake up asshole," but when he finally forced his eyelids open there was no one to be seen. He wasn't sure if the kicks and curses had been the bitter end of a dream, a hallucination, or reality.

Hairline cracks and spider webs on an unfinished cement ceiling came into focus above him; he could feel that he was lying on a cold rough cement floor. Familiar smells of concrete dust and some kind of smoke filled his nose. He rolled his head to the side and saw that an entire wall was missing, wide open to airy blue nothing only a yard from him. A breeze stirred white papers around the room and out to the sky, one page dipped as it fluttered past his face. He thought for a moment that he saw those crazy Arab worm letters on it, those worm letters he vaguely remembered from his time in the desert.

After years spent in and out of veterans' hospitals and homeless shelters, Jimmy Shifflett was no stranger to waking up in strange places. He had come-to along the sides of highways, half in rivers, once even across the tracks on a railroad bridge. Randomly chosen construction sites and unfinished buildings were familiar surroundings. He raised his right arm to block the sun from his eyes, and saw a desert camouflage sleeve, something he could not remember wearing since his discharge from the Marines over a decade earlier.

The problem was that the damned nurses at the VA hospital put new drugs in your orange juice and never told you what to expect. They fed you new "study" pills by the handful like they were jellybeans. Some made you shake, some made you sweat, some brought nightmares and some brought peace. That's what happened to a sick and broke vet: they used you for a damned guinea pig. Some of the nurses were nice though. Some were real angels come down from heaven. But they made you take the pills anyway.

There was a weight across his chest. His hands fell across something hard and hot, his fingers traced old half-remembered shapes and contours. Even for a hospital dream, this was a real doozy. "Any time now," he thought, "I'm going to wake up in the VA hospital."

In the meantime he used his elbows to push himself up into a sitting position, and looked down upon a strange rifle lying across his lap: black steel and brown wood, with a gray metal tube the size of several beer cans fixed onto the end of the barrel. There was a short black scope attached to a home made mount not straight on top of the rifle, but offset high on the left side. The scope was not only mounted off to the side, but seemed to be pointing downward, totally misaligned. A fat pad or pillow bulged out from the stock where a shooter's face might rest; it was attached with wrappings of gray duct tape. A pair of bipod legs was attached to the barrel just behind the long gray can. A long curved ammunition magazine stuck out of the bottom of the gun.

It was without a doubt the ugliest and weirdest rifle he'd ever seen, as befitted a hospital dream, and after he finished looking at it he tried to set it aside but found it was attached to him by a sling made of green cord caught behind his neck. To get the cord over his head he needed to lift the heavy rifle up off his lap. If he wasn't careful he could fall right out through the missing wall, but in a dream such as this he sometimes could fly. The dreams where he could fly usually started out scary but ended up happy, with him soaring like a bird over soft green meadows. Out the missing wall, past woods and fields and roads, way out in the distance stood some kind of huge multi-colored building. It looked for all the world like the mothership had just landed on earth to take him home. Or maybe they were just going to just do more experiments on him, poking and jabbing and injecting.

Suddenly dropping in front of the missing wall there appeared an insect-like blue and white helicopter, which slowly turned until its side was to him, its rotors invisible and unheard. "It's not right they put the damned drugs in your juice and don't tell you," he thought, still trying to lift the rifle's string over his neck.

"**Roger that base,** I have the shooter in sight. Confirmed shooter is in sight, he has a rifle, he has a rifle! He's moving, take him out Billy, take him out!"

SWAT sniper Sgt. Bill Paxton spotted the subject only by his slight movement. The shooter was hard to see, wearing clothes which matched the bare concrete of the half-finished office building which hid his sniper's lair. A telephone tip from a civilian had alerted the police to the suspected sniper's location, the tip was passed to the Maryland State Police helicopter, and they located him in under a minute after leaving their tight orbit around the stadium.

The shooter had found an A-1 position. Paxton had to give him professional credit: his hideout was hundreds of yards beyond the stadium's outermost security perimeter. No one had ever considered the fans inside the stadium to be in danger from such a distance, well over a thousand yards away. It had always been believed that any rifle shots fired from such a distance would either impact the stadium's outer walls, or sail safely over it. This brainy marksman had somehow figured out a way to precisely drop his shots just over the near side of the stadium, and down into the opposite upper deck. Nobody had ever thought of it before—it was one for the books. This shooter had used a rifle for indirect plunging area-fire, almost like a mortar.

So Sgt. Paxton didn't underestimate the shooter's skill, and he quickly settled his scope's mil-dot reticle on the man's head. At 150 yards it wasn't a challenging shot, even restrained by a harness while sitting half out of the vibrating helicopter. The pilot held the chopper steady as Paxton squeezed his rifle's trigger and fired a single .308 caliber hollow point, then flicked the bolt and reacquired his sight picture. There was no need for a follow up: the gruesome evidence of his accurately delivered head shot was clearly visible on the walls. The dead body of the shooter was sprawled flat on his back, and lying perfectly motionless.

1

Two hundred miles south of the stadium at the bottom of the Chesapeake Bay, thirty year old Brad Fallon sat alone in the tool-strewn cabin of his mastless 44 foot sailboat, staring at a small black and white television. A breaking news bulletin on the radio had caused him to put down his work and dig out the rarely watched portable 12 volt television. He sat transfixed, numb, the same way that he had up in Alaska when he had first seen the replays of the jetliners flying into the World Trade Center on another September day. No words spoken on the radio could duplicate the impact of seeing the actual events, even on a nine inch black and white screen.

His garage-sale Panasonic only received four broadcast channels, but it didn't matter, because the network anchors had been found and brought to the studios, preempting all other programs. All of them wore similar black suits and maintained a funereal demeanor as they read the latest updates, interspersed with frequently repeated replays of the worst imagery of the disaster. The usual network talking heads were inset in the corners of aerial views of the stadium in suburban Maryland, near the Washington Beltway, where a full blown mass casualty triage and evacuation was underway. Familiar sports announcers provided grim eyewitness accounts from inside of the stadium.

The full proportions of the disaster were still emerging, but it appeared that a sniper shooting from outside had fired dozens or perhaps hundreds of bullets into the packed stadium, killing and wounding many directly, and precipitating a panic stampede. Many of the exit ramps and tunnels were still choked with tangled victims presumably both dead and alive. The seating areas beneath the upper decks which had become falling body impact zones were too gruesome to show on television. The whispered casualty estimates ran from hundreds to thousands depending on which expert was asked.

Military and civilian helicopters were landing directly on the football field. Charter buses which had come to the stadium full of cheerful fans were being pressed into service to augment the hundreds of arriving ambulances in removing the injured. Frenzied police struggled to open passable routes through the gridlock around the stadium. Commercial tow trucks were pressed into service clearing lanes, and abandoned cars were being pushed and pulled out of the way without regard to damage.

The stadium's PA system continuously advised fans to find a seat and wait while rescuers removed the trapped victims. Some listened, but others crawled through exit tunnels over the heaps of dead and injured, searching for a way out, increasing the crushing weight on those struggling for their last breaths while buried alive far below.

Across America and around the world hundreds of millions of television viewers were once again absorbing the impact of mass casualty terrorism, not as the result of crashed jetliners or smallpox or anthrax or a suitcase nuke, but all apparently as the result of one sniper armed with an "assault rifle." And this time, the carnage was ongoing, as the trapped continued to succumb to asphyxiation.

Two more weeks, three at the most, and Brad Fallon was sure that he'd be gone, right over that blue horizon, leaving America to work out its latest agonies without him. He had $75,000 banked after his last six month contract working in the Alaskan ANWR oil fields, a bought and paid for boat, and a mast and engine just waiting to be installed. If domestic events now unfolded the way he suspected they might, he guessed that he had picked an opportune time to leave the States for a few years of cruising the world's tropical oceans and islands.

The networks broke simultaneously for an impromptu press briefing. The Governor of Maryland, the mayor of Washington, and many recognizable national politicians stood behind the local chief of police, taking the opportunity to get their deeply concerned faces on national television. The uniformed police chief was handed a wallet by a helmeted SWAT officer wearing black tactical gear, cameras jerked as the press pushed forward. Microphones cut in and out and the grandstanding Chief of Police, making the most of his fifteen minutes of national fame, began a short statement.

"This wallet was just taken from the sniper's body and brought directly to me by the commander of our tactical unit." He slipped on reading glasses, and then he opened the shiny black wallet, oblivious to his contaminating possible evidence. He examined it for a moment, and then he turned it around to the cameras, which zoomed in on the ID cards behind two clear plastic windows. He cleared his throat and said "James R. Shifflett. The ID found on the sniper is in the name of one James R. Shifflett, of Norfolk Virginia." Fallon's TV picture zoomed in on the ID cards; a Virginia driver's license and a military card of some sort. The tiny photos were too blurry to make out anything other than that Shifflett was a white man with light brown colored hair and a stringy mustache. Most of the printed information was too small and grainy to read.

It was a sign of the deep cynicism Fallon felt that he was not surprised that they put the sniper's name and photo on national television right away: he seemed to be a garden variety Caucasian male. When an act of terrorism occurred and the suspect was from the Middle East or had a Muslim name, that fact was usually concealed for days, in order to dampen anti-Muslim anger. The way that the broadcast television networks strived to "protect" their viewers from politically incorrect news was one reason Fallon's TV set usually stayed buried in a locker. He listened to AM news-talk radio to find out what was really going on.

Brad Fallon had hoped that he would get his new 80 horsepower Perkins turbo diesel aboard Guajira today, or at least from the dock over onto her deck, but as the afternoon wore on he resigned himself to waiting until Monday. The news that the sniper was from Norfolk gave him a sense of unease, drawing the day's horrific events uncomfortably close.

The Suffolk Virginia police department needed less than thirty minutes to discover James Shifflett's last domicile, a dilapidated thirty foot camper trailer located at the end of a long dirt driveway. The trailer was tucked back among pine trees and was almost invisible from the paved state road, where the first TV vans were sending up their microwave antennas. The hundred yard long driveway and dusty weed-choked yard was already packed tightly with marked and unmarked police cars, a SWAT truck, and mobile crime scene vans.

The SWAT team and bomb disposal technicians quickly examined the trailer for booby traps; one of the local TV crews with a lucky camera angle captured the sight of SWAT officers carrying out rifles in each of their hands. This damning evidence was laid on top of the hood of a police cruiser as a temporary exhibit, and camera crews were permitted in to film them. By two PM the entire world knew that James "Jimmy" Shifflett was a fanatical gun nut, who had lived in a trailer containing an "arsenal" of five rifles and shotguns and over two thousand rounds of ammunition. His small library contained books on sniping, bomb construction, and white supremacist hate literature.

Even as millions of TV viewers were still watching and rewatching video clips of the day's bloodbath in the stadium, and while the residents of southeastern Virginia were absorbing the fact that a local man had gone berserk and caused it all, the never-stopping gears of the federal government were turning out reactions, responses, and contingency plans. The new and untested president, in office only eight months, called an emergency meeting of the Homeland Security Team in the White House Situation Room beneath the Oval Office. One of their first decisions was to ask the national television networks for a prime time slot to give a brief presidential address to the country at nine PM eastern time.

All afternoon millions of families sat quietly in front of their televisions as the toll of dead and injured mounted. They watched as the triage of victims continued on the stadium parking lots. They saw an unending stream of departing ambulances, and helicopters flicking in and out. In several areas around the stadium the steadily increasing ranks of the dead were laid side by side covered with blankets and sheets. Over and over Americans watched replays of the fateful moments after the kickoff when something strange began to happen in the western end zone upper deck, which in two minutes became a life and death stampede for 6,000 desperate fans.

That false rush to nonexistent safety ended cruelly as the lowest fans were pushed ever downward by the sheer weight of the fleeing crowds above them, until their broken bodies collapsed the railings at the bottom. At last they tumbled over the edge in linked clusters, falling nine stories down onto the disbelieving fans below them. This horror show then triggered a general panic throughout the stadium, and even though the sniper had fired only a limited number of bullets into one section, the entire stadium dissolved into a nightmarish bedlam with hundreds and thousands of trapped fans jamming every exit tunnel. The stronger behind climbed up over the weaker ahead until every way out was plugged with choking and groaning masses of crushed and suffocating humanity.

The video clips of the hundreds of fans tumbling from the upper deck to their deaths before the unblinking television cameras became the indelible image of the day, even though far more victims died trampled and asphyxiated and unseen in the exit tunnels.

"Get me the gun! I want to have the gun during the address," President Gilmore told his Assistant Chief of Staff.

"Mr. President, I don't think that's a good idea. I think we can emphasize the enormity of the tragedy without resorting to any... theatrics which may detract..."

"I said get me the damn gun! Where is it? Put it on a chopper, do what it takes, I want that damn gun here by nine PM, is that clear enough?"

President Edward Gilmore sat behind his Oval Office desk in a black suit and a charcoal tie, the lights hot on his makeup-caked face. It was funeral director's attire, he thought, his eyes on the teleprompter, and a funeral director is what I am tonight. The clock ticked down to nine PM.

"Good evening my fellow Americans. I come to you tonight with a heavy heart, a broken heart. As of my latest information over 1,000 of our fellow citizens have died since today's catastrophic events. Thousands more lie in almost a hundred hospitals up and down the coast, many near death or on life support, as our wonderful doctors and nurses work into the night to save them. My prayers go out to all of the victims and their families, and to our heroic medical staffs who are working so hard to save lives even as I speak.

"I have received over one hundred telegrams and letters and calls of condolence from leaders around the world on this terrible day, and it is difficult for me to find the words with which to answer them. Difficult because this was not a natural disaster which befell us today, nor was it an accident, nor even an act of war by a hostile power or a foreign terrorist group.

"No, my fellow Americans, this was an act of sheer malice, a calculated act of evil springing from the darkest pit of our own national heart. This was an act made possible only because of a peculiar sickness in our American culture. Today's tragic event resulted from our inexplicable national love affair with firearms and weapons of war, like the assault rifle which was used today to mow down our friends and neighbors."

Jimmy Shifflett's murder weapon had been placed upright against a wall, at a sufficient distance from the President that the camera would not place it with him in the same view. President Gilmore pointed toward the rifle and another camera cut briefly to it. Across America and around the world viewers saw the ugly black and brown rifle, with its long menacing home made silencer, and its curved banana clip magazine. It had a telescopic sight mounted on the left side and pointed down at the exact angle which would raise the barrel just enough to loft its bullets over the stadium walls from 1,250 yards away. As ugly as it was, the obsolete Russian-surplus military rifle exuded menace. It had been cheaply but effectively customized into a long range crowd killer. It was clearly the product of a cunningly evil mind.

"I am told that this is an SKS assault rifle, manufactured decades ago in the former Soviet Union, and legally sold in any gun store in America for about one hundred dollars. It was built to hold ten bullets at a time inside it, but it has been modified to accept thirty round magazines. It can fire the thirty bullets automatically, as fast as the trigger can be pulled. Three of those magazines, ninety bullets, created today's massacre.

"Apparently Mr. Shifflett was a former Marine, and served his nation with honor in 1991 during the first Iraq war. Since then he has been beset by numerous health problems, including mental health problems, and he had been hospitalized for both physical and psychiatric reasons many times. Yet in spite of that troubled personal history, Mr. Shifflett was able to acquire a virtual armory of assault rifles, including the one responsible for today's carnage.

"Something is very deeply wrong in our country, when a long-time mental patient is able to obtain a private arsenal of assault rifles. Something is very, very deeply wrong, and now it is time to correct that wrong.

"So I have asked the leaders of both parties, many of whom witnessed the horrific Stadium Massacre today in person, to take up this issue without delay. It is long past time to acknowledge that our gun laws, which utterly failed to keep assault rifles out of the hands of a dangerous psychotic, are not sufficient to provide for the safety of our people. It is long past time that the United States of America addressed its unholy love affair with weapons of war and death. We must join the ranks of all other sane and civilized nations in keeping these awful instruments of death away from criminals and the unbalanced. Let Congress address this cancer eating at our soul without delay, so that there will be no more assault rifle massacres.

"Good evening, and may God bless and have mercy on the United States of America."

2

That Monday morning Washington was appropriately overcast and gloomy, with an intermittent drizzle just keeping the streets and sidewalks slick. Cynthia McFadden was the National Firearms Organization's chief Capitol Hill lobbyist, and although she dreaded today like no other in her memory, she squared her shoulders and walked through the metal detectors, had her purse and briefcase checked by the armed security guards, and entered the atrium of the Hart Senate office building. She had no real prospect of turning the tide threatening to sweep most of the Second Amendment out of the Bill of Rights today, but she hoped to at least stiffen a few backbones and prevent a complete rout.

Congress was meeting in an extraordinary emergency session, and a radical new gun control bill was to be introduced, debated, and possibly voted on this very day. With a little luck she thought she might encourage a handful of stalwart Republican Congressmen and Senators to pull a tricky rules maneuver, and have the final vote delayed until the heat and anger resulting from yesterday's events had time to cool.

Her first objective was Congressman Wilson Packard of Utah, the minority chair of the House Rules Committee. Although she had no appointment (and none of her calls had been returned) she hoped to lean on their old friendship for a moment or two of his time. Anyway, hopeless or not, lobbying Congress was what she was paid to do.

Mrs. McFadden walked up the marble steps to the second floor; the offices were all on balcony corridors overlooking the central atrium. On all of the floors grim-faced staffers hurried from office to office, bearing hastily-written gun control bills she imagined. The offices were allotted on the basis of seniority, Republicans were intermingled with Democrats. Halfway down the balcony corridor she passed a group of five or six young staffers, with possibly a freshman Congressman among them. She couldn't put a name to all of them but she knew most of the key players by sight. This group was all wearing dark suits with black armbands.

"Excuse me," she heard behind her, and she turned around. "You're Cynthia McFadden from the NFO, aren't you? I've seen you on TV," said a twenty-something blond female in a black pants suit.

"Yes I am" said Cynthia, extending her right hand.

The young lady recoiled as from a rattlesnake, her face turning into a mask of rage. "What are you here for you NFO whore, paying off your bounties? Paying your blood money for all those people you killed? You put that machine gun in Jimmy Shifflett's hands! You might as well have aimed it and pulled the trigger! I just wish that some day all you gun whores would be shot, instead of innocent people!"

Cynthia McFadden knew from long experience that it was counter-productive to debate with hysterics, so she smiled gamely and turned around again to continue her walk toward Congressman Packard's office.

"Don't you DARE turn your back on me, you murdering bitch!" the young woman shrieked, launching herself and grabbing Cynthia from behind, raking her neck with long red fingernails. A score of faces leaned suddenly out of office doors, people up and down the corridors turned to watch the angry outburst.

Cynthia McFadden was not only an ardent defender of every woman's right to have the choice to defend herself against attack with firearms; she was also a dedicated martial artist who had earned her brown belt in Aikido. When the young blond jumped her from behind she reacted instinctively, grabbing her attacker's wrists, bending at the waist, and throwing her headlong down the corridor. The blond landed on her back with a thud, the wind knocked out of her. Two uniformed Capitol Police bounded up the stairs. Oh crap, I've really done it now, McFadden thought. She had no doubt that a dozen witnesses would now swear that she had just launched an unprovoked assault upon the congressional staffer, who was now being helped up from the floor, livid with wrath and gasping for breath.

"You bitch! I hope you die! After today the NFO is finished! You'd better start packing for your compound in Idaho, you NFO whore!" The young woman then hocked and spit at Cynthia McFadden from a few yards away, missing her target but effectively ruining her case with the two uniformed policemen, who were now being joined by two more.

"You ladies care to tell me what's going on?" asked the police sergeant.

"Officer, if I may…" said a distinguished looking older gentleman. "I'm Congressman Delante. I heard the altercation begin and I came out in time to witness this young lady attack Mrs. McFadden from behind, you can see the scratches on her neck. Mrs. McFadden was merely defending herself. No one can be expected to passively accept being choked and scratched from behind, even here in the Hart building. Mrs. McFadden, do you wish to press charges of aggravated assault and battery?"

Cynthia was now shaking slightly, her mouth having gone cotton ball dry as she weighed her options. She shook her head slowly. The day was an unsalvageable disaster.

"No? Then if we're finished here I'll walk you out, and we can all continue with our days, if that's all right with you officers? Excellent."

Congressman Delante took Cynthia's arm and guided her back to the steps; they were both of an age when such gentility was customary.

"What a day my dear, what a day. I've never seen anything remotely like it in twelve terms, not even the impeachment, and it's still only nine o'clock in the morning."

"It was a mistake even coming down today. Now I know how Custer felt. James, what's going on? Have you seen the proposals yet?"

"Oh yes, indeed I have. We're all looking at several bills, but Senator Schuleman has been the busiest. His bill will ban the possession of all semi-automatic rifles, right down to your grandson's .22. We might be able to save the .22 rimfires, but it's doubtful. Most of the ignoramuses around here are positively proud that they don't know a rifle from a shotgun, so it's pretty hard to educate them. They think .22s are what the Beltway Snipers used! They have no clue that there's a difference between little bitty .22 rimfires and the .223s that an M-16 shoots. Anyway, I don't see any lines of resistance anywhere; every last Democrat will sign anything today, and so will a lot of Republicans. They're all just scared to death of voting against any bill that promises no more so-called assault rifles."

"Is there any chance of getting enough votes to send it to committee?"

"None. Not a prayer."

"What about you?" asked Cynthia. "What will you do?"

"Oh, I'll vote against it, if we vote today. I know what the good old boys in my district think: they think the Shifflett thing was a set up from the git-go. Even today my emails are three to one saying this was a put-up job, and they won't accept any law passed in reaction to it."

"Thanks James, thanks for the heads up. And thanks for not getting stampeded with the rest of the herd."

"That's what this whole thing was if you ask me, a stampede job. Fire some shots, and get the herd to run off the cliff, just like the Indians did with the buffalos. First in the stadium, and now here in Congress."

"Well thanks, I'll pass that along. And good luck."

Congressman Delante stayed inside the atrium while Cynthia McFadden passed through the security points and went back out onto the dreary street, giving up for the day. She would go back to her National Firearms Organization office and watch the day's events in Congress on television like the rest of America.

Senator Ellsworth, the elderly senior Republican Senator from Montana, was the last of a very short list to speak against the bill. He had been in poor health for a few years, and it was no secret that he did not plan to run for reelection.

15

"Thank you Senator Prescott, for extending to me your time to deliver these last remarks before we vote. And I am grateful to my party's leaders, who allowed me to speak in their place." This was an oblique jab; most of the senior Republicans were attempting to hide under their antique Senate floor desks. There had been precious few volunteers lining up to speak against the proposed law.

"I am not grateful that the majority party leadership has seen fit to pack the gallery with hooligans who have behaved like a street mob today, apparently with the majority leadership's blessing. We will all live to regret the day that this august chamber was turned into a Roman Circus."

Catcalls, whistles and chanted jeers came down from the gallery along with a hail of wadded up paper. All day the Democrat Senate leaders had made only token efforts to control the strident and obnoxious behavior of the public gallery, which had frequently joined in chanting "Shame! Shame! Shame!" and "The NFO has got to go," drowning out the few Republican speakers willing to speak against the bill.

The packed gallery was the result of it inexplicably being opened to the public an hour earlier than the usual time. Activists from Gun Control Inc., Stop Gun Violence, the Gun Safety Policy Center and other anti-firearms groups had "somehow" found out about the early opening, and had filled the gallery with emotional supporters. This was their day, they would not be silenced, and the majority leaders would not have them ejected despite repeated demands from the minority. Senator Ellsworth was one of the few with the heart, not to mention the lungs, to stand against the organized jeering and catcalling.

"My fellow Senators, I beg you one last time to consider what this well-intentioned but terribly conceived law will mean. To begin with, millions of Americans will be forced to give up valuable property without recompense, an unconstitutional taking of lawfully obtained private property." This statement was greeted with a chorus of boos.

"Many millions of Americans will be stripped of the ability to defend themselves against criminal marauders, who will surely applaud the passing of this bill, which should be called the 'Safety for Violent Criminals Act.' In this era of terrorist attacks on our home soil, it is almost unbelievable that the Congress wants to make our citizens more vulnerable to terrorism, and not less.

"Veterans who fought and bled for this country from Germany to Viet Nam to Iraq will be forced to surrender their old M1 carbines and M1 Garands, surplus rifles which for many decades the federal government itself provided to veterans and other law abiding citizens for a nominal fee! Now a few short years later, the federal government is taking them back. Honorable weapons with which those veterans defended our nation and our Constitution, they will no longer even be entrusted to own! Our veterans fought and bled for our nation. They took an oath to defend our Constitution, and that Constitution says clearly in black and white 'a well regulated militia being necessary to the security of a free state, the right of the people to keep and bear arms shall not be infringed.'

"George Mason, the father of the Bill of Rights, said about this very subject: 'What is the militia? It is the whole people, except for a few public officials.' This has now been stood on its head! The whole people are to be disarmed, and only a few public officials are to be entrusted with the very types of weapons which are suitable for the 'militia of the whole people' of which Mason spoke! He wrote it my friends, you can check it yourself, if you care about what is actually written in the Constitution.

"My fellow Senators, I beg you to reconsider. There are millions of Americans who will never in their lifetimes accept the Second Amendment being torn from the Constitution and burned. The Second Amendment was included right behind the freedom of speech, assembly and worship, to stand guard over and protect all of the rest of our God-given rights. With the Second Amendment ripped from the Bill of Rights, there will be no final check to encroaching tyranny, and I am certain, dead certain, that millions of Americans will not be willingly disarmed.

"It is my worst fear that the passage of this misbegotten and blatantly unconstitutional law will lead inexorably to a terrible conflict within this nation. You may choose to believe that your radical Supreme Court will have the final word on the constitutionality of this law, but I assure, I promise you, indeed I warn you, they will not have the final word! Five left-wing activist judges who believe that the simple words printed on the paper of the Constitution do not mean what they clearly say will not have the last word!

"There is still time my friends, blessed time, to enact reasonable legislation which will help to prevent the type of national tragedy which we witnessed yesterday. But we must all recognize that in a free society, we will always be at the risk of madmen in hijacked jet airplanes, or madmen armed with truck bombs, or a vial of germs, or a rifle. If we are searching for 100% guaranteed safety, we will not find it in this law, or any other. Instead, we will all be swallowing a sweet tasting poison, and not some utopian panacea. In the words of Ben Franklin, let me remind you that 'they that give up essential liberty to obtain a little temporary safety deserve neither liberty nor safety.'

"My fellow Senators, please hear my words and my warning: millions of Americans will never consent to being disarmed without a great and terrible struggle. For millions of Americans, this law will be their Rubicon. This foolish bill demands that in one short week all semi-automatic rifles must be turned in for destruction, or their owners will face five years in federal prison for each weapon. I tell you now that in one week, millions and millions of those arms will not be turned in by loyal and law-abiding citizens. What then? I ask you, what then?"

Senator Ellsworth gathered his papers and left the podium among an outpouring of curses, boos and wads of paper thrown from the gallery.

The last to speak before the vote was Senator Jack Schuleman, the senior Democrat Senator from Connecticut, and the primary author of the bipartisan Schuleman-Montaine Firearms Safety Act. His short brisk walk to the podium was greeted with thunderous applause and a standing ovation by most of the Senate.

"My fellow Senators, Congressmen, and American citizens, I don't want to debate the constitutionality of the proposed bill before us tonight, we have been through various Second Amendment cases all day today ad nauseum. So let's just blow away the gun smoke: all reasonable people agree that the Second Amendment only protects a state's right to maintain a well regulated militia, and not an individual's right to possess any type of firearm. In ruling after ruling, the courts have stated that the Second Amendment refers to a collective right of the states, and not the right of an individual to own a machine gun or semi-automatic assault rifle!

"Ultimately, it will be up to the Supreme Court of the United States to rule on this law, and I am confident that they will uphold its constitutionality. And when they do, we must all join together and respect their decision, as the last word and the final law of the land.

"But let us leave all that tortured legalese for the future, and return to the real world where this law will affect all Americans. Yes, some will be asked to make a small sacrifice for the greater safety and security of our entire society. They are being asked to give up their rapid-fire semi-automatic assault rifles and submachine guns and so on.

"For the life of me, I could never understand the need for these military assault rifles in the first place! What sort of hunter needs to shoot a deer or a rabbit thirty times, as fast as he can pull the trigger? Maybe what that type of 'sportsman' needs is more target practice, one shot at a time!" This quip was greeted with laughter and cheers and applause.

"This bill does not in any way affect the vast majority of legitimate hunting rifles and shotguns owned by genuine American sportsmen. Let me repeat that: this bill does NOT in any way affect genuine American sportsmen. So what need then is there for individuals to own semi-automatic military assault rifles? Let's examine this question. Do some of our own citizens harbor the paranoid delusion that we may someday suffer a foreign invasion by enemy armies? Should anyone so delusional even be allowed to own any kind of firearm at all?

"Yet far more dangerous, it seems to me, are the paranoid fanatics who harbor a secret hatred for their own democratically elected government. Some of these demented souls even compare their own government to the Nazi regime, and attempt to peddle the sick lie that gun control in America will lead somehow to gas chambers. In America! As if America is in any way comparable to Nazi Germany! As a Jew and the descendent of Holocaust survivors, I find that argument particularly repugnant, and it must be rejected by all sane and intelligent Americans.

"I can tell you the name of one American who was filled to overflowing with that extreme right wing anti-government and anti-Muslim fervor: Jimmy Shifflett. Besides the arsenal of assault rifles that madman was able to assemble, his home was a virtual library of racist hate literature, and books on sniping, booby trapping, and bomb making.

"Perhaps worst of all were the letters he intended to be found in his sniper's lair after the massacre, laying the blame for the attack on our honest, hardworking and loyal Muslim American brothers and sisters. Thank God that at least Shifflett did not escape, to leave behind a black cloud of false blame. His organization clearly intended the massacre to lead to vigilante violence against those of our fellow citizens who follow the teachings of Mohammed, along with the teachings of Jesus and Moses.

"Now although the mass murderer James Shifflett is dead, we know all too well that there are thousands more like him still hiding in cabins and basements and garages all across America. Shifflett may have been the poster boy for the paranoid right wing militia movement, but there are many more like him waiting to take his place. By passing this law tonight, you will be voting to take these military assault rifles out of their hands, before they can perpetrate another massacre like the one which wounded our national soul yesterday.

"So I ask and I beg you not to forget the nearly twelve hundred victims of Jimmy Shifflett's assault rifle. Our unholy American love affair with weapons of war must be ended. We must announce our final divorce from that evil witch called gun lust! We must finally learn to care more for the victims of assault rifles, than for the lovers of those completely unnecessary military weapons!

"So please, do the right thing tonight. Please vote to put an end to this national scourge, and take the assault rifles out of the hands of the next Jimmy Shiffletts. Pass this bill so that we may all live in a safe and sane America, free from the threat of assault rifle violence. Thank you."

Waves of stormy applause fell upon Senator Schuleman, who was mobbed by throngs of ecstatic hand-pumping and back-slapping colleagues as he left the podium.

The cable television news channels and C-span carried the House and Senate debates live all through the day and into the evening, alternating with the ongoing Stadium Massacre investigation, fatality reports, and updates on the hundreds of other victims lying in hospitals. Many survivors were expected to suffer permanent brain damage from oxygen deprivation, after finally being extricated from under the human log jams. When the Senate vote appeared imminent the broadcast networks also joined in live coverage through the roll call. All 51 Democrat senators and 17 Republicans voted "aye," and the Schuleman-Montaine Firearms Safety Act passed with an unneeded veto-proof supermajority. The session was gaveled to a close as the bill's advocates all shook hands, grinning and high-fiving. The opponents quietly gathered their papers and departed.

The no longer young Canadian who was the long-time anchor for a major American network turned to his in-house legal expert. "So, Jeffrey Bootkin, tell us in practical terms, layman's terms if you will, what does the passage of the Schuleman-Montaine Act mean? Just how many Americans will be directly affected, and how will their soon to be outlawed assault weapons be collected?"

"Well Desmond, estimates of the total number of semi-automatic rifles in circulation range from thirty to fifty million, but they are very, very rough estimates. Most of them are small .22 caliber target rifles."

"Didn't the notorious Beltway Sniper use a .22 caliber rifle?"

"Umm, no actually that was a .223; I think that's a much larger bullet. The case is bigger, I mean, the .223s hold a lot more gun powder, I believe. The .22s, I mean what most people call .22s…they are those very tiny bullets, like we used to shoot for target practice at summer camp."

"Really! Shooting guns at summer camp! Imagine! That was certainly a different era. But let's not get sidetracked. How many of the rifles that are banned are there? Military assault rifles I mean."

"Well, actually, not all of the banned guns are what you might call assault rifles. The .22s are certainly not assault rifles. And many of them you might say are legitimate hunting rifles that happen to be semi-automatic. The rest might to one degree or another be called assault rifles, although there is a large gray area. Actually, there's quite a big ongoing dispute over what exactly constitutes an assault rifle. Previous laws focused on some of the um…exterior features, such as pistol grips and folding stocks. The manufacturers got around those laws rather easily, that's why this law just goes after all semi-auto rifles. It eliminates all the loopholes in one fell swoop."

"I see." The news anchor looked doubtful. "The new law says the weapons must be turned in for destruction by next Tuesday at noon.

How will this be accomplished, with so many banned rifles still in circulation? How does the law actually deal with the logistics of this?"

"Well Desmond, the actual wording on the collection side of this are a bit vague, but according to the bill—I should say the law—all semi-auto rifles must be turned in at the police station nearest the owner's home. Fifty million dollars has been allocated in the law to provide for their collection, in, I believe, large dumpsters. I understand the dumpsters will be taken to central collection sites for destruction."

"How will the actual destruction occur? Is that specified?"

"No, in some cases the rifles will be taken out to sea on trash barges and dumped, in some locations they will be crushed or shredded or melted. The bill leaves that to the individual states to accomplish."

"And what again are the penalties for failing to comply with the law? I'm sure that many die-hard advocates of the so-called 'individual right' interpretation of the Second Amendment cannot be too pleased with the prospect of turning in their rifles?"

"Well that's right Desmond. In order to ensure compliance, the penalties for possession of any semi-automatic rifles after noon next Tuesday will be quite harsh. Holdouts will receive a five year federal prison sentence, with no parole, for each rifle they fail to turn in. And large cash rewards, I believe it's $10,000 per rifle, will be offered to anyone who provides information leading to violators. So anyone considering holding back will have to consider very carefully everyone who might know about their banned rifles. Plus, we know from the 2002 Beltway Sniper case that even without an actual 'national firearms registration list', the FBI and ATF are very good at finding out exactly who does own these rifles, just from computerized sales records and ammunition purchases and so on."

"But Jeffrey, I would imagine that after yesterday's horrific tragedy, most gun owners will be glad to get rid of their assault rifles, to dispel any doubts about their...I should say...to convince their neighbors and law enforcement that they are not dangerous people, not a danger to their communities. Are any major problems foreseen with the turn-in? As you said, the law is a bit vague on the details."

"I don't know Desmond; we really are sailing into uncharted water here. But I might mention that thousands of licensed gun dealers are going to have to forfeit much of their inventory, this law may ruin or bankrupt many of them. Not that there will be much sympathy for gun dealers who are forced out of business, not after what happened yesterday."

"Indeed. Thank you Jeffrey Bootkin."

"Thank you Desmond."

3

Monday evening **Brad Fallon** succeeded in moving his new diesel marine engine from the dock into the engine compartment of his sailboat Guajira. This was accomplished using ropes and pulleys, and a hand-cranked wire winch "come along" attached to a branch of the live oak tree which spread above his boat. Determined not to lose another day to the wall-to-wall TV coverage of the Stadium Massacre, he followed the congressional debates on the radio. He worked through the afternoon and into the night, and his Perkins turbo diesel was finally bolted to the engine bed under the harsh yellow glare of clamped-on work lights.

In celebration of this critical milestone he took Tuesday morning off to drive the mile into the nearby town of Highpoint for a sit-down breakfast at Lester's Diner. He justified this extravagance by coupling breakfast out with a visit to the local hardware store.

At age 30 Brad was single, never married, and had no marriage plans even on the distant horizon. He had a long term plan which he had carried out faithfully, and now he was nearing the payoff. He'd worked the ANWR oil fields two months on and one month off for the last three years, he'd banked his payroll, and bought Guajira. The pay had been excellent, but the social life was nil, since he was not interested in one hour romances with toothless and tattooed Arctic boomtown whores.

Compared to the ANWR oil fields, the small town of Highpoint was a tropical Club Med, with some very pretty local girls working at the Dairy Queen, Lester's Diner, the auto parts store and a few other places. Brad always looked forward to some flirtatious banter with the Highpoint girls, it made him feel a little less like a forgotten marsh-dwelling hermit.

Realistically, he knew that a mastless sailboat on a nameless creek at the edge of the Great Dismal Swamp was not going to attract girls like his purple bug zapper light attracted mosquitoes. Brad was a six-footer and he thought he was a reasonably good looking guy, the quick smiles and easy laughter of the local girls told him that. From time to time, out of nowhere, waitresses and cashiers told him that he had beautiful blue eyes. But Guajiras current interior dé cor of paint cans, power tools, electric cords, tarps, bare plywood and a dozen epoxy products was not apt to appeal to any girls Brad could imagine being attracted to, so he had invited none to visit. Anyway, the pretty local girls were almost all too young, married, or spoken for.

The girls would enter the picture later, on his extended tropical voyage. By late September or October Brad planned to be ready to leave Virginia for Florida, and then the Bahamas and the Caribbean. If he didn't find a girlfriend in Fort Lauderdale or Miami, he would find one in the islands.

Brad pulled his red Ford F-250 pickup onto the paved road for the quick spin into Highpoint. Lester's Diner was between the Virginia National Bank and the A & J Auto Parts store, but today it was completely surrounded by television vans and trucks, with their microwave antenna dishes telescoping skyward. He knew at once that the Stadium Massacre must have had a local angle, very local, to draw such attention. Brad had seen on TV that the killer's trailer was located in Suffolk County, but it must have been very close by to rate such a media blitz in Highpoint. He gave the circus at Lester's a pass. He'd find out what was going on at Dixie Hardware and Lumber, where he had some items to purchase.

The media caravan had not yet aimed their lenses at Dixie Hardware, so there was plenty of parking on the gravel lot out front. Brad always felt at home inside the hardware store in the company of farmers, plumbers, welders and carpenters. The usual customers were men with sun-chapped faces and hard leathery hands who looked you straight in the eye when they talked to you. The owner of the place was a middle-aged cracker running to fat named Cecil Towers. He was holding court behind his counter as a half dozen locals drank free coffee and picked donuts from an open box.

"Help yourself Brad; it's worth your life to go near Lester's this morning. I was just telling Barney here how those news boys would all crap their pants if they knew that Jimmy Shifflett had swept this very floor not two months ago! Drank coffee from this very same pot! Hey Barney, you're not going to try to sell this story to the tabloids are you? If anybody makes anything off this, it should be me! I must be the last employer Jimmy ever had, even if it was just sweeping and sorting for petty cash."

"How do you even know he's dead?" asked a short man in mechanic's overalls. "That boy up in Maryland had his head blown clean off. Who's to say it's Shifflett?"

"Well Fred, they got his wallet, they got his ID and they got his fingerprints and I'm sure they got plenty of his DNA, so I'd say it was our Jimmy Shifflett," replied Cecil Towers. "But I still can't believe it. Jimmy's old Datsun ain't run in years, and don't tell me he rode his bike up to Maryland! He always took the bus over to the veteran's hospital in Hampton, or he got a van to pick him up. That Gulf War disease just tore that boy up. I mean, he could hardly hold a broom to sweep! Yeah, Uncle Sam really screwed him good, just chewed him up and spit him out. He lived like a dog on that little disability check they paid him, and he just wasn't bright enough to work the system and get it raised up to anything decent."

The mechanic said, "Yeah, I can see why he was pissed off. He never was too bright before he went into the Marines, but at least he was strong for his size, he played high school football even. Shit, the last time I saw him he couldn't have weighed much over a hundred pounds. You'd think he had cancer or AIDS or something he was so skinny, but I think it was that Gulf War Syndrome thing that screwed him up."

Brad asked, "So where'd he get all the guns they found in his trailer? How'd he get mixed up with all that white racist militia stuff?"

Another man entered the store, but no one paid him any attention as he pretended to shop. He was wearing dress pants, a dark windbreaker, and a ball cap which was fitted with a tiny pinhole video camera. The camera was transmitting to a plain white van parked outside. Where the man looked, the camera recorded. Today he was collecting faces all over Highpoint, faces which would become names when linked to the license plates he had already recorded outside. If any of the men's faces being filmed were already in the criminal, military or DMV data bases (and almost every face was) then digital face mapping technology would also provide rapid identifications. Jimmy Shifflett had been a right wing militia nut case, and the man with the video camera hidden in his hat was a local FBI Special Agent, who had been sent to find out which of the local rednecks were his militia buddies.

Cecil Towers said, "Bradley, you're new around here, so maybe you haven't figured this thing out. And anyway, you're leaving soon on that sailboat of yours, and you'll forget all about us anyway, but listen to me a minute. Jimmy Shifflett didn't have a racist bone in his body. He'd split a beer or a cigarette with a black man or a Mex any day, and I seen it. And he couldn't spell 'militia' or tell you what it meant. Shifflett had no politics at all. He just had lots of pain and lots of forgetful spells, and that's all he had. He worked as an auto mechanic after the Marines, until he got too weak and tired and shaky all the time."

"Yeah," said the man with Fred embroidered on his coveralls, "and just how the hell did he pay for all those fancy rifles they found in his trailer? Shifflett couldn't hardly afford to buy himself lunch at the Dairy Queen, much less all that firepower. And why would he use that piece of shit SKS instead of one of those nice rifles they showed on TV? It don't make no sense at all."

The man they had called Barney, a wiry older fellow with a trimmed gray beard and military style wire-rimmed glasses said, "I went hunting with Jimmy a couple times, a few years back before he got so bad. I had to lend him a rifle, all he had was a .22. And that boy would NOT climb a tree stand! He was scared to death of heights, afraid he'd get dizzy and lose his grip and fall. Now the TV has him climbing four stories of scaffolds to get up into a half-built office building, like he was some sort of Rambo, but it's all a crock. He was just a mechanic and a truck driver in the Marines, not Rambo."

"They said on TV he shot expert with the M-16, that he was the top gun in his boot camp company at Parris Island," Brad said.

Cecil Towers replied, "maybe so, but that was what, 15 years ago? Anyway that boy was a Shifflett. They're from Green County, and they grow up shooting down there. They all learn to shoot down there just like you and I learned to read. Him shooting expert in boot camp don't mean nothing. I'll lay odds his little sister could shoot expert her first try, and so could his momma. Anyway, you can't hardly miss a stadium full of folks, can you? Not even from 1200 yards, not if the scope's been dialed in. And all those books they hauled out of his place? That's another steaming load of bullcrap too. I never seen Jimmy Shifflett read so much as a comic book in his entire life."

"So what was all that stuff doing in his trailer?"

"You tell me Brad, you're the smart one here, all ready to retire on a yacht and you're still just a pup. You tell me, cause it makes no damn sense to us at all."

The oldest of the network anchors had gotten his big break while covering a presidential visit to Dallas four decades earlier. Now in the waning twilight of his career he found an eerie symmetry in covering this latest epochal event in American history, which was also launched from a former Marine's rifle barrel.

For the past two days Pete Broker had been in front of a camera almost continuously, as he had been for a week after 9-11. This time he realized that he didn't have any more reporting marathons left in him. He looked older than makeup or new hairstyles could cure, it showed, and he knew it. Besides producing his own nightly network news broadcast, he had been covering the congressional debates and the first of the hundreds of memorials and funerals which went on seemingly around the clock. In his gut he knew it was time to retire, but not just yet, at least not until after this story played out.

He had led the Tuesday nightly news with the congressional decision on the assault weapon ban, and then he cut to a funeral Mass for over fifty of the dead with the sermon presented by Cardinal O'Malley of the Washington Diocese. The Cardinal's sermon centered on the need for all Americans to change their hearts, and the need for American Catholics to rid themselves of the sinful blight of gun lust. Pete Broker had selected these sound bites himself.

When the old news man brought the program back to his anchor desk, he read the results of the latest telephone poll commissioned by his network. "Our scientific poll conducted today shows that 62% of Americans strongly support the Schuleman-Montaine Firearms Act outlawing assault rifles, 19% support it with some reservations, and 15% oppose it.

"Perhaps most interesting in this poll was the answer to the question, 'would you turn in a neighbor or acquaintance whom you knew to be concealing an illegal assault rifle?' 59% said that yes, they would turn in neighbors or acquaintances for owning an illegal weapon. That must be a very sobering thought indeed, for the estimated ten to fifteen million Americans believed to currently own weapons which have been banned.

"We now take you to our reporter Juan Salazar in Virginia, at the Norfolk police headquarters, for a report on the progress of the rifle turn-in near the center of the storm. What can you tell us Juan?"

"Peter, I'm standing in front of police headquarters here in downtown Norfolk, not far from the home of stadium sniper Jimmy Shifflett. As you can see, a large truck-sized dumpster has been placed on the parking lot. I'm speaking now to Ms. Luanda Johnson of Norfolk. Ma'am, what are you turning in today, and why?"

Ms. Johnson was holding a cheap bolt-action .22 rifle by the barrel like a broom, flanked by a uniformed Norfolk police officer. "I have my ex-husband's old rifle. I'm not sure if it's on the list or not, but I'm not taking no chances, and anyway I don't want no guns in my house around my childrens no more."

"I see. Officer, how long has the dumpster been here, and how many semi-automatic rifles have been turned in so far?"

"Well, we've had the drop site up and running here since early this morning. So far there's maybe about twenty banned rifles, and quite a few other guns that people just want to get rid of, and of course we're encouraging that civic mindedness."

"What kinds of records are being kept? Are you providing any type of receipt, or taking any information from people as they turn rifles in?"

"No Juan, that's not covered by the law as it's written. We're taking any and all rifles, no questions asked, under general amnesty conditions. We just want to encourage the widest possible response."

"So these weapons will not be tested for their 'ballistic fingerprints'?"

"No, that's not in the law, there are no provisions for any ballistic testing. We're on a rigid schedule and a tight budget here. The aim is to get as many assault rifles off the street as possible by next Tuesday, and that's what we're doing."

"This is Juan Salazar in Norfolk, back to you Peter."

George Hammet was working on his neglected hedges with an electric trimmer when he felt the pager vibrate on his belt. It wasn't the same pager that he was issued at work, but a separate one he had purchased prepaid with cash at a mall. After another ten-plus hour day at the office he didn't much feel like yard work, but the unruly shoots sprouting from the top of the hedges made it look like he was white trash, something he could not abide. A neighbor passing by might have observed a similarity between Hammet's flat topped hedges and his blond flat top haircut, but Hammet himself was not one to notice such parallels.

Dusk was settling over his Virginia Beach neighborhood and he needed to use the backlight to read the pager number. He went inside through his side door to the living room, where his wife and eleven year old daughter sat planted on the sofa in front of the television. An aerial view taken from a helicopter showed a long candlelight procession winding its way through Washington streets, led by police cars with blue flashing lights. No matter what channel you put on, you could not escape coverage of some aspect of the Stadium Massacre. George Hammet just avoided it as much as possible. Yard work was a welcome respite from his job, and the media deluge.

"Laura honey, I have to pick something up at Home Depot. I'll be back in a little while." He thought he detected a slight grunt from his wife, but she didn't look up as he left the house.

Instead of driving to Home Depot, George Hammet pulled his red Jeep Cherokee into a small strip mall off Independence Boulevard in front of a convenience store. On a scrap of paper while waiting at a red light he had written down the seven digit number from his pager, and then added two to each digit, creating the actual number he needed to call. In this code eights became zeros, and nines became ones. The area code he had already memorized. George Hammet enjoyed this aspect of his new secret life, this "tradecraft," as it had been explained to him.

He used an untraceable prepaid phone card, one of a pack he had been given, to pay for the call which was picked up on the second ring.

"Hello."

"Hi boss, that you?"

"It's me. I have new instructions, memorize them, and don't write anything down. Got it?"

"Sure, no problem. Go ahead."

"Okay, things are tracking well here. If anything, we're ahead of schedule. I want you to execute the next phase this Friday night, the fourteenth, as close to midnight as you can, but not before ten PM. How many targets have you identified? And how many teams do you have ready?"

"I've got eleven targets, and three teams. I've got one primary contact. He used to be an informant, he's perfect for this, he's recruiting all the muscle. He's good for ten or twelve men, easy. Yeah, Friday night is good."

"Fine. Use the cash to get what you need for the job. Make sure the drivers aren't assholes; make sure they keep their speeds down in and out. Do it exactly like we discussed. You can do all this, right?

"No problem boss, I'll get it done. In fact, it'll be a pleasure."

"I'm depending on you, big guy. After Friday everything's going to really take off, and you're going right to the top with me. I know you'll work it right."

"Yeah I will, but, umm...one thing..."

"What?"

"Did you figure it would be...so many? It's just a lot more than I ever thought it would be."

There was no reply for a moment. "Yeah, well, I must admit the number kind of took me by surprise. But what's done is done, and if anything, it's helped to accelerate the timetable."

"Uh huh, right, that's about how I feel too. What's done is done. In the long run, it'll work out best all around."

Brad was down below on Guajira, hiding behind his hatch screens from the mosquitoes and no-see-ums which ruled the Tidewater twilight. He switched off his portable TV after the national news finished. More massacre coverage continued on every channel, but he couldn't stand to see another funeral with scores of sobbing wives and husbands and children. As he had flipped between his four broadcast channels he'd had to adjust his rabbit ears antenna each time. He'd gotten the gist of what little hard news was presented. Jimmy Shifflett was an ex-Marine, and an expert marksman who was a psycho, a white racist, and a right wing gun fanatic. The clips of the SWAT team carrying assault rifles out of his trailer were played over and over.

Short segments of lengthy hand-scrawled letters from Shifflett threatening violence against the directors of the Hampton Virginia Veterans Administration hospital were shown and discussed. The expert consensus was that he had been a desperate man veering toward losing control for a very long time. It was hinted that other letters existed in which Shifflett threatened various other politicians concerning their neglect of his alleged "Gulf War Syndrome" caused illnesses. These letters seemed to provide a solid background for his rage.

Nothing that Brad saw on the network news squared with what he had heard earlier in Highpoint at the hardware store. The Jimmy Shifflett the locals knew did not sound like the same man the networks were so convincingly portraying as a hate-filled loser venting his rage with an assault rifle, while conspiring with shadowy others to lay the blame at the feet of the Muslim American community. One network even sandwiched Shifflett's haunting photo between pictures of Lee Harvey Oswald, Charles Whitman, Timothy McVeigh and John Allen Mohammed, describing them all as military-trained sharpshooters who had gone over the edge. Why hadn't the networks found a single person in Highpoint who really knew Shifflett to interview? All of their TV trucks had been there.

Brad knew who to call to ask about this mystery. He picked up his cell phone and called his mom in Fort Lauderdale Florida. He knew that she was an internet news junky, and she would be up on the very latest inside scoop. She answered on the fifth ring. "Mom? Yes it's me. I'm fine, are you online? Are you following the Stadium Massacre story?"

"Is the Pope Catholic? I've hardly been out of this chair since Sunday! Your father says he's going to buy me a porta-potty and just slide it under me! Can you believe it? I haven't seen anything like it since 9-11. And you're right in Suffolk County! Right where he came from!"

"Mom, what's the word you're hearing on Shifflett? I just saw the network news and they all have him as a confirmed right wing militia kook, but I've talked to some folks here who knew him well, and they all say that story is pure BS. They say he was a nice guy, harmless, who just got weak and shaky after the First Iraq War. And he was just a Marine Corps truck driver anyway. He was so broke he couldn't keep up a car, and he had to take a bus to get himself over to the VA hospital. They say he was so broke he had to do odd jobs for spending money, but he could barely hold a broom he was so shaky! He was kind of a dim bulb; he wasn't smart enough to get his disability money raised. Nobody here believes those other rifles were his, he was too broke. They think they were planted. And nobody believes those sniper books were his either, he didn't even read comic books. Plus, they said he wasn't any kind of racist at all, not in the least!

"And get this, he was afraid of heights. It's all flat land around here, they hunt from tree stands around here, but he wouldn't climb up one, and now he supposedly climbed up four sets of scaffolding with that SKS rifle! Now he's supposed to be some kind of Rambo! A guy who hunted with him had to lend him a rifle, all he had was an old .22. Can you believe it? Can you believe the crap they're putting out on TV?"

"Of course I believe it, it's just the mainstream media doing what they do best, telling PC lies and feeding the sheeple garbage. Bradley, I can't wait to post what you told me! I've been on Free Americans dot net since Sunday, the Stadium Massacre threads are unbelievable, and we keep crashing the server! It's the biggest story since 9-11! On the Shifflett threads everybody's debating whether he pulled the trigger at all. Most folks think he did, but that he was probably drugged out of his mind on painkillers and antidepressants. Most folks do buy the "right wing gun nut" story though... Wow! I can't wait to post what you said! Listen; tell me what you heard about Shifflett again. Everything, let me write it down."

The "FreeAmericans," as the thousands of regular visitors to the FreeAmericans.net website called themselves, lived in an entirely different nation than that inhabited by the ordinary "sheeple." The "sheeple" trusted the liberal news networks to give them all the information they needed to know, while they were switching between worn-out sitcoms and insipid game shows. Once again the politically astute FreeAmericans formed a real-time cyber think tank, which was far ahead of the usual network news "experts." The broadcast television networks only seemed interested in painting Shifflett as a stereotypical Hollywood version of a "deranged right wing gun nut." Any facts about Shifflett which did not fit their simple predetermined story template, they simply did not run.

Within twenty minutes Margaret Fallon, the middle-aged suburban housewife known as PerfectStorm on FreeAmericans.net, had written and posted her first original report. She titled it "The Real Jimmy Shifflett," and she attributed her information to "folks in Suffolk Virginia who knew Shifflett for years, up until last month."

Ten minutes after she posted her report, it had been read by over a thousand "Free Americans," and the reply thread had grown to over 100 responses. By the time "PerfectStorm" logged off of her computer and went to bed well after midnight, her original report had garnered over 2,000 responses in a free-wheeling debate over the story's stated facts and lack of substantiation.

Some additional new information on Shifflett was also posted on PerfectStorm's thread. "GulfWarArmyVet" had seen a local television report in Alabama, where a black former Marine who served in Shifflett's Motor Transportation Company had sworn up and down that Shifflett was no way and no how a racist. "BoatChick" claimed to be the close friend of a nurse at the Hampton Virginia V.A. hospital. This nurse had reportedly told her friend that Shifflett had been admitted voluntarily to the hospital in the middle of August as a walk-in, but that he had signed himself out against medical advice after he was visited by an unknown "old friend" over the Labor Day weekend.

And so it went on FreeAmericans.net. As report piled on report, the overall consensus emerged that if Shifflett had been the shooter, it was only under some kind of drug-induced mind control. Another faction believed that Shifflett was a patsy pure and simple, and the rifle had been put in his hands only after the real sniper finished his deadly work.

A smaller group stuck with the "official" government-media story line: Shifflett was a right wing gun nut with a grudge against Washington because of his condition, which he blamed on mistreated "Gulf War Syndrome." This group further believed that Shifflett, the white racist, was hoping to turn his anger into violence against Arab Muslims. To this group the "blame the Muslims" theory was "proved" by the Arab language leaflets found near the sniper's lair. This group accused the other factions of being paranoid anti-government wackos themselves, the types of paranoids that allegedly wear hats made of tin foil to prevent "CIA brain control waves" from invading their minds. In return, the other factions derided the "Shifflett did it" group as unthinking government shills.

Most but not all "FreeAmericans" came to believe that the Stadium Massacre was a phony put-up job designed to railroad Congress into passing extremely restrictive gun control laws, exactly as they had done. The fifty thousand registered FreeAmericans had no illusions about what was coming next, and they did not have the slightest intention of turning in any rifles at all. One way or the other, they were determined not to repeat the (as they saw it) fatal error of the "law-abiding German Jews," who voluntarily turned in their firearms when they were ordered to do so in the 1930s.

On FreeAmericans.net the Stadium Massacre was frequently called the "The Reichstag Massacre," after the 1932 arson attack which the Nazis blamed on their communist enemies. The Arabic language "Death to America" leaflets found around Shifflett seemed too contrived, too obvious an attempt to instigate violence against Muslims in America. The leaflets seemed to be too complex for the likes of Shifflett, even after the Arabic phrases were shown to have been photo-copied from earlier Jihad pamphlets which had been published widely.

Most of the FreeAmericans were simply not accepting the pabulum which the government and the major news networks were trying to spoon-feed them.

4

Thursday morning Brad drove into Norfolk to make the rounds of boat stores and marine chandleries. He returned after lunch time with his truck bed loaded with coils of thick nylon dock and anchor lines, cardboard boxes full of assorted cruising gear, and a pair of giant deep cycle batteries that could easily power a golf cart through 36 holes. His tires crunched down the oyster shell driveway past the empty farmhouse and outbuildings of his seldom-seen absentee landlord, and as he neared the river he saw that he had visitors. A dusty black Chevy Suburban and a burgundy Crown Victoria were parked in his turn-around circle under the oak tree. Both vehicles had opaquely tinted windows and sprouted numerous small antennas.

Brad pulled off to the side of the drive to allow them room to leave and stepped out of his pickup. The four doors of the Suburban opened at once and four men got out, white men wearing sport coats and ties in the Indian Summer heat. Another pair of similarly attired men got out of the Crown Vic. There were only two reasons Brad could think of why anyone would wear a jacket and tie and long pants in the almost ninety degree weather: because it was departmental policy, and to conceal firearms. Brad was wearing his standard khaki shorts, polo shirt and boat shoes. He stood by his truck, and they fanned out as they walked toward him. He noticed that all their jackets were hanging open, presumably for fast access to their hidden pistols. Half of them were wearing dark sunglasses, the very image of the bad-ass detective.

"Bradley Thomas Fallon?" asked the oldest man, the only one over fifty judging by his lined face.

"Who's asking?" Brad had a watery feeling in his gut but tried to give no sign of his unease.

"FBI. I'm Special Agent James Gibson. We'd like to talk to you." Gibson held out his credentials briefly for Fallon to see: a gold badge and a laminated ID in their own leather wallet. One of the younger agents walked behind and around Brad. He had an unseen device on his belt that resembled a cell phone; if Brad Fallon had been carrying a firearm it would have begun vibrating. It didn't, so he nodded an "okay" to his superior.

"Mr. Fallon, why don't we sit in our truck and get out of the heat while we talk?" asked the oldest agent.

"I'm fine out here thank you."

"Please Mr. Fallon, we'll only take a few minutes of your time, and then we'll be on our way."

Brad looked around him at the six agents. One of them, a tall man with weight lifter's shoulders straining against his jacket said, "Don't be an asshole Fallon. If we were arresting you today, you'd already be handcuffed. So do everybody a favor, and let's have a short talk in the air conditioned truck. Please." He smiled bemusedly at Brad and they locked eyes. He had blue eyes like Brad, brush-cut blond hair, and a neck like one of the oak tree's branches.

He gave up and walked with them to their Suburban; its motor was idling noisily. He briefly wondered if he was going to be hauled away as soon as the door was closed behind him, but he didn't see any alternative. He warily climbed into the backseat of the Suburban like a rabbit visiting a python's cage. Gibson sat in the front passenger seat, the burly blond sat in the back seat next to him.

The third bench seat had been removed. The back half of the truck was full of aluminum and plastic lockers and boxes, weapons cases, body armor, communications gear, and other police and military items. The two agents settled in, closed the doors, and turned in their seats to face their "person of interest."

Special Agent Gibson surprised him with his first question. "Well Mr. Fallon, how much longer until you sail off into the sunset?"

Brad tried not to express any astonishment at their knowledge. Perhaps Gibson was simply making an educated guess, trying to spook him. After all, there was a 44 foot mastless sailboat tied up at the dock. "It depends on how many problems I have getting the boat ready."

"Well you should be able to go rather far on $68,000, I'd say. And I understand that the Adalaska Corporation has a very generous transportation policy, so you can always fly back to the oil fields if your account gets thin. Really, it's a remarkable achievement for a young man hardly thirty years old. But I'm guessing your parents in Florida would prefer that you finish college, instead of sailing off around the world."

Brad took a deep, slow breath, feeling flushed in the face, and said, "Okay guys, I'm impressed. You know all about me. What do you want?"

The muscular agent next to Brad said, "Maybe it's your assault weapons. Maybe it's the AR-15 rifle you bought at; let me see here, A&A Sporting Goods in Missoula Montana in 1996. Maybe it's the Mini-14 you bought in Jacksonville Florida in 1995. You've heard about the new law, haven't you?"

"I think I might have heard something about it."

"Uh huh. So do you still have the rifles? They'll get you ten years hard time after next Tuesday."

"I sold both rifles years ago. 223 isn't my caliber."

"Is that so? Can you prove it?"

From the front seat Agent Gibson said, "Settle down gentlemen. We're not interested in your old rifles, bought or sold. Not until next week anyway. We're only interested in some friends of yours." Gibson opened a cream-colored folder and handed several grainy black and white photos to Brad. Brad could see that several of the pictures had been taken inside the hardware store in Highpoint. There was a picture of the store owner Cecil Towers, along with two of the men who had been part of the conversation at the counter, and a few others.

"Of course I know him; he's the manager of Dixie Hardware. The old man with the beard I've seen around, the other man I only saw once at the store. Am I supposed to know them?"

"Don't play stupid Fallon," Gibson replied. "We know you're a bright guy. I'll lay our cards on the table. We need to know everything about Shifflett's friends and acquaintances, and we need to know it ASAP. We need to know the extent of militia activity in southeast Virginia, and if any of Shifflett's old militia buddies helped him at the stadium. We need to know if they're planning any more actions, and we need to know about it like right now."

Brad was stunned by their questions. "How the hell would I know? I've been here less than two months! The only way I know anybody around here is running into them in a store."

The crew cut agent said, "So you've never been shooting with any of them?"

"Of course not. I don't even know them."

"I see…" continued the agent. "Fallon, have you ever been to the Mineral Springs Rifle Range, down by the Carolina border?"

Actually this blond agent did not carry FBI credentials, because he was the Assistant Special Agent in Charge (or ASAC) of the Norfolk Virginia Field Office of the Bureau of Alcohol Tobacco Firearms and Explosives, formerly the BATF, and still commonly called that or simply the ATF. Since the massacre he had been temporarily attached to the newly formed MD-Rifle Task Force, which fell under the Joint Domestic Terrorism Task Force, answering to the Department of Homeland Security. The federal "alphabet agencies" were playing Scrabble as they responded to changing terrorist threats. Supervisory Special Agent Gibson had come down from Washington with additional agents to augment the Joint Task Force in the Tidewater Virginia area as they ran down Shifflett's militia connections.

The muscular blond ATF agent knew that Brad Fallon had been to Mineral Springs because he had reviewed videotapes showing Fallon there two weeks earlier, participating in a monthly rifle shooting competition which drew serious shooters from several states. ATF agents routinely trolled the parking lots of gun shows and shooting ranges covertly taping license plates and people's faces. The tag numbers were crunched by computers, revealing the regional and national patterns behind the ebb and flow of militia and so-called "patriot" groups and their hangers-on. The faces were scanned into digital biometric data bases and matched with vehicles, addresses, and many of the weapons these individuals had purchased.

It was a well-established fact that extreme right wing gun nuts and militia kooks were devoted attendees of gun shows and rifle shooting ranges. Fallon's Ford truck had indeed been filmed at Mineral Springs, along with those of several members of a group called the Black Water Rod and Gun Club. This was a group that Jimmy Shifflett had once belonged to. This was a group which the local ATF Field Office suspected of being a cover for a clandestine militia organization based in Tidewater Virginia.

"Sure, I've been there twice. Once to sight in rifles, and once to shoot in a match."

"What kind of rifles Mr. Fallon?" asked Gibson. "There are rifles... and there are rifles."

"I thought you already knew, Agent Gibson. I thought you knew everything about me. Don't you already have it written down?"

"Don't be a smartass Brad, don't go getting an attitude. We're not in a joking mood. After the Stadium Massacre, a lot of things changed, a lot of things. The American people have had it with you gun nuts, so you'd better buy a clue and get with the program while you can! Special Agent Hammet has already started an investigation into the disposition of your assault rifles, and that's just for starters. We can freeze your bank accounts, or we can invalidate your passport with one phone call, do you understand me? We're not playing for match sticks here! We've only got to say the magic word 'terrorism' and you'll be put into a whole other category, and you won't know what hit you! We'll drop you into a cage with the other terrorists, and you'll never even see a lawyer!"

Brad couldn't make words form; his mouth had gone bone dry.

"We know things about you that you can't imagine. We know you shot 294 out of a perfect 300 with your Swedish Mauser over iron sights at Mineral Springs, and took second place against folks who shoot competition every weekend of their lives. We have the entire roster of shooters; we know their scores, where they live, most of the guns they own, how much ammunition they bought last year.

"We know that after two good semesters in college you suddenly quit and enlisted in the Navy to try to make it into the SEALs, but you washed out on some sort of oxygen test in a pressure chamber. So you served the rest of your enlistment as a machinist's mate and got out. I've got your DD 214 discharge paper right here in this file. Then you went up to Alaska to make a ton of money, and now here you are on the verge of sailing away on your own boat.

"Well if you want to get that boat finished and sail away, you need to do your patriotic duty and help us out. I can't put it any more clearly than that. Now if you'll excuse me I have other places to go today." Gibson climbed down from the Suburban, leaving Brad alone with the younger agent, who except for his northeastern accent reminded him of a Russian boxer, with his blond flat top, pale blue eyes and broken nose. Gibson got into the burgundy Crown Vic, which departed immediately. The remaining agents had climbed aboard Guajira in their black-soled street shoes, shed their jackets, and made themselves comfortable in the cockpit under the shade of the oak.

The blond Special Agent had recruited and run dozens of confidential informants during his 12 years with the ATF. Frequently his CI's were parolees eager to avoid a return trip to prison, which they knew could easily be arranged if they failed to cooperate. But from Hammet's point of view even non-felons typically had 'hooks' attached to them: a struggling business which could not endure a microscopic federal regulatory 'rectal exam', a critically needed job and paycheck which could not be lost, or young children and pretty wives which could not be left behind while Daddy went off to prison. Among the federal law enforcement agencies, the ATF had always been known for ruthlessly manufacturing federal cases out of thin air where necessary, usually in order to create a needed informant as part of an ongoing investigation. The 20,000 plus federal and state gun laws on the books, which were often vaguely written or even contradictory, made gun owners and especially licensed gun dealers an easy target for extra-legal arm twisting.

In Fallon's case his 'hook' was his eagerness to finish his boat and get away sailing, after years of working steadily toward that goal. Once he accepted that his bank accounts and his passport could be frozen at their whim, Fallon would come aboard, the veteran ATF agent was certain of it.

"So what's it like sailing across an ocean on something like that? You could never get me on one. Fishing on the bay is all the ocean I can handle." This was just an ice breaker; he knew that Fallon was still somewhat in shock.

Brad was slightly disarmed by the innocent question. "It's not for everybody. But it beats the nine-to-five and a house in the suburbs, at least for me."

"Oh give me the suburbs any day. I just wish I could cut back to nine to five! Okay Fallon, here's the deal: you want to go sailing, and we want you to help us for a little while. If you help us, I'm sure that we'll find that no investigation is needed into your assault rifles. We'll give you a clean bill of health, forget we ever heard of you, and you'll be on your merry way. If you try to move your money offshore before that, you'll find that it's been blocked. Screw with us, and you'll find out what it's like to live in a six by nine cage. That's just the facts of life Brad, those are the ground rules.

"Now what we want you to do is get close to the folks on this list. You're a big deal shooter and hunter, so they'll trust you. All of these guys belong to the Black Water Rod and Gun Club, which is a cover for a secret anti-government militia group. There's no formal membership roster, no dues, and the members come and go, but these men here seem to be the core.

"The club was formed right here in Suffolk in the 80's, but it really grew in the mid 90's. That was the same time that most of the open militias were fading away or moving underground after Oklahoma City. Most of the members of this 'club' are ex-military, most of them own and shoot assault rifles, most of them have four wheel drive trucks and a lot of them have boats. We want to know what connection they had to Shifflett and the Stadium Massacre, and if they have plans to commit any more terrorist acts in the future.

"That's it. Now here's where you come in. Most Friday nights some of them have what passes for a meeting in the back room at Lester's Diner in Highpoint. They eat dinner and drink a lot of coffee, and then they pile into their trucks and go off into the swamps to shoot some damn animals or something. We want you to meet them at Lester's and buddy up to them. We just want you to get an invitation to do whatever the hell it is they do. They've seen you around town for a while; they've seen you at the range, so it won't be a problem. We know how these groups operate. Any shooting or fishing or hunting that comes along, you want to go, tag along. That's it. Easy stuff. Then you call and tell me about it. Any questions?"

Brad had too many questions to count, but settled for, "What's your name? Who do you work for?"

"Yeah right! You can just call me George, and I work for your government. Any more questions?"

Brad was studying George's face, committing the small blue eyes and sprinkling of old acne scars and bent nose to his memory. He thought he had heard his last name but could not remember it. "H" something. If he ever met "George" on equal footing in the future, free of coercion and official blackmail, he wanted to deal with him personally. Threatening his freedom and his boat was threatening the very core of Brad's existence.

"No, no questions."

"So that's it then, we'll be in touch. Use this cell phone to contact us at any time. Just hit star twenty nine, and a duty officer will contact Gibson or me. Identify yourself as Bradley Fallon, and one of us will call you back. The phone has unlimited minutes on Uncle Sam's dime, so feel free to use it for any calls you want to make in the fifty states. Remember star twenty nine gets us 24/7, but don't call at night unless it can't wait, like if you hear of any plans for violence. Okay? You can get out now, we'll be in touch.

"And remember Brad: if you screw with us in any way, we'll screw you for good. We're not messing around: domestic terrorism is serious business, just like the Muslim kind."

Brad opened the door and stepped down with the cell phone and a large manila mailing envelope containing the names, addresses, brief biographical sketches and photos of the gun club members. The other agents who were relaxing on Brad's boat climbed off onto the dock and smirked at him as they passed, then they got into the Suburban and it went crunching back out the oyster shell driveway. He watched it until it was gone from sight, and he continued to stare after it until he could no longer hear its tires on the oyster shells.

"Shit...shit...shit..." thought Brad, climbing aboard his boat. Guajira's companionway hatch padlock had been cut and was laying in the cockpit well. They were very up front about invading his private property; they didn't even bother to toss the broken lock overboard. He looked below; he could see that his boat had been searched. Nothing looked broken and there was no obvious malicious damage; no slit cushions, no broken locker doors, so at least they hadn't been in a foul mood. Just a friendly warrantless search to demonstrate their disregard for the Constitution, and their complete power over him. The only weapons he had on the boat were standard bolt action rifles, not covered by the new law, and his Smith and Wesson .44 magnum. The rifles were still safe in their hidden locker, but Brad could tell they had been removed and handled and then replaced. Brad figured that if they meant for him to infiltrate a gun club, they knew he'd need his guns.

He climbed back into the cockpit and lay on his back staring up through the oak branches at the sky, as beams of sunlight flickered through the shifting leaves. They really have me by the balls, he thought. He knew that he could not ignore their demands. Randy Weaver had tried that approach with a BATF blackmail operation and refused to turn informant, and in the end the feds killed his son and his wife for his defiance. They shot his young son in the back, and they shot his wife through the head while she was holding a baby in her kitchen. The new federal police had somewhere crossed the line and become a super mafia. When they offered you a deal, you couldn't refuse.

After 9-11 the feds permitted themselves to go after foreigners in the U.S.A. without regard for normal due process, all in the name of fighting the "War on Terror." Now the War on Terror, with its special rules and constitutional exemptions, was being widened to include American citizens under "domestic terrorism." The cut padlock left flippantly as an insult on Guajira's cockpit floor told Brad that much in clear language.

Now in the wake of the Stadium Massacre, Brad had no doubt that the feds would extend the same harsh war-time measures against any suspected "militia" terrorists, that they had taken against suspected Islamic terrorists, who had been rounded up and put into secret detention facilities without any trial. Ignoring the feds' demands was not an option. As the famous phrase had put it, "You are either with us, or with the terrorists."

Twenty miles up this river on a mastless sailboat Brad felt as helpless as a turtle flipped on its back: trapped and vulnerable.

But Brad Fallon had one slight edge which had not shown up on the FBI's computer screens, one stealth weapon which did not show on their radar scope: he was something of a self-taught student of espionage, law enforcement and special warfare techniques. During his long months working on the ANWR, he had devoured literally hundreds of paperback novels, biographies and histories. During his stints in Alaska he worked twelve on, twelve off, seven days a week. Informal paperback libraries in the dormitories were well stocked with the works of LeCarre, Seymour, Ignatius and many others. There were also plentiful non-fiction works covering every dirty war and covert operation from Southeast Asia to Northern Ireland, and from Central America to the Middle East.

By analyzing and comparing the information in these books he had developed a strong instinct for determining what was critical fact, and what was hyperbolic nonsense. His informal education in special warfare and covert intelligence operations would not register on George's biography sheet, an advantage which Brad hoped to use if he could.

Brad had not developed an affinity for reading about espionage and clandestine operations by accident. For years he had watched the federal government's rising tide of well-meant tyrannical power, which always tightened one click of the handcuff ratchet at a time on American freedom, without ever reversing direction or loosening. First in the name of the "War on Drugs," and then in the name of the "War on Terror," the federal law enforcement agencies had carved out their own special rules of engagement. In the name of national security, these rules superceded and bypassed the Bill of Rights where ever it stood in the way.

For the sake of expediency, pleading dire emergency, exceptions and exemptions were granted to federal law enforcement agencies, but the "exceptions" then quickly became the accepted norms. Each new graduating class of agents came into the federal law enforcement world learning that they were somehow above the Bill of Rights, because their calling was higher, and their mission too important, to be hamstrung by strict adherence to outdated rules of legal conduct.

Brad could connect the dots into the future: he had studied the pattern in many nations where the secret police gradually became empowered to break the law with impunity, and for a long time he had seen the same trends at work in America. Years ago he had wanted to become a Navy SEAL, in order to learn the dark trades from the inside. That plan had been torpedoed in the hyperbaric dive chamber when the Navy doctors discovered he had no taste for pure oxygen at a simulated depth of sixty feet.

So Brad did the best he could by teaching himself, and so he used his off-duty time in Alaska reading everything he could find on spies, commandos, and terrorists. Now that he was planning to become a world traveling sailor, Brad considered a sophisticated understanding of how secret police agencies worked to be an important tool for avoiding the kinds of mistakes which could cause his boat to be seized, or himself to be tossed in a foreign jail. In most nations, and increasingly in America, it was becoming crucial to be able to discern where the actual lines of power ran, as opposed to the overt public lines. The public lines of authority were often public lies, just polite window dressing, and often a trap for the naïve and unwary.

He had expected to use his special knowledge to help him to navigate through the Byzantine channels of third world politics, to tell him when to shut up and pay the mordida bribe, and when to demand his rights; when to seek a local patron, and when to pull up anchor and flee in the night.

Brad understood very well that the world was increasingly becoming more complex and dangerous for the serious traveler. He just didn't foresee that he would be trapped by secret police right here in America, before he could even cross his first ocean on Guajira!

One thing he knew for certain was that the standard retirement plan for a dirty war informant was a rural safe house torture session, followed by a bullet in the brain and being dumped in a roadside ditch. The Black Water Rod and Gun Club might or might not be a cover for a secret militia group, but if they were, he was dead certain they would immediately suspect him, the stranger, if he suddenly showed a desire to follow them on their outings.

In fact, his position would be so exposed and obvious that he felt fairly sure that there must already be a government informant in the club, and that he was intentionally being dangled as a cover for the existing spy. If bad things suddenly began to happen to members of the gun club, suspicion would immediately fall on Brad Fallon, leaving the real informer or informers undiscovered and unsuspected. Fallon thought that he would most likely be playing the role of the feds' intentional sacrificial pawn, a common last role for a duped informant.

Brad was not going to pull a Randy Weaver and refuse the feds outright. He didn't want to have his money seized or his boat sunk at the dock, or to wind up living in a six by nine cage. But neither would he become an informant. He had just over 24 hours to come up with an alternate plan.

He picked up his broken padlock and threw it far out into the river, where it made a soft thunking splash and disappeared.

5

George Hammet was riding shotgun in the front of the FBI's black Suburban, on their thirty mile drive back from Suffolk to the federal building in downtown Norfolk. The three FBI Special Agents with him were among the fifty or so federal law enforcement agents rushed into the area to augment the Tidewater end of the MD-Rifle investigation. Local FBI and ATF agents were riding with new arrivals to familiarize them with the area. The visit to Highpoint had primarily been an orientation run for them. In the morning they had toured Shifflett's trailer, and conducted field interviews of Cecil Towers and several other Highpoint residents, but without indicating any interest in the Black Water Rod and Gun Club.

The task of actually making the recruitment pitch to Fallon had been given to the ATF's George Hammet because he was assigned locally, and would run the new "militia informant" long after the Joint Task Force had departed. The FBI's own high-profile Counter Terrorism Division was focused primarily on foreign based Islamic terrorist cells. The ATF was left with the less glamorous task of investigating domestic "militias" and other mostly right wing groups, because these investigations were often based on firearms law infractions.

From the front seat Hammet turned to the others and said, "One more stop and we'll call it a day. We're going to visit a gun store for a compliance check. You can see the kind of crap ATF is up against every day. Take a right after the Union 76, then head south on 32."

Virginia State Road 32 was a two-lane blacktop cutting due south through pine trees and soybean fields, with asphalt heat mirages shimmering in the distance. "That's the place up there on the left," said Hammet. The gun store was a white one-story cinderblock building set behind a gravel parking lot. An American flag flapped softly atop a pole out front. "FREEDOM ARMS" was painted in blue letters across the top of the building above the front door and a pair of windows. Behind the store across a football field sized yard was the owner's tan-colored one story ranch-style house. Pine woods bordered a wire fence around the yard and behind the house.

There was a jeep, a pickup truck and a motorcycle parked in front of the store. The muffled staccato popping of a handgun could be heard from within, someone shooting on the indoor range. Virginia was a "right to carry" state and many of the citizens who carried a licensed concealed handgun practiced regularly.

A heavy wrought-iron burglar gate was latched back against the building, allowing access through a plate glass door. The two small windows in the front of the structure were set high and covered with iron bars. From the outside the place looked almost like a small bank.

The four federal agents got out, adjusted their jackets over their concealed pistols, and went inside. Decals from firearms and reloading supply companies were stuck all over the glass door. Cowbells jingled and a chime rang when the door was opened. Inside the store the air conditioning was refreshingly chilly. A young man, perhaps a military reservist judging by his haircut and demeanor, stood behind a long glass-cased counter talking to a wiry older customer who was wearing jeans and boots and a black Harley Davidson t-shirt and leather vest. Out of sight, another string of shots was fired on the indoor range. Typical for a gun store, the young man behind the counter was wearing a holstered pistol on a wide leather belt. George Hammet noted his pistol, and it occurred to him that he could not remember a single case of a gun store ever being robbed during business hours. Hammet never connected this fact to any larger issues involving citizens being allowed to carry firearms more generally.

The three FBI men browsed through the crowded non-firearms merchandise display areas, examining holsters, books, boxes of various calibers of ammunition and other shooting accessories, all while discreetly watching Hammet handle the "compliance visit." As it would be expected of FBI agents, all of them were at least proficient with firearms. They carried their own .40 caliber pistols in shoulder rigs or belt holsters hidden under their jackets. They all considered themselves "shooters" and bore no particular animosity toward the owners of gun stores, since they were themselves frequent customers in them. Gun stores were strictly the ATF's beat as far as the FBI agents were concerned.

On one knotty-pine paneled wall there was a large black and white poster of Adolf Hitler with bull's-eye rings printed over him. Hitler had his arm raised high in a stiff Nazi salute. Across the poster, "All those in favor of gun control, raise your right hand," was written in large Germanic letters. In smaller print was written, "After Hitler was elected Chancellor in 1933, the Nazis used existing German gun registration lists to disarm the Jews. The rest is history."

One young FBI agent pointed the poster out to his colleagues and they all chuckled. FBI agents generally looked down on their ATF cousins, referring to them as the BATF and now the BATFE. The ATF agents had a serious inferiority complex and wanted to be considered a first-tier "three letter agency" like the CIA, FBI, DEA and NSA, and never referred to themselves as the BATF or BATFE. The BATF had spent sixty years within the Treasury Department as glorified tax collectors, or "revenuers," before most of their law enforcement functions were transferred over to the Justice Department, following the homeland security reorganizations in the wake of 9-11.

With the transfer had come the new letter, the E for Explosives, and the only four letter agency had become the first five letter agency. Behind their backs, BATFE agents were still called "F-Troop" by the FBI for their tendency to screw up major cases, such as the initial attack at Waco. (Not that the FBI had covered itself in glory ending the standoff.)

It was fair to say that the FBI and ATF had shared a long, complex, and often troubled bureaucratic relationship before these three G-men found themselves watching an ATF gun store compliance visit on this particular Thursday afternoon in Virginia.

George Hammet went to the counter and presented his credentials, the black leather wallet containing his gold badge and laminated BATFE identification card. The conversation between the young store employee and his customer halted in mid-sentence.

"ATF. I'm here for a compliance check. Where's the owner, Joe Bardiwell?"

"In the back, wait one." The employee pushed a button concealed behind the counter, and in a few moments a heavy steel door to the back rooms of the building opened. A middle-aged man wearing a leather machinist's apron and clear safety glasses stepped out. Before the door closed behind him a few louder shots could be heard from the range. Bardiwell had thick dark hair and a mustache, and at first glance might have been said to resemble Antonio Banderas or Omar Shariff. Besides owning the store and its indoor range, he was a highly respected gunsmith, well known for his custom modifications to standard grade hunting rifles. His work shop and reloading room was in the back, along with his office, storage rooms, and the four lane pistol range.

"The ATF again? And there're four of you today? What's the big problem? I just had a check last week, and everything was in perfect order."

Agent Hammet already knew this to be factually correct. As the Norfolk ASAC (Assistant Special Agent In Charge) he was responsible for scheduling the compliance check Bardiwell was referring to. "I see that all of your semi-auto rifles are gone," he said, pointing to the nearly empty gun racks behind the counters. As in most gun stores, the pistols were in glass cases beneath the counters, the rifles and shotguns were lined up in vertical racks along the back walls. "Have you turned them in, or sold them? Where are they?"

"Oh, I guess I sold just about every one of them. It's been a busy week."

"Sold them? All of them? Why would anybody buy a rifle that's about to be prohibited? Did you inform the purchasers of the new law?"

Bardiwell tried not to smile. "They all know about the law, everybody does. And why they want the rifles is their business. This week selling them is still perfectly legal, there's nothing in the law which comes into effect before next Tuesday."

"But the weapons will be illegal in five days! You're aiding and abetting criminal activity!"

"I don't see how. I didn't write the law, and there's nothing in the law about not selling them this week, not one word. Call your Congressman if you don't like the way they wrote the law."

"But buying an assault rifle a week before they're illegal clearly shows intent to break the law!"

"First, they're semi-automatic rifles, not assault rifles. Assault rifles have a fully automatic capability. You know that. And I didn't ask them about their 'intent.' They were all qualified buyers who passed the instant background check. I just sell legal firearms to qualified buyers for a living. And this week they're still legal."

"Let me see your form 4473's, let me see all your paperwork for the last week." Hammet was asking for all of the yellow federal firearms purchase forms filled out by each purchaser, which by law were retained at the gun stores. Theoretically this was to prevent the information from being centrally collected, which would constitute national firearms registration. The ATF routinely collected information from the forms in the conduct of actual criminal investigations, which was permitted. Lately they had taken to bringing in their own laptop computers and scanners, and copying forms wholesale, which should not have been permitted. The "Beltway Sniper" case in 2002 had finally buried the pretense that the ATF could not go on wide-net fishing expeditions. They had collected and culled through every 4473 in Maryland and Virginia on that case, and a new precedent had been set.

Joe Bardiwell went to his back office and returned in a minute with a stack of yellow cards. Usually an ATF agent would try to slip into the office to mine data in privacy, but Bardiwell had built a heavy hinged section into his counter to prevent his offices or storage rooms from being rushed by armed robbers, (or federal agents without a warrant). The seemingly unbroken counter top served its purpose, and Hammet remained on the public side of the store. Bardiwell laid the forms on the counter top in front of the ATF agent. "The last sales are on top, they go back in order. Rifles, pistols, everything."

George Hammet quickly flipped through the cards. "AR-15, SKS, Bushmaster, FAL, an AR-180, two Ruger Mini-14s, a Dragonov, another FAL....Jesus, you sold all of these yesterday! Did you think these guns were bought by people who intended to comply with the law?"

Joe Bardiwell shrugged. "How would I know? And why should I be left with unsold inventory I already paid for?"

Hammet picked up the entire inch-thick stack of forms and turned to leave the store. Bardiwell said, "You can't take them out of here, you know the law! Those are my records, and they have to stay secured in my office, that's the law. You can copy pertinent information in pursuing an investigation, but you can't take the forms out of here as long as I'm in business."

Bardiwell was making that statement for the record in front of witnesses, and knowing as well that his video surveillance cameras would catch the ATF agent in clear violation of the statutes if he left with the forms. It would not be above the ATF to take the forms on one day, and then arrest a firearms dealer for not having them as required by law on the next. Bardiwell's store had two video cameras that were meant to be seen, and two more that were hidden. The ATF had been known to remove surveillance videotapes after harassing and abusing firearms dealers.

"And just exactly how long do you expect to stay in business Bardiwell? Maybe not as long as you think, if you've been selling assault rifles with the intent to evade the law! That's conspiracy, at the very least! You'll be hearing from us, Bardiwell!" Hammet held onto the entire stack of yellow cards and turned for the door.

The older customer, who had been at the counter watching and listening to the entire exchange, suddenly blurted out, "Hey Mr. BATF man, I thought there was no federal gun registration? But there you go, walking out the door with the 4473's."

Hammet stopped and shot a withering look back at the civilian who had unexpectedly challenged him, but the man continued.

"Let me ask you something Mr. BATF... excuse me, Mr. BATF-E man. After next Tuesday, are you going to be kicking down those peoples' doors? Waking up the babies with concussion grenades? Stomping on their kittens and shooting their dogs? Throwing pregnant women around and causing miscarriages? Isn't that what you do, in your black ninja suits, hiding your faces behind masks? We've got Muslim terrorists running around loose, but all you can think about is taking away regular peoples' guns. Now why is that?"

George Hammet, the Norfolk ATF Assistant Special Agent In Charge (ASIC) was accustomed to receiving obsequious courtesy in gun stores and was momentarily stunned into silence by the outburst. His face had turned an instant shade of red. When he regained his voice he called back, "and just who the hell are you, Gomer?"

"Gomer? Just who the hell am I? Who the hell am I? I'm just somebody that was bleeding in the jungle for this country when you were still in diapers, that's who! 'Killin' a commie for mommy', so she could raise you up to be a BATF man! Yessir, above the law, taking the yellow forms away, so you can go smash down their doors next week. But hey, you think it's all fine and dandy if the lawyers up in Washington decide to tear up the Bill of Rights! That's just fine by you, as long as they sign your paycheck, isn't it?"

Hammet was in the middle of the aisle, and turned back. "I'm going to need to see some ID, and I'm going to need to see it right now!"

"I'm sure you would, and I'd like to see your ID too while we're at it, so I'll know who to file the lawsuit against."

"Shut up you asshole! Leave it alone, if you know what's good for you! Leave it alone, or else!"

"Or else what? You'll arrest me for impeding a federal agent in the breaking of the law?" The two men were now standing only feet apart. The older man, the civilian in the black t-shirt and vest stayed by the counter, he had carefully made no threatening move toward Special Agent Hammet. Two of the FBI agents approached Hammet from the side, whispering for him to cool it and leave. The situation could easily have escalated into a full-out armed confrontation right there in the gun store, and the out-of-town FBI agents didn't want to be dragged into a protracted snafu of the ATF agent's creation.

The civilian had more to say, he wouldn't leave it alone. "I earned the right to say my piece over in that jungle, and I've got the scars to prove it! And let me tell you something: all of us that went over there, we all took an oath to defend the Constitution from ALL enemies, foreign AND domestic, do you read me sonny?"

"I don't need a lecture on defending the Constitution from you!"

"No? Well maybe it's time you read up on it! Maybe it's about time to figure it all out again, figure out just exactly who's defending the Constitution, and who's crapping on it! So my question to you is this: just exactly who wants to disarm us all so bad, and why?" Long harbored thoughts were flying through the old veteran's mind now, and he couldn't stop his mouth from firing off wild shots. "Let me tell you something else, whoever wrote that damn law is either the biggest fool who ever lived, or he just flat-out wants to start a civil war in this country."

The three FBI agents looked at Hammet and at the old crackpot with some amusement, but mostly they just wanted to get out of the store while they could, without the situation escalating to a level which would require them to fill out reams of unwanted paperwork.

"You don't believe me huh?" the old veteran continued, now addressing all four of them. "Then why'd every decent rifle in Tidewater, and probably everywhere, get bought up this week? Look around in here. There's not a rifle or an ammunition magazine left, and not hardly a box of rifle bullets. Now why do you think that is? So people can throw them all in dumpsters come next Tuesday? You federal boys better think about it long and hard, and pick which side of the Constitution you're going to stand on!"

Hammet said, "Put a cork in it old man, or we'll arrest you for threatening federal officers!" His bulging neck was practically splitting his shirt collar, his face was almost purple. He was trying to regain his composure and his control over the situation. Threatening arrest usually did the trick: nobody wanted to be handcuffed and taken away to jail.

But the angry man just sneered. "I'm way too old for you to scare me that way sonny! Now the VC and the NVA, they scared me plenty back in the day, but not you, oh no, not hardly! And let me tell you something else: Charlie taught me a thing or two over there, things I ain't never forgot! And not just me, no sir, not just me by a long shot!"

George Hammet spun and headed out the door, still red-faced with anger, the three FBI men trailing behind him in line. The last FBI agent turned back around at the front door, nodded slightly, flashed a 'thumbs up' sign against his chest in the old man's direction and shot him a wink. Then they were gone.

In the shop the ranting man's anger immediately turned to regret. "I'm sorry Joe, I guess I really crapped in the coffee pot this time. I mean, I really put you in the shit with those assholes. But seeing that BATF guy hauling out your 4473s, knowing what that means, what's going to happen to those folks now…damn. I just don't know what's happening in this country any more. I feel like a war's coming. I don't quite know how I know it, but I can feel it coming. And now I went and got the BATF all pissed off, right in your store."

"Ah, forget it Phil, you spoke the truth. You said what you thought had to be said, don't ever be sorry for that. That's why we live in a free country." Joe Bardiwell spoke with a slight foreign accent, one hard to place.

"I really thought they still weren't allowed to take the 4473s out of the store."

"They're not, but they do what the hell they like. Especially after 9-11, and the Beltway Sniper, and now the Stadium Massacre…. Yeah, they're a law unto themselves; they just do what the hell they want. If they can say it involves national security or terrorism, they get a blank check and a free hand, and no questions asked. It's difficult times my friend, difficult times. Muslims are running around shooting people and blowing themselves up, and the feds pick right now to disarm honest Americans."

"Well Joe, I'm sorry for any trouble I caused you with the ATF, I really am."

"Hey, don't worry about it. What's going to happen is going to happen. Don't let 'em drive you crazy. We'll get through this if we stay cool." The two men shook hands across the glass topped pistol display counter, and then the older man left the shop, mounted his Harley, fired it up and took off fast to the south.

Joe Bardiwell went back into his office and began making phone calls. He felt it was his duty to call his customers and tell them that the ATF had just pulled their 4473's and taken them away, which was highly unusual, and indicated certain trouble. In order to avoid any ATF concocted conspiracy charge he carefully told each customer or customer's answering machine the safe and truthful statement, "The ATF just pulled your yellow form, make sure you comply with the new law and get rid of your semi-auto rifles by next Tuesday."

In reality Bardiwell knew that virtually all of these rifles had already been "gotten rid of." They had already been buried in watertight plastic containers or otherwise well hidden. He had heard talk of stockpiles and caches and large diameter PVC pipe all week long, as rifles and ammunition had flown off the shelves. Customers wanted to know what kind of grease or lubricant to use for long term storage, and if they should take apart weapons to relieve spring pressure.

Bardiwell stayed away from talk of weapons caches and resistance, he heard it but didn't join in it. However, in point of fact Joe Bardiwell had himself already cached a significant amount of arms and ammunition. Storm clouds had been gathering for a long time, and he intended to be ready for whatever came next.

Joe Bardiwell was not a born American. He had lived until his late thirties in a Christian town in the hills east of Beirut Lebanon. He knew better than most people that if and when the storm broke, America could quickly be divided into two classes: armed survivors, and disarmed victims. He had seen it and he had lived it from 1976 until 1981, when he finally immigrated to the United States with his American-born wife.

His entire village had been ethnically and religiously cleansed by the far better-armed invading Muslim PLO. The poorly-armed Christians were all murdered or forced to flee, after two thousand years of their people living in the same town. After leaving Lebanon and embracing freedom in the United States, he had decided that he would never again, under any circumstances, be disarmed.

ATF agent George Hammet was livid, slamming the heavy door of the Suburban shut behind him. "Do you see now, do you see now, the kind of shit we have to take from these stinking gun nuts every damn day in and day out? You guys saw it! Those bastards hate the government, they hate us, they're armed to the teeth, they're crazy and they're itching for a fight! They think their almighty Second Amendment is some kind of holy writ, something Charlton Heston brought down from the mountain like the Ten Commandments! You just cannot get it into these stupid crackers' skulls that the only real 'militia' today is the National Stinking Guard! These gun nuts all think they're Thomas Stinking Jefferson, and we're the God damned redcoats!"

After a moment of embarrassed silence in the truck as they drove off, one of the FBI men said, "Well, uh, George, it looks like you won't have to go all the way to Idaho or Montana to find the militias any more. It looks like you've got them all over your own backyard these days."

"You've got that right. They're everywhere. Right wing loonie-tunes have been stockpiling guns and ammo like you wouldn't believe. If you saw the amount of .223 and .308 that's been getting bought every month, it would blow your mind. These gun nuts, they don't buy a hundred rounds at a time any more. They buy a thousand, they buy ten thousand, they buy it by the case and the truck load, I kid you not!

"But we've got some tricks up our sleeves too, believe you me! They talk about resisting, they talk about a fight, well…they'll see. They call us 'jack-booted thugs', right? We're going to show them our jack-boots, right in their damned teeth!" Hammet was banging his fist on the door ledge by the window as he shouted.

"Who's this 'we' George?" asked an FBI agent sitting behind Hammet. He was the one who had flashed the secret 'thumbs up' while leaving the gun store. "Don't try to enlist the FBI in your war against gun owners! My Dad's a gun owner, and so are all my brothers. Hell, so am I! Don't you know, every year ten or fifteen million Americans buy deer stamps and go off into the woods with scoped rifles? Have you ever thought about that? I'm not so sure it's a great idea to piss off millions of 'gun nuts' with high-powered scoped rifles. I mean, they've got us out-numbered about a thousand to one."

Hammet was laboring to control his breathing so that he could speak normally. "That's the hunters, they're okay. I'm talking about the wackjobs with the assault rifles."

"Okay… So exactly how are you going to find the wackjobs in the middle of those 15 million hunters?"

"Oh trust me. We've got some ideas. We've been working on that problem for a long, long time. We'll be able to sort them all out when the time comes."

6

The remaining ATF Headquarters offices on the eighth floor of the Treasury building were normally deserted by six o'clock on a Friday evening, except for the duty sections. With the Stadium Massacre investigation running at fever pitch, and the assault rifle turn-in deadline looming over them, more officials than usual were still in their offices. But one by one the last remaining supergrades were slipping away, leaving their secretaries and admin assistants to close up shop. The field agents would be beating the bushes around the stadium and down in southeastern Virginia all weekend, and nationwide the Field Offices would be coordinating the procedures for the collection of the banned weapons, but the senior officials were going home. They preferred to be "reachable" at home via cell phones and email. As they rationalized it, they were "on duty 24 hours a day," so there was no need for them to physically be at Headquarters over a weekend.

Frank Castillo, the Deputy Director of the BATFE, was on the phone with his wife and clearing some items on his desk when his secretary called him on the intercom.

"Mr. Castillo, Mr. Malvone is here to see you."

Frank Castillo sank into his black leather high-backed swivel chair and stared at the ceiling. Then he punched the button on his intercom. "Nancy, give me five minutes, and then send him in." The five minutes was just to make Malvone cool his heels in the outer office. He said to his wife, "Honey, I'll see you at home; I've got to go now. Bye."

Wally Malvone was the Deputy Assistant Director of the ATF's Office of Firearms, Explosives and Arson, but in reality he was much more that that, primarily because he was politically very well connected. Malvone also had a rough charisma which charmed many of his seniors, all the way up to the Attorney General's office. At the same time he was seen as a macho field operator who commanded unflinching loyalty from the troops. He had come to the ATF after an unusual career path which led from the FBI to a senior staff position with Senator Schuleman in the 1990's, and then back to federal law enforcement at ATF as an early-promoted GS-15. The promotion was widely considered to be a result of his political drag over on Capitol Hill.

In spite of the fact that he had spent most of his middle-grade years as a senate staffer and not in federal law enforcement, he was the only ATF GS-15 ever to regularly show up on the eighth floor in a black tactical uniform, dirty and smelling of gun smoke. It was his style to let them know that he had personally been out on the firing ranges with his experimental unit. After moving to the Office of Firearms, Malvone had quickly pushed for the creation of a new tactics development group, the generically named "Special Training Unit." This effort stalled initially, but in the post 9-11 federal law enforcement environment, funding for many types of novel counter-terrorism groups had been allocated. After the ATF had moved most of its functions from Treasury to Justice in 2003, Malvone had worked his political contacts to secure some of the added transitional funding, and his small experimental unit grew once again.

Castillo had not supported the creation of this oddity, but Malvone obviously had clout in high places and the unit had been formed anyway, drawing most of its original personnel from ATF's Special Response Team. The STU members were officially still carried on the SRT for accounting purposes, even though they were virtually independent, and answered only to Malvone.

The STU also became a collection point for ATF Special Agents on administrative hold following incidents of excessive force, or the repeated "misapplication" of evidence in pursuing investigations. In a short period of time, the STU had become an ATF-wide dumping station for a certain species of unwanted "problem children" that Malvone thought were deserving of a second (or third) chance.

Some of the STU personnel had been among those reprimanded in the 1990's for their involvement in the overtly racist "Good Old Boys Roundup." This was the whites-only law enforcement barbecue and picnic weekend held every summer in Tennessee, which was traditionally organized by ATF agents on their own time. Malvone claimed in justification that the salvaged "good old boys" had unique knowledge of, and contacts within, certain white supremacist fringe groups, which were connected to various right wing militias. Frank Castillo never doubted the veracity of that claim for a moment.

Promptly after five minutes the door opened and Wally Malvone entered, thankfully in a suit and tie. As usual his face was sunburned below the level which would be covered by sunglasses and a ball cap, giving him an unusual two-tone look: red from the nose down, white from his eyes up and over his shaved dome. Malvone's bald head always reminded Castillo of his own rapidly receding hairline. Soon he would have to decide if he was going to continue the comb-over, get transplants, or just shave it all off like Malvone.

The only hair showing above Malvone's collar was his shaggy walrus-sized brown mustache, which he deliberately kept hanging over his lip a half-inch beyond regulation length. This was just enough to irritate the more conscientious ATF senior officials, but not quite enough to make an issue of. Flaunting dress and grooming standards was one of the many ways Malvone ingratiated himself with the rank-and-file agents, and at the same time tweaked the noses of his superiors.

"Have a seat Walter, what's on your mind? Something come up?"

"Yes sir, I'm afraid so. We're getting some new intell reports from southeastern Virginia... Apparently it's been confirmed that Shifflett belonged to a hardcore clandestine militia group down there. This group's nothing at all like the open militia buffoons we usually deal with; they're the real deal. Ex-Green Berets, that sort. Now some of them have dropped out of sight, and we believe they may be planning some kind of violent response to the new assault rifle law. I'd like permission to send the STU Team down there, but to operate independently of the Joint Task Force."

Operate independently of FBI control and oversight is what you mean, thought Castillo. Malvone had created the Special Training Unit to develop new operational concepts and tactics to aggressively and proactively go after domestic terror groups, instead of merely waiting and reacting to terrorist incidents the way the FBI and ATF's "conventional" special response teams did. It was understood that the purpose of the Special Training Unit was to develop new tactics which might at some time in the future be used by the ATF's SRT. The STU itself would only be activated and "go operational" in the event of a serious domestic terrorism crisis.

For the past year the unpublicized STU Team had cross-trained with the FBI's Hostage Rescue Team, the Army's Delta, the Navy's "Development Group," and other elite units. The rest of the time it was conducting its own in-house training under Malvone's direction. Much of their training took place at private commercial academies set up to teach advanced skills to selected military and law enforcement units and personnel. Selected STU Team members learned to fly small planes out of rough fields, use cars as weapons both in pursuit and in defense, and pick locks in order to conduct black-bag "information retrieval" operations. All of the STU personnel received the latest and most advanced training in how to fire submachine guns and pistols, equipped with both visible and invisible lights and lasers, to "clear" buildings in pitch darkness.

Frank Castillo had observed some of their "CQB" or close-quarters-battle training at Quantico. The STU men were real pit bulls, straining at the leash and eager to bite. They wore non-regulation length hair and were not often seen in either a jacket and tie or the standard black tactical gear. They preferred to conduct most of their training in a variety of casual civilian attire, in order to always retain the element of surprise. Conventional hostage and terrorism response situations would still be handled by uniformed and helmeted FBI Hostage Rescue Teams or ATF Special Response Teams. The STU was created to develop the tactics needed to take the war on domestic terrorism to the next level: the preemptive attack.

And now, thought Castillo, Wally Malvone wants to send his Special Training Unit down to southeastern Virginia to go after a clandestine militia group. Not to arrest them, but to "take them out." This was not going to happen on Frank Castillo's watch! Not even in the wake of the Stadium Massacre.

He kept his composure and answered evenly, "Not yet Wally, we're not there yet, and with luck, we never will be. Let's wait and see what happens down there with the Joint Task Force."

Malvone seemed nonplussed at being refused, and replied, "Okay, but if the balloon goes up, I mean if the shit hits the fan, the STU is ready to go. And if the situation really gets bad, I think we'll need to think about designating more 'proactive' units in a big hurry. The SRT is fine, as far as it goes, but we both know it has a certain...institutional mindset. I mean, it can't just switch modes of operation and be as effective as a unit trained from the start for preemption."

"Walter, we've been over this before, it's old ground."

"I know, but the situation is different now, since the stadium. I'd like to show you something... I've written up a proposal covering how the STU could be used in an emergency situation. It's a concept of operations for preemptive operations, for when we're faced with a domestic terrorist threat, and we've got an idea who the players are. I'd appreciate it if you'd pass the copies on to the Director and the Attorney General's office."

Malvone passed over three copies of his proposal. The cover sheet was titled "The Special Projects Division: Preempting Domestic Terrorism."

"Thanks Wally, I'll read it over the weekend." Castillo left the three copies on his desk untouched.

Malvone thanked Castillo for his time, rose and left.

Where does the ATF find guys like that, Castillo wondered, spinning his chair around to look out over the White House. In his Army days men like Malvone were derided as "snake eaters," and it was a matter of constant debate whether they were more of a danger to the enemy or to their own side. Today it seemed like the military was practically run by the Special Forces and SEALs, and the special operations "commando mentality" was beginning to permeate law enforcement as well. Malvone was not unique in seeking harder-edged military-type solutions to domestic problems. He was just an extreme example.

Malvone's personal choice for the STU Team's operational commander was a prime example of the type of knuckle-dragging Neanderthal he preferred. Bob Bullard actually made Malvone seem like a refined gentleman by comparison. Although on paper Bullard was a highly decorated ATF career veteran, Castillo privately considered him to be a psychopath, and so did many others with access to the restricted files. He had been at the ATF's botched raid in Waco, and ever since he had hated right wing gun nuts with a burning passion.

Bullard had also led several pre-dawn raids against homes where the suspects were machine gunned in their beds, supposedly while reaching for a pistol. In the community it was widely believed that these consistently deadly raids were the result of Bullard settling old scores, against criminals who had humiliated him by beating his cases in court. It was said that Bob Bullard had a very long memory, and a very short fuse.

To Frank Castillo's thinking, the entire STU was a waste of funding. It was a unit in search of a mission at best, and a ticking bomb at worst. Obviously Malvone had "guardian angels" much higher up the food chain than the Deputy Director of ATF, probably going back to his time as a staffer for Jack Schuleman, the powerful Senate Judiciary Committee Chairman. Castillo, who had been promoted on time and risen through a conventional federal law enforcement career path, despised the political pull that fast-track outsiders like Malvone brought with them.

He threw Malvone's proposals into his open briefcase, snapped it shut and got ready to go home, dreading the long bumper-to-bumper drive down I-66 into northern Virginia.

As dusk was spreading Brad pulled into the parking lot of Lester's Diner in Highpoint. He didn't see any four-wheel-drive trucks carrying ATV's or portable kennels for hunting dogs, or any camouflage-painted river boats on trailers. Lester's didn't appear to be the staging area for any "rod and gun club" outing on this particular Friday evening. There was just a typical assortment of cars and trucks and a few motorcycles.

Since his visit from the feds Thursday afternoon Brad had carried the cell phone they had given him at all times. He had no way to be certain, but he was fairly sure that the offer of the "free" phone had been an enticement to encourage him to carry it with him. Brad knew that the phone could be used as a tracking device, and possibly even a remotely activated microphone and transmitter. In the days of universally-carried cell phones, there was less and less need to put a "wire" on an informant, because the cell phone carried in plain sight could often do the same job. As an occasional ocean sailor (crewing on other people's yachts) Brad had kept up with developments in Global Positioning System technology. He knew it would be a simple trick to modify a phone to silently receive and transmit GPS location data.

Brad discreetly checked the parking lot and up and down the street for dark Suburbans or possible surveillance vans, but he knew that the absence of such a vehicle meant very little. The cell phone he carried in his shirt pocket could very likely do the same eavesdropping job, at far lower cost, and with a huge savings in manpower for the feds.

He could have left the phone on his boat or in his truck, but he had a plan in mind for it. If the phone was indeed a tracker, he wanted to assure his unseen federal monitors that he was indeed routinely carrying it. Then when he truly needed to disappear, he might gain some head start time by leaving it on the dock while he fled down the river or out to sea on Guajira.

Of course, the cell phone might just be a cell phone, in which case all of his worrying and scheming was for nothing. He had often read that a healthy dose of paranoia was a necessary virtue for any intelligence operative, but that paranoia taken to extremes could be paralyzing. Now Brad truly understood those words.

Since his forced recruitment in the black Suburban, he had been seeing hidden cameras up in power pole transformer boxes, and surveillance teams in every van on the street. He was even feeling the gaze of cameras high above him in small planes or unmanned drones. The military had provided air surveillance assets during the Beltway Sniper case, and there was every reason to believe that they were still doing so when requested. Overhead watchers could be tuning in on his "free" cell phone, to keep him under their unblinking eyes...

Brad forced himself to shake off the mounting paranoia, and walked across the parking lot to Lester's Diner.

He had given this meeting with the Black Water Rod & Gun Club a great deal of thought, planning out the possible permutations, considering his best options and approaches. He wore long blue jeans held up with a wide leather pistol-shooter's belt, made to hold competition holsters firmly in place. Such pistol belts were a subtle marking recognized within the fraternity of serious shooters, but they went unnoticed by outsiders. On his feet he wore his Gore-Tex-lined water proof Danner boots, which were equally at home in the woods and swamps, or a country bar or pool hall. Topping it off he wore a brown Western style long sleeved shirt: if he was under observation by his handlers they would see that he had come dressed and ready to join the gun club on whatever kind of outing they had in mind, in the woods or on the water.

In each of his pants pockets he had a different carefully written and folded note. Which note, if any, that he used would depend upon whom he found at the back tables of the diner, and his appraisal of the situation. He had studied the member list and the information given to him on the key members of the club, along with pictures taken from their DMV photos, and committed it all as best he could to his memory.

Brad Fallon walked up the front steps to the landing, pulled open the stainless steel and glass front door and stepped into Lester's Diner.

The place was busy; some folks were sitting in the waiting area waiting for tables to be cleared. No one paid any attention to him except a young brunette waitress, who made eye contact and flashed a brief smile as she went by with a tray. He walked past the counter and the front room tables, passing salesmen and truckers and farmers with their wives and kids. He continued all the way around the "L" shaped dining room to an extra-large circular booth in the furthest corner. Six men sat around the table, sharing draft beer from pitchers. To Brad, beer instead of coffee and iced tea meant there would be no hunting tonight.

He walked directly up to the table, nodded to them, gave a half smile and said, "Mind if I join you gentlemen?" All six faces turned to the stranger. Thank God, he thought, he recognized one of the men he had already met. It was Barney Wheeler, the old guy with the short gray beard that had been in the hardware store Tuesday morning. Even before that, Brad had already seen him on his creek: Wheeler had a small blue houseboat which could fit under most of the highway and railroad bridges throughout Tidewater Virginia and on into the Carolinas. Many houseboats wound up as permanent fixtures tied to the same dock year after year, but Wheeler used his boat for serious inland cruising. Wheeler had passed Guajira's dock in his houseboat a few times and they had exchanged hand waves.

It was a relief to find Barney Wheeler at the table, he felt certain that no old guy who lived on a river houseboat could possibly be an ATF or FBI informant. At least, it hardly seemed likely. A few years before he had read that five out of the six leaders of the Aryan Nations white supremacist group in Idaho had been paid informants for different government departments, spying on one another and making their separate reports. The feds strongly believed in using multiple informants to determine the truthfulness of each other one, or when their loyalties might be drifting off course. In the case of the Aryan Nations, the BATF and FBI informants had in effect constituted the core of the Aryan Nations leadership, unknowingly spying on each others' spies for several years.

Brad could only hope that if there was in informant already sitting at the round table, it was not his fellow boater Barney Wheeler.

"Pull up a chair Brad. Fellas, this here is Brad... I didn't catch your last name..."

"Fallon. Brad Fallon."

"Right. Fellas, this here is Brad Fallon. Brad's got a big old sailboat way up Little Nansemond Creek, except it's not much of a sailboat, being as it's got no mast, but then it never would have fit under all those bridges. Brad, you've been working in the oil fields up in Alaska, isn't that right?"

"That's right, the ANWR. I'm a machinist, but mostly I've been doing pipe fitting."

"Brad, you having a beer?" asked a tall red haired man. "It ain't against your religion is it?"

"Hell no it ain't! Sure I'll have a cold one, thanks." Brad dragged over an extra chair from an uncleared empty table and sat at the opening of the booth. Wheeler gestured to their waitress, and another glass and a fresh pitcher of beer was quickly brought over to the table of the well-known regulars. Brad slipped her a ten dollar bill before anyone could beat him to it, establishing right away that he was not a moocher.

He got right to the point, ahead of their questions. "I heard in town that you guys know the hunting scene around here, and I'm up for just about any hunting or shooting you got going."

A stocky balding man wearing gold wire rimmed glasses introduced himself. "Nice to meet you Brad. Gary Milford." He leaned across the table to shake Brad's hand. "You get to do much hunting up in Alaska?"

"When I could, between contracts. I've taken moose and caribou, and I've been out for brown bear once."

"What are you using on the big game up there?" asked another man.

"Nothing too special, just standard stuff. 300 Winmag and .338."

"Now that's some hunting!" said Milford. "Damn, that's real hunting! I'd like to get up to Alaska some day and go after a brownie. I saw you at Mineral Springs last month, I know you can shoot," he said, filling Brad's beer glass from the new pitcher.

Brad slipped the tiny folded-up note from his left back pocket and palmed it. Then he reached with his right hand across the table for his beer just a little too quickly and "accidentally" tipped it over away from Barney, who was next to him on his left. The spill spread across the table, the men jumped back in their seats laughing and cheerfully berating him. While all eyes were on the flowing beer spill Brad quickly slid the note under Barney Wheeler's hand and whispered "read this." No one noticed, the diversion worked as intended.

Wheeler put the note on his lap and peeked at it while their laughing waitress mopped up the spilled beer with a bar towel. She was blond and fairly young and still attractive, so with her tight white blouse and friendly smile and perfume hovering closely over them no one cared about the beer, or thought it was strange that a crack shot like Brad could be so clumsy with his hands, especially when he was still cold sober.

Barney glanced at the note; in tiny print on both sides it said "IMPORTANT! READ THIS IN THE MEN'S ROOM NOW! NOT A JOKE!" Barney slipped the note into his own pants pocket, and after the

58

table was dried off and their waitress was gone he said, "Excuse me Brad, nature calls."

In the men's room he locked himself in a stall and sat down, carefully unfolding the paper over his knees, and then he slipped on his reading glasses and read it:

> "I was visited at my place yesterday by 6 FBI agents. I was shown one FBI credential. They had a black suburban and a maroon crown vic. The truck was full of assault gear in the back. They are blackmailing me and forcing me to infiltrate the BWR&G club. They think it's a secret militia front. Please tell me 'no thanks' and brush me off, tell me to get lost in a way that the FBI will believe. You may already have an informant in your group. I'm dead serious about this. Tear up and flush this note."

Barney Wheeler re-read the note twice, and then he did tear it up into small pieces and flushed it and returned to the booth. The note seemed to fit with the phone call he had gotten from Joe Bardiwell at Freedom Arms yesterday. He'd have to stop by the gun store and talk to Joe about it all. He could hardly believe that the FBI would be investigating the rod and gun club!

Back at the table the men were all discussing the Stadium Massacre, Jimmy Shifflett, and the new gun law. No one thought that Shifflett had acted alone. They even doubted whether he was the actual shooter. Shifflett had come along on a few gun club coon hunts years back, but even then the boy was too weak and he couldn't keep up, and he had stopped coming. Then the subject shifted over to the semi-auto rifle ban. Each man in various ways mockingly stated that he had either turned his rifles in already, intended to do so, or had lost them overboard on a fishing trip. This was all said with winking and rolling of the eyes.

Brad finally asked, "So what's the hunting look like this fall?"

Wheeler said "Looks like we won't be doing any hunting or shooting for a while, not until this mess with the new law gets sorted out. Bow season won't open for a few more weeks, you still going to be around then?"

"I hope not. As soon as I can get my boat ready to go down the river I'm putting my mast up, and then I'm heading for the islands."

"That sounds like a hell of a good plan about now, the way things are going," replied Wheeler. "I don't think any of us will be doing much shooting for a while anyway, not until things settle down. Things are just too damn crazy now. It's a bad time to be a hunter around here."

Brad had another beer with them, finishing the pitcher. Then he excused himself and left, again seeing no visible signs of surveillance teams inside or outside. If Wheeler was an FBI informant, then he was truly 100% screwed. Otherwise he felt optimistic that he had a chance of wriggling out of the federal grip, having demonstrably given the infiltration attempt his best shot to no avail.

He wondered if their table conversation had been recorded or transmitted, or if one of the men he had shared the table with was a government informant. He wondered if "George" was somewhere analyzing tapes of what had transpired in Lester's, but he needn't have worried. George had other plans for his Friday night, and Brad Fallon was not even faintly on his mind.

7

The Special Training Unit supervisors had been playing poker and drinking in the basement club room at Wally Malvone's house for a few hours. This was their normal Friday night routine when they were in Washington. Malvone lived in a moderately sized older home, on the Maryland side of the Potomac River, a few miles south of the DC beltway. What his house lacked in size it made up in location, with water frontage on a small bay which opened onto the Potomac. His long narrow property bordered large wooded estates on both sides, so he had no close neighbors to complain about raucous party noise no matter what the hour. All night blow outs with twenty or more STU members and sometimes their wives or girlfriends were not uncommon, because Malvone believed that both hard training and hard partying promoted team camaraderie.

Bob Bullard turned over the last card in his hand. "Three ladies Joe. Looks like you're sucking hind tit again." He raked in a pot of well over four hundred dollars in red white and blue chips.

"That's all for me gentlemen, I'm finished," said a younger agent across from Bullard, pushing back from the table. He was a good looking young man with light brown hair.

"Count on Hollywood to bail out first," said Joe Silvari. Silvari was the second in command of the Special Training Unit, and was the leader of its ten man technical support team. "Hollywood" was Tim Jaeger, one of the two team leaders.

Malvone said, "Joe, if you had a hot piece of ass like Cindy's warmed up and waiting in the sack for you, you'd be bailing out too."

"That's the truth," Silvari replied, laughing. "Hell, you would've never seen me here tonight at all! I mean, I haven't had anything like that in oh….well I guess I never did, dammit! Nobody as hot as Cindy anyway! Don't get old Hollywood, what ever you do, don't get old."

The rest of them stretched, scratched, yawned and began to get up. Malvone said, "Look, before you and Michael take off, I've got some goodies for you."

Tim Jaeger, the one they called Hollywood, and Michael Shanks, who with his beak-like nose and weak chin would never be mistaken for a movie star, were the leaders of the STU's "Blue" and "Gold" teams. Each was a former military junior officer with specops qualifications. Jaeger had been a Navy SEAL, and Shanks an Army Ranger. Both were hard chargers in their early thirties, and both had seen action in Iraq and Afghanistan.

"I've got a couple of bags for each of you." Malvone went to a closet under the stairs which led up to the kitchen, and dragged out two heavily-loaded green canvas military duffel bags. Then he went back into the closet and carried out two black vinyl gym bags. The duffel bags were lashed into stiff bundles with green parachute cord cinched around them.

He said, "The big ones each have ten assault rifles in them. We got them from a couple of militia nut-jobs. None of them were ever logged in, so they'll all trace back to their original point of sale, and then to the morons we took them from. The dumb jerks always think they're catching a break, just having their guns confiscated! If they only knew… And don't ask me how I wound up with them, you don't need to know."

"The gym bags each have ten pistols, same story. Here's the deal: when we start going after these militia groups, these guns will be our insurance policy. No matter what else we get, we can always pin possession of the guns on them, and the serial numbers will connect them to other militias. That way, we'll tie them all into one big national militia network, and once that happens, it'll be a lot easier to start getting really proactive on their asses and taking them out."

Jaeger and Shanks were smiling as they easily lifted the heavy bags, hefting their weight and imagining the cool toys inside.

"Dirty tricks are what I'm talking about boys, dirty tricks. We're taking the gloves off. We know who the enemy is, and we're going to hunt them down and destroy them! We're going to fight fire with fire! We're not going to sit around waiting for them to hit us first any more."

Tim Jaeger flashed his movie star grin and exclaimed "Hoo freakin' ya! It's about time!" He gave Shanks a casual high five.

Malvone said, "We're not going to Norfolk for now, not just yet, but stand by, I have a feeling things are moving down there. Keep these little bundles safe and handy, and remember: they've never been logged in, so be careful. All right guys, that's all I've got for now, see you on Monday. And Tim, give Cindy a wet one for me… okay you assholes, beat it, and take care of those bags."

Shanks and Jaeger went out the basement door, which exited at ground level to the backyard on the river side of the house. Each of them toted a duffel bag over a shoulder by its carrying strap, and a gym bag in their free hand. The duffels weighed nearly a hundred pounds each, but both operators handled them like they were full of Styrofoam packing peanuts. Nobody in the Blue or Gold Teams bench-pressed less than 250 pounds, including the team leaders. The STU operators were all seriously muscular guys, able to climb scaling ladders like gorillas while wearing full tactical gear and body armor, and of course carrying their weapons. It was not a job for pencil neck geeks to say the least.

When they were gone Joe Silvari said, "Wally, I've got to take off too. We've been on the road training for I don't know how many weekends, and I can't be sneaking in at zero dark thirty smelling like a brewery when I'm finally in town. If I keep this up, what's left of my marriage is going to go straight down the shitter."

"Well Joe, I guess it's just a question of your priorities." Malvone said this only half jokingly. "I was married twice, how many was it for you Bob, three times? Yeah, if you can stay married to one woman for ten years in this business, either you're not working hard enough, or you have one hell of an understanding woman."

"Or a woman who can't wait for you to hit the road, so that she can step out on you," said Bob Bullard, who was now sitting on the couch channel surfing with the sound muted on the big screen TV. They were still showing replays of the football fans going over the railings, and showing survivors in hospitals, and more funerals than anyone could keep up with. Unlike in the aftermath of 9-11, the bodies of the Stadium Massacre victims were all very much available for funerals and burials.

"Yeah, well, maybe. Anyway Wally, I can't push it, I've got what I got and I don't want to lose it."

Malvone walked with Silvari out through the back door, around the house and up the path to his car. "Joe, I gave Castillo my proposal to activate the STU and turn it into the Special Projects Division today. You know he's by the book, so he won't go for it, but he'll pass it on up to Boxell. Wilson's already got a copy; he's just waiting for it to come through channels." David Boxell was the Director of the BATFE; Paul Wilson was the Deputy Attorney General. "Boxell's a dip shit, but he'll see which way the wind is blowing and go along. Wilson's already in our pocket, he's going to be our pitchman to the Attorney General and the President."

"Is Wilson still banging that little senorita in the hot tub?" asked Silvari.

"I guess so. I think she's still at his place. Who'd have ever guessed that an old goat like Wilson would go for a teenage taco like her?"

"Did Wilson's wife ever find out?"

"No, and she won't as long as he does his part," said Malvone.

"You sent him a copy of the video tape?"

"Damn right. It's my favorite movie; I've only watched it about a hundred times."

"Yeah Wally, that was a nice morning's work."

The STU had its own single-engine Piper Lance, and had obtained a BigEye surveillance pod for it. The BigEye was a gyro-stabilized combination video camera for daytime use, and infrared camera for night use. An operator up in the plane could put the camera's cursor mark on a stationary or moving ground target and the camera would lock on to it even as the plane circled high above, out of sight and sound of its quarry.

The extensive use of light planes was a tradition in the ATF going back decades; from the time when the "revenue agents" had flown them to spot bootleg liquor stills from the air. These pilot-qualified agents bragged that for them ATF stood for 'agents that fly.' The numerous flying special agents and ATF light planes often permitted them to reach the scenes of federal crimes involving illegal firearms or explosives before any other agencies. Any one-horse Podunk town with a dirt landing strip nearby could usually have ATF agents on the ground in a few hours at most. The ATF was independently air-mobile to a greater degree than most other agencies at the light plane end of the aviation spectrum.

After a brief familiarization period with the BigEye Malvone gave his air team the addresses of a dozen senior government officials who were in a position to help the STU. They hit pay dirt on a Sunday morning in June when the Piper was flying lazy eights over Fairfax County Virginia, and they noticed activity at the estate of Deputy Attorney General Paul Wilson. A Mercedes arrived with a young couple who turned out to be Wilson's daughter and son-in-law. Mrs. Wilson then left with them to attend church services.

Soon after the driveway's automatic gate closed behind the Mercedes, Paul Wilson had appeared in a bathrobe on the back patio of the mansion by the swimming pool, accompanied by someone else. The stabilized zoom lens of the BigEye then recorded in intimate detail the white-haired federal official and a black-haired girl playing in the Jacuzzi, with no detail left to the imagination for the next fifteen minutes. Upon further investigation the girl had turned out to be the 16 year old daughter of the Wilson's Costa Rican housekeeper, who had taken the day off.

Malvone was smiling broadly at the memory. "As soon as I saw that tape I knew we'd own Wilson, we'd have him in our pocket. When the time comes he's going to go to bat for us, big time, and we'll get the Special Projects Division approved."

"The FBI's going to fight it. They'll never let ATF have a new division with that much power."

"That's where you're wrong Joe, the STU or SPD or what ever we end up calling it is going to be seen as a dirty outfit for dirty jobs, and the FBI won't want any part of it. If the SPD falls on its face, the stink won't rub off on them. They'll be glad to let the ATF have it, and let the ATF take the hit if things go wrong. By the time they figure out what's really going on, the Special Projects Division will be too big for them to stop."

Silvari said, "Yeah, that's one of the things I love about this the most: sticking it to the FBI. For once the ATF is out in front."

"When I got that jerkoff Boxell to authorize the STU, he never dreamed what kind of 'Special Training' we'd be doing. And once we got Wilson's 'nanny problem' on video tape I knew I'd be able to push the

SPD through, it was just a matter of time. And you know what? I've got a feeling it's going to finally happen this week."

"And all because of Shifflett."

"Yep, all because of Shifflett. I guess there really is a silver lining in every dark cloud. Sometimes good things even come out of tragedies. Take it easy Joe, see you Monday."

"See you Monday."

Malvone went back into his house through the front door on the first floor, then into his kitchen and down the stairs to the basement club room. Bob Bullard had switched from beer to Wild Turkey, and held out another smoke-colored glass for his boss. Malvone sipped it, but he was more of a scotch drinker himself, when he wasn't having a martini. He went over to his stereo and turned the volume up on a twangy country music station. Silvari had swept the basement for bugs earlier, demonstrating some new gadgets for the other STU leaders, but Malvone and Bullard were old school and still liked to crank up the music before having a sensitive private conversation.

"Since the stadium, we're right at the critical point," said Malvone. "We just need to give a little push, and the President will be ready to let the STU Team go hot. I've seen some reports that covert militia groups in Virginia are planning more actions, but their timetables are unknown, and we don't know their targets. What we need to do is disrupt them, throw them off balance and put them on defensive. What I've got in mind is an 'accidental' premature explosion. I've got a list of three possible subjects for you. I want you to head down to Norfolk tomorrow morning, but don't check in with the Field Office, obviously. Use the credit card I gave you for your expenses, and use this prepaid cell phone to call my pager and I'll call you right back. Don't use your own cell phone down there, okay? Don't even take it. Don't leave any tracks."

"When does it need to happen?"

"No later than Monday morning."

"A house or a car?"

"A vehicle if possible, but a house if you have to."

"Do you have a device, or should I put one together?"

"I've got one." Malvone went back into his storage closet under the stairs and brought back two small brown cardboard shoe boxes. "There's ten pounds of C-4 in this one; the caps and firing assembly are in the other one. It's a radio firing device: dual frequencies, multiple safeties. The old garage door opener; nothing tricky. Check it out, you'll see." One of the advantages of working for the ATF in the firearms and explosives division was ready access to demolition materials for training purposes.

After a day at the Fort A. P. Hill demo range blasting holes in the ground, it was impossible for anyone to ascertain just how many pounds had been detonated, and how many pounds had gone home in the trunks of cars.

"I got the picture Wally. An unlucky stray radio emission, and a dangerous militia terrorist goes kaboom on his way to planting a bomb."

"That's it exactly—kaboom too soon." They both chuckled at their witticism. "You provide the 'stray radio signal', and America breathes a sigh of relief that the incompetent bomber blew himself up, instead of his target. Same old-same old. I'll admit it's not original, but it always works."

"What about bystanders?"

"Well, just use your judgment. Try to avoid collateral damage, of course, but it's got to happen by Monday morning. When it's done, call the pager number I gave you with the prepaid phone, I'll call you back. Don't get sloppy; do it right, okay?"

"Wally, you know I'm a professional."

"I know you are Bob. By Monday, right?"

"You got it. By Monday morning." Bullard swallowed the rest of his bourbon and left through the basement door with the two shoe boxes.

Malvone glanced at the wall clock over his bar; it was after one AM, early Saturday morning. He'd been prowling between his first floor office (where he was checking a few news-oriented websites while keeping an eye on the cable news channels) and his kitchen, where he was grazing on the honey ham and roast beef left over from his party. By now things should be happening in Tidewater Virginia, and any time he'd be getting the first situation report.

Nothing was being reported on the television from southeastern Virginia yet. CBA news was rerunning an old documentary on right wing militia types firing fifty-caliber rifles on a farm in Wyoming. It was at least the second time Malvone had seen that five year old "special report" aired since the stadium. Any piece of videotape showing middle-aged white men in camouflage uniforms firing "assault rifles" which had been shot in the last decade had been dusted off and re-aired as if it were breaking news. These clips were always accompanied by dire warnings from Malvone's old boss Senator Jack Schuleman, or other perennial gun control advocates such as Senator Geraldine Randolph of Maryland, or Senator Ludenwright of Delaware.

Over on FreeAmericans.net, the usual paranoid anti-government right wingers were spouting their usual conspiracy theories. The beauty of these conspiracy nuts was that their ravings totally discredited any factual information that surfaced which could point to an actual conspiracy. As long as these "tin foil hatters" (as they were called) continued to weave everything from the JFK assassination to Oklahoma City to 9-11 together in grand plots, no "serious" reporter would ever pay attention to what had actually happened 1,250 yards east of the stadium last Sunday.

Some of the many posters on FreeAmericans.net were treading dangerously close to what had actually happened, but their bits of information, mainly on Shifflett's background, were still submerged in a sea of absurdity. Anyway, Shifflett had already been analyzed, discussed, and dealt with in the media. The "fact" that he was a white racist militia kook was accepted as gospel truth on all the networks, even on the right wing TOP News.

At 1:35 AM a "FreeAmerican" with the screen name of SwampFever posted a self-generated news story that there had been several arsons in Tidewater in the past two hours, and that according to information gleaned from police scanners and eyewitness accounts, the arsonists seemed to be targeting gun stores.

Malvone's pager chirped. Hammet was contacting him. It was a pager he had bought for thirty dollars cash at a mall kiosk, good for a year, with no contract required and no information given. He jotted down the number, converted it to the number of the pay phone he would call, and punched the new number into his prepaid throwaway cell phone. The call was picked up after the first ring. There would be no trace of the call that could ever be connected to Wally Malvone.

"Hello."

"Hi boss, it's me," said George Hammet

"Uh huh. I've been watching the news. Nothing's on TV yet, but there's something being reported on the internet. Tell me about it."

"It looks like we went eleven for eleven. Clean sweep."

Malvone replied, "I see…great. Well, we've really jammed a sharp stick in their eye now. We'll just have to wait and see what happens next. Any loose ends? Any problems? Any exposure on our side?"

"No, none. The cars were all wiped down and abandoned; everybody used gloves, no problems. Say boss, I've been watching the local news down here today; I might have a nice target of opportunity."

"Hmm… tell me about it."

"We've got sort of a local Louie Farrakhan down here. He's on all the local news, raving that Shifflett was a white Christian racist, the 'militias' are trying to start a race war, the usual stuff. He goes everywhere with armed guards. You know, 'we're going to defend ourselves by any means necessary' and that kind of talk. He's a very intimidating guy, and he's a pretty big player in the local black community."

"What did you have in mind?" asked Malvone.

"He has a storefront 'mosque' over in Portsmouth. I was thinking a drive-by might liven things up."

"Hmm... Well, that has potential. Sure, why not? Keep this one to yourself, and definitely don't use any of your local contacts. Do it solo. Use one of the, ah...items...I gave you, and then leave it there. Just hit the property, keep your exposure to a minimum, and don't take any chances. Don't do it unless it's just right. This sounds pretty good, it sounds like you're doing some great work. Keep it up, and we're going to go far together."

"Thank you sir, I won't let you down."

8

Ranya Bardiwell had made the 150 mile ride from Charlottesville to Suffolk at least forty times during her three years at the University
of Virginia. Saturday morning, after her first full week back at school, she
had returned from a three-mile run up Observatory Hill to have a phone
thrust into her hands by her frantic roommate, with a number to call
immediately. Upon calling she had been connected to a Suffolk police
sergeant who informed her that there had been a fire at her house, and she
needed to come home as soon as possible.

Why were the police calling about a fire? Could she speak to her
father? "Not right now, just come home as soon as possible."

Without changing out of her running clothes, she threw on jeans
and her jean jacket and boots, tossed her purse and a few items into a
daypack, pulled on her helmet and in minutes she was screaming down I-
64 on her Yamaha YZF 600. On her many trips between school and home
she had found the hidden locations of every radar trap that the state police
had ever dreamed of, but today she didn't even bother looking. The angels
were riding with her and she made the 150 miles in less than 80 minutes.
The road was wide open and where it wasn't she slalomed around cars as if
they were parked, sometimes splitting lanes between pairs of shocked
drivers like a streak, rarely dropping below one hundred miles per hour.

On her last half mile Ranya cut through the Union 76 to shave the
corner and shot down 32, downshifting rapidly in succession as she saw
the fire truck and all the police cars on the parking lot and along the road
next to her family business. There had been a fire all right, the walls of the
store were scorched black, and the Freedom Arms sign was barely visible
under the soot and charred paint. As she drew nearer and cleared the last
stand of pines, she looked across to her house, but it was gone!

She braked to a hard stop by the side of the road a hundred yards
away to survey the unbelievable scene: the store was burned and her house
was gone. On the lawn between where the house had stood and the store a
cluster of men were huddled over a black lump on the ground, and a darker
awareness took hold. Ranya kicked her bike into gear and shot around the
outside of the wire property line fence, just inside the trees to the open
back vehicle gate, and almost dumped the bike as she spun through the
turn. She dropped the bike with the engine still running and threw off her
helmet as the huddled men scattered before her, and she saw him.

It couldn't be him, it mustn't be him, but... She fell to her knees
and then onto her face, her eyes shut against upwelling tears, her wet face
in the burnt grass next to the charred body of her father. She had only
looked closely for a moment, her father's corpse had almost no face, little

of his head at all, just burned teeth and bones, but she had seen the silver cross he had worn around his neck and she was certain.

The Suffolk policemen who had been so surprised by her motor-cycle charge reacted quickly, covering the body with a blanket. An older uniformed police officer sat on the ground by her, pulling her face from the ground, pulling her away from the body, cradling her against his chest, his own tears falling on her neck.

"Oh Ranya darlin' I'm so sorry, I'm so sorry, I never would've... you never should have seen him that way, never, I'm so sorry. I thought for sure you'd be another hour getting here from school, you must have broken every record getting here...thank God you're safe, but what a thing for you to see..." Her arms were clenched tightly to her chest; her hands covered her face as she sobbed against him.

Suffolk police lieutenant Jasper Mosby had known Ranya since she was a toddler and he was a patrol officer. He had bought shooting supplies and a few guns at Freedom Arms over the years and had considered Joe Bardiwell a friend. Young Ranya had been a fixture around the shop as long as he could remember.

An only child, she had tried to fit into the macho world of the gun culture which revolved around her family business, but her amber eyes and long brown hair and ready smile had always betrayed her femininity. Countless boxes of ammunition had been purchased over the years by wistful men who had stopped by Freedom Arms secretly hoping to win a laugh from the increasingly curvaceous "tomboy" Ranya Bardiwell. During her teenage years customer visits to the store seemed to increase during the after-school hours when Ranya did her homework and helped at the counter.

Hundreds of cartons of reloads had been bought two at a time by customers willing to spot Ranya a free box, in exchange for an impromptu match on the indoor pistol range. As a teen she had mastered all calibers, and customers would buy her boxes of .45 and .44 magnum just to see her out-shoot grown men. She was considered a minor celebrity within local shooting circles, and she was the secret sweetheart of most of the men who knew her, including Jasper Mosby.

A similar pattern developed for her in the world of motorcycle riding. Customers who saw her zipping around the property on her lawn mower engine powered mini bike offered her rides on the back of their Harleys and Gold Wings, and this fine addiction also grew deep roots from an early age. Ranya was racing motocross by the time she was 13, and she was winning her share, but serious talks by her father and her orthopedic surgeons convinced her to give up competition, before her knee and shoulder damage became permanent and debilitating.

So Suffolk police lieutenant Jasper Mosby didn't care what anybody thought as he sat on the grass in his uniform with a young woman crying herself out against his chest. It was the least little favor he could give to his friend Joe Bardiwell, and he did not hurry her. After a while the sobbing stopped and he pulled her up and walked her away from the covered body.

"What happened Jasper? How did it happen?" Ranya's hair was full of grass, her eyes reddened and her face smeared with dirty tear tracks. "After midnight. It was an arson attack. Not just here, all around Tidewater. About a dozen gun stores were burned. It looks like your dad came out, I don't know, maybe an alarm went off, and he was shot. From the looks of it he was shot four or five times, then the arsonists burned him and burned your house. And they shot your dog too."

"Armalite? My dobie's dead too?

"Yep. He's over there, by the fence. You just rode by him on the way in. He must have heard them and alerted Joe. They were both shot... If Joe had a weapon, they took it."

"...I can't believe this is happening, I talked to him yesterday... I just can't believe... My father, my house, everything..."

"I know it darlin', I can't believe it either."

"What's going to happen to my father now? I don't know what to do." Ranya forced herself to talk as her tears kept falling. "Do I have to make...arrangements today? You know, I'm the last of my family, I'm the last one. The last one." She was trying very hard not to completely break down again.

"Not today Ranya. The M.E. has to take him first, it's the law. It looks like they tried to burn him to hide the gunshots, or maybe who ever did it was just crazy."

"God, I just can't believe this, any of this." She sighed deeply, and wiped her face with the sleeve of her denim jacket. "Well, I've got to bury my dog. I can do that can't I? Do they have to take my dog too?"

The dog had been killed by a single through-and-through bullet wound, and Mosby told her that she could have him.

"And Jasper, can you please get my father's silver cross? It was from my mother, from her family..."

"Hey, anybody have a shovel in their unit?" Mosby asked around among his subordinates and colleagues on the parking lot. Nobody did. Some friends of Bardiwell stood behind the yellow police line tape, and Mosby asked them too. A tallish young man with light brown hair standing alone behind the tape said that he did, and retrieved a soldier's folding shovel from the cab of his red pickup truck.

"Are you a friend of the Bardiwells?"

"I knew him," said the man, a steady enough looking fellow in his late twenties or early thirties, one that Mosby did not recognize as a local.

"The owner's daughter wants to bury her dog. Her dog was killed too. You mind helping her out? It's up to you."

"Sure, why not?"

"What's your name?"

"Brad Fallon."

"Fallon... you have a sailboat with no mast?"

"That's me."

"What were you doing here? Today I mean." Mosby had to ask, he couldn't leave a loose end like that hanging. Everyone who showed up at a crime scene had to be looked over carefully, especially arsons. In this case, with eleven gun stores burned, it was more a matter of professional habit than real suspicion that he asked.

"I heard the ammunition cooking off, and the sirens. Joe Bardiwell was working on a rifle for me."

"Okay Brad, I appreciate your help. Her name's Ranya Bardiwell. Let me grab a blanket from my trunk and we'll go around back."

Ranya was sitting cross-legged a yard from her dog, staring across the field to the smoldering wreckage and ashes of her house, and the silent pine woods beyond. Lieutenant Mosby crouched by her and put the silver cross into her hand. He had needed to clip the chain to remove it from Joe Bardiwell's remains.

"Ranya, this fellow volunteered to help you bury your dog." She said nothing, and after a few moments Mosby left them to return to his police business. Brad stood off a little to the side with his shovel and Mosby's gray army blanket.

After an uncomfortable minute she asked, "Who are you?"

"I'm just the guy who had the shovel. My name is Brad Fallon."

"What are you doing here?"

"I knew your father. As a customer I mean. He was working on a rifle for me."

"Looks like your rifle got burned up."

"It doesn't matter."

"What a great dog. I raised him from a puppy, he was nine years old. There was never a better dog. We named him Armalite, like the rifles, because he was skinny and black and fast. He was the best dobie there ever was, and he died trying to defend my father. I guess you can't ask for more in a dog." She began to quietly weep again, tearing up little pieces of grass and staring at the doberman.

"I'm sorry. I'm just real sorry about all this."

Another pause, another deep breath, and she said, "...Yeah."

"Looks like he was shot right through. It would have been quick anyway."

She said, "That's what they do. They shoot the dogs first."

Brad didn't know how to respond to that remark, so he unfolded the blanket next to the dog's back, rolled his stiff body onto it, and covered him in wrappings of gray wool. Then he slid his arms underneath like a fork lift and picked him up.

"Where are we going?"

"Into the woods behind the house. What used to be our house." Ranya carried the little shovel and they walked together through the back vehicle gate into the trees, walking across brown pine needles until she found a little shifting pool of golden morning sunlight which seemed right.

"Do you mind? I hate to ask, but I don't think I could do it." She was getting numb, still crying but no longer shaking.

"No. It's all right." Brad gently placed the stiff bundle on the ground and then unfolded the shovel and locked it in position and began to dig. Ranya stared deeper into the woods, her arms crossed, squeezing the cross tightly in her right fist. Brad didn't disturb her reverie. When the grave was deep enough he laid the wrapped bundle into the hole, and then covered it with sandy earth, and finally a covering of pine needles. "Listen," he said gently when he was done, "if you need anything, I'd be glad to help. I've got a truck, and you might need to move something from your house or the store, I don't know...but I'd be glad to do what I can."

Ranya didn't answer, her mind was a whirl of images and memories, so many happy memories, and some painful ones, now all burned to ashes like her family picture albums in the house. She hurt. And she knew from experience that the pain would not go away. But she had been well-trained over the years to endure pain, to focus on her target, to strive for her goal, and not to collapse under pressure. Her mother had died of brain cancer when Ranya was only eleven, she knew about grief and despair and survival. She had worked two summers as an ocean lifeguard on Virginia Beach, and she had saved lives and she had seen death. But this time she was alone.

"I need to talk to some people, there's so much to do... I didn't bring anything from school... I go to UVA, and now my whole house is gone..." She fought off her need to collapse again in tears. She could not permit herself that indulgence, she was a woman, she was twenty one, she was all that was left of the family and she needed to take care of her father and his affairs. There was no one else, she was the last, so she had to carry the burden or it would not be carried. She would not let her father down. The only way to honor the memory of her father and mother now was to be strong, and take care of business. She could cry later.

While they were in the woods burying her dog the crime scene investigators finished with Joe Bardiwell's remains and released them to the medical examiner. His body was gone when they walked back to the ruined gun store. All that was left was the burned section of grass, which was now marked by four little yellow flags. The CSI's had left them marking the spot where he had been killed, in the unlikely event that they might come back to look for more evidence. The fire truck and some of the police cars had also departed. Her motorcycle had been picked up and pushed across to the parking lot.

Lieutenant Mosby met them at the back of the ruined gun store. The heavy wooden back door had burned away, but the iron-barred burglar door was still locked firmly in place. "The M.E. took your father to his office in Suffolk. You'll have a few days at least, or as long as you need to make the arrangements. Your mother is buried here isn't she?"

"Yes, at Saint Charles."

"Okay, that's Father Alvarado, right? He'll take care of you. Ranya, do you want to hear what we know so far, about what happened?"

"Yes. I can do it, I can listen. I want to know."

"All right then. The arson investigator is gone, he's got a lot to do today with all the fires, but he had some good information. There were eleven gun stores burned across Tidewater last night from Suffolk to Virginia Beach. They were all hit between eleven and one. Figuring the times and distances, we're looking at several groups working together in coordination.

"Gasoline was used at all of them. Molotov cocktails made from old liquor bottles were found at several sites. Arsonists screw up a lot with these things, that's what the arson investigator said. When they drop one or it bounces back, they don't tend to pick them up for another throw, not when they're lit. So they've recovered enough gasoline bombs all made from the same kinds of bottles to know it was a planned, coordinated attack.

"And we found long pieces of half-inch iron rebar at several sites, they were used to smash in the windows through the burglar bars. Gasoline was then poured in using jerry jugs with long spouts, we recovered one of them, and then Molotovs were dropped in. Simple, but very effective. We're guessing no more than a few minutes were taken at each site. By the time the fires flared up, the arsonists were gone.

"And your father wasn't the only one killed. A husband and wife who lived over their store in Norfolk were trapped and burned alive. And another owner who lived near his store was killed in Portsmouth, and another was wounded in Virginia Beach. So we're looking at three groups of arsonists, based on the geography and the times. Each probably consists of a driver, at least one armed lookout, and at least one arsonist. That makes it at least nine bad guys, but probably more."

Ranya had no reason to disbelieve Jasper Mosby's hypothesis, but it couldn't explain her father's death in the open over a hundred feet from both the house and the store. She could understand armed lookouts, but they would have been on the parking lot side of the store. Her father would have been approaching in the darkness with his twelve gauge pump shotgun, unseen by them on the other side of the store. How could he have been shot so easily in the darkness, over a hundred feet from any cover which could have hidden his killer? Before he died he would have killed or at least wounded some of his assailants, Ranya felt certain of that. It all made no sense.

Brad, the grave-digging volunteer said, "I guess this is all about the Stadium Massacre, like some kind of retaliation, but by whom? Liberals, I mean your typical gun control liberals, they don't normally go out on midnight arson raids with armed lookouts. None of this makes any logical sense. It just doesn't add up."

"Nope," said Mosby, "none of it makes much sense. But whoever did it likes cheap wine and 32 ounce malt liquor, if that narrows it down any. And now there's four people dead and eleven gun stores and a couple of houses torched, and that most definitely adds up."

A news truck from a local television network affiliate had parked on the shoulder of the road near the parking lot, and a perky blond reporterette climbed down from the passenger seat while the telescoping microwave mast ascended into the sky. Brad walked over to the young male producer type who was talking to his camera man behind the truck. He smiled at them and made the "come here" gesture with his finger, the folded shovel held casually in his other hand. The producer, eager for a local tip, walked out of earshot of the cameraman who was busy getting his gear ready.

Brad said, just audibly, "Do you see that attractive young brunette in the tight jeans over there talking to my good friend Lieutenant Mosby? You do? Great. If you point a camera in her direction today, you'll be walking back to Norfolk, do you get my drift? And if a microphone happens to get put in her face, it'll take an operation to get it out of you. Okay? She's not part of your story." Brad smiled again at the shocked young man with slicked-back black hair, and then he turned and tossed his shovel into the back of his truck where it bounced with a clang. He rejoined Ranya and Lieutenant Mosby, and when he looked again at the TV truck the antenna was going back down.

Mosby was talking to a fire department official about the arsons at Freedom Arms and the Bardiwell residence. By midnight fire trucks were already working two earlier arson attacks, and there was some confusion as to whether a new fire was being reported, or the same fire was being called in twice. As a result Bardiwell's store and home burned for nearly an hour before the first drop of water reached them. The decision was then made to put the available water onto the gun store, and let the wood framed house burn: it was already far beyond saving. Only much later were the lingering embers of the house fire quenched.

Although the gun store was built with cement block exterior walls, there had been ample fuel inside in paneling, flooring, interior walls, furnishings and so on. The roof had collapsed, adding fuel, then ammunition and gun powder had cooked off or burned, causing the fire fighters to spray their load from an ineffective distance. (In fact, in a fire uncontained gun powder does not "explode," and loose ammunition does not fire itself, and they present no greater danger than other types of common household products.)

The store and its contents were a total loss, and the fire department would not permit anyone inside until it was totally cool, due to the perceived risk of more ammunition cooking off in the cinders. The doors and windows were still covered by burglar bars, so security was not an issue. Inside the gutted cinderblock walls the debris and ashes still let out steam and a little smoke while they peered inside through the iron bars, trying to visualize where everything had been before the fire.

Mosby asked "Ranya, where did your father keep his important family papers, like his insurance and bank documents?"

She snapped back into the present. "Oh, in a firebox. Actually it's like a safe built into the floor of his bedroom closet."

"Do you think you can find it?"

"Um, yeah, sure, I guess so."

"Then that's where you should start. You'll need those papers, the sooner the better."

"I'll get my shovel," offered Brad.

He scraped and cleared and dug in the corner of Ranya's former home until he found the square cutout in the cement slab where the safe had been hidden. A flush-fitting concrete plug had protected the top of the safe from the heat, and once it was lifted out the combination dial still turned. Ranya had no trouble remembering the combination; it had been set to her mother's birthday. She loaded the contents of the safe into her black daypack, a few folders and envelopes and some small wrapped boxes which weighed a few pounds.

They walked around the burned home site looking for anything salvageable. Ranya poked and prodded around in the ashes with a piece of metal conduit but there was nothing. Beds and furniture were reduced to blackened springs and scrap metal. A five foot tall gun safe stood alone, burned to bare metal with buckled sides, it had clearly surpassed its rating, and the contents would be ruined. Her father's pickup truck and car were blackened hulks resting on their chassis where the car port had been. The odors of burnt wood and plastic and paint and rubber were nauseating.

Behind the house but inside the wire fence there was a little barn-like shed which had escaped the fire with only blistered paint. Ranya suppressed a bitter laugh. "I've got no father and no house, but at least I have three motorcycles." She used her keys to remove the padlock, and swung open the plywood double doors. Inside there were two motorcycles under a green dust cover. She lifted it up and gave them a look. "They seem okay."

"I don't have a house either," said Brad.

"Oh? Where do you live?"

"I have a sailboat up the east fork of the Nansemond, not far from here. I've been working on it."

"A sailboat? Up this far? How'd you get it under the bridges?"

"Well, at the moment it's got no mast. I've got the new mast at a yard in Portsmouth."

"What are you doing so far up the river?"

He laughed. "I got a great deal on the dockage; it's free. And I can use power tools day or night, because there's no one around to bother. I've been rebuilding the interior, and I just put in a new engine. None of the commercial boat yards want to let you 'do it yourself' any more. They make you hire their yard labor for fifty bucks an hour, no thanks!"

"Don't the mosquitoes drive you crazy up the river?"

"Those aren't mosquitoes. If you want to see real mosquitoes, go to Alaska! That's where I've been working for a few years."

"What do you do?"

"I'm a machinist, but up there I've mostly been bolting big valves and machines together. But I'm done with that for a while; I'm getting ready to take off sailing. That's been my goal forever."

"You're lucky. Almost achieving your goal I mean."

"I guess so. I've been working on it for a long time."

Ranya snapped the lock back onto the shed's hasp, and then she turned around to face Brad. "You're a shooter, right? You said you had a rifle in our shop. Do you shoot much?" Ranya knew that many hunters fired less than ten rounds a year at deer or elk, and then put their rifles away until the next hunting season.

"Oh sure, I'd call myself a shooter."

"All rifle? Any pistol or shotgun?"

"Both. I've spent some time stomping around the boonies in Alaska and the northwest, and I usually carry a .44 magnum for bear protection. I've owned a few shotguns, but none right now."

"Okay, fine. I just wanted to throw some ideas at you, things only a shooter would understand. I'm trying to figure out how it happened last night, because it just doesn't add up, it doesn't make sense to me. Say my father hears our dog barking like crazy after midnight. Or he hears the alarm from the store—it was set up to go off quietly in the house. Either way, he's armed and ready when he comes out. He'd have his twelve gauge shotgun for sure. The house would be all dark, inside and out, so he wouldn't be backlighted, and he wouldn't be carrying a lit flashlight or anything stupid like that. The arsonists are on the other side of the store, the road side, smashing windows and pouring in gas and lighting Molotovs. My father is on this side, in the dark, almost 200 feet away, and these drunk and probably stoned home boys managed to hit him four or five times? In the dark, on the other side of the store? I can't see how."

Brad looked all around the property. "Do you remember where we found your dog, over on the side near the fence? Why was he over there, and not by the store going after the bad guys, or by your father?" They walked back to where the doberman had died, a hundred feet from the state road near the front corner of the Bardiwell's fenced in property. Just over the fence was the narrow dirt road which Ranya had ridden her bike around when she had arrived, and beyond that the brush and pine woods began.

Ranya went to the wooden fence post closest to where her doberman had been found, and climbed the square-checked wire with practiced ease. Brad followed after she jumped down on the other side. From the tree line they had a clear view of the burned home site, the back and side of the gun store, and the places where both the dog and Joe Bardiwell had been shot and killed.

The morning sun was slanting across the narrow road into the woods. Ranya looked around her and moved to an ideal shooting position under a cedar tree with widely spaced lower branches. She laid her arms across a thick limb jutting out at shoulder height, and with her hands together in a pistol grip she sighted from the home site across the yard to the gun store. Then she looked around her on the forest floor, she walked in a small circle around the cedar tree, and found nothing. She expanded her search area, and twenty feet from the tree, off to the right from the possible shooter's perspective, she caught the glint of gold.

"There's the brass! There it is! The shooter was here!" Ranya crouched over the gold metal and brushed away some leaves, then picked up an empty shell case with a twig in its open mouth. She looked closely at the head stamp, the imprinted manufacturer's markings around the base of the shell case. "Oh shit... Look at this, ten millimeter. And see these marks on it, these little lines? And this dent on the lip?"

"What's that mean?"

"It means the feds killed my father. That's what it means."

"The feds again! The feds! Everywhere I go, it's the feds!" Brad took a deep breath. "Ranya, do you have a cell phone on you?"

"What? A cell phone? No, it's back on my bike. Why, do you need to make a call?"

"No, I don't need it. But before we say anything else about the feds, I think you should know something about cell phones. Sometimes cell phones can be used just like microphones, even if they're turned off. As long as the batteries are in them they can be switched on to track you, and even to listen to you." Brad's own "free" government cell phone was safely back in his truck's glove box.

"Are you serious? They can do that?"

"Hell yes they can."

"How do you know that?"

"It's not exactly a very well-kept secret; they just don't talk about it. I mean they don't announce it, but the word gets out. The technology is built right in; they put in all kind of 'back-doors' for the government to use. They've tracked and killed terrorists just by their cell phones, tracked them and killed them."

"That's right, I've heard about that. They can shoot rockets from drones now, and I remember reading about how they homed in on their cell phones."

"And not only that, they can listen to what's being said around the phone, even when it's supposedly turned off. So be careful. Don't keep your cell phone too close if you're talking about the feds, and yank the battery out if you're going somewhere you don't want to be tracked."

"Big Brother is really here, isn't he?"

"Yeah he is, and that's one of the big reasons why I'm taking off. You wouldn't believe how easy it is for the feds to track you any more, to know every damn thing about your life. Anyway, how did you know about the ten millimeter ammo?"

"Because I know guns! I mean, I was raised in the business."

"Oh right, sorry."

"Don't worry about it, nobody ever expects a girl to know about guns. Look at the brass, see these little black lines? Heckler and Koch uses a funny grooved chamber, it leaves those marks when the shell is extracted, and it dents the lip like this too. So these shells were fired from an MP-5, no doubt about it.

"A few years ago, even before 9-11, the FBI bought thousands of brand new Heckler and Koch MP-5 submachine guns, right from the factory in Germany. They made a special production run in ten millimeter, just for our feds. Nobody else has ten millimeter sub guns. Don't ask me why, but the FBI was hot on ten millimeter for a while. It's a great caliber but it never really caught on with civilians, because it's a little too hot for most pistols. It's sort of a .40 caliber magnum. Hey, there's another shell case!" Ranya scooped up several more empty brass shells in succession in the same area until she had collected five.

Brad said, "If these guns are so unique, isn't it almost like leaving a calling card? It wouldn't be very professional for a killer to leave that kind of brass around, would it?"

"Who ever said the feds were professional? Remember 9-11, and all the warnings that they ignored? Besides, who gets to do all the forensic analysis? They do! Do you really think the feds ever worry about leaving evidence around? They don't care about evidence; they can do anything they want with it. Do you remember Waco?"

"I read about it."

"Well, some guys that used to come into the store had some books and videos about it. It's really amazing what the feds got away with. Like the sheet metal front doors, they were critical evidence, absolutely critical. They'd prove who shot first by which way the bullet holes were going. Guess what? The FBI 'lost' the doors. Lost them! Big steel doors! They have pictures of them at Waco, after the fire, and the FBI 'lost' them! Can you imagine that? Lots of evidence that goes to the FBI lab gets 'lost.' And what they don't lose, the FBI labs get to work on it until it comes out just the way they want it.

"Anyway," she continued, "I'm guessing the killer used a government-issue ten millimeter MP-5 for a good reason: because it'd already be set up with a night vision scope and a sound suppressor. The feds have all the best gear; they use suppressors all the time. They even buy some submachine guns with suppressors built right in. And the killer wouldn't have any trouble tracking my father across the yard if he was using a night scope. A silenced submachine gun with a night scope…my father never had a chance. He was an easy target."

She stared across the fence, imagining the government assassin aiming at her doberman as the dog streaked toward him. Armalite could have cleared the waist-high fence in a bound, but killing the dog would have been simple using a night scope. And then her father came out of the house with his pump shotgun, heading for the back of the store. He would have been moving right across the killer's line of fire, just fifty yards away from this very spot. The entire fatal exchange unfolded in her mind like a movie. Her grief and shock were still present, but a new kind of quiet rage was flowing into her heart on top of the sadness. She stood behind the fence with her arms folded, staring at the four tiny yellow flags that marked the location of her father's murder.

After an awkward minute, Brad said, "Ranya, did you ever hear of the Blackwater Rod and Gun Club?"

"Sure. Why?"

"Well you're not going to believe this, but Thursday afternoon when I drove back to my boat, the FBI was there waiting for me. By my boat. You know why? Because I was at Dixie Hardware in Highpoint on Tuesday morning, and someone filmed everybody there with a hidden camera. They were looking for accomplices of Jimmy Shifflett in Highpoint. I'm not kidding. I was in the pictures from the hardware store.

"So Thursday the FBI came to my boat and showed me a bunch of pictures of men from around here. Here's the kicker: they think the Blackwater Rod and Gun Club is a militia front, and Shifflett was part of it. Really, that's what they think."

"That's a joke," Ranya retorted. "Anybody from around here knows that's a joke! The rod and gun club is just what it says it is, it's just a bunch of local rednecks who like to tear around the woods on ATV's, fish and shoot and drink beer. And mostly drink beer! They're no more a 'militia' than I'm G.I. Jane. It's got to be a joke; somebody must be goofing on the FBI, feeding them that kind of bullshit."

"I don't think so. They're convinced Shifflett was one of them. They think the gun club might have helped Shifflett do the Stadium Massacre."

"That's a crock! A total crock!"

"The FBI sure doesn't think so. They wanted me to join the gun club, just because I'm a shooter. They put the squeeze on me, big time. They want me to rat out the gun club and be an informant. They threatened to freeze my bank accounts and take my passport if I didn't cooperate! They had me meet them at Lester's last night. They think I can just walk up and join the gun club, like it's joining the Elks or something, just because I'm a shooter."

"The FBI doesn't have a clue. So what happened?"

"I went and I had a few beers with them in the back room of Lester's, and I made sure they brushed me off. I had to go in case the feds were watching, or getting a report from somebody else. You can't just tell the FBI to go to hell, not when they've got your bank accounts and your passport in their hands! Believe me, all I want to do is get my boat finished and get the hell out of here before it all gets any crazier, and now I've got the FBI on my back."

9

A black and chrome motorcycle idled slowly down state road 32 in front of Freedom Arms, stopped for moment, then bumped onto the dirt side road and rolled up toward them, its engine rumbling out the staccato signature of the Harley Davidson. The rider looked for a hard spot to put down his kick stand, then climbed off and walked straight to Ranya who began crying again as they embraced. He was an old man to be riding a big Harley, wearing a sleeveless denim jacket over a black sweat shirt, with a small visorless black helmet and gold-rimmed aviator sunglasses. The man pulled off the helmet, revealing short-cropped gray hair. Brad stood by feeling awkward, and turned away from them as they held each other. The man was between Brad's height and Ranya's, maybe about five ten, and seemed to be in good shape for his age.

Ranya and the old biker separated, and she made the introductions. "Brad, meet Phil Carson. He's an old family friend, kind of like an uncle. Phil, this is Brad Fallon. I just met Brad today. He's been helping me. He buried my dobie Armalite for me."

"They killed your dog too?"

"Yes."

"Those bastards."

The two men shook hands cautiously and checked each other out, the weathered fifty-something biker and the young man in jeans and an ocean blue polo shirt which matched his eyes.

"I've seen you around; you're fixing up a sailboat on Sodermilk's old farm, right?"

"That's me. You know the place?"

"I sure do, I almost bought part of it once."

Ranya asked, "Phil, didn't you used to do some ocean sailing?"

"Where'd you hear that? Your father? Yeah, I did some sailing, a long, long time ago, but I got it out of my system. So Brad, you're the guy from Alaska who shook 'em up at Mineral Springs last month? I heard you came within one point of knocking off the best open-sight rifle shot in Virginia and the Carolinas."

Brad looked directly at the man. "It seems like my life's an open book around here."

"Don't get your feathers ruffled son. Suffolk's a big county, but the serious shooters are a small group, just like any place. And let's face it, your story's more interesting than most, coming from Alaska to buy a boat and all that. These days, people pay a lot of attention when somebody new shows up with a big interest in shooting. Folks are paranoid, and they should be. Just look at what happened here last night."

Ranya said, "So you already heard about it?"

"Well, I wasn't just riding by. Sure, I got a call. So now tell me, what are you youngsters doing standing way over here outside the fence? I know there's got to be a reason, so tell me what's really going on. Come on Ranya, don't hold out on Uncle Phil if you found something."

The old biker had a warm smile, and for a moment it allowed Brad to see him as he must have looked as a younger man.

She handed him an empty ten millimeter shell case, its head stamp facing up. Carson had to squint hard to make it out, holding it at arm's length. "Ten mill. I knew it; I knew it, the feds! So your father was shot over there by the little flags?"

Ranya nodded yes.

"So that's forty or fifty yards from here, at midnight, and almost pitch black. The moon didn't rise until after one AM, I checked. Somebody shot him at that range, in the dark, and nobody around here heard the shots. What's that tell you? You already know what it means, don't you Ranya?"

"Yeah. Ten millimeter with these marks on the brass and the dent on the lip means the 'FBI Special Edition' MP-5. A night scope on top, and a sound suppressor. I'm guessing subsonic loads, for no sonic crack. It was the feds all the way," said Ranya.

"That's about how I already figured it, and as far as I'm concerned the brass you found proves it. They're pretty slick: they used the home boys to do the dirty work with the gasoline out by the road, and take the rap if it goes sour. Meanwhile they're waiting in the tree line for Joe—for your father to come out. They knew he'd be coming out, and they were waiting in ambush."

Brad asked him, "How did you know it was the 'home boys'?"

"I've got my friends on the force. When I heard the news I made some calls. Who else makes gasoline bombs out of 32 ounce malt liquor bottles? You don't need to be Sherlock Holmes to figure that one out. But now you know something the cops don't know: that's the ten millimeter secret Ranya's got in her pocket." He paused, suddenly uncomfortable. "And I know something nobody knows, nobody at all. I know who killed him."

"What?" Brad and Ranya exclaimed at the same time. "Who? How can you know that?" asked Ranya.

"Because I think I talked to him right inside your store Thursday afternoon. The BATF came by for a compliance check, four of them in a black Chevy Suburban. One of them did all the talking at the counter, a BATF agent, a real asshole, a big crew-cut gorilla with a Yankee accent like maybe Boston or New York. He wanted all the 4473's from the last week. He was having a fit about your father selling semi-auto rifles last week after they passed the law. Turns out it's not illegal to sell them, not until next Tuesday, but the BATF guy got all bent out of shape. He took the 4473's right out the door, no pretense at all about just copying down information for an investigation. We had some words... I blew up like a big asshole and gave him a major ration of shit...

"I feel like crap Ranya, you don't know how bad I feel, I feel like I set your father up, like I set the feds onto him. If I hadn't of pissed that BATF guy off so bad, your dad might be alive. They might have just burned the store and left it at that." Phil Carson was speaking quietly now, staring down at his boots with his hands at his sides. "I had to tell you, I had to tell you that it's my fault."

"Shit... Shit... Well, geez..." Ranya was crying again. "God, this is so messed up. Phil, you can't blame yourself...and you don't know if they shot him on purpose, if they planned it. They might have had the same kind of security at all the arsons, and my father just walked into their line of fire, they just saw him coming with a shotgun and... Oh shit." She sat down heavily on the ground, staring blankly.

"Well anyway, I'm sorry if I had anything to do with it. I know I feel like I did." Carson stood next to the cedar tree, looking over the limb the assassin had most likely used to steady his weapon while he shot Joe Bardiwell. Brad was the outsider again, his back to them, leaning against the wooden fence post. All of them were staring out across the field to the little square of yellow flags which marked the burnt spot where Joe Bardiwell had been murdered.

Carson took a deep breath and sighed. "Aw hell... You know, a war's coming. I can feel it. Thirty years and I haven't killed anybody, and as God is my witness I had some good reasons to! But now it feels like it's all coming around again, like a big wheel... Only this time I'm just an old guy with bad knees and weak eyes. Man oh man, I sure wish I was your age and had eyes like you youngsters again. Now that I finally know what's going on, I'm just about too damn old and busted up to do anything about it. I guess this is going to have to be your generation's fight."

Brad turned around and faced this stranger, wondering where he was coming from with his war talk. "I can't speak for 'my generation', but as far as I'm concerned, it's not my fight. I'm sorry, but I just want to get on my boat and go travel for a while, and see the rest of the world."

"You're just going to take off? Now? Damn. You seemed like maybe you'd be a fighter to me, being a crack shot and all, but I guess you never can tell. And if somebody like you isn't going to fight back, I guess there's not much hope that the purple-haired nipple-ring crowd is either."

"Look, Phil, I'm sorry, but America...it went off the tracks a long time ago. I can't fix it, and I'm getting out while I can."

Phil Carson paused, looking between Brad and Ranya. She was still sitting on the ground, staring across her property. "If America goes down the tubes, where are you going to run to? Where will you find the kind of freedom we had here? Argentina? Brazil? That's a laugh. Or will you just keep running? Because if America goes down, then the whole world goes down. And then there's not going to be anywhere safe to hide, not anywhere. Not for years, maybe not in our lifetimes."

Brad said nothing. He knew the old biker was grieving and bitter, and there was already enough bitterness and sorrow to go around today without adding any of his own. He certainly didn't want to argue with an old friend of Ranya's in front of her, when she had already suffered so much.

"Ah, what the hell," Carson said. "Maybe you're right Brad, get out while you can. You're young, you want to explore the world. We all did at your age… I guess I'm just an angry old man, and my clock's ticking down. I've only got time for one more battle, maybe one more war. It's just a damn shame we won't have a young man that can shoot like you on our side."

"Am I missing something?" asked Brad. "What are you talking about? Another civil war?"

"Hell yes another civil war, or maybe a dirty war like they have in South America. What do you think that bullshit act in the stadium was about? What do you think these gun store attacks are about? You think they just 'happened'? Somebody, the feds, maybe the BATF, I don't know who, but somebody's trying real hard to pick a fight. It's like they're standing between two armies shooting both ways. They're trying to start a war, and I don't know why. Maybe so they can crack down and bring in martial law, I haven't figured that part out. But somebody sure as hell's trying to start a war in this country. Liberal against conservative, city against country, pro-gun against gun control, pro-government against pro-freedom, black against white against brown, Christian against Muslim… There's no other explanation that makes sense."

Brad replied, "But every poll says most people believe Shifflett had militia help. They see the militias behind all of this, that's what the news people are all saying." Brad didn't believe the polls or the media; he just wanted to hear the old biker's reaction.

Carson snorted. "Let's face it Brad, most people in this country are stupid and getting stupider by the year. The public schools are practically designed to crank out stupid people! Stupid people will believe any stupid story; stupid people are easy to control. You already know that. I mean, we all know the militia story is horse shit. It's just nice easy-to-understand baby food to feed the morons, to get them to support the gun ban and all the rest that's coming. And we're outnumbered; we're way outnumbered by the morons."

Ranya stood up again and turned to join their discussion. "That's true, sure we're outnumbered, but don't forget one thing: we have all the guns. The nanny-state sheeple-types hate guns. They've been brain washed for years, so even though they out number us, they can't hurt us because they've basically got no weapons. It's the government itself that's going to be the other side in this war. They have guns too, all the guns they need. It's the government that's going to come after us, and the sheeple are going to cheer them on every step of the way."

"How in the hell did we wind up on the other side from our own government?" asked Brad. "That's just about the worst part of it. That's why I'm getting out while I can."

"Brad, you were in the military, weren't you?" asked Carson.

"Four years in the Navy."

"You remember the oath we took when they swore us in? 'Raise your right hand' and all that? Well we didn't swear to defend the federal government, or any damn government. No, we swore to defend the Constitution, from 'all enemies, foreign and domestic.' So now is when it gets sticky: what if 'domestic enemies' of the Constitution are running the government? Do real patriots roll over and play dead, or fight back? That's the big question, because for sure anybody who resists isn't going to win any popularity contests with the sheeple.

"And you can bet the government's going to call anybody who resists either a traitor or a terrorist. They can just make up any damn laws they want now, because we've got a Supreme Court that'll say two plus two equals five hundred, as long as it's politically correct. And then they expect us to just salute smartly and go along with the program, while they tear up the Constitution! They think they can just say 'war on terror' and 'national security' and everybody will just shut up and obey orders…well I'm just about finished obeying orders. There's some lines that won't be crossed, and one might be coming next Tuesday at twelve noon!

"Listen you two, I'm sorry I got all worked up, but it just breaks my heart to see what's happening to this country. It breaks my heart to see good men like your father killed by our own government. Now I guess everybody has to decide for themselves what to do about it… Ranya, if there's anything you need, just give me a call, and let me know about the services for your father, I want to be there." Carson handed her an old business card with several numbers penciled in on the back, and she put it into a small compartment on the outside of her black daypack. "One of these numbers will get me. If you need anything at all, just give me a shout, all right?" He gave her another hug, then held her by her shoulders at arm's-length and looked at her.

"I will. I'll call you."

Carson returned to his bike, mounted it and tugged on his helmet. "And Brad, Ranya's just about the only 'family' I've got in these parts. I'm sure you'll be a gentleman, won't you?" He smiled when he said this, but his concern for her welfare was evident.

"I'm going to be gone soon. You won't have to worry about me." Carson answered him by firing up the engine, and then he snapped his bike into gear and turned back toward the state road. He stopped on the edge of the pavement behind Lieutenant Mosby's patrol car, and Mosby walked over and briefly spoke to him. Brad and Ranya watched as the two men shook hands, and then Carson took off riding his black Harley toward the south.

"**Man, he's a trip**" said Brad. "Is he serious about all that war talk? I mean, I expect a lot of problems, the country's going to crap, but a war?"

"Sure he's serious. He's the real deal, that's what I always heard. I used to hear some other customers at the shop talk about him; they said he was into some pretty crazy stuff in Viet Nam. Special Forces, that deal. Phil never talks about it, but some other guys, they told my father some pretty amazing stories about him. So yeah, if he's talking about a war coming, I'd say he knows what he's talking about."

"I don't see how a civil war can happen in this day and age, but I definitely feel the hate, it's right under the surface. I can see all the dividing lines. America really is two countries today. One half still loves freedom, and the other half's already socialist, even if they don't call it that. The free half is keeping them from going all the way to having the kind of socialist government they want, but they can't quite shove us out of the way while we've got so many guns. I think that's what all this is about: once they've got our guns, they'll just pass all their damn socialist laws. They'll just increase our taxes until we're like Sweden, and if we don't like it, tough shit. Anybody that fights back will get a free ride to a special camp for problem children. That's where it's all heading, and that's why I'm leaving now, before I need to get permission to go."

"Brad, I think your plan's pretty smart, get out of Dodge while you can. But as far as what he said about a new civil war goes, well, it's already started for me. I don't know about the rest of the country, but somebody sure as hell declared war on me when they killed my father."

"Listen Ranya, I didn't mention this when your friend was here, because I didn't want to bring up the FBI coming out to my boat, or the thing at Lester's. The only credential I saw when the FBI came to my boat was from an older agent named James Gibson, but the main guy who dealt with me said his name was George, just George, and he didn't give his last name. He didn't show me any ID, so I assumed he was FBI too like Gibson, but now I don't think so. He was definitely a crew-cut gorilla, and he had a Boston kind of accent, just like the ATF agent Phil saw in your store. It's got to be the same guy."

"So the FBI and the BATF are working together down here. Probably because of the Stadium Massacre," she replied. Her tears were gone for now, pushed back, replaced by a new steely-eyed interest. "So Gibson is an older FBI agent who was at your boat, and George is the crew cut BATF gorilla who was at your boat, and at Freedom Arms."

"Right. I think so," said Brad.

"Well, that's good to know, that's something anyway."

"What are you going to do next?" he asked her.

"What do you mean next? Today?"

"No, I mean are you going to stay in Suffolk, or go back to Charlottesville?"

"I'll stay a few days, maybe a week, I don't know. I don't even know all the things I have to do. I've got some high school friends around here. I can stay at somebody's house."

"Okay, well, if you need anything, let me give you my cell phone number, and if you need my truck to move your other motorcycles, any thing like that, just call me, and I'll be glad to help. Do you know where my boat is?"

"I think so. I can find it."

"Well, if there's anything you need, just call me. And Ranya, I'm really glad I met you, I'm just so sorry about what happened to your father, about everything." They walked down the dirt road and along the fence by state road 32 until they were back at the gutted store. Brad climbed into his truck, jotted his number on an old receipt, and handed it to her. Then he said once again, "If there's anything I can do…"

"I'll call you. Thanks Brad, thanks for all your help today."

There was nothing left to say, so he pulled out of the parking lot and headed back to Guajira. Ranya was still standing on the parking lot; he could see the American flag waving in his rear view mirror.

10

After Phil Carson and Brad Fallon departed, long after her father's body had been taken away, there was nothing left for Ranya to gain by lingering on her property except more painful memories. At the age of twenty-one she was burdened with the crushing knowledge that she was utterly alone in the world. She had no living relatives in America that she was aware of, and only scant knowledge of any family left in Lebanon. All that she knew of her family history in Lebanon was that many of the Christians in their native village had been wiped out during the civil war in the 1970's, and the survivors had been forced to flee in an unlamented modern-day Diaspora. Now, thirty years later, the last remnant of her tribe was again faced with extinction.

She would have had an older brother named Michael, but he did not survive to see his sister born. He had been killed when only a toddler by a car bomb in East Beirut, where her parents had taken refuge. He was buried somewhere over there, somewhere Ranya could now never know. Her mother, Elise, was buried in a Catholic graveyard here in Suffolk County Virginia. As for her father, she could not bear to think of where he was, because then the agonizing images of the morning stormed back into her mind and paralyzed her with another layer of grief.

Only the clarity of onrushing asphalt could push back the images, so she twisted her ponytail up under her helmet and blasted up state road 32. She passed anonymously through Suffolk's business and commercial district, and a few minutes later she parked near her mother's grave in a sunlit granite-studded meadow. Her entire family was now lying in graveyards, or even worse, in some cold stainless steel drawer. On the short walk to her mother's grave, Ranya knelt to pluck a few yellow wild flowers which were growing at the base of a hedge, ashamed that she had not remembered to stop at a proper florist's shop.

She had last seen her mother alive a week before Christmas in 1992, bald and puffy after months of radiation and chemo. Her mother had always been beautiful, with Ranya's hazel colored eyes and thick brown hair, but her last months on earth were a horror show. Ranya extracted a pair of small color snapshots of her mother and father from her wallet, and set them in the grass at the base of the grave stone. On the left side of the rose-colored marble was chiseled "Elise Marie Bardiwell, Beloved Wife and Mother, Eternal Peace." The right side of the stone was smooth and uncarved; another task to add to my list, Ranya thought.

She sat on the lawn facing the marker, and then gently placed her father's silver cross between the two pictures. The cross had come from her mother's family, one of their few family keepsakes to be brought out of Lebanon.

There was no one else nearby, and Ranya spoke softly. "Hi Mom, I'm sorry I haven't visited in a long time. I guess you already know what happened... I hope that Dad has found you and you're together again.

"I'm trying to keep it together here. I'm trying to hold up. I'm trying to understand everything, but I don't know if God hears my prayers at all. Mom, what happened to our family, why am I left all alone?"

There didn't seem to be much of a future in being a Bardiwell, and not much point in trying, when they all died so young. She fell asleep crying on the warm grass above her mother's grave.

The afternoon sun moved behind a nearby stand of Poplar trees. A burial service awakened her, and she sat up and brushed the grass from her hair, and put away the cross and their pictures. She knew she looked awful, and she was grateful to get on her bike and be able to hide again beneath her full visor helmet.

A mile from the graveyard, at the northern edge of the 'city' of Suffolk, was the brick and plaster Saint Charles Catholic Church. Ranya parked in front of the small adjoining rectory and hesitantly rang the doorbell. She had stopped attending weekly Mass when she went away to college three years earlier. The white-painted door finally creaked open and to her relief Father Alvarado greeted her.

Ranya Bardiwell had been blessed with a face which was not easily forgotten, not even by an elderly parish priest, not even after hours of crying had taken their toll. It took him only a few moments to recall her name. She had attended Saint Charles Elementary School through the eighth grade, and her father Joseph Bardiwell never missed the nine o'clock Mass on Sunday.

"Ranya? How are you? Come in, you don't look so well. What's the matter?"

"My father's dead. He was killed last night."

"Oh, God help us all! I saw something on the news, gun stores were burned, was he...?"

"He was shot, and he was burned. Oh Father, it was terrible what they did to him!" She fell against the frail priest, sobbing again. There was no end to her tears today.

After leaving the church rectory, Ranya rode north to the home of a high school friend. She had only vague ideas of where she might stay, so she was letting her Yamaha pull her along rural lanes remembered from happier days. Valerie Edmonds was in her senior year at nearby William and Mary, and spent most weekends at her family home in northern Suffolk County. Her house always seemed like a mansion to Ranya, located on a dozen acres of high ground overlooking a bend in the

Nansemond River near its mouth on the Chesapeake Bay. Valerie's house had numerous guest bedrooms, and Ranya hoped that they would offer to put her up for a few days while she sorted out her father's affairs.

Valerie's father Burgess Edmonds had been one of Joe Bardiwell's best customers over the years. He was a prolific gun collector, with tastes running mainly to custom-made hunting rifles in the latest ultra-magnum calibers. Joe Bardiwell had done much of the customizing himself, delivering rifles that were not only works of art to behold, but were invariably capable of astonishing accuracy. All of Bardiwell's rifles were delivered with proof targets, demonstrating that they had been zeroed in to shoot groups of well under one inch at one hundred yards. This was the minimum acceptable level of accuracy for a rifle out of Bardiwell's custom shop, and most of them could produce half-inch groups, which on a paper target produced a single ragged hole resembling a cloverleaf. Joe Bardiwell charged a lot for his custom work, and Burgess Edmonds had been happy to pay the premium, often while waiting months for the gunsmith to work through his back orders.

Ranya had been a guest of Valerie's on social occasions from grade school birthday parties, all the way through high school to their senior prom pool party, complete with a band. They had been friends, but Ranya was always aware of the social gulf between them. Upper class Valerie had her horses and piano lessons, middle class Ranya had her motorcycles and shooting. Something they had still in common were their dogs. The Edmonds had two dobermans from the same litter which had produced Armalite; they had been sold to both families by another regular customer of Freedom Arms. Ranya expected to see the two black dogs come sprinting down the hill to meet her, and then lope alongside her on her ride up to the house, and she knew it would hurt.

So Ranya reached the Edmondses' private road with mixed hope and dread, but she stopped far from the big white house when it became obvious that a social event of some kind was taking place. A dozen or more gleaming luxury SUVs, convertibles and foreign touring sedans were parked on the circle and the lawn in front of the house, and there was a white canopy tent the size of a tennis court visible on the lawn. Music from a live band drifted down the long private driveway to her.

Ranya held in the clutch, standing over her bike, imagining her entrance: a poor ash-smeared Orphan Annie, sweat streaked, her hair pulled back in a dirty ponytail, wearing boots and jeans. She pictured the smiles and whispers among the satin-gowned debutantes as they struggled to recall Ranya What's-her-name, the gun dealer's daughter. Perhaps they would sit her in the big trophy room on one of the stools made from an elephant's foot, place her between the stuffed lion and the polar bear rug as a new exhibit: "wild Arab girl." Maybe they would let her earn her room and board in the kitchen, or perhaps she could help the caterers, but suitably behind the scenes.

No. She was resigned to being the outsider, the loner. It was part of her inner core anyway, why else had she owned seven motorcycles, but never once a car? Ranya Bardiwell had always been able to stand her own company, and now she would have to. First she had been an only child, then she had lost her mother, and now there was the final loss and she was alone. Alone.

She drove to the outskirts of the city of Suffolk to the Super K-Mart, and bought what she would need for a few days: toiletries, shorts, running shoes and plain black t-shirts, a conservative black dress for church and the funeral, and a nylon zipper bag to hold it all on the back of her bike. She ate as an afterthought, a tasteless sandwich she picked up at a fast food place next to the K-Mart.

Ranya bypassed the Suffolk Holiday Inn and drove to the old motel located at the intersection a mile north of her former house on state road 32. The "Colonial" hovered between quaint and seedy, with twelve units in a straight line, set well back from the road under towering loblolly pines. The Indian manager in the office did not stare at her or ask questions; his sari-clad wife was also behind the desk.

The air conditioner in her unit was loud but at least it pumped out a steady stream of cold air. The bed was not too soft, the sheets and the room were clean. The austerity matched her spirit. She showered, glad to shed her very stale running clothes and sports bra, then she changed into entirely new clothes from the skin out: black nylon running shorts, a black bra and a black t-shirt, and mostly-black running shoes. The shower and new clothes gave her a lift, and at last she felt ready to examine what she had taken from her father's floor safe. She sat cross legged on top of the bed, and spread out the contents of her daypack.

A sealed business-sized envelope was on top of the stack, on the front her father had hand written "Ranya, read this first." She opened it carefully with her folding pocket knife, which had been in her jacket pocket when she had thrown it on back at her apartment in Charlottesville. She withdrew the single sheet of stationery and unfolded it slowly, savoring her father's imagined touch.

Hello Ranya My Love,

If you are reading this letter, then I have either died or I otherwise cannot communicate with you, so I am terribly sorry for leaving you all alone my beloved, please forgive me. I have prepared a list of all of our bank accounts and insurance agents and attorneys to call now.

In the small yellow envelope you will find a bank safe deposit box key and instructions. The deposit box contains some items and papers which you may find useful as well as some family photographs and records. The white envelope contains some emergency money to hold you over temporarily. The box wrapped in brown paper contains my graduation gift to you.

Now that I am gone, there is a good chance that our family business is gone as well, or Freedom Arms is no longer under your control. In that event, I have prepared some items and put them into a safe location for you. Do you remember where you separated your shoulder, and where I found you? Go there. Going west, take the left fork, and stop at the stone tower. From the tower walk 200 feet (80 paces) at 300 degrees by the compass. Look under the southwest corner.

Ranya, if you are reading this after my passing, always remember your Mother's undying love for you, and try not to forget your father, who loved you so dearly.

Ranya read the letter a second and third time, and then she folded it into a small square and put it into her wallet next to her parents' pictures. She slit the fat white envelope with her folding pocket knife and riffled through the cash; there was a half-inch thick stack of fifty dollar bills.

In her mind Ranya tried to picture the location of the arms cache her father had described in his personal code. At age fifteen she had slammed into a hole on her 125cc Enduro and badly dislocated her left shoulder. She clearly remembered the accident and thus the general location of the cache. She knew she could reach it in twenty minutes on a dirt bike, or a bit longer on her Yamaha.

Finally she turned to the wrapped gift box, which was as big as a medium sized text book. Under the brown paper was a polished rosewood box. She lifted open the top and saw a gleaming blue-black pistol set into red velvet padding, along with two spare magazines, and a plastic compass the size of a large coin. She understood at once that the compass was to guide her way to her father's arms cache. He was a methodical man, and he had left nothing to chance.

The pistol was a highly customized compact .45 caliber "Colt Commander." Ranya lifted the pistol out of its velvet bed: it fit her hand perfectly. She noted all of the improvements: the extended beavertail grip safety for softer felt recoil, the checkering cut into the front of the grip, the glow-in-the-dark tritium sights, and the extended slide release for quicker reloading. Importantly, the pistol had safety release catches on both sides just above where her thumbs would rest for ambidextrous use. She was right handed, but if she needed the pistol while riding her Yamaha she would have to draw and fire left handed. Her father knew this, and put safeties on both sides.

The .45 was a beautiful piece of custom gunsmithing, right down to its sharply checkered rosewood grip panels, which matched the presentation box. Ranya stood by the bed and jacked the slide back with her left hand, verifying that the chamber was empty, and then eased it forward with a smooth metallic rhythm. She tested the safety, clicking it up and down with her thumb, and then she took aim at a mark on the wall and slowly squeezed the trigger. The hammer snapped forward crisply with a loud click.

There was no ammunition stored with the pistol, a wise precaution because it might have cooked off from the heat of the fire and ruined the rest of the contents of the safe. But without its cargo of ammunition, the pistol was no more useful for self-defense than a brick or a hammer. After seeing what men had done to her father, and feeling extremely vulnerable alone in the motel, Ranya put obtaining ammo for the pistol at the top of her list. It was out of the question that she would spend the night in the motel room defenseless and at the mercy of anyone who wanted to kick in her door.

Ordinarily Ranya traveled with a smaller Kahr 9mm pistol, to defend herself if she broke down or ran out of gas in an isolated rural or dangerous urban area. Today she had been in such a hurry that she had left the pistol still hidden in her apartment back in Charlottesville. She did not yet have a concealed pistol permit, she had only recently turned twenty one, but she had "carried" for several years anyway with her father's knowledge and approval. The 9mm pistol was purchased in his name because she had been officially under age.

Ranya Bardiwell had known she was attractive ever since she had been a young teenager from the way men often gazed at her. Sometimes leering men stared hard at her while unconsciously licking their lips, like a starving lion contemplating a gazelle. She knew what these men wanted, and that some of them would take it by force if they could.

Both Ranya and her father had nothing but contempt for law makers who would prefer to see a young woman raped and strangled, than to see her carry a pistol for her own self-protection against much larger and stronger men. At five foot eight and 120 pounds, Ranya harbored no delusions about her ability to fight off a 200 pound rapist in a bare-knuckles contest. She much preferred the idea of presenting a would-be rapist with the choice of instant flight or sudden death, after being confronted with her unexpectedly drawn pistol.

But without ammunition, the .45 was just a pound of steel. She tried to think of where she could buy ammo nearby late on a Saturday afternoon. The big national discount chain stores had stopped carrying ammunition, after repeated protests from gun control advocacy groups, and the other local gun store had also been burned out the night before. Then it occurred to her: the cache. She could get there easily before dark, and besides, she was curious to see what her father had left in it.

Ranya dressed again in her jeans and tan boots, and as she closed the door she left a "tell-tale," a small wad of rolled-up paper on the carpet which would be moved if anyone entered while she was gone. She felt it was a somewhat paranoid thing to do, but after what had happened to her father, she felt justified in her fears. The unloaded .45 was wrapped in a new t-shirt in her daypack.

The last afternoon sun was slanting through the pines when Ranya parked her Yamaha near the "stone tower," which was actually a chimney from a long-vanished house. The abandoned homestead sat in the middle of thousands of acres of immature new-growth pines belonging to the Federal Camp Timber Corporation. She had cautiously steered her street bike around the gate off the paved state road. It was only a heavy chain hanging between two steel posts, sufficient to keep out a car but not a motorcycle. After a mile of cautious riding on the dirt road (her low slung café racer was not suited for rutted terrain to say the least) she found the old stone and mortar chimney, which ironically was the only remnant of another house fire generations before.

Compass in hand, she set out through the forest underbrush on an azimuth of 300 degrees. It was not easy counting off precisely eighty paces while trying to walk a straight line through brambles and bushes and around trees, but she finished the course in short order, arriving at what she hoped was the correct location.

"Look under the southwest corner." The southwest corner of what? She hung her daypack on the stub branch of a pine tree and began a spiral search around it, studying the needle and leaf covered forest floor until she found a tiny clearing with only weeds and a few hardy saplings struggling to emerge. The clearing was a little higher than the surrounding ground, and when she brushed away the pine needles she found part of an old concrete foundation. She kicked the dirt and leaves away until she could see the edges of the fifteen by twenty foot slab; the earth beyond the south west corner was lower where the ground sloped downward.

That's got to be it, she thought, scooping away at the weedy soil beneath the corner. She wished she had brought a shovel, but still she made steady progress working her way under the cement until she came to a wall of rocks, which she quickly pulled down. There under the slab was a metallic case, with a folding handle facing her. She dragged the box out from under the concrete slab. It was green-painted aluminum, about four feet long by about eighteen inches high and wide. It had faded white Cyrillic lettering and numbers stenciled on it, and Ranya had no doubt that the case had once carried shells or grenades for the Soviet military. Now it contained another type of ordnance, for one private American citizen.

The lid of the metal case fit over the bottom with metal clips around its perimeter. Ranya unsnapped them quickly, eager to see the contents. She had spent her entire life around hundreds of guns and now they were all reduced to the contents of this one aluminum locker. She lifted off the lid and set it aside. Inside she saw three rifles nested together on their sides: two 5.56mm AR-15 variants similar to the military's M-16s, and an FAL in the heavier 7.62 NATO caliber. The AR-15s lacked the usual M-16 style carrying handles. All three of these semi-automatic military-style rifles had small scopes mounted on top. One AR-15 variant was a short-barreled carbine with a collapsible stock and the other was the standard length. They were set in their own plywood rack with magazines and ammunition boxes packed between them. These so-called "assault rifles" definitely had their uses, and perhaps she would need them one day, but for now they did not suit her motorcycle lifestyle. Even taken down into its two parts, the carbine was too large to carry inconspicuously in a back pack, and anyway Ranya had no intention of engaging in shootouts with better armed and more numerous enemies.

She lifted out the plywood shelf carrying these first three rifles and placed it on top of the locker's lid on the ground. Next there were another three rifles, these were bolt-action hunting rifles mounted with large telescopic sights. All three of them had black synthetic stocks. These rifles were not just lying on their plywood shelf, but were raised above it on precisely-made notched wooden stands with nothing else touching them. Their steel parts were coated in a thin layer of some type of clear grease. There was a paper and string tag hanging from each of their trigger guards, noting their calibers. They were in the utilitarian high-powered calibers of .243 Winchester, 7mm Remington magnum, and 7.62 NATO. Ranya admired the rifles without touching them, not wanting to disturb their protective coatings. She understood that these powerful and accurate long range rifles might prove very useful in the future, but again she knew that it would be ridiculous to try to transport any one of them on her motorcycle.

So she lifted out the plywood shelf containing the three sniper rifles and set it aside as well. The bottom of the aluminum box was jammed with cartridge boxes and bags and fabric zipper cases. Ranya rooted among the boxes until she found what she had come for: a bright yellow plastic carton labeled ".45 caliber." She snapped opened its lid; each of the 50 hollow-point cartridges was standing in its own little compartment like so many tiny brass eggs in a crate. Right away she loaded seven rounds into each of her three magazines, then slid one of them into her new pistol and jacked the slide to chamber a round, and finally snapped the safety up with her thumb. Her .45 was now "cocked and locked," perfectly safe to carry but ready to fire in a fraction of a second. This simple process provided an immediate sense of comfort and relief to her. Loading the pistol transformed her from a basically helpless female, at the mercy of the next pack of toothless hicks or hostile home boys to cross her path, into a warrior who could confidently take care of herself in almost any situation. Anyone who had grown up around guns knew that the world was starkly divided into two groups: unarmed potential victims, and armed survivors. Most of the unarmed potential victims didn't have any awareness of this dichotomy. Like sheep grazing placidly in a pasture, they optimistically hoped that they would simply slide through life without ever being confronted by a violent criminal.

As an added measure, Ranya dropped the magazine out and loaded one more bullet in it to replace the one she had chambered, providing her the full complement of eight rounds which her .45 could carry. Other pistols carried more rounds, but her eight fat .45 caliber bullets were each show stoppers, and would not require more than one shot delivered per attacker. Being a "single stack magazine" pistol, with its bullets resting one directly on top of the other in the magazine, the overall width of her .45 was still slim enough that she could carry it stuffed halfway down inside the front of her jeans. Held firmly in place by her leather belt, it would be virtually invisible with her jacket hanging over the exposed grip.

It was growing dark and Ranya had accomplished the task of acquiring ammunition for her .45, but she was still curious to see what other useful items were in the small cases at the bottom of the locker. These zipper cases also had paper and string tags tied to their carrying handles. She saw tags for various pistols, but one tag in particular caught her eye and she pulled out its black nylon case and unzipped it. Inside was an unusual type of firearm completely unknown to the vast majority of people, a single shot Tennyson Champion long range target pistol. These pistols looked like a cross between an antique dueling piece and a science fiction movie prop gun. This one had a walnut grip and a fourteen inch long blued steel barrel. A telescopic sight was mounted on top of the rear of the barrel, and the muzzle end was threaded to accept a compensator or other devices. The Tennyson Champions were unique in that their grip and trigger assemblies could accept a wide variety of interchangeable barrels in literally dozens of calibers. These ranged from .22 rimfire, to rifle cartridges capable of taking down an elk, if the shooter had wrists capable of handling the heavy recoil.

This particular Champion's barrel was chambered for .223 caliber, also called 5.56mm, the same cartridge fired by the military M-16 and its civilian version the semi-auto AR-15. With a quality scope and superior ammunition, and fired from a steady rest position, the Champion was capable of rifle-like accuracy. Best of all, the Champion would fit easily into Ranya's daypack. If and when she ever found the federal agent who killed her father, she intended to pay him back in kind, and the Champion could be exactly the right tool for the job. Her new .45 was a fine pistol for close range defensive use, but it would be nearly useless beyond 50 yards, the range at which her father had been killed. And Ranya had no desire to engage in a close-quarters-battle against agents armed to the teeth with the latest German submachine guns. The 5.56mm Champion could give her a rifle's long range stand-off distance, but in a portable low profile package.

The black pistol case had three pockets on the outside, and Ranya glanced into each. Two contained special ammunition in red plastic cases the size of cigarette packs, but the third Velcro-flapped pouch contained the real prize, a black sound suppressor no bigger than a fat stogie cigar. Sound suppressors could not remove the cracking sound of a supersonic rifle bullet flying through the air, but they could remove most of the sound of the muzzle blast as the bullet cleared the barrel and the expanding gases hit the air. Anyway, the "sonic crack" did not point to a shooter's position, since it was created by the passing bullet. Even when firing supersonic rifle bullets, a good sound suppressor would serve to keep a shooter's position from being discovered by greatly reducing the far louder muzzle blast.

Ranya decided to take the Champion with her, so she loaded the big pistol case into her daypack along with the rest of the .45 ammo and two more spare .45 magazines. She stuck her cocked and locked .45 into her jeans just inside of her hip on the left side, its grip toward her right hand in the "Mexican carry" position. As soon as she could, she intended to get a decent inside-the-pants concealment holster which would hold the gun more securely.

The rest of the cache would await her return on another day. She replaced the stackable rifle shelves in the locker, gasketed down the aluminum lid with its metal latches, and shoved it back into its hole under the cement slab. She quickly rebuilt the concealing wall of rocks, then heaped dirt against it and finally covered everything she had disturbed with a layer of pine needles.

Now Ranya not only felt the security of being able to defend herself with her pistol, she also enjoyed the new power of being able to reach out and touch an enemy at any distance out to several hundred yards away. With her better-than 20/20 vision and her steady hands, combined with what she now carried in her pack, she began to entertain thoughts of turning the tables on her father's killers, and hunting the hunters. Left alone in the world, she had no other remaining goal.

In a half hour she was back at her motel room. Her tell-tale wad of paper had not been disturbed.

11

Just after nine PM, after another scan of the "top of the hour" news summaries on the cable news channels, Ranya was pacing back and forth in front of her television. Even the coverage by the ordinarily more balanced TOP News Network was disappointing. The local Norfolk stations were teasing the gun store arsons for their late news programs, but there was no film footage of Freedom Arms or any mention of her father by name. His death was only referred to indirectly, as one of the victims killed in the Virginia attacks.

Ranya held her unloaded .45 pistol in her hand and practiced racking the slide and dry-firing it, aiming at television talking heads the instant a new face came into view. She practiced dry-firing right and left handed, with both single and double handed grips, frequently spinning around and drawing from inside her belt. She was working on acquiring a perfect sight picture on each newly appearing reporter as swiftly as possible, using them as convenient reaction targets. Besides becoming familiar with the pistol's sights, she was committing the pistol's operation to instinctive "muscle memory."

She stalked her drab room like a caged animal, constantly drawing, turning and shooting at the TV. Snap down the safety as the sights settle on the target, squeeze the trigger dropping the hammer, rack the slide, safety on, over and over. She was imagining the federal agent she knew only as George. She was visualizing blowing his brains out with a 200 grain hollow-point.

At 9:30 she clicked off the television and sat cross legged on the bed, staring at the cheap seascape print on the wall of waves crashing on a rocky beach. Enough. What next? She didn't remember to bring her phone and address book with her from her apartment in Charlottesville, and anyway most of her Virginia Beach lifeguard crowd had scattered after Labor Day. Then she remembered the new phone number she had on a scrap of paper.

Brad Fallon picked up on the second ring. "Hello?"

"Hi, Brad? This is Ranya…Ranya Bardiwell."

"Ranya! Hi, what's up?"

"Remember you said to call you if I needed anything? Well, I'm staying in a crummy motel and I'm going nuts. Do you… are you busy tonight? Anyway I'd like to see your boat, can you handle a visitor on short notice? Just to talk…"

"Sure, why not? No problem. Do you know how to get here? Sodermilk's farm at the end of Old Cypress Road, all the way around the back."

"I'll find it. Can I bring some beer or something?"

"No need, I'm testing out my new fridge even as we speak. It's loaded with cold beer already."

"I'll be there in twenty minutes. Just to talk, okay?"

"I've been such a hermit lately I'm kind of out of practice, but sure, come on over."

Brad pushed the end button and set the cell phone down on his dinette table. His phone, not Hammet's, which he had left in a Tupperware box on the dock. It figures, he thought, that when I finally get a nice looking female visitor, she's involved in the local trouble and has personal problems up to her eyeballs. Ever since last Sunday's Stadium Massacre he had felt as if lighting bolts were landing in succession closer and closer to him, and he wondered just how wise it was to invite a lighting rod like Ranya Bardiwell aboard Guajira.

He wasn't much of a believer in fate, but he still found all the coincidences beyond merely bizarre. Two months earlier he had almost closed a deal on a sailboat in Fort Lauderdale, and had also taken a close look at one in Charleston. Both boats were under forty feet long, which was more in his price range, and were available almost "cruising ready." If he had bought either one, he'd have been in the Bahamas by now, sailing and snorkeling in warm clear turquoise-colored water.

Instead, he had chosen Guajira, a larger ex-racing boat which needed a new engine, a new mast, and an interior makeover. And so here he was, as far up the eastern branch of the Nansemond River as a mastless forty-four foot sailboat with a seven foot draft could get. Now he was landlocked and trapped under the FBI's thumb.

So far his credit cards and bank accounts seemed unaffected, and on Monday he'd motor Guajira down the river and over to Portsmouth, to the boat yard where his mast was already waiting. Once she was rigged and ready he planned to haul ass out onto the Atlantic just as fast as he could. The thunderbolts were already landing too close to him, and he didn't want to be waiting around for one to land on his head.

Brad had showered but not shaved today, after completing the installation of a new 12 volt compressor for his built-in icebox. He checked himself out in the mirror of his cramped "head," or bathroom, and rubbed his one day whiskers. Not too bad, not bad enough to warrant a high speed shave, which might leave him with a nick that could still be bleeding when Ranya arrived.

He didn't look thirty, he thought. He had just the first hint of lines around his blue eyes, and he believed he could still pass for twenty-seven or so, not that he really wanted to. He wondered if he seemed old to a college-age girl. He didn't feel old, in spite of hitting "the big three-oh."

He considered cologne, but decided against it. This was not a date; this was comforting someone who had lost her father. But he did change from his old paint and varnish-stained cutoffs to clean khaki shorts, and a nice blue and white Hawaiian shirt. Then he did a quick straightening-up of his boat's interior, grateful that his refurbishing was nearly complete, and the power cords and paint cans were gone. He didn't want Ranya to think that he was an actual ogre, even if he lived alone on a boat on the edge of the Great Dismal Swamp. Not that he was considering putting the moves on her, not on the day her father was killed...

Still...she was young and she was attractive, with a pretty face and a cute figure, at least what he had been able to see of it. She certainly filled a tight pair of blue jeans very nicely. He had a vivid image of her climbing over the fence before him, and he'd liked what he had seen, very much. Best of all, she rode motorcycles and knew her way around guns, so she was certainly no "princess," a type Brad had no time for. Who knows, maybe she'd like to sail to the islands, and forget her sorrows under the warm Caribbean sun...

No, she was just coming over because she needed to talk, and had no one else to talk to.

But there was no denying it. Whether she was in mourning or not, she was a very attractive girl...

Ranya steered her way carefully down the oyster-shell road in second gear until she came around the last big tractor shed, and Brad Fallon's boat came into view in her headlight beam. It was bigger than she had imagined, long and low and gleaming like an ivory dagger beneath the limbs of an oak. Soft golden light glowed from a row of oblong portholes along the sides of the low cabin, and shined up from the deck hatches. The river was only about a hundred yards wide here. Marshland and Spanish moss-draped cypress trees extending into the Great Dismal Swamp began on the opposite shore. A steady breeze from the north moved the oak tree's branches, and the yacht shifted restlessly against its dock lines.

Brad stood up in his cockpit in her headlight's glare as she shut down her machine. She pulled off her helmet, shook her long hair down over her shoulders, and walked onto the small wooden dock which ran along the river bank.

"Welcome to Guajira, my humble home. Please come aboard. And yes, she really is a sailboat, or at least she will be next week, I hope."

"Should I take off my boots? I don't want to leave any marks on your deck."

"Don't worry about it. Who's going to notice any more marks, with all these leaves and crud from the tree?"

Ranya stepped across onto the boat through an open gate in the white lifelines. Soft jazz music was playing, coming out of speakers in the cockpit and from down below.

"Can I get you something to drink? I have beer, but I can open bottle of wine, or make a drink, whatever you'd like."

"Rum and coke?"

"That sounds great; I think I'll have the same thing." Brad slipped down below. His galley was by the companionway steps, and while he fixed their drinks Ranya sat on a cushioned cockpit bench seat looking around at the outside of the boat and also down inside.

"What does Guajira mean? Did you name her?"

"No, she was named Guajira when I bought her. Sailors are pretty superstitious, and some say that it's bad luck to change a boat's name. But I liked the name anyway, so I kept it. Plus, I really like the way it's painted on the transom. Guajira means a few different things. It means a kind of a peasant girl, and it's also the name of a wild Indian tribe in South America. The Guajira Peninsula is where they live; it's sort of a no-man's-land between Venezuela and Colombia. Did you ever see the movie Papillon?"

"No, I don't think so."

"Well, it's in the movie. It's one of the places that Steve McQueen stayed, after he escaped from Devil's Island."

"I guess you're lucky that you bought a boat with a name you like. I like it too. But what if it was named 'Rust Bucket' or something? Would you have changed it? Are you superstitious?"

"Not really. Well, maybe a little." Brad laughed. "I mean, I'll put a silver coin under the new mast when I raise it next week, that's pretty much mandatory!"

Ranya thought he had a great smile, and his blue eyes seemed to light up. She had made the right decision to visit his boat; he was cheering her up in spite of the ache that she felt.

"Cheers!" He passed up her rum and coke in a tall glass. "You wanted to know if I'm superstitious. Well I'll tell you one thing I won't do: I won't start a voyage on a Friday. Any sailor that does that is tempting fate. That's just asking for trouble."

"Are you serious?"

"Absolutely. I'm not really superstitious, and I don't care about black cats or walking under ladders, but no real sailor ever starts a voyage on Friday. That's not a superstition, that's a whole other thing... You just don't mock King Neptune. Out there, he's in charge. Starting a voyage on a Friday, well, that's just not something you do."

"You're kidding, right?"

"Sort of. But I won't start a voyage on a Friday. That's just begging for trouble. Ask any ocean sailor, they'll tell you the same thing." Ranya couldn't decide if he was pulling her leg or being serious. "Mind if I see down below? I'm curious to see what a sailboat like this is like inside"

"Of course, come on down. I've done a lot of work on her, but I'm not much of a carpenter, and I'm definitely not Martha Stewart. Guajira's a K-44, a racer-cruiser, but more on the racer side. There wasn't too much of an interior to begin with, and her owners raced her hard, and well, she needed some home improvements."

Ranya went below, Brad moved out of her way from the galley to give her room. There were four wide steps on a varnished teak ladder with hand rails on the side. The interior was mostly cream-colored surfaces with varnished teak moldings and accents, softened with cozy royal blue cushions and curtains.

Across from the galley and a little forward, on the right side of the main cabin, was a teak dinette table in its own little nook, with cushioned seating around it on three sides. On the tabletop there was a large chart of the Caribbean under a thin sheet of plexiglass, which was cut to exactly fit inside of a little wooden rail which ran around the edge of the table. Ranya correctly guessed that the little rail was to keep dishes from sliding off the table at sea. Even though she could feel the boat moving, rolling slightly at its dock, it didn't make her feel uncomfortable. She took her jean jacket off and hung it on a hook. She intentionally exposed the butt of her pistol, which was sticking out above her wide black leather belt against the black t-shirt she was wearing. She was curious to see Brad's reaction, it would tell her a lot about him.

He made a joke about it. "Hey, you won't need that around me, I promise!"

"Sorry, I guess I'm kind of paranoid lately."

"I wouldn't call it paranoid, not after what you've been through. I'd call it intelligent. I keep my .44 ready too. Up there." He pointed forward to his V-berth sleeping compartment.

Ranya eased out her .45, still cocked and locked with the hammer back, and laid it carefully into a narrow shelf full of paperbacks and CD's, which was built against the boat's hull above the dinette table. This shelf also had a teak railing on its open side, as did most of the tables and shelves on the boat. She thought it was handy; it kept a pistol or anything else that size out of sight but within easy reach. She was rapidly becoming impressed with how cleverly the built-in furnishings on the yacht were arranged, like the parts of a 3D puzzle.

She sat down behind the dinette table to look at the chart. Brad carried over their drinks and sat along the forward side of the table, careful not to crowd her. She wanted company, but not closeness, and Brad was being careful to give her some space, which she appreciated. The chart covered the Bahamas, and the Caribbean Islands from the latitude of Florida to Venezuela. "That's going to be my universe for a while, maybe a year at least. Cheers." They both sipped their dark rum and cokes from matching heavy glass tumblers. The smooth jazz sounds filled the interior of the yacht, occasionally their glances met above the chart, their eyes locking briefly and then quickly looking away. Ranya thought he had gorgeous eyes, dazzling deep blue. In another time and place she would have loved to stare into them.

"The last two summers I've worked as an ocean lifeguard in Virginia Beach," Ranya said. "I'd sit up in my stand and watch sailboats going past. I always wondered what kind of people were on them, and where they were going."

"Most of them are just out for a day sail, for just a few hours. But some of them might be setting out to cross an ocean, or even to sail around the world."

"Are you? Setting out to sail around the world?"

"I don't know... First I want to cruise the Bahamas and the Caribbean, and then sail on down to Venezuela. After that, I'll have to decide if I'm going through the canal to the Pacific, or staying in the Caribbean, or maybe heading down to Brazil...or coming back to the States. I'm going to play it by ear. And then you have to factor in the hurricane season. That's a big part of the planning, because Venezuela is just under the hurricane belt."

"But isn't it hurricane season now? Aren't you going to wait until it's over?"

"Good question. I was planning on taking it slow and coast hopping down to Florida, staying close to safe harbors until after hurricane season, but with the feds on my case...I'm kind of getting anxious to get out of their reach. Ever since last Sunday a lot of really weird stuff has been happening, and its getting way too close to me."

"Not as close as it got to me."

"I'm sorry, that was really stupid of me..."

"...Forget it."

"It's just... None of this seems accidental any more. Ever since the Stadium Massacre, it just hasn't, it's just, I don't know... It's just not what it seems, it's not what people think it is."

"Well that stadium job was pure bullshit, you do realize that, don't you?" asked Ranya.

"Yeah, of course, I mean, well anybody with a three-digit IQ knows that. I think it was all done on purpose, it was a set-up. To get the herd stampeding, the way that Indians used to stampede buffalo herds over cliffs. The sniper stampeded the herd in the stadium, and now the whole country's getting stampeded the same way."

Ranya sighed and leaned back against the cushions behind her. "Oh thank God, I'm glad to hear you say that. I thought I was the only one who thought that way. Everybody I know at school, at UVA, they all believe what they see on TV is the gospel truth. They all think the 'militias' did it, and they all support the gun ban one hundred per cent. They think the semi-auto ban's a great idea, only it doesn't go far enough! They'd ban everything! They think only cops and the army should have any guns at all, can you believe it? If they only knew my father was a gun dealer…"

"Ranya, this just isn't the same America I grew up in any more. I mean, we have all these Arab terrorists running around, but instead of focusing on the real threat, they'd rather be politically correct, and take everybody's guns away."

"Hey, I'm an Arab, did you know that? I'm Christian Lebanese, but I'm 100% Arab. But I know what you meant to say, you meant Muslims."

"I'm sorry Ranya, again. I'm really putting my foot in my mouth tonight… I'm not really as stupid as I must sound. I know the difference between Arabs and Muslims. Not all Arabs are Muslims, and not all Muslims are Arabs."

"That's right. And nobody's suffered under the Muslims more than the Christians in Lebanon. That's why my parents moved to America in the first place… But the government's still stuck in the PC mode, it's still in denial. They're afraid to come out and say what we all know: a hell of a lot of Muslims are just plain crazy."

Brad asked, "So do they really want to stop terrorism, or just turn America into a police state? If they really wanted to stop terrorism, they'd go after the real threat, and they still won't even say there's a problem with Muslims! And now they're trying to frame up white 'militias' as the next big terrorist threat. Why? I just don't understand it, and I'm not sticking around to find out what's going to happen next."

"Where are you going to go that's any better? Some banana republic where they'll take your boat and throw you in jail if you don't bribe the right people?"

"They'll do that here! The FBI or the BATF or whoever George really works for, they're threatening to take my money and my passport if I won't be an informant. What do you call that? And just look at what they did to your father! Face it, America is turning into a banana republic right here, just a great big banana republic. Laws don't mean anything any more, and the Constitution's become a joke. Laws are just whatever a couple of left wing radical judges say they are. I think this country's gone past the point of no return."

"Well that may be so, but I still think we should fight back."

"How? You can't stop it."

"You might be right, but I'm still going to try! I mean, it's like what Phil Carson said: if America goes down, there won't be anywhere left to hide. Anyway, I'm not leaving. My parents escaped to this country, and it's still the freest country there is. If America goes down..."

"America IS going down, isn't that obvious? And if Americans want to live in a police state, I can't stop them."

"Well I'm still going to stay and fight it. Maybe because there's one big difference between us."

Brad looked straight at her. "What's that?"

"They killed my father! I'm not letting it slide, and I'm not running away. Somebody's going to pay for killing my father!"

"I'm not 'running away', I'm just giving up on this country, for a while anyway. There's a difference."

"If you say so. But I'm staying, and I'm fighting, somehow... Hey, it's about time for the news, does that little TV work inside of here?"

Brad got up and moved across the boat and retrieved the little Panasonic from a shelf, and then he set it on the dinette table and plugged its cord into a 12 volt "cigarette lighter" style outlet in the galley.

The Friday night outbreak of arson attacks against the gun stores was the lead story on all the local stations. Ranya twisted the dial between the local network affiliates, wondering if Freedom Arms would appear, but it didn't. The in-studio anchors were alternating with younger "stand up" info babes and blow-dried hunks in front of burned and ruined stores. The operative word on all channels was "backlash." It was accepted at face value that the attacks across Tidewater Virginia were a result of fed-up local citizens on an anti-gun vigilante rampage.

Brad and Ranya caught part of a middle-aged black man's impassioned tirade. The title on the screen identified him as "Imam Sheik Ali bin Muhamed." The station was running some video taken earlier in the day of the Imam standing in front of a storefront mosque in downtown Portsmouth, just to the west of Norfolk. He was wearing a long white robe and a white caftan and was surrounded by a dozen grim-faced young black men in dark conservative suits and sunglasses wearing long overcoats, who were standing at what looked like the military "parade rest" position. The Imam gestured wildly as he shouted.

"These so-called attacks, they were not attacks; they were purely self-defensive in nature! Certainly they were at least as self-defensive as when the mighty United States Air Force bombed innocent Muslim cities in Afghanistan and Iraq, killing old men, women, and helpless baby children! What happened last night was self-defense by the community against the vile and vicious merchants of death, merchants of death who have been feeding on the blood of our people, pushing the tools of death on our people! So I feel no sorrow for their loss, for they can not ever repay the sorrow and pain which they have inflicted on our people with their white devils' tools of death! Now they have met their righteous fate, all praise be to Allah, peace be upon him!"

Ranya was burning inside. "Look at those bastards! 'Merchants of death'! All of those guys are packing, they say they hate guns, but they're all carrying them!"

"How can you tell?" asked Brad.

"Trust me, I was raised in a gun store, we sold holsters every day, we taught the concealed carry license course, I can spot a gun. But those guys are packing serious stuff, big stuff, pistol grip shotguns I'd say. They're hardly bothering to hide it! And you don't see the cops hassling them either. I wonder if any of them were the same guys who burned our place down? I wonder who paid them, the FBI or the BATF?"

She was livid, and violently twisted the channel dial. She stopped briefly on the next local channel. They were replaying for the hundredth time the signature video footage of the massacre: victims tumbling in a human avalanche from the upper decks of the stadium.

"Less than fifty people were hit by bullets," Ranya said, "but it's still called a gun massacre. They should blame it on penning up thousands of people like cattle in those upper decks. Anything could have caused that panic: tear gas, smoke grenades, anything! But every single victim gets blamed on the gun." She switched it again, and on the next channel it was also "backlash" night. A pretty Asian-American female anchor was introducing her next piece.

"Today at the state capitol in Richmond, Commonwealth's Attorney General Eric Sanderson held a news conference and fielded questions about the 'night of rage' against Tidewater gun stores." The camera cut to a handsome man somewhere in his forties, with a luxurious growth of thick dark hair graying at the temples. He was standing at a podium in some formal briefing room, flanked by an American flag and the flag of Virginia.

"While I regret the violence which swept through southeastern Virginia last night, I do understand the intense outrage felt by most of our citizens toward those gun dealers who have made a handsome living by selling the tools of murder and death. And although the mass murderer James Shifflett does not appear to have personally bought his deadly assault rifle at one of the gun stores which was destroyed last night, the sad truth is, any of those gun stores could just as easily have sold it to him, or a wide variety of other assault rifles which are every bit as deadly. And as incredible as it may sound, gun stores have continued to sell assault rifles, even after the Stadium Massacre, even up until today!

"So I do wholeheartedly support the Schuleman-Montaine Firearms Safety Act, and all of its provisions. And I most seriously warn any persons in Virginia, anyone who might be tempted to hold onto an illegal assault rifle after next Tuesday, that the full force of the Commonwealth will be brought down upon you if you make that mistake! I will have zero tolerance for any other Jimmy Shiffletts lurking among our law-abiding population!

"I have also been asked if I shall vigorously pursue and prosecute those criminals who participated in last night's arson attacks, which resulted in the deaths of four gun dealers. My answer is that in Virginia, we already have dozens of open murder investigations under way, and most of those murders were committed with guns sold by gun dealers like the ones who were attacked last night. So no, I will not assign a higher priority to investigating last night's attacks, than to all of the other unsolved murders caused by the firearms that these gun dealers sold! These dead gun dealers, these merchants of death, well, they'll just have to get in line and wait their turn behind all of their dead victims, who were already killed by the guns they sold for blood money!'"

Ranya switched off the TV set. She had passed beyond angry to morosely reflective. "Blood money. A merchant of death. That piece of shit just called my father a merchant of death, just like the Muslim guy did. What's his name, Eric Sanderson? He won't even investigate. He just declared open season on all firearms dealers, he just drew a target on all of them. Shit."

"You want another rum and coke?"

"Just hand me the damn bottle. This is the worst! Sanderson just called my father an enemy of the people, and practically praised his murderers. And did you hear what he said about next Tuesday and the full 'force of the state'? It sounds like he's getting ready to deal with a lot more enemies of the state. I guess that's me too, I mean, I'm the daughter of a merchant of death."

Brad poured an inch of Captain Morgan's into a fresh tumbler and handed it to her. She drained half of the dark spiced rum in a gulp and made a sour face and coughed.

He said, "This country is finished. The America we knew is gone, and now it's time to get the hell out. It lasted for two good centuries, that's something, but now it's over."

"Maybe so, Brad Fallon, maybe so. But they killed my father and burned my house, and I'm not going to just let it go! I'm not! Somebody's got to pay!"

"So what are you going to do?"

"I don't know yet. I'll think of something. Find George, start there I guess." She finished her rum and poured herself some more. Ranya was developing the germ of an idea, if not quite yet a plan. She wasn't going to forget George, she'd still look for him, and through him try to find out who was really pulling the strings behind the Stadium Massacre and the arson murders. She was going to find George, but that might take a long time. In the meanwhile, she was going to make somebody pay for her father's murder. Somebody who was making political hay from his death, somebody who didn't think his death was worth investigating. Somebody who was glad he was dead.

First she was going to kill Virginia Attorney General Eric Sanderson, the politician who had just put the government seal of approval on her father's murder. A slight smile curled across her lips as a delicious irony occurred to her: instead of using one of those ee-vil semi-automatic assault rifles with their high-capacity magazines, she was going to kill him with a single shot target pistol. Oh yes, she had just the tool for the job.

Now that she had decided on who, and she knew how, next it was just a matter of finding out where, and deciding when she would do it. And she would do it.

Ranya slid down on her back on the sofa-like "settee" behind the dinette table. The low ceiling above her began spinning as the sailboat rolled gently at the dock, so she closed her eyes. She was still smiling as she contemplated Sanderson's face in her crosshairs, with her right index finger increasing its pressure on the trigger one ounce at time.

Brad pulled a soft blanket out of a locker and spread it over her, then untied her tan hiking boots and gently pulled them off without causing so much as a stir. Finally he placed a pillow next to her where she would find it if she rolled over. He studied her while she slept; she was at peace for the first time since he had met her. Ranya was attractive, but in a girl-next-door way; she had no fashion model's angular features or swollen bee-stung lips. She did have stunning eyes. Even in her sadness and her anger they were beautiful, sometimes appearing amber, sometimes hazel or even pale green depending on the light. Asleep, he could see a touch of the orient in their cast, which recalled to him an old girlfriend he had loved to kiss, just to see her eyes closed in passion. Ranya's eyebrows were not plucked into thin lines, but neither were they bushy, they were just perfect the way that God had made them. He hadn't really seen her smiling, but he imagined that she would have a terrific smile on a happier day. She was taller than average, which appealed to Brad, with a nice figure that he had enjoyed seeing tonight after she had removed her jacket.

She was pretty, yes, but she had more than her share of personal problems, to say the least. Even so, from their first meeting Brad had been unable to avoid considering her as a possible partner for his tropical sailing adventures. She was certainly more than sufficiently attractive and intelligent, and when she mentioned that she had been an ocean lifeguard, that had sealed it for him. For Brad, swimming, snorkeling and scuba diving were a large part of his enjoyment of the sailing lifestyle, and his ultimate dream was to find a spirited mermaid to share it with. He had little use for porcelain princesses or mere boat adornments.

But he knew that it could never happen with Ranya, she was finishing college, and she had her father's murder to deal with at the same time. To top it off she appeared to have a quixotic streak, and she planned to stay in America and tilt at windmills, while Brad was going to sail away far and fast.

Well, it didn't matter that she wasn't the one. He knew that the Caribbean islands were full of pretty girls, tourists on holiday from Holland and Germany and Scandinavia, and further south he intended to discover the beauties of Venezuela and Colombia and Brazil.

Brad closed the hatches, turned off the music and the lights, brushed his teeth and crawled into his triangular V-berth double bed which was all the way forward in the bow of the boat. He was trying to compare the qualities of the blond northern European girls to the raven-haired South American lovelies, but he couldn't stop thinking about the motorcycle-riding brunette lifeguard named Ranya Bardiwell, who was sleeping only fifteen feet behind him.

George Hammet, the ASAC of the Norfolk Field Office of the BATFE, spent Saturday night drinking beer and swapping lies with visiting ATF and FBI colleagues at the Ship's Bell. This was a bar-and-grill close to Norfolk's Little Creek Naval Amphibious Base, a place which was much favored by the local Navy SEALs. Some of the fifty or so out-of-town agents supplementing the Joint Task Force were staying at the amphib base's Bachelor Officer's Quarters, and a few had called old buddies who were still in the service. The Ship's Bell had come highly recommended as a meeting place; it was tucked discreetly into the back corner of an obscure second-rate shopping center. By ten o'clock the parking lot was packed with dark full-sized SUVs; Suburbans and Excursions with discreet government bumper and windshield decals, known only to federal law enforcement insiders.

George Hammet enjoyed the fact that his unpredictable work hours meant that he never had to explain his comings and goings or whereabouts to his wife Laura, and he was free to spend his night drinking with other agents and flirting with the waitresses and "frog hogs" or SEAL groupies who frequented the place. The juke box was cranking, the beer was flowing, and the testosterone level was sky-high in the Ship's Bell, with its walls covered with photographs and memorabilia of past Underwater Demolition Team and SEAL Team glory. More girls were arriving by the minute as the word went out by cell phones and instant messengers that a real live crowd was in town at the Bell.

These impromptu parties and the easy women that gravitated to them were either a fringe benefit or an occupational hazard, depending on the outlooks of the federal agents who spent weeks at a time "in the field" on cases. Very frequently their gold wedding bands were left behind in their motel rooms as they became "out of town bachelors," and this propensity to play the field was reflected in sky-high divorce rates.

George Hammet was a local though, and he had a strict policy of not fooling around in Tidewater: he wasn't stupid. Tonight he was also limiting his alcohol intake, and he excused himself from his circle of new and old buddies just after midnight. As a local, he had his own personal vehicle, and was not dependent on anyone for a ride.

He drove his red Jeep Cherokee across Norfolk, through the downtown tunnel and into Portsmouth, the location of Imam Sheik Ali bin Muhamed's "Al Fuqra Mosque." The mosque occupied several store fronts taking up an entire block along King Street. Hammet allowed himself one casual pass in front of it and saw that the lights were out and there was no activity around it to be seen. The rest of the neighborhood was zoned for commercial use, but all of the businesses were closed, and not a soul was to be seen walking around.

He drove along the side streets across from the mosque south of King to establish his walking route in and out, and then two blocks away he found a dark and hidden place to park his Cherokee behind a shuttered laundromat. He pulled on thin black driving gloves and a dark ball cap, and exited the Jeep carrying a black gym bag. At this hour, no one was going to fool with a burly guy in a leather bomber jacket, even a white guy. Just in case, Hammet carried his Glock 19 in his shoulder holster rig with his jacket open. The ball cap was pulled low over his eyes, to make identifying him harder in case someone did happen to see him.

He walked in the shadows in the alleys and foot paths on the way to his preselected position across King Street from the mosque. Crouching behind a hedge, against the cement wall of a discount shoe store, Hammet unzipped his gym bag and withdrew an ugly little Ingram MAC-11 machine pistol, the smaller .380 caliber version of the infamous MAC-10. A suppressor the size of a paper towel tube was screwed down onto the stubby barrel until it met the rectangular body of the gun. This MAC-11 was one of the "dirty tricks" guns Malvone had given him a month earlier when they had finalized their plans. It was a gun which had been seized from a member of one right wing group or another in Idaho or Montana or Arkansas, but never entered into any law enforcement log or registry. A trace on the MAC's origins would quickly prove that the "militia movement" was a serious national security threat, with "militiamen" and weapons flowing freely from state to state.

Hammet inserted a long 30 round stick magazine into the pistol grip under the blocky weapon, then with his left hand he grasped the knob on the MAC's flat top and pulled the bolt all the way to the rear until it caught. That's all there was to it; the MACs were, as they said, "crude but effective." The rough sights on top were a joke, and he ignored them as he raised the weapon above the waist high bushes. He sighted down the long suppressor at the big crescent moon painted in white on the plate glass front of the mosque. Hammet pulled the trigger and swept from right to left as he emptied the entire thirty round magazine in one three second burst, holding the MAC down with his left hand gripping the suppressor. The sound suppressor on the MAC-11 was fairly effective, and the puny low velocity .380 caliber rounds were subsonic so there were no sonic cracks to deal with, but in any case the sound of his firing off the magazine in one burst was completely drowned out by the plate glass exploding and crashing down across the street.

He dropped the warm MAC-11 machine pistol into the middle of the hedge, where it would soon be recovered as evidence. Then he reached into the gym bag again and withdrew a sheaf of a hundred pages, which he tossed over the hedge onto the sidewalk, to be scattered by the wind and found later by citizens, reporters, and police. His task complete, he crept along behind the hedge, until he reached the pathway which led to the alley and back to his hidden Jeep.

In five minutes he was driving west at the speed limit on I-264. He did not want to have his Cherokee filmed going back through the tunnel right after the shooting. He was an experienced lawman, and he knew that the tunnel had cameras which recorded every vehicle passing under the Elizabeth River, so instead he took the long way home, circling around and returning to Virginia Beach on Military Highway. He banged on his steering wheel in time with the country music on his radio; it had been a great night's work. The shooting had gone without a hitch, and the anxiety of operating in the danger zone dissolved into post-mission euphoria. He even felt good for the "imam," because after tonight, Sheik Ali bin Muhamed was going to be as famous as Al Sharpton or Louie Farrakhan. He was actually doing the "sheik" a favor, as he saw it.

Ranya was walking down a sodden forest trail between steep fir-covered slopes. She was following twenty feet behind a trail guide, or perhaps a ranger, who was dressed in green and brown with a pack on his back. Going around a bend in the trail the guide suddenly froze, then turned and ran, shucking his pack, and began climbing up a medium-sized larch just ahead of a pair of onrushing yearling brown bears. As soon as Ranya saw the bears she looked for her own tree, and in only moments she was twenty feet above the ground, looking directly across at the trail guide, as both grunting and huffing bears sniffed the air and raised up on their hind legs, and tested the trunk of his tree with swipes of their paws.

The smaller of the bears then hugged the tree, and inch by improbable inch it lifted itself up until it was snapping and snarling only scant feet beneath the trail guide, who was attempting to climb ever higher up the swaying boughs, until under the weight of bear and man it began to bend. Finally the man could climb no higher, yet the bear kept hunching up the sagging tree, an inch at a time. The trail guide was trying to lift his feet and legs above the snapping maw of the yearling bear, holding them up with no branches left to support them, holding them up for dear life. At last he began to slide down the slender trunk, and the brown bear snatched his booted ankle as easily as a river-running salmon, then jerked him in one smooth motion out of the tree to the ground where he landed with a thud, and where the larger bear was waiting with open jaws.

Ranya stared in rapt horror as the two bears then pulled at the man, thrashing him between them like two terriers playing bloody tug-of-war with a broken squirrel, and when the man was ripped apart they began to loudly eat the pieces on the ground, holding them down and tearing the flesh into bloody strips with their great fangs, then bolting down the shredded meat, chewing and gnawing at his bones until no flesh remained, and then all at once they were finished and without a single look up the other tree at Ranya, they both turned and lumbered into the brush, leaving only cracked and scattered bloody bones.

12

Ranya Bardiwell was relieved that no one recognized her, sitting alone in the last pew of Saint Charles Catholic Church. She didn't particularly want to be there, but felt obligated to make an appearance. She had awakened suddenly on Brad's boat in the first light, with a cutting headache and vague nightmare images still rolling through her consciousness. She had to piece together where she was, and why she was there, and suddenly all of yesterday's unimaginable events came flooding back in a rush. But she didn't allow her grief to paralyze her. She dragged herself off the boat and onto her bike without waking up Brad, and didn't come fully alive until she was under the shower in her motel room. She inhaled a McBreakfast in Suffolk, and made it to church in time for the nine o'clock mass wearing her jeans and denim jacket.

Ranya sat, and stood, and kneeled with the rest of the congregation, her lips half-moving along automatically with long memorized prayers, but she did not hear the spoken words of the readings or the sermon.

Instead, she sat in church behind a hundred dutiful and faithful parishioners and she plotted a murder. She schemed and figured and planned several of the ways that she might be able to sneak undetected within three hundred yards of the highest law enforcement figure in Virginia, and snipe him from a hidden place.

"Give us this day our daily bread, and forgive us our trespasses, as we forgive those who trespass against us," rose from a hundred throats, but not from hers. No, she would not forgive, not now, and maybe never. If there was a hell, perhaps she would go there, but she would not forgive. If God wanted to forgive her, if there was indeed a God, forgiveness was going to be up to Him.

Anyway, hadn't she earned up some special consideration, some surplus of blessings to weigh against her sins? She rarely lied, drank practically no liquor for a University of Virginia Cavalier, didn't do drugs, and most of all she had remained true to the pledge she had made to her dying mother, all those years before. Ranya Bardiwell, with the amber eyes and the swelling hips, almost a decade beyond puberty, was still a virgin. Beside her mother's death bed it did not seem like a difficult promise to make or to keep, not for a girl of twelve, to take no boy into her bed before marriage. "True love waits," her mother said, and Ranya had made the promise and had waited all these long years.

She had become an expert at fending off the clumsy hands of horny boys, as well as detecting counterfeit promises of undying love. She had steeled herself to wait for the Right Man, and she was still waiting.

And now, a twenty-one year old virgin, she was plotting murder in church during Mass. She was going to kill a man, even before she had slept with one.

So be it. Sanderson had publicly and proudly spit on her father's murdered body. Her father who had been shot and burned by government agents, and now Sanderson was going to pay.

She guessed that she would never be able to get a long range shot in Richmond anywhere near the capitol: Sanderson's schedule would be confidential, and his precise path a mystery. She could stalk him, and get close enough to use her .45, but escape would then be impossible, and her plans didn't end with the death of the Attorney General of Virginia.

On short notice it would be impossible to find out where he lunched or clubbed or golfed or played tennis, not without making herself conspicuously nosy.

That left his home. Even the Commonwealth's Attorney had to have a home where he went most nights, and he was likely to own a nice chunk of property that would have adequate hiding places within range of her scoped .223 caliber Tennyson Champion. If she could locate his house, she could get him. After three years of doing university undergrad research on the internet, she knew she could easily find his house. She made a mental list of the things she would need for the operation, and where she could obtain each item on a Sunday in Tidewater.

Ranya did not join the line to walk up to the altar to take Holy Communion, but she did wait until the end of Mass before leaving, so that she could speak to Father Alvarado as he greeted his flock outside of his church. She had to do it, to pretend, for the sake of ensuring her father's proper burial in the family plot next to her mother. Her own belief in God was very much in doubt, but she could not extend that doubt to her father, who had been a devout Catholic to the end.

After returning to her motel room, Ranya changed into jogging clothes, pulled her hair into a pony tail with a colored band, and ran the mile down the gravel shoulder of state road 32 to her property. As she approached she could see a man in a gray suit talking to a deputy who was leaning against his patrol car. Ranya was amused by their surprise when the female jogger they had been watching suddenly stopped in front of them. She held her hand out to the fortyish man in the suit, catching her breath. "I'm Ranya Bardiwell, Joseph Bardiwell's daughter. Who are you?"

"Nice to meet you Miss Bardiwell. I'm Fred Pybus, from Atlantic Property and Casualty." He handed her his business card. "We underwrote the store and the house, the whole place. I'm real sorry about what happened, to your father, everything...but you'll be glad to know that he had excellent coverage with Atlantic. You're the, uh, only living relative, correct?"

"That is correct. I'm the last, the bitter end."

"Well that will certainly simplify things. I've been in touch with your father's attorney... Say, you don't happen to have a key for the burglar doors, do you?"

"No. They might be back there," she pointed to the ashes and ruins of her house, "if you have a rake."

"That's okay. It's better locked up. I was thinking about getting a dump truck tomorrow, and having the place cleaned out. The truck can yank the burglar doors off with a chain. It shouldn't be a problem."

"What do you mean a dump truck? There's a lot of valuable stuff in there, it can't all be burned."

"Well, Miss Bardiwell, we'd like to call it a total loss, and just write it off. It's not worth it to try to assess the condition of each firearm. With the high temperatures a gun that seems okay might not be safe to shoot. They could never be sold; it's a question of liability. We'll inventory them as they go in the dump truck for the claim, but we're going to clean the place out. It's best for everybody."

"All right, what time?"

"Say, make it ten?"

"I'll be there Mr. Pybus."

Ranya left them and walked around the store and across the big lawn, stopping at the scorched and blackened earth marked by the little yellow flags. Once again she was hit with a painfully vivid image of his burnt and ruined body, and she looked skyward beyond the clouds, deep into the blue and said, "It's not over, Daddy. I'm going to find them, and I'm going to make them pay. I've got your guns now, and I'm going to go after them."

She unlocked her little shed by the back fence, swung the two plywood doors open wide, and pulled the green canvas cover off of her two old motorcycles. Sometimes she would accept a ride in a car down from UVA, so she kept her spare street bike's tag and registration current, to have transportation around Tidewater when her Yamaha FZR was back up in Charlottesville. Ranya admired her still-gleaming "black cherry," her 1986 450cc Honda Nighthawk, which she had found unwanted and unridden in a Freedom Arms customer's garage and bought for a song. It didn't have the blinding speed of her 600cc café racer, but the Nighthawk was a perennial classic, a sweet ride, and a lovely all-around bike. It was the first street-legal bike she had ever owned, and she would never give it up.

The 250cc Enduro next to it was as ugly as the Nighthawk was beautiful, built up from parts, and painted in flat tan primer. It was a screamer that could run trails flat out and catch more air than anyone could handle, but despite its dirt-eating look it had been made street legal with a bolted-on light kit. When Ranya needed to cover any distance on the highways on it, she just switched the tag over from one of her other bikes, and she had never been pulled over or had any problems.

Ranya backed the Nighthawk out and locked the shed up again. She folded up the green cover and strapped it over the back of the saddle with her bungee cord net. She was taking the canvas cover because she already had a use for it in her steadily evolving plan. The black motorcycle had her extra helmet hanging from a handlebar. She checked it for spiders, (she'd made the mistake of not looking carefully inside her stored helmet before), then twisted her ponytail up with her left hand and trapped it under the white plastic "brain bucket." The Nighthawk's motor caught as soon as she turned the key and pushed the start button, living up to its reputation as her "black cherry," and immediately settled into a rhythmic purr.

While nowhere near as fast as her FZR at its top end, the Nighthawk was plenty fast enough for what Ranya had planned, and it had sufficient range in its gas tank. The FZR had an eye catching (and memorable) red white and blue "slash" paint job over its full fairing, but the black and chrome Nighthawk was handsome in a more classic, but rather generic and less memorable way. Finally, the Nighthawk had much higher ground clearance beneath it than the low-slung FZR, and if necessary it could be carefully ridden off of the pavement.

Ranya took an old trail through the woods to a small back road to return to her motel, because she didn't want the cop to remember seeing her on the black bike. She parked it behind the end of the Colonial's twelve units away from the office.

"Danny, I think we'd better bring the Jeep" off the street, and back it right up to the garage. We need to be extra careful today."

"Can I do it Dad?"

"Do you think you can reverse it straight up the driveway without plowing into Mom's rose bushes?"

"Aw Dad, that's easy. I'll get it."

Mark Denton pushed the button inside the garage to roll the door up out of the way, while his son Danny went down to get their black Jeep CJ. His wife's Lexus occupied one side of the two-car garage, while the other side had been surrendered years before to their eighteen foot ski boat on its trailer, and a small mountain of recreational gear. Sixteen year old Danny Denton had a learner's permit, and he reversed up the driveway slowly and carefully until the back of the jeep was flush with the open garage door.

If any of their neighbors on the adjoining half-acre properties had been watching very closely, they would only have seen a large igloo cooler, a few plastic storage crates, and a golf bag being loaded into the back of the Jeep. In reality, the boxes contained ammunition and cartridge magazines, and the golf bag contained four semi-automatic rifles.

"Dad, can I drive today, please?"

"Son, I'd say yes, but we can't risk getting pulled over today, not with what we're carrying."

"Why not? The ban's not until Tuesday."

Mark Denton, gray haired at 57, but still an imposing figure with ever present military bearing, shot his son the withering "no way" look. "You ready? Let's roll."

"Will we be back in time for supper?"

"Nah, it's eighty miles down, a couple of hours to bury this stuff, then eighty miles back. We'll eat on the road. Just us men today kiddo, no split tails, so maybe we'll eat at a real truck driver's diner on the way home. The kind of place your mother hates."

"That sounds cool dad."

Mark Denton weaved his way out of his Virginia Beach subdivision and swung onto West 44, the Virginia Beach Expressway. They both knew every inch of the route which would take them down into North Carolina, where they had a cottage near Harvey Point along the Albemarle Sound.

Danny said, "At least they're letting us keep our shotguns and bolt actions. We'll still be able to go hunting this fall."

Mark Denton stared at his son through his green-lensed aviator's sunglasses. "Isn't that special. They're 'letting' us keep some of our guns. 'Letting' us. For how long? What ever happened to the second amendment? What ever happened to 'shall not be infringed'? Danny, when I was twenty-two, just a few years older than you are now, the government handed me a fully-automatic M-16, and all the ammo I could carry, and sent me out to kill as many NVA as we could find. No tag limit, and no season!

"And now I can't keep the semi-automatic AR-15 that I bought twenty years ago. Your grandpa Denton hauled an M1 Garand from Guam to Okinawa, and our own government sold me that surplus Garand in the golf bag for 250 bucks. Now they don't trust me with it any more, and I'm supposed to just throw it in a police dumpster. Same thing with your M1 carbine: your Uncle Herbie brought it back from Korea, no problem. It was okay for Herbie to bring it back on a troop ship in '51, but now we can't keep it any more. They don't trust us any more, because of what one lunatic supposedly did up in Maryland. Supposedly. And now all of the semi-autos have to go. Danny, you do understand what's happening, don't you?"

"Well, at school they said it's for everybody's safety. It's for the common good."

"For the common good my ass! Danny, it's all about power: who's got it, and who doesn't. Just about the only weapons a SWAT team is afraid of are these semi-auto rifles. They'll cut through Kevlar vests, and they put out plenty of firepower. Shotguns won't penetrate their body armor, and bolt actions are too slow. With the semi-autos out of the way, the SWAT teams can go anywhere they want and pick up anybody with no trouble. No muss, no fuss. Anybody, anytime."

"But only if you're a criminal, dad. We don't have to worry, because we don't break the law."

"Are you kidding? We're getting ready to break it today! And the way things are going in this country now, anybody can be arrested for breaking one damn law or another just about any time. If you do your taxes wrong, or you step on a rare endangered cockroach, or if you fill in a puddle without the EPA's permission, your ass'll be hauled in front of a judge. And if you won't go, they'll send the SWAT boys to bring you in… or kill you."

"Dad, I'm not saying you're wrong, but…you know, you're sounding kind of…paranoid. That's what mom says."

"Yeah? She does? Paranoid? Well maybe getting shot a couple of times in Viet Nam and Laos will do that to you! Danny, I saw a lot of good men die, better men than me by a long shot, and I killed some folks too, and I learned something important: the big difference between coming home alive or in a tin box is firepower! Smooth talking lawyers and preachers and congressmen won't save your ass when it gets down to brass tacks! When it's really crunch time, when you're right down in the mud and the blood, there's only two kinds of people: the ones with the fire power, and the dead ones. Fancy words don't mean crap when some-body's pointing a gun at you!

"You know, when I was shot on my second tour, that's the purple scar across my hip, we were almost out of ammo. We were hauling ass to a landing zone near the Laotian border, and I was down to just my .45. I was getting carried along by my buddies like you help your grandma. Now a .45's a great handgun, but don't let anybody kid you, AK-47's will trump it every time. That is, until a friendly Huey with a pair of mini-guns shows up and trumps their sorry asses! Oh yeah!" Mark Denton smiled at the old memory of the sudden reversal of fortune which had saved his life.

"That's what it always gets down to Danny, trump the chump. And if you've got no firepower, you're the chump."

"Then why are we going to bury these rifles?"

Mark Denton had to pause and think about that one. "Well, I guess I'm afraid one of our brainwashed commie neighbors might call the snitch line, and we can't take the chance. We'd lose the house, I'd go to jail, hell, they might just shoot in the pyrotechnics and do a Waco on us, and burn us out. You know, when the SWAT boys find out they've got an old Special Forces guy holed up, they come in hot and heavy. They probably know about these rifles, at least the Garand. Hell, they sold it to me! I'm sure they have it all in a data base somewhere. They might decide to pay us a visit, and maybe come in the hard way, at oh-dark-thirty. We can't risk it."

"But Dad, they can't do that, that's against the Fourth Amendment, right? No search and seizure without a good reason and all that?"

Mark Denton shook his head slowly. "Danny, you've got a lot to learn. That's how it used to be, when the Bill of Rights used to mean something. But between the war on drugs and the war on terror, they can basically smash down anybody's door and find a reason later. After Tuesday, they'll have 'probable cause' to come charging into any gun owner's house any time they want to, searching for illegal semi-autos."

Their Jeep approached the I-264 cloverleaf interchange just after crossing into Norfolk, and Mark Denton signaled and moved to the right lane, slowed down and got ready to exit. A moment later there was a blinding flash and a fireball accompanied by a crashing thunderclap, and the Jeep, which had been traveling west at sixty miles an hour, was sent cart wheeling end over end down the highway in chunks. Pieces of the Jeep, pieces of Mark and Danny Denton, pieces of rifles, and thousands of bullets and ammunition fragments rained down and rolled along both sides of the highway for three hundred yards.

Several other cars were destroyed or knocked out of control by the force of the blast, and a fifty-car pileup resulted in seconds. This happened on a warm September Sunday just before noon, when tens of thousands of tourists were flocking to the beaches, and in minutes both major highways were backed up in solid gridlock for miles, to the north, south, east and west.

"**Hey boss, it's me.** I'm in Norfolk. It just went down."

"Oh? All right. It's sooner than I expected. Everything cool?"

"Very."

"Which one?"

"Number two."

Wally Malvone looked at a copy of the potential target list he had given Bob Bullard at his house, after the poker game broke up Friday night. "Number two" on the list meant Mark Denton, a fifty-seven year old corporate attorney who lived in Virginia Beach. Denton was an avid hunter and NRA match target shooter, who at one point several years ago had been associated with the Blackwater Rod and Gun Club. It wasn't a tight connection, but it would be enough to stick in the public mind. Most important of all, Denton was a combat veteran who had done two tours in Viet Nam with the Army Special Forces. Mark Denton was a former Green Beret, and therefore, he was obviously an extremely dangerous "angry white man."

"Any collaterals?"

"Oh yeah, big time. He was turning off the highway. He'd have been heading away from downtown if I waited any longer. Traffic was kind of heavy, so it's a mess. But on the plus side, we really lucked out and scored some major bonus points! You should see the crash site. There's pieces of rifle ammo all over the place, and I saw a cop carrying half of an AR-15. It sure looks like Denton was moving weapons! I saw .223 and 30 caliber ammo, so you can bet he had more rifles in his car, and the cops are bound to find them."

"Hey, well, that sounds great! Okay, get on back up here, oh, anytime tomorrow. Have a big night out on the card I gave you, just stay out of trouble. We're really looking good on this one. Oh, and make sure you watch CBA News tonight. I think they're about to get a major scoop."

Ranya Bardiwell changed into her disguise in a stall in the women's bathroom on the first floor of Old Dominion University's main library. She had spent a productive hour shopping in the downtown Norfolk Goodwill Store, and now she admired her new look in front of the long mirror above the row of sinks. Her hair was pulled back and pinned in a tight bun and covered with a crocheted Jamaican-style Rastafarian cap, and an oversized pair of orange-tinted glasses obscured her eyes. Her jeans, boots, t-shirt and bra were now in a large hemp shoulder bag, and in their place she wore a calf-length Mexican peasant's dress, with a deeply-scooped front and tight elastic gathers under her breasts. She bounced on her Birkenstock clogs and was satisfied with the jiggle it produced.

In less than five minutes Ranya located her quarry, a pimply-faced freshman web-surfing on a library computer, in an isolated corner of the stacks on the second floor. There was an untouched tower of books beside him on the desk at his carrel, all of them concerning the Civil War.

"Oh, wow, are you a Civil War buff?" she asked, leaning over as she pretended to study the titles on the book spines. "Or should I say, the War of Northern Aggression?"

"Uh, yeah, sure, I guess so," he stammered, his eyes darting between her face and her exposed cleavage. He had a slightly deeper voice than she had expected.

She said, "Nathan Bedford Forrest was the greatest Confederate general, even though he was a slave master and he started the Ku Klux Klan, don't you think?"

"Uh, well, probably, but he was just in Tennessee. I think you have to consider the generals in Virginia to be much more important."

"Hey, that's a great point! Are you a history major?"

"I haven't declared my major yet, but I think so."

"Say, can I ask a teeny favor from you? I'm down here visiting friends at ODU; I go to Georgetown. Are you online? Do you mind if I check my email for a few minutes?"

"What? Oh, not a problem, be my guest." The pizza-faced frosh got up, offering Ranya his chair. "I need to go outside for a cigarette anyway. Take your time."

Mission accomplished, thought Ranya, clicking to her favorite search engine as soon as he walked off. The tricky part was not finding Eric Sanderson's home address: the tricky part was doing it from a computer that could not be traced back to you. Her queries of real estate sales, property tax and mortgage records would leave an electronic trail, and after Sanderson was shot Ranya knew that investigators would be checking those data bases for anyone who had shown recent interest in his home and property. It was unlikely that even skilled cyber sleuths would get beyond the library's computer network to find her unwitting accomplice, and even if they did, she was certain that he would not be able to provide a useful description above her neck.

It only took a few minutes to find Sanderson's address and a bit of biographical data, including the fact that he had a ten-year younger wife, and two college-age daughters of his own. She went to a free satellite imagery website and zoomed in on the area around his house and made a quick hand-drawn sketch, because she had no capability to print out the overhead picture. Then Ranya deleted her computer "cookies" showing the sites she had visited, logged off, and was gone before the freshman returned to his empty chair.

Before leaving the library, Ranya made a stop in the reference section and located the U.S. Geological Survey elevation contour maps. She found the paper map covering the area around Sanderson's house in complete detail, down to every stream and fence and dirt road. Each house and barn was marked on the map by a tiny black square. She slid the map out of its wide steel drawer, folded it up unobserved, and put it into her shoulder bag. Then she returned to the ladies' room and changed back into her jeans; the peasant dress and shoulder bag and clogs went into her black daypack. She let her hair down, brushed it out, and left the library. She found the process of becoming another person to be quite enjoyable, the first diversion she had enjoyed since learning of her father's death.

Bob Bullard was halfway through his bottle of room service Chivas Regal. He was staying on the seventh floor of the Virginia Beach Sheraton overlooking the Atlantic. Wally Malvone had said to enjoy a big night out on the credit card he had provided, and Bullard was not one to turn down such an offer. Access to shady unaccountable credit cards to cover operating expenses in the field was one of the attractions of leading the Special Training Unit.

The escort service he had called assured him that his "date" would be equipped to handle the card, and while he waited for her ("blond, long legs, big knockers") to arrive, he lay on the king-sized bed in his boxer shorts chomping on a cigar and channel surfing between the cable news shows. Call girls loved his huge muscles and thick black chest hair; he could hardly wait for his "date" to arrive.

The Stadium Massacre and its aftermath was still the lead story, but now the rash of gun store arsons, the machine gun attack on the mosque in Portsmouth, and the breaking-news freeway car bombing were competing for the top billing. Bullard was proud that the freeway explosion was not only dominating the local news, but it was getting major play on the nationals.

It had been a good night's work. He had quickly settled on Mark Denton as his target when he saw that Denton drove a Jeep that he parked on the street in front of his house. It had been a simple matter to jam the ten pound bomb up under the chassis between the gas tank and the rear axle. He secured it in place with wire coat hanger rods which stuck two feet out of each end of the duct tape wrapped package.

Bullard knew that eventually fragments of the radio firing device and the coat hanger wire might be discovered, but it didn't worry him. For one thing, the analysis would not be completed for weeks if ever, and by then it would be old news. But Bob Bullard mostly didn't need to worry because the bomb analysis would be done by ATF's own Arson and Explosives Division, and he knew everybody that mattered down there.

Finally it was time for the CBA nightly news. Bullard sat cross legged on the king-sized bed, a glass of Chivas in one hand and a stogie in the other as the show began.

The blow-dried CBA weekend news anchor was visibly excited to be breaking a fast moving story ahead of the other networks, even ahead of The Sledge Report for once! This had not happened to him in more months than he could remember, and he was lucky that the senior anchor was fly fishing in Montana, or he would have been dragged in to claim credit for the CBA exclusive. This was a big break for the weekend anchor's career, and could push him ahead of his backstabbing colleagues in the cutthroat race to replace the doddering senior anchor. He relished his coup as he was given the countdown to air time.

"Good evening. CBA News has been covering the deadly car bomb explosion on the highway in Norfolk Virginia which claimed seven lives today. Now CBA News has learned from a senior federal law enforcement official that the driver of the vehicle which exploded was until recently a member of a shadowy anti-government militia group in southeastern Virginia. James Shifflett, the stadium sniper, may have also been a member of the same militia group.

"The driver of the Jeep, Mark Palmer Denton of Virginia Beach Virginia, was a successful corporate attorney with connections to the Republican Party. Interestingly, three decades ago he was a 'Green Beret' officer in Viet Nam. Denton was traveling with his son when their Jeep exploded at the interchange of the Virginia Beach Expressway and I-264 in Norfolk. Both of them were killed, along with five others who had the horrible luck to be traveling near them at the same time. Twenty seven more were injured, many critically."

The camera switched to an aerial view recorded earlier showing a scene of unimaginable gridlock stretching to the horizon in all directions. At the center was a highway cloverleaf strewn with cars, trucks and rescue vehicles.

"In the wreckage of the fifty-car pileup which followed the explosion, police found an entire arsenal of assault rifles, and literally thousands of assault rifle bullets scattered on the highway. All of the assault rifle bullets recovered are said to be deadly 'cop killer bullets' capable of penetrating any police officer's bulletproof vest. Several of the rifles which were recovered have been positively identified as belonging to Mark Palmer Denton."

Bullard laughed out loud at these inane comments. Virtually all rifle bullets made in the last century or two would penetrate Kevlar vests, so in the view of the network news writers, they were now all "cop killer bullets." And thousands of bullets, which sounded on the news like enough for an army, would fit in a few shoe boxes and could be shot on a single weekend at a range. It was great to see that the networks were still singing from the ATF's music sheet.

"Now our sources within federal law enforcement tell us that they have very strong information from informants within the Virginia militia movement, that Denton was on his way to plant his powerful bomb inside the Norfolk federal building. Our sources believe that the attempted bombing of the Norfolk federal building is related to the Stadium Massacre, and that the bomb was going to be detonated on Tuesday, when the assault rifle ban comes into effect.

"Our sources tell us that a faulty detonator, or old degraded explosives, possibly stolen years ago from an Army Special Forces depot, may have caused the premature accidental explosion. Forensics experts from the Bureau of Alcohol, Tobacco, Firearms and Explosives are now on the scene investigating all the evidence.

"Meanwhile the entire Tidewater Virginia region is a literal powder keg of fear and anger. Earlier today CBA reporter Beverly Bronwyn interviewed Muslim leader and community activist Sheik Ali bin Muhamed, whose Portsmouth Virginia mosque and community center was heavily damaged in a machine gun attack early this morning. Here is her report."

An attractive blond reporter was holding her microphone in front of Sheik Muhamed, who was wearing a green military-style flak vest over white robes. Behind him were the shattered empty windows of his store front mosque. All around him stood more than twenty bodyguards, angry-faced young African-American men in black suits and dark sunglasses who were openly brandishing pistols and shotguns.

"I'm telling you, I'm telling America, I'm telling the whole world that if these white-devil racist militias want a war, we'll give them a war!"

He held up one of the leaflets which had been found after the attack. The visible headline of the pamphlet said in large block letters:

NIGGERS GO BACK TO AFRICA!!
MOSLEMS GO BACK TO HELL!!

"I was right back inside there last night when we were attacked," the Sheik lied, pointing behind him to the open windows, which still had shards of broken glass hanging from the edges. "The machine gun bullets flew all around me, but Allah, peace be upon him, saw fit to protect his servant, to save him for his work, and I was not struck, all praise be to Allah, peace be upon him!

"These disgusting papers were left behind after the cowardly machine gun attack. Now you can see the kind of genocidal murdering butchers who are trying to exterminate us! Jimmy Shifflett was just the tip of the white devils' iceberg! This paper says it is 'Communique Number One from General Lee of the White Christian Militia of Virginia', now what does that tell you? I cannot even read to you all the filthy, evil, disgusting, vile, racist, anti-Muslim insults written on this so-called communique!" Ali bin Muhamed's hand was shaking; he held the paper by a corner with a thumb and one finger, as if it was infected with a deadly contagion. "Today we are demanding, demanding that the President send the Army into Virginia to smash these rampaging white-racist militias!"

The news cut back to the weekend anchor in the studio, a look of deep worry on his face. "There is a further development in the Stadium Massacre investigation. Experts from the BATF's firearms tracking program have positively identified the SKS assault rifle used by Jimmy Shifflett as having been purchased by a founding member of the White Identity Militia group in Idaho. The rifle was purchased at a gun show in Coeur d'Alene Idaho in 1993 by Frederick Fultz, who was later convicted on federal weapons charges in 1999, and sentenced to fifteen years confinement at Leavenworth Kansas. In a strange twist of fate, Fultz hanged himself with a towel in his prison cell just one month ago, on August 16th.

"Tonight I am joined in the studio by Rutherford Cavanaugh, an expert on militia groups and domestic terrorism. Mr. Cavanaugh is the founder of 'The Center to Study Militia Violence' in Chicago, and is a leading consultant to the federal government on domestic terrorism. Mr. Cavanaugh, were you surprised to learn that Shifflett's SKS assault rifle came from the White Identity Militia in Idaho?"

Cavanaugh was a morbidly obese balding man in his forties, with rolls of fat completely obscuring his shirt collar. "I'm not surprised at all, because we have found that there is a constant flow of militia members and assault weapons from state to state and from region to region. Working closely with federal law enforcement, we have discovered a nationwide network linking the most dangerous right wing militia fanatics, who frequently hide within the so-called 'gun show circuit.' So no, it's no shock that Shifflett's assault rifle came from the White Identity Militia."

"What do you expect next, Mr. Cavanaugh? The assault rifle ban goes into effect less than 48 hours from now, on Tuesday at noon eastern time. Are the militias going to comply with the new law?"

"Well, just today we have seen a machine gun attack on a mosque in Portsmouth Virginia; that was clearly a white-racist militia attack. And we have seen the attempted bombing of the federal building in Norfolk. So I certainly don't see the militia violence stopping before the Tuesday deadline. But I hope and I believe that the right wing violence will end soon after the deadline, as even the most rabid gun fanatics come to accept the new law of the land. After all, Europe and the entire civilized world have accepted common sense gun laws for decades, and so will all good and decent Americans, given time."

"Thank you Rutherford Cavanaugh."

"Thanks for having me on."

Back in his room at the Sheraton, overlooking the ocean, Bob Bullard couldn't stop grinning. Wally Malvone, the unnamed "senior federal law enforcement official," was a genius! He was playing 3D chess when the rest of the country was struggling to learn checkers. Bullard was certain now that the President would give the green light to upgrading the Special Training Unit into a larger and permanent Special Projects Division, just the way that Malvone had laid it out. When that happened, he would get some of these magic credit cards of his own to keep.

There was a knock on his door; his "date" had arrived. Life was great. Bob Bullard was on a solid winning streak with no end in sight, and it was only going to get better.

"Come on in Sugar Darlin', and say hi to your new Sugar Daddy!"

13

Ben Mitchell was in the middle of pouring several gallons of clear liquid plastic onto a new mahogany tabletop when the phone rang in his garage workshop. The table had taken him several days to build and he could not stop now: the catalyzed liquid was going to harden in a few minutes. The clear plastic would forever capture an "underwater" scene of sea shells, realistic looking "gold doubloons" and other pirate loot and artifacts. The ten foot long table was going to an upscale seafood restaurant on the Rappahannock River south of Fredericksburg, and they were paying him twelve hundred dollars for it. If they liked it (and they would) they would order more.

After seven rings the answering machine kicked in with his taped message, and Ben Mitchell heard a familiar voice, cracking with emotion. "Damn it Ben, are you there? This is Terry Shriver, pick up the phone! They blew up Mark Denton, Captain Mark Denton! Pick up the phone damn it, or turn on the TV, it's all over the news!" The voice ended, the line went dead and the answering machine clicked off.

Mitchell finished pouring his bucket of clear liquid plastic, pulled off his rubber gloves and apron and air filter respirator and went back into his house. Terry Shriver was another retired Special Forces NCO, but Ben hadn't heard from him in a few months. Mark Denton was blown up? What was that about?

Mark Denton! Now there was a name from the distant past! Mark Denton had been a young lieutenant back in 68 or 69 when Ben was running a Studies and Observation Group recon team out of Kontum back in the Operation Prairie Fire days, jumping the fence into Laos on a regular basis. Denton had gone along as a straphanger on some ops with Mitchell's Recon Team Utah, although he was actually a staff officer of a much larger SOG "Hatchet Force." In the SOG it was not an exaggeration to say that when it came to cross-border operations, rank came in a distant second to skill and experience. Even junior NCOs were made recon team leaders, based strictly on their aptitude and talent. When an officer was crazy enough to want to tag along, he went as a junior man: he followed instructions and he kept his mouth shut.

This inverted rank structure was unique to the SOG, and unique to that time and those classified missions. Later in the states Denton and Mitchell had both briefly served at the Special Forces Training Group, as a staff officer and an instructor, and the seniority relationship of course returned to the conventional one. But both men remembered their times together jumping over the fence into Laos when the Sergeant had led the Lieutenant. The ties forged on those classified missions, missions which were never officially recognized until decades later, were particularly strong and deep. No one knew about those do-or-die missions, about their shared dangers, and the friends who didn't make it back. No one knew except the men who had suited up and climbed aboard the lone Hueys to go places they could never talk about publicly.

Mark Denton was a fine man and a good listener for an officer, but he hadn't been career Army, and he'd gotten out a few years after the war as a captain. Ben still knew of Denton through the Special Forces Association, and periodically had run into him at SOG reunions at Fort Bragg and elsewhere over the years, but Denton wasn't one to make a life out of being a former Green Beret, like some did. He'd moved on.

Ben Mitchell looked up Terry Shriver's number and called him back, but the line was busy. Terry was probably calling up other old SF buddies of Denton, so he took the phone into his den and snapped on the TV, which was already set to TOP News, the only cable news channel he considered worth watching. They were showing an overhead shot of a huge highway smashup in Norfolk; dozens of cars were piled up on both sides of a highway overpass. The title at the bottom read "Highway Car Bomb in Norfolk Virginia."

Ben hit redial and got right through. "Terry, Ben Mitchell here, what's going on?"

"Have you been watching the news Sergeant Major?"

"I just turned it on."

"Mark Denton, you remember him?"

"Sure, I know Mark. What's going on?"

"His car blew up right on the highway in Norfolk, killed him and his son. Now they're saying he was in some kind of militia, and he was carrying a bomb and it went off early. They say he was going to bomb the federal building in Norfolk, and it looks like he had some rifles and a bunch of ammo in his car, they're all over the road is what they say. I tried calling his house, but the phone must be off the hook. I just can't believe it Ben, I just can't believe it."

There was a long pause while neither man spoke. Ben Mitchell said, "It's a crock. It's bullshit Terry. There's just no way, no way at all."

"It's a setup Ben. It's got to be a setup."

"Yeah, it has to be. Thanks for calling Terry, and keep your powder dry—there's something mighty strange going on."

"You watch your back too, Ben."

Ben Mitchell had retired from the Army after putting in 25 years, most of it in the Special Forces. One wall in his den was covered with military plaques, unit memorabilia and framed photographs. He walked over and took one large picture down off its hook and brushed his fingers gently over the glass. The faded black and white photograph showed a group of ten smiling men, half of them Americans and half Asians, dressed in tiger-striped jungle uniforms and wearing all types of non-regulation head gear. They were carrying a mix of CAR-15s, M-60s, AK-47s, and an assortment of other weapons. They still had a faint smear of camouflage paint left on their faces; they had the look of happy, exhausted warriors.

"Recon Team Utah, Kontum RSVN, 9-29-68," was written across the bottom of the picture. Lieutenant Mark Denton was in the center of the photo, holding one end of a captured NVA flag, a wide grin on his face. Staff Sergeant Ben Mitchell was holding up the other side of the flag, also grinning at the camera. He was the only black man in the picture, a largely immaterial detail which was totally irrelevant in the Special Forces community, which was a large part of the reason he had stayed in for 25 years.

Mitchell did three tours in Viet Nam, in 66, 68 and 71, but his time with the SOG had always been what he remembered most intensely, running covert ops into Laos and northern Cambodia against the NVA on the Ho Chi Minh Trail. The SOG recon teams' primary mission besides gathering intelligence was calling in air strikes, which sometimes rained death and destruction on NVA troop concentrations. More frequently however, they were themselves discovered by NVA hunter teams and had to flee under pursuit to landing zones for hot extractions.

LT Denton had ultimately gotten shot during a Hatchet Force rescue mission, a clean "million dollar wound" which finished his tour without ruining his life.

And now he had been blown up on a highway in Norfolk, along with his son and five other people, and he was being called a fumbling "militia terrorist."

Ben Mitchell, Sergeant Major (Retired), tried to watch more of the news, but he was too disgusted by all the lies that he heard.

Number one, Mark Denton was not going to bomb a federal building, or anything else, period.

Number two, he wouldn't involve his son in anything like that, period.

Number three, he would not in any way be associated with white racists, period. The "Niggers Back to Africa" leaflet from the Portsmouth mosque, which was being tied to Denton's alleged "militia" activities, looked like a very crude and amateurish attempt at psyops. Mark Denton would not in a million years be involved in any way with that sort of racist crowd, whether or not the "Niggers Back to Africa" leaflet was a fake.

Number four, Mark Denton would never "accidentally" blow himself up with his own C-4 bomb. Your average civilian might buy that line of horse crap about "old unstable C-4," but no professional demolitioneer ever would. During his decades of handling demo, Ben had often used hard-cast blocks of TNT left over from World War Two. It had been as safe and stable after forty years as brand new stuff, and C-4 was much better than TNT in every regard. Like all military demo, it was built to last just about forever. It didn't just "go off by itself," and Mark Denton was not some goofball who would throw together a Rube Goldberg firing device and blow himself up. Impossible.

Clearly, someone had murdered Mark Denton and his son and the others. Clearly, it was meant to be tied together with Jimmy Shifflett and the Stadium Massacre. Clearly, someone or some group was trying to panic the American people and make them believe in a right wing "militia" boogie man plot, and so far it seemed to be working.

But to an old pro, it just didn't wash. Ben Mitchell knew all about "black ops." The Special Forces and SOG had run them all the time in Southeast Asia, such as leaving doctored exploding ammunition and mortar shells in NVA caches along the trail. The CIA would then insert manufactured rumors into NVA communications back channels saying that poor quality control at Chinese munitions factories were to blame for the "accidental explosions." This was an attempt to make the NVA and VC distrust their ordnance, and their Chinese suppliers.

Later in El Salvador and elsewhere in the 1980s he had been aware of programs to leave doctored weapons and field radios for the communist guerrillas to "find" after what they considered to be successful attacks. Sometimes the weapons and radios were fitted with tiny beacons, to lead the government forces to guerrilla hideouts. Other times they simply exploded when used by the guerrillas.

He knew from friends serving in the Balkans in the 90's that it had been practically SOP for one side to occasionally blow up some of its own civilians, in order to score propaganda points and win world sympathy, by blaming their own atrocity on the other side. It was real nasty business, the worst form of black op there was.

Yes, Ben Mitchell knew all about black ops, and everything from the Stadium Massacre to Mark Denton's death said black op to him. He was not fooled for one minute. The so-called assault rifles and incriminating books immediately found in Shifflett's trailer proved that the Stadium Massacre was a false-attribution operation as far as Ben was concerned. The rifles conveniently being carried out of the trailer an hour after the massacre just screamed "made for TV." It was all too pat, too perfectly scripted, just like the "Niggers Back to Africa" leaflets. No, the week's events had all the hallmarks of a black operation to Ben Mitchell.

The only question was who was running the operation, and why?

Whoever was running the operation was probably in the government, it was the only source which made logical sense. It made no sense for any "militia" to be doing it; it would be suicidal for them to go head to head against the FBI. Besides, the only "militias" Ben had ever heard of were composed of middle-aged wannabees playing Rambo and drinking beer. The only "militias" he had ever heard of couldn't organize a successful gas station heist, much less get Shifflett up in that building, hit the stadium upper deck eighty or ninety times from a thousand yards, and then get clean away.

What made Ben Mitchell certain that the operation was being run from somewhere inside the government was the one glaring anomaly: the gun store arson attacks Friday night. All of the other actions could plausibly be explained as having originated in a right wing militia conspiracy. They wanted to blame the Stadium Massacre on Muslims, they shot up a mosque, and Mark Denton was being portrayed as a militia terrorist on his way to bomb a federal building.

But the gun store arson attacks didn't fit the pattern in any way. They were obviously done to create the illusion of a vigilante reaction to the Stadium Massacre, but who ever heard of violent anti-gun vigilantes? It made no sense; it was the flat note in the song. The anti-gun crowd would hold candlelight vigils, or pay for anti-gun TV ads, but attack gun stores with gasoline bombs, and kill some of their owners? No way. The most violent thing the anti-gun crowd ever did was scream and throw trash down onto the Senate floor during the debate. They preferred to let paid agents of the federal government handle their anti-gun violence for them, in the form of the black-clad ninja storm troopers of the BATF.

The gun store arsons were probably designed to provoke a genuine violent reaction from the right wing gun rights crowd, and to make it appear that some type of dirty war was starting up in southeastern Virginia. But they just didn't add up. Little old ladies in tennis shoes made up the anti-gun crowd, and they were hardly the types to throw gasoline bombs. So if it wasn't them, it was the government, or some group inside the government. After serious reflection, Ben Mitchell grew sure of it.

But if it was all a government sponsored black operation, what was their motive? He had some ideas.

Ever since the early 1990s, Ben had been watching the militarization of American police forces with growing dismay. Increasingly, young Special Forces officers were doing their minimum time in the Army, and then getting out and going directly into the FBI and other federal agencies' special operations teams. SF enlisted men, without college degrees, were getting out in droves and joining local police department SWAT teams. It was the same thing with the Army Rangers, and he also heard from his Navy buddies that young SEALs were frequently serving one hitch and then going on to law enforcement SWAT teams, where they could still enjoy "the action," but without having to spend months and years in third world shit holes like Iraq, Afghanistan, Haiti and Kosovo. SWAT teams had the latest gear and the best training, at least as good as the military equivalents, but they didn't have to deploy overseas. A civilian SWAT team operator got to kick down doors and shoot guns for a living, and then go home and sleep in his own bed with his own woman in his own town.

Along with the increasing militarization of the police came a militarization of the police mindset. Military specops personnel who were routinely involved in covert ops and dirty tricks overseas had to be bringing their "total war" mindset back to the states when they left the military and joined a SWAT team. There was no way to avoid it. Military specops troops and civilian SWAT personnel often practiced side by side at the same training academies, learning the same skills from the same instructors.

The flow was constant, back and forth, between the military and civilian special tactics units. They first learned their skills in the military, and then they got out and joined SWAT teams. Then they typically stayed in the military reserves, where they were periodically activated to serve on deployments overseas again, keeping up their military skills. Back and forth they went, until there was virtually no noteworthy distinction between the military and the civilian special operations troops.

Everything from the Stadium Massacre to what was happening in Norfolk smelled like a covert operation to Ben Mitchell. Perhaps it was part of the military covert ops mindset trickling over to the civilian law enforcement world? That mindset said that the only thing that matters is results, and how you achieve them isn't important, as long as you're not caught red-handed flagrantly violating the rules of engagement. If a civilian law enforcement unit in this gung-ho "war on terrorism" era felt that it was being hampered by overly strict rules of engagement in carrying out its missions, it was predictable that they would simply bypass the rules. It's what they were encouraged to do overseas in the war on terror on a weekly basis, with a wink and a nod from the highest authorities. "Do what you need to do, just don't get caught," was the new unofficial motto of American specops units.

At the outer fringes of the specops covert action mindset, framing and killing the innocent could even be rationalized in the pursuit of their greater mission. Perhaps the Stadium Massacre had indeed been meant to be blamed on Muslim terrorists. In that case, the war on terror might have been turned into a war on all Muslims in America…. Special ops troops who learned to hate Muslims fighting them overseas might be getting eager to ratchet up the battle against their perceived enemies at home. It was a possibility.

Or perhaps the goal was to incite an armed reaction from the pro-gun crowd, in order to begin a new crackdown in that direction? Either motive was plausible.

But whoever was behind this campaign stepped over a very personal line when they blew up Mark Denton, forever damning his good name as a racist militia terrorist. Denton's honorable combat service for his country in Southeast Asia all those years ago was now being twisted into some kind of evidence of his terroristic tendencies, just background material to turn him into a convenient fall guy for a black operation.

And so far, from what he had seen and heard on the television, it was working. Denton was already being uncritically accepted as some sort of incompetent militia bomber. Well, Ben Mitchell wasn't accepting it. If whoever was running this operation thought that they could use an old Special Forces officer in this way and get away with it, well, they had better think again. By blowing up Mark Denton and his son and the others on the highway, they had made the fight personal.

After 25 years in the Special Forces community, Ben Mitchell not only knew about black ops, and he not only knew about C-4 plastic explosive, he actually had forty pounds of it. And he already knew where he was going to put it.

If the President of the United States didn't know what was going on in his government behind his back, well then, Ben Mitchell was going to tell him. Once his C-4 calling card made its mark, the President would listen to him, with his complete and undivided attention.

And if the President knew what was going on in Virginia and approved of it, then to hell with him: it would be war.

By the time it grew completely dark Ranya Bardiwell was in position overlooking Eric Sanderson's three story brick Colonial-style home in the exclusive Fox Hills area ten miles east of Richmond. The Virginia Attorney General's desire for seclusion and privacy now worked against him: once she had found his address, his isolation and lack of close neighbors made her approach to within range a simple task.

She had ridden the Nighthawk up Route 460 almost to Petersburg, and once in the area she stayed on back roads until she found the best place to leave her bike while she stalked into position. A dirt road ran parallel to a small stream a quarter mile west of his property, it was county watershed land and there were no houses built on the wooded slope which ran up to Sanderson's hilltop property line. She left the bike hidden in a thicket under the green canvas cover while she put on her sniper's garb in the last light. An old set of brown mechanic's coveralls went over her jeans and jean jacket. They were big enough to pull on over her boots, which she then covered with a pair of men's galoshes, which would leave false footprints if she could not avoid leaving footprints at all.

Over her head she wore a dark green t-shirt, with the neck hole pulled up around her eyes. The two short sleeves were then tied together behind her head to create an instant camouflage mask. This left a clear horizontal slit for her vision, and gave the overall effect of an irregular misshapen stump with the shirt draped loosely over her shoulders. This was a trick an old turkey hunter had showed her, from the days before there were store-bought camouflage head nets. It worked just as well, and left her with no incriminating mask in her possession, just an ordinary t-shirt.

On her hands she wore thin brown driving gloves, supple enough to load and fire her .223 caliber shells while hiding the shine of her hands, and of course preventing the leaving of any possible fingerprints.

The quarter mile uphill approach from the dirt road was easy traveling through mostly open forest floor, beneath a mix of fir and deciduous trees. The woods ended on the ridge along the property line above Sanderson's house. His house had been featured in an on-line architectural digest. It was almost two hundred years old and was a registered landmark, so there was no question of misidentification. Five minutes on a college library computer was all it had taken to direct her to his home with the accuracy of a GPS-guided cruise missile.

Ranya moved slowly along the inside of the tree line until she had a clear view of the front of his house, facing the side of the long driveway which descended away to her right. There were security lights on the corners of the house and over the front and back porch landings, bathing the immediate area in bright light. Ranya thought they should be called "false security lights," because they put anyone near the house into her clear view, and at the same time blinded them to anything beyond their brilliant circle of illumination. She was certain that the top of the hill and the woods which concealed her would just be a black void to any light-blinded people in or around the house.

Fifty yards from the house a dark sedan was parked under some small trees along the side of the driveway. At 7:35 PM by her wrist watch another car came up the driveway, a Chevy Caprice or Ford Crown Victoria by its look, and after a few minutes the first car drove away. So Sanderson has a detail guarding his house, Ranya thought. Probably plain-clothed state troopers. She wondered if the security detail had been added since he had made his "merchants of death" speech; no doubt he'd received some threats after going high-profile with that gem. But certainly not from Ranya Bardiwell: she was light years beyond making anonymous threats.

She shifted around until she found a comfortable shooting position sitting behind a low deadfall pine trunk. The top of the log was at the level of her ribs while she sat cross-legged with her knees just under it. She moved some rocks from under her, because she knew she had to be comfortable enough to stay in her position for hours if necessary. Finally she took off her black daypack, unzipped it and withdrew the long pistol case, laid the case across her lap, and removed the Tennyson Champion. From one of the case's outside pouches she slid out the suppressor and screwed it onto the threaded end of the pistol's fourteen inch long barrel. From another pocket she took out the plastic cigarette pack sized case which held her father's hand-loaded .223 caliber match quality cartridges. She put the half-zipped gun case back in the daypack, which she also left unzipped beside her. She planned to take only one shot, and then hit or miss, she was going to unscrew the silencer and drop it in the bag, then plunge the Champion muzzle-first into the pistol case within the pack, zip it up and throw it on her back, and escape down the hill to her motorcycle.

Ranya knew that she had to be down the hill, out of her sniper's garb, packed and on the bike and out the area within five minutes of the shot. With state police bodyguards on the scene, she could not depend on confusion to delay the pursuit. The call would go out over police radio almost immediately. Any police in the area might begin to block key intersections, which is why she had a route planned out that used only local neighborhood streets. She had a yellow-highlighted section of road map already cut out and taped onto her gas tank to assist her. Her worst fear though was that a police helicopter would already be airborne over Richmond, which seemed likely, and in that case it could be over Fox Hill in mere minutes. Her escape would be a narrow run thing at best.

She snapped open the top of the plastic cartridge case, and selected one bullet, pulling it out by its sharp conical tip. She closed the case and put it into the breast pocket of her coveralls and buttoned the pocket: it was critical that she not drop, forget or leave behind anything at all.

Enough light from the house reached her position to permit her to examine the single .223 cartridge. It was made of gleaming golden brass, a bit over two inches long, thicker than a pencil, then necked down in two sharp angles to hold the narrow .223 inch wide projectile. A half inch of the sharp copper-coated projectile extended from the mouth of the brass case, at its tip was a tiny hole, opening into a small internal cavity. The 50 grain-weight projectile would leave the Champion's fourteen inch barrel at almost 3,000 feet per second, and when its hollow tip struck flesh or bone it would virtually explode, dumping over 600 foot-pounds of energy into her target. This was more destructive energy than her .45 pistol fired at point blank.

If Sanderson was getting death threats, he might be wearing a Kevlar vest, and he might even be wearing a thin armor plate in a pouch in the front of the vest, a plate which would stop the tiny high velocity .223 hollow point. Because of this possibility, Ranya decided to go for a head shot if possible. She knew that from its steady rest across the pine log the Champion would absolutely be able to hit an apple-sized target at the house 250 yards away, but Sanderson would be moving. Her best chance would come right at his front door, when he might be expected to stand still for a few moments. If she could not get a head shot, if he didn't stop, she would go for his torso.

But Ranya really wanted to take the head shot, because she wanted to erase Sanderson's self righteous smirk forever. In death her father had not been permitted the dignity of an open coffin viewing, and Ranya had been left scarred with the hideous memory of what she had seen on the ground between her house and the store. Ranya meant to give Eric Sanderson the same gruesome sendoff that federal agents had given her father. She wanted to blow his telegenic face and head into shreds, so that there could be no public viewing of his formerly handsome corpse in the capitol in Richmond. She wanted his bodyguards and aides to experience some of the horror she had been forced to endure, when they saw Sanderson's head disappear. Besides, their shock might slow down their reactions and their radio calls, and every second of their delay was a second added to her escape.

Ranya wrapped her long fingers around the carved wooden grip of the Champion, pulled back the trigger guard extension tang to unlock the breech, tipping the long barrel down so that she was looking into the empty chamber. She lifted the barrel back up and snapped the breech shut, and then laid the barrel across the pine log. On top of the long barrel there was mounted a 2.5 to 7X variable magnification pistol scope. Ranya flipped up the small hinged lens covers at each end, and rotated a knob on the black scope to turn on its internal reticle light. She had already adjusted the magnification to its 7X maximum, now she adjusted her sitting position again so that she could comfortably examine the house through the scope with the pistol resting across the log.

The crosshairs glowed red-orange, and the front porch filled the ocular lens as she sighted on the brass and iron door knocker, which when it was magnified seven times appeared to be only 100 feet away. With a two-handed grip, she settled the thin crosshair on the center of the door knocker, and began to slowly exhale while softly touching the trigger with the pad of her right index finger, only squeezing when the crosshair was directly on the center of the knocker. At three pounds of pressure she felt and heard the sharp metallic click as the hammer dropped on the empty chamber, a certain hit within an inch of where she was aiming. An experienced shooter like Ranya could generally "call" her hits or misses as soon as the trigger was pulled. Dry firing, Ranya hit the knocker and door bell again and again with imaginary shots, practicing for Eric Sanderson.

When she was satisfied that she had adapted to the Champion's crisp trigger, and she was comfortable shooting the 250 downhill yards to the house from her sitting position behind the log, she loaded a single .223 caliber hollow-point cartridge into the chamber and closed the breach for the last time. She laid the heavy pistol, with its fourteen inch barrel and scope and seven inch long suppressor across her lap and waited, studying the house, the driveway, and the car with the unseen bodyguards.

No lights had come on in the house after it had grown dark outside, and she was fairly certain it was empty. Perhaps Sanderson was out of town; there was no way Ranya could know. She had a small water bottle in her pack. She drank a little, putting it away carefully each time in case she had to flee with no warning. She shifted and stretched her muscles to keep from getting too stiff, but she never left her position sitting behind the log with the Champion across her lap. An occasional mosquito buzzed around her eyes; crickets accepted her presence and chirped close around her. At 9:00 PM she washed down a caffeine tablet with some of her water. She thought about Brad Fallon and his lovely white sailboat and his escape plan of sailing to the islands. She wondered about Phil Carson and his civil war talk. She wondered if Phil was also in the woods tonight, and whether he was burying or digging up his serious weapons. She remembered a saying she had heard, that when it gets bad enough to have to bury your guns, it's time to dig them up. She thought about snorkeling with Brad in transparent blue-green tropical water over coral reefs.

At 9:55 she saw several sets of headlights bouncing and turning up the road from the right and onto the driveway. He's home!

Her pulse and breathing quickened as she laid the Champion across the log, holding it securely in her two-handed grip. She thumbed back the hammer. A full-sized SUV was in front, a sedan behind. The SUV stopped momentarily by the unmarked car which was parked down the driveway; they were getting the "all clear" no doubt. If they only knew!

The SUV pulled into the circular driveway and came to a stop facing Ranya, its headlight beams aimed into the hill. Then the dark sedan, a Lincoln or Cadillac, came to a stop at an angle partly hidden from her view behind the SUV.

The Champion's pistol scope had a long eye-relief distance. Ranya's face was a foot behind it; she switched between looking over the scope at the entire scene and through it at the vehicles. According to the ballistic data card which her father had prepared and placed in the case with the pistol, the scope had been zeroed in at 200 yards. Its bullets would drop barely an inch from there to the 250 yards which Ranya estimated was the distance to the front porch. She only needed to hold the crosshairs on the center of his head, and squeeze the trigger.

Car and truck doors clunked open and shut. The sounds of talk and music and laughter floated up the grassy hillside, to where Ranya Bardiwell sat holding a long range target pistol. A female stepped out in a full-length sequined gown; it was blazing gold in the home's security lights. Then some men in dark suits—aides or bodyguards—were getting out of the SUV. Finally Eric Sanderson himself came into Ranya's view from around the SUV. He was wearing a tuxedo, his blow-dried black mane with the silver sides giving him away.

Moving...get the crosshairs on him. Stand still Eric, oh what now? He's back behind the SUV, no shot. Now here he is again, and two more ladies are with him; stand still Eric! They're all moving to the porch, he's behind them, find his head, lay the crosshairs on his head, move with him... The other two ladies are in front of him now; young blondes, a matched-set in black mini-dresses. They must be his daughters, up from college for the weekend, they matched his bio.

The group walked to the front porch and up the steps. His wife, his aides, his daughters, his bodyguards; all of them milling and turning and blocking her view of Sanderson. They stopped at the front door, his body obscured but not his head, his black and silver hair a beacon. On the door step now, the women smiling, no doubt full of fine food and wine. All four of them now in a tight shifting knot, aides trailing on the steps below. Sanderson's back to Ranya for a clear shot, her finger on the trigger, one pound of pressure taken up. His head between his two daughters, in front of his wife's face. A blond daughter leaning on his shoulder, tipsy and laughing; Ranya's crosshairs on the back of his head. Two pounds of pressure on the trigger, the crosshairs jiggling faintly in time with her heartbeat. Steady...exhale...aim...squeeze...the sequined wife facing him, smiling in her scope...

Stop. Pressure off the trigger, finger clear.

I can't do it, not in front of his daughters. Ranya closed her eyes, her head down, uncocking the hammer with her thumb and easing it forward and putting the pistol on safe. She looked again, but not through the scope. She looked down at the contented family scene as Eric Sanderson, his wife and his two daughters disappeared behind their front door, and the lights came on inside.

Sanderson was a pig, he was filth, and his hands were on her father's murder one way or the other. He was using her father's murder to advance his own political career, all that was true, but Ranya just could not splatter his skull and brains all over his wife, and especially not in front of his daughters. In the end she found that she just couldn't do it, there was a line that Ranya discovered she couldn't cross. She unscrewed the suppressor from the muzzle, slid the pistol into its case inside her back pack, and checked the area for anything left behind. Then she crept back into the brush, stood up and walked carefully in the darkness down the hill through the trees to her Nighthawk.

Okay Eric, you son of a bitch, you just got a reprieve.

Enjoy your father's company, girls. Your presence tonight saved his miserable life.

14

Ben Mitchell was retired at more than half of an Army Sergeant Major's pay, but he earned even more than that as a craftsman and artist. He had started his second career by building military plaques for other soldiers, and that had evolved into building exotic custom coffee tables topped with an inch of clear Lucite which contained linked ammo, medals, fighting knives and other souvenirs; all made to the customer's order.

From his military customer base his reputation had somehow spread to restaurants, and he was usually back-ordered for months. He knew that he could expand his operation and take on employees, but he didn't want the hassle of dealing with all the government paperwork and oversight that employees would bring. As a sole proprietor, he could work right out of his garage workshop in Reston Virginia, twenty miles west of Washington DC.

He was long divorced, living alone, and able to set his own hours. He worked when he wanted, and he took off and vacationed when he wanted. Since Sunday night when he had found out about Mark Denton's murder, he had stopped building custom tables and gone completely into the "operational" mode. Even at 58 years old, Ben still considered himself to be an "operator." Without a doubt he was slower and weaker than he had been on active duty, but he believed that what he had lost physically he somewhat made up for by becoming smarter and sneakier with age.

Like most career specops guys he had made a near religion out of being ready for any conceivable contingency. Off of his bedroom his former wife's old walk-in closet had become his "war room," shelved on both sides and containing every piece of gear and uniform article that might be required to operate in any terrain and climate from the arctic to the desert to the jungle. He had a free fall parachute, packed and ready and unused for a decade. He had early model night vision goggles, he had skis, and he had enough rope to rappel down the Grand Canyon. Inside a standing gun safe he had firearms ranging from a .22 caliber Colt Woodsman pistol (threaded to take a "hush puppy" silencer) to a scoped bolt-action Remington 700 in 7.62 NATO. Most of the contents of his war room were just gathering dust as the years passed and Ben grew older and further away from being an operator, and in reality his war room was becoming more of a private museum than anything else.

Ben thought of everything in his war room as simply the tools of his former trade. Like many of his generation of soldiers, he could not accept the possibility of being caught unprepared for any eventuality, in peace or in war, even in the good old USA. If the "balloon went up" Ben would be ready to do… something. Maybe he would be called back to help rush a new crop of youngsters through Special Forces training, and maybe he would be asked to do something more. No matter what happened, Ben Mitchell would be ready for it, just as long as he could fend off the doctors and their lying lab reports...

Two of the most useful tools which Ben had acquired over the years he did not dare to keep in his war room or anywhere else on his property. Ben had long ago filched a pair of satchel charges, each with twenty pounds of military high explosive compound C-4 in a green canvas bag the size of a child's knapsack. C-4 was the magic stuff that gave an ordinary soldier Superman's fist. It could knock down a large tree, reducing its trunk to splinters, or blast a concrete wall to rubble in the blink of an eye. It could dig an instant trench, or launch a steel manhole cover like a blazing meteor, which could burn a hole clear through a locomotive.

The white plastic explosive was just too damn useful not to include in his personal load out. Once a soldier became accustomed to having Superman's fist available, it was hard to envision going through life without some of it set aside...just in case.

Along with the forty pounds of C-4 he had collected an ample supply of waterproof time fuse, fuse igniters, detonating cord, and electric and non-electric military blasting caps. All of these items came packed in vacuum-sealed heavy foil bags, and had a much longer shelf life than Ben Mitchell expected of himself.

Although explosives were tightly controlled in the civilian world, they were simple to come by in the Special Forces. Once a few hundred pounds of C-4 were signed out of a demo bunker, there was no way for anyone to know how much had actually been blown up at the end of the day. When properly used as it was designed, C-4 simply disappeared in a loud bang and a cloud of dust. Demo ranges were typically sprawling tracts on vast Army bases, and it was no problem to set aside a few bricks of C-4 here and there without drawing any attention.

Ben Mitchell's forty pounds of C-4 had been cached nearby in Great Falls Park by the upper Potomac, where he had thought it would probably lay undisturbed for centuries after his own eventual demise. But now here it was again on the work bench in his garage... He threw away the dirt-encrusted heavy plastic lawn and leaf bags which had protected them.

Inside each green canvas bag there were eight 2.5 pound bricks of C-4, shaped like foot-long sticks of butter. Each brick of C-4 was contained in its own green canvas "sock," and each brick was connected to the others with folded lengths of waxy yellow detonating cord. The satchel could be detonated as a single twenty pound charge, or the eight bricks could be pulled out and strung around a large target, all of them connected into one "shot" by the det cord which ran through them.

If it was needed for a technical application, the raw blocks of C-4 could be removed from their green socks and inner paper wrappings, and molded into any shape. The white C-4 which Ben examined on his work bench looked, felt and smelled exactly as if it had been issued yesterday, and not fifteen years ago.

Ben's sunset tour before retirement had been at the Pentagon, and he was familiar with every section of Washington and the DC suburbs. As an intellectual exercise during long commutes, Ben had often theorized about where someone could place forty pounds of C-4 to leverage the greatest impact, looking at Washington from the point of view of a foreign saboteur. Years ago he had decided on that hypothetical target. He never imagined that he would ever actually be planning a one man demolition raid to strike a symbolic blow at his own government, but here he was, with forty pounds of raw C-4 lying on his work bench in sixteen white bricks.

By Monday afternoon, Ben had constructed five linear shaped-charges designed for cutting through thick steel. Each of them was two feet long by three inches square, rigidly cased in thin sheet metal and wrapped in gray duct tape. Ben was a craftsman and he took pride in his work, under different circumstances he would have proudly shown the prepared charges to a demo class in Special Forces Training.

Monday morning Brad Fallon was hosing down and scrubbing Guajira's dirty leaf-covered decks with a long-handled brush, while his new Perkins turbo diesel was chugging steadily, throwing hot river water and exhaust smoke out of the stern at the water line. AM talk radio was turned up loud enough to be heard all over the boat; Brad was trying to stay up with the events which could affect his departure. His escape plan was serious business now, and he had switched over from music to more useful news radio. After weeks of sweaty and often filthy work at the dock way up the Nansemond, and after all the craziness which was descending around him, he was finally ready to motor downstream to the boatyard, where Guajira's mast lay waiting.

Ranya had left the boat early Sunday morning while he was still asleep, and he hadn't heard from her since. Maybe when he was underway going down river he'd give her a call, from his own cell phone of course, and not the one George had given him. Or maybe to be on the cautious side he'd just wait to call her from a land line pay phone around the boatyard. Or maybe he wouldn't call her at all. She probably wasn't interested in hearing from him anyway, or she wouldn't have left without saying goodbye or at least leaving a note.

After months of celibate bachelorhood, weeks of it up the river at the Sodermilk farm's dock, he had finally had a pretty girl sleep over aboard Guajira and he hadn't even touched her, which seemed typical of the way his love life had been going. But in Ranya's case this was probably just as well, because she was carrying such heavy emotional baggage. Brad wished her well, but he knew that he had to steer clear of any close personal attachments now, with the blue horizon beckoning him and the feds dogging his heels.

He just needed to wait for a few more weeks, and then he would glide into an anchorage near one of the big Caribbean resorts and have his pick of the Scandinavian girls on holiday, many of them predictably eager to find a way to avoid returning home for another frozen and sunless northern winter. He had been working on this plan with single-minded determination for years now, and he could wait for a few more weeks, and do it right.

Brad was intently scrubbing at a series of purple stains left on his cabin top by a bird that had obviously been digesting wild berries in the oak tree above Guajira, when he happened to glance aft. A narrow silver boat was coming up river, steered by someone wearing a khaki-colored shirt and long pants. The boat was an aluminum canoe with a square transom mounting a small outboard motor. Brad couldn't make out who was steering, the man was wearing a wide-brimmed straw hat and sunglasses.

Instead of passing in mid channel and continuing upstream, the man steered for Guajira's port side, popped his motor into neutral and grabbed onto the toe rail by the cockpit. The visitor looked up at Brad, who was standing in the cockpit, tanned and glistening with sweat, wearing only a pair of old cut-off jeans.

"You know who I am, right? We've met before."

Brad could see the short gray beard and recognized the voice. The man's hat and sunglasses and zinc oxide covered nose hid the rest of his face. It was Barney Wheeler, from Dixie Hardware and Lester's Diner.

"I know you."

"We need to have a chat, grab my bow line. Do you have a gas can handy? I should have a reason to be stopping here."

"What? Sure, I have a gas can." Brad walked the canoe's thin bow line a little way forward and tied it to a life line stanchion, casually scanning the Sodermilk farm property behind Guajira and the marshland across the river. Then he lifted open the lazarette locker at the aft end of the cockpit and retrieved a brand new and still empty red plastic fuel jug. Wheeler's cautious approach had caused Brad to wonder yet again if he was under observation, but he realized that his watchers, if there were any, would be invisible to him. The feds could have mounted a remote video camera up in a distant tree or electric pole, or they could be watching from an airplane or conceivably even a drone from thousands of feet above him, far higher than he could either see or hear.

Barney Wheeler was not behaving so carefully for no reason. If they were under observation, the gas can provided a plausible "cover for action," and if he was asked about his visitor later, Brad could reasonably say that he had merely been providing a little extra fuel to a passing fisherman who was running low. The canoe's outboard, Guajira's diesel engine, and Brad's talk radio would render a directional microphone useless, but ultimately each man had to trust that the other was not an informant in the first place.

"Here you go," said Brad, passing over the empty red container, and then sitting in Guajira's cockpit close by Barney Wheeler in his canoe. Wheeler went through the motions of pulling out the pouring spout and transferring imaginary fuel into his own red metal tank.

"I assume you've been following the news, and you heard about Mark Denton and his son and some folks getting blown up on the highway?"

"Sure, it's been all over the radio and the TV. They're talking about it on the radio right now."

"Well, have you figured out yet that Mark Denton used to be in the Black Water Rod and Gun Club, the same as Shifflett, the same as you met at Lester's Diner Friday night?"

Brad was stunned again to hear the confirmation of his fears. Here was yet another lightning bolt landing too close. "Damn, that figures. The news just said that he might have been involved in militia activities with Shifflett, but it didn't mention the Black Water club."

"Quite a nasty string of coincidences, don't you think?" asked Wheeler. "First Shifflett, who was half-dead and afraid of heights, climbs pipe scaffolding up a building and shoots at a stadium twelve hundred yards away with a tricked out SKS. Now Mark Denton 'accidentally' blows himself up. And in between we have gun stores burned by so-called anti-gun vigilantes, which is an oxymoron if I ever heard one."

Brad leaned back and sighed, staring across the river into the distant marshland. "You know, I almost bought a boat in Fort Lauderdale… I mean, I'm just minding my own business, I'm just trying to finish this boat and get out, and the next thing I know the FBI is right here, right here on this boat, threatening to take my money and my passport, forcing me to infiltrate the Black Water club, and all I want to do is get the hell out! And believe me, the last thing I want to be is an informant for the feds! That's why I passed you that note at Lester's."

Barney placed Brad's gas tank in the bottom of his canoe and sat back down on his thwart seat. "It's a good thing you did; that was a nice move. I don't think a real FBI informant would have pulled that trick with the note. And I didn't tell any of my friends about it; that's between us. After what happened to Shifflett, and now with Mark Denton getting blown up, I think if some of my buddies even heard Fallon and FBI in the same sentence, they might take a shot at you on general principle. You know, some of my friends were thinking back to Friday night at Lester's, and started wondering about just exactly who the stranger was with the sudden interest in the club. I sure didn't mention what you said in the note, about the FBI being interested in them."

"Thanks. I've already got the feds on my case, and I sure as hell don't need your friends coming after me too."

"No, I wouldn't think so. Brad, I know I wouldn't want to be in your spot, but look at us! Somebody's gunning for our club, picking us off one at a time. And I include Joe Bardiwell too, even if he was supposedly killed by gang bangers."

"Yeah, it sure seems like the feds have it in for you guys. Listen, Barney...I've really thought this out, and if you ask me, I'm being used as a diversion, a 'dangle.' I mean an obvious informant, sort of a red herring, and that probably means somebody wants to draw attention away from a real informant."

Wheeler cocked his head and looked up with new interest after that observation. "Brad, I checked you out, as much as I could, and it looks like you really were working up in Alaska. But that could all be faked too, backstopped with false records... So now I'd like to know how you know about things like informants and agent dangles?"

"You'll have to take my word for this, but I read a lot, really a lot. Up in the ANWR you have plenty of time to read. There's no where to go and not much to do on your twelve hours off, and I guess I've read too many spy books. Now where did you learn about using a gas can for a cover for action?"

"Cover for action...now that's a term of art I haven't heard in a while. Maybe I'll tell you some day, if we live through this. Not in books, I can tell you that much. Anyway, I figure you're clear of all this. Shifflett and Denton hadn't done anything with our group in a couple of years. We're not any kind of formal organization, so whoever fingered Denton and Shifflett had to have one of our old telephone lists to work from. Those phone lists are about all the 'organization' the club has ever had, so if there's a real informant, he has to be one of my own hunting buddies. Ain't that a pisser? One of my old friends, giving up Shifflett and Denton to the feds. Or giving them an old phone list anyway."

"Well let me tell you, the FBI can be very persuasive when they have your nuts in a vice.

"I can imagine that's true. You know, Jimmy Shifflett, he didn't amount to much, but he was a good kid. Maybe the first Iraq war ruined anything he might have become. I don't know about that Gulf War Syndrome stuff, but something happened to that kid over in the desert. Something. But Denton… Mark Denton was a real hero, and I don't use that term lightly. He was the real deal, and he was as fine a gentleman… That they'd kill him and his son, and all the others in the stadium, just to…" Wheeler looked down at the water, hiding under his wide-brimmed hat while quietly choking with emotion.

"Anyway Brad, I'm getting out of here. I've got some creeks down in Carolina calling my name. What about you? You look like you're about ready to go too."

"I'm leaving the farm today, and as soon as I can put up my mast, I'll be out on the ocean and I won't be looking back. But listen, there's something else." Brad was grateful for the information that Wheeler had given him, and on some level he felt that he should return the favor. "The feds killed Joe Bardiwell, not gang bangers or vigilantes. I was at Bardiwell's place Saturday with his daughter Ranya. I met her there. I buried her dog for her, they shot her dog too. I was the only one there with a shovel…

"Anyway, we found ten millimeter brass in the woods right across from where Joe Bardiwell was shot, definitely from a fed's submachine gun. They had those stripe marks an MP-5 leaves, and the dented-in lips. So for certain, the feds killed him, and that means all the gun store attacks were done by the feds too, probably using gang bangers as contract muscle, judging by their brand of Molotov cocktails. It's feds on all sides of this equation. Look at that mosque in Portsmouth, isn't it mighty convenient that a MAC-11 just 'happened' to be left at the scene, a MAC-11 that just 'happened' to trace back to some guy that belonged to a militia group in Montana? Now just who might get their hands on a gun like that, a gun with that kind of pedigree, and then just might 'accidentally' drop it at the scene of an anti-Muslim hate crime?"

"Well, I'd say the BATF could do it for sure. Or the FBI, I guess."

"That's how I see it too."

"Brad, I hope we get to talk some more about all this some day. I've been here too long already as it is. Here, let me give you your gas tank back. Take it easy son, I hope you make it clear of the feds and out on the ocean real quick. Good luck, keep your powder dry, and watch your back."

"Maybe we'll be able to sit down and talk about all this over a few beers some day."

"Maybe, I hope so. Just don't spill the beer next time, and no more notes."

"No more notes. Good luck to you too, Barney." Brad slipped the bow line off of his lifeline stanchion and tossed it into the front of the canoe. Wheeler snapped the gear lever ahead on his outboard and waved back to Brad, and motored up the river. In a minute he was out of sight around the bend. Brad coiled up his water hose and unscrewed it from the tap on the dock, and stowed it away in his aft lazarette with the empty plastic gas jug. Guajira's deck was clean enough. He had to get the hell away from this place that the feds knew so well, and get down river to the boat yard and his mast.

The squat gray mile-long Woodrow Wilson Bridge, which crossed the Potomac River just below the bottom diamond-point of Washington DC, never won an award for design or engineering. But if such records were kept, it would have retired the gold medal for headache creation among the motorists forced to use it on a daily basis. The Wilson Bridge completed the circle of the I-495 beltway around Washington at the six o'clock position, joining the state of Virginia to Maryland. The next bridge across the Potomac to the south was thirty miles away, and the next bridges to the north ran straight through downtown Washington. The Wilson Bridge also formed a critical link completing I-95, the primary interstate highway running from Maine to Miami.

The Woodrow Wilson Bridge was built cheap and fast for a paltry fifteen million dollars in 1961, during the rush to complete I-95. At that time the bridge was seen as a temporary solution, to be replaced within twenty years by a permanent and superior structure. As a temporary solution, it was engineered to carry only 75,000 vehicles a day.

In 1961 almost no one could have predicted the explosive growth which would occur in the Washington metro area, most of it the result of the exponential growth of the federal government during the following decades. Instead of 75,000 vehicles, the Wilson Bridge had been carrying more than 200,000 vehicles every day for twenty years beyond its originally predicted twenty year working life. Every tenth vehicle was a heavy truck, and the bridge was literally shaking to pieces.

On its best day the Wilson Bridge was the worst bottleneck in the Washington area. The mile long bridge was the only six lane constriction on the eight lane I-495 DC beltway. Every single day of the year from before dawn until long after dark unlucky commuters forced to use it could expect to spend at least an extra half hour creeping up to and over it. Accidents on or near the bridge instantly resulted in backups stretching for miles, and the Wilson Bridge had more accidents occur on it than any other single mile of the Washington Beltway. Even after midnight, when the bridge opened its draw spans for the passage of large vessels, the road traffic was heavy enough to instantly cause long backups.

In 2001, construction began on a two billion dollar twelve lane replacement, a sweeping monument of architectural excellence, but it would not be completed for years into the future. Until then, highway engineers and the Governors of Maryland and Virginia would keep their fingers crossed, hoping that the new bridge would be finished before the patched and re-patched Wilson Bridge inevitably shook apart and collapsed into the river under the relentless stampede of traffic.

For Ben Mitchell, the Wilson Bridge was the obvious choice for his target. He had often been forced to sit parked in choking exhaust fume gridlock on its approaches and on the bridge itself during his Pentagon tour, and when delivering tables to Maryland after he retired. He had spent what seemed like weeks of his life creeping along at a walking pace, in the middle of a sea of cars locked bumper to bumper to the horizon, trying to get across the bridge. He had often wondered what would happen to the federal government, if the old bridge finally did collapse into the Potomac, and tens of thousands of federal employees simply couldn't get to work.

Now, at 0235 hours on Tuesday morning, if his demolition shot went off as planned he wouldn't have to wonder any longer. He glanced again at the luminous digital timer on his wrist watch. He had pulled the rings on the fuse igniters thirteen minutes earlier, while standing on the catwalk under the Wilson Bridge. His linear shaped charges were in place against one of the twelve foot tall "I" beams which supported the road bed. The entire mile-long bridge was held up by 32 quad sets of concrete pilings; each set of four pilings was 165 feet from the next four. From piling to piling, twelve foot high steel I-beams carried the weight of the road, four of the giant I-beams for each 165 foot span of the bridge. Ben Mitchell only had enough C-4 to cut eight feet of one single steel I-beam, including the horizontal web at its bottom.

After the fuses were burning, he packed up his gear and rappelled fifty feet down to the small inflatable kayak which was waiting below him at the end of his rope, hidden in the darkness directly below the bridge. Once he was away from the bridge and paddling south on the ebb tide, he paused and called the Coast Guard on a handheld VHF radio, using a micro-cassette recorder to repeatedly send the electronically distorted message that there was a bomb on the Wilson Bridge, and it needed to be cleared of cars immediately. Seven minutes after pulling the fuse igniters, he saw flashing red and blue lights at each end of the bridge, and by ten minutes after there were no more vehicle lights visible crossing it at all. A helicopter was slowly flying down its length at a safe altitude, scanning the roadway with its "night sun" spot light.

At thirteen minutes Ben reached the shore a mile south of the bridge on the Maryland side at Fort Foote Park, having already discarded all of the tools which he had used for the operation, including his rope, his caulk gun loaded with fast-bonding adhesive which had stuck his shaped charges to the steel, his VHF radio and all the rest. At the river's edge he slit his kayak tubes with his old Randall knife and pushed the deflating remains out into the current, to be carried away and sink in deeper water.

Fourteen minutes. Ben crouched in some bushes, oblivious to the mosquitoes. There was no moon and the river and the park around him was inky black to his eyes, but he knew that to an infrared equipped helicopter his body heat would stand out from the background like it was daytime. Still he waited, watching the bridge, checking his digital timer.

At fifteen minutes and twenty five seconds, there was a flash of light under the bridge, at the center of the span between his chosen pilings. Ben counted off the seconds, on "seven one thousand" a loud boom reached him across the water followed by several resounding echoes. The charge had gone off, but the bridge didn't move.

Then, almost imperceptively slowly, the road between his pilings seemed to sag ever so slightly, as a low grinding and moaning sound was heard across the still water. Ben's span, one of the 32 comprising the Wilson Bridge, began to take on a distinct shallow V-shaped appearance. His linear shaped-charges had in fact cut cleanly through the bottom eight feet of the twelve foot tall I-beam which supported the southern edge of the roadway. The hundreds of tons of steel and concrete above the cut steel would not be denied, the cut I-beam slowly spread apart, and at the top of the eight foot cut the steel suddenly ruptured and the I-beam split all the way through.

The untouched second I-beam, one of the pair supporting the center of the roadway, could not carry both its load and that of the now unsupported and sagging southern quarter of the span, and it too began to stretch and twist and droop, as if in final refusal to say goodbye to its faithful brother of more than four decades. This second old steel girder, after decades of sustaining the double traffic load, offered its own collection of small stress fractures to the demands of the suddenly compounded weight above it and it too buckled and split from bottom to top.

This process repeated itself more quickly with the third and fourth I-beams, and the entire 165 foot long span broke in the middle and collapsed into the river, dragging the ends of the I-beams off of the concrete towers at either end. Finally the last echoes of the tortured metal grinding and groaning stopped and the night was silent again. Power lines within the bridge had snapped, and much of Alexandria on the Virginia shore opposite Ben went dark, as neighborhoods blinked out in succession.

15

The President and his advisors were getting the latest information on the sabotage of the Woodrow Wilson Bridge the same way that millions of other Americans were: they were watching the local and national television news programs. The Homeland Security Team was assembled in the Situation Room beneath the Oval Office watching a bank of four enormous TV screens, all of them depicting the bridge from various angles. From above, the bridge resembled a long row of teeth with one tooth knocked out. An unseen aide in harmony with the President's tastes kept the four televisions tuned to whichever four stations were running the best images, or had the most interesting expert being interviewed. President Gilmore sat in his black leather recliner (with the Presidential Seal on the head rest) holding the remote control, bringing the sound up on the channel he wanted to hear moment by moment.

A dozen news helicopters buzzed around the bridge like gnats, focusing their cameras on the mid-river gap where the span had been dropped. No one spoke as the President switched the sound from channel to channel. Television voices fired out random comments.

"That's right Katie, if you're in a hurry in Washington today, you'd better have a helicopter!"

"...looks like a laser-guided smart bomb hit the bridge Tony, or at least a very smart bomber!"

"The other downtown bridges are completely overwhelmed. People are abandoning their cars and walking to metro stations, which is compounding the gridlock..."

"...DC Beltway is at a total standstill from the Baltimore Washington Parkway around to I-66, so stay away from Washington is all I can say."

"This is Bob Margate, your eye in the sky. We're taking a break from the bridge for a moment to show you the National Mall, where smaller than expected crowds are gathering this morning for the countdown to the assault rifle deadline..."

The President muted the sound entirely. "Turn 'em off, I've seen enough." Walnut panels quietly slid across the television screens. "What a total goat screw! How long until that section is repaired and the bridge can be reopened?" The President glared at the Secretary of Transportation, who had just entered the Situation Room disheveled and out of breath, part of his "comb over" hanging the wrong way across his ear.

"Me? Uh, well sir, I'm just getting up to speed on the particulars on this sit..."

"Then tell me what you do know, dammit!"

"Well, the part that's down was 165 feet between the cement columns on each end. The bridge spans all rest on four long I-beams between the columns, and we might be able to get new I-beams in a couple of weeks, at least..."

"Weeks! Weeks! Don't tell me that! That bridge can't be out for weeks!"

"Uh, sir, we're checking everywhere, they don't build bridges that way any more, and I-beams like that, well they're not lying around anywhere, they have to be manufactured in a foundry, and we're checking everywhere. Also sir, I need to mention, the engineers are telling me the support columns have been damaged, they were cracked when the girders tore off. This is going to be tricky to fix if we use the same columns and don't replace them. If we go that way, we'll have to keep the speeds down, and, um, well, no more trucks. What I'm told is the Wilson Bridge was a wreck to begin with, and the damage goes well beyond what we can see."

President Gilmore sank down in his recliner. "Oh that's just great. And the new bridge is still what, two years from completion?"

"Yes sir, maybe a bit less."

"Does anybody have any good news? Wayne, what's the FBI got so far? Is this an Al Qaida job? Is it Muslims?"

"Mr. President, no one has claimed this one yet. We do have a preliminary report from our dive team."

"Did they find anybody? Did any cars go over when the bridge went down?"

"The dive team reports no vehicles sir. The Coast Guard received a warning call at 2:25, and police were able to clear the bridge before it went off."

"So can the divers tell what happened? Was a car bomb parked on the roadway?"

"No sir, it looks like explosive charges were placed underneath on the supporting steel itself. I'm told it's very sophisticated work, definitely the work of pros. We'll know what kind of explosive was used in a few hours. And we have some photos taken by the dive team." FBI Director Wayne Sheridan signaled to another audio-visual assistant, a Navy Senior Chief in a white dress uniform, and murky color images appeared on a large screen for the Homeland Security Team to examine. The clean cut young FBI director slipped a laser pen from his suit pocket to point out the areas of interest with its brilliant red dot. "This picture shows the precise area of the original explosive cut, on one half of the I-beam that was on the southern side of the span. You can see how clean the cut was, like an axe hit it. Next picture please."

"What's this one showing Wayne? Letters?"

"Yes sir, the letters D.O.L. are spray painted next to the cut. Possibly the name of a new terrorist faction, we're checking it out against all known groups. Possibly it's an authentication code: in case the terrorists try to contact us, they can use the letters to prove who they are. We don't know yet."

"What's your feeling? Is this a Muslim job, or a militia job? Is it Shifflett's old gang? Is it the same people as that car bomb in Norfolk? Is it related to the Stadium Massacre?

"We don't know yet sir. With the assault rifle ban coming in three hours, it could possibly be some type of protest over that. It might be an attempt to disrupt the ceremony on the Mall. We really don't have a handle on how these things are tied together yet, or even if they're connected at all."

President Gilmore stared hard at the giant image of the broken steel under murky water with the initials spray painted near the cut. "D.O.L.... Okay, that's all everybody, thanks for your time." More quietly he said, "Harvey, you stay," to his most trusted advisor. His Chief Staff Officer and old friend Harvey Crandall pulled his chair closer to the President. Crandall was a nearly obese man with an uncanny ability to calculate political fallout.

After the others had filed out, the President asked him, "Any ideas? How do we play this?"

"It's a tough one. If all of these...incidents after the Stadium Massacre are unrelated, if they're just spontaneous, then we'll take a big hit for asking for the gun ban and provoking the gun nuts. You know, the Second Amendment fanatics. Pushing them beyond their limits. I thought we'd just hear the usual carping about "trampling on the Constitution," like we heard after we passed the Universal Surveillance Act, but this might be something much deeper. We might have really struck a raw nerve.

"So no matter what, we have to spin it all as a planned and coordinated militia terrorism campaign, from the Stadium Massacre on. We need to play the domestic terrorism angle all the way. The people will rally against terrorists, even domestic terrorists. That'll play bigger than the gun nuts' anger over the assault rifle ban. The people always rally against terrorism, that always comes first."

"Okay...that makes sense. Tell Mickey to spin it that way." Mickey was Mickey Flanagan, the White House press spokesman. "And you can leak it the same way to your usual reporters, from the 'unnamed senior white house official.' Now what about my making an 'unscheduled appearance' on the Mall for the deadline ceremony, like we discussed yesterday?"

"Absolutely not, not after this bridge fiasco! Let Schuleman and Montaine have their day in the sun. Let them catch the laurels today, and then they can catch the brickbats if this situation blows up any worse."

"Is that statue made out of guns finished?" asked the President.

"What? Yes, it is, that's my understanding. Schuleman and Montaine are going to unveil it at noon. They've got white doves and about a million white balloons ready to go. It's going to be a real dog and pony show."

"What kind of crowd are they going to get with the traffic fouled up like this?"

"They've already got a few thousand true believers there, the 'million mom march' types, and more are coming in on the Metro. But it doesn't really matter. As long as they have at least four or five thousand show up, the networks will shoot it close and tight and make them look like a million. Anyway, they can blame a low turnout on the traffic, and they can always say there was fear of a right wing militia attack."

The President sighed, sinking even lower into his presidential recliner. "What a day."

"And it's only nine o'clock."

There were two men in a silver Toyota 4-Runner, a father and son, trapped on a highway which had become a vast parking lot.

"We should have driven all night Dad, then we'd have been at the launch point hours ago, instead of being stuck in this mess!"

The older man slammed his hands against the dash board. "You're beating a dead horse Joel, I know it already! So what's the absolute maximum range on that thing?"

"Round trip like we planned it? Or one way?"

"No, still round trip, back to here. Can I launch from here and fly to the Mall and make it all the way back?"

"With a full tank, you might get 25 miles total range, depending on the wind. So sure, you could theoretically launch from here and make it back. But I don't think you should fly it Dad, not from here. You've only had a couple of hours on it."

"So what? I can fly it, can't I? It's easy. Like you said, it's the safest flying machine ever invented. You're already under your parachute, right?"

"That's not the point Dad. Sure, you could fly straight down the Mall, turn around and come back. But from here? I don't think you have enough control. It's not like flying the Cessna."

"Right, it's a lot easier! More throttle, you go up, less throttle, you go down. Pull right, pull left. How hard is that?"

"Dad, I know this whole thing is your idea, but I don't want you flying into a bridge or a building, or getting messed up with a jet coming out of Reagan National. It's too far, and I won't be able to help you if you go down. If we have to start from here, I'll fly it."

"Joel, this was my idea, I should do it. You're young, you just got married…"

"Look, Dad, this traffic is completely stopped. Face it, we have to launch from here, or we have to abort the mission and drive back to Knoxville. You can't fly it from here, not safely. I've got over a hundred hours on the power chute, it's my rig. Either I fly it, or we abort the mission and go home."

The sixty-something year old man and his thirty-something son studied each other across the front seats of their SUV. They had spent the last three days working on this plan, printing 5,000 leaflets and training Michael Friedman to fly his son's motorized parachute.

Now, with less than an hour to go until the twelve noon assault rifle deadline, and the ceremony on the National Mall, they were hopelessly stuck in traffic gridlock on I-66 just inside the DC beltway near Falls Church Virginia. The National Mall was only ten miles due east, but the traffic had finally stopped creeping and come to a complete halt an hour before, due to the spillover from the Wilson Bridge sabotage. All of the other Potomac River bridges going into Washington had frozen tight with traffic detouring around the Wilson Bridge, and the ripples continued extending outward and intersecting with each other until the entire DC Metro area was locked up tight.

"Okay Joel, you fly it. We can't go back now, we've come too far…we have to see this through." Michael Friedman paused and cleared a lump in his throat. "We owe it to all the Jews that went quietly."

"I know. We have to do it… I'll fly. We can set up and launch from that field over there. Everybody's pulling U-turns across the median, so let's roll."

"I've got the bail money Joel, just in case."

"Just in case."

"**All right Mr. Fallon**, your check is good to go, are you ready to ring it all up now?"

"I think I've got everything I need today, let's do it."

The manager of the Boat America marine super store had several employees help carry Brad Fallon's selected products to the front of the store by the checkout lanes. "We've got the twelve foot Avon inflatable dingy, the 25 horsepower Yamaha motor, the ICOM single sideband, the Furuno radar, the Garmin GPS color chart plotter, the lap top, the salt water rods...then we have everything in those shopping carts... Is this everything?"

"I believe it is, I don't think we left anything back on the shelves! Let's start ringing it up and I'll write the check."

"Well that's fine by me, let's get to it." The other employees carried Brad's selections to the counter, and as they were scanned they placed his items into large cardboard boxes and placed them under the windows along the front of the store.

Several customers in the other checkout lines and a few plain gawkers stared in awe as Brad racked up his titanic order. You never could tell with yachties: a millionaire or a trust fund baby could walk in wearing shorts and old boat shoes, and buy enough gear to outfit a brand new sport fisher in one shopping spree. This young fellow seemed to fit that mold. Or he could just be the hired captain of a big yacht simply doing his job, working off the boat's expense account. And of course it was impossible to rule out that the young fellow with the big order might be spending the profits made running an illegal cargo from Colombia or Jamaica. Boaters were hard to pigeonhole that way.

All Brad Fallon cared was that Boat America would accept his personal check, and that the bank had given them its blessing in advance. The feds had threatened to freeze his accounts if he fled, but it appeared that he still had the ability to write substantial checks against them. If they were going to freeze his accounts after he took off, he planned to leave them as little as possible of his savings to freeze.

The cashier at the register scanned the last small item from the fourth shopping cart and deducted fifteen percent, a discount that had been worked out in advance with the manager, and then added the state sales tax. The paper receipt ran several feet along the counter from its printer within the register. The cashier tore it off and circled the bottom line figure with a ball point pen and pushed it across to Brad. He took the receipt and sat in a wood and canvas folding deck chair and spent several minutes checking the listed items. The store manager waited patiently until he was finished, and then invited him into his office off to the side of the checkout counters.

In the private office, sitting across the desk from the manager, Brad wrote the second biggest check of his life, for twenty-six thousand four hundred and eight dollars. His only larger one had bought Guajira.

The store manager shook Brad's hand as he accepted his check. "Thanks for choosing Boat America Mr. Fallon, let me give you some store coupons. These are our big ones, and there's no expiration date. And of course, since your order is so large, we'll be happy to provide free delivery anywhere in Tidewater."

"I really appreciate the offer, but I have my own truck. I'll pull it in front." Brad had no intention of unnecessarily disclosing the location of Guajira to anyone if he could help it. He felt fairly sure that "George" would soon be hearing about this big purchase, and he might come to Boat America trying to find Brad's current location.

"We'll be glad to help load up your truck Mr. Fallon."

"That would be fine." Tomorrow Brad planned to do it again at East Marine, and what he couldn't use he would sell or trade down-island, or later in South America.

"**William Peter, William Peter,** this is Henry Niner. I have visual on what looks like a red white and blue motorized hang glider, repeat hang glider, flying southeast over the Roosevelt Bridge, estimated altitude 500 feet, how copy over?"

"Uh… Roger, copy all Henry Niner, you have visual on a red white and blue motorized hang glider, what's your location over?"

"William Peter, I'm at two grand over the Lincoln Memorial. William Peter, is this guy on the program? He's turning east toward the Mall at ten to fifteen knots. Is he on the program over?"

"Henry Niner, stand by, we'll contact the Park Police and the Secret Service, wait out."

Joel Friedman had stopped worrying a few minutes into his flight, and was enjoying his aerial view of the Capitol from 400 feet up. The 180cc motor on his back sounded like a chain saw so he really couldn't hear anything else, but the skies were clear, the winds were light and manageable, and the scenery passing below was stunning. Hundreds of motorists who were standing around their gridlocked cars on Potomac Parkway waved up to the man in the red white and blue "power chute" as he buzzed over them. Before he reached the Lincoln Memorial he added throttle on his chest mounted control panel, then gently tugged his left riser to turn left over the Viet Nam Veterans Memorial. He straightened out over the Reflecting Pool, and finally began his approach flight down the National Mall.

He checked his watch, it was 11:51 and he had just two miles to fly before he would be over the temporary location of the still unnamed "gun statue" at the Capitol building end of the National Mall. His timing was nearly perfect, the national media would all have their television cameras rolling for the twelve noon unveiling of the statue, which had reportedly been welded together from thousands of turned-in assault rifles.

No one knew what it looked like yet. The sculpture had been brought to the Mall covered in tarps on a flat bed trailer before being erected. Joel Friedman passed along the north side of the Washington Monument a hundred feet below its apex; more people looked up and waved at the red white and blue canopy and the man with the noisy little screen-enclosed gas-powered fan on his back. With only a few minutes to go, he undid the Velcro flaps on his canvas sack full of 5,000 leaflets. He could see the crowd milling on the grass at the far end of the Mall, he could see the several story high statue at their center which was covered in light blue canvas.

"Henry Niner, this is William Peter, Park Police advise that the parachute man is not, repeat not on the program, over."

"Roger William Peter, I copy parachute man is not on the program. Break break, Sierra Four, do you have the parachute man visual, over?"

"Roger Henry Niner, the parachute man is passing my location down the center of the Mall, he's over 9th Street now over."

"Sierra Two, Henry Niner, do you have him visual Sierra Two, over?"

"That's a roger Henry Niner, we have him from our location on the Art Gallery. Break, William Peter, request instructions over."

"Henry Niner, this is Sierra Three, we have him from the Air and Space Museum, clear shot over."

"Break Break! All Sierra Teams, this is William Peter Control, do not, repeat do not fire unless he crosses First Street approaching the Capitol. First Street is the red line; do not take a shot without authorization, over."

"William Peter Control, this is Secret Service One, we'll take this now, request you stay off this channel at this time, break, Sierra…"

"…William Peter, this is Sierra Two. I copy are we green light to shoot east of First Street, please confirm, over."

"Sierra Two, Secret Service has opcon, advise…"

"…calm down people, this is Hotel Niner, we don't know this guy's intentions. Parachute man appears to have a large package strapped to his waist, but both of his hands are visible up on his parachute lines over."

"…Service, Sierra Three. Copy and confirm large package strapped on parachute man's waist, parachute man is approaching 4th Street, he's almost over the crowd, request instructions, over…"

Senators Schuleman and Montaine were standing front and center on the temporary stage, holding the ropes which would pull away the sky-blue canvas coverings to unveil the gun statue. They were surrounded on the stage by other politicians, film and television stars, famous network media personalities, and other well known gun control advocates and activists. On a smaller stage to the side, a rag-tag collection of aging folk singers with gray pony tails and frayed bell bottoms were strumming acoustic guitars and leading the crowd in singing, "How many times, must the cannonballs fly, before they're forever banned? The answer my friend, is blowin' in the wind…" All of them: the folk singers, the politicians and stars and the crowd below them were swaying back and forth as they sang, tears of joy rolling down their cheeks, euphoric smiles on their faces. The law had been passed! They would be free forever from the scourge of assault rifle violence!

At a minute past twelve the two Senators pulled down on their ropes, and the pale blue canvas fluttered free of the forty foot tall statue. At the same moment a hundred white doves were released from unseen wire cages beneath the decorated platform supporting the statue. The doves winged off in all directions as a thousand white balloons ascended at the same time, released from giant white boxes behind the main stage.

The forty foot tall statue was obviously meant to be a person with his arms reaching skyward, holding up a large golden ball, which closer examination revealed to be a representation of the one united world. The gun-man statue was constructed entirely of hundreds and thousands of rifles and pistols of all types, welded tightly together along with odds and ends of scrap metal to fill the gaps. The hands and fingers were constructed from rifle barrels; it was possible to identify the front sights of AR-15s and AK-47s as the very finger tips supporting the world.

Joel Friedman watched the unveiling as he crossed 4th Street, flying above the outer fringes of the few thousand people surrounding the statue. He flew through a cloud of white balloons as he neared the center of activity, but with the chain saw motor on his back he hadn't heard any of the speeches or the folk songs. Descending slightly, down to three hundred feet above the crowd, and using the gun statue as his release point, he let go of his risers and reached into his open sack and grabbed a double handful of leaflets.

"William Peter, Sierra One. Parachute man is almost over the stage area, he's reaching into his bag, I can't see his hands, request permission…"

"Henry Niner, Sierra Two. Confirm if the bag contains a bomb over?"

"… bomb, William Peter…"
"…Peter, Sierra Two has a clear shot…"
"…William Peter, Sierra Three clear to shoot, request…"
"…William Peter, Sierra…"
"…this is Hotel Niner, break, Sierra…"
"…this channel, repeat, stay off…"
"…Sierra Two…"

On televisions across America, the views were alternating between the crying and hugging gun control advocates on the stage, and the white balloons and doves lifting into the clear blue sky above the gun statue. Some of the skyward-pointing cameras captured the unscheduled entrance of the rainbow shaped red white and blue parachute, and the man in the white jumpsuit suspended in a harness beneath it, being pushed along by an oversized fan on his back.

The parachute man was reaching into a sack tied around his waist when he suddenly arched backwards, throwing both hands high and releasing a blizzard of confetti which fluttered through the air. Then he fell limp in his harness, his chin on his chest and his arms dangling as he flew on towards the Capitol.

"**…shot? Who shot? Cease fire!** All Sierra teams stand down, stand…"

"…William Peter, Sierra Three. Sierra Three shooter has, uh, discharged his rifle. Uh, wait one, over…"

The parachute man had been shot by a .308 caliber Remington 700PSS bolt-action police sniper rifle firing a 165 grain-weight lead and copper hollow-point bullet. The slug entered his right side just above his pelvis at 2,600 feet per second, slewed sideways, and exited under his left shoulder. Instantly dead in his harness, his white jumpsuit filling with blood and blooming into crimson, Joel Friedman flew on, gently descending until his body thudded into the south portico of the Capitol building. His red white and blue parachute snagged a black wrought-iron balcony railing and stopped there, draping it almost like patriotic bunting.

His chain saw motor continued running, swinging his body back and forth like a pendulum against the whitewashed wall, leaving a red smear. He continued swinging to and fro while amazed Capitol police on the balcony looked down, conferring on cell phones and radios, until ladders were extended up the wall from below. Finally Capitol workers were able to tear out his motor's rubber fuel line, and silence the tiny engine. They lowered his limp body down to the ground, under the unceasing gaze of the network television cameras.

Ten miles to the west, Michael Friedman watched his son Joel's last act play out on a wall of televisions in the electronics department of a Falls Church Target Store, along with other shocked and speechless customers.

Then Michael Friedman's very own leaflet was suddenly the hottest item on television, framed in close-up detail on every channel. It showed an old black and white picture of a nameless hollow-eyed Jewish man kneeling by the edge of a vast body-filled pit, staring directly at the camera in helpless despair, in the last moment of his life. Behind him a grinning Nazi soldier in a slouch cap aimed a pistol at the back of his head, while other smiling Nazis with rifles and sub machineguns slung casually on their shoulders looked on in approval. Millions of Americans simultaneously read the captioned headline printed above the strange picture, puzzling out its meaning.

**WHEN GUNS ARE OUTLAWED
ONLY GOVERNMENTS AND CRIMINALS HAVE GUNS.**

Beneath the picture of the doomed Jew and the smiling Nazis, this was printed:

**DURING THE 20TH CENTURY, OVER 100
MILLION CIVILIANS WERE KILLED BY THEIR OWN
GOVERNMENTS, MORE THAN IN ALL 20TH CENTURY
WARS COMBINED. IN EACH CASE, EXTERMINATION
FOLLOWED GUN CONFISCATION.**

1911: Turkey established gun control. From 1915 to 1917, 1.5 million Armenians in Turkey, unable to defend themselves, were exterminated.

1929: The Soviet Union established gun control. From 1929 to 1953, 40-60 million "class enemies," unable to defend themselves, were exterminated.

1935: China established gun control. From 1948 to 1952, 20 million Chinese "class enemies," unable to defend themselves, were exterminated.

1938: Germany established gun control. From 1939 to 1945, 13 million Jews, Catholics, Gypsies and others, unable to defend themselves, were exterminated in Nazi controlled Europe.

1956: Cambodia established gun control. From 1975 to 1977, one million "class enemies," unable to defend themselves, were exterminated.

1966-1976: China still had gun control. Millions of more "class enemies," still unable to defend themselves, were exterminated in Mao's "Cultural Revolution."

1990s: Rwanda established gun control. In 100 days in 1994, over 800,000 Tutsis, unable to defend themselves, were exterminated by machete-wielding Hutus backed by armed government militias.

NEVER AGAIN!

WE WILL NEVER AGAIN BE LED LIKE LAMBS TO THE SLAUGHTER, BECAUSE IN A MOMENT OF NAÏVE OPTIMISM WE ALLOWED OURSELVES TO BE DISARMED!

16

Ian Kelby watched the incredible events unfolding upon the Washington Mall on a portable television in his Rockville Maryland law office. His office occupied a storefront in a small shopping center which he shared with a pet store, a beauty salon, and a national real estate franchise. Kelby specialized in real estate law, but he also did divorce and DUI and just about anything that walked through the door. It wasn't glamorous, but it paid the bills. Most important of all, he didn't have to kiss anybody's ass, and he was able to set his own hours.

He watched the entire painfully farcical celebration of the official termination of the Bill of Rights (as he saw it) on the stage packed with ecstatic left wing politicians and movie stars. He groaned and cursed as he watched the unveiling of the so-called "peace statue," and the release of the white balloons and the doves. And like millions of Americans, he had noted the unplanned appearance of a man flying a motorized parachute. He had shared the confusion of the reporters, and he had watched in disbelief as the man was shot dead. Like the rest of America, he had been shown the now-famous leaflet. He had seen the haunting image of the doomed Jew, forced to kneel at the edge of a mass grave, with a pistol aimed at his head by a grinning Nazi soldier.

Kelby was soon informed by a network talking head that Joel Friedman, whose identity and home town had just been released, was like himself also 34 years old. He was dead, killed by a police sniper, but his leaflet had been seen and read by millions of Americans who had never given the "right to keep and bear arms" a minute's thought in their entire lives. Joel Friedman had been willing to risk his life to put that leaflet in front of the American television viewing audience, he had succeeded beyond his wildest dreams, and now he was dead.

Like Joel Friedman, Ian Kelby was an ardent believer that the Second Amendment served as America's last-ditch insurance policy against the steadily creeping approach of federal government tyranny. Kelby had watched in mounting frustration as the perversely named Patriot Acts (One and Two) had become law. Then came the Total Information Awareness program, which was renamed the more palatable Terrorist Information Awareness program, which collected every knowable fact about every American, and placed it all into searchable data bases. Then finally, under President Gilmore, had come the hideously named Universal Surveillance Act, and America's streets began to be laced with a seamless spider's web of digital face-mapping cameras.

All of these new "Big Brother" laws had been sold under the guise of combating terrorism and increasing security, but none of them dared to address the specific threat posed by Islamic terror. Instead the federal government seemed to prefer to increase security by treating all Americans equally: equally as criminal suspects in a vast open-air penal system.

To Ian Kelby, the obviously contrived Stadium Massacre, and the resulting semi-automatic rifle ban, seemed like the final bricks in a wall of tyranny being quietly built up higher and higher by the federal government over the course of many years. Kelby had seen the wall rising brick by brick and layer by layer, but instead of merely staring up at it in pessimistic acceptance, he had been quietly making his own plans, and pondering when the wall would, for him, go up one brick too far and then no farther.

Like Joel Friedman, Ian Kelby also had a private protest plan. But Kelby's plan was nothing as elegant or creative as dropping leaflets in front of the network television cameras, while they were recording the celebration of the death of the Second Amendment. Ian Kelby's plan was more direct, and simply involved a century-old Russian rifle made for the Czar's army, and a United States Senator who had shared the stage with the gun-grabbers on the Mall. He considered and he reconsidered, and then he irrevocably made up his mind: the time had come. He clicked off his television and flipped open his cell phone.

"Roy, this is Ian. How ya doing man? You watching the TV?"

"I sure am. I just about threw up. You saw the guy with the parachute?"

"Yeah I did, I couldn't freakin' believe it! Hey Roy, how's your schedule look the rest of the day? Can you spring loose?"

"In a couple hours maybe. Give me a little time to make up some lies." Roy Millard was a junior partner at a "real" law firm in Chevy Chase, and he needed to create a fictional client-related reason to be away from the office, in order to skate out early without raising senior partner eyebrows.

"The Brew Pub at 2:30?"

"Make it 3:00, and you got it."

"Roy..."

"Yeah?"

"You know what the lady said about the awkward time? ...I think it's just about over."

"Ian, it's been over. It just took us this long to admit it."

The two old law school friends were referring to an increasingly famous quote by the libertarian writer Claire Wolfe: "America is at that awkward stage. It's too late to work within the system, but too early to shoot the bastards."

Ranya Bardiwell rode her Yamaha FZR back up I-64 to Charlottesville in the morning, spent an hour punting the rest of the semester at the registrar's office, and went shopping for used vans in the afternoon. She almost gave up and rented a U-haul truck, but after several tries she got lucky with a classified ad and found a cream-colored 1988 Ford Econoline. It had been owned by a husband and wife catering service. They were quitting the business, and the van was available for cash on an expedited basis. They assured Ranya that the engine had been rebuilt only the year before. She sweet-talked them into a solo test drive, and once out of their sight she torture-tested it by blasting up the steep mountain road to Monticello. The engine and transmission were outstanding for the van's age, so she bargained them down to $2,500 cash, took the title and kept their tags.

At a construction site on the university grounds she bought a short piece of scaffolding plank for literally a smile, and she had her motorcycle ramp. The construction foreman even tossed in a thirty foot long piece of dirty but serviceable nylon rope, and her Yamaha was quickly cinched up tight inside of the van.

The van was crucial to her steadily evolving plan. Everything she cared about that she owned could fit inside it, she could transport her bikes with it, and she could even sleep in it. The van could be her mobile base of operations, yet it was low-key enough to be left anywhere without attracting undue attention.

In another lifetime, just before her father's murder, Ranya had lived for one week with another fourth-year student in an apartment on Jefferson Park Avenue, a few blocks from The Grounds. Her new roommate wasn't home when Ranya arrived to collect her belongings. They shared a small two bedroom furnished apartment, and Ranya was able to fit everything she wanted into some cardboard boxes and hanging bags.

She left a note for her roommate saying that she was sorry, but she had to go. She had family business to attend to in Suffolk after the death of her father (that was certainly true) and then she was going to do some traveling and think things out. She'd be in touch.

In less than an hour Ranya was gone from the apartment that she had just moved into, with almost everything she owned in the world contained within her new-old Ford van. For now that suited her perfectly: she was anonymous, mobile, and armed. In another hour most of her currently unneeded worldly possessions were packed in a five-by-eight mini storage unit, paid up in cash for the next six months.

On her way out of Charlottesville she passed down University Avenue, and briefly pulled the van to the curb across from the Rotunda. In front of the Rotunda, a tall and imposing bronze statue of Thomas Jefferson stood silent guard over his "academical village." UVA was unquestionably still Thomas Jefferson's University; his unmistakable mark was left indelibly on every yard of "The Grounds." Well, Ranya thought, hadn't he said it all, two centuries earlier? Hadn't Jefferson written, "Rebellion to tyrants is obedience to God?" Hadn't he also written, "The tree of liberty must be refreshed from time to time, with the blood of patriots and tyrants?"

By 4:40 PM Ian Kelby was in his preselected sniper's lair across a small valley from the back of Senator Geraldine Randolph's home, located in rolling countryside near Potomac Maryland, a dozen miles south of Rockville. Kelby had put the U.S. Senator from Maryland on his personal "to do" list years before, because of her consistent and vocal support for every proposal that ever floated through Congress which served to diminish or deny freedom in America. There was not a gun control, "anti-terrorism," "computer security" or "hate crime" bill which did not include her name near the top. She had just led the charge in the Senate for the passage of the President's new "Universal Surveillance Act," with its painfully insulting USA acronym. In short, any law which lessened liberty and freedom in America, Senator Geraldine Randolph strongly endorsed.

When it came to firearms ownership, Senator Randolph was among the rankest of hypocrites. She was on the record saying she believed that only the police and the military needed handguns at all, and that she supported totally banning their possession by the general public.

Yet she herself had one of Maryland's extremely rare concealed pistol permits, which were given only to the power elite with the very best political connections. Not only did she have a concealed permit, it was well known that she carried a revolver in her purse at all times. She claimed she needed the Smith and Wesson .38 due to all of the threats she had received from angry gun owners, and she perceived absolutely no irony in her position. Marylanders who owned businesses in high-crime areas had virtually no chance of obtaining a concealed permit, but evidently Senator Randolph felt that her need was greater than theirs, even though she was escorted everywhere with her own detail of heavily armed bodyguards provided by the Secret Service.

To Kelby's way of thinking, all of this clearly made her one of the "domestic enemies" he had once sworn the military officer's oath to defend the Constitution against. Today, now that the "shooting phase" had more or less officially begun with the sniper's shot on the Mall, Kelby saw her as just a piece of low-hanging fruit which could be picked off with relative ease, before he moved on to more difficult targets.

Notoriously unsociable, Senator Randolph could usually be depended upon to return home by six PM, unless an important vote was scheduled. She was independently wealthy, a multi-millionairess with her own family money, and she did not need to cruise the usual fund-raising receptions groveling for campaign contributions. She had inherited everything of value in her life. She had even inherited her Senate seat, taking it over when her husband had died in a plane wreck a decade earlier. Later she had used her vast inherited wealth to fund her easy reelection.

Ian Kelby was aware of her personal schedule and habits, because he had come to this exact spot on "dry runs" without a weapon several times before, armed only with binoculars, a field guide to North American song birds for cover, and a pocket note pad. Most weekday afternoons and evenings in nice weather, Senator Randolph would spend some time reading or meeting with key assistants on the raised patio deck behind her angular brown-painted "ecologically harmonious" home, which Kelby, the real estate lawyer, considered a multi-million dollar eyesore. The deck did afford a magnificent view of her own little section of Glen Falls Park and the hardwood forest on the opposite slope. Some mornings deer would even slip from the woods to graze in the valley beneath her house.

Ian Kelby knew about the deer, because he had occasionally watched her place while appearing to take a break on completely plausible morning jogs, up the old fire trails on the other side of the state park from her house. Ian's old buddy from the University of Maryland Law School, Roy Millard, had also taken a few turns surveilling her, but today Roy was handling the transportation and logistics end of the operation, because he had not had as much preparation time. His turn to shoot would come on another day. Together they had compiled an extensive list of "domestic enemies of the Constitution" in the capital region.

For this operation Ian Kelby had selected from his seldom-entered garage attic an antique Russian bolt-action rifle, a Mosin-Nagant in 7.62 by 54mm, an obsolete rifle designed for the Czar's army. The example which Ian owned had been manufactured before his similarly blond and blue-eyed grandfather had been born in Holland, and to a modern eye it was bizarre looking, with a wooden fore stock extending all the way out to the end of its thirty inch long barrel. Obsolete or not, Viet Cong snipers had been capable of hitting unlucky American sentries at well beyond 600 meters with them, and communist bloc shooting teams had always performed well in international target competitions with accurized versions.

Ian had bought his Nagant for $75 cash, outside of a flea market that he'd stumbled across in West Virginia, while on a kayaking trip with Roy. He'd sensed its deadly potential, and had never shown it to anyone else but his best friend. Once he'd shot it a few times and discovered how uncannily accurate it was, he'd made the effort to put a cheap 3X9 variable magnification Bushnell scope on it. This cost another $175 cash, including a special Nagant scope mount. For $250, he had a rifle which could hit ten-inch-diameter paper plate targets, taped to cardboard boxes a paced-off 550 yards away. Every time—just as long as he was firing from a steady rest position.

And a steady rest position is exactly what he had here, 550 yards across Glen Falls Park from Senator Randolph's back deck. Ian's antique Nagant was lying balanced across a rotten tree stump. Without his even touching the rifle it was aligned so that her house could be seen when he leaned over from his sitting position and looked through the bright ocular lens of the scope.

Kelby had never attended a military sniper school, and he was not wearing a bushy burlap rag covered "ghillie suit." He didn't lie frozen in place in the prone-position ready to shoot for hours on end, perfectly disguised as a six foot long patch of weeds. He just sat behind a tree stump surrounded by bushes, wearing a faded green sweat suit, and waited for her to come home. Except for his skin-colored latex surgical gloves and the rifle, he could have just been a hiker or a bird watcher taking a rest.

By 5:45 pm the sun was dropping low into the woods behind him, but it was still shining on the Senator's deck when he saw the colorful flash of vehicles rushing up her private drive and disappearing out of his sight on the other side of her house. He put his binoculars and his water bottle back into his brown daypack, and hunched up close behind his rifle as his heart raced from sixty to well over a hundred beats a minute.

He was sitting Indian-style with his shins against the base of the tree stump. The low wooden stock of the Nagant didn't provide a good "cheek weld" to Ian's face when he was looking through the scope, which was raised well above the original iron sights, but this kept his skin, and his DNA, from being left on it. He squirmed his body into a tighter position behind the rifle and the Senator's house leaped out through the light-grabbing ocular lens of the scope, which was already turned to its maximum 9X magnification. At that range and magnification, the Senator's house filled the entire diameter of the lens from side to side. With the rifle so well supported along its length by the decayed stump, and his body position so steady, the crosshairs remained fixed and unmoving on her back doors.

A sturdy-looking waist-high wooden railing prevented people from tumbling off the deck and fifteen feet down to the ground behind the Senator's house. Kelby saw the railing as an obstacle which could potentially deflect his shot if she came out and sat down right away. It would be chancy to try for a shot over or through the rails if she were sitting, but it was doable as a last resort with the heavy 180 grain bullet he had in the chamber.

Ten minutes after Senator Randolph's party arrived home, Kelby saw the curtains move behind her large sliding glass doors, then they slid open and a man in a dark jacket and white shirt came out, holding his own pair of binoculars. He spent barely a minute scanning the valley and the distant woods, and Kelby had to stifle his laughter at the man's feeble effort at counter-surveillance. His shooting position was in deep shadows and quite invisible from the house; while the Senator's back deck was a floodlit stage in the late afternoon sun.

At 6:05 the Senator herself finally came out, wearing blue slacks and a beige cardigan sweater. Her chin-length dyed auburn hair was as stiffly styled and coiffed as it always was, moving with her face like a medieval helmet. The Senator and a different man, this one in a gray suit, walked over to the railing. She was pointing with her arm to the stream with its little foot bridge, and other features visible to her in the meadow.

Kelby steadied the Bushnell's thin black crosshairs on her left armpit to account for the slight cross breeze, and began squeezing the Nagant's trigger while slowly exhaling. His heart was racing wildly, his blood was surging with such force that he could hear nothing but its whooshing in his ears, but the crosshairs remained steady while his right finger gently squeezed.

Suddenly with a deafening BLAM the rifle's hardwood stock launched itself back into his right shoulder, and the thin metal rim at the back of the scope struck him just above his right eye. He quickly reacquired the back deck through the scope for one last quick look: somebody was down, and there was a flurry of activity around his or her body. Randolph wasn't visible, so logically it had to be her lying on the deck behind the railing.

He retracted the bolt slowly to extract the single shell case by hand; he didn't want to leave that particular piece of evidence behind. The empty brass shell went into his brown daypack, and then he gently tossed the rifle into a patch of thick ferns. It was just an untraceable single-use throwaway, and he had others. He peeled off his latex gloves and stuffed them into his pack.

After a quick scan of the area for anything left behind, Kelby put on his pack, jogged a short distance to where a cheap mountain bike was stashed, and pedaled hard and fast down the fire trail to where his friend was waiting a mile away.

Roy Millard popped the trunk from inside of his burgundy Chevy Malibu when he saw Ian pedal into view. He was parked behind an abandoned gas station on a bypassed and seldom-used rural blacktop behind the state park. Ian Kelby threw his bike inside the open trunk, slammed it shut, and got in on the passenger side. He high-fived his friend, who then handed him a cold bottle of Gatorade, started the engine and slowly drove off.

"I heard it. You get her?"

"Yeah." Kelby guzzled half of the bottle of green liquid in one long drink. There had not been a molecule of moisture in his mouth since he had seen the cars arriving at her house.

"You sure?"

"Positive... I think. Yeah, I got her."

Roy was laughing. "Dude, you got scope eye, you got a cut there! What, did you get buck fever and crowd up on it?"

"Damned rifle's stock is too low for a scope. I should've taped a cheek pad onto it like you said. Is it bad? I've got court tomorrow." Kelby screwed the top on the Gatorade bottle and set it on the seat.

"Nah, no problem. I've done worse shaving, just not up that high! So who's next on the hit parade, what do you think? Courtney or Silas? Or maybe Schuleman, if we can find him."

"Well Roy, it's your shot, so I guess it's your call."

"Yeah, okay. Anyway, we don't have to decide right now. Hey, are you hungry after your big afternoon?"

"Yeah man, let's eat. I'm starving."

"Well I'm buying." Roy turned north onto Falls Road, heading back to Rockville.

Kelby wiped his temple with the back of his hand. "You know, I probably left some blood on the scope. Shit."

"DNA, you mean? You're not in any data base, are you?"

"I don't think so...but there's nothing I can do about it now."

They drove in silence a few minutes, Ian Kelby staring vacantly out of his passenger window at the passing scenery. Then he got back on track with the plan, and took off his old sneakers and socks and peeled off his green sweats. He already had black dress shorts and a preppie red alligator shirt on underneath. His entire sniper suit, including his latex gloves, went into a garbage bag for disposal in a distant dumpster. He was not willing to have a single fiber or shoe print ever traced to him. He pulled a pair of brown Docksiders boat shoes from under the seat and slipped them on.

"It's finally started," said Roy Millard.

"Yeah, it sure has." Kelby picked up the Gatorade bottle again. His hands were shaking and they slipped as he unscrewed the top.

"Got the heebie-jeebies huh? Well who wouldn't? There's a pint of Rebel Yell in the glove box. Go on Ian, haul it out."

Kelby fumbled with the glove box latch and got the bottle of hundred-proof bourbon out and twisted off the cap. He took a long pull, and passed it to his friend Roy, who looked across at him, lifted the bottle in a toast and said, "Sic semper tyrannis Ian," before taking his own drink.

"Yeah buddy, sic semper tyrannis. One down, and a bunch more to go."

17

President Gilmore called an emergency meeting of the Homeland Security Team when he was informed of Senator Randolph's assassination. The story was just breaking on the internet: the Sledge Report had a one-sentence headline announcing her killing with no other details. The cable news networks were just breaking into their programming to announce her shocking death. The team met as usual in the Situation Room beneath the Oval Office, where the President was pacing in front of the mahogany conference table, running his fingers through his thick gray hair.

"Okay folks, we're losing control of the situation. First the bridge, then that absolute fiasco on the Mall! They're beating us like a drum in the media! That damned parachute guy's pamphlet, now this 'D.O.L.' letter… The wrong side is setting the agenda! And now this! A United States Senator has been shot and killed! A United States Senator!"

Copies of the Friedman mass-grave leaflet and the bridge bomber's letter had been passed around the conference table where some of the Homeland Security Team now scanned them, as if searching for some hidden meaning missed on their first dozen readings. No one wanted to meet the President's gaze. He was on a tear, veering toward heart attack territory.

"Folks, we can't have any more days like today! The bridge was bad enough, and then that parachute thing, but, but, killing a United States Senator? That is UNACCEPTABLE!!" President Gilmore was practically screaming, his face scarlet. He spun his black leather recliner around and rested both hands on the head rest, closed his eyes and dropped his head, and attempted to slow his breathing and regain control.

If Senator Randolph could be killed at home within hours of sharing that stage on the National Mall, any of them might be killed, except for possibly the President and Vice-President. Senators were provided the same level of security as the rest of the Cabinet and other Homeland Security Team members seated around the conference table in the Situation Room.

"Wayne, what's the FBI got so far on her assassination?"

"Mr. President, Senator Randolph was shot while standing on the patio behind her house near Potomac. She had just arrived home and was talking with an admin assistant when she was killed instantly by a single rifle shot. She was evidently shot through her heart and spine. The shooter's rifle has been recovered; he fired from the woods opposite her house from 600 yards away."

The President looked at his FBI Director, shocked. "Damn! What's 600 yards, about a third of a mile? Does that mean this was a professional job, like a trained military sniper? You said you have the rifle, have you picked up any suspects?"

"No sir. The rifle was left behind, but we don't have any leads on the shooter. We're working with the Maryland State Police, we're combing the area with dogs and helicopters, but it's almost dark...and all we have is the rifle."

"Well, what kind of sniper rifle can hit someone in the heart from a third of a mile away? You said you have it, is it a military sniper rifle?"

"No sir, not at all. It's actually a Mosin-Nagant, a Russian rifle made around the First World War."

"It's a what?"

"A Mosin-Nagant. It was the standard-issue Russian shoulder arm from the 1890s until World War Two, sort of the Russian equivalent of our old Springfields. Did you ever see 'Doctor Zhivago?' No? Well, anyway it's a bolt-action, the kind where you pull a bolt handle back and forth to load each bullet." The FBI Director mimed pulling the handle of a bolt-action rifle.

"Is it some kind of super-accurate rifle? Is it rare? Expensive?"

"No sir, not at all. Millions of them were produced. Today they're sold for about a hundred dollars. But obviously, with a telescopic sight... Well sir, the result speaks for itself."

"Okay then, if this particular rifle is so accurate, why was it left behind? Does that mean the sniper is quitting after one attack? Or that he panicked and fled?"

"That's possible sir, but I don't think so. I think, I think the sniper is...begging your pardon sir, but...I think the sniper is...mocking us."

"Mocking us?!"

"Yes sir. I think he's telling us that our top leadership can be assassinated even with, um...a trash rifle. I'm told that that rifle and scope probably cost the sniper less than $300. And there may be a message in the Russian origin of the rifle. It might be related somehow to the Russian SKS used by the stadium sniper."

"Well even an old Russian rifle has some kind of serial number doesn't it? We should be able to trace it, right? Doesn't the ATF have some kind of program for that? Isn't the ATF in the Justice Department now?" The President turned to the newly confirmed Attorney General, Lynn Axelmann. Today she was looking sharp, if a little butch, with her mannishly short brown hair, black-framed glasses and a severe navy blue pants suit. "Lynn, who's the ATF Director? ATF is part of Justice now, isn't it?"

"Um, most of it is sir. The law enforcement parts are. And the ATF Director? That would be David Boxell, sir."

"Well, I want him to sit in on these homeland security meetings from now on. It's all about these damn guns, this plague of guns! He's our gun expert right? Guns and explosives?"

"Yes sir, that's correct. I'll have Director Boxell contacted right away," said Attorney General Axelmann.

"So can we trace this rifle or not?" asked the President.

Lynn Axelmann got busy whispering to her Deputy Attorney General who was sitting beside her. He was the much older Paul Wilson, who had been brought over from the Treasury Department after the most recent Department of Homeland Security reshuffle.

Wilson in turn whispered to an aide behind him, presumably to have the aide call Boxell over from the Treasury building. Some of the senior executive ATF offices were still in the Treasury building just across from the White House, some divisions had moved to the new ATF Headquarters on New York Avenue, and still other divisions were slated to be moved into the new multi-billion dollar Department of Homeland Security building which was still under construction. As always, the ATF was an unwanted bureaucratic bastard stepchild, with its divisions, functions and office space divided.

The President almost shouted, "Does anybody know the answer? Can we trace this rifle or not? Wayne?"

All eyes returned to FBI Director Wayne Sheridan, mostly to avoid the President's wrathful gaze.

"Yes sir, I'm sure that ATF is already working on it, they've got some terrific firearms tracing programs. They've really been making great strides towards a comprehensive national data base, but frankly sir, I'm not very hopeful. The rifle could have been in private hands for the last, well, who knows how many decades…and it could have been privately resold a dozen times."

"Well, we're going to have to do something about that! We just can't allow every Tom Dick and Harry out there to sell guns to each other without sending in proper records to the authorities! And we need ballistic fingerprints for all guns, all of them! Put that on the action list Harvey," the President said to his Chief Staff Officer. "What about the scope, does that have any way to trace it?"

"I'm sorry Mr. President, I'm afraid the scope isn't much better. It's a very common, inexpensive model, one of millions really… I think we're going to find that the sniper left us a sterile gun, virtually impossible to trace. And that could conceivably be part of a message the sniper might be sending us."

"Message? What message? Expand on that."

"Mr. President, there's probably ten million high-powered hunting rifles floating around out there, with telescopic sights that are capable of hitting somebody at five hundred yards. It's anybody's guess how many of them have been fine-tuned enough to hit somebody at a thousand yards or more. That's over half of a mile. And I don't just mean hit a section of a stadium, I mean hit one particular person, like Senator Randolph."

The Situation Room fell dead quiet. All of them knew Senator Randolph, and several of them had been to her house at one time or another. The sniper had obviously planned the assassination well in advance, and if the sniper could get her, he could get any of them. A dozen minds were imagining what their homes looked like from distant vantage points, and wondering whether anyone had already done assassination planning at the distant edges of their lives.

The President said softly, "Ten million? Ten million potential sniper rifles?"

"Or more," replied the FBI Director.

"So Senator Randolph's assassination wasn't some incredible feat by an...an Olympic-level target shooter, or a trained military sniper? It was just an ordinary shot by some yahoo with a...junk rifle?"

"I'd say it was better than ordinary, but basically, yes, I'd agree with that assessment Mr. President."

"Then all of our emphasis on the semi-automatic assault rifles has been misplaced? We're in greater danger from...ordinary hunting rifles?"

"So it would appear, I'm sorry to say."

"And Senator Randolph had a standard Secret Service protective detail for her personal protection? And they were unable to prevent this?"

"That would also appear to be correct. Pistols and submachine guns aren't much protection against a sniper hidden 500 yards away."

"Then we're going to have to totally revamp how we provide security for the senior leadership, ASAP!"

The FBI Director paused, studying his fingernails, considering his words carefully. "Mr. President, I would say that it would be just about impossible to put a five hundred yard moving security perimeter around all of the national leadership. Or even one hundred yards for that matter... We just don't have anything like that amount of trained manpower. You know what's involved in your own protection...extending that kind of protection to the Senate, to the Senior Executive Service...to hundreds of key personnel...I don't think it's possible."

The President dropped into his black leather presidential recliner facing the conference table. "Wayne, you paint a grim picture, very grim, but I appreciate your candor. One last question: is this some kind of militia uprising? Just what in the hell do you think is going on?"

"I wish I knew sir, I wish I knew. Believe me, we're pushing all of our militia and right wing fringe groups hard, very hard. We're really stretching the constitutional envelope, even under the Patriot Act. We're treading right on the line, you might say... But in the end the full-court press may prove counter-productive. It may not have the conventional results we would normally expect to see, say, if we were going after the Mafia, or even our own American Muslims."

"Why not?" asked the President, tapping a water glass with a pen.

"Frankly, it's those millions of deer rifles sir. There's just too many of them, and too many folks who know how to shoot them. The harder we push on what we consider the fringe groups, the more we might be provoking the rest of them into doing something...something like what happened to Senator Randolph today."

"Well then, what will work? What other solutions do we have?"

The FBI Director paused, and said, "Have you seen the pictures we're getting mailed to us? The assault rifle pictures?"

"I've seen some of them. Kooks and criminals have been mailing them to us. So what?"

Someone on a conservative internet forum had suggested mailing in photos of the assault rifles they did not plan to turn in, and the idea had snowballed. The White House, the BATFE and the FBI were being inundated with thousands of anonymous envelopes a day, containing pictures of people holding various semi-automatic rifles, which they claimed they would never surrender. The pictures all had the gun owners' faces cut off, so there was no way to trace them. Most of them said something along the lines of "from my cold dead hands!" and other things that were a great deal more threatening. "Come and take it!" and "You can have my rifle as soon as I'm finished shooting the bullets!" were two common sentiments.

"Mr. President," the FBI Director continued, "we might want to ease up a bit, maybe extend an amnesty period on the assault rifles, maybe grandfather some of them back in..."

"Screw that!" returned the President angrily. "Wayne, you've been a great help today, but that idea's a non-starter. That would be seen as a surrender to the terrorists, and that will NOT happen on my watch! We will NOT back down one inch! Not one millimeter! Any other bright ideas?" The President's voice dripped with scorn at the idea of retreating.

FBI Director Wayne Sheridan slowly shook his head no, while studying his fingernails.

"Well, does anybody have any ideas? Unconventional ideas, out of the box ideas? Come on people, you're supposed to be my best and brightest!" President Gilmore glanced quickly at his "Homeland Security Czar," Art Mountjoy, the former Governor of Ohio. He was the well-meaning dolt who had been hand-picked to be the President's lackey and potential fall-guy in the domestic security arena. Now is when I need idea men, thought the President, and I'm saddled with that moron. It was often said that Art Mountjoy had "Peter Principled" 35 years earlier as a linebacker for the Ohio State Buckeyes, and the President believed it. Mountjoy was attempting to look busy by reading a copy of the bridge bomber's letter, the furrows deep across his wide brow beneath his oily Grecian Formula black pompadour.

"Anybody?" asked the President. "We're stuck behind the eight ball here; we're getting our asses handed to us! We're just reacting, and we need to take back the initiative!"

The FBI Director cleared his throat and spoke. After he had been rebuked for going soft, he had clearly seen which way the White House wind was blowing, and he quickly decided to trim his sails accordingly. "Just an idea Mr. President, but all of those rifles are really only a serious threat with scopes mounted on them. Not many shooters can hit much past one or two hundred yards without a telescopic sight... Just outlaw the scopes. Let the hunters keep their bolt-action rifles for legitimate sporting purposes, but ban the scopes. Rifle scopes are already illegal in most countries around the world, and for a damned good reason! Banning them will bring us closer into line with international law, and that'll help us up at the UN with the International Small Arms Convention."

"Well that's a hell of a fine idea Wayne! It shouldn't be a problem to get that passed and signed right away. Harvey, contact Senator Schuleman. Tell him and Montaine I want something workable on my desk tomorrow. They can name the law for Senator Randolph. Do you have anything else Wayne?"

"Yes sir. Checkpoints. We should set up a comprehensive system for conducting vehicle inspections for illegal firearms and explosives, like they did during the Beltway Sniper case. We can greatly diminish the threat if the terrorists can't use the roads for transporting weapons. The courts have always sided with us here, so I don't really see any Fourth Amendment problem with checkpoints, given the emergency."

"Okay, let's talk about that. Can we do that with just a Presidential Decision Directive, or do we need a law?"

Attorney General Lynn Axelmann chimed in. She spoke as if her jaws were wired together, and behind her back she was called "Doctor Strangelove" by junior staffers. "Absolutely sir, you can do it with a Presidential Decision Directive. You have the authority under Patriot Two and the Homeland Security Act. It's all there. It grants you blanket authority to enact 'other measures as may be required', etcetera, etcetera. Don't worry, the wording's all there, it covers just about anything. In fact, I don't see any problem with doing the telescopic rifle sight ban the same way, with a Presidential Decision Directive, not after Geraldine—er— Senator Randolph was shot with a scoped rifle. Just decree that scoped rifles can't be transported on the federal highway system, that'll certainly hold up as a first step. If you want Schuleman and Montaine to get credit for a comprehensive bill, that's fine, but you don't need it. All you really need is the Patriot Act, all the authority you need is already in there."

"Thanks Lynn, I was leaning that way already. You don't see any problem from the Supreme Court?"

"No sir. It's a slam dunk, six to three our way, no matter what."

"Well, that's good news for a change—at least we can count on the Supreme Court. Transportation, what's the latest on the bridge?"

"We're on track sir. The reroutes and detours are making progress, and most of the gridlock is cleared away. I would recommend that we ask non-essential government employees to stay home tomorrow, so we can test the new traffic patterns, and see how it holds up."

"Like a snow day?"

"Exactly sir. Like a snow day."

"I'll consider it. I'm hesitant to let the...hell, who are they? The 'domestic terrorists' I guess, I'm hesitant to let them see us forced to stop the normal workings of the federal government on their account. They'll see it as a victory for them and a defeat for us. What's the latest estimated time to fix the damn bridge anyway?"

"Four weeks sir, if we can get all the parts we need as fast as possible. The long girders are the problem. The only place that can make them needs to retool."

"Christ! Four weeks?" The President turned to his Homeland Security Czar. "Art, do we have a plan for protecting our other key bridges and tunnels? Really protecting them, not just making a show?"

"Bridges? Well yes, local police departments are notified, they already have contingency plans. That was done this morning. But after 24 hours we'll need to call out the National Guard, there's literally thousands of critical bridges on the interstate highway system alone."

"Then we'd better do it. Wayne, did you get anything out of the D.O.L. letter?" The Wilson Bridge bomber had mailed copies of his manifesto to a dozen television and print media offices around Washington very early in the morning, some of the copies had been delivered by the late afternoon and the cable news channels were already running it. Mickey Flanagan, the President's press spokesman, was refusing to confirm or deny that the letter was genuine or that it was from the bomber. He was also denying any knowledge of the D.O.L. mentioned in the letter and spray-painted on the cut steel girder.

"Mr. President," said the FBI Director, "the D.O.L. letter was hand-typed on an old Smith-Corona electric typewriter. We might get lucky, but I'd assume it's already on its way to a landfill in pieces. We're working on marks left on the letters by the photocopier, and we're trying to trace the bomber's vehicle by the time and location that he made his mail drop in southeast DC, but those are long shots. As you know by now, the current assumption is that D.O.L. stands for the Green Beret motto 'De Oppresso Liber', so it's a fair bet the bomber is another Green Beret like the guy who blew himself up in Norfolk. That's our best angle; that narrows down the field of suspects considerably."

"Wayne, are you going to find this guy, the bridge bomber?"

"Yes sir, we'll find him."

"Well I sure hope so. We need some good news; we need to make visible progress. Find that guy and bring him in fast, all right?"

"We're doing our best sir."

"Okay. Anybody have anything else?" asked the President, looking up and down the conference table.

The white-haired Deputy Attorney General cleared his throat and spoke. "Uh, sir, a few minutes ago you were asking Director Sheridan if he had any...fresh ideas for dealing with this rather...unconventional situation that we have been thrust into. Actually I recently read something very interesting, something promising. It's come up from within the ATF, actually. I've seen a proposal, a position paper by one of the ATF Assistant Directors...well you might find it interesting reading. Actually I found it quite thought-provoking, and possibly worth considering."

"Well thank you Paul, I'm sure I will. Fresh ideas are what we seem to be lacking at this juncture. So far everything we try seems to blow up in our faces like a trick cigar! Give the proposal to Harvey."

Harvey Crandall, the President's old friend and current Chief Staff Officer, accepted the slim report which Paul Wilson slid to him across the polished mahogany conference table.

Homeland Security Czar Art Mountjoy finished rereading his copy of the bridge bomber's "D.O.L. letter" sitting at the conference table, while the others were collecting their effects and getting ready to leave the Situation Room. It made no sense at all to him. It had to be some kind of trick, some kind of sneaky underhanded psychological warfare trick by the right wing militias, designed to throw the government into confusion.

To my fellow Americans:

I regret the inconvenience that my action is causing to drivers around Washington, but today I am a very angry man, angry that a bogus false flag terror campaign is being conducted by unknown elements within our own government, a false flag campaign being blamed on innocent men for evil purposes.

I am angry that Mark Denton, his son and five others were murdered in Norfolk in a covert operation, designed to falsely portray him as a terrorist who "accidentally" blew himself up on the way to plant a bomb. Mark Denton was a brave soldier who won two Purple Hearts and a Silver Star as a Special Forces officer in Southeast Asia. He was a true patriot who sacrificed greatly and served his country well in wartime, and now his honorable wartime service is being twisted into "proof" that he had become a terrorist bomber.

This outrages me beyond words, which is the simple answer why there is a gap in the Wilson Bridge today.

If you cannot take my word that Mark Denton was a loyal and upright American every day of his life, then take my word on this: if he had wanted to, he could have demolished the Wilson Bridge or any other target of his choice as competently as I did, also without injuring anyone. He did not "accidentally" blow himself up.

My fellow Americans: all that I can ask is that you search out the facts which most of the media seem reluctant to give you, from the very questionable stadium massacre to the more recent events across southeastern Virginia. Don't be led like sheep, stand up on your own hind legs and look around at the facts for yourself!

To the FBI: I realize that most of you gentlemen are honorable and loyal Americans, doing your duty trying to defend America from terrorists, while also upholding your oath to "defend the Constitution of the United States from all enemies, foreign and domestic." Please study all of the evidence carefully: James Shifflett was a patsy, Mark Denton and the others in southeastern Virginia were murdered. The events at the stadium and in Virginia are certainly connected, but not in the way they are intended to be seen. Follow the evidence wherever it leads, even if it leads to "domestic enemies" concealed within our own government, who are running a destabilization campaign for their own evil purposes.

If this letter is widely printed and read on television and radio, you will not be hearing from me again.

D.O.L.

18

Guajira was dragging anchor and being swept by breaking waves onto a boulder-strewn coast. Brad was all the way forward on his belly in the chain locker, trying to untangle an armload of fouled ¾ inch diameter anchor line. He was attempting to prepare a second anchor in order to save the boat, but the spare anchor line was knotted and twisted into a solid mass with dock lines and sail halyards mixed into its coils and loops. He opened his folding rigger's knife to cut and remove the other lines braided into this all-important backup anchor line, but when he pulled the blade against a dock line it was as dull as a butter knife, and when he sawed against the line even harder in desperation, the blade broke free from the handle. He was digging into the rat's nest of fouled lines for the blade when Guajira's keel and hull first slammed against the unseen rocks. He heard and felt the splintering fiberglass as the cold ocean rushed in.

Brad awakened suddenly in his forward V-berth, prepared to leap to his feet to save his boat, but then he oriented himself, and checked the glowing green dial of his diver's watch. It was 4:15 Wednesday morning. The shipwreck dreams were not unexpected. Moving Guajira down the river to Portsmouth meant that she had taken on entirely new motions, which could spark his sleeping fears. Being tied alongside of a rusty barge on the Western Branch of the Elizabeth River meant that Guajira was exposed to the industrial-strength wakes of passing tugboats as they hurried between jobs. Without the inertia of a mast to dampen her rolling, her hull snapped hard from side to side with each passing tug, and then gradually returned to the stillness which he had grown accustomed to up the narrow and almost untraveled Nansemond.

Mile by mile Guajira was moving closer to the open ocean, and his stormy shipwreck dreams were born of the increasingly lively salt water the yacht floated in. It couldn't be helped, it simply had to be understood and endured. In a month Brad knew he would be sleeping soundly down below, while Guajira bashed along at nine knots, under autopilot control in typical ten foot mid-ocean waves. The mind and body could adapt to almost anything; it just took time.

He slipped on a gray sweatshirt against the chill and went topside to check his fenders. Lying against an old barge and being subjected to strong wakes he had to frequently check that his yard-long white rubber bumpers had not worked themselves up out of position. Without his four sausage-shaped fenders in place Guajira would be hurled violently against the steel barge with the next strong wake, gouging and scraping her gleaming white fiberglass hull, and Brad had not allocated any time for hull repairs in his getaway schedule. The passing tugboat which had awakened him with its nightmare-producing wake was already gone from sight.

On the land side of Guajira the only nearby lights were affixed over the boatyard's business office. Workboats and fishing trawlers and a few pleasure craft stood propped up on the ground, awaiting the next day's scraping and welding and painting. Alongside Guajira on the barge her new mast gleamed like a white lance, resting atop a half dozen sawhorses. Two more days of measuring and cutting the last of her ten wire stays, of running the internal electrical wiring and mounting lights and hardware and masthead instruments, and her mast would be ready to put up.

Brad had bought Guajira with a frozen engine, an overly Spartan racing interior, and a broken mast with questionable, undersized rod rigging. It was the only way he had been able to afford a fast 44 footer with such a thoroughbred pedigree. Now after months of hard work she had a brand new 80 horsepower Perkins turbo-diesel engine, a cozy interior, and with luck on Friday he'd step her new mast. This sixty foot spar would carry Guajira's sails, and send her flying across the oceans. Once the mast was up, its extra mass and inertia would also help to steady her from rolling so violently, when the tugs sent their wakes slamming against her hull.

In the boatyard, it was easy to forget the FBI and BATF agents who had visited him at his old dock up the Nansemond, but Brad still worried and he reflexively looked around for signs of surveillance. Crosby's Boatyard was a dump, a third-rate yard at best, but it was cheap and it was secure. Beyond its few acres lay waste ground, scrap yards and derelict warehouses. The only landward access was through a single chain link vehicle gate, which was locked after business hours. Due to the proximity of several railroad tracks, the street route leading to the yard was extremely confusing, with several long maze-like detours to navigate in order to get over the crossings.

Neatly attired FBI agents would stand out like strobe lights if they managed to find their way into this gritty world of welders and marine mechanics and painters. Since moving Guajira to the yard on Monday, Brad had detected no sign of the feds. He had let the battery on their cell phone run down and he had deliberately not recharged it. If he was pressed about it, he hoped to tap dance around the issue by pleading ignorance of the state of the battery.

Dawn's first tentative glimmers began to reveal the low Portsmouth skyline across the Elizabeth, as the river's blinking red and green buoy lights faded and disappeared. Today he'd finish mounting all of the stainless steel hardware bits on the mast and boom, and put the last end-terminals onto his wire stays. He'd work late, under lights and into the evening if necessary, to get ahead of his schedule. Thursday he would take the morning off to go to Joe Bardiwell's funeral in Suffolk. On a certain level he genuinely wanted to pay his respects to the gunsmith, who had been shot dead simply because he wouldn't take the hint, and leave the firearms-selling business quietly.

Really though, most of all, he just wanted to see Ranya again. He knew he had no possible future with her, because in a week's time he'd be sailing out of U.S. waters, probably for years. Still, he wanted to see her, and find out how she was getting along since her father's murder. She had been an only child, now she was an orphan, and Brad didn't want to leave her by herself to bury her father. He knew a great deal about being alone, even if it had been mostly by his own choice, and he could well imagine her utter desolation.

Dale Gunnison completed twenty years with the Bureau, and had taken his retirement from government service just months before 9-11 to open his own private investigative agency in Philadelphia. After the terrorist attacks he had been offered a job at Headquarters in Washington to come back in, and he had been glad to do his patriotic duty and return to service under a certain set of new understandings. He had been roundly assured that the era of political correctness within the FBI was finally over, and that they would take off the PC gloves and aggressively battle the Islamic terrorists and their supporters hiding throughout America.

Unfortunately, he had been disappointed once again to discover that this had only been hot air and wishful thinking. The Bureau continued to tip-toe around the Muslim issue, denying the obvious reality which they all knew. Once again he was disillusioned with the Bureau, and he was thinking of putting in his papers to retire a second time, permanently.

Gunnison was ascending in an executive elevator within the Hoover Building after taking his mid-morning cigarette break outside, when the doors opened and two colleagues he knew by sight joined him. They nodded to him, and then continued their hushed conversation. He stood apart from them, but could still hear some of their talk.

It was widely considered that the bridge bomber or bombers had come from within the Army Special Forces community. The bomber's letter focused on the allegedly accidental car-bombing death of the ex-Green Beret officer Mark Denton. Also, the bomber signed his letter "D.O.L." which in the Special Forces context meant De Oppresso Liber, or To Liberate from Oppression.

Dale Gunnison knew this before almost anyone else in the bureau did. In fact it leaped at him off the page, because Gunnison had been an Army Special Forces officer himself in the 1970's, before getting out to pursue a career in the FBI. The Army had paid for his college education with an ROTC scholarship at Villanova, and Gunnison had both enjoyed and benefited from his five years in the military. But since childhood he had set his mind on becoming a Special Agent, having grown up watching the television heroics depicted on "The FBI" starring Efrem Zimbalist, Jr. When his obligated service was up, he left the Army for a career in federal law enforcement. He found that the reality of the FBI had rarely approached the idealized fictional version.

Dale Gunnison overheard words and phrases spoken quietly between the two men sharing his elevator, enough to catch the essence of their conversation. The bridge bomber's mailbox had been located, and a pickup truck had been filmed by a nearby security camera just before 3 AM. The pickup was later tracked from camera to camera as its route was reconstructed across Washington. The plate was traced, and the tag number had produced a hit: the truck belonged to a retired Green Beret named Ben Mitchell.

Gunnison exited the elevator on the seventh floor, went straight to his office and closed the door behind him. Sergeant Major Ben Mitchell was the bridge bomber! Jesus! Ben Mitchell had been a legendary combat veteran and all around stud at Fort Bragg when Gunnison had been just another young Special Forces lieutenant in the early 1970's. Mitchell would almost certainly not remember First Lieutenant Dale Gunnison, one of the dozens of neophytes he had impacted during his long SF career, but Dale Gunnison sure remembered him!

Mitchell had been an unforgettable presence, the black Sergeant First Class with the chiseled face and the body builder's physique, exuding the kind of magnetism born of supreme self confidence. SFC Mitchell taught parts of the demolition phase at the Special Forces Training Group when Gunnison was a trainee. He had hung on every word and look and movement from the decorated veteran, one of the rare breed of men who had led the "Studies and Observation Group" recon teams deep into Laos and Cambodia. In the 1970's the very existence of cross-border outfits like the SOG was still classified top secret, and Gunnison had felt extremely privileged to learn guerrilla warfare techniques from masters of the art like Ben Mitchell.

Dale Gunnison only stayed in the Army for five years and got out as a Captain, but he had maintained his membership in the Special Forces Association through the years, and had seen Sergeant Major Ben Mitchell's name come up from time to time. Gunnison recalled their brief professional contact with great pride.

So Ben Mitchell was the bridge bomber! Damn! On one level he could understand Mitchell's anger over the death of Mark Denton. Dale Gunnison also considered that "accidental detonation" to be highly suspicious. So the Sergeant Major had dropped a span of the Wilson

Bridge as an expression of his displeasure! From a purely professional standpoint, Gunnison had to admire the operation. I-95 and the DC Beltway had been severed with one demo charge, paralyzing Washington traffic, and all without injuring a single person. And Mitchell was what, in his late fifties by now?

Gunnison paced back and forth in his tiny office. His SF days had been among the best in his life, and he often wished that he had stayed in the Army and "lifered out," instead of leaving to join the FBI. In the 1970's, there was no war on the horizon, only an endless series of Mobile Training Team missions to third world backwaters, and the FBI had appeared more attractive to him at the time. He had soon learned that he had left the honor and clarity of the Special Forces, for the venal office politics of a Bureau which was far more concerned with grooming its media image, than with catching mobsters or spies, or as it had finally turned out on 9-11, than with catching Islamic terrorists.

He knew perfectly well what would happen next, now that a case was being built against Mitchell. An arrest warrant was being filled out and signed by a judge, and an FBI "Enhanced SWAT Team" was studying the plans of Mitchell's house and doing dry runs on mockups. An advance team was already reconnoitering his neighborhood, his phones were being monitored, and his computer was being remotely examined.

Soon, very soon, possibly tonight, Sergeant Major Ben Mitchell would be awakened by stun grenades, and at the very best he would be cuffed and manacled and dragged out onto the street in his skivvies.

If he went for a gun—and he would—he'd be trapped in the beams of a half dozen incredibly bright gun lights and riddled with submachine gun bullets.

And if he managed to get himself into a barricaded position, flaming tear gas canisters would be shot through his windows until his house caught on fire, and he was roasted alive inside. These were the only three possibilities left open to Ben Mitchell.

Dale Gunnison sat down at his desk and stared at a wall and meditated on the twin virtues of honor and loyalty. The warriors of Mitchell's era had fought and died to defend Montagnard villages which had later been abandoned, to be slaughtered by the communists when the Americans were pulled out. The Green Berets had gone into Laos and Cambodia on their government's orders, but they all too often had to depend only on each other to get themselves out, because officially they were never there at all. When things went wrong they fought to their last bullets, but they never, ever left a wounded comrade behind.

After leaving the military he had spent his career in the FBI, where the "elite commandos" of this group, the Hostage Rescue Team, were most famous for roasting civilians alive at Waco, and sniping a mother holding a baby at Ruby Ridge.

There was no comparison between the two worlds, the world of the Special Forces and the world of the FBI.

He would not let Ben Mitchell be burned alive.

Wednesday Ranya went apartment hunting, dressed innocuously as a student in her jeans and a peach-colored top, with her hair brushed back and held primly in place behind a matching plastic band. She hoped to pick up George's trail near the downtown Norfolk federal building, but she didn't want to live too close to it, so she ruled out the student-infested areas near Old Dominion University. There were tremendous off-season bargains to be found along the Atlantic in Virginia Beach, but that was a long drive from downtown Norfolk, and there was too great a chance of being seen by someone she knew from her summer lifeguard job.

So she headed out in her loaded van for Ocean View, a short stretch of coast running east to west along the bottom of the Chesapeake Bay. Ocean View was the northern-most part of Norfolk, sandwiched between the giant Norfolk Naval Base to the west, and the Little Creek Naval Amphibious Base to the east. She cruised around a few blocks from the beach, looking for vacancy signs. In a once-genteel working class neighborhood now in decline, she found the Alcazar Apartments at the dead end of a shady street. Older single-family homes and duplexes lined the street leading to the Alcazar, which was a gray and pink stucco two story structure built in the shape of a "U," with the open end facing up the street.

The manager's office was at the end of one of the two legs of the building; a small sign out front on the wall announced that a one bedroom apartment was for rent. Ranya rang the doorbell, and in a minute she was greeted cautiously by the apparent landlady, a heavily accented middle-aged woman of indeterminate Central Asian origins.

"Yes, what do you want?"

"I'd like to see your one bedroom apartment, is it still available?"

"It is, yes, but it is very small, you live by yourself? Are you student or dancer? I don't want no dancers, dancers give trouble. I don't want that here."

East Ocean View had far more than its share of strip tease clubs, well supported by the thousands of sailors on the nearby bases.

"No I'm not a 'dancer.' I'm a student at Old Dominion. Can I please see the apartment?"

The short woman looked hard at Ranya, evaluating her. Not finding any needle marks, missing teeth, tattoos or evidence of silicone breast implants, she relented. "Okay, come with me."

The apartment was on the ground floor in the back of the courtyard formed by the "U." Its front door was under the open stairway leading to the second floor balcony, to the right of the door was a narrow passageway leading through the ground floor to an alley behind the Alcazar. The place showed promise. The landlady opened it up, it was a bit musty but Ranya had seen worse during her years as a student. The furniture seemed functionally adequate. The tiny front room was a combined kitchen, dining room and living room with one window looking out to the courtyard garden, which would permit her to see anyone coming. The small bedroom at the back had a window which opened to the alley; it could be a rapid escape hatch if necessary.

"It's fine, I'll take it. How much?"

The landlady seemed a bit surprised. "Six hundred a month, includes electric."

"I want it the rest of the year."

"I give only for six month or year."

"I'll pay cash, all in advance."

"Okay, come to the office."

There was an ironwork gate at the back of the passageway by the alley. Ranya asked, "Is that locked?"

"I lock every night six PM. I give you key, all right?"

"That will be fine." In fact, it was almost perfect. She could park her van out front and her Yamaha in the alley. She could exit or enter either way, so no one could easily keep track of her coming and going. Her front door was obscured in shadow by the stairwell above it, and she had a back window for an emergency exit. With the electricity included, she wouldn't need to register with the electric company. Paying cash, she didn't have to provide references or submit to any kind of background check. Her van would be registered to her family address in Suffolk at the end of the month, but for the time being she'd use the old tags. There would be virtually no record at all of her at this East Ocean View address.

She'd done it, she thought, she'd become a ghost. And after her father's funeral tomorrow, she'd start hunting.

Ben Mitchell was clicking through the cable news channels in his den in the early afternoon, when his back porch doorbell rang. It was his neighbor Mrs. Mendoza, so he opened the door.

"Hello Mr. Mitchell?" (He loved how she said Meester Meechel.) "I'm sorry for to bother you, but a delivery man give me a package, and I think it's a mistake. Inside is just another little package for you. And a little time before, a man he called me by the telephone, he said he was an old friend of the Army, and the present was a surprise for you. Anyway I don't understand these things, but here is your present, all is okay?"

Mitchell was very surprised, but he made an effort not to show it. "Well, muchas gracias Guadalupe, thanks. I have some real crazy Army amigos. Muy loco amigos. Sometimes I don't understand them either."

Ben went back into his kitchen and carefully slit open the securely wrapped and taped package, which was the size of a compact disc box. On the outside it just said "For Ben Mitchell" in magic marker block letters. Folded inside was a note on a plain piece of printer paper, also in block letters like a first grader had written it.

SERGEANT MAJOR, YOU HAVE BEEN MADE.
EXPECT VISITORS SOON. GET OUT. GOOD LUCK.
"D.O.L."

He trembled, reading the short message over and over. Damn, damn, damn he thought. He'd been totally 100% careful. He'd left no fingerprints, no fibers, no nothing. The typewriter was an old piece of junk, and now it was gone without a trace, smashed to bits and scattered. What could it have been? He'd told no one.

Certainly he had realized they would focus on the old SF'ers who had served with Mark Denton. Even though Denton had never officially been rostered on one of his recon teams, no doubt his name had been in some of the old after-action reports covering the missions he had tagged along on. And there were bound to be old photos, in Denton's house and elsewhere…

Well at least it looked like he had a friend in the FBI, someone who knew that his house was already under surveillance. Someone clever enough to send the warning message through his neighbor, in order to avoid detection.

Shit. Oh well Ben, you knew you wouldn't live forever anyway. Six months, or a year at the outside, and he would have to make the decision to have his balls cut off, or get ready to die. At least, that's what the doctors all said, and he'd never had any intention of letting them castrate him. Prostate or no prostate, his gonads were going to stay right where they had always been. Ben Mitchell was going to live, die and be buried as a complete man.

He'd felt the same way about blowing up the bridge. Live or die, some considerations just went beyond how many more years one could bargain out of God to keep breathing the air on His sweet blessed planet. So what was the point of running now, of going on the escape and evasion?

He needed too much medicine, which he couldn't possibly get on the run, so what was the point? He was too old, too tired, and soon he was going to be too sick to run.

He walked into his living room and peeked out a front window. Sure enough, a cable television truck had a cherry picker going up a utility pole diagonally across the street, installing some new gadget. Cable truck my ass, he thought. "Smile, you're on candid camera," is more like it.

What to do, what to do? Just don't let me burn, sweet Lord Jesus, that's all I ask, just don't let me be burned alive. He knew all too well what happened when the FBI's "Hostage Roasting Team" went the pyro-technic tear gas route: a house burned to ashes was the preordained result, along with anybody trapped in it.

Ben Mitchell had seen, heard and smelled men who had been burned alive, and even 35 years later they were something he had never forgotten. They were some of the worst of the many indelible scars he had on his memory.

There was no worse way to go. Death didn't frighten Ben Mitchell, but burning alive did.

Okay, he thought, if they call me on the phone, or send somebody to walk up to my front door and knock politely with a warrant, maybe I'll just go with them. Then I'll get a chance in court to explain exactly why I blew up the bridge. And that could last for years, maybe for all the years I've got left.

But what if they attack? If they attack, I'll fight. So let's think about this. Let's sit down and start making a plan…

What the hell Ben, you always knew you weren't going to live forever.

19

Wednesday afternoon Virginia Attorney General Eric Sanderson was in his natural element, chairing a high-profile conference convened to organize a new multi-jurisdictional law enforcement program. President Gilmore had just signed Presidential Decision Directive #87, and in one paragraph of his directive he had "requested" assistance from the Governors of Maryland and Virginia. They were "requested" to immediately implement a program of highway checkpoints, in order to prevent terrorists from transporting illegal firearms and explosives through their states. These two states, flanking the seat of federal power in Washington DC, would provide the test programs which would then be analyzed and modified and put into effect nationally, if the evolving security situation warranted such measures.

The Governor of Virginia had passed the ball to his hot-shot Attorney General for him to actually devise the plan and put it into action. Eric Sanderson was the obvious choice. Before becoming Attorney General he had been an FBI Special Agent, a congressional staffer, an assistant district attorney, and a federal prosecutor. The inner workings of a complicated joint task force were as familiar to him as springs and cogs to a clock maker.

The checkpoint program was being touted as a temporary measure, a response to the outbreak of right wing militia violence which had begun with the Stadium Massacre. Semi-automatic assault rifles (banned on Tuesday) and telescopically-sighted sniper rifles (banned in the Presidential Decision Directive) would no longer have free run of the highways. Once the message was received by the gun crazies that the government was serious about controlling the movement of firearms, it was hoped that the problem would become manageable.

In the immediate aftermath of Senator Randolph's assassination, the President was under enormous pressure by the members of both houses of Congress to take any steps necessary to lessen their chances of becoming the next target. These politicians understood the utter impossibility of assigning to each of them the twenty or more highly-trained bodyguards, working in three shifts, which would be required to afford them security out to beyond the range from which Senator Randolph had been killed.

Senators, Congressmen and other senior federal officials were literally running scared, dashing from vehicles to buildings obscured by clouds of black umbrellas held aloft around them by staffers. Their personal bodyguard details, with their close range pistols and submachine guns, suddenly seemed as useless as life jackets in the desert.

The tragicomic sight of famous politicians ducking and weaving and running for cover was being shown on television, and it was making a mockery of their prestige and authority. Some politicians instead went the television hero route, boldly walking in the open (just as long as television cameras were on hand to record their bravery). In truth, the almost casual assassination of Senator Randolph had them all petrified down to their marrow, particularly those who had in the past been vocal advocates of restrictive gun control measures.

So a comprehensive system of mobile highway checkpoints had been suggested as a viable means of increasing their physical security around Washington DC at least, and there was not a Senator or Congressman in either party who raised the issue of the Fourth Amendment, and the right of the people to be secure from arbitrary search.

Eric Sanderson had immediately grasped that the successful implementation of a bold new anti-terrorism program, with the broad national exposure it would bring, would be a major feather in his political cap when he ran for Governor in two years. He had to rein in his excitement at the prospect of all of the favorable media coverage he would garner, and force himself not to constantly smile.

The meeting was held in the main conference room in the Virginia Attorney General's office, overlooking Richmond's Capitol Square across 10th Street from the Federal Court. Also present were the Commanding General of the Virginia Army National Guard, the Commandant of the Virginia State Police, the Assistant Director of the ATF Office of Firearms, Explosives and Arson, the ATF's Resident Agent In Charge from the Richmond Field Office, and various other Virginia chiefs of police in full dress uniforms.

The conference dragged on most of Wednesday afternoon, and after a period of haggling between the ATF and the State Police, it was decided that each mobile highway checkpoint team would consist of two ATF agents, four Virginia State Troopers, six to eight National Guardsmen, and a number of local police to be determined on a case-by-case basis depending on the jurisdiction.

The checkpoint teams would be under the operational control of the ATF agents, they would communicate on State Police radio frequencies, and the State Troopers would be permitted to depart the checkpoints temporarily to respond to local emergencies, but they would not leave less than two troopers on scene.

The use of camouflage-uniformed National Guard soldiers driving Humvees in domestic anti-terrorism roles no longer created a public perception problem in the aftermath of 9-11, the Beltway Sniper case, and the Stadium Massacre. In fact, citizens had come to expect to see M-16-carrying camouflaged soldiers in and around airports, train stations, and government buildings. It provided them with a feeling of reassurance to see that the government was taking every step possible to ensure their safety. The National Guard soldiers would provide overall control and perimeter security around the lines of detained cars, permitting the law enforcement officers to focus on searching the vehicles. No one was likely to bolt from the holding area to try to make a run for it with machine gun mounted Humvees at each end of the control zone.

The actual searching of vehicles for illegal concealed firearms still raised some residual constitutional issues. Sanderson and the state law enforcement officials in the end agreed with the ATF to simply go the "consent search" route. Any drivers deemed suspicious by the law enforcement officers present would be asked to permit a voluntary "consent search" of their vehicles. Recent Supreme Court decisions had upheld the admissibility of evidence found after suspects had given their "voluntary consent" to squads of heavily-armed police to search their cars. It was not required of the police that they inform the suspects that they had the right to refuse to give "consent." It was not the job of the police to give roadside lessons in constitutional law.

Any suspicious cars (suspicious in the opinion of the police, based on their training and experience) which refused to give "consent" to be searched would be directed to a holding area. In the present high-threat environment, refusal to give "voluntary consent" would be construed as "probable cause" for the police to request a search warrant. One of the state police on the scene would be swiftly dispatched with a pre-formatted warrant, which would immediately be signed by a judge waiting nearby and returned to the checkpoint.

In effect, any and all vehicles stopped at the checkpoints could be searched at the discretion of the police, one way or the other. This apparent "Catch 22" search strategy had been used with great success for years in the war on drugs, and thus far it had always passed constitutional muster. After 9-11, police were given even greater latitude in conducting vehicle searches.

The 2002 Beltway Sniper attacks in Maryland and Virginia had further pushed back the constitutional envelope, as hundreds of white men had been unceremoniously dragged from white vans by police at ad hoc checkpoints. This occurred after law enforcement officials leading the investigation issued erroneous instructions based on a wildly incorrect psychological sniper profile, as well as incorrect witness testimony concerning white vans. The actual killers were two Black Muslims firing from the trunk of an old brown Chevy, who had passed unhindered through many of the temporary highway checkpoints set up to catch the imagined sniper, the legendary but nonexistent "white man in a white van."

No one at the conference dwelled on the basic constitutionality of conducting mass searches on the public streets and highways of Virginia. These officials were so accustomed to getting their way on vehicle search policies that they assumed that there would be no serious challenge to their authority to pull over dozens or hundreds of motorists, any where at any time, and search their vehicles.

The subject of the use of police K-9 units in the searching of the vehicles was also brought up and discussed. There was some debate between the ATF and the state police representatives about the effectiveness of "gun-sniffing dogs" in an environment where a dozen police officers and soldiers were themselves already carrying firearms and ammunition. The eventual consensus was that dogs would still be quite effective at sniffing for hidden firearms under seats and in open trunks, saving the police time and effort on each search.

As an added benefit, the K-9 advocates half-jokingly mentioned that the mere presence of snarling German shepherds usually caused otherwise smart-mouthed "curbside lawyers" to just shut up and go along with the program. It was their contention that the presence of gun-sniffing dogs in the search area would cause most drivers concealing contraband to admit to any weapons hidden in their cars. It was decided that the state and local police would contribute their K-9 units to the greatest extent possible, and that the feasibility of borrowing additional K-9 teams from the Customs Department and other federal agencies would also be explored.

The overall checkpoint process was compared to the routine vehicle and body searches now being given to airline passengers and their vehicles in and around airports. By and large the public had stopped griping and grown accustomed to these searches, and there was no reason to believe that they would not do the same with random highway checkpoints. After all, it was for the greater safety and security of the entire population.

The final policy decision reached was to immediately field ten mobile checkpoint teams, five each in Northern Virginia and in Tidewater. They would be working in two twelve hour shifts initially, and then go to three shifts as the manpower stream was brought on line. The required number of National Guardsmen would be called up for periods of 90 days, the state police would be shifted around as needed, and the BATF would bring in additional agents from out of state. The BATF Special Agents who would actually be conducting most of the searches would wear their tactical uniforms, helmets and external body armor to enhance their personal security. The National Guard soldiers would also be deployed in helmets and body armor. The composition and deployment patterns of the checkpoint teams would be modified as experience was gained and lessons were learned.

The meeting wrapped up for the senior officials after two hours. They had other important places to be, so they let their aides and staffers remain to hammer out the details and put it down in black and white for the Governor's signature. Eric Sanderson allowed a brief "media availability" outside the conference room, and returned to his office.

Once he was back at his desk overlooking Richmond's Capitol Square, the Attorney General tilted back in his leather executive's chair and gloated for a few minutes. By moving so quickly, he would get his checkpoints into operation days before Maryland did, and capture the lion's share of the national press coverage!

He then pondered the two most critical aspects of the program. First, how to present "his" checkpoint program to the media in the most effective way, to put himself in the best possible light, and second, the creation of a snappy and easily remembered name for the new mobile units. Coming up with the right acronym was of primary importance to the success of any new law enforcement program. A powerful nickname like "DARE" or "SWAT" or "CAGE" could almost ensure a program's success, regardless of its actual merits. The key was coming up with a clever acronymic slogan which looked and sounded terrific on promotional t-shirts, ball caps, coffee mugs, and of course on billboards and on the local television news. A successful new high-visibility anti-terrorism program with a memorable name could very well launch him into the Governor's mansion in two years, and from there to the U.S. Senate, and from there....

Sanderson spent the next half hour at his desk doodling on a yellow legal pad, juggling likely words and letters like a dyslexic Scrabble player.

The quiet Reston Virginia neighborhood had finally gone to sleep, as indicated by the last remaining lights of the late night television viewers blinking off one by one. Inside a bogus electrical contractor's van, men sat staring at grainy green-tinted night vision video monitors, with headphones on their ears and microphones on slender stalks in front of their lips. Down the tree-lined street rolled an unlit windowless club-sized van. It slowed almost to a stop, and from its far side and open back doors shadows spilled out and flowed across a yard and up to the front door of a middle class house.

On both sides of the paved walkway and the small landing in front of the door there were chest-high hedges; the shadows sank below them and disappeared. Eight men in black, wearing black uniforms, helmets, body armor, soft-soled boots, gloves, balaclava masks, ski goggles and

MP-5 submachine guns were crouched in perfect silence, stacked tightly in two files on either side of the door, ready to charge into the house.

The split-level wood-framed house had presented a bit of a problem. The lower elevation backyard was fenced in chain link, and the high back porch was a rickety-looking wooden affair, and totally exposed. One adjoining neighbor had a pair of alert Labrador Retrievers in the back yard, and maintaining the element of surprise on an approach from that direction was doubtful. Under each ground floor window there was a thick hedge which would impede entry, so the front door was the choice by default.

Into the front hall and living room, turn left, 25 feet straight ahead, master bedroom. Flash-bangs through the bedroom window first for a diversion, and in seconds it's over, one way or the other, with a deafened and stunned man in his bed pinned down under a half-dozen blinding gun lights. That was the plan, rehearsed until it was second nature.

The leader beside the front door whispered, and his voice was picked up by the microphone built into the elastic band he wore around his head beneath his helmet. Beside him the door breacher swiftly applied his small charges. No mere battering ram would do in this outfit; this was not some local Podunk PD SWAT team busting a crack house. This was an FBI Enhanced SWAT team, making a violent felony arrest on a federal warrant.

"Romeo, Fox One ready," went the whispered call.

"Romeo, Fox Two ready," came back from one of the wraiths under the bedroom window.

"Fox One, this is Charlie. All quiet, no movement inside," said a man in the electrical contractor's van, watching his screens and listening to his headphones.

"Okay Fox One, this is Romeo. Show time Fox Two, give us a countdown." This was the go-ahead from the on-scene supervisor.

"Copy Romeo. We are going in five, four, three, two…"

From his small window perch up on top of a heavy table in his attached garage workshop, Ben Mitchell had a clear view of the front of his house between slightly opened curtains. As expected, they had come, and as hoped they had been channeled into his front walkway. He had set a timer to turn off the television and lamp in his den at 11:35 PM, and another to turn off his bathroom light at 11:45. When they had approached he was already in his guard position, sitting on a chair placed atop his cleared-off workbench, where he could see out of the small garage window across the front of his house and out to the street.

Ben was wearing an old BDU uniform he'd dyed black in his washing machine. Underneath he wore civilian clothes, a gray suit for Washington camouflage. Over his uniform he wore an old military kevlar vest covered in pouches and pockets, and an old Kevlar helmet on his head. He had spray painted all of this black, to closely match what he guessed an FBI assault team would be wearing. He wore clear parachuting goggles to protect his eyes and obscure his face, and green Nomex aviator's gloves on his hands.

The pouches and pockets attached to the vest were packed with escape tools and getaway gear. In the end he just couldn't bring himself to formulate a plan which didn't include a provision for his escape, no matter how short or long term it might prove to be. One of the pouches on his chest had been modified into a holster, and in it he carried his government model Colt .45 pistol. If he could escape, he would.

Beginning at eleven PM the same dark Crown Victoria drove slowly up and then back down his street at even 15 minute intervals. Ben wondered why the supervisors didn't just go with the video imagery that they were undoubtedly getting from all angles. Perhaps the older supervisors just couldn't bring themselves to trust the technology, and had to personally lay their eyeballs on the house to reassure themselves. He wished he had a radio scanner, he could only imagine the web of radio traffic swirling around his house.

At 2:30 a dark van with all of its lights out rolled up and slowed in front of Mrs. Mendoza's house, almost beyond his sight. A half-dozen or more dark figures poured out of it and scurried low across her yard and into his. They moved to his front door where they sank down to hide out of sight below his bushes. Two of the men continued across his yard to a position below his bedroom window, no more than twenty feet from Ben's garage lookout post. They were just visible in the glow from the streetlight on the distant corner of the block.

That old intense rush came back over him, flowing through him stronger than any drug, that never forgotten thrill of waiting motionless in ambush, to be rewarded by the appearance of the unsuspecting enemy in the kill zone...

They wouldn't wait now. Their snipers and rear security team would already be in position, ready. Ben knew what was coming next, and he was ready too.

He held in each hand a small green electricity generating "clacker" the size of a computer mouse. Each trailed a long thin wire tail. They had originally come packaged with claymore mines, the mines were long gone but the clackers remained.

Ben had chosen to use the old military hand generators as much out of nostalgia as for any other reason. Some of the most intense memories of his life had revolved around those spring-hinged claymore clackers, sending squads of NVA soldiers to their doom in a steel hailstorm. If tonight was going to be his last combat action, he wanted to feel something comforting and familiar in his hands. He had tested them on small light bulbs and they had worked perfectly, and this had saved him the trouble of putting together a battery-powered switch.

The FBI SWAT team members crouched on each side of the low front porch and looked away, ready for their small breaching charges to blow the door inward. A pair of SWAT team members waiting outside the master bedroom was going to initiate the assault by "breaking and raking" his window with a long handled sledge hammer, and then immediately tossing in two def-tek flash-bang grenades with two second delay fuses. The front door breaching charges would be fired the instant that they heard the window shatter, and they would be on top of their man in less than five seconds. They knew just how long it would take, because they had already run through the maneuver a dozen times today in full assault gear on their base at Quantico. They trained and trained, but arresting a violent felon never became routine, and now their adrenaline was surging as it always did.

Each crouching man held his MP-5 with its sound suppressor and barrel-mounted gun light in front of him, their stocks tucked into their shoulders. Their gloved right index fingers all rested just outside their trigger guards, their right thumbs rested lightly on the safety selector switches above their pistol grips.

A thirty round magazine fully loaded with ten millimeter bullets was in the well of each of their MP-5s, a second magazine was snapped alongside it for a faster first reload, and more magazines were ready in the pouches on their tactical vests. In each left ear a tiny radio speaker kept them synchronized to the plan as Romeo Two counted down from five to one. In a matter of seconds the entry team could fire hundreds of devastating ten millimeter slugs into any person presenting a threat to them, but they fully expected that a pair of flash-bang grenades and eight retina-searing gun lights would make shooting their quarry unnecessary.

Ben Mitchell stood peering out between the curtains of the garage window, his hands holding the twin claymore mine clackers firmly, waiting for the assault team to move first, waiting for them to initiate the violence. He saw one of the men below his bedroom window stand tall, leaning over his hedges with a sledge hammer held back over his head as his partner stood up behind him.

The long hammer came down through his window, exploding it, and then was raked in a swift circle clearing the screen and the glass shards away as the second man tossed in two small cylinders, flash-bang grenades. At the moment the glass shattered there was a flash of light and a boom from his front porch, and then more booms from his bedroom and the stacked assault team rose up and went flooding through the front door.

Ben paused a moment to let them all get inside, then he squeezed both spring-hinged clackers hard and electrical charges shot down the thin green wires to the blasting caps at the other ends.

The electric blasting caps were embedded into golfball-sized chunks of white C-4 military high explosive, saved from the Wilson Bridge demolition charges. Mitchell had plenty of blasting caps. They were smaller than cigarettes, made of aluminum with a pair of thin red and white wires trailing from one end. And it had been no particular problem to cook up crude high explosives, not with his garage workshop full of solvents and other chemicals that he routinely used in his business, along with a few items from his medicine cabinet, his bathroom and from under his kitchen sink. The technical problem was in reliably initiating a clean high-order detonation of his kitchen explosives using only blasting caps, which was why he had saved a little C-4 for just this type of contingency. The caps would detonate the C-4, and the C-4 would detonate his kitchen demo mines, no problem.

The FBI Enhanced SWAT team poured into his foyer, lighting up his living room with the amazingly bright Sure-Flash flashlights mounted under their gun barrels as the boom of the flash-bang grenades reverberated from his bedroom down the hall. Fifteen feet away from them, against the opposite foyer wall, was a kitchen chair with a towel draped over it. Hidden under the towel was a square plastic Tupperware casserole dish the size of a large text book, which was duct-taped on its edge to the back of the chair. The casserole dish, with its lid snapped tightly on, had a small green wire leading into a tiny hole in its back. Just in front of the casserole dish on the seat of the chair was standing a cardboard box full of a common household cleaning item, and in front of that box was a one gallon plastic milk jug that was not filled with milk.

The entire SWAT entry team was within fifteen feet of the towel-draped kitchen chair when the electrical impulses reached their blasting caps and Ben's living room exploded outward in a massive fireball. That end of the house was an immediate splintered inferno; it went from zero to Armageddon in one second, and nobody came out.

Behind Ben's house, just beyond his backyard fence, his other improvised mine had detonated in the gulley where he had guessed that the assault team's rear security element would be lying in wait. As soon as he squeezed his two hand generators Ben dropped them and jumped off his table and crossed his workshop to another table. Here a row of high capacity military smoke grenades the size of spray paint cans were waiting, with their pins pre-straightened and partially pulled out. The small window on the back side of his garage was already open; he pulled the pins and threw out four smokes in rapid succession. Ben drew his cocked and locked .45 while he paused to let the smoke bloom, and then he pushed his side garage door open and dove through it, rolling sideways into his yard lest the snipers find him. The flames from the other end of his house were already hot on his back. He scrambled to his feet and ran through the billowing clouds of fire-lit purple and yellow smoke, reached his waist high chain link fence and vaulted over it, and then rolled down into the drainage gully running behind his property.

FBI SWAT team member Weston Thatcher was lying prone at the top of the ravine, peering over the berm watching the back of the suspect's house and listening to the assault team's countdown in his earphone. The door-breaching charges detonated exactly as he expected, then there was a massive explosion just off to his right side. The concussion of the blast rendered him senseless momentarily, but much of its force was absorbed by the other three rear-security team members to his right. Two of them had been kneeling or hunching upright for a better view instead of lying flat, and so they had been blown over Thatcher, who also was hurled some distance. He of course remembered none of this, but when he could see again through one eye he saw a helmeted figure in black moving through radiant yellow smoke just past where he lay. The man paused and looked directly at him, holding a pistol in his hand.

Thatcher tried to say, "Who are you," through his smashed teeth and bloody lips but no sound came out, anyway he could not have heard a reply with both of his ear drums ruptured. Anyone fleeing the house in this direction would be a Bad Guy, and it was Thatcher's sole mission tonight to stop anyone from fleeing. The man crawling past him was dressed like a team member, but not quite. The man was dressed in black, with a black helmet, but this man wore no black face mask. This man was black; this man's face was black, black, black. The suspect was black, and nobody on his team was black. Black. Black face, black. Thatcher slipped in and out of sensibility as bands of pain tightened their grip around him. Anyone coming in this direction was a Bad Guy. Anyone coming in this direction had to be stopped, and even in Thatcher's semi-delirious state his mission tasking rose to the front of his mind. Anybody who was black was the Bad Guy tonight. The Bad Guy.

Ben Mitchell looked briefly at the broken bodies of the SWAT troopers, covering them with his pistol. One was still alive, moaning, his face was a bloody wreck, his left arm was bent impossibly, a compound fracture. He scrambled past them and got to his feet and began to run up the slope toward the protection of the bushes and woods and the fence line which led away to safety.

Special Agent Thatcher, lying on his back, felt for his MP-5 but he could not reach it, and that's when he discovered that his left arm didn't work at all. His MP-5 was trapped under him still connected by its sling, so he reverted to training without thinking and drew the .45 caliber pistol from the black tactical holster which was still strapped to his right leg. He raised it one-handed across his stomach, flicked the safety down and then depressed the gun light's pressure switch with his thumb.

The light mounted to the rail under the pistol's slide threw a harsh yellow cone out into the swirling smoke and its brilliant center found the running man's back, wavered and fell and found him again. He couldn't hold up the heavy pistol any longer as the beam wavered from side to side across the man's back. Thatcher squeezed the trigger twice, and then he passed out.

20

The President couldn't sleep and had refused the offered pill. He was wearing his blue robe with the gold Presidential seal, pacing back and forth in a study off of his bedroom, rereading the proposal written by a mid-level BATF official named Walter Malvone, with his half-glasses low on his nose. His on-duty Secret Service liaison entered through the partially open door to the corridor and spoke to him in hushed tones, handing him a telephone. It was more bad news: the Director of the FBI was on the phone from the Hoover building, where he was pulling another all-nighter.

"Mr. President, we've got a situation underway in Reston Virginia. Actually it's a total disaster, I'm sorry, it's…" Director Sheridan was choking with emotion.

"Give it to me straight, Wayne."

"We have an FBI SWAT team out there in Reston; they were serving a warrant on the prime suspect in the Wilson Bridge sabotage. They were ambushed… They were blown up and burned, the house is burning… It's a total mess, and it'll be on TV any minute. It's going to be bad sir, real bad."

"Jesus… How many casualties?"

"We don't know yet, most of the team I think. It looks like nobody got out of the house… The on-scene commander is working it; I'm watching some of our own video. We've got some bad burns and a lot of missing at this point. I'm hearing eight missing and three dead, and it doesn't look good for the missing. They were in the house…"

"Okay Wayne, thanks. Keep me informed." Lost deep in thought, President Gilmore handed the phone back to the Secret Service agent. Gilmore was still holding the heavily underlined, highlighted and margin-noted Malvone paper. He gestured to the liaison; he was as always fully alert, pulling his normally quiet midnight duty. "Get me my CSO. I need Harvey Crandall here as soon as possible."

"Yes sir, right away sir." The Secret Service agent backed up, spun on his heel, and left the study.

The phone call Wally Malvone had long been anticipating came at 4:30 AM on Thursday morning, eleven days after the events at the stadium. He was tersely instructed to be at a certain entrance to the Old Executive Office Building, on the other side of the White House from the Treasury Building, promptly at 8 AM.

Malvone's driver dropped him off on 17th Street. He passed through numerous security points where his various ID cards and badges were closely examined, and his briefcase was inspected. Upon entering the building he was scanned with a metal detecting wand, and handed a receipt in exchange for his SIG 220 pistol. He was given an escort of both a uniformed Secret Service officer, and someone in a suit with a laminated badge clipped to his jacket pocket, who did not bother to identify himself. They led him deep into the building to an executive elevator, and finally down a hall past another security checkpoint where his briefcase and cell phone and PDA were taken, and he was once again scanned closely with a wand and patted down thoroughly.

His minders directed him to a small windowless conference room where he was left alone and told to wait. They closed the door behind him without any other instructions. He sat at the unadorned narrow mahogany table, enjoying himself immensely, while endeavoring to maintain a poker face in the event that he was under observation. The walls were bare white. The unusually thick door through which he had entered was also painted white on the inside, and now that it was closed it blended with the walls so as to be scarcely noticeable. Sitting absolutely still he could hear nothing, not the faintest rumble or vibration from the building, not even the sound of an air duct. He was obviously in some sort of a quiet room, well protected from eavesdropping devices or methods.

At 8:15 Harvey Crandall entered through another almost indiscernible door on the other side of the room and sat across the table from Malvone. The CSO was older than Malvone, probably mid-sixties, with a thin fringe of white hair. He was overweight, with a fat white face which evidently rarely or never saw the sun. More than anything, Crandall reminded Malvone of an older Pillsbury Dough Boy, and it was easy to see why he avoided the Sunday morning talking-head circuit. He reached across the table and offered a flaccid handshake, but his piercing ice-blue eyes locked onto Malvone's with an electric intensity.

"This room is as secure as possible Mr. Malvone, as secure as possible. If we are ever asked, we have never met, and no one will ever be able to say different, am I clear?"

"Perfectly." Malvone suppressed a sardonic grin with difficulty. He had often wondered just how this contact would be handled, if and when the call finally came. He had considered the possibility of park benches and dark restaurants, but had ruled them out as improbably melo-dramatic at the National Command Authority level.

"Mr. Malvone, the President has already seen your proposal, the red notations are his. We'll go through them now, and I'll keep this copy. All other existing copies will be collected and accounted for and destroyed. Is there any reason that this might present a problem?"

"None, there's no problem." The copies were numbered, and there were only five in existence. Malvone had written the proposal himself on an ancient IBM Selectric typewriter, and made the copies himself on a Xerox machine. There was no computer involved at any point to conceal an unseen copy on its hard drive, for possible later recovery.

"Mr. Malvone, the President wishes me to convey to you his extreme reluctance at…setting this plan of yours into motion. But desperate times call for desperate measures, and the President feels that we have no other recourse than to move forward with your…concept of operations. He accepts the necessity of going ahead with your ideas, as you have outlined them here in points one through seven, but he does not give permission for your steps number eight or nine at this time."

"I see."

"Is that a problem?"

"No. We can proceed, we can operate effectively just working up to number seven…as you've seen they're in graduated steps."

"Yes. It's very well thought out. Rather disturbing, but quite well thought out. The President is authorizing you to go forward with a pilot program, a test program in Virginia, which seems to be where most of these problems are originating. You will take your team to southeastern Virginia for a period of one month. After that we will evaluate the results, and then the President will decide whether to terminate the test program, continue it at its present level, or expand it. You may operate at your discretion in Virginia, within the limits of your outline up to stage number seven. You may also operate, when necessary, in Maryland and North Carolina, but not in the District. If later on you feel that these boundaries are too restrictive, you may contact me personally by secure means. Are we on the same page so far?"

"Exactly the same page. I really don't see a need for us to operate outside of Virginia at this time, unless it's a case of hot pursuit, or we're acting on extremely perishable intelligence."

"That's just how we understand your operational constraints as well. Good. For the time being we think you should try out your concept of operations with the present group already under your command, the 'Special Training Unit.' After a month, if everything is going well, we'll discuss augmenting your unit with more agents from the ATF and the FBI and other agencies as you have proposed in section three paragraph four. But we will exclude any recruiting from within the Secret Service, the President insisted on that personally. Any personnel augmentation will be based on the performance of the S.T.U. during the first month, is that understood?" Crandall spelled out the initials, he was not an insider, and did not pronounce it "the stew" the way Malvone and the operators did.

"Of course. We can work with what we already have personnel-wise during the demonstration period, and then we'll go from there."

"Right. Now, I've already obtained the services of a contract specialist, an expert at finding, shall we say, creative solutions to the financial and logistical challenges you will be facing. 'Mr. Emerson' will be your point of contact; he is quite experienced in these matters. Arranging discreet sources of operational funding will not be a major problem. He'll be in touch with you today."

"Thank you sir."

"Now this was not covered in your proposal of course, but the President and I agree that you should be promoted commensurate with your…unique responsibilities. Mr. Malvone, understand, we have simply not been receiving any worthwhile solutions from the conventional sources, nothing at all really, so your proposal has reached the President at an extremely critical time…

"We have 'think tanks' from here to Christmas, and none of them have put anything on the President's desk remotely as promising as your proposal. I'm sure you understand that since your overt position and title as Deputy Assistant Director of your division will not be changing for the time being, we can't officially have you promoted at this time, but be assured that your promotion to SES-1 for seniority and back pay will begin as of today. Congratulations Mr. Malvone, and welcome to the Senior Executive Service. Your promotion will have to remain unannounced for now I'm afraid, but I'm sure that you understand why." Crandall reached across the table and offered Malvone another limp-fish handshake, but his smile seemed genuine.

"Yes, perfectly sir." Malvone did understand perfectly. Today's promised promotion to the federal inner sanctum, the Senior Executive Service, was meant to be his motivating carrot, and of course it had cost the President nothing. He'd put on SES-1 officially, permanently, if and only if the Special Training Unit obtained the desired results, without creating any disasters like the FBI's fiasco in Reston. The STU was to be a ghost BATF division, its actual operations were to be strictly unofficial, off the books, written of nowhere and absolutely unacknowledged. If a STU operation blew up into a flap on the front pages of the Washington Post or the New York Times, the President and the CSO would deny ever hearing of him or the STU, and as far as that promised promotion to the SES…

"Does that cover everything, Mr. Malvone? Can you think of anything else we need to discuss?"

"Yes sir: air assets. To be fully effective, we need both fixed wing aircraft and helicopters. The STU has one single-engine aircraft available to it, but we'll need the flexibility of controlling our own helicopters, full time, with crews answering to us 24/7."

The CSO waved his hand as if shooing away a fly. "That can all be arranged. Mr. Emerson will take care of it to your satisfaction I'm sure.

Really, you don't need to be overly concerned about budgetary constraints. Anything else?"

"Access to current intelligence. We'll need to be plugged directly into Trilogy, NCIS, TIA, EPIC...all of the federal data bases. We'll need to see the raw product of the Joint Task Force in Virginia in real time, and we'll need the drag from your end to make them give us what we need. It's been my experience that the kind of cooperation we'll need is often promised, but it's not given willingly, and I'll need that level of cooperation for the STU to operate up to its potential."

"Mr. Malvone, if you meet any resistance in accessing the data bases or intell products you need, contact me on one of the secure phones that Mr. Emerson will provide you, and I will have it taken care of personally. We have high expectations for your group, but you also have the right to obtain the tools that you require to do your job effectively. Of course, this cooperation must be obtained with more than a bit of...subtlety. I'm sure you understand."

Again, Malvone did understand. The STU was going to be operating in a hazy gray area, completely outside of the normal bureaucratic organizational flow chart. Getting the intelligence product was going to be an interesting challenge, and in the end the push would have to come from the White House. How the President's men handled this without leaving a paper or electronic back trail would be up to them. More than likely, the key decision makers in control of the intelligence flow would be given their orders one at a time in secure rooms like this one. No memoranda, no emails, no witnesses, and every spoken instruction totally deniable.

"Is there anything else we need to discuss now?" asked the CSO.

"No sir, not that I can think of at this time."

"Fine then. I don't expect that we will be meeting again, Mr. Malvone. From now on you will deal with Mr. Emerson, or in extremis you may contact me on the secure phone."

"I understand sir."

"Yes, well, I'm sure we both understand. Mr. Emerson will be contacting you shortly." Harvey Crandall rose, weakly shook Malvone's hand one more time, thanked him for his time, and left through the door on his side of the table.

After lingering a few moments to savor the ultra-secure "quiet room," Malvone departed through his own door. He knew that if he was ever asked, Crandall would deny ever having met him in his life, and there would not be one independent witness who could ever prove otherwise. Neither man's official calendar would reflect this brief meeting in any way. It was simply the way this kind of dirty business was conducted.

21

Virginia Attorney General Eric Sanderson was in his favorite place, standing in front of a bank of television cameras. There was nothing he loved better than being in the public eye, and today he was taking personal credit for pushing through a brand new anti-terrorism program. While his aides gave him a countdown to air time, news producers were shoving five dress-uniformed chiefs of police around behind him like movie extras, framing the television shot for the best effect. These medal-wearing law enforcement officials went along passively with being grabbed and pushed like stage props: they were also aspiring politicians, and they cheerfully suffered the indignity of the moment in fair trade for the free television face time.

It had not been a simple matter for Sanderson to pull together a television-ready demonstration checkpoint team in 48 hours, but he had done it. He had the gift, he was going places and all of the important people knew it. Doors opened themselves magically in front of him as they had all of his life, from Harvard Law up until today, because success was Eric Sanderson's birthright.

Now it was 11:59 AM on Friday, and a dozen television cameras were bore-sighted on his powdered face and perfectly arranged hair. Behind him and the police chiefs, spreading across the west-bound lanes of I-64 in Norfolk, Virginia State Troopers were directing cars at a walking speed through channels of orange traffic cones. "Randomly selected" vehicles were being directed onto the shoulder of the highway to park and await inspection. Desert camouflage painted Humvees at each end of the control zone provided the military "bookends" commanding the scene and framing the camera shot.

A careful television viewer might have noticed fully automatic M-16A2 assault rifles slung on the shoulders of the half dozen camouflage-wearing National Guardsmen posted evenly along the hundred-yard length of the control zone. Unseen were the dozen Norfolk Police SWAT Team members concealed around the area with their own 7.62mm sniper rifles pointing outward, protecting the publicly-gathered VIPs from the fate of Senator Randolph. Unseen were the three police helicopters orbiting high above with their zoom video cameras scanning the surrounding neighborhoods. Unseen were the Glock and SIG pistols beneath the suit jackets of the undercover Virginia State Police bodyguard detail, standing just off camera on both sides of the Attorney General, looking stern and almost Secret Service-like with their sunglasses and earpieces and coded lapel buttons.

Standing behind a simple podium jammed with a cluster of microphones, Sanderson began his prepared text at exactly 12:03 PM, precisely timed to give TV producers and mid-day news anchors a chance to begin their shows and then cut to him as the "live and local" breaking news story. Besides all of the local network news affiliates, several of the national cable news channels were also present, preparing to send words and images of his highway checkpoint program from coast to coast. Already his staff had been approached by producers from several network news magazine shows. One weekly show was already referring to him in a promotional piece as the "national gun safety crusader."

Down the front of his podium there was a printed sign:

1-855-GUN-STOP

F irearms
I nspections
S top
T errorism

"Good Afternoon. On behalf of the Governor of the Common-wealth of Virginia, and at the direction of President Gilmore, I'm here in Norfolk today to announce the launching of a new anti-terrorism program. On the highway behind me you are seeing the very first of Virginia's 'Firearms Inspections Stop Terrorism' mobile units, working to ensure the safety and security of all Virginians." Sanderson paused to give the cameras a chance to pan across the checkpoint area.

"Beginning with the Stadium Massacre twelve days ago, we have all witnessed an unprecedented outbreak of domestic terrorism, much of it, tragically, originating here in Tidewater Virginia. Fortunately, the true home-grown militia origins of the Stadium Massacre were discovered, otherwise we might have placed the blame for that atrocity on our Muslim countrymen, as the conspirators had obviously intended. The Stadium Massacre, as horrible as it was, would have been even worse if it had been falsely blamed on an innocent and too often maligned segment of our diverse multicultural society.

"The Stadium Massacre was caused by the easy availability of assault rifles in America. Since the passage of the Schuleman-Montaine Firearms Safety Act that flood of weapons has been stopped, but realistically we know that there are militantly reactionary segments of our society who do not intend to comply with our new firearms safety laws. The sniper rifle murder of Senator Geraldine Randolph on Tuesday, the day the new law went into effect, is an indication of the lengths that a small but extremely dangerous number of gun fanatics will go to in order to sabotage effective gun safety legislation.

"We have also seen a local wave of firearms-related violence, such as gun store arson attacks, and the drive-by machine gun shooting of a mosque in nearby Portsmouth Virginia. The very location of this checkpoint where I am speaking today is itself less than one mile from where militia leader Mark Denton's car bomb exploded, before he had a chance to plant his terror bomb in the Norfolk federal building. As we know, Denton was also transporting a virtual arsenal of assault rifles and high powered cop-killer bullets when his bomb exploded prematurely on the highway, taking the lives of five innocents.

"So today I am announcing that the highways of Virginia will no longer provide a safe avenue for terrorists to transport their illegal firearms and explosives." Sanderson pounded his own fist on the podium for effect. "Starting today, mobile FIST units will be in operation around the Commonwealth of Virginia, and they will soon be adopted by other states as well, beginning in Maryland next week. These FIST units will provide much-needed security to all of us, by preventing terrorists from getting a free ride on our freeways!

"Now I am asking all of the decent law-abiding citizens of Virginia to assist our law enforcement officers by cooperating fully when you come upon a mobile FIST unit. Courtesy will be returned to our cooperative citizens, and only a few moments of your time will be required if you are asked to pull over for a brief inspection. I'm confident that the good people of Virginia will consider showing this cooperation to be an opportunity for them to play their own part in our 'war on terrorism.'

"Additionally, I wish to assure those of you in our immigrant community that FIST units are not intended to harass or intimidate you in any way. The Commonwealth of Virginia respects and welcomes all of our hardworking immigrant population, regardless of their technical documentation status. FIST units will only be looking for illegal firearms, and not for immigration papers.

"In conclusion, I would like to remind my fellow Virginians that all semi-automatic rifles are now illegal, and should have been turned in for destruction already. Also, I would like to remind the hunters of Virginia, and I am proud to say that I am one of that group, that tomorrow, Saturday at midnight, the transportation of sniper rifles will also be forbidden. This is following the President's last decision directive, which he made under the provisions of the Patriot Act of 2001, based on an 'imminent terrorist threat.' A sniper rifle is now defined as any rifle with a mounted telescopic sight. After midnight tomorrow, it will be a felony punishable by five years in federal prison to transport a scoped sniper rifle on the highways of the United States.

"Since the Stadium Massacre and the assassination of Senator Randolph, both crimes committed using scoped sniper rifles, we find ourselves in dangerous new territory, unfamiliar to law-abiding Americans. As I said, I am a hunter myself, and I am aware that many Virginia sportsmen will perhaps feel that they are being unfairly burdened by this law. But since this war of snipers and terrorists has been brought to us by a handful of gun fanatics, all of us must now unfortunately share in the burden of increasing security, for the benefit of all of our society. So you hunters, don't forget to take off those scopes by tomorrow night! There's still plenty of time to get to the range and practice with those old iron sights before deer season starts next month. I'll be at the range doing just that myself, and I don't think it's too much to ask, as our small contribution in the war on domestic terrorism.

"Now I'll take a few of your questions."

An older male reporter called out, "Attorney General Sanderson, how many FIST teams will there be and where will they be located?"

"I think for rather obvious reasons I can't discuss all of the operational details of the program, but there will be plenty of FIST units, you may be certain of that. Enough to do the job." Sanderson pointed to a middle-aged African American reporter next.

"Will the FIST units use racial or ethnic profiling in determining who they are going to pull over and search?"

"No, the FIST unit commanders will select cars completely at random, in accordance with constitutionally tested precedents." Sanderson did not even crack a smile as he uttered both of these blatant lies.

A reporter in the middle of the gallery called out, "Are you going to run for Governor?" and Sanderson replied, "I plan to serve the people of Virginia to the best of my ability." When the same reporter called out again, "Is that a yes?" Sanderson ignored his question and pointed to a perky young blonde reporterette who had been waving her hand frantically.

"Mr. Sanderson, isn't 'FIST' a rather... harsh name?"

This question drew chuckles and guffaws from the other reporters, and from the police chiefs still dutifully standing shoulder to shoulder behind the Attorney General. But Eric Sanderson didn't laugh, instead he pounded his own fist down hard on the podium, and the sound boomed through the microphones.

"Is the FIST program harsh? You're damn right it's harsh! We intend to be very harsh with domestic terrorists and militias and illegal gun runners! Very harsh!" He brought his tightly-balled fist up in front of his chin for effect and held it there, suddenly aware in that instant that it would be on the front pages of tomorrow's papers across Virginia, and that he had just created the six second sound bite which would sweep him into the Governor's mansion, and then into the U.S. Senate. His harsh visage slowly melted into an avuncular smile, and finally he brought his hand back down and gripped the sides of the podium.

"Now before I go, I'd like to remind everyone about the toll free, totally confidential illegal firearms tip line, 1-855-GUN-STOP."

Sanderson pointed to the number displayed across the front of the podium just beneath the cluster of microphones. "You can serve your state and your country by calling this number if you have knowledge of anyone in possession of semi-automatic rifles of any kind. Calls which result in arrests for possession of semi-automatic assault rifles will be rewarded with up to $5,000 for each illegal rifle which is recovered, so you can serve your country and yourself at the same time, if you know anyone who is holding onto an illegal rifle.

"And wives, if your husband is still holding onto an assault rifle, ask yourself: is it worth it to your family to have him sent to prison for five years? For the good of your whole family, get rid of those illegal semi-automatic rifles! You can't be sure who knows about them; they're probably already listed, and it's only a matter of time until they're found. So for your family's sake, get rid of those illegal assault rifles now!

Ranya Bardiwell had hardly been out of her one-bedroom hideout in East Ocean View since returning from her father's brief funeral and burial the day before. Phil Carson, Brad Fallon and a handful of former friends and customers (often one and the same) had made the effort to show up for the services, but Ranya had been brittle and distant and had not planned for any kind of wake after her father's casket had been lowered into the ground. Brad Fallon and Phil Carson had both offered to take her out to lunch, but she had declined and returned alone to her seedy apartment to brood.

Friday morning she walked to breakfast at a Waffle House on East Ocean View Avenue. On the way back she bought a portable radio and CD player in a People's Drugstore, so that she could follow the news, and listen to some music in her room to relax. She tried reading a paperback novel that she had started over the summer, but gave it up and went for a three mile run down to the Little Creek Inlet and back. After showering and changing she just flopped on the bed and stared at the ceiling, and in time she slept, but her dreams repelled her from that refuge. Brad Fallon had mentioned where his boat was now, and she considered riding over to Portsmouth to check it out. He had said that his mast was going up on Saturday, and so he would be busy getting it ready today, and could probably use some help. But she didn't go.

At lunchtime she was fooling around with her portable ten-inch color TV, seeing what kind of reception it would get inside the apartment with its whip antenna. She had no interest in daytime network television, but felt that she should keep up with the domestic terrorism news, since her father had been a casualty, and because she had her own scores to settle. She was sliding the television along the chipped red formica-topped kitchen counter and playing with the antenna, when the 12 o'clock local news came on. The sound was muted while an attractive Asian anchor woman was chatting soundlessly with her dutifully nodding sandy-haired male co-anchor, when suddenly Ranya was looking directly at the face of Eric Sanderson! The last time that she had seen that face, and the blow-dried hair and gleaming teeth, she had been looking through the scope of her Tennyson Champion target pistol!

The news caption on the screen underneath him said "ATTORNEY GENERAL BEGINS GUN CHECKPOINTS." Ranya jabbed the volume button and his firm and fatherly voice spilled out into her kitchenette. On the front of his podium a sign read "1-855-GUN-STOP" and "Firearms Inspections Stop Terrorism" arranged vertically to spell FIST. Behind him police and soldiers were directing slow-moving traffic along the side of a highway. Sanderson was talking about the Stadium Massacre, about the assassination of Senator Randolph, and about gun inspection road blocks—FIST checkpoints—and how they would increase public safety. Then he said "We have also seen a local wave of firearms related violence, such as gun store arson attacks, and the drive-by machine gun shooting of a mosque..."

The meaning of these words suddenly hit her, and she screamed at Sanderson's face on the television. "What!? 'Firearms related violence, such as gun store arson attacks'? Your goon squad killed my father and it's just 'firearms related violence'? My father and the others were shot and burned, and they're not worth mentioning? 'Firearms related violence', like the firearms did it, like the gun stores just burned themselves down? Like it was their own fault?"

And according to Sanderson, the answer to this 'firearms violence' was going to be the creation of 'FIST' checkpoints on the highways? As if now that the Second Amendment had been ripped out of the Bill of Rights, it was also safe for the government to rip out the Fourth Amendment as well?

The FIST checkpoint was evidently on I-64 right here in Norfolk, near where the old Green Beret and his son and some others had been blown up, (which was another highly dubious 'accident' to Ranya's way of thinking). So Sanderson was in Norfolk right now, Sanderson who would not investigate her father's murder, Sanderson who had called her father a 'merchant of death' and all but applauded his murder by a government death squad... Sanderson who should have died last Sunday night, Sanderson who had already been in her crosshairs....

If he was currently in Tidewater, she might get another chance to finish what she had set out to do.

Now Sanderson was talking about scopes being outlawed. That was simply rich. As if anyone (like herself) contemplating sniping a public official would bother to obey that law! 'Gee, I was going to assassinate the state Attorney General, but now that telescopic sights are illegal, I'll have to cancel my plans.' Ha! What a joke, what imbeciles! They deserve to be shot, just for being that stupid!

Anyway, the law would not come into effect until Saturday at midnight... She thought of the hysterical irony of shooting him on the last day that scopes were legal. Perhaps she would send the Governor a note: 'I was going to kill the jerk next week, but I didn't want to violate the new scope law, so I killed him today.' That would actually be pretty funny!

Well she would do it: she just needed a time and a place. If she knew where Sanderson was going to be, and she could arrive nearby first, she could get him. When Sanderson was finished the Asian news anchor moved onto her next story: an Arlington National Cemetery memorial service was scheduled for the FBI agents slain in Reston.

She switched off the television and began to plan.

Ranya made the call to Sanderson's Richmond office from a pay phone in Virginia Beach, using a pre-paid calling card that she bought with cash from a third-rate convenience store. She rode her Yamaha that far from her apartment because she knew that the pay phone would eventually be traced, and she parked it at a distance from the phone so that no one could ever connect the caller to a motorcycle. She wore masculine sunglasses, and a black ball cap with her ponytail twisted and tucked completely underneath to obscure her identity. This was on the chance that she might be caught on a digital face-scanning camera. She wasn't positive, but she suspected that the government was able to tap into just about all of the cameras scattered across the modern urban landscape: in ATMs, in stores, traffic cameras, all of them. So she went to great lengths to reduce her risk of video identification at some later time.

"Attorney General Sanderson's office, how may I help you?"

"Hi, I'm Liz Courtney, I'm the managing producer for Channel 14 Action News in Norfolk; may I speak to Attorney General Sanderson's media representative?"

"Oh, um, that would be Samantha Jeffers, I'm sorry but she's in Norfolk with the Attorney General today. May I take a message?"

"Oh, Darn! I'm out of the studio right now, I'm on another story, perhaps you can help me. I'm afraid I left the Attorney General's itinerary back at the studio, can you be a dear and go over his appearances the rest of this afternoon? I'm really pinched for time, we're running between stories and we really do want to squeeze in an interview for the five o'clock news...if it s not too much trouble?"

"Well, um, certainly, let me see...at one he's visiting the federal building, he's speaking to the FBI and the Joint Task Force, but that's a closed meeting, there's no media availability. At 2:30 he's speaking at

Norfolk State in Mandela Hall, that should be a great event, his gun safety initiatives are really very popular in the minority community, as you know. At four he's going to be attending the re-dedication of the Al-Fuqra Mosque in Portsmouth. The rest of his schedule is private I'm afraid."

"Is he staying in Norfolk tonight, then? Perhaps we could schedule an interview for tomorrow morning?"

"I don't think so; the Attorney General is playing golf in the morning with friends, and then he's returning to Richmond."

"Which golf course would that be? Will there be a media availability, or at least a photo opportunity?"

"Um, I believe it would be... here it is: the Greenspring Country Club. But I don't see any media event listed."

"Well perhaps we can do the interview in Richmond next week. I'll call Samantha Monday morning and set it up. And thank you so much, you've been a dear."

"Glad to be of help. Did you say you were from Channel 14 in Norfolk?"

"That's right, Channel 14 Action News."

"Okay, thanks."

"Bye now."

"Bye."

Click.

Ranya hoped that the conversation hadn't been automatically recorded; she had found and called an interior office number, and not Sanderson's main switchboard. But if it was recorded, so be it, it was necessary: there was no opportunity that did not come without an element of risk. Anyway, they'd have to catch her for the tape to do them any good; her voice was not on any computer data base that she was aware of. And she didn't intend to be caught.

So Sanderson was a golfer...

This was a very nice hobby for him to have, to Ranya's way of thinking.

22

Friday after lunchtime Malvone called George Hammet directly on his cell phone, and found him in the ATF offices in the Norfolk federal building, where he was holding down the fort. Hammet's nominal boss, the Norfolk Field Office's totally ineffectual Special Agent In Charge Kayla Coleridge, was out with the Attorney General's traveling FIST checkpoint media circus. She was totally absorbed in sucking up to the rising-star Attorney General and to the ATF honchos who had come down from Washington and Richmond, and had little time to bother with her deputy, Assistant Special Agent In Charge George Hammet.

Malvone broke the news to him that the STU was going operational and heading down to Tidewater over the weekend. He invited Hammet up to his house in Maryland for a Friday night STU Team party, informing him that the time was finally right for him to join the STU. He would officially be taken aboard as the next team leader, when they expanded to three tactical teams in the near future. The party would be an opportunity for him to meet the rest of the team in an informal setting.

This was welcome news to George Hammet, the culmination of his clandestine working relationship with the ATF Deputy Assistant Director. It was no problem for Hammet to break away from the Field Office. Kayla Coleridge was out tagging along with Sanderson's entourage and was not even aware that he took off early. The normal Friday afternoon office routines were discarded as the "Eric Sanderson Show" took precedence over everything else, including supporting the Joint Terrorism Task Force and the MD-Rifle investigation.

So George Hammet was able to take credit for keeping his nose to the grindstone and staying back at the nearly-deserted ATF office. He finished some work and left at four PM. He had made the 200 mile drive up I-64 and I-95 to DC so many times that he could do it in his sleep, and he arrived at Malvone's place before seven.

Malvone had a narrow waterfront property overlooking a small bay just off of the Potomac, about ten miles south of DC. Hammet parked his red Jeep Cherokee on the grass under some trees out front with a dozen other SUVs, pickups, sports cars and motorcycles. Then he walked down-hill around the side of the house to the backyard as he'd been instructed, following the sound of loud rock music. Malvone's property had woods along both sides all the way to the river. The house was at least eighty years old, with dark wood-shingle siding, and dormer windows protruding from the sides of the roof.

Malvone met him coming around the back of the house, greeted him cheerfully and quickly put a cold Heineken in his hand. Most of the other STU men were milling around on the patio, gathered around a brick barbeque cooking steaks over mesquite wood. It was obvious to Hammet that they were quite a few drinks ahead. He sipped from his Heineken and shook hands with the other STU leaders, while Wally Malvone made the introductions.

"George, I'm glad you could make it on short notice. I thought you should meet the gang up here socially before we get to work. You already know Bob Bullard from Headquarters, right? Bob's the STU commander on paper, even though we all know I'm the one that runs the show."

Bullard was at least a decade older than the rest of the team, in his late forties, but he was obviously still an operator just the same. He was a hard-looking man with a hawk face and very little evidence of middle age-spread. He accepted Hammet's hand and gave it a firm shake, making direct eye contact. "Don't listen to him George; Wally's just our headquarters admin puke. He likes to pretend he's an operator, and as long as he keeps buying us new toys we let him hang out with us. Plus he throws pretty good parties, so we put up with him."

Malvone laughed good naturedly at the ribbing and continued with his introductions. "This old cripple here is Joe Silvari. We call him 'Half Ass.' He tried to sit on a flash-bang grenade once and blew off most of his right ass cheek…it's a long story. Now he's our number-one support puke, and he's the second-in-command of the STU Team. You need anything wired, Silvari's little band of geeks will take care of it for you. Night vision, phone taps, special weapons…anything the shooters are too dumb to figure out."

"For once you're telling the truth Wally." Silvari was one of the smaller men gathered around the barbeque, with stringy brown hair combed straight back and a face which resembled a rodent, with a weak chin and a protruding nose.

More burly young men began to filter in, coming around the house and down to Malvone's backyard overlooking the water. They were wearing an assortment of loose casual clothes, such as Hawaiian shirts, Latin-style guayabera's, and a few biker-style leather vests which hung over their belts to conceal their pistols. These days, federal agents didn't walk to the mailbox without at least carrying a serious pistol, and their submachine guns were also never very far from reach. Hammet noticed that there were a few Hispanic-looking guys, but no blacks.

Malvone said, "Friday nights I usually have just the team leaders over for poker, but since the whole STU is finally moving out and going operational I decided to throw a party for all of the troops. You'll get to know all of these assholes pretty soon. Before you know it, they'll be stealing your gear and hitting you up for loans like the rest of us. Almost everybody's here tonight except Michael Shanks. He's the Gold Team leader, and he's already down in Chesapeake with the advance party, they're setting up our new forward operating site. This pretty boy here is Tim Jaeger, we call him Hollywood because he's so cute. Tim's an ex-SEAL, and he's the Blue Team leader. He's also our official team chick magnet, so just hang around with Hollywood if you want a shot at sloppy seconds."

Jaeger ignored Malvone and said, "Welcome aboard, George." Then offering his right hand he went for a short grip around Hammet's fingers to try to innocently crush them, but Hammet was quick and sober and ready for the old trick. He shot his hand all the way in and they locked brutal grips like a pair of vises for a solid ten seconds. Both men were serious power lifters, and both liked the measure of the other, grinning at one another as they recognized kindred spirits. Given the chance, both enjoyed the game of crushing the average pencil-neck weenie Special Agent's hand, and tonight both respected the strength of the other man.

It was one of George Hammet's recurring fantasies that someday he would be able to play the handshake trick on his Norfolk SAC Kayla Coleridge. In her presence he often imagined pulverizing her tiny kitty-cat paw into little crunched up girly bone fragments within his powerful hand grip, leaving her on her knees screaming in pain, while he just smiled pleasantly. Of course, this could never happen. In the ATF the real hard-ass operators had to treat the little princesses with complete PC deference, or they would run shrieking and boo-hooing to Human Resources to file an EEOC complaint. Then a good agent would be written up and charged with sexual harassment or even assault, and his career would be ruined for no damn reason at all. Hammet had seen it over and over again.

Obviously, none of that PC bullshit applied here in the STU Team. Clearly the STU was composed of hard-cases only: pencil-necks, fairies and princesses need not apply! This was one of the reasons Hammet wanted to join the STU: to escape the ridiculous upside-down PC world in the rest of the ATF and federal law enforcement, where hundred-pound Miss Prissies pretended to be Special Agents. They were usually masters at office politics and sucked up most of the promotions, but they always hid way in the back on raids. Or they simply avoided the danger and hardship of raids altogether, with well-timed PMS sick days.

Just about the only occasion when George enjoyed having the lady agents around was on the outdoor firing ranges. That's when watching them getting knocked on their butts firing the 12-gauge shotguns was always good for a knee-slapping laugh riot by the male agents, and there was nothing the lady agents could do about it except turn beet-red and endure the humiliation of their exposed weakness.

The lady agents weren't much better when it came to firing the "MP-Five and Dimes," the ten-millimeter version of the MP-5 submachine gun commonly used in federal law enforcement. Most of the female agents Hammet had seen handling the MP-5/10 flinched so badly burst-firing the powerful rounds that they were unable to hit the paper at 25 yards, and had to accept the snickering behind their backs.

"So here's the deal George," Malvone said. "The entire STU is moving out tomorrow. We're setting up shop way down in Chesapeake on the old South River Naval Auxiliary Landing Field. It's almost down to North Carolina. You know the place?"

"I know where it is, but I've never been on it. Isn't it closed? I thought they shut it down a few years ago."

"It is, but it's going to be open for us. Anyway, we're setting up down there this weekend, and we're going to start operating right away. Then, next month, we're going to bring aboard another dozen or so operators, mostly from ATF, but some FBI and DEA too. When we get them all we're going to muster in another STU tactical team, the Red Team, and you're going to be the Red Team leader. For now you're going to be the assistant Blue Team leader and strap-hang with Tim here, just to learn our SOPs, and pick up how we operate. But this is going to have to be un-official for a while…on paper you'll still be the ASAC in Norfolk, until we get the Red Team pulled together. But you can come out and play with the STU at night." Malvone winked at Hammet, and the men exchanged casual "high fives" all around.

By now most of the STU Team members had gathered in Mal-vone's backyard around the beer and the barbeque, taking guarded stock of the new guy who Malvone was going to bring in, untested, as a new team leader. Tim Jaeger said, "Well George, there's one more tradition we need to take care of to formally welcome you into the STU."

George Hammet wasn't sure what was coming, probably a beer chugging ritual or some other frat-boy type prank he thought, for about one second. He thought wrong.

With no warning most of the fifteen or twenty STU Team members nearby lunged at him all at once, tackling and burying him under a dog pile of muscular bodies. Then he was hoisted roughly off the ground, face down, with three men pinning each leg under their arms, with others locking his elbows and wrists in painful jujitsu "come along" holds, and one more standing by his shoulder, with a powerfully biceped arm around his neck in a choke hold. Before he could react, much less put up resist-ance, he was hauled through the backyard between the trees and shrubs toward the bay.

Carried face down and head first, Hammet only saw the water coming when they got him to the end of the yard where it fell away in a steep bank. Most of his carriers had to peel away as they neared the edge to allow the others room to give him a proper heave-ho into the water, and

Hammet literally seized this opportunity to turn the tables. Just when he was being thrown over he managed to seize hold of Wally Malvone's belt, and his momentum and his grip sent them both over together. Instead of flying out into the water, the two men tumbled down the eroded dirt slope into the shallow water at the bottom.

The two soaking-wet slime-covered men rolled around, yelling and swearing, and then they stood up in the knee-deep water at the bottom. With great difficulty and much back-sliding they both climbed up the crumbling seven or eight foot high mini-cliff to Malvone's backyard, while the rest of the STU operators above them whistled and howled and poured beer down upon them.

Once they were back on top, they were both presented with fresh bottles of beer and back-slaps all around. Hammet and Malvone, dripping bay water and covered in black river mud, casually rejoined the party by the barbecue as if nothing at all unusual had just happened. The macho rite of passage had been successfully accomplished. The new guy had been baptized into the STU, and Malvone had been reconfirmed as their boss.

After that the music was cranked up even louder, and then the serious drinking began. Wives and girlfriends were specifically excluded from this STU Team pre-deployment party, and anyway a man would have been insane to bring a lady anywhere near this joyful mob of foul-mouthed knuckle-dragging drunken good-old-boys.

Two hundred miles south, Brad Fallon was also celebrating with a cold beer in his hand, a can of Miller Genuine Draft from his 12-volt refrigerator. In the dying light he was walking slowly beside his mast, which was lying horizontally across five wooden sawhorses on the flat-decked steel barge that Guajira was tied alongside. The gleaming white-painted sixty-foot long aluminum tube was finished from the tip of its VHF whip antenna on the masthead, to its hollow oval base.

The masthead, which was now within casual reach at Brad's waist level, sprouted a collection of antennas, a combination red green and white running light, wind speed and direction instruments, and other devices required for safe and efficient ocean sailing. Each item was machine-screwed to the mast, into holes Brad had drilled and tapped and threaded into the raw aluminum. After tomorrow morning, if Brad wanted to inspect his masthead or replace a part, he would need to sit in a bosun's chair and haul himself sixty feet above the water with a five-part block and tackle.

Two pairs of white-painted aluminum spreader bars stood five feet out from the mast like outstretched arms, one third and two thirds of the way along its sixty foot length. Ten stainless steel wires were ready to hold up the mast. Four were attached just below the masthead, and the others near the bases of the spreaders. Tonight the wires sagged loosely along the spar and between the spreader tips, but when the mast was raised they would be securely fastened to Guajira's decks at her sides, bow and stern until they were all bar-tight. The heavy stainless steel turnbuckles and end fittings of the ten wires were now tied together with yellow twine into a single bundle near the mast's base, ready for the mast to be raised in the morning.

There was nobody left in the small boatyard except the night watchman, who was watching television in the back of the business office. There was no one to share Brad's pride in completing the mast, the last and most complex of the tasks he had undertaken in getting Guajira ready for sea, more difficult even than the engine installation. He walked along beside it, running his hand down its glowing "Matterhorn White" poly-urethane paint finish.

The oval aluminum mast section had been extruded in a factory in Connecticut horizontally, had its fixtures cut and welded on while lying horizontally, and had been sanded and primed and painted and trucked to Virginia horizontally. Tonight was the last night that it would spend hor-izontally. In the morning the mast would be lifted to vertical by a crane, and lowered through a hole in the cabin top and over the mast step on the keel. The ten wire stays would be pinned to the deck chain plates, the ten turnbuckles would be screwed down tight, and Guajira would become a sailboat again. With luck, the mast would remain vertical for many years to come.

In a few days he would leave the Chesapeake Bay and sail out onto the open Atlantic at last, a free man, free to set his own course and choose his next landfall.

Later, Malvone and Hammet were standing on the open balcony deck which ran the width of his house overlooking Tanaccaway Creek, which was in fact a small bay in its own right, a mile long and a half mile across. The creek jabbed eastward off the Potomac where the river made its last dog-leg turn before running straight north into Washington. Malvone's property descended downhill to the creek, so the first floor on the landward side was the second floor in the back. Maple and sycamore trees in his backyard partially screened his house from the water side. It was fully dark now and the backyard was lit by small floodlights mounted under the deck.

Both men were in clean, dry, government-issue navy blue sweat suits while their clothes were in the dryer. They stood by the wooden railing watching other STU Team members below them who were engaged in a raucous game of 'simunition' quick draw with their pistols. This game being played by intoxicated federal agents broke every gun-safety rule in existence, but the men lived with their guns, and their guns were virtually extensions of their bodies, whether drunk or sober. The STU men literally did not walk out of their front doors without carrying their loaded Colts and Kimbers and Glocks and SIGs. To do so would have been as unthinkable as walking outside bare-ass naked, if not more so.

They shot countless hundreds of rounds a week on ranges and in close-quarters-battle facilities at Quantico and elsewhere. They could fire right or left handed, they could fire hanging upside down from ropes, they could fire and reload and fire again with their eyes closed, so it was not entirely unexpected to see them playing quick draw with simunition after more than a few beers. When the operators got drunk they got rowdy, and they did what they wanted to do. To try to intervene with a Mickey Mouse gun safety lecture at this point would only have earned a team leader a quick trip to the water. Bullard, Silvari and Jaeger were wisely out of sight, inside the club room most likely, getting started on the scotch and the cigars and the cards.

"Look at 'em," said Malvone. "Complete freakin' animals. I love these guys."

"They're all shit-faced. You let them engage in horseplay with guns when they're drunk?"

"Are you gonna tell 'em to stop?" Malvone laughed, toasting his team with the tall glass in his hand.

A pair of STU men below them were standing twenty feet from the cement and brick barbeque, using beer bottles placed on top of its chimney as targets. Their hands were at their sides, their pistols holstered and covered by their loose shirt tails while other team members watched, offering rude comments and free advice. A third man called out, "Ready—set—BLOW!" One of the duelists drew and fired and knocked over a beer bottle with his paint-filled plastic simunition bullet. The bottle fell from the barbecue and shattered on the cement patio, while the others hooted and jeered at him.

One yelled, "Frank, man you really 'blow'!"

Frank quickly hand-loaded another simunition round into his SIG and without warning turned and fired it offhand at the kneecap of the man who had joshed him, causing him to grab his knee and hop around cursing in pain. They were really drunk, nearly out of control, and a simple mix-up between live ammunition and simunition could result in a serious or even fatal negligent shooting. Wally Malvone took a sip from his gin and tonic and said, "George, when they get like this, they're an unstoppable force of nature. You just stay out of their way."

"I see your point. But will they be ready to go in the morning? How many vehicles are you—are we moving to Chesapeake?" In this case, Chesapeake referred to the name of the almost completely rural county stretching from Norfolk south to North Carolina.

"We're taking everything we've got George. Everybody's driving something, even their own cars. The more vehicles we have down there, the better cover we'll have on our ops. And don't worry about them being ready; they'll all be ready to roll when we muster at eight. Most of 'em are ex-Marines, Rangers...they don't need to sleep. They think sleep is for pussies that can't hack operating. And right now they're just about out of their skulls with the thought of busting caps on real live terrorists! Just the thought of no more simunition training, no more cardboard terrorists and CQB houses...hell they'd run barefoot all the way to Norfolk for the chance to put live rounds into real terrorists! Kids train that long and that hard, by God they want to kill somebody! You can't blame 'em, you know how that is.

"Anyway, they won't be hanging around here too long tonight. They're young studs, and they've got better places to be on their last night up here than hanging around with us. They'll be drinking and screwing all night right up until muster time no matter what we tell them to do, but don't worry, they'll be standing tall at 0800. If they weren't that good, they wouldn't be in the STU."

"Wally, you said I'll be paired with Jaeger to pick up your team SOPs. How long until you see us actually forming the Red Team? And how are you going to man the new team? Not with all new guys I hope."

"You're all business, aren't you? What I'm planning is to take four operators each from Blue and Gold, plus three more new guys besides you to make twelve for the Red Team. Then more new guys will backfill into Blue and Gold to bring them back up to twelve each. That'll be next month if things go right, but first we have to operate with what we've got down in Tidewater.

"We should start getting the new guys after about a month down there. Once we've got the Red Team on line, I want to bring all three tactical teams up to sixteen shooters and four support guys each. My basic idea is that these twenty-man teams should be able to travel and operate independently. They'll go to the hotspots and stamp out the fires, all on their own, without having to be supported by the Field Offices. All covert, all deniable. Hell, we could have ten or fifteen new teams up and running this time next year, who knows?"

"How are they taking all this up at Headquarters, and at Justice?"

"Oh, we're still flying under the radar, for the most part. We're still just an inconsequential 'training unit' hardly anybody ever heard of.

But George, we're working directly for the National Command Authority now." Meaning the White House. "So Headquarters doesn't matter."

"Does he understand what we're going to be doing?"

"Who, the President? He knows some of it, I'm assuming, but he's using a cutout. It's not like he talked to me personally! He probably doesn't want to know, that's my guess. He just wants results, that's what his contact said."

"You know if it goes sour, they'll hang us out to dry in a microsecond."

Malvone laughed. "So what else is new? Hey, they might try, but I'm taking precautions, I've got some insurance... And they're desperate! They've tried everything else, and nothing's working. The Joint Task Force is going nowhere. So it's been left up to us resolve it."

"You know, it's kind of funny. We get to resolve it, after...you know. But the stadium thing seems to be holding up just the way you planned it. And everything else flowed out of that, just like you said it would. But Wally, does the rest of the team accept everything as...legit? On its face legit I mean, like it's covered on TV?"

"Oh hell yes, absolutely. 100% legit."

Senator Randolph's assassination and the Wilson Bridge sabotage were indeed 'legit.' Malvone knew that they had nothing to do with any STU operations, that they had occurred unexpectedly. These 'legit' attacks were quickly becoming the best possible camouflage for the stadium operation, and the other "pump priming" operations by Hammet and Bullard in southeastern Virginia. There were too many attacks coming now, one after the other, to afford law enforcement the manpower to minutely dig for the well-concealed truth about what had happened at the stadium. When a Senator is assassinated, even a Stadium Massacre can fade somewhat in importance, at least at the federal decision-making level.

Events were now unfolding spontaneously, the way he had predicted. There was no longer a need for false acts of terrorism to be blamed on the right wing militias; the gun nuts were now fully provoked and taking actions on their own. Senator Randolph and the Wilson Bridge were proof of his basic concept. He had done it: like switching on a nuclear power plant, Malvone had initiated a continuous chain reaction.

And the beauty of his concept, the sheer elegance of it, was that the more aggressively the STU and other federal law enforcement teams operated, the more new 'domestic terrorists' there would be to fight, and the more STU Teams they would need to bring on line to do the fighting! He had created a positive feedback loop, a working perpetual motion machine. His unique genius was that he understood both mindsets across the great ideological divide, the yin of gung-ho federal law enforcement agencies and their supporters, and the yang of the Constitution fanatics.

The engine of action and reaction was speeding up, and he was harnessing that limitless energy to ride into the Senior Executive Service and far beyond.

"Wally, I'm just glad to be aboard, I'm proud that you chose me to be a team leader. Now we'll finally get to operate against these assholes without our hands tied behind our backs!"

"Well George, I'm real glad to have you aboard too," Malvone lied. In fact, Malvone had no intention of ever letting Hammet lead a STU Team. George Hammet was the only other person alive who knew everything about what had happened at the stadium. Promising to reward him with a STU Team position was simply the carrot he had been using to string Hammet along, and ensure his faithful obedience and continuing loyalty.

This promise had so far induced Hammet to locate an ideal patsy, and carry him up into the empty building 1200 yards east of the stadium. The promise also motivated him to organize the gun store arsons and pull the mosque attack. But Hammet knew far too much, and he would present a mortal danger to Malvone as long as he was alive, which was why he planned to keep him very close and buy his happiness with false promises. For a little while longer at least.

Fortunately for Wally Malvone, George Hammet worked at a very dangerous occupation, where job related fatalities happened frequently in the line of duty.

23

Ranya was sitting on a flattened cardboard box, her arms wrapped around her knees for warmth. Even wearing several layers of clothing which were topped by a gray track suit, she was chilled through and sometimes shivering after sitting nearly motionless for over three hours. She was stiff and sore, peering through the vertical gap where she had pulled out a wooden slat in the trash can enclosure that concealed her. Since three AM the six foot square cypress-wood box had been her hunting blind, open to the stars above on the unseasonably cold night. There had been no moon at all, and no wind. After occasionally nodding off, she was watching the first hints of dawn seeping through the black forest wall across the lake, until branch by branch the individual trees emerged from the gloom into a new day.

Ranya had picked the back of this two-story brick home on the street lined with luxury sedans and SUVs after seeing two newspapers lying by the front door, and no lights on inside, during her scouting trip Friday night. She strolled up and rang the doorbell several times, noticing at the same time a half dozen pizza delivery and carpet service fliers jammed inside the screen door. After hearing the loud doorbell chime inside the house she walked quickly away to observe from a distance: there was no reaction within and she was certain the house was unoccupied.

When she returned at three in the morning, dressed and equipped for her mission, she settled into the trash bin storage area on the back side of the house. It was an ideal hiding place, with an unobstructed view across the lake. The upscale red brick home she had selected was directly across a finger lake from the fifth hole of the Greenspring Country Club, in the southwestern corner of the county-sized and mostly rural city of Virginia Beach. The water hazard ran north to south for hundreds of yards in each direction from her position, forming the western border of the golf course's front nine.

At 6:20 an early morning jogger ran down the cinder golf cart path near the water's edge, and Ranya could hear his footsteps crunching across the still water from 200 yards away. Mallards paddled by in a line, moving to their morning feeding grounds, leaving a series of V-shaped wakes. Ugly moscovy ducks with their red deformed bills wandered on the grassy lawn near the water's edge, unaware of Ranya's presence only twenty yards away. A little breeze from the north riffled the treetops and set tiny wavelets into motion down the lake, causing the mallards to change their course in formation.

At 6:35 the first golf cart of the day drove down the path. The cart's passenger was holding a cell phone or a walkie-talkie, and had a pair of binoculars hanging on a strap around his neck. The two men in the cart were wearing dark suit jackets and ties, not golfing attire. The golf cart stopped in the open near the fourth hole's putting green, and the passenger stepped out and scanned through 360 degrees with his binos, then he climbed back in and they drove further down the cinder path and repeated the process in the middle of the fifth hole.

They had to be Sanderson's advance team making a security sweep. This was a very positive sign to Ranya, strong evidence that her information had been correct, and the Virginia Attorney General was indeed on his way. She had been hopeful that Sanderson and his powerful friends would use their VIP clout to move their party into the first tee time, and this security check was the first evidence that her assumption was correct.

She took up her final shooting position, sitting with her back against the wooden boards across from her vertical firing slit, and pulled her shooting platform into position in front of her. This was a small two foot high black rubber garbage bin, turned upside down to make a steady shooting table to rest her Tennyson Champion across. She placed an old telephone book from the blue recycling bin in the middle of her 'table' to support the barrel and sound suppressor of her scoped target pistol. Her Champion was already loaded with its single .223 caliber hollow-point cartridge.

Ranya placed the insides of her feet against the upside-down black plastic bin, with her knees bent sharply upwards. Her elbows rested on the tops of her knees, both of her gloved hands were wrapped around the carved wooden pistol grip. The bottoms of her fists rested on the curved edge of the trash bin, with the weight of the Champion on the old telephone book.

With her face a foot behind the pistol, she scanned across the lake through the scope. Even in the early light the vivid emerald-hued clarity of the short-cropped turf around the fifth tee leaped out through the ocular lens. At 7X magnification, looking across the trash enclosure through the slot where she had pulled out the board, Ranya only had a narrow sliver of a view of the country club, just covering all of the area around the fifth tee. A golf cart zipped quickly past her field of view from left to right, just a blur. Perhaps more security, or country club course wardens.

Another cart rolled into her sight and stopped, she was looking over the scope now, watching with both of her eyes. Two men climbed out, and then one more cart parked partly behind the first. There were four middle-aged white men, old frat brothers perhaps, or former law partners, or possibly campaign contributing corporate lobbyists. To Ranya it didn't matter which: it only mattered that Eric Sanderson was one of them.

Ranya lowered her head to scan through the scope again, checking faces, and there he was! Sanderson appeared to be standing only a hundred feet away when she peered through her seven power scope. He looked the same as he did on television, with his youthful black hair trimmed with distinguished gray at the temples. Today he was wearing tacky lime-colored pants and a yellow V-neck sweater. Ranya never could understand men and their bizarre tastes in golfing outfits, but she quickly banished her extraneous thoughts.

The decision had already been made; the time for doubt and emotion was in the past, now was the time for only a stable body position, proper breathing technique, and precise trigger control. She squirmed her bottom into a better place further back, the small of her back against the rough cypress boards. Then she welded her elbows into her knees, stretched out her fingers and remade her grip. Finally she thumbed the sharply-checkered hammer all the way back, and both felt and heard its metallic treble click as it locked to the rear.

An overweight gray-haired man in a pale-blue sweater went first, facing her shooting blind 220 yards across the finger lake. Magnified, he appeared to look directly at Ranya from only a hundred feet away for long seconds, sending a chill through her. Then he bent over and planted the ball on its tee in one smooth motion. He stretched and twisted his torso with his arms straight up, his driver held between both hands, and then he slowly and with exaggerated flourishes assumed the position over the tee and took a practice swing. Finally he settled his twitching club head down near the teed-up ball, and as he bent over Ranya laid the thin black cross-hairs on the top of his head. It's not your day you fat jerk, it's not your day, she thought. But you'll never forget this day for as long as you live, I guarantee it.

The chubby older man swung, the ball was smacked beyond her view. The foursome all stared after it, their clubs resting lightly over their shoulders, loose and relaxed. Their unintelligible words and laughter floated across the still water as murmurs. The first to tee-off had sliced his ball into the lake, judging by their amused reactions.

Then Eric Sanderson stepped up and planted his own ball on its tee. Ranya sucked in a deep breath and watched him through the scope as he stepped back and took a practice swing. Next he dug his spikes in, shifting his weight around, his lime-green legs shoulder width apart, his arms in a rigid "V," his face down with the top of his head pointing directly at her.

Ranya slowly exhaled while putting light pressure on the Champion's trigger with the pad on the end of her right index finger. The thin black crosshairs danced ever so slightly in rhythm with her pulse as they quartered the top of Sanderson's head, while he stared straight down at his waiting golf ball. Sanderson was as motionless as a marble statue at the moment that the Tennyson Champion spat out its muffled shot.

The fifty grain lead and copper projectile was the weight of a dime, and the size and shape of the first half inch of a ball point pen. It left the barrel and the suppressor at almost 3,000 feet per second and covered the distance to Sanderson in one-fifth of a second, hitting him near the center of the crown of his head while he was bent over. The high velocity hollow-point slug pierced his skull, mushroomed open and shredded into pieces, releasing more energy than her .45 caliber fired point blank, literally exploding his head as his cranial vault failed to contain the overpressure from the supersonic shockwaves.

The slight sound of the suppressed muzzle blast arrived a half second after Sanderson's head exploded. His three golf partners and the security detail never heard it; their minds were overloaded with the sudden sound and images of flying blood, brain, flesh, hair and bone. The snap of the supersonic bullet passing over the lake was as loud as a bullwhip's crack and it startled the mallards into sudden flight, but neither this sound nor the flight of the ducks was noticed by the other men, they just stared, slack jawed, at what had been the Attorney General's head.

The fat golfer's heart went into instant tachycardia as they watched Sanderson's body, headless above the exposed jawbone and fountaining blood, crumple forward and bounce once off of the smoothly manicured turf. One of the other men golfing that day, who had served in combat in Viet Nam, hit the ground only a second later, his old survival reactions coming to the fore after lying dormant during three decades of peace.

The other two men stood frozen in their places, their eyes wide and their mouths agape, their clothes splattered with blood and tissue. One of them had a dark stain spreading down the front of his khaki trousers. After more long seconds of shock the Attorney General's two-man bodyguard team jumped from their own cart and pulled the two golfers who were still standing transfixed down to the ground between their golf carts, like cowboys seeking the protection of circled wagons during an Indian attack. Only then did they begin babbling semi-coherently into their cell phones and walkie-talkies, staying well hidden to avoid the next bullet from the unseen sniper.

After Ranya's utterly quiet three-hour wait in her sniper's lair, the echoing sonic crack of her shot seemed certain to wake up any neighbors who were sleeping in on the weekend morning, and sure to attract the attention of those already up for the day. But she could not pause to worry about that, and immediately went into the escape plan she had thought out and mentally run through over and over while waiting for daybreak and Sanderson's arrival.

Still sitting, she broke her Tennyson Champion into its three components: the suppressor, the barrel with its mounted scope, and the grip and trigger assembly. She withdrew the empty brass shell case and dropped it into the unzipped black fanny pack lying on the cement next to her. The suppressor and grip went into the fanny pack next. The fourteen inch barrel she slid up under her t-shirt and layers of clothing and beneath her sports bra, where its smooth blued-steel came to rest snuggly between her breasts. The chamber end of the barrel and the scope she pushed down inside her track pants and the blue jeans she was wearing underneath. She then snapped on the fanny pack and pulled it around in front of her, where it would cover the lumpy bulge under her layers of clothing.

Ranya wore a cheap blond wig under a pink and gray knitted wool Icelandic cap, pulled down so that six inches of golden hair fell on her shoulders. The track suit, knit cap, wig and fanny pack had cost her less than ten dollars at the Salvation Army thrift store in Norfolk.

She turned the small trash can she had used for a shooter's bench back upright, and as she pushed the missing cypress wood slat back into its place she heard a police car's siren across the lake. She took one more look around the trash can enclosure for any items left behind, saw none, took a deep breath, stood and reached over the boards to unlatch the gate and she stepped out.

Just under one minute had passed since her muffled shot, enough time, she hoped, for anyone already up at this hour to look out a kitchen window, and then return to their newspaper or television. Her goal was to be clear of the neighborhood in less than two minutes. Her fear was a police cruiser that might already be in place, blocking the way out to Greenspring Avenue. Her .45 pistol was locked under the seat of her motorcycle where she had left it. She had not declared war on society at large and would not shoot a local cop like Jasper Mosby in order to escape.

Ranya didn't hesitate. She strode purposefully back up the path beside the brick home, her face turned away from the neighbor's house a hundred feet away across a dividing hedge. While she walked her thin beige driving gloves went into her fanny pack, and she brought out and slipped on the large pair of orange-tinted glasses she had worn in the library, back when she had begun her search for Eric Sanderson. When she reached the street she turned right on the sidewalk and began "power walking," her arms pumping, just another slightly overweight young suburban housewife burning up the calories while the children were still asleep. A block further on she passed an elderly man across the street, but he was intent on his cocker spaniel's bowels and didn't even look at her.

Ranya turned left at the stop sign, and then walked two more blocks out of the tree-lined subdivision and crossed the four-lane avenue at the traffic light. She continued past the Quick N' Go convenience store, and ducked into the strip shopping center's 24 hour laundromat and went straight through the rows of washing machines to the narrow corridor in back.

In the bathroom of the laundromat, with the door bolted shut behind her, Ranya unzipped her fanny pack and dug out of it a blue baseball cap and a carefully folded department store shopping bag. She pulled off her itchy synthetic blond wig and stretch cap and dropped them into the bag, along with her orange glasses and the fanny pack. She unzipped and removed her gray warm-up jacket, then slid out the barrel and scope from against her body, wrapped it in the jacket, and placed it in the bag. Her gray warm-up pants had zippers at their ankles so that she could pull them off over her running shoes standing up.

With the gray suit peeled away Ranya was dressed in blue jeans and a red long-sleeve sweat shirt. Her brown hair was already in a pony tail, she twisted it and piled it on top and pulled the blue ball cap down over it. After a quick look in the mirror she picked up her shopping bag, stepped out of the bathroom, and left the laundromat through the glass rear exit door to the alley which ran behind the row of shops.

Police sirens were screaming down Greenspring Avenue from both directions, just on the other side of the shopping center, while she walked down the alley with her heart pounding furiously. Two blocks down the alley and partly around the corner her faithful red white and blue Yamaha FZR was waiting for her. It was half-concealed by a green dumpster alongside a cinder block wall, outside the back entrance of a closed tavern. As she strapped down her shopping bag under the black bungee net on the back of the bike she could hear more than one helicopter. She didn't look up until she had removed the cable locking her black helmet to the bike's frame, and pulled it down over her head.

She kept to her planned route, using only secondary streets through suburban neighborhoods, until she was clear of the immediate area. She heard many more police sirens. Less than seven minutes after the fatal shot, she was on I-64 heading west at sixty miles per hour in the slow lane. She desperately wanted to twist the throttle wide open and eat up the asphalt pavement in front of her, but she forced herself to remain as inconspicuous as a twenty-one year old female assassin on a motorcycle could be. She felt certain that her guilt was flashing like a beacon, that her disassembled sniper pistol was glowing within the bag behind her, that her obvious guilt would immediately be noticed by any passing policeman on the highway or up in a helicopter.

As she covered the miles with no destination, she saw Eric Sanderson on the 5th tee of the Greenspring Country Club again, his club across his shoulder, smiling and relaxed, laughing with old friends, enjoying his perfect life which was one continuous ascending arc of personal success and political victory. He had not minded if his latest political victory was gained over her father's charred body. In fact he had publicly, gratefully welcomed her father's death. Joe Bardiwell's dead body was just a convenient stepping stone placed before him to advance his career, a minor help in establishing his national reputation.

Whether Sanderson had personally sent the killers to the gun stores and to her house or not, he had certainly been using the murders to advance his political fortunes, which in Ranya's mind made him a legitimate target. Someone had to pay for her father's murder, and Sanderson was a good place to start, at least until she could find George, and hopefully learn from him who was actually giving the orders. Anyway, Ranya knew that whoever was actually behind the Stadium Massacre and the arson murders and all the rest of it was now clearly on notice. In a country where the people are armed, politicians who employ or benefit from government killer squads, well they too can be killed.

Eric Sanderson was not going to run for higher office on the ever-popular Constitution-shredding platform. He was not going to dance on top of her father's grave.

All the way down I-95 and I-64 to their new base of operations, the STU Team members in the 36 vehicle convoy were tuned to National Public Radio's "Weekend Edition" and later to AM talk radio, listening as each new detail about the Virginia Attorney General's assassination was reported. All 36 of them, the operators and tech support guys in their mix of government and private vehicles skipped from station to station, relaying the latest news to each other on their VHF tactical radio net.

Listening in on Virginia State Police frequencies they learned that Virginia Beach police were searching for a white male, approximately 45 years old, who had been seen in the area fishing. It was believed that he may have carried a rifle to a black pickup truck concealed in a long white tube and escaped from the area. Police were stopping and searching all white men in black pickup trucks moving in southeastern Virginia, unceremoniously pulling their drivers out and to the ground at gunpoint.

Attorney General Sanderson had been nailed by a sniper while golfing, teeing off on a private Virginia Beach country club. The golfers among the STU Team couldn't help thinking 'what a way to go.' There you are, concentrating on one of your favorite activities in the world, and in the next second your head is melon salad and you're talking to Saint Peter…or Lucifer…or to nobody at all. Not a bad way to go, even if it's messy for the cleanup crew. Messy but painless.

The sniper had not been captured or for that matter even seen or heard, so he was a pro. He'd known where Sanderson would be, and was waiting for him. Unlike Senator Randolph, Sanderson had not been sniped at home, but on the move, at a private and unannounced event, so the shooter obviously had a good source of inside intell. This was a strong indication that the sniper was part of a well-coordinated team, which lined up perfectly with what they had already been briefed about.

Inside and unspoken all of the STU Team members, alone in each vehicle, felt a great deal of respect for the assassin. Obviously he was a kindred spirit on some level, even if he shot for the other team. "One shot, one kill," and a clean getaway: you had to admire that...strictly on a professional basis. Probably ex-military or ex-SWAT or both. The bad guys obviously had some pretty decent shooters, who would demand their utmost attention and respect.

Sanderson had foolishly taken a high profile on guns recently, hoping to gain publicity for his run for Governor. Just yesterday he was all over television promoting his "FIST" checkpoint teams. Well, obviously, someone had not liked the idea of submitting to random highway firearms searches, and had taken him out...

The killing brought a new sense of urgency to their mission in Tidewater, energizing the STU Team as they rolled down the highway in their anonymous mixed convoy. They drove black Chevy Suburbans, "Bell South" and "Virginia Power" vans, motor homes, utility trucks, a small fuel truck loaded with aviation gas, some of their own private vehicles, and actual rental trucks hired to haul their lockers and crates and boxes of bulky equipment.

They knew that hard-core domestic terrorists were loose in Tidewater Virginia, spreading fear and death and havoc. But unknown to these domestic terrorists, a new kind of ass-kicking undercover sheriff was coming to town. The covert operators of the secret STU Team were on their way, and the evildoers were about to find out that their only easy days were yesterday.

All of them to a man could not believe their good fortune, that they were members of the STU Team on that crisp clear Saturday morning. They'd trained and planned and sweat and bled for years, mostly beginning way back in the military, and now the battle had finally come to American soil. On that day not one of them would have accepted a transfer to the FBI's Hostage Rescue Team, or even to the almighty Secret Service. For once the Fibbies of the Joint Domestic Terrorism Task Force would be playing the supporting role while the deviously named Special Training Unit would do the shooting and killing.

And they all knew exactly who to thank for their great good fortune on that blue-sky Saturday as they rolled south to Tidewater: none other than that genius and visionary, Wally Malvone. Only Malvone had the insight, only he had foreseen the coming need for the Special Training

Unit. He had pushed for the creation of the STU Team, just in time for them to go into action when they were needed the most.

The President's Homeland Security Team met in the White House Situation Room at ten o'clock and the mood was beyond grim. As usual President Gilmore sat in his swiveling black leather recliner by the center of the conference table, and used the remote control to switch the sound among the bank of big screen television screens.

The eight FBI SWAT agents slain in the Reston Virginia ambush were being memorialized at Arlington National Cemetery with full military honors, a first for federal law enforcement agents killed in the line of duty. Seven of the eight had prior military service, so it was not much of a stretch when they were brought to the cemetery on flag-draped caissons. There were bagpipes playing Amazing Grace, and a bugle playing Taps, and weeping children and stoic wives veiled in black, being handed American flags folded into tight triangles.

"Damn… I should be there," said the President bitterly. He hated the idea of missing the solemn and dignified national television exposure which attending and speaking at such an important ceremony would have brought him.

No one corrected him. They all knew that the Director of the Secret Service had admitted that they could not absolutely ensure his safety during outdoor appearances for the time being, while new procedures were put into effect. The completely expendable Vice-President had gone in his place. The Reston ambush had been the worst single day's disaster to ever befall the FBI, even worse than 9-11.

"Wayne," he said to his FBI Director Wayne Sheridan, "what do we know about Sanderson's assassination?"

"We're on it Mr. President. He was killed by a single high velocity rifle bullet which struck him in the head. The assassin has thus far eluded detection, but local police have some solid leads. They're looking for a thin white man with a goatee-style beard who was seen carrying a long white tube back to a black pickup truck. They believe the sniper was posing as a fisherman, waiting at the end of the lake where Attorney General Sanderson was shot. We have an eyewitness working with FBI sketch artists, and we think we may be able to use hypnosis to recover the license number of the getaway truck. We'll nail this guy. We're hot on his trail."

"How far did the sniper shoot from this time? Did he use another antique 'trash rifle'?"

"We're searching the area where the fisherman was seen, it's 500 yards away at the north end of the lake. It'll be a while before we can tell what kind of rifle he used; apparently they've only recovered a few tiny fragments of the bullet so far. They can't even tell what caliber it was yet."

"Did anybody hear where the shot came from?"

"Well sir, the initial reports from his security detail, they're inconclusive. They're still in shock, Sanderson's head… Well it happened right in front of them, and they're pretty shook up. They might have just missed the sound, or the sniper could have used a sound suppressor."

"A what? You mean a silencer?"

"He may have. Used a silencer I mean."

"But they're illegal, aren't they?"

Wayne Sheridan looked over at David Boxell, the Director of the BATFE. ATF's profile had risen considerably in the federal hierarchy since the Stadium Massacre, and he had been asked to attend the HST emergency meetings. Boxell was a rather slight man wearing horn-rimmed glasses. Sometimes his subordinates called him Barney Fife, after the timid deputy from the fictional town of Mayberry, because of the way he spoke.

Boxell said, "Silencers? Uh, no Mr. President, actually they're not illegal, as long as one pays the tax, a fee, $200 I believe. That's the same as it is for fully automatic weapons, one pays a $200 tax and they're legal."

"Wait just a minute! You're telling me that silencers and machine guns are legal, if you pay $200?"

"Well, yes. That's been the law for decades. One registers them with ATF of course, and there's a background check, and the $200 tax…"

"That's insane!" the President shot back. "I can't believe what I'm hearing!"

Boxell stuttered, "W-w-well, the Schuleman Montaine Act, th-that only addressed semi-automatic weapons. It didn't address Class Three weapons, that's silencers and machine guns that have had their tax paid…"

"That's ridiculous! I'll just fix that situation with another Presidential Decision Directive!" He looked over at U.S. Attorney General Lynn Axelmann, who nodded her head up and down in assent. "I just can't believe the whole situation! The day after Sanderson announces the new road block plan, the plan we pushed on Virginia, he's killed by a sniper! The very next day! This situation is out of control! These secret militias have got to be stopped!"

The FBI Director cleared his throat and said, "Sir, if I may…"

"Go ahead Wayne, what? What?"

"It's the Second Amendment people."

"The who?"

"It's more than just 'militias' sir. I wish it was just militias! Militias we could handle…but it's the whole Second Amendment crowd.

Ever since we passed the assault rifle law, we've been getting death threats mailed to us, emailed, telephoned… They're calling us traitors, threatening to kill us…and they're not only threatening. Yesterday in Dallas somebody put a round through the FBI Special Agent In Charge's window. Luckily the room was empty, and we've kept it quiet, but the shooter obviously knew exactly which office was the SAC's.

"And in Phoenix a package was found Thursday. It was placed, we don't know how, right inside the ATF Resident Agency. They got a phone call telling them exactly where to look. It was twenty pounds of bricks in a plastic file box, and it had a note inside, it said, "The next one will be C-4." It came with a blasting cap and a little bit of C-4 explosive in a baggie, so it was no prank."

The President said, "You see Wayne, you're making my point: they're just terrorists, they're no different from Muslim terrorists or any other kind."

"Perhaps on one level it's the same, but this is different too. For one thing, they didn't explode a bomb in Phoenix, they just sent a warning. Muslims don't warn: they just blow you up. And we're getting hundreds of letters and calls a day, and they all say the same thing: 'you took an oath to defend the Constitution, now you're destroying it' or 'you're a traitor, you're a domestic enemy of the Constitution.' Hundreds of them, thousands of them, every day."

"All over the Second Amendment?" asked the President.

"Yes sir, and the Fourth, with the checkpoints now, but mostly the Second. They feel…strongly…that we've stepped over the line with the assault rifle ban, that we've crossed a point of no return. They're threatening outright violence."

"They're doing more than threatening. Remember, that militia nutcase Shifflett started all this with the Stadium Massacre! They shot Senator Randolph, they shot Sanderson, they blew up the bridge, and they killed eight FBI agents. They've gone way, way beyond threatening! They're just terrorists, plain and simple. They're no better than any damned Muslim terrorists."

"I agree sir…"

"We need to crush them, ruthlessly, without mercy! There's over a thousand dead Americans because of them, and they've got to pay. I'm going to make them pay!"

"Yes sir, but, but that may not be a very simple task. Sir, I'd like to show you some film that was just shot within the hour by an FBI surveillance plane in North Carolina. It shows the extent of the problem we're up against."

The President paused, catching his breath, and nodded.

The FBI Director made a hand signal to an Air Force audio-visual aide, and the center television screen cut to a grainy black and white aerial view with time and date numbers on the bottom. Director Sheridan said, "We're looking at the funeral of Ben Mitchell in Dunn North Carolina."

The President said, "The retired Green Beret who blew up the Wilson Bridge and wiped out the FBI agents."

"Correct. Now you'll note the hundreds of vehicles parked here." Sheridan circled the area on the screen with his red laser pointer. "Quite a crowd turned out for the man. He seems to have been well known in the Special Forces community. Watch this group when the picture zooms in."

The video was taken from an overhead angle. An open grave, a white tent and a coffin became visible, surrounded by a crowd that was comprised almost completely of men. Some of them wore suits and jackets, many were dressed casually, and a few were wearing jungle fatigues, but most of them wore berets.

"Mr. President, here's where it gets really interesting. Now watch right here, this group." He circled an area in the crowd with his laser pointer. All of the members of the Homeland Security Team were leaning forward, staring intently at the four foot wide video screen.

From the center of the densely packed milling group of several hundred men, black sticks emerged, aiming skyward. The video taken from the circling FBI Cessna jerked and zoomed in and recentered on the sticks, which under greater magnification were obviously rifle barrels. Even the senior officials in the room, who had never held a rifle in their lives, could identify them by their distinctive triangular fore sights as M-16s of some type, along with others that were also obviously assault rifles.

"Oh my sweet Jesus," whispered the President in the silent room. "Didn't the I.R.A. used to do that?"

The seven men carrying their rifles vertically in front of their chests at the "present-arms" position formed into a single rank, the crowd around them melted back to give them room. All seven of the men had dark triangular rags wrapped around their heads masking them below the eyes like Wild West outlaws. They all wore dark sunglasses, and they all wore berets.

"Jesus H. Christ… They're giving him a 21 gun salute."

"That's exactly right Mr. President. I've been informed that the bandanas are from combat field dressing kits, the kind the Army uses to tie bandages in place. They're giving Mitchell the Special Forces version of an I.R.A. funeral."

While they watched the rifles were shouldered in unison, aimed skyward at a 45 degree angle, they were fired, brought down to present-arms, then returned to their shoulders and fired again. The members of the Homeland Security Team watched the display in mute wonderment.

The President spoke first, with a sarcastic scoff. "Well, it appears that they haven't all turned in their assault rifles."

After a moment to see if anyone else had a response, the FBI Director said, "No sir, it doesn't appear so. To say the least."

"And they're doing all this for a bridge bomber and a murderer?"

"They're doing it for Sergeant Major Mitchell, yes. And they're doing it for the other old Green Beret, the fellow who was killed with his son in the jeep in Norfolk. Denton? Mark Denton. From what we've been hearing, these Green Berets are pretty ticked off about both of them."

"Didn't that one in Norfolk blow himself up accidentally? Wasn't he part of that militia ring with Shifflett?" asked the President.

"Well, we think so, but the Green Berets…they're another story. They think the fellow in Norfolk, Mark Denton, was murdered, that's what our sources say. Apparently they agree with Ben Mitchell, with what he said in his D.O.L. letter. They think Denton was murdered."

"Oh come on, murdered by whom? Those people are paranoid. They're conspiracy nuts! They're the black-helicopter crowd!"

"Maybe so Mr. President, maybe so, but there's thousands and thousands of them," said the FBI Director.

"Well I don't see thousands of them on your video; hundreds maybe, but not thousands. Don't you have FBI agents on the ground down there? Don't you cover these things? These men have clearly broken the law! Blatantly! Why can't you move in and make arrests?"

Director Sheridan squirmed in his seat, clearly uncomfortable. "Yes sir, we did know about the funeral in advance and we did have several teams on the ground. It's S.O.P to cover funerals like this, the same as mafia or motorcycle gang funerals."

"And? Did they make any arrests?"

"Uh, no sir, they did not. Evidently our Special Agents on the ground were discovered. The last word I have is they haven't been hurt, but they were disarmed and sent away, with messages. Threats, actually."

"Sent away? Disarmed? What are you talking about?"

"We assigned six agents to monitor the funeral on the ground, in three vehicles. Pretty standard, but we had no idea that hundreds of old Special Forces guys were going to show up…and well, our agents were 'made.' Spotted. There was nothing they could do. We're lucky they were let go; some of the hot-heads in the mob wanted to lynch them."

"Lynch them! I don't understand?" The President was growing more and more incredulous.

"As traitors sir. They called our Special Agents traitors. Some of them were mentioning ropes and trees, that's my understanding sir. Ropes and trees… But calmer heads prevailed, and our agents were released…

but without their pistols or submachine guns or credentials. Or their video cameras."

"FBI agents carry machine guns now?"

"Well yes, in their vehicles. They carry MP-5 submachine guns in their vehicles, yes sir."

"And they let them be taken away? Just like that?"

"I'm sure it'll be investigated. It just happened, but judging from the film we just saw, they had no choice. They were outnumbered and outgunned a hundred to one."

"And they called our agents traitors? Traitors?"

"Yes sir, it's that Second Amendment thing again. They told our agents they were violating their oaths, and they were 'domestic enemies of the Constitution.' It's all of that Constitution business..."

"Traitors!" The President had slowly been building toward a rage, and his voice was raised almost to a scream. The FBI Director forced himself to meet the President's scathing glare, but the other members of the Homeland Security Team were watching the FBI Director, or looking down at their papers.

"They're the traitors! They're the ones sniping at Senators! They're the ones blowing up bridges and shooting up stadiums! And they have the brass balls to call us traitors!" The President was leaning against the conference table, looking up and down at them all. "Now listen people, and get this real clear: I want those roadblocks doubled, tripled! I want them in all 50 states, I don't care what it takes, mobilize the National Guard, I don't give a damn! If they think they can just drive around on our highways with guns and bombs in their cars like these God damn Green Berets, well, well, they're not! They're not! I won't have it!"

The President brought his voice down and said in a hushed voice, "Make it happen people. Make it happen. That's all I'm going to say." Then he pointed his finger at his CSO Harvey Crandall and indicated that he should follow him out. The President swept out of the Situation Room through his own door, a Secret Service agent scrambled to open it without causing him a single moment's delay, afraid of incurring his wrath.

In the walnut-lined passageway President Gilmore said to his friend, "Harry, get in touch with that Malvone. Find him now, right now. Tell him we're taking a beating, and we can't let these assassinations just stand out there with no response. We're losing control of the situation, this fire is spreading fast, and we need to stamp it out now, right now. Tell Malvone we need to see concrete results, and we need to see them now, like to-day!"

24

The grimy yellow and black mobile hydraulic crane was set up perpendicular to the quay wall, with its unextended boom jutting over the barge and Brad Fallon's mast. For a 25 ton capacity crane which usually earned its keep doing jobs such as lifting out and installing massive Caterpillar and Detroit Diesel fishing boat engines, lifting 400 pounds of sailboat mast and rigging was not going to be a challenge. Brad was going over the mast hoisting plan with the boatyard's crane operator Ramon, and his brother Salvador. They were standing next to the crane by the quay's edge and Brad was pointing out various aspects of the job, using a mixture of English, Spanish, and hand signals.

Brad was holding a wooden paint roller's extension handle as a stand-in for his mast. He had tied a piece of string around its middle and was showing them how he expected the lift to proceed. Crosby's yard rarely handled sailboats, and this was unknown territory for the brothers. Although the mast was light and would be easy for the crane to lift, it would be vulnerable to expensive and time-consuming damage while it was swinging in the air. All together Brad had put over $12,000 into the mast and rigging, and he needed the job to proceed smoothly to stay on his departure schedule.

The crane operator's brother spoke virtually no English beyond yes and no, and Brad's Spanish was uncertain at best, so they had to find the key words they would need to direct the soon-to-be vertical mast into place on Guajira. Brad was wearing paint-stained khaki shorts and boat shoes and a t-shirt with the semi-profane name of a bar in Fairbanks Alaska on it. The two brothers were wearing long blue jeans and work boots and tan Crosby's Boatyard work shirts with the sleeves rolled all the way down, even though it was sunny and almost 80 degrees out and growing warmer by the hour.

The three men halted their discussion in mid-sentence when a stranger on a red white and blue Japanese café -racer style motorcycle appeared from around the big corrugated steel paint shed, heading slowly their way. The two Guatemalan brothers looked back to Brad to see if the interloper was someone he knew. The motorcyclist, whose entire head was concealed under a black helmet, was looking less and less like an hombre the closer he came. The short-statured brothers reflexively straightened up to their full heights and ran their fingers back through their black hair. When the biker parked her Yamaha close by them and pulled off her helmet and shook down her brunette ponytail, Ramon and Salvador glanced between Brad and the young woman, grinning broadly. The younger brother, Salvador, asked Brad, "Es tu amiga, esta guapa?"

Before Brad could think up a clever or diplomatic answer to the question "is this babe your girlfriend," Ranya retorted to Salvador, "Brad no tiene amiga, es un solitario." Meaning, Brad doesn't have a girlfriend, he's a loner. The brothers erupted in laughter and began to pepper Ranya with friendly questions in rapid-fire Spanish, but she said, "sorry, lo siento muchachos, pero mi Espanol es terrible." This wasn't exactly true, her Spanish was better than adequate, but she thought it would be rude to exclude Brad from any of their conversation. Besides, she was not here to chat with boatyard employees.

Ramon said, slowly and carefully, "Brad, you are the capitan of this yate Guajira; you are going to have many amigas I think!" At this remark Brad and Ranya made direct eye contact, and neither of them hurried to look away.

Brad could not hide his complete joy at her totally unexpected arrival; he was beaming and made no effort to conceal his delight. She looked sexy in her tight jeans and red sweater, and there was something else: she was actually smiling back at him, something Brad had only imagined before. "Ranya, oh my God, it's so great to see you again, I can't believe you're here! And just in time to see the mast go up!" He extended his hand to her and she shook it willingly, still holding eye contact with him.

"So this really is the day when Guajira becomes a sailboat?"

"Right now!"

"Is there anything I can do to help out?"

He reluctantly let go of her hand in order to point out the elements of the task ahead of them. "There sure is. We have to get the bottom of the mast through that hole in the cabin top and down over the mast step. Well it's easy to get it through the hole in the deck, but it's very tricky to line it up exactly vertically, so that it'll go right down over the step. See, look at the lifting strap: the mast gets lifted from the middle, not the top, and it won't really want to go perfectly straight up and down. If you go down below on Guajira, when the mast is over the step on the keel, just call up to me if it needs to come right or left or front or back, then I'll yell over to Ramon how to move the top of the crane. Simple right? And when it's perfectly lined up, tell me, and I'll tell Ramon to lower it down."

Brad continued, with instructions to the brothers. "And Salvador helps me on deck. Tu conmigo en el barco, okay Salvador? You with me, okay?" The arrival of Ranya was fortuitous. Brad had not been excited about the prospect of depending on the eager but non-English-speaking Salvador to be a part of the chain of communication, where a botched order to Ramon at the crane's controls could result in a bent and ruined mast.

Salvador nodded solemnly and said, "Si capitan, I with you."

Brad continued instructing his little team, using his wooden pole and string to demonstrate. "Okay Salvador, we'll stand on the barge while the mast is lifted to vertical, then we'll hold the bottom and walk it across, while Ramon booms out the crane." Salvador was nodding assent as Ramon translated Brad's words. "All right? Everybody understand? Let's do it then."

Ramon climbed up on the mobile crane and into the operator's compartment and fired up the diesel engine which powered the hydraulics, revving it with earsplitting blasts and belching smoke. It was parked facing the river by the quayside with its outriggers planted on the cement on each side for stability. The steel boom whined as it telescoped out and up to its full length, eighty feet above the center of the horizontal mast. Brad, Ranya and Salvador jumped across the gap from the seawall down onto the barge.

When the crane's hook with its steel "headache ball" came down within reach Brad grabbed it. He had previously duct-taped a carpet remnant around the steel ball as padding to keep it from scarring up the mast's paint. Brad had already fastened a nylon lifting strap around the mast just slightly above its mid point, and now he placed the nylon webbing loop over the crane's hook, looked all around him on the barge and on board Guajira for a final check, then he walked back to the base of the mast where Salvador was waiting.

"Everybody ready? Todos listos?" Once the fragile sixty foot mast was lifted off of its five saw horses and was swinging around it would be very susceptible to damage.

Brad looked at each of them in turn. "Listo Ramon? Listo Salvador? Ready Ranya? Everybody ready?" Brad pointed his right hand straight up and made a circling motion with his index finger and called out, "Okay Ramon! Arriba! Take her up!"

The hook took up the slack from the long nylon webbing sling, then without even pausing it smoothly lifted the mast up a few feet into the air over the saw horses. The mast flexed and quivered slightly along its 60 foot length. As the mast continued ascending Brad and Salvador held down its base, and it rotated smoothly to the vertical, almost touching the crane's wire along its top half. The base of the mast came to rest suspended in mid-air at shoulder level by the two men. The mast swayed and turned as they struggled to control it from the bottom.

"All right, let's walk her across. Ramon, ready?"

Ramon nodded, concentrating on his controls. He slowly lowered the angle of the crane's boom, while he extended its telescoping sections outward. The precisely coordinated movements sent the now-vertical mast out across the barge, its base held by Brad and Salvador. The two men hopped one at a time across onto Guajira's deck; Ranya had already gone aboard the boat and disappeared down below.

When the mast was directly above the hole in Guajira's deck, Brad gave the finger circling down signal, and Ramon spooled out wire to lower it slowly until it was only a foot above the deck, where he stopped it again. The two men twisted and rotated the oval shaped mast to align it properly with the hole, then Brad gave the slow finger circling down signal to Ramon again, and the base of the mast was smoothly swallowed by the deck.

There was a band of blue electrical tape around the mast which marked what would be its final position at deck level. When the mast was a few inches from the blue tape, Brad made a sudden fist and the mast stopped short, swaying slightly.

"Okay Ranya, how's it looking?" Brad called down to her through a small open deck hatch aft of the mast.

"It's got to go left an inch and back a half inch," she replied.

Brad did the quick geometric conversion in his head and yelled loudly to Ramon, to be heard above the crane's diesel, "Bring it back this much!" He held his hands a foot apart to show Ramon the distance he needed to pull the top of the crane back toward the land.

After a few adjustments front and back and side to side Ranya called out, "Stop! That's it! Let it down!"

"Okay Ranya, watch your fingers, here it comes!"

The mast slid the final inches down through the deck and Ranya called up, "That's it Brad, she's on the step!"

"Fantastic! Okay, come on up and help us pin the stays." Brad smiled a little nervously and said, "Now we get to see if I'm a complete idiot or not." He used his folding pocket knife to slice away the yellow cords which held all of the wire ends together in a single bundle. This awkward bundle had been covered in a piece of bubble wrap plastic and tied to the mast to keep it in place while it was lifted.

"Each turnbuckle has three inches of adjustment, and if I did my math correctly, each wire will fit tightly. If not..." Brad shrugged and smiled at Ranya, putting a brave face on his apprehension.

This was crunch time, the pass-fail acid test, and all four of them knew it. The mast was completely new, and Brad had cut the wires to their lengths entirely according to his own mathematical calculations.

"If they don't fit, then what?" asked Ranya, helping Brad to separate the wires from the bunch and lead them in their correct directions.

"If they're too short, we'll have to pull the mast back out and put it back on the sawhorses. Then I'll have to go buy some more hardware to add on a few more inches. If they're too long, I'll have to take the end fittings apart and whack off a few inches of wire, and do them over.

That'll take time, and the crane's not free! Okay, let's start with the four lower shrouds…"

In just a few minutes all ten of the rigging wires were pinned to Guajira's deck chainplates with thumb-sized stainless steel cross pins, and all ten did indeed fit. Brad went below and came up with four cans of cold beer to celebrate this milestone, in spite of the morning hour. They toasted Brad and drank some beer; they were all in high spirits, happy to share his victorious moment with him.

Salvador went back up onto the quay and helped his brother with the crane. Its hook spooled all the way up, the boom's telescoping sections slid back down, and the steadying outrigger legs were withdrawn. Brad tipped them a twenty dollar bill each for coming in and doing the weekend job, even though he had already paid the yard the $240 minimum for the crane service. They drove the machine away grinning, winking at Brad about his "guapa chica" back on Guajira.

When they were gone Ranya was left alone on the sailboat with Brad to help him tighten down the turnbuckles and tune the rig evenly. As they moved around the deck from bow to stern and side to side, alternately tensioning the stay wires a little at a time, Brad had numerous opportunities to observe just how pretty a girl Ranya actually was. He wondered why she was out riding her Yamaha wearing only running shoes and a thin sweater besides her jeans. She had always worn hiking boots and a jacket before.

"Well I guess this proves you're not a complete idiot," she told him with a warm smile. They were both all the way aft, behind the cockpit crouched on either side of the backstay wire's turnbuckle, making the final adjustments. A few times when they handed each other tools or cotter pins or rolls of white rigger's tape they brushed fingertips, and each time Brad felt a little electric charge...

He couldn't remember seeing her smile before today. He thought she was actually beautiful when she was smiling. She had perfect teeth, absolutely flawless, straight and white. He'd never appreciated this before, because he hadn't seen her smiling until now. He'd always loved her mysterious eyes, which were sometimes amber, hazel or even green, and now she had the dazzling smile to match them.

He accepted her praise about his rigging job. "Thanks. I guess I was a little lucky too, going ten for ten."

"I'm impressed Brad, this is really an accomplishment. And not just the mast. All of Guajira…everything. I guess this is really an important day for you, isn't it?"

"Oh yeah! Very important! It's huge. Guajira is a sailboat again, almost."

"So what's next?"

"Let's finish tuning the rig, and I'll make sure the mast is nice and straight. Then let's put on the boom and the mainsail and go sailing!"

"Just like that? That's all there is to it?"

"That's it! Don't you want to go sailing? I know I do! It's going to be a perfect day on the bay. Warm, sunny, nice westerly breeze... You know, I spent a long, long time up that river on Guajira without a mast. I really want to take her out; you don't have any idea how much I want to take her out sailing! I've been planning for this day for so long..."

"But I'm not dressed for it! I'd need to get changed; I can't go like this in blue jeans..."

"Oh don't worry about it; I've got some things you can wear. We'll figure it out, come on, let's go sailing!"

They worked steadily to complete the rigging work and install the boom. Then together they partially unfolded the giant white mainsail across the cockpit, and slid the plastic slugs which were sewn along its front and bottom edges into the slots on the back of the mast and the top of the boom. Finally the entire mainsail was flaked down and secured along the boom with red nylon straps, ready to haul up the mast and catch its first breeze. They cast off from the rusty barge at Crosby's Boatyard before noon.

When the President's CSO called, Wally Malvone was skimming two thousand feet above the Virginia countryside in "his" new helicopter, flying south. The royal blue Eurohelo VK-100 was smaller than what he had envisioned for transporting his STU Teams, but it represented a remarkable start on such short notice. "Mr. Emerson" didn't tell him who the helicopter and the tight-lipped pilot actually belonged to, and Malvone didn't ask. Mr. Emerson didn't think there would be a major problem getting the larger choppers with greater troop carrying capacity that Malvone was requesting, but it would take a little time.

Wally Malvone understood that it was not a simple process to create and activate fictitious "proprietary front" companies and covertly interface them with secret government black-budgets. This required engineering invisible wheels within bureaucratic wheels. Just how many layers of real and phony corporations and holding companies, Malvone couldn't begin to guess. That was Mr. Emerson's bailiwick. Neither did Mr. Emerson ever inquire as to exactly what the STU Team's mission was going to be. "Don't ask, don't tell" was the guiding principle of the relationship between Malvone and Emerson in both directions. They both had the authority they needed to do their jobs, and that was enough for each of them.

Among the items Mr. Emerson had given to Wally Malvone when they met in an anonymous office in an unmarked building in Alexandria was a special telephone. It was a real "brick" and came in its own gray metal box, but it was supposed to provide secure encrypted voice communications between the Malvone and the White House from almost anywhere in the USA. Malvone didn't know how it worked and he didn't care. Cell, satellite or radio, that wasn't his department.

It rang with an urgent double buzz from within the green nylon aviator's helmet bag on the seat next to him. He had to dig out a notebook computer, a PDA, binoculars, a digital camera, his Sig Sauer 9mm pistol in a brown leather holster, night vision goggles in a green plastic case and other loose gear before he could get to the phone-in-a-box. If the gum-chewing pilot with his headphones and aviator sunglasses noticed the comedy taking place on the seat behind him, he didn't give the slightest indication.

As he had been instructed, Malvone extended the thin silver whip antenna out two feet, then placed the urgently buzzing phone box on his lap and pushed a five digit code on its small touch pad. Mr. Emerson had explained that if he ever entered the access code incorrectly three times in a row, there would be nothing left inside the metal box but acid and melted electronics, so he had better remember the number, and not screw it up. He held the ungainly brick-sized phone to his ear, tilting it to the side so the antenna cleared the helicopter's padded ceiling

"Mr. Brown, this is Mr. Green. Can you hear me all right?"

Malvone thought that the CSO's idea of adding a layer of security with "Mr. Brown" and "Mr. Green" was rather silly, but he was willing to play along since "Mr. Green" was paying the bills.

"I can hear you just fine Mr. Green." His voice was actually coming through like it was bubbling up out of a deep well, and it was warbling up and down in tone, but he was understandable.

"Mr. Brown, what is the status of your company, and how soon will they be ready for customers?"

Company? Customers? This was evidently more childish code-talk. Malvone imagined that the CSO was a fan of cheap espionage thrillers. "Well Mr. Green, they're unpacking at their new location right now, and they could be open for business any time."

"I'm glad to hear it. The CEO is very, very upset by current events, and especially by this morning's golfing accident. You don't know how upset he is. We've really had a nasty couple of weeks, and now with what happened this morning…well the boss finds this totally unacceptable and intolerable. He wants you to put your business plan into effect immediately, right away if that's at all possible. Do you have any of those types of jobs we discussed already lined up yet?"

"Well sir, frankly we had expected to have a chance to get organized at our new location for a few days, sort of get the lay of the land, do some interfacing with our local affiliates…but if the boss wants us to move up our timetable…"

"Yes, he does. He urgently wishes to see results, tangible results. You might say that we need to visibly start taking market share away from our competition right away, do you understand me Mr. Brown?"

"Yes sir, loud and clear."

"So I can tell the boss that he's going to see results, say, inside of 24 hours? Or better yet, in time for… early Sunday morning?"

He knew at once what this meant: in time for the all-important Sunday morning network television talking-head shows. As things presently stood, the shadowy right wing terrorists were seemingly striking at will, and to a certain extent this was actually the truth: he had had nothing to do with the Wilson Bridge, Senator Randolph, or this new Sanderson shooting. Now it was being left up to his STU Team to dramatically alter the growing national perception that the government was powerless to stop or even identify the domestic terrorists responsible.

Malvone got into the spirit of the CSO's childish code talk, knowing that the phone's warbling encryption would not allow the man to hear him almost laughing out loud as he spoke. "Yes sir, you can inform the CEO that he'll be seeing a sharp uptrend in our company market share within that time frame."

"Good. That's what I wanted to hear, and that's what I'm going to tell him."

"Do you want me to submit a plan for your approval before we conduct the first transaction?"

"No! Just get it done, within the parameters we discussed, but get it done by morning!"

The connection broke after a series of clicks and whistles and hums in Malvone's ear. The pilot in front of him was still chewing his gum, his hands steady on his yoke and cyclic controls, his headphones over his ball cap and sunglasses, guiding the Eurohelo over the green fields and coffee-colored tributaries of the Chesapeake Bay watershed.

25

The morning spent in the boatyard had been exactly what Ranya needed. She was too busy helping Brad to get Guajira ready for sailing to do much futile brooding. There was no chance to watch television or listen to talk radio as they got the mainsail ready; instead Brad played music CDs on the boat's stereo. But she didn't need to hear the news to know what a hornet's nest she had kicked open: the police sirens and helicopters converging on the golf course had told her that already. No official confirmation was necessary to be certain that Sanderson was dead. Ranya had known a second after her shot that she had center-punched the top of his head while he was leaning over his golfball.

After they cast off from the barge they motored out of Crosby's side-creek and north up the congested industrial sections of the Elizabeth River, past a mile of bulk cargo terminals and container handling facilities. They finally caught a fair breeze as they passed Craney Island on their left, but they continued motoring north until they were in sight of the world's largest naval base off their starboard bow to the east. Security vessels patrolled back and forth in front of the long line of submarines, destroyers, cruisers, and two aircraft carriers which were docked at the Norfolk Naval Operations Base.

Ranya was wearing a set of light green hospital scrubs which Brad had lent her, with the ankles rolled up around her calves. It felt nice wearing Brad's clothes; the wind made the light cotton flutter around her legs and her waist. She was steering, standing in the back of the T-shaped cockpit behind the four-foot diameter silver wheel, while Brad moved around the decks getting the mainsail ready to hoist. The center of the wheel was attached to a white pedestal in the middle of the cockpit, on top of the pedestal there was a black compass floating in clear liquid beneath a glass dome. Sometimes Brad gave her a compass course to sail, such as "steer three fifty," or 350 degrees, almost north. Sometimes he pointed to a distant landmark and asked her to aim for that point: "head for the smokestacks."

When he was ready he said, "Okay Ranya, put her into the wind, and I'll haul her up."

Brad stood a few feet from her in the front of the cockpit, one hand on each side of the open companionway hatch which led below. She turned the wheel until Guajira's bow was facing west, directly into the wind, and Brad began hauling in on the mainsail halyard line. This white and red flecked rope led from the back of the cabin top, to the base of the mast and up inside of it, to the top of the mast and over a pulley sheave, and then back down the outside of the mast to the top corner of the mainsail. With each of Brad's two-handed pulls back on the halyard line the entire mainsail slid a yard up the slot on the back of the mast. In half a minute it was all the way to the top and flapping furiously in the wind. He wound the rope around a soup can sized silver winch, and put a handle into the top of it to ratchet in the last few inches, and stretch the sail tightly up the mast.

She privately admired his physique from her position behind him at the wheel. He had a nice strong back and broad shoulders, his muscles were visibly rippling under his t-shirt as he hauled back on the line and then winched it in.

"All right, turn to starboard. Steer to the northwest until the sail fills." Brad moved from side to side in the cockpit and used other winches to adjust the thicker white and blue lines, the main sheets, which pulled the aluminum boom at the bottom edge of the mainsail in and out. Guajira leaned over and increased speed as the triangular main sail stopped fluttering and suddenly took on a single smooth tight curve from bottom to top. The boat continued to pick up more speed under the press of the wind, and the faster they went, the more breeze Ranya felt against her face.

"Now we're going to hear the sweetest sound in the world, a sound I've never heard on Guajira!" he said, standing just in front of her and beaming, holding onto the front of the compass pedestal. They both had to bend one leg to stand upright as Guajira motor-sailed along to windward, heeled over under the force of the wind.

Ranya smiled back at him and asked, "What sound is that?"

"Just listen." He turned back toward the front of the cockpit, turned the engine key to "off," and held down the kill button. The diesel motor, which had been steadily droning in the background since they had left the boat yard, coughed and died. Its persistent clatter was suddenly gone, replaced by the smooth hiss of the fiberglass hull being driven through salt water under wind power alone.

"That's the sound, that's the sweetest music there is," he said. "Turn a little more to the north, steer about 330 degrees for now." Brad climbed up onto the high side of the cabin top and stood leaning against the slanting mast, sighting up along it, checking that the new rigging wires were still holding it straight and true under the full weight of the wind. The white mast and main sail made a stunning picture against the blue sky, this was the very first sailing mile Brad was making of what could be a life time of ocean voyages aboard Guajira.

"See that mast and sail? It's the most beautiful thing in the world to me, because it means freedom! It means crossing whole oceans, and not asking for permission, or buying tickets, or standing in lines and getting questioned and searched! It's tropical islands and warm clear water, and skin diving any time you feel like it! It's staying as long as you like and leaving when you want, it's the real freedom of choice, the choice to live where you want, just the way you want!" He paused, staring up the mast again as it swung against the sky.

"It's all of that?" asked Ranya. She wasn't sure but she thought she saw him turn and brush away a tear with the back of his hand, but maybe it was just the wind in his eyes.

"It's all of that and much more. It's days and weeks completely by yourself to think and read and write, if that's what you feel like doing. Or time to spend with only your very best friends, if that's what you feel like, getting to know them on a deeper level than you ever could anyplace else. It's moonlight across the water, and trade winds pushing giant cotton ball clouds along, and whole tribes of porpoises that stay with you for days on end, playing around your boat. It's all of that every time you hoist up your mainsail and catch the wind, because it's the same wind that'll carry you to any place you want to go."

She just stood behind the wheel, watching him, the compass, and the sail. He was elated; his long years of planning and work were coming together in these last few minutes, and she was genuinely happy for him and wanted to let him savor his triumphant moment. She kept watching her compass course, the angle of the wind, and the shape of the mainsail. She noticed that when she steered a little more away from the wind the boat gained a few tenths of a knot, according to the digital speedometer by the engine panel.

"Brad, we're making almost seven knots under the mainsail alone. How much faster will she go when you have both sails?"

"I don't know, nine I hope, maybe ten. But you don't get this kind of a breeze all the time. She should make 150 mile days in the trade winds, that's what I'm hoping for. That means crossing a thousand miles of ocean on a good week, averaging everything out."

"When's the new jib going to be ready?"

"Oh, it should have been ready weeks ago! Never, ever believe a sail maker. They'll promise anything to get your business! Anyway, he swears it'll be ready next week."

"Is that the last thing you need before you take off?"

"That's the last big thing. Are you getting tired of steering yet? You're really a natural, you know it? You have a knack for keeping the sail full."

"I'm just steering 330, like you asked me to."

"No, it's more than that. You've got a feel for it, I can tell. You must have salt water in your blood."

The STU Team's new forward operating base was located deep in rural Chesapeake County Virginia, south of Norfolk and only a few miles from the North Carolina border. Through a murky and undefined mechanism they had been given access to a small annex of the old South River Naval Auxiliary Landing Field, which had been abandoned a decade earlier during a round of base closings. The annex adjoined the primary airfield, and at some point in decades past it had been used in training Navy helicopter pilots.

Since the base closure, the landing field and the annex had been used periodically for military exercises and law enforcement training. Navy SEALs, Marine Recon, Army Special Forces, Delta and the Rangers, and certain law enforcement agencies including the FBI and the DEA had used it both as a staging area, and at other times as a target, in various training scenarios. At different times the base had pretended to be an Iraqi chemical weapons depot, a POW camp, an enemy airfield and barracks, and a Colombian FARC guerrilla cocaine factory.

The few civilians living within earshot were used to blacked-out C-130s roaring in as loud as freight locomotives for midnight landings and immediate spin-around takeoffs. They were nonplussed by off-target parachutists in camouflage uniforms dropping into their soybean fields by day or by night. They paid no mind to all types of helicopters which came and went without any discernable pattern, including many that were painted the military anti-infrared color, which to most civilians appeared to be black. (This had given rise to the much-derided "myth" of black helicopters, which of course actually did exist by the hundreds, flown by U.S. Army pilots.)

So the assorted STU vehicles coming in from several directions at different times passed without notice. The vehicles all fit into one of the two rusting and decrepit 50 yard by 50 yard helicopter hangars on the landing field annex, with plenty of room left over for their gear.

Malvone had his pilot circle the old base at 1,000 feet in order to get a look at his team's new home and the area around it. The Naval Auxiliary Landing Field was bordered on three sides by branches of the sluggish black water South River, and tidal marshland beyond that to the edges of dry farmland. A narrow canal off of one branch separated the annex to the south from the runway and most of the abandoned buildings of the landing field to the north. The two parts of the base were joined by a single one-lane vehicle bridge, which was semi-permanently barricaded by a row of refrigerator-sized concrete blocks. The entire base and its annex were surrounded by a rusty chain link perimeter fence.

Scrawny pine trees covered most of the higher ground which was interspersed through the marshland around the old Navy property, and covered most of what was not paved over on the base itself. The concrete runways and service roads and aircraft aprons were webbed with cracks from which grew weeds and bushes and even small determined trees.

The annex was located on the southern end of the base, a mile from the old control tower and the primary cluster of buildings which had supported the landing field operations. The annex had its own separate gates and service roads leading to the state roads. The base was as remote and private a place as was likely to be found only twenty miles from an east coast city as big as Norfolk Virginia.

Besides the two primary hangars, the annex contained several cinderblock workshops and offices, and some smaller metal-sided storage sheds. While he orbited the old base in a bank, Malvone spotted a couple of STU vehicles on a narrow black top state road heading in: a thirty-foot motor home and a blue conversion van. The convoy had, as planned, been arriving in staggered intervals to maintain a low profile. Finally he had the pilot set the Eurohelo down on a faded yellow-circled "H" landing spot in front of one of the large hangars. An old windsock which had once been orange swung from a rusty pole, and that was the extent of the working airport landing aids.

Blue and Gold Team leaders Tim Jaeger and Michael Shanks met him as he stepped down from the chopper. They were dressed casually in jeans and t-shirts and ball caps on the warm day. Their pistols were worn holstered high on their belts on their right sides, concealment being unnecessary on their new base.

"Tim, Mike, how'd the move go? What's the place like?"

Jaeger answered, "No problem, except it's a bitch finding your way in here right at the end. The paper road maps don't agree with our electronic maps, and neither ones match what's really here. Some real morons made those maps, let me tell you. But we're thinking that if we had a hard time finding the way in, so will anybody else."

"Was the gate open? How did that work?"

Shanks had come down first with the advance team on Friday. He said, "No, it was chained shut. Some Navy guy in civvies was waiting for us in a white van. He unlocked it and got the power turned on, showed us around, and left. We've got our own lock on it now, and that's it."

"Did he ask who you were with?" It was essential that the presence of the STU Team leave no ripples upon the local waters.

"He asked if we were SEALs."

"What did you say?"

"I gave him the old 'I'd love to tell you, but then I'd have to kill you' line. He laughed and then he took off, and that's the last we've seen of anybody from the Navy, or anyone else for that matter."

The Navy's long-haired and civilian-attired counter-terrorist SEAL team was based fifteen miles northeast of the auxiliary landing field on the Fleet Combat Training Center at Dam Neck, right on the Atlantic. This unit had been commissioned in 1980 as SEAL Team Six, and had been renamed the "Development Group" in the 1990s in a rather lame attempt to disguise its identity and its mission.

Many clandestine and covert units gave themselves generic-sounding bureaucratic names as camouflage, much as Malvone had done in naming the Special Training Unit. One of the STU's commo techs had served with the Army's Intelligence Support Activity, which was later renamed a half dozen times in an attempt to hide between Pentagon cracks. In more recent years, even such nondescript bureaucratic names had given way to entirely classified nomenclature. These classified units, when they were known of at all by outsiders, were referred to by informal tags such as "Gray Wolf" and "Lincoln Gold." When their true unit names made it into the press, their names were changed, and the very existence of the units was denied once again.

Along with the propensity for classified government units to turn chameleon, had come a certain acceptance of the necessary murkiness of the sources of their funding, a fact which Malvone had noticed and exploited in his creation of the STU. In the aftermath of 9-11 even more special-operations funding spigots opened up, and Malvone used his Capitol Hill connections to ensure that a good-sized piece of this invisible financial pipeline was directed his way. In the atmosphere of secrecy and compartmentalization prevalent after 9-11, Malvone was able to shield the total amounts and sources of his funding even from his own nominal chain of command within the ATF and the Justice Department.

And the fruit of all of his bureaucratic cunning was that today he had his own domestic special operations unit, answering virtually only to himself, operating as he had envisioned it operating, and all with the President's knowledge and complete blessing.

STU operational commander Bob Bullard met up with them as they walked into the nearest of the two large hangars. The fifty-foot high overlapping sliding panel doors had rusted into place in their tracks at each side, leaving the hangar permanently open for a hundred feet of its 150 foot width. Inside were five long trailers, lined up with their ends facing the hangar opening. They were generic white-painted government models similar to mobile homes, the plain vanilla types which were sent by FEMA to disaster areas for emergency housing and services. In recent years the sixty-foot trailers had intermittently provided temporary quarters for soldiers, spooks, SEALs and spies.

"Hey Wally, welcome to STUville," said the hatchet-faced Bob Bullard, smiling for a change. "The vehicles are all stashed in the other hangar. In here we've got two barracks trailers full of bunk beds, a classroom trailer for briefings, a kitchen and chow-hall trailer, and one trailer with bathrooms and showers. All the comforts of home."

"STUville...I like it," said Malvone. "Home away from home. And I couldn't see anything from the air, just a couple of the guys outside walking around. The hangars are perfect, it's a great setup."

"Yep, and next to the hangars we've got a couple of smaller buildings for offices, secure storage, whatever we need. Club Fed it's not, but it'll do," added Bullard.

"Well the important thing is keeping operational security, and this place looks about as secure as anyplace we could ever find. Is everybody here yet?"

"Yeah Wally, the last of 'em are just rolling in now, you must have seen the motor home from the air. It's kind of confusing; the last turns to get in here don't match the map. But what the hell, even that's good for opsec." As Bullard spoke the thirty foot Winnebago which contained the bulk of the STU's computer and communications capability rolled around the front of the other hangar to the west and parked just outside of it, followed by the blue van which disappeared inside the hangar.

"All right then," said Malvone, "muster the troops in the briefing trailer in ten minutes. Operators and support pukes. Everybody. We've already got a short-fuse real-world mission, and that's no bullshit."

Just after four PM, when the sun was still high enough to make the day a hot one, they anchored Guajira in twenty feet of water inside the mouth of the Nansemond River.

All afternoon Ranya had been learning a new vocabulary in the language of sailing. She learned that there were no ropes aboard Guajira, only lines, and each line had a precise name to match its location and function. There were sheets and halyards, vangs and preventers, outhauls and downhauls and a dozen more. She learned about cam-cleats and jammers, traveler tracks and Harken cars and two speed Lewmar winches.

They practiced tacking and gibing and running and reaching and beating to windward. She learned what the numbered red and green buoys signified, she learned about cans and nuns and channel markers. Very importantly, she learned that while all of the water of the Chesapeake Bay looked the same greenish brown from shore to shore, only certain parts of it were deep enough for Guajira's seven foot deep keel. All afternoon they sailed back and forth across Hampton Roads and the lower bay, using Guajira's mainsail alone. The area forward of the mast would remain bare until Brad's sail maker finished his new genoa jib.

She was thankful for this nautical education, to occupy her mind. It gave her a reason to stop her from constantly scanning the sky for helicopters (of which there were many in this Navy town) and to prevent her from being tormented by each approaching Coast Guard cutter and patrol boat. They were sailing within a few miles of the largest naval base on the entire planet, and security was thick and omnipresent.

Any of the helicopters and patrol boats that she saw could even at that moment be receiving the word, that the prime suspect in the Sanderson assassination was named Ranya Bardiwell, and that she had been seen leaving Portsmouth on a sailboat named Guajira. She didn't think that she had made a mistake; she didn't think that she had left any clues or forensic evidence behind. But she also knew that she could very well have inadvertently done so, starting with her computer searches in the ODU library, or perhaps yesterday with her pretext phone call to Sanderson's office in Richmond.

So she was content to fill her mind with the world of sailing and navigation. All day, in the boatyard and while sailing, they had listened only to music CDs. Ranya had not heard a single news bulletin since Friday evening. She didn't underestimate the police or the FBI, and she could only hope that even now they were not faxing around blown-up college yearbook pictures of her face. But despite her fears, she was glad she'd done it, proud that she'd tracked him down despite his security, found the smarmy self-righteous bastard, and killed him. She had fears for herself, but no regrets for what she had done.

When they decided they had had enough of sailing, they headed for a spot which Brad had previously marked on his chart as an ideal temporary anchorage. He had seen it Monday while motoring down the Nansemond to the James River, on his way to the boatyard. The mouth of the Nansemond was a mile wide where they dropped the hook; it was open only to the northeast with the point of Newport News six miles away on the distant horizon. The other three sides of the little bay were well-protected by bluffs, with stately mansions scattered along their green fields and oak studded crests. The wind from the west meant that the anchorage area was calm and sheltered, and Guajira rode easily at anchor without rolling or pitching.

Infrequently a ski boat or wave runner passed within a few hundred yards of them, but by and large they possessed their own broad expanse of water, under a nearly cloudless sky on that Indian summer Saturday afternoon. The wind had died under the cover of the surrounding slopes, and Brad had stripped down to a pair of blue swim trunks. They were a little tight on him, Ranya thought, not that she was disappointed... He had wide shoulders and a nice back, which narrowed where it disappeared beneath his blue shorts, and like her own, his skin was not marred or disfigured by so much as a single tattoo.

She sat across from him on the other side of the cockpit, watching him while he dug under the lifted-up starboard cockpit seat into the locker below. Finally he pulled out a net bag with a mask and snorkel and fins in it, and dropped the hinged cockpit seat back down. The snorkel was not attached to the mask, and he left it in the yellow mesh bag.

"I need to go down and see how the anchor's set. I've never used this kind before. It's called a Delta, and it's supposed to be good for all kinds of bottoms. Anchors might not seem very exciting, but when the wind's howling at midnight a good anchor is worth its weight in gold, and a bad anchor can get you killed, or lose you your boat." He was adjusting the clear silicone strap on the mask while he spoke. "So I really want to see how this one sets. I need to know how well it works on all kinds of bottoms; it should be soft mud here. Are you coming in? The water's nice and warm."

Ranya was still wearing the pastel green hospital scrubs that he'd lent her, with the pant legs rolled up. "Sure I'd love to, if you don't mind me looking like Old Mother Hubbard going for a swim in 1905." They were now sitting across from each other on opposite cushioned cockpit benches, their toes and knees just occasionally brushing, their eyes and smiles sparkling at one another. The backs of the cockpit seats rose up almost to their shoulder heights, and the sheet handling winches that were bolted on top lent them even more privacy from any passing boats.

Earlier Brad had put in a mix of beach and summer music CDs, and following Jimmy Buffet, the Beach Boys were singing about an island off the Florida Keys, a place called Kokomo, where you wanted to go to get away from it all. Ranya was sipping a rum and coke from a glass tumbler, looking into Brad's blue eyes, imagining that they were anchored off of one of the islands spoken of in the song: Aruba, Jamaica, Bermuda, the Bahamas... It was a dream that Brad was going to live.

"You can go swimming in the scrubs if you want, but I think I might have something a little better in the bathing suit department." Brad got up and disappeared below, and in a few moments he returned holding a small clear plastic bag containing a bit of folded red fabric, which he handed to Ranya.

"Oh, and what have we here, Mr. Fallon?" She tore open the sealed bag. "Your basic one-size-fits-all spandex bikini, that you just happened to have on board? Well aren't you full of surprises! You're just like a Boy Scout aren't you, always prepared?" She was trying to sound like she was scolding him, as if she somehow disapproved of his forethought in purchasing a woman's swim suit, but she was laughing too hard. "And just how many bikinis DO you have on board? Well I guess I should be honored to be the lucky girl to try it on first. Hmm...50% off clearance sale, good job Brad, there's hope for you yet! So was this going to be a present for some lucky island girl?" Ranya held the red triangle-top up over the green scrubs, teasing him.

Brad was blushing and grinning at the same time. "You never know who might decide to come sailing without bringing along a bathing suit... like today. It's sort of like having a new toothbrush on board for an unexpected guest."

"And do you have a new toothbrush on board too? For an unexpected guest?"

"Of course..."

She stood up and 'accidentally' brushed the shimmering red fabric across Brad's face as she slid past him and went below. She was a little surprised, but glad at the same time, that he'd had the new suit. She wondered if he had more of them in different styles and sizes and colors, or only this one which seemed to be in her size, meaning that she was the size of girl he was hoping to meet in the islands? She wasn't exactly huge in the boob department, rather nice she thought though, somewhere between a B and a C cup, depending on the bra.

Plenty of young men had certainly been interested in them since she had developed a figure at about age fifteen. She could never quite understand why, but she knew that she had been forced to remove the octopus-like hands of enough boys from her breasts on dates over the last few years to know there must be something magical about them. She certainly was aware that most guys developed some sort of spontaneous eye spasm when talking to her; their eyes tended to acquire an involuntary downward twitch. Men were such pigs, but she still loved them, crude behavior, rough edges and all. She understood that it was simply the way that they had been designed by God and nature.

She changed in the small second bedroom behind the galley, located half under the cockpit on the port side of the boat. It was a strangely shaped room, with the bottom of the cockpit dropping into it over the middle of the oddly truncated bed.

The green hospital scrubs and her underwear were quickly off and she dropped them on the bed, then she immediately stepped into the stretchy red bottom and pulled it up. It was going to be so embarrassing if her butt was too big for it! But it fit nicely; it was high cut on the sides, and had almost full coverage in back. Thank God he hadn't given her a thong! She just wouldn't have worn it. Not that she was totally against thongs, but for what it would have said about her, borrowing a thong! And at least I still have my summer tan, she thought.

The simple wireless triangle top was easier, she tied it together and spun it around, then tied the strings up behind her neck, and she was glad to see that she filled it out more than adequately. She had been briefly terrified that he might have inadvertently given her some gargantuan DD sized top. She would not have been able to show herself on deck if there had been droopy folds of excess fabric, which her breasts were too tiny to fill out! But she did fill the two soft red triangles, and quite nicely, as she admired herself from different angles, in the small mirror in the micro-sized toilet compartment next to the bed.

Ranya's big department store shopping bag, with the Tennyson pistol, her .45 and her gray track suit was wedged in the back corner of the bed where she had put it before they left the boatyard. She took out her fanny pack, found her brush, pulled the rubber band out from around her pony tail and quickly brushed out her shoulder length brown hair. She checked her face closely in the mirror, and retrieved the tube of lip gloss from her bag. She applied it looking in the mirror again, and rolled her lips together, satisfied with the subtle improvement. She considered wrapping a towel modestly around her hips, but discarded the idea, and at last she took a deep breath, squared her shoulders and climbed up the teak com-panionway ladder and back into the sun-drenched cockpit.

Ranya tried to be casual and blasé , she was ready to feel Brad's eyes devouring her, but he played it cool and tried not to look below her neck, at least not too obviously…

He said, "I don't have another mask, but I've got some swim goggles, if you want to try them. I thought you might like to see what Guajira looks like underneath."

"Sure, I'll use your goggles, I'm pretty used to them. I usually swim laps a few times a week at school to stay in shape. You know, the lifeguard thing."

"Let me get some towels and fill the sun shower before we go in."

"What's a sun shower?"

"This thing." While Ranya was below Brad had pulled a square vinyl bag with a spray nozzle on the end of a hose from the cockpit locker. "It's clear on one side and black on the other, so the sun heats it up pretty fast. You use it to rinse the salt water off." Brad went below and filled it with a few gallons of water from the galley sink, and then he laid it in the sun on the outside of the cockpit between the winches and the toe rail along the edge of the deck. Ranya appreciated that he had waited until she had changed and come back up to the cockpit, before he went below to the galley. He wasn't taking liberties; he was a gentleman…so far. She ad-justed the strap on the goggles and pushed the two black-tinted lens caps tightly down over her eyes.

"I'll race you," she said.

"What?"

"I'll race you to the anchor." She gestured to the digital depth display inset above the engine instrument panel, to the right of the companionway hatch. "We're in twenty feet of water. You put out about seventy feet of rope and thirty feet of chain, that's what you said, and I'll race you to the anchor." With that she sprang out of the cockpit past him to the starboard side of the Guajira's deck, and dived over the lifelines and into the water. As soon as she surfaced she began a fast free-style stroke forward along the side of the boat.

Brad grabbed his mask and ran up the side deck all the way to Guajira's bow, scrambled onto the stainless steel bow pulpit which wrapped around in front of the forestay, and dived far out ahead into the water. When he surfaced he pulled on his mask, he was already a little ahead of Ranya after his running forty-foot short cut. The three-quarter-inch diameter white nylon anchor line leading off of Guajira's bow disappeared into the water at an angle, as Ranya swam past him he took a few deep breaths and surface dived, grabbing the rope and pulling himself along it hand over hand.

On the surface Ranya kept on going with her fast free-style, she lost sight of the white rope halfway out to the anchor when it disappeared into the muddy bottom, but she could see the path it cut by the disturbed silty water above it. She thought that she was comfortably ahead of Brad, but then she saw him below her, pulling himself out along the rope much faster than she could swim on the surface! No fair!

He's cheating again, she thought. She took a deep breath and surface-dived down after him, her ears squeezing with pressure as she passed ten feet, so she did a quick nose blow to equalize pressure. He was already slightly ahead of her, so she grabbed the only "handle" she could find, the back of his blue swim trunks, and yanked them hard, pulling him in surprise off of the anchor line lying along the muddy bottom.

He spun around, shocked to see her right behind him, and while he was turned away from the rope she kicked past him, pushing his shoulder backward with her foot. She reached for where the anchor line was shackled to the chain, grabbed it and pulled herself through water and silt hand-over-hand the last thirty feet to the anchor, with Brad in hot pursuit. He tried to grasp her by her ankle, but she easily wrenched her foot free.

She touched the gray anchor first; it was buried like a plow in the mud except for the tops of its flukes. She held on until he touched it a second later, they were looking at one another through swirling clouds of silt. The water was glittering all around them as the sunlight pierced down into the depths and turned the particles to radiant gold dust.

They broke the surface together, gasping in lung-fulls of air, their legs kicking to hold them up, touching, their bodies close. Brad pulled his mask back up onto his forehead and said, "That was cheating, no fair pulling down bathing suits!"

"Oh, you're a sore loser, are you? You cheated first, running up and diving off the bow."

Brad lunged for Ranya's hips and grabbed the sides of her bikini bottom, Ranya tried to pull away his wrists, but they were too thick and slippery in the water, so she reached across to tickle his sides instead. But he didn't yank her swimsuit down, and the next thing Ranya knew their arms were around each other, they were laughing like children, grinning toothy smiles at one another, their wet noses touching, knees and legs and feet treading water and bumping together clumsily. Then they were kissing, submerging when they stopped treading water in their embrace, kicking their way back up, and all the while laughing, and kissing.

Wordlessly they found a slow rhythm of gently kicking with their legs that kept them at equilibrium, with just their chins above the water. They stopped laughing altogether as they kissed more deeply.

"Let's go back to the boat," she suggested, softly.

They swam back together, touching, and at Guajira's stern Brad pulled a rope handle and the boat's hinged swim ladder flipped down into the water. He let her go up first, following closely behind her, the water streaming off her smooth skin in the warm sunshine as she climbed aboard and pulled off her goggles.

She sat back down on the cushioned cockpit seat, and Brad sat across from her, their knees and toes touching. They were still catching their breaths from their race, their eyes and noses and lips only bare inches apart. Brad's eyes were so blue, it was like looking through to the sky. "You're a pretty good kisser…" she said, brushing her nose over his.

"You're not so bad yourself."

"What do you think we should…do about it?" she asked, leaning even closer to him, her hands on the blue seat cushion beside her hips, her bare knees demurely together, her face tilted upward toward his. A scarcely known feeling of animal passion was sweeping through her with waves of electric shivers. The only other times she had felt anything approaching this wild abandon she had been consciously forcing herself to hold back from the edge. Today she felt like she was running for the abyss with something like desperation. This time she was not going to stop.

Brad placed his hands gently on each side of her face, then slid his fingers behind her head and neck under her wet hair and drew her lips to his. Ranya's eyes fluttered closed as her lips parted and met his, then his tongue found hers and this time they didn't have to tread water, this time they didn't need to come up for air.

She felt something entirely new taking over her will, she felt like a helpless but willing witness as this strange new Ranya pushed Brad onto his back on the long blue cockpit cushion, kissing his face and his neck, her knees astride him, grinding herself frantically against his sudden hardness, then he was pulling aside her red bikini top and kissing her right…there…

It never hurt her, not for even one second, it was pure sweet pleasure for Ranya from his first exquisite invasion to their all-too-swift first climax. She fell asleep in the sunshine, rising and falling on his chest, her face buried in his neck, breathing him in, capturing his scent forever.

The sun was much lower in the sky above the western bluffs when they finally disentangled. Brad hung the sun shower from the mainsail boom above the cockpit, and gently washed every inch of her salty-tasting tan skin and hair with coconut-scented shampoo, then he rinsed her with the warm fresh water, and she blissfully returned the favor.

After they dried each other off with the sun-baked towels, Brad led her more than willingly by her hand down below and forward to his triangle-shaped V-berth in the bow. He made love to her again, his face above hers this time, their eyes wide open, drinking in each trembling reaction, each breath interrupted by a new stab of pleasure.

Within the confines of his small forward compartment, with its oddly slanted hull-side walls and its low ceiling, Ranya discovered that she could place her feet and legs in countless positions. But when he began to move steadily and increasingly deeply, she could only clutch her arms and legs around his back and hold on for dear life as waves of ecstasy rolled and crashed through her again and again.

When they finished his face lay over her shoulder, his lips gently kissing her neck. She was looking up through the open foredeck hatch at wisps of high stratus clouds, which were painted in stripes across a sky which had never been so blue, because now it was the color of Brad's eyes.

A while later she awakened, and a comforter was pulled over them. She was snuggled against his side with her leg over his, and her warm cheek pressed against his beating heart. Turning her head slightly, she could see the three bright stars of Orion's belt and a million others, through the open deck hatch above them. The constellation was slowly wheeling first clockwise, and then back, as Guajira swung on its anchor.

So much had happened in one day. She wondered how it came to be that she had killed a man, and at long last she had made love to a man, and both on exactly the same day, and that she had killed first. And both inconceivable events had happened precisely one week to the day after the one other man that she had loved had been killed. Killed by agents of the man who she had then killed in return. How unlikely was that? How often do things like that happen?

Three stars on Orion's belt: one for her father, one for Sanderson, one for Brad. Then falling in love with the man you met on the day you found your father...that terrible Saturday. And making love for the very first time with him, on the same day that you took another man's life.

How can this not be fate? How could there not be some greater, hidden purpose being served? Or were the gods merely toying with her idly, for their amusement?

She thought of her father's gifts, and of his hidden arms cache. The disassembled Tennyson Champion sniper pistol was still wrapped in her gray track suit and hidden back in the aft cabin. The Tennyson was now accompanied by her loaded .45 pistol, another gift from her father. A graduation gift...if he only knew. Or did he know? Could he know? Even after his death her father was playing a role in this drama, handing her the tools she needed to find justice.

She considered how easily she could slip out from Brad's bed and give the Tennyson sniper pistol the deep-blue goodbye. She could just throw the pieces far out over the side, where they would drop through the water and sink into the soft river mud and disappear forever. She could be done with it, and put Sanderson's murder safely behind her. After a minute's deliberation she dismissed the idea, because she knew she was not yet finished with her mission.

Ranya wished that she could discuss all of her dark secrets with Brad, but she knew she could never tell him what she had done, at dawn across the water from the golf course. Telling him would draw him in as a conspirator, and it was already bad enough that she had left the murder scene and come to his boat with the killing weapon. She wondered what keeping the secret bottled inside of her would do to her soul, or if there even was such an ethereal entity within her. She had committed the very worst of all the sins, and she could never erase that black stain.

Looking up at the stars turning in the sky above the open deck hatch she thought, I'm sorry Mother; I didn't wait until I was married...

But coming after the mortal sin of murder, that broken vow seemed much less important now.

She had not even told Brad that she was a virgin, and she had not told him that she was not on birth control, which must have been Brad's reasonable assumption about a 21 year old college girl... Well neither of them had been asking any questions earlier in the cockpit... And anyway, she had practically assaulted him...so whatever happened, it was her fault.

Staring up at the three bright stars of Orion's belt, one star for each man, Ranya pondered the crushing realization that in one week she had become an orphan, a murderess, and a tramp.

26

Fifteen year old Danny Edmonds was sitting at his desk hunched over his computer keyboard typing furiously when his father walked into his bedroom. "Danny, do you know what time it is?"

"Uh, hi Dad, let's see... zero one hundred hours."

"Affirmative. Time for lights out son."

"But Dad, it's Saturday night!"

"So what's the battle tonight?"

"Stalingrad."

"Which side are you?"

"I'm Russian this time."

"So what time zone is Field Marshall Von Paulus in? Maybe it's not one AM in his command bunker."

"Actually, his bio says he's an Army major at Fort Campbell, so it would be midnight his time. But I'm still kicking his butt clear back to the Ukraine."

"An Army major huh? Well, one more hour then, until two AM, and that's it. Tell the Field Marshal that General Zhukov's father ordered him to go to bed by then."

"Oh Dad, give me a break, he doesn't know I'm a kid." Danny's voice cracked, halfway between boyhood and manliness.

"So you're whipping an active duty Army major in military tactics?"

"Strategy Dad, strategy. It's corps level warfare."

"Right. Pardon me. And you still want to enlist in the Marines in three years?"

"Not three years Dad, two years."

"You know I won't sign for you at seventeen, we've been through this... Three years and you'll be eighteen, and free to make your own mistakes."

"Dad, I'll still become an officer eventually, but a mustang officer! The greatest Marine officers are mustangs, prior enlisted."

It was an ongoing battle between them. Burgess Edmonds could get Danny an appointment to Annapolis or West Point with two or three phone calls, but at fifteen Danny was determined to enlist in the Marines, "ASAP" as he put it, and get into the action as a "mud Marine" in the ongoing war.

Danny's room told the story. Where other fifteen year old boys had posters on their walls depicting rock groups and basketball stars, Danny seemingly had every Marine Corps recruiting poster ever made. He wore tan suede USMC combat boots to school, he had a camouflage poncho liner for a bed spread, and sitting at his desk he was wearing bright red USMC sweats, with the gold "eagle, globe and anchor" on the front.

Danny was already fifteen, and Burgess had no complaints about him, not really. He was carrying a 3.7 GPA at Saint Paul's while lettering in wrestling and lacrosse, and he could have his choice of colleges. He just hoped that his son would come around and see the benefits of accepting an appointment to a service academy after high school, instead of enlisting straight away in the Marines.

Danny was afraid that the war would be over before he could get into it if he waited for four more years after he finished high school to join the military. Burgess Edmonds did not share his son's belief that the war would be over any time soon, and after what he had been through in Viet Nam, he had no wish for his son to experience combat. Still, he knew better than to push the issue with the headstrong and determined fifteen year old. Danny and 21 year old Valerie were his second family, and this time he was not going to blow it like he had the first time around. Maybe he'd mellowed, or maybe he'd just learned from bitter experience not to push them too hard.

"Okay Danny, whenever and however you do get your commission, you'll be the greatest officer the Marines ever had. Two AM, all right bud?"

"All right Dad."

Burgess Edmonds turned to the hallway before Danny could see the tears welling up in his eyes. Then he slipped down the hall to Valerie's room, Valerie who was spending the weekend down from college, his little girl Valerie who had so quickly grown up to become a woman. Her door was slightly ajar, so he looked in and watched her sleeping under her quilted comforter, her golden hair spilling across her face and pillow. Where had his little girl gone, the little girl he had tucked in among teddy bears what seemed like only last week?

He quietly went back downstairs. His wife Glennis, his second wife, was already long asleep in their bedroom, at the other end of the second floor hallway from the kids' rooms.

George Hammet was in the shotgun seat of the lead vehicle in the Special Training Unit raiding convoy, a black Chevy Suburban SUV with heavily tinted windows. It was parked on the shoulder of a dead-end county service road under a covering of oak trees a mile from the Edmondses' driveway. Next to him in the driver's seat was the Blue Team leader Tim Jaeger. Behind them in the back of the truck six more STU Team members were sitting on the carpeted cargo deck. Both the middle and rear bench seats had been removed for the operation to give them more room and allow faster exiting. Nearly all of them had prior service overseas with military specops units, and the stripped-out Suburban was just a "low flying helo" taking them to their latest battle zone, as far as they were concerned. They were all wearing black tactical gear, with black kevlar helmets, black balaclava face masks, black gloves, black boots, and even black Heckler and Koch MP-5 sub-machineguns.

Three more black Suburbans were lined up behind them. Tonight the STU Blue Team was the lead element and was taking down the house, and the Gold Team was providing the snipers, the recon team, and the perimeter security. STU Team on-site commander Bob Bullard, in the trailing Suburban, was not masked or helmeted and was remaining as the "blocker" at the bottom of the driveway. He would badge any local law enforcement which might arrive unexpectedly with his fake FBI credentials. Nothing about the STU Team tonight would connect them with ATF.

They all sat silent as death, watching the subdued lighting of the various screens in the front between the leaders, straining to hear their radio earphones which were turned down to a barely audible hiss. The snipers and the recon team had gone out hours before the raiding party had arrived at the forward staging area, dropped off by the STU's blue Dodge conversion van and the phony Virginia Power van, which was now hidden nearby serving as a commo relay and electronic support unit. Their bogus power company van was already monitoring the house's telephones and electrical usage, and would cut off the Edmondses' ADT alarm system connection just before the raid.

Cutting the complete electrical power to an up-scale home in advance of a raid came with a risk, because such homes typically had emergency backup lights and alarms which would activate and alert the residents if the power was cut. In this case the STU Team decided to leave the electrical power on, and rely on their speed to get themselves in before the Edmonds could react. Once inside, they would then be able to use the house lights to assist them in safely clearing it.

Unknown to the sleeping family, three of their cell phones had been covertly switched on, providing the STU with interior audio listening devices paid for and put in position by the Edmonds themselves. To the STU Team members, what civilians didn't know about their own cell phones was simply mind boggling.

The two man sniper teams and the recon team carried advanced 3rd generation night vision rifle scopes, thermal imagers, electronic "big ears," and electronic field detectors. If the Edmonds had infrared or microwave or other alarm systems on their property, then recon team Romeo would find and neutralize or bypass them before the raiding convoy arrived. The sniper teams with their night scopes and thermal imagers were in position to cover the flanks of the Edmondses' 100 acre property, as well as the rear of the house towards the bluffs and the river.

The radio crackled in Hammet's ear; all 24 STU Team operators heard the report at the same time. "Blue Leader, Romeo. All clear. Condition status: zebra zebra, hush puppy times two."

"Zebra zebra" was a STU brevity code slang for "z's," meaning a sleeping house. The ATF and other federal law enforcement special response teams preferred to raid in the early hours when people were most deeply asleep. This was safest for everyone, providing the maximum shock for their "speed, surprise, and violence of action." This caused people to quit before they even had the first idea of resisting.

"Hush puppy times two" meant that the recon team had taken care of the Edmondses' two watch dogs, with sound-suppressed weapons.

Blue Team Leader Jaeger then checked the sniper teams, code named "Daniel Boone" and "Davy Crockett."

"Delta Bravo, Blue leader: sitrep."

"Blue Leader, Delta Bravo ready."

"Blue Leader, Delta Charlie ready."

"Blue Two ready?"

"Ready" came from the Suburban behind Hammet and Jaeger. Gold Leader and Gold Two reported in immediately after.

Blue Leader Tim Jaeger flipped his helmet-mounted night vision goggles down over his eyes. All four vehicles' engines were switched on. Jaeger punched the gas pedal and all four blacked-out vehicles ran up the service road to the county road in tight formation, fast but silent with their custom mufflers. They'd all studied aerial photos of the Edmondses' estate taken earlier that day from Malvone's borrowed helicopter. They knew exactly where the snipers and the recon team were hidden, they knew exactly where to park and the order in which they would jump out, they knew the locations of the doors and windows and who was assigned to each.

It was 2:45 am, and the STU Team was conducting its first "real world" operation. They were primed, cocked, and coursing with adrenaline and testosterone. Payback for the Stadium Massacre, and the Reston Virginia ambush of the FBI team, and the assassination of Senator Randolph and Attorney General Sanderson was starting in one minute. They had all been briefed that Burgess Edmonds was the leader and financial kingpin of a shadowy right wing terrorist organization loosely hidden behind the cover of a hunting club in southeastern Virginia, an organization which was primarily responsible for the past weeks' acts of domestic terrorism. And they all believed it: all except for George Hammet in the lead Suburban, and Wally Malvone, the founder of the Special Training Unit, orbiting high above in the helicopter.

Burgess Edmonds was still awake, down in his windowless basement "gun room." He sat at his workbench, wearing magnifying eyeglasses while using a tiny gunsmith's screwdriver to carefully remove a $4,000 US Optics 8X44 scope from one of Joe Bardiwell's custom hunting rifles, a 7mm Ultra Mag built up from a Winchester Model 70. There were already a half dozen long black scopes lined up neatly on the table. It broke his heart; every rifle had been meticulously crafted and matched with the best possible scope for each caliber and use. Looking around his gun room, he could remember when and how and with which rifle he had taken each of the mounted trophies on his walls, back when he was interested in collecting game trophies. But by far his greatest trophy, his crowning achievement, had been his second wife Glennis, the beautiful blond South African whom he had found and married when she was only 23...

Each rifle and scope combination was a work of art worth nearly ten thousand dollars, and sometimes more. It was a crying shame, but it was all over; it was the end of an era. As he looked around at his mounted Eland and Elk and Cape Buffalo and the many others, Edmonds reflected that the riflemen would be missed most of all in Africa: entire villages, whole regions, depended on the hard currency brought in by the safari trade. He'd personally dropped hundreds of thousands of dollars into African hands over the past 25 years. It was a shame, but he knew that nothing lasts forever... Sure, there'd be some big game hunting in America over iron sights, and some Americans would go over to Africa on safari to hunt with rented scoped rifles, but not very many. It was just not as appealing as building up your own scoped hunting rifles and hand loaded cartridges; that was half of the fun of the sport. Maybe more than half.

Anyway, none of his serious hunting rifles had iron sights mounted on them, and with his 59 year old eyes, Burgess Edmonds wasn't going to put them on now. He reflected once again how Joe Bardiwell, his gunsmith, his custom gun maker and his friend had been killed just last week, and buried only days before. Truly it was the end of an era, in so many ways.

Suddenly the red warning light flashed on the wall over the door leading to the steps, and the alarm buzzed in rapid-fire succession an awful lot of times! Each buzz was a pair of tires crossing a pressure pad buried an inch under his driveway down by the county road. It was old fashioned, but 100% reliable, and not subject to outages or false alarms like the fancy new infrared and ultrasonic stuff.

Damn! This was at least three or four cars, really moving fast up his driveway! His brain scrambled to make sense of it. Why weren't his two Dobies Pluto and Blackie barking? They should be going crazy! Then in a clear flash of insight he guessed: it was the BATF. It was after midnight Saturday, and he still had scopes on some of his rifles! Damn the ATF to hell, they'd killed Vicki Weaver and her boy over a "sawed-off shotgun" that was one-half inch shorter than legal, and now here they were, just a few hours after midnight, the night the new scope law went into effect!

Edmonds didn't want them smashing down his front door: he'd meet them and open it instead. He was reasonably sure the new sniper rifle law, or "Presidential Decree" or whatever it was, only covered the transportation of scoped rifles, and not their private possession on your own property, at least not yet.

Thank God he'd gotten rid of his semi-automatic rifles last week before the ban on them went into effect! Semi-autos were never his thing, ultra accurate bolt-actions were, but he had still collected two AR-10s and a National Match M1A over the years, and an FAL he'd picked up as a souvenir in Zimbabwe, back when it was still Rhodesia. But he'd gotten rid of them all in time before the ban went into effect last Tuesday, even Danny's semi-auto .30 caliber M1 carbine and his little Ruger 10-22. He wasn't going to risk losing everything he'd built over 40 years to hold onto an illegal semi-auto rifle, no sir! He didn't need that headache, and that wasn't his style of shooting anyway.

He hurried up the cellar steps to meet them at the front door. He felt fairly certain he could reason with them, show them around his gun room, and convince them he had no semi-auto rifles. Anyway, here he was at this very hour, this minute, taking off all of his scopes, in full compliance with the new emergency Presidential Decree. They'd listen to him, they'd understand! At least, he sure hoped they'd understand...

Danny was lying awake in bed, still reviewing his recent victory at Stalingrad in his mind and planning the rest of his life when the motion-triggered halogen lights around the front of the house flashed on at the same time he heard vehicles skidding to a stop out front on the gravel. How could cars get up the long drive without Blackie and Pluto giving chase and warning them with their barking? He shot up from bed and looked out his bedroom window: three long black SUVs were parked on their circle in a line, and shadowy black figures were running silently toward the house!

They disappeared under the roof of the front porch, and then Danny heard a crashing splintering boom and his Dad hollered. Damn it was all so fast! He jerked open his closet and grabbed his Marlin .22 lever action rifle. He knew it had 12 of the tiny rimfire bullets loaded into its tubular magazine under the barrel. Shit! He wished he'd still had his old

M1 carbine with its fifteen-round magazines, or even his Ruger 10-22, but Dad had taken them away last week!

No time to think, no time to plan, he only knew that he had to protect his parents and his sister, so he headed out the door into the dark hall in time to see his mother in the dim light, running across the landing and down the steps, her little chrome-plated .38 revolver gleaming in her hand, her long white nightgown flowing behind her.

Then his father was yelling and men were cursing and screaming, there was an earsplitting boom like a shotgun and flashes of light like an arc-welder from downstairs, sounds like a jackhammer and his mother screamed just one time. What should I do? What should I do? What's happening down there he thought, his mind reeling, suddenly dizzy on his feet.

Then brilliant beams of light were coming up the stairs, a lot of them, super bright! He had to protect Valerie. In the hall was a heavy dresser piled high with folded laundry on top. Danny jumped behind it crouching low, his rifle barrel laid across a stack of clothes, hidden. Something thumped against the wall and a man yelled "flash!" and Danny buried his face in the clothes and covered his ears with his hands as a stun grenade detonated down the hall. A man yelled "clear!" and Danny took up his position again, he could hear them, feel them, and with his left hand he reached for the hall light switch, God had placed it right in his reach, he thought momentarily, and he flicked it on.

There was a huddle of men in black on the landing at the top of the stairs, holding submachine guns with the super bright lights under their barrels. Two were facing his way down the hall; they were taken by surprise by the chandelier suddenly turning on right above them. Danny put the Marlin's white bead front sight under the closest man's black helmet and ski goggles and squeezed the trigger, threw the lever and fired again. The man's hands flew to his throat but his black machine gun with the light stayed hooked on his chest. Danny fired again each time he thought he saw a face, the men wore black helmets and masks and goggles and he knew they wore bulletproof vests. The goggles and black masks under the helmet visors were all he could see of their faces.

The man clutching his throat was grabbed by the next man from behind and dragged away backwards on his heels. The two men who had been facing the other way towards his parents' rooms spun around on either side of them and they both let loose firing full auto bursts, their bullets tearing into the walls around him, but Danny remained unseen and unhit behind the dresser.

Both shooters went empty at the same time, and were switching to full magazines which were clipped parallel to the empties. Danny aimed and fired again when their bright lights turned aside, he couldn't tell if he had made a hit or not, but then he pulled the trigger and dropped the hammer on an empty chamber. At the same time one of the men in black fired another burst, splintering the dresser to kindling and stitching Danny Edmonds across his chest.

The boy who dreamed of becoming a United Stated Marine fell backwards, his head bouncing off the hardwood floor. The Marlin .22 rifle came to a rest on the floor next to him with his right hand still clutched around its stock. Danny Edmonds blinked and looked up through the ceiling to the starry sky, and saw his beautiful mother reaching down for him with warmly inviting hands, her white nightgown and long blond hair flowing in the wind.

George Hammet sprinted up the staircase after the shooting erupted in time to see the Edmonds kid go down. The wounded Blue Team member was already being dragged away, his blood pouring down the wooden steps. Hammet advanced down the hall with his HK at the ready-shoulder position next to the STU man who had shot the boy, and he kicked the rifle away from the kid's hand. Good looking boy, wearing a red sweat suit and staring at the ceiling with flat dead eyes.

More STU operators stormed up to the second floor and they began the ritual of clearing each room: a flash-bang grenade followed by a two man buttonhook inside, quartering the rooms with their barrel-mounted Sure-Flash lights, shouting "clear left!" and "clear right!" Then they switched on the room lights and checked under the beds and in the closets for anyone else who might be hiding.

Hammet helped to clear a girl's room; the bed was unmade and recently slept in. He yanked open the closet door with his black-gloved left hand, his right hand still controlling his submachine gun. He swept away a rack of hanging clothes and found a blond girl with her eyes tightly shut and her arms crossed in front of her who was sliding down the far corner to the floor, crying and choking out over and over "Hail Mary, Hail Mary, Hail Mary…"

The STU operators carried hard rubber wedges in their tactical vests for securing doors behind themselves. Hammet pushed shut the closet door, grabbed a wedge with his left hand and shoved it into the crack of the door frame at shoulder height and hammered it in with the butt of his MP-5. He dropped a second wedge on the floor and kicked it under the door with the steel-reinforced toe of his black SWAT boot. The girl was still whimpering "Hail Mary" when he left, and the second floor was cleared.

Downstairs all the house lights were now turned on. A STU Team man was leaving the house with a duffel bag containing some of

Edmonds's rifles and scopes, but they weren't being collected for trial evidence this time, because there was not going to be a trial, that was not the STU Team's mandate. The "sniper rifles" were being collected by the STU Team for future mischief and dirty tricks in actions which would then be blamed on Edmonds's so-called clandestine militia organization. Hammet knew that the same man carrying out Edmonds's rifles had been tasked with taking in and leaving a variety of fully automatic weapons, .50 caliber ammunition, 40mm grenades and even a few mortar rounds to be "discovered" later. These would "conclusively prove" that Edmonds's organization was tied directly to right wing militia groups in several Western states, with ready access to prohibited military weapons and explosives. This was another classic STU Team black operation, another of Wally Malvone's most deviously inventive ideas.

Hammet left the house to return to his Suburban. Malvone's helicopter, showing no lights, had landed on the front lawn a hundred yards away. Burgess Edmonds was being dragged like a side of beef across the grass towards it by two men. A heavy canvas sea bag had been pulled over his head and torso and was cinched tightly around his knees. The two black-uniformed STU Team members were pulling him by the sea bag's carrying straps, his stocking feet dragging across the lawn. When they reached the open side of the chopper they both picked the human bundle up and heaved it inside and the door slid closed. The blades spun up their RPMs as the unseen pilot pulled pitch, sending out a sudden rush of wind, and the chopper lifted from the ground. Then it dipped its nose, and took off over the cliffs and dropped from sight, disappearing down low across the mouth of the Nansemond River, leaving silence behind.

Hammet climbed back into the passenger seat of the lead SUV and stripped off his helmet and black balaclava face mask. Jaeger climbed in beside him and began to check his troops on the tactical net.

"Blue Two loaded up?"

"Roger that."

"Gold Leader?"

"Ready to roll."

"Gold Two?"

"That's affirmative."

"Gold Two, you got the dogs?"

"Roger that."

"Deltas and Romeo in?" The snipers and recon team checked in, they were departing in Gold Two with Bob Bullard.

"Silver Team?"

"We're ready." Tonight the "Silver Team" was two Gold Team men driving Burgess Edmonds's silver Mercedes. Malvone already had a plan for it: Edmonds was "not going to be home when the fire struck."

This way he could "stay on the run" committing more acts of terrorism with his organization....as far as everyone outside the STU Team was concerned. Actually, after his interrogation was finished in a day or two, Edmonds was going to be Vince Fostered with his own pistol, put into his Mercedes, and dumped in a lake. This way, as long as he was missing he could seemingly be kept alive as a fugitive terrorist kingpin bogeyman, using his sniper rifles in future assassinations to be blamed on members of his illegal clandestine organization. The rifles could be left where convenient to be found by the forever intentionally out-of-the-loop FBI, as dependably "Famous But Incompetent" as always.

If and when it suited the STU Team's evolving mission, Edmonds would be "discovered" in his car in the lake, with his own suicide weapon by his side, closing the circle. No doubt Edmonds had been very depressed over losing his family in the tragic fire, feeling especially guilty that the fire started in his own gun room... Some headlines just wrote themselves, Hammet reflected. It was almost too easy, spoon feeding the media what they already wanted to believe.

"Poppa Team?" asked Jaeger.

"We're coming out." Poppa was the pyrotechnic team. These last two men came running out of the house and jumped in the back of Blue Leader's truck through the open rear doors.

"How much time?" asked Tim Jaeger.

One of the pyro team replied "anytime." There was a muffled boom from within the old mansion, and suddenly fire erupted into the first floor.

"That asshole sure had a lot of gunpowder in his cellar, very dangerous stuff! He should know better than to store it next to gasoline and paint thinner!"

They all laughed at that one. Without a doubt the arson investigators would fall back on blaming the fire's start on faulty electrical wiring, that was the old stand by. Somebody in the back passed up two open bottles of ice cold Tuborg beer. "They're from Edmonds's double-wide fridge, you shoulda' seen the size of it! No point in wasting good beer!"

Hammet took a long drink, holding Jaeger's for him in his other hand as they flew down the drive in the dark, relying on NVG's again. Hammet always got a kick out of rushing blindly through the pitch darkness, trusting the driver with the night vision goggles, but this time their way forward was partially illuminated by the flames behind them.

One of the men in back asked, "How's Robby?" Robby Coleman was the STU operator the Edmonds boy had shot.

"Robby's dead," Jaeger said. "He's on the helo, but he bled out. Shot in the neck—must have got an artery. Bad luck."

They were all quiet after that. "God damn gun nut bastards," one of them muttered.

The Edmondses' old wooden house was well on its way to being fully engulfed in flames as they turned onto the county road and headed back to their new temporary base, on the annex of the closed Naval Auxiliary Landing Field. A few hundred yards from the Edmonds's estate the vehicles switched on their headlights and split up for the return trip.

George Hammet wondered if that blond girl was still saying Hail Mary over and over again in the closet. It was a shame he had to leave her there, but Malvone's instructions had been clear: take Burgess Edmonds alive, swap the weapons, burn the place, and leave no witnesses. It was a shame, because she looked like she might have been a real hottie. She could have been a sweet little morale booster for the troops, while they were stuck in isolation at STUville.

But Malvone had been clear on the matter: no witnesses.

27

The westerly breeze had gradually diminished and then disappeared after sunset, leaving the water a dull mirror reflecting the lights of the houses around them on the shore. Later, as the night air cooled and sank across the Virginia countryside, the wind returned from the northeast, pushed by the expanding atmosphere flowing away from the warmer Atlantic Ocean. During the afternoon Guajira had been sheltered beneath the bluffs on the western side of the Nansemond River's mouth, now the sailboat had turned through almost 180 degrees and was riding nervously at her anchor, facing into choppy wind waves built up after being driven across the seven miles of open water from Newport News.

Before three AM Brad was wide awake and on deck, barefoot and dressed in his old gray sweat suit, enjoying the simple pleasure of being far away from the barges and docks to which Guajira had been shackled like a prisoner. After months spent mastless and hobbled, tied up in fixed directions while lashed securely to wood or steel or concrete, Guajira was finally free to swing her bow into the wind with each shift of the air and water currents. His 44 foot sloop was held in place only by a hundred feet of rope and chain, not touching the earth except with its anchor, floating nearly free with twenty feet of salt water under her keel.

In less than a week he would be taking the big leap, and Guajira would not be touching any ground at all, not even with an anchor line. He would leave the land and its troubles behind. Even better, if he could convince her to come he would take Ranya along with him, or at least arrange for her to fly down to meet him in the Bahamas. But either way, he was leaving. He could count the days on one hand.

The night sea breeze was no more than fifteen or twenty knots, and Guajira was riding the chop and slight swell easily. There was no moon, and the land was only discernable as a black smear wiping out the stars down low. This void was punctuated only by scattered porch lights and street lamps, and the lights across the Route 17 bridge spanning the Nansemond River where it narrowed behind him. The southward pointing peninsula of Newport News was a single swatch of bright lights marking the horizon seven miles to the northeast.

The glowing green face of his GPS navigational unit, located among the instrument displays on the back of his cabin top beside his companionway, told him that his Delta anchor was holding fast. If the anchor had been dragging backwards through the mud, it would have triggered an alarm after moving 100 yards beyond his predetermined safety zone. The combined length of only 100 feet of anchor line and chain in water twenty feet deep was marginal for the conditions, but Brad wanted to see what kind of holding performance the Delta anchor was capable of.

Even if the anchor did drag tonight, he would have ample time to start his engine and motor upwind and reset it in a new location. In the worst case, if a sudden gale swept down on him from the open northeast, Guajira could conceivably be blown ashore. But he had been monitoring the marine weather channels on his VHF radio, and knew that there was virtually no chance of such a surprise.

Brad welcomed the old familiar satisfactions and worries of standing watch at night, even anchor watch, but this time he was not crewing on someone else's boat, this time he was the skipper, "Capitan Brad." And on his very first night away from the land on his own "yate," Brad did indeed have an amiga on board, a beautiful young lady, but for how long was an open question...

He enjoyed the test presented by being anchored in open water, exposed to the wind-driven waves. Guajira was dancing on the anchor line, pitching slightly in the chop, swinging twenty yards to port and starboard every few minutes. Sixty feet up on the top of the mast, a bright white anchor light marked the sailboat's position, to avert the slight risk of collision with any late-traveling boat. The anchor light's shine illuminated the masthead antennas and the wind direction indicator arrow, and the mast traced arcs across the star-filled sky as Guajira pitched and rolled. On another night in another anchorage, he could be staring down a full gale or even an approaching hurricane. He knew he would look back on this first night's conditions as idyllic, so he savored the experience to store it against the storms that surely would come.

At its worst the open ocean's fury could sink your boat or even kill you. Even at anchor the shoreline could snatch your boat away if you were the least bit careless or stupid. But these were honest and eternal dangers, known and understood, and nothing like the concealed and shifting dangers to be found on the land.

A few days more, and he'd leave the land and its hidden perils and secret treacheries astern...

The white Dacron mainsail was flaked down and tied along the top of the boom, its idle halyard line was hanging down the back of the mast. As Guajira swung back and forth across the wind the halyard was lifting off the mast, and beginning to make a rhythmic slapping clang against the hollow aluminum. Brad grabbed a bungee cord and climbed up on the cabin top to the mast. He reached high up the flapping halyard and hooked on the bungee, and then he pulled the halyard away from the mast and hooked the other end of the tightly stretched cord to one of the wire stays which supported the mast.

A trivial job he thought, silencing a clanging halyard, a task neither possible nor necessary yesterday. But in another week I'll be standing in this same spot reefing down the main in big ocean swells, grappling vast yards of flailing Dacron sail, with Guajira heeled over and the spray flying as we slam across the waves...

The salt air Brad smelled and felt on his skin had been sent as a messenger from the Atlantic only twenty miles away, whispering to him to flee the narrow confines of the Chesapeake Bay for the open ocean. He thought, just give me 360 degrees of clear horizon around me, and 500 deep blue fathoms under my keel, and I'll take any weather that comes! The risk of encountering storms at sea would be a fair trade for escaping the land's clutches.

He stepped lightly down off the cabin top onto the forward deck, to check where his anchor line passed over the grooved black rubber wheel of his bow roller. Since he'd bought Guajira, he'd beefed up the size of all of the bow hardware and the foredeck cleats that the anchor line was now tied to. The rest of the anchor line passed down the hawsehole to where it was stored in the anchor locker just forward of his triangular bed, the bachelor sailor's bed which tonight warmed Ranya, his new lover. She was the first girl he had slept with in months beyond counting, and the first girl that he had cared deeply about in years.

Guajira's bow was facing to the northeast, out of the mouth of the river, easily taking the chop coming down the Hampton Roads. Even so, it was enough to bring her hull to life and make her spring like a new colt against the anchor line. Brad stood on Guajira's bobbing nose, just behind the bow roller, holding the forestay tight against his shoulder to steady himself with the ocean breeze pouring against his face. Next week, he thought, if I need to work up here it will be in full foul weather gear, as Guajira flies off of waves and slams down into troughs, sometimes burying this foredeck half under water, with green wave tops breaking across this spot where I'm standing so dry and comfortable tonight...

But hopefully he wouldn't need to work on the bow while sailing off shore at all, especially since he would be sailing solo with the boat under auto pilot control. If he tripped or fell or was swept off of Guajira's decks, the sloop would not turn around for him or even stop. Instead, she would sail mercilessly over the far horizon while he treaded water and watched in despair. Even if he was restrained by a safety harness and a stout line clipped securely on board, he would probably be dragged alongside Guajira's hull until he drowned. It would be virtually impossible for him to climb back up the side of the hull against the force of the ocean, not while Guajira sliced through it at eight or ten knots.

This was the greatest danger of ocean sailing: the unexpected lurch of the deck beneath your feet, the missed step, the slip and stumble and plunge over the side and into the briny blue racing astern. The unlucky solo mariner could drown while being dragged along by his safety tether, or if untethered, he could drown after watching his boat sail out of sight. The result would be the same in either case: a prolonged watery death.

Just behind him he heard a little metallic hardware rattle and a squeak as the closed foredeck hatch lifted slightly, and Ranya's sleepy face appeared in the faint starlight.

He asked, "Did I wake you up, stomping around up here?"

"No...I don't know... I just woke up. Do you want some company?"

"Of course, come on up. But it's chilly; you'll want to put on your sweater."

The hatch dropped back down, Brad went along the side deck to the cockpit and slipped down below, and slid a few of his favorite night-time-on-the-water CDs into his machine: some Cowboy Junkies, Enya and Enigma. Now that he was finally on the verge of sailing away, he wanted to make her fall in love with every aspect of this cruising life that he could. He wanted to seduce her into sailing away with him. He briefly thought of opening a bottle of wine but rejected the idea only because of the hour. They had been making love and sleeping and making love again since the afternoon.

She walked aft through the main salon, a little unsteadily since she had just awoken and the boat was rolling and pitching a bit, and this disequilibrium was magnified inside the boat, where she could not fix her gaze on the land to balance herself.

"I'm so...disoriented. I had some of the craziest dreams..."

"That always happens on your first night on a boat." He was standing by the companionway ladder after putting the music on.

"It's not my first night on Guajira, remember?" She walked right to him until she was pressed against him, her head against his chest, and his arms slipped around her waist. She was wearing just her red sweater and panties, and he slid his hands onto the hollow of her back beneath her clothes.

"That's right; it's not your first night. But it's your first night away from the land. Guajira's moving around a bit, it's a little choppy. How do you feel?"

"I'm fine, if you mean am I seasick. Just a little disoriented."

Brad retrieved a fuzzy yellow blanket from the aft stateroom and followed Ranya up into the cockpit. He spread the blanket around his shoulders and sat down next to the open companionway, just behind the back of the raised cabin, to keep them out of the wind. Ranya sat in front of him and pressed her back against his chest, her head resting on his shoulder, sitting with her knees drawn up to her chest, encircled by the blanket. He wrapped his arms around hers and intertwined her fingers in his own, and she squeezed his in welcome return.

Ranya snuggled back into him, his arms and legs around her keeping her warm, with just her face peeking out above the warm blanket that cocooned them both. The Cowboy Junkies' Margot Timmons was singing in her languid haunting style, so softly and so moving, with words that seemed written for them and for this night, and they didn't speak for a long time.

Brad kissed her gently on the nape of her neck and her ear, soft baby kisses while they both cuddled under the blanket. He was striving to spin his web tightly around her, trying to set his hook deeply.

"It's so beautiful," she whispered at last. She was holding his hands close to her face and kissing each of his fingers in turn.

"I know. I feel so sorry for people, most people really, people who never get to experience this. The music, the stars, the lights across the water; it's just something so...special. It's something magical."

"Are you going to have many nights like this? Anchored I mean? Or will you be staying in marinas? Or just sailing most of the time?"

"Not too many marinas. They cost too much, and anyway that's not the kind of life I'm after. I could live in marinas here. I want to sail and explore until I find perfect places. Tropical lagoons and little bays with warm clear water, and I'll stay there until I get tired of them."

"How long are you going to be gone? How long can you live like that? Just wandering the oceans?"

"Mmm... I don't know, exactly. At least a few years I guess. I don't have a schedule, there's really no set plan. But I know one thing: I'm not coming back to a police state."

"But how long do you think America is going to be like this?"

"I don't know...years maybe, I guess. I can't see it just going back to the way it was...at least not anytime soon. What about you? You only have another year until you get your degree, then what?"

"Well, I'm punting this semester. Maybe I'll go back to school in January, I don't know. I have to decide if I'm going to rebuild on our property, or just sell it. I have, well... There's pretty good insurance."

"You don't have any family at all in the states? Nobody at all?"

"Family? No one. Not in America. And I have no desire to go to Lebanon. That place means nothing to me. I'm an American, and that's it. Bad as it is, America's all I've got left."

"Well why don't you come sailing with me? And if you can't come right now, then fly down and meet me in Nassau in a few weeks, when everything's settled for you up here."

"Brad, I'd love to, I really would. But my father didn't pass away, he was murdered, and the people who did it haven't been punished.

Nobody's even looking for them. I'm not leaving before I find out who did it. I can't leave before I do at least that much, it would be like deserting him. I can't leave before that."

"It won't bring your father back."

"It doesn't matter. I have to do it."

"Then you have to find George. The George that Phil Carson met at Freedom Arms, the same George who wanted me to spy on the Black Water boys."

"That's right: George the Fed, George the G-man, George the BATF agent."

Without any warning a helicopter shot past them, a black shadow that for an instant blocked the lights on shore as it whipped across the Nansemond River almost at wave top level, heading north up the James River.

"Jesus he was low!" exclaimed Brad. "He could have hit my mast!" They both strained to follow the helicopter with their eyes but it was already gone from sight, and the sound was fast diminishing to a distant whine. "Military, he had to be. He wasn't showing any lights."

"I don't think so; he was too small for a Blackhawk or a Navy Seahawk. They fly low level up and down the beach all the time, just out over the ocean. I know what they sound like, and that was no military helicopter."

"Well if it's civilian he's taking a big chance joyriding with no lights on this close to the Navy bases; it's all controlled air space. Unless he was too low for radar to pick him up." The sound of the helicopter was already gone.

Ranya said, "SEALs from Little Creek are out here all the time training; parachuting into the bay, or just jumping out of real low-flying helicopters, and climbing back up rope ladders. And the pilots all fly with night vision goggles, so they don't care about the darkness. It's not dark for them, it's bright green, so they could see Guajira, they could see everything. We sold some night vision stuff in the store, and what they've got is a lot better. Around here, the military is training all the time, you never know what they're up to."

"But on a Saturday night? I mean three AM on Sunday? I was in the Navy, and I don't remember any training at three in the morning on Sunday, not on shore duty." Brad was about to tell her how he had enlisted in the Navy to try to get into the SEAL teams, but he decided to skip it. Why tell her that? It was too long a story, and so what? He hadn't made it, and it was long in the past. He changed the subject instead, trying to get her to think beyond George, so that she might consider sailing with him later.

"So if you find George, what then? If he killed your father, will it be enough for you to take revenge on him?"

"I don't know; I'll cross that bridge when I come to it. I'd like to ask him some questions… Sure, I'd like to find out if he shot my father, and why he did it. But who was behind all the gun store attacks? George didn't do them all. Who gave the orders?"

"But what do you expect to find out? If our own government is behind it, then what? You can't fight the entire government. I mean it might be admirable, but it's not exactly realistic, don't you think?"

"But just what's realistic any more? So much is happening that I wouldn't have ever thought was realistic a week ago."

"Well that's sure true. But what about after you…deal with George, why don't…"

Brad was interrupted by an orange bloom of light a mile to the south on the high ground, which was followed a few seconds later by a dull boom. "Did you see that? Look over there!"

"I saw it, what is it, a bonfire? Sometimes people throw parties on the shore and they light up driftwood bonfires."

"At three o'clock in the morning? And it's not on the beach, it's up higher." It was becoming more obvious by the second exactly what it was.

"It's a house fire." Ranya stood up in the cockpit, holding onto the silver grab-bar in front of the compass pedestal. "What's with all the fires around here?" She was crying, Brad stood up to hold her, and she wept against his chest. The sight of the distant blazing house took her back to what she had found after her high-speed ride down from school.

Brad said, "It sure started fast! There was nothing, then wham! Flames everywhere." He let go of her and reached inside the companion-way for his binoculars, popped off the lens caps and took a quick look, then passed them to her.

"Brad, I know somebody that lives over there on that point. There's not very many houses over there, I might know them! We should call 911."

"I'll get my phone, but I think it's too late." The distant fire had grown to an enormous size in less than a minute. It was obvious that anyone who had not gotten out of the house would not get out now. He said, "There's been too many fires around here lately. Fires and explosions and killings."

"Brad, do you remember at the funeral, the older man who was at Mass, who came by himself to the burial? The one with the nice black suit, with the gray hair and glasses? He drove a Mercedes, remember him?

"Who? Yes, I think so. Why?"

"That man was one of my father's best customers for years and years, Mr. Edmonds. Burgess Edmonds. I went to high school with Valerie Edmonds. Brad, that's where they live, right around where that fire is! I'm not sure, but it's got to be one of those houses on the point!" Ranya was getting hysterical, shaking and crying.

"Burgess Edmonds lives over there? Ranya, I know that name."

"You do? How do you know him?"

"I don't know him, I mean, I only saw him at the funeral, but I know his name! Burgess Edmonds was on the list that George gave me last week, the list of people to spy on in the Black Water Club! He was on the list, and Mark Denton was on the list, and you know Jimmy Shifflett, he used to be in the club too!"

"My father knew them all, from the store. And they're dead." She had put the binoculars away and was holding him again, while they both stared across the water at the distant house fire.

A feeling of doom, a feeling of being fatally caught in a trap descended over Brad. He held Ranya tightly and they rocked together slowly. "I need to get away from here. Tomorrow. From this side of the James River I mean. If George is still keeping tabs on me, this is where he'd look, on the south side of the bay. My sail maker's over in Newport News, I'm going to take Guajira up the bay and hide out in the wildlife refuge in Poquoson until the genoa's ready. Then I'll have a straight shot out to the ocean."

She was watching the fire through her tears, watching the yellow flames licking upwards, illuminating its own roiling cloud of smoke. The flashing blue and red lights of a police car were visible near the house now.

"Ranya, this is crazy, we have to get away from here! Come up to the peninsula with me, stay with me on Guajira."

"You want me to stay with you until you get your sail, and you leave?"

"No! I want you to go with me! Come with me, please, let's get out of here before they find us! Please, come with me... I don't want to say goodbye to you, I don't want to leave you, I don't want to lose you, but I've got to go, I've got to get out of here!" Brad was trying not to join her in crying, but it was a losing effort. "I've been threatened, I've been blackmailed, they said they'd put me in a cage with the terrorists! It's not like it used to be, you don't get lawyers anymore if you're called a terrorist, you just disappear! Ranya, they're not joking, they're not kidding, they're not playing games!"

"You think I don't know that? They killed my father! They burn people alive! They shot up a stadium and framed Jimmy Shifflett for it! But I'm still not going to run away! I don't care, I'm not running away! Screw them, screw them all, I'll kill all those bastards before I run away, I swear I will!" They were both crying now, holding one another, and the pent-up words poured out of her in a torrent. "You think I don't want to sail away with you? Do you think I'm crazy? Of course I want to go sailing with you, you big moron! Of course I do! But I swear to God, I'm going to kill those bastards first!"

They just stood in the cockpit sobbing together for a long time, watching the fire. There were more muffled sounds of explosions. Periodically flaming embers flew out from the fire almost like rockets or Roman candles.

As the fire gradually diminished in intensity, Brad took a deep breath, and said, "All right. All right. Okay… If you can't come with me now, then I'll stay and help you. I'll help you find George. And I'll help you find out who sent him to your house."

She squeezed him even more tightly. "You don't have to…you don't have to…you've worked so hard to be ready to go…"

"It doesn't matter. I don't care, I won't leave you. I won't go if you can't come with me."

"After we find George, after we find out what he knows…"

"Ranya, after that, we can't do any more. We just can't. What ever we find out, who could we tell? Not the FBI. If the people who are doing it are inside the government, they'd find out about us. Maybe there's a reporter we could tell, maybe TOP News would put it on television…and we could put it all on the internet and hope it gets out… But that's all we can do! After George, will you come with me? Will that be enough?"

She only hesitated a few seconds. "All right…I will. After we find George, after we deal with him and find out what he knows, I'll come with you."

And all the while the Cowboy Junkies played on undeterred, their silky rhythms just as tight and hard driving as ever. The house fire was a horrible thing, but Brad still couldn't help having the unforgivable thought that it was beautiful too, in a terrible way, illuminating its own rust-colored cloud on this moonless night, and reflecting a path of golden shards across the black water to Guajira.

28

Ranya parked Brad's truck down the alley two blocks away from her Ocean View apartment. She had circled the neighborhood once already looking for signs of surveillance, trying not to stare at every vagrant, delivery truck and parked van. Since watching the house burning, and becoming certain in the day's new light that it was indeed the Edmond's house, her paranoia had ratcheted up to stratospheric levels. It became a certainty in her mind that whoever was killing members of the Black Water Rod and Gun Club would sooner or later turn their attention to her, if they had not already. She already knew that the FBI would be moving mountains trying to discover the identity of the Attorney General's assassin, and she was intelligent enough to realize that it was impossible that she had not left a single clue.

They never went back to sleep after the fire, they stayed up and watched the hopeless efforts of the fire engines until the fire burned out, and they talked until after dawn. They decided that Ranya would take Brad's truck to her apartment, and get the things she would need for a few days. Then they would rendezvous up in Poquoson on the other side of Hampton Roads, after Brad had anchored Guajira. It was windless and flat calm again in the early morning hours after they left the anchorage, and they brainstormed ideas for finding George on the two hour motor run back from the Nansemond anchorage to Portsmouth.

Brad dropped her off at the boatyard, nosing up to the barge just close enough for her to jump off of Guajira's bow. Then he put the diesel into reverse and backed away, turned, and motored up the Elizabeth River toward the bay again. She had her .45 pistol safely in her fanny pack for the leap ashore. The disassembled Tennyson was hidden in Guajira's aft stateroom, in a locker under sheets and towels. Its existence was still a secret from Brad. She had dropped the thrift-store track suit, wool hat and wig overboard on the motor run back to Portsmouth, while he was down below. No fiber left behind at her sniper's lair would be allowed to betray her.

Ranya went straight to his truck, leaving her Yamaha parked out of sight behind the business office for the time being. After Brad found his new anchorage by the wildlife refuge, she would meet him ashore at a restaurant they both knew, and then they would drive back together in his truck for her to retrieve her Yamaha. That was the plan.

Nobody had ever seen Ranya in the red Ford F-250, so if her apartment was under observation, she might have a chance of spotting them before they recognized her. On the other hand, they might have Brad's license plate on a watch list already... There was no end to the spiral of paranoia. Her stomach was twisted into a hard knot, and she could feel that her mouth was so parched that if she had to speak she would not be able to do so without betraying her fear. All she could do was tug her ball cap down low over her sunglasses, keep her head down, and walk along the side of the alley toward the iron back gate of the Alcazar Apartments. It had already been unlocked for the day and she went right in through the breezeway.

If they were lying in wait, if they were going to ambush her, it would be here. For the walk from the truck to her apartment her cocked and locked .45 was stuck inside her jeans on the left side, its butt toward her belt buckle, covered by her red sweatshirt. Two spare magazines were in the back left pocket of her blue jeans. On her way into Norfolk she had stopped and bought a fat Sunday newspaper out of a curbside coin box, now she held the paper over her waist with her left hand, covering the pistol; her right hand was under the paper, on the pistol's grip, with her thumb resting on the safety.

She had made the decision that if any plain-clothed men tried to grab her, she would draw and shoot, and shoot for the head since they would certainly be wearing kevlar. Her thinking had evolved over the past 24 hours since she had walked out of the neighborhood by the lake without her .45 pistol. Keeping the Jasper Mosbys of the world in mind, she had decided that she still would not shoot a uniformed local cop, but any other armed undercover agents who tried to stop her would be fair game. Watching the house burn last night, and imagining the Edmonds family trapped and burning, had pushed her toward these new personal "rules of engagement." But she saw no one at all as she walked through the breezeway. She unlocked her door and slipped inside of the one bedroom apartment without incident.

Once the door was locked and dead-bolted behind her she stripped down and enjoyed a much-needed shower and shampoo. She left her always-loaded .45 on top of the toilet tank within easy reach.

On the drive from Portsmouth to Ocean View she'd tried to catch what radio news she could. The house fire in northern Suffolk County had not even rated a mention, and there was only follow-up reporting on the assassination of the Virginia Attorney General on the news at the top of the hour. She found it highly interesting that the police were pursuing a white man driving a black pickup truck.

National Public Radio's "Weekend Edition" spent only a minute on the Sanderson killing; it was sandwiched into a long feature story on "the militia movement and domestic terrorism." The NPR special report was describing as established fact a vast right wing militia conspiracy theory. The plot ran from Shifflett and the Stadium Massacre, through the mosque shooting, to the attempted bombing of the Norfolk federal building, the sabotage of the Wilson Bridge, and the assassinations of Senator Randolph and Virginia Attorney General Eric Sanderson.

For most of this lead story the NPR reporter was interviewing Rutherford Cavanaugh, a so-called expert on militia violence from some anti-gun left wing think tank. Not even mentioned in their story were the gun store arson-murder attacks...par for the course for the left-tilting "Nationalized People's Radio." The conclusion of their "experts" was that the solution to the outbreak of right wing domestic terrorism would lie in much tighter restrictions on gun ownership by the general public, especially "sniper rifles," and a harsh crackdown on fanatical "anti-government groups," who took a dangerously literal view of the Bill of Rights.

They just don't get it, Ranya thought. They're standing in a hole up to their necks, and their solution is to dig faster. They want to put out a raging fire with buckets of gasoline.

After drying and brushing her hair and changing into a clean black t-shirt and black nylon running shorts, she fixed a breakfast of orange juice and cold cereal. Finally she spread the Sunday paper out on the small kitchen table. On the bottom of the front page there was a wide-angle overhead photograph of the lake by the golf course, and the 5th hole where Sanderson had been killed. An "X" was printed on a brushy spot several hundred yards north of her firing position at the end of the finger lake; a dotted line marked the presumed trajectory of the fatal bullet. The "X" was located on a public swale between the residential neighborhood and the Greenspring Country Club; it was where the "fisherman" had been seen by an eyewitness scurrying to the black pickup truck.

The incorrectly identified sniper's location pointed out an advantage to using a light high velocity hollow-point bullet like the one she had fired from her .223 Tennyson. Not enough of Sanderson's head, or the fatal bullet, would be left sufficiently intact to accurately indicate the direction the shot had come from. With the bullet fragmented into tiny bits, the police would be hard pressed to even narrow down its caliber, much less recover a so-called "ballistic fingerprint." The fact that the paper did not mention the caliber of the rifle which had killed Sanderson seemed to confirm her theory.

With so little evidence to go on, most of the articles focused on the remarkable life and many achievements of the fast-rising Attorney General, who had been cut down in his prime, just when he was standing on the edge of greatness and ready to take his place on the national stage. Foremost among his recent accomplishments had been the enactment of the FIST program for highway firearms inspections; this was described as only the most recent effort of his lifelong crusade against gun violence.

Nowhere in the article did it mention the phalanx of bodyguards armed to the teeth with high-capacity pistols and submachine guns which had surrounded him everywhere he went in public. Instead he was portrayed almost as a Gandhi-like figure, a proponent of peaceful conflict resolution, and a martyr who had bravely faced down gun-toting right wing terrorist gangs with the last breath of his life.

A martyr my ass, Ranya thought. A "martyr" who had spoken approvingly of the murder of the "merchants of death," gun dealers like her father. She closed the paper in disgust and pushed it aside, then turned on her little color television. It was time for the Sunday morning talking head shows.

Shortly after ten she found "Face the Press" on CBA. The host was gently interviewing Art Mountjoy, the Department of Homeland Security "Czar" with the bull neck and the greasy black pompadour. Who gets that man ready for TV, Ranya wondered?

"That's right Tom, we do see this as an organized conspiracy, there's nothing at all 'spontaneous' about these killings."

"Then who is actually behind it, pulling the strings? Since the Stadium Massacre we've had a United States Senator assassinated, the Attorney General of Virginia was shot and killed yesterday, and last night Clarence Wilkerson, the Philadelphia police chief, was killed virtually on his own door step. Who's behind these assassinations? Who's giving the orders?"

"Well Tom, we all know that Senator Randolph was a long-time advocate of strong common sense firearms laws, and she was murdered in cold blood last Tuesday only hours after the assault rifle law went into effect. Attorney General Sanderson was also very strong on gun safety issues, and he was in Norfolk kicking off the new highway inspection program when he was murdered. And Chief Wilkerson was the driving force behind the 'Philadelphia Anti-Gun Enforcement' division, which was very successfully taking firearms out of the hands of individuals who had lost their right to possess them."

The homeland security czar failed to mention that the PAGE Team had been working in close partnership with the BATFE as part of a national pilot program together with ten other large cities. The PAGE Team and the ATF were culling through an extensive network of data bases going back over 30 years, ferreting out firearms owners who had committed misdemeanors years or even decades earlier. Recently passed laws in Pennsylvania and other states stripped the right to keep and bear arms from broad categories of non-violent misdemeanor offenders, and the PAGE Team was pursuing them with a vengeance.

Using convoluted and highly-parsed legalisms, the PAGE unit was systematically taking away the right of armed self-defense from thousands of law abiding Philadelphians, many of whom lived in rough neighborhoods where nonexistent "police protection" was a bitter joke.

The PAGE Teams did virtually nothing to disarm actual violent armed felons, who never bought firearms through legal channels, and who therefore never showed up on the PAGE Team's data bases of firearms owners. In the end the PAGE units had virtually no effect on actual rates of street crime, except to make it easier and safer for violent felons, who had less to worry about from their more and more frequently unarmed and defenseless victims.

The homeland security czar also didn't mention some other information that he was privy to, which had not been made public. On Friday Senator Carly Weiner of Oregon had had her armored Lincoln Continental limousine drilled by a high powered rifle bullet, possibly from a .50 caliber sniper rifle. The bullet had pierced the inch-thick bullet resistant Lexan glass of one side window, passed within inches of the homeliest female nose in the Senate, and exited out the opposite window. This had happened at a red light on Fox Hall Road in posh northwestern Washington DC, and the clear implication was that her schedule and route had been compromised in advance, by someone with inside knowledge.

In addition, the Governor of New Jersey had a brush with death Saturday afternoon in his helicopter, as it lifted off from the pad behind the Governor's mansion. It was 100 feet in the air when the tail rotor hub exploded. He was seriously injured in the crash landing, and the pilot was killed. The cause of the "accident" was being kept a secret, but it was known within law enforcement that the "mechanical failure" had in fact been caused by a rifle bullet.

And finally, the homeland security "czar" didn't mention the countless reports pouring in of bullets shattering windows in federal office buildings in almost all 50 states, putting them practically under a state of siege, with nervous counter-sniper teams hunkered down on their rooftops behind hastily filled and stacked sand bags. These incidents, when they were reported at all, were still being treated as local events, but the homeland security boss knew that they were spreading like an epidemic.

So far no arrests had been made in any of these shootings, although several untraceable junk rifles had been found a few hundred yards from the scenes. Some of the rifles were left with highly disparaging and often obscene notes directed toward the federal government. Art Mountjoy didn't mention any of this.

The host pressed on: "But how are these shootings connected? Other than the obvious, that high profile advocates of gun control have been targeted?"

"Well Tom, we're working aggressively to nail down the answer to that question. We've directly linked the stadium sniper James Shifflett to both the Norfolk car bomb explosion and the Wilson Bridge sabotage, through what appears to be a secret militia group in Virginia."

"The two bombers were both Green Beret combat veterans, isn't that true?"

"That's correct Tom."

"Are all of these terrorists military veterans?"

"Most of the ones that we've identified, yes."

"Is their motivation simply hatred for gun control laws? Didn't Shifflett attempt to blame the Stadium Massacre on Muslim radicals? And of course, the mosque in Norfolk was attacked…"

Ranya switched off the television. They were so far from the truth that they were living on another planet. Whoever was actually behind the attacks was artfully doing it in such a way that the so-called "militia movement" would be blamed, most likely to pave the way for a further government crackdown against gun owners. They had killed her father, a gun dealer, and they had killed several members of the Black Water Rod and Gun Club, a bunch of harmless old coots if there ever was one. It was obvious that the Black Water boys were now going to be painted as dangerous anti-government extremists, when they were simply convenient patsies like Jimmy Shifflett. This operation had already sideswiped both herself and Brad Fallon, and they could both be in extreme danger, as "loose ends" to be disposed of as the killers worked their way down their list. Not even to mention the efforts the FBI would be making to catch Sanderson's killer…

It would be so easy to forget about "George the Fed" and take off with Brad…just forget all of this insanity and head out into the Atlantic, sailing south for the tropics. So simple to hoist up Guajira's sails and leave all this madness behind. So tempting, to spend years of days swimming and diving and sailing and making love with Brad Fallon under the warm tropical sun on Guajira...

Guajira blended in with the usual weekend pleasure boat traffic, as she motor-sailed up the lower bay past Hampton. Under her full 500 square foot mainsail, and assisted by the Perkins turbo diesel, she was making over seven knots of boat speed through the water to the north-northeast on the ten to fifteen knot westerly breeze. It was a perfect mid-September day, combining warm air temperatures with just enough wind to form tiny whitecaps on the sun-lit green water. Random clouds left vast shadows dappling the bay, as they drifted away to the east. From the cockpit stereo speakers, the Counting Crows were singing about Mr. Jones.

To the west, buildings on the paper-thin Hampton shoreline jutted like broken teeth above the horizon. To the north there was a clear horizon all the way up the bay, and on the eastern horizon Brad could just make out four black dashes. These dashes were the man-made rock islands of the 20 mile long Chesapeake Bay Bridge Tunnel, where the causeways plunged into the tunnels under the two separate ship channels. The "bridge-tunnel" spanned the open mouth of the Chesapeake from Virginia Beach on the south to the Delmarva Peninsula on the north.

Guajira's sixty foot tall mast prevented her from being able to pass under the low causeway sections of the bridge-tunnel. When the time came Brad would have to escape from the confines of the bay through one of the two ship channels over the tunnels, or through the smaller North Channel under the high bridge section just below the Virginia Eastern Shore.

These three choke points controlled access into and out of the Chesapeake Bay for any vessels higher than 20 feet above the water, and since 9-11 they were closely watched by the Coast Guard. Considering the alternatives, Brad wondered if it might not be wisest to wait until next Saturday to leave, when the largest number of boats would be moving in and out, and the Coast Guard would be their busiest. Guajira could hopefully leave inconspicuously on its one-way voyage mixed in with scores of day sailors...unless the feds had put Guajira on a watch list. He considered the pros and cons of painting a false name on her transom, which might improve his chances at binocular inspection distances. But if Guajira was nonetheless stopped and boarded for an inspection, a name which did not match his vessel documentation papers and hull iden-tification numbers would be tantamount to an admission of guilt. This was yet another Catch 22, another aspect of the ever increasing dread he was feeling.

As he motor-sailed up the bay under autopilot control he sat in the open companionway, his bare feet on the top step of the teak ladder, his arms resting on each side of the cabin top. This is where he would primarily keep his lookout at sea. When he was sailing solo he would come up here for a check every so often at night. He had a marine radar detector to tell him when Guajira was being painted by a ship's radar; this would provide an extra measure of safety offshore at night. He also had a Furuno radar still in its box below, bought during one of his account-depleting shopping sprees. He intended to install it down island when he would have the time. Given his time constraints he felt that the radar was a luxury, not a necessity, and it could wait.

If Ranya came with him, they could take turns on watch, or just stay below together while the boat looked after herself...

Guajira was close-reaching along, the wind just forward of her port beam, her mainsail eased out a bit on the starboard side to translate that wind into forward drive. For a few minutes Brad had been watching a big two-masted ketch running before the wind, sailing eastward for the open Atlantic. The ketch appeared to be about sixty feet long, with a royal blue hull. She had a traditional-looking hull shape with a clipper bow and bowsprit up front, a low pilothouse on top, and a gray zodiac-type inflatable hanging from davits across her stern.

Brad reached inside the companionway to the rack where he kept his binoculars and his hand held VHF radio. His handheld VHF and Guajira's more powerful hard-wired VHF with its masthead antenna were one area where Brad considered older to be better: the newer models were all digital, and sent out an identification code every time the microphone was keyed, making anonymity an impossibility.

He hailed the other vessel on channel 16. "Eastbound ketch off my port bow, this is the northbound sloop over."

A few moments later a female voice crackled from his hand held. "Northbound sloop, this is the sailing vessel Mariah, switch and answer on 71, over."

He punched in channel 71. "Mariah, this is..." Brad hesitated to name his vessel on the open radio waves, because he knew that any of the channels could be monitored by the Coast Guard. "Mariah, this is the northbound sloop. You're looking mighty good, captain. I just wanted a radio check, over."

"We read you loud and clear skipper."

"Thanks Mariah...out."

The big ketch passed a quarter mile in front of Guajira's bow. Looking through his Steiner binoculars, this was close enough for Brad to see a middle-aged couple in the center-cockpit between the masts, under a blue canvas Bimini-top awning. They exchanged arm waves in the distance, and the ketch kept sliding and rolling along to the east, sailing wing and wing with her mainsail out to port, her genoa jib poled out to starboard, and the mizzen sail on the smaller second mast down and furled on its boom.

Part of Brad wished he were following her out onto the Atlantic, right now, today! He had full water and fuel tanks, and enough canned and boxed and refrigerated food on board to make it nonstop to South America, much less the Bahamas. There was nothing to stop him from easing out his main sheet and turning the wheel to starboard, and following Mariah out onto the ocean.

Down below he had an old working jib which had come with the boat, a tan kevlar blade which would fit up Guajira's roller furling jib's slot, but it would only fill half of the fore triangle back to the mast. It would be an easy matter to bring it on deck after clearing the bay, and haul it up by himself while sailing downwind in these light conditions. It wouldn't get him the 150 mile days he expected with his 600 square foot mast-overlapping genoa, combined with the 500 square foot main sail, but it would do, it was a viable option. The bridge-tunnel was just seven miles away, dead down wind to the south-southeast, and beyond it was the open Atlantic and freedom.

Instead he was sailing north to hide Guajira up a creek in Poquoson, to wait for his new genoa jib.

But of course the missing sail was hardly the primary reason he was sailing up the bay instead of out to sea: Ranya Bardiwell had changed everything. The red bikini she had worn yesterday was still hanging by a pair of clothespins from the top lifeline on the starboard side, between Brad and the open Atlantic. He laughed at the idea, he laughed at the frailty of his determination, that an ounce of shiny red spandex could so totally cloud his vision.

The bikini had been dry since minutes after it had been hung up yesterday, but Brad would not take it down. It was a tangible reminder of Ranya's presence on board Guajira, and now in his life. Looking at the miniscule patches of red fabric he could see and feel the soft skin which it had barely concealed on their swim, and after...

He wanted her back on board. He wanted to see that red bikini stretched over her sexy curves again, he wanted her sitting in the cockpit touching-close to him, he wanted to see her standing behind the wheel with a smile on her face in the sunshine. He wanted her in his forward V-berth; he wanted to make love to her again under the open foredeck hatch, with gentle breezes pouring down to caress their tangled bodies...

The two red triangles could also be interpreted as storm-warning pennants: Brad recognized the signs. He was falling for the girl; he was no longer thinking clearly, he was sailing toward danger. But danger was the price that she asked, and that was the bargain he had struck.

In another month that red bikini might have been stretched around an eager young Dutch or Danish tourist, or a raven-haired Colombian or Venezuelan beauty, and with no entangling snares or trip wires leading back to the USA.

Well that was done, and it no longer mattered. He'd found a girl who was gorgeous, smart, and tough enough to endure the frequently uncomfortable life aboard an ocean yacht; a girl who could match him in swimming and diving, who rode motorcycles, and was even a shooter. She was practically perfect for him in every way, except for that one detail: she was determined to find and interrogate and in all likelihood kill a certain federal agent before she would go. And, incredibly, he had agreed to help her!

Her red bikini fluttered on the breeze, pointing the way to the Atlantic. Now that he had enjoyed an afternoon and night with Ranya, he couldn't imagine sailing away without her. He was thrilled inside just knowing that she would be waiting for him at their rendezvous point, he was going to crush her in his embrace, he could not wait to be kissing her again…but he could only hope that she would want him as much as he wanted her. "Morning afters" could bring cold reevaluations, they could vex and surprise with mixed emotions, second thoughts, bitter regrets…

Brad had no second thoughts, he was crazy about Ranya, and he wanted to see her again, to hold her, to swim with her in warm clear Caribbean water, to make love to her again and again beneath the sun and the stars on Guajira. He just hoped that she would still want him, the day after… Would she even show up in Poquoson? Brad knew from painful experience that a night filled with passion and promises could be followed by an unexplained no-show the next day.

The blue-hulled ketch Mariah slid off to the east, sailing down wind through sun lit whitecaps. That should be Guajira he thought, and in another week it will be, but I won't be sailing solo, I'll have a lover and a partner to share the sea miles and the lagoons and the coral reefs. He nudged the silver throttle lever on the side of the steering pedestal forward until the tachometer read 3,000 RPMs.

29

Liddy Mosby's husband Jasper pulled their Ford Expedition on
to the shoulder, and they waited for the second and last fire truck to make
the wide turn back onto the county road. When it was out of the way he
proceeded up the Edmondses' long curving drive. The Expedition was
their own vehicle, but it had a department-issued police radio installed in
the ceiling console above them, turned down so that the dispatcher's voice
was just barely audible.

The off-duty Suffolk police lieutenant parked on the grass away
from the mud-tracked parking circle overlooking the smoldering pit. A
layer of wet ashes and mud covered the area around the pit for a hundred
feet. A pair of soot-blackened chimneys standing ninety feet apart marked
what had been a local landmark, on the bluffs where the Nansemond River
spilled into the James.

Liddy Mosby was a handsome woman with well-coiffed brunette
hair who did not show all of her 49 years. She was wearing her yellow
floral-print church dress with matching yellow high heels, and she had no
desire to tramp around in the ashes and mud left behind by the fire fighters.

She said, "I'll just wait here honey. You take your time." She
was listening to AM talk radio out of Norfolk, with the windows up and
the engine and the air conditioner still running. Once Jasper stepped out,
she turned the volume up to a more comfortable level.

Usually Sunday talk radio was a boring series of computer,
gardening and quack herbal remedy shows, but because of the recent chain
of events stretching back two weeks to the Stadium Massacre, the topic
was still domestic terrorism. The Sunday garden show had been
preempted again, and in its place the regular local weekday afternoon host
was in the studio. He was beginning his third week of daily shows, which
had started immediately after the Stadium Massacre had been connected to
Tidewater, in the person of one Jimmy Shifflett. As they had been for two
weeks without a break, the phone lines were jammed with callers pushing
their pet theories and spreading rumors and half-truths.

Liddy Mosby was an independent thinker with strong opinions,
which is why she listened to talk radio, and never watched the network
television news programs, (with the exception of TOP News). It was her
belief that the liberal TV networks were controlled by closet Marxists, who
in their secret hearts wanted to brainwash Americans into accepting a
socialist government, controlled by the one-worlders at the UN.

Other than her family and her church, the only things that Liddy
Mosby enjoyed more than AM talk radio were her favorite conservative
internet web sites, and above all of them she loved FreeAmericans.net.
Writing under the name "Tin Lizzy" she was able to put forward her own

theories on any subject, and mix it up in the ideological free-for-all with the best of them.

Jasper still read the daily paper, the Norfolk Star, but Liddy hadn't touched newsprint since she had discovered the internet years before. Why read one paper, when you can read them all on the web? She was too polite to ever say so, but she considered herself far better informed than anyone she knew in her personal life, because she was mentored by experts in every field on FreeAmericans.net. But the computer was at home, and she was in the Expedition, so she settled for listening to AM talk radio as the best substitute, while her husband went to do a little after-church police business.

Jasper Mosby got out and walked over to see the North Region weekend shift supervisor, Sergeant Bob Price, who was talking with Suffolk's arson investigator. "Good morning Bob, morning Henry. Anybody heard from the family yet?" There was a chance that they had been out of town when the fire struck.

The uniformed sergeant answered, "Nope, afraid not Jasper. They have a daughter who goes to William and Mary, but her sorority says she was home for the weekend, right here. It's looking like they were probably all inside: Burgess, his wife, and both kids."

"Damn... Fine family, fine people. Henry, are you going to be able to get down in there today?"

"Hi Jasper, sorry about calling you on your weekend. No, it's still too hot. It's still smoldering down there, the whole house is right down in the cellar. That's lot of lumber; and now it's like a giant charcoal pit. The trucks brought what water they could; they contained it, but..."

"Sweet ever loving Jesus... Down in there... It must have been like hell itself." Mosby asked, "So how come we're treating it like a crime scene? You really think it's arson already?" He gestured to the crime scene investigators who were lifting out white plaster tire-track molds.

Sergeant Price said, "Let's take a walk, Jasper." He led them down the drive a hundred yards to where thick hedgerows crowded one side of the asphalt, and then he took them through a break in the hedges and pointed underneath. Small numbered plastic markers indicated where evidence had been recovered. "We found blood trails over on the slope, and drag marks leading to the driveway. And we found some fresh brass under here."

"The Edmonds had guard dogs didn't they?" Mosby already knew the answer to this question. He knew that the Edmondses' two dobermans had come from the same bitch that had produced Joe Bardiwell's dog. Mosby could already see where the evidence was leading, but he wanted to hear what Price had found on his own, and he didn't want to reveal too much about his own friendly relationship with the Bardiwells and Burgess Edmonds, a relationship developed by being a long-time regular at Freedom Arms.

"That's what their neighbors say, two dobermans. Nobody's seen them. But we've got blood that's probably from the dogs, and we've got the brass."

"Let me take a wild guess: ten millimeter?"

"Good guess Jasper, how'd you know?"

"Just a hunch." Actually it was more than a hunch, because he already had his own ten millimeter shell case. Phil Carson had given it to him when he was leaving Freedom Arms Saturday a week ago, the day they had found Joe Bardiwell murdered and his house and his store burned.

He had never logged the shell in as evidence. He knew what it meant, and he knew that reporting the ammunition, which was used by the feds in their subguns, would have caused more problems than it would have solved.

Price pointed across the grassy slope and said, "Judging from the blood, it looks like the dogs were shot over there and dragged to the road about here and carried away in a vehicle. Whoever did this went to a lot of trouble to kill the dogs and take them away, but they left a lot of blood and they left their brass."

"So Lieutenant, you agree with us then, somebody shot the dogs and torched the house?" asked the arson investigator.

"That's as good of a working theory as any I can think of."

"But why'd they bother to take the dogs? If they weren't trying to conceal the crime, why not leave the dogs out there? They left the blood and the brass, that's almost as good, so why take the dogs?"

"Good questions Bob, I don't know. Maybe he was in a hurry, maybe he just made a mistake. Why did you say 'they'?"

"Tire tracks. We got a couple of castings where they went off the circle. Different vehicles; trucks or SUVs it looks like. Fresh from last night. So why would they take the dogs when there's so much other evidence?"

"Bob, maybe they just didn't care. Maybe they weren't worried about the investigation. Maybe they have a reason not to worry about the investigation. You know, a lot of things don't make sense any more." Mosby was wondering how far he should go in sharing his own theory with Price.

On the way back up the hill they were overtaken by a black Crown Victoria. The car pulled to a stop next to them and a rear window slid down. A slight blond female in the back seat asked Price, who was in uniform, "Hello, um, Sergeant? Can you tell me who's in charge around here? Who's the supervisor?" She spoke with a sing-songy Texas twang, like a lost Dixie Chick asking for directions.

Price and Mosby looked at each other; Mosby was senior but he was technically off-duty. *Lucky I'm still in my church suit*, he thought. Some feds would sneer at him as a local hayseed cop if he was in his usual weekend boots and blue jeans, working an active crime scene.

"I'm in charge. Lieutenant Mosby, Suffolk PD. What can I do for you?"

Three of the doors opened and a lady and two men climbed out; the men wore jackets and ties, the lady a blue pants suit. Mosby guessed they were all in their late thirties. The woman was fairly attractive, if on the small side for a federal agent. Their driver stayed behind the wheel.

The lady briefly flipped open her credentials, then snapped them shut. "Hi Lieutenant, I'm Kayla Coleridge." Her voice went up on the last syllable, turning her sentence into a question like an air-headed southern sorority sister. "I'm the Special Agent In Charge of Norfolk ATF. We're asserting federal control over the Edmonds property."

Mosby was taken aback. "Now, why would that be?"

"Sorry Lieutenant, but that's protected information. It's terrorism related. Suffice it to say it's part of an ongoing federal investigation." A muscular agent with short-cropped hair stood apart from Coleridge, leaning against the car with his arms folded.

"Will you be needing our assistance then?"

"No, we'll be bringing in our own team. Turn over anything you've got to Special Agent Hammet, he's the ASAC, my assistant. If you have any questions, you can reach our office here." She handed Mosby her business card, it had "ATF" and a thumb-print-sized gold representation of her badge embossed on it.

"Okay then Ma'am, we'll pack up and clear out." He handed her his own Suffolk PD business card in return, and she slid it into her waist pocket without looking at it.

"All right then Lieutenant, Sergeant; thanks for your cooperation." The federal agents climbed back into the Crown Victoria and drove the rest of the way up the hill.

"Jasper, why didn't you tell them about the dogs, or the brass?"

"Why? Screw the feds. They asserted federal control; let them do their own damn leg work. Let them find out about the dogs. You have the brass? Keep some of it. And don't give them all of the tire molds." The Feds would see the left over plaster on the dirt and grass, and would expect to take the track imprints, but there was no reason to give them everything.

Price looked a little confused. "Why are we holding out, Jasper?"

"Let's just say that I have less than total faith in the ATF conducting a thorough investigation."

On the way back down the driveway Mosby had to pull his Expedition off the pavement onto the grass, to let a convoy of vehicles climb up the hill. Another pair of Crown Victorias and a dark green Ford Excursion were escorting a low-boy tractor trailer to the site of the fire. On the trailer was an enormous yellow backhoe excavator on caterpillar treads. Following the tractor trailer and bringing up the rear of the convoy was a Toyota Four Runner SUV, colorfully painted with the logos of Channel 14 Action News, the Norfolk affiliate of CBA.

As they passed by Liddy Mosby blurted out, "Beware of the government-media complex. That's what Michael Savage always says."

"What?" Jasper Mosby snapped back to the present, from being lost deep in his own thoughts. He had a new 10mm shell casing to compare to the one found at Joe Bardiwell's. He knew who used 10mm cartridges in their submachine guns, often sound-suppressed submachine guns, with night vision scopes. He's seen them. It was all leading him to some extremely disquieting conclusions.

Liddy said, "They're not wasting any time, are they? The Feds are bringing in a backhoe and a TV crew on a Sunday. They must have a really good idea of what they're going to find down there."

"Yeah, a really good idea." Jasper was thinking about the dead dobermans, the 10mm brass, and the multiple large tire tracks. He mentioned them to Liddy, and they discussed their perceptions of the overall situation on their way home.

Even while they were talking, internet news forum devotee Liddy Mosby was scheming and planning ways to post everything that she had just learned on FreeAmericans.net without compromising Jasper. Over fifty thousand "FreeAmericans" were reading the forum every day, posting every scrap of news about the recent outbreak of so-called domestic terrorism, and intensely debating its meaning.

The consensus was that most of the incidents, and in particular the Stadium Massacre, were bogus and had been stage-managed for effect. This was seen as part of a planned effort to disarm all Americans, prior to a crackdown on civil liberties and constitutional rights, all in the name of fighting the ever-expanding "war on terror."

She knew that she had to be cautious and circumspect, and she could not directly post her original information about the Burgess Edmonds family arson-murders under her own "Tin Lizzy" screen name. By the time they arrived home, she knew exactly how she would do it, using several email contacts as insulation.

Down in rural Chesapeake Virginia, not far from the North
Carolina border, and cut off by meandering rivers and streams and miles of
marshes and farmland, the Special Training Unit was relaxing on their
temporary base after their first "real world" operation. The annex of the
former Naval Auxiliary Landing Field was arranged around a dozen acres
of cracked concrete; on the south side were two large hangars which
concealed their vehicles and their habitation trailers. At mid day some of
the operators were cleaning weapons, some lifted weights, a few tossed a
football and others went on conditioning runs around the perimeter roads.

On the east side of the hangars, also fronting onto the concrete
helipads, were a pair of one story cinderblock buildings, seventy feet on a
side, that had at one time been painted white. The building closest to the
hangars was divided into rough offices; the other had once been a
workshop. A heavy steel door led from the tarmac into a large open room
in this workshop building. The dirty cement floor was marked where the
drill presses and lathes and milling machines had been removed when the
landing field was closed. A long rusty workbench remained, which ran the
length of the back wall of the room. In its center was an industrial-sized
stainless steel sink.

A pale Caucasian man in late middle age, wearing only boxer
shorts, was lying on his back tied to a wooden door. The door had been
placed on the workbench with a cinder block raising the end beneath his
feet. The man's head was at the lower end of the door next to the sink; his
face was half covered with a piece of cloth, a dish towel or rag, which
covered his eyes and nose but not his mouth. Pairs of large holes had been
drilled through the solid door so that the man's ankles, wrists and neck
could be tied down securely with short lengths of rope.

Tim Jaeger stood by the man's head and refilled a plastic sports
bottle with water from the sink. Bob Bullard, Mike Shanks and some other
operators stood around him, watching. They were all dressed casually in
shorts or blue jeans and t-shirts.

"So, where'd you learn this trick?" asked Michael Shanks. With
his weak chin and bulging eyes and nose, he looked right at home in the
makeshift interrogation center. "I've heard about it, but never seen it."

"Afghanistan. The locals did it, we just watched. Works like a
charm; a few minutes on the water board, and good old Mohammed starts
blabbing every time. And you don't even need a door; you can do it on the
ground just fine. It just works better with their feet up, for some reason.
You'll see."

Bob Bullard asked, "Did you ever try electricity? If this doesn't work out, I'll show you how to use an ordinary extension cord for electro-shock therapy."

"Don't worry, this'll work." Jaeger said, "Mr. Edmonds, can you hear me?"

Burgess Edmonds, tied to the door at five points with his hands by his hips, nodded and sputtered out a weak "yes." His lips were cut and swollen in several places; his body was scraped and bruised. Prisoners were not treated like fine china when they were brought in for torture, not when they were going to be killed anyway, and especially not after a team member had been killed. Robbie Coleman, the dead STU operator, was already being out-processed by Malvone as the victim of a training accident, and the STU Team was not in a merciful mood.

"My family? What happened to…"

Jaeger pulled the towel completely over Edmonds's face and poured a stream of water onto it from his open-topped sports bottle. Edmonds's body convulsed, jerking up from the table as he gasped for air through the water-saturated cloth. The water board torture gave the victim the actual physical sensation of drowning; the degree of water or air reaching his lungs could be closely controlled by the interrogator.

Jaeger stopped pouring the water and pulled the cloth back from Edmonds's mouth, but left it over his eyes and nose. Edmonds choked out water and gasped in air, his chest wracking up and down. Jaeger said, "You listen asshole: you don't ask the questions here. You just answer the questions, do you understand me?"

Burgess Edmonds caught his breath, still panting, and nodded as well as he could with his neck tied tightly to the door.

"Mr. Edmonds, I have a list of names. We're going to talk about some of them now, all right?"

"…All right…"

"And after we talk, we'll take you back to your family, and then my friend won't have to use his electrical wires, okay?"

Edmonds was crying, choking, the rope marks were livid red around his throat from his convulsed movements. "But I don't know…"

The towel went back down over his mouth, completely covering his face. Jaeger poured some more water on the towel and Edmond's body began to thrash spasmodically against the door, his wrists and ankles and neck rope-burned and raw where they held him down. He struggled to hold his breath and couldn't, and in desperation tried to breathe through the cloth but he sucked in only a painful mixture of mostly water and a tiny bit of air instead.

The STU Team leaders formed a semi-circle around Jaeger and Edmonds, watching the process with detached professional interest. Jaeger had learned this "field expedient" interrogation technique by watching friendly Afghans applying it to captured Al Queda and Taliban. Considering some of the other more fiendish tortures the Afghans regularly used, the water board seemed positively humane by comparison.

Often the key to operational success was to extract information rapidly from new prisoners, in order to act on the intelligence while it was still very fresh, before the enemy could react and disperse or go to ground. American specops troops often conducted new missions only hours after a successful interrogation, so they tended to overlook the brutal methods sometimes used by the friendly Afghans to gain the critical information.

Prisoners were frequently captured in remote regions far from the eyes of senior officers, and there was nothing to gain from passing them back to the rear echelons for a brief internment and then inevitable release. Prisoners were often squeezed and disposed of by friendly Afghans within a short time and distance of their capture, with no records kept of what transpired in the mud rooms and hidden ravines. Tim Jaeger hadn't personally done the water board on anyone before today, but he had seen it done, and he had learned of the enormous benefits to be reaped from acting on extremely fresh intelligence, however it was gained.

Today in STUville he was merely utilizing what he had learned in Afghanistan about the most effective ways to defeat terrorists. The only difference to him was that these terrorists were home-grown, and he didn't have to fly 5,000 miles to find them.

Brad Fallon was halfway through his second mug of draft beer, sitting on a bar stool in Lloyd's Crab Shack and keeping an eye on the double doors which led to the parking lot. Lloyd's was decorated in a funky rustic nautical style, with crab pots and oars and nets hanging from the ceilings and walls, but in this case they were not props purchased from a seafood restaurant warehouse. They were the genuine items.

Some of the tables looked like they had been made from old wooden hatch covers, but they were topped with an inch of clear Lucite which covered an "undersea" landscape of sand, seashells, starfish, and authentic-looking "gold doubloons." Each table was different, they were obviously hand made, and Brad admired the creativity and workmanship which had gone into building them.

Sliding glass doors at the back of the dining room opened onto a wooden patio deck overlooking Lloyd's Creek, a minor branch off of the Poquoson River between Yorktown and Hampton. In a corner of the patio deck a three piece band was belting out Jimmy Buffet and Bob Marley tunes, for an audience of a few dozen yachties and yuppies and hippies and college students. Guajira was only 25 miles up the bay from Portsmouth and Norfolk, but listening to Buffet at the bar in the Crab Shack, sitting between friendly drunks who were wearing loud Hawaiian shirts, Brad was beginning to feel as if he was already part way to the Caribbean.

The twin front doors opened. Ranya walked into the restaurant and looked around, letting her eyes adjust to the relatively dim light. Brad saw her at once, but did a double-take. She was wearing her tight jeans again—she was going to go fetch her Yamaha after all—but this time she was wearing a very tight and sexy pink sleeveless top, with spaghetti straps and a scooped neckline. She was also wearing her black fanny pack, turned to ride on her right hip: Brad could guess what was in it. He didn't want to push himself on her if she was having second thoughts, and he held back slightly as he went to greet her, but Ranya settled his doubts permanently by meeting him halfway across the room, wrapping her arms around his neck and shoulders and pulling him in close for a kiss.

"I missed you," she said, "I really missed you. Did you have a nice sail?"

"I cheated, I motor-sailed. I was in a hurry to get here and see you. Are you hungry? They've got incredible crab cake sandwiches."

"No, not really. Where's Guajira?"

"She's a couple miles from here, on a side creek."

Ranya pulled him more tightly against her, kissed him tenderly while looking into his eyes, pressing her soft body against him. "Why don't we go back to the boat? We can get my bike later."

His hands were resting on the small of her back, just brushing over the swelling curvature of her hips with his fingertips. She was wearing perfume and makeup, and her hair was brushed down over her shoulders; she was truly more beautiful now than he had remembered. She certainly didn't seem much like the tough 'biker chick' he was used to... "You sure you don't want lunch?"

"No sir. That's not what I'm hungry for."

Brad left his unfinished beer on the bar and they walked out into the bright sunlight hip to hip, with their arms behind each other's backs, both of them grinning at one another. She retrieved her black daypack and a small blue zipper-topped duffel bag from the front of Brad's red pickup. She slung on the daypack, he carried her bag, and they walked holding hands around the side of the restaurant down to the creek.

Brad's brand new twelve foot gray Avon inflatable was tied to a floating pontoon dock next to the boat ramp. Teenage boys on the other side of the dock who were loading a ski boat for a day on the water all stopped their chores to gaze at the sexy brunette. Ranya stepped onto the Avon's hard aluminum floorboards and sat down on the fat port-side tube. Brad tossed her bag down into the bow, hopped aboard and started the new 25 horsepower Yamaha outboard with his first pull on the cord. He sat on the starboard tube opposite Ranya where he could control the engine by holding its tiller, but with his right hand he reached over and held her hand across the boat.

They left the boat ramp area at low speed, and after a minute they cleared Lloyd's Creek and its marinas, restaurants, private docks and "no wake zone" signs. Brad twisted open the throttle and the Avon jumped up onto a fast plane, skimming over the smooth waters of the Poquoson River heading east along the shoreline. He had to almost shout to be heard above the motor. "Grab the bow line and stand up in the middle!" She did as he suggested, holding the line tightly in her left hand for balance with her legs apart and her knees flexed, smiling deliriously like a surfer riding a never-ending wave.

In a few more minutes he smoothly turned south onto the unnamed creek where he'd anchored his sailboat. Towering cypress and loblolly pines flew past them on both sides, cormorants disappeared under the tea-colored waters at their approach, mallards ran across the water and took wing to get out of their way. As they came around a final curve Brad slowed to an idle for the last hundred yards, admiring his yacht, enjoying the sight of her floating all alone in the natural setting. He did a complete circle around his sailboat to appreciate her from every angle.

Ranya said, "She's… so beautiful. Guajira looks fast even when she's at anchor. You've really done a magnificent job getting her ready." She was still standing, holding onto the bow line for balance.

"Thanks, but she was a great boat to begin with. I didn't have to do that much. I've always loved her lines; she looks like she's trying to leap forward. I think the designer drew her sheer line perfectly, and he got all the angles just right. See how the angle of the bow matches the angle of the transom? That's what gives her that fast 'leaning forward' look."

He nudged the gray Avon alongside Guajira's hull by the cockpit and Ranya climbed aboard first, stepping onto the toe rail and climbing over the lifeline, where she tied the bow line off on a cleat. She looked all around the narrow creek, no more that 75 yards across, surrounded on all sides by tall pines so that the entrance behind them was not even visible.

"I can't believe we've only gone a couple of miles from the Crab Shack; we might as well be way up the Amazon here! I never knew there were places this secluded, this pristine, so close to the cities."

"That's the idea. It'll be a good place to lay low for a while." He tossed her duffel bag over, climbed aboard and joined her in the cockpit.

"I'll show you how to lay low, Brad Fallon." Ranya looked around once more, and then gently pushed him down onto his back on the cockpit cushion. A mottle-feathered osprey glided just above Guajira's masthead and alighted on the blunt top of a dead lightning-struck pine; the early afternoon sunlight flickered through the shifting tree tops.

30

Brad was driving his red pickup with Ranya snuggling against him as they crossed the five mile wide I-664 James River Bridge-Tunnel from Newport News. They covered in only a few minutes the same water which they had sailed upon yesterday at a tenth of their present speed. It was a little past four PM on the warm Sunday afternoon when they passed back onto the northern shore of Suffolk County, almost within sight of the burned ruins of the Edmonds house. Neither one of them spoke of it, although they both stared in that direction.

Driving down from Poquoson they had been listening to the news on AM talk radio. The latest shock to hit Tidewater was an accidental police shooting. Either Virginia Beach police or an FBI team—it wasn't clear which—had shot a man in the head at a dramatic felony traffic stop. The man, whose identity had not been released yet, had been pulled over in his black full-sized pickup truck on Laskin Road, misidentified as a possible suspect in the shooting of Attorney General Sanderson.

Blocked in by their patrol cars and surrounded by uniformed police and undercover agents, the unlucky driver had been simultaneously ordered both to "freeze!" and to "get out!" of his truck. The man had slowly reached for his seat belt buckle to comply with the order to get out, and this had been seen as a "suspicious movement" by one of the police or undercover agents who had heard him ordered to freeze.

He had been shot in the face point blank through the windshield, with either a police or FBI assault rifle or submachine gun, that wasn't determined yet. This had happened two hours ago in broad daylight, in front of numerous witnesses, some of whom were already angrily calling in to the radio talk shows. Apparently the police and FBI undercover agents had been seen whooping it up and "high-fiving" over the bleeding body of the man they had thought was the sniper. No firearms or weapons of any kind were recovered from his vehicle.

As they entered Suffolk they were in a grim mood, the magic of their afternoon aboard Guajira already shattered. The news of the man's death hit Ranya with another spiritual hammer blow. She felt personally responsible, because instead of pursuing her for Sanderson's murder, the police had killed an innocent person instead. Her stomach knot twisted another turn, but of course she couldn't share this secret pain with Brad...

In a few minutes they would arrive back at Crosby's Boatyard in Portsmouth, where she had left her Yamaha the day before, and then they'd return once again to Brad's sailboat. She was looking forward to wrapping herself around the bike and snapping it into gear, using its clutch and throttle to fly over the highway at three digit speed. She hoped the wind blast and the onrushing pavement might clear her mind of its accumulation of guilt, pain and fear.

"I need to get gas," Brad told her, and he pulled over onto the exit lane for Hoffler Boulevard. The exit ramp cut through a break in the wall of pines alongside the highway, then curved off out of sight to the right and sloped gently downward. "Oh crap, what's this?" he said, braking quickly.

Ranya bolted upright and buckled her seatbelt. There was a police cruiser on the side of the ramp just beyond the trees, and a cop was standing in the middle holding up both hands, blocking Brad's truck and two cars in front of him.

"Checkpoint!" Ranya said. "One of the FIST checkpoints, it's got to be!" The FIST program, the brainchild of Virginia Attorney General Eric Sanderson, was intended to stop the transportation of illegal weapons. Sanderson had come down to Norfolk to announce and promote the program on Friday, he had been shot and killed Saturday morning, and Sunday afternoon they had driven straight into one of his FIST checkpoints. There just seemed to be no escaping his reach, she thought.

Thank God she'd left her Tennyson Champion .223 sniper pistol hidden back on Guajira! But she still had her father's gift to deal with: the new .45 pistol was in her fanny pack on the floor.

Hopefully they would be able to slide through the checkpoint unmolested. The police would readily verify that the pickup carried no long guns of any kind. On the other hand, Ranya was sure that if the pistol was found, its serial number would be called in to some national data base, and she would be taken aside and cross-examined closely. She would be questioned about the legal ownership of the gun, leading to more questions about her murdered father. She would be questioned about Brad, about their relationship, their destination, what they were doing together...

Maybe they would be questioned separately, and there was no way to know how such a split interrogation session would turn out. Should she admit to the police that she had the pistol if she was asked, or deny having a firearm in the car and hope it wasn't found in a search? Fear constricted her throat, instantly turning her mouth desert dry yet again. But at least she didn't have the Tennyson, that scoped .223 pistol would have linked her directly to Sanderson's death as neatly as a signed confession.

She had to tell him she had the gun. While they had time, they had to quickly get their stories lined up together, in case they would be questioned apart.

"Brad, I'm sorry I didn't tell you, but I've got my .45 with me. What should we do?"

"Ahhhh...Crap. Okay, it should be all right. I think they're just looking for rifles. I hope."

"Me too."

The exit ramp made a slight right then left "S" curve as it descended through brush down to Hoffler Boulevard. There were large stop signs on both sides at the end of the ramp at Hoffler, which passed under the I-664 overpass off to the left. Halfway down the ramp, parked along the right shoulder, there was another police car, then a line of eight or ten civilian cars and SUVs, then two more police cars. Orange traffic cones divided the wide asphalt ramp down the middle. Police and camouflage-clad soldiers were walking alongside the row of parked cars; some of the cars had open doors and trunks. A single slow-moving motorcyclist was being waved past the line of cars to proceed on his way, a fact which Ranya noted with great interest. Obviously, the police did not think a motorcyclist could be concealing a banned semi-auto or sniper rifle.

Two hundred yards away at the bottom of the ramp, parked off to the left in the weeds and facing uphill towards them, was a desert-painted Army humvee.

"Damn, look at that!" said Brad. "The humvee's got a machine gun on it. I've never seen that before, not in America."

"I've seen it up around DC sometimes, they put them near the Pentagon and Reagan National during security alerts. They were there all the time after 9-11." A helmeted soldier's head and torso was visible, sticking out of the humvee's roof behind the pintle-mounted machine gun.

"They picked a perfect spot for a checkpoint. I didn't see anything until it was too late," said Brad.

"Yeah, they can be damned sneaky. I've seen them set up this way a few times when they're searching for drugs. It's just like a trap: by the time you see it, you're caught in it."

"I wonder if they're checking every car, or if they're letting some pass around? I wonder if they're going to hassle us?"

"A thirty year old white guy in a red pickup truck? What do you think Brad? They're not looking for guys named Mohammed down here; they're looking for guys named Bubba."

"I guess we'll find out in a minute."

The young father in the white Ford Taurus, the second car from the front of the line, said, "No sir, I won't open my trunk, not without a warrant, and I do not 'consent' to be searched."

The even younger Virginia National Guard corporal standing outside his driver's side window looked around, confused. This situation had not come up before. Could this guy just refuse? Was that allowed?

The holdout's young blond wife said, "Martin, please, just do like he says. Don't make trouble; the girls are frightened."

"Honey, it's the point of it. This is still America, and there's still a Constitution."

"Daddy, why are there soldiers here? Is there a war?" asked seven year old Danielle from the back seat. Her four year old sister Ashley, next to her in her booster seat, sucked her thumb, afraid without knowing why.

"No sweetie, there's no war. The soldiers are helping the police to look for some bad men."

"Criminals daddy?"

"That's right sugar plum, criminals."

Another man walked up to their window. Martin Powell could not tell if he was from the military or the police: he was dressed in black from his helmet to his boots, with no badge or insignia in sight. The man in black rapped on his driver's side window with the steel muzzle tip of his black submachine gun. "Open up! Get out! Now!"

"Officer, do you have a warrant? What's your 'probable cause' to search our car?" Martin Powell was trying very hard not to show the fear he felt, holding onto the wheel to keep his hands from visibly shaking. He hoped he did not sound as afraid as he felt. He remembered reading about the Eagle Scout in Maryland, who had his face shot off a few years ago by an FBI agent with an M-16 rifle, after a mistaken traffic stop. Powell had not yet heard about today's accidental police shooting in Virginia Beach of the man in the black pickup truck. His wife could not stand listening to news talk radio and they played soft rock music CDs instead.

"My 'probable cause' is you're an asshole who refuses to give consent for a search, that's what! Now get out! Out! Out!"

ATF Special Agent Alvin Bogart was having a bad day, and now he was angry enough to chew up barbed wire and spit out nails. He was angry because it was Sunday afternoon, and he was pulling the absolute shit duty of all time manning a FIST checkpoint, instead of kicking back on his recliner in his den, with a cold Budweiser in his hand, watching the Eagles play the Carolina Panthers. For this he had become a Federal Law Enforcement Agent?

He was angry because he was pulling his second consecutive day of twelve hour checkpoint shifts, which really meant a 14 hour work day, only with no overtime pay like the State Troopers were raking in. And worse, he knew that he had to do it again tomorrow and the next day and it looked like forever. If he had wanted to pull this kind of shit duty, he would have joined the Border Patrol like his brother Daryl!

He was angry because he had to walk around all day in full tactical gear in almost 90 degree heat, including his Kevlar helmet and black body armor, carrying his MP-5 as if they were expecting a head-on terrorist attack right here in Hicksville Suffolk Virginia! This had been at Sanderson's direct orders. Sanderson, that preppie douche bag who was not even in his Federal chain of command. Sanderson, who had never sweated like a pig beneath heavy body armor and tactical gear on a hot day in his life. Just for this alone, Bogart was glad that Sanderson had had his head blown off on the golf course yesterday! But unfortunately, the FIST checkpoints had not died with the state Attorney General; instead they had been stepped up.

He was extremely angry because earlier today he'd heard through unofficial federal law enforcement back channels that a brother ATF agent had been killed in the line of duty last night, shot in the neck by some punk-ass redneck during a raid not three miles from here.

And now Alvin Bogart was positively livid because this curbside Allen Dershowitz in the old piece of shit Taurus wanted to give him a lecture on the 4th Amendment, consent searches, and probable cause! As if he needed to hear that shit! Like all ATF men, Alvin Bogart held a special burning hatred for "Constitution fanatics."

"So, you refuse to give voluntary consent for a search of your vehicle, is that correct?" Bogart smiled pleasantly at the man in the car.

"Yes sir, that is correct. Under the 4th amendment of the Bill of Rights of the Constitution..." The driver's side window was rolled halfway down. Turned slightly sideways, ATF Special Agent Alvin Bogart had casually slipped the small can of pepper spray from his tactical vest unnoticed, and then he snapped it up and sprayed Mr. Martin Powell, U.S. citizen and taxpayer, straight in his shocked face.

As Martin Powell screamed and dug at his eyes, Bogart snaked his arm down inside the half open window, grabbed the handle, and jerked open the door. As Powell's wife and daughters screamed both in terror and from the effects of the pepper spray being released inside the car, Agent Bogart grabbed Powell by his hair and shirt and pulled him halfway out, until he snagged up on his seatbelt. Bogart unsnapped the belt, and then used both hands to jerk Powell all the way out onto the asphalt, where his head landed with a satisfying smack.

Active duty Navy Lieutenant Commander Ira Jacobson was sitting in his mint-condition 1971 red Mustang Mach One just behind the Taurus. He was not in uniform, returning from a visit to his mother's house in Alexandria. His ship, the Burke class destroyer Winston Churchill, was at the Norfolk Naval Base. He was the ship's Operations Officer.

He had sat patiently in the line awaiting his turn, fully intending to cooperate. But seeing the black-uniformed policeman, (if he was really a policeman, it was hard to tell), abuse the civilians in front of him was getting him steamed. When the black-clad policeman had maced the interior of the car Jacobson couldn't believe it; he clearly heard a woman and children screaming!

When LCDR Jacobson saw the man in black pull the driver out of his car and slam his head down onto the ground, it was time to take action. LCDR Jacobson would have intervened automatically if he had seen a Chief Petty Officer abuse a junior sailor even half as severely; he'd write the Chief up for Captain's Mast in a heartbeat! For assault! So Navy LCDR Ira Jacobson, not in uniform, stepped smartly out of his red Mustang. It was his nature and his training to take action, to render instant decisions and intervene in such a situation. LCDR Jacobson did not skate away or tap dance around when dealing with out-of-control junior personnel, and he did not shrink from his perceived duty today.

"Just what the HELL do you think you're doing to that civilian?" he barked, using his strongest officer's "command voice" to impose order and gain control of the situation.

ATF agent Alvin Bogart was kneeling on Martin Powell's chest, one hand around his throat, getting ready to pepper spray him again with the other.

The other ATF agent was at the uphill end of the line of cars when he saw and heard the fracas. He was working with a State Trooper K-9 dog handler and his German shepherd, searching the trunk of a Volvo.

Six National Guardsmen and women and three other state troopers were spread out along the line of cars and past it in both directions, directing traffic and generally trying not to be jerks, avoiding actually searching the cars as much as possible. None of them wanted to be there. The two ATF agents were the gung-ho ones, pushing them to search more cars, to find contraband weapons.

None of the state troopers or soldiers was certain about what had happened in the white Taurus, to cause the driver to be pepper sprayed and pulled out, but they assumed an illegal weapon or maybe drugs had been spotted: after all, that's what they were there for. Suddenly they saw a tall civilian with short black hair jump out of a red Mustang and go after ATF Special Agent Bogart, screaming something. Bogart's ATF partner shouted, "Turn the dog loose!" to the K-9 handler. He immediately did as he was told, pulling the 100 pound beast back short on his leash, crouching down close to his canine partner to direct his attention, aiming the dog like a missile, and releasing him with the command "Hansie! Attack!"

The German shepherd cleared the thirty yards to Jacobson in a blur and knocked him down from behind, biting him viciously on the buttocks and in the groin area. Ira Jacobson screamed, Martin Powell was still screaming, and Powell's wife and little girls in the car kept screaming as shocked state troopers and soldiers converged on the scene of the melee.

From Bogart's first rap on Powell's window, to the dog attacking LCDR Jacobson, only sixty seconds had passed, but they had been a long sixty seconds! The next sixty seconds were going to be far, far longer.

Two cars behind Jacobson's red Mustang, 83 year old Luke Tanner's hands were locked in a death grip on the steering wheel of his cream-colored 1986 Cadillac Eldorado. His teeth were grinding, his breath was short and labored, his heart was racing, and his skin was so flushed that the liver spots on his bare arms were nearly invisible.

The last time that Luke Tanner had seen that black uniform and peculiar black coal-scuttle helmet in person had been six decades earlier. It had been in the Ardennes Forest in Belgium, trying to hold out against the 6th SS Panzer Army, during the defining days of his life in The Battle of the Bulge. Tanner had fought regular German Wehrmacht across France, and he'd fought the Waffen SS in Belgium, and he still held a burning hatred for them even six decades later.

But he had never imagined that he'd see the God damned black uniform of the SS here in America! Then he watched as a young man was pulled from his car by the storm trooper, and he saw his head bounce off the pavement, he heard a lady and children screaming, and his hand fell to the seat beside him.

He'd lost his wife Edna in 1997 after almost fifty years together. She had been dragged to her death alongside her own Buick, the victim of a botched carjacking in Richmond. After that, Luke Tanner always kept his old Government Model .45 caliber pistol under a folded newspaper on the seat beside him, with a round in the chamber. He didn't know what the particular legality of that was, and he didn't care: a man had a right to defend himself, law or no law. It was the very same .45 automatic he'd brought back on the hospital ship in 1945. Every year since then he had fired one box of ammunition through it at the National Guard Armory range where he knew people, then he cleaned it and reloaded it with fresh bullets. He'd never fired it in anger in over sixty years.

The last time Luke Tanner had fired a weapon at anything except paper targets had been around frozen Ettebruck, Belgium in 1944, and it had been at a God damned Nazi storm trooper in a black SS uniform!

Who could ever have dreamed that sixty years later, Nazi SS storm troopers dressed in black would be running loose right here in Virginia! Certainly not Luke Tanner. All those good men of the 28th Infantry Division had died in the Ardennes fighting the Nazis, and now here they were again, in the flesh!

Then a brave young fellow got out of a red Mustang in front of Luke and proceeded to give the SS Nazi hell for what he was doing to that man on the ground. Good for him! But an instant later a dog, a big German shepherd no less, had that fellow on the ground thrashing like a whirlwind and biting him to pieces, then more soldiers and police were hollering and screaming and running from all over!

Another of those black-uniformed Nazi SS storm troopers ran past Luke Tanner's Cadillac and began kicking the man on the ground with his black boots, and that's when Luke Tanner had seen enough! Too much! The 28th Infantry "Bloody Bucket" Division had not killed all those God damned Nazis in France and Belgium just so they could regroup here in America! He'd long ago seen far too many fine young Americans killed and crippled at the hands of the Nazis, way more than enough to last many lifetimes.

Luke Tanner had always considered every day since December 23rd of 1944 to be a gift from God, a bonus day, springing from the pure dumb luck which had for unknowable reasons deserted so many better and more deserving young men than him. December 23rd of 1944 was the day that he earned a Purple Heart, a Bronze Star, and a trip home all during one fire fight near frozen Ettebruck, Belgium.

He'd lost his left eye and part of his stomach over there, and more recently he'd lost his wife, and that was enough. To Luke Tanner, it was not going to be worth living in America another year, if the last vestige of freedom was going to be lost too. What had all those guys died for in France and Germany and all across the Pacific? What for? What for?

Somebody had to teach the youngsters how to fight Nazis, and Luke Tanner figured he knew about as well as anybody. There just weren't many of his generation left, who'd had the good fortune to still be alive so many years after those bitter-cold never-forgotten days at the end of 1944. He wrapped his leathery old hand around his heavy slab-sided Colt .45, thumbed back the hammer, opened the door all the way, and stepped out into the sun.

The police and soldiers and Nazi SS storm troopers were all busy, focused on the tangle of confusion beside the white Ford when Luke Tanner walked up along the red Mustang, his .45 held down beside his right leg, hammer back, safety off, finger on the trigger. When he'd picked up that .45 and thumbed back the hammer, the last six decades cleanly disappeared. But no one paid any attention to the frail-looking old bald man with the thick black-framed glasses, in the yellow short sleeve shirt. Not until he unexpectedly grabbed one of the Nazi SS storm troopers by his black shoulder strap.

ATF Special Agent Alvin Bogart spun part way around, saw yet another civilian interloper and yelled "Now what the hell do YOU want, grandpa?"

Luke Tanner, chronological age 83, and the survivor of more than that number of deadly skirmishes and battles with Nazis as a much younger man, smiled unexpectedly and said, "I want to see you dead, Fritz!" He held Bogart off with his once-again strong left arm still gripping the black shoulder strap, quickly raised the .45 from behind his leg, and fired once.

The .45's report was like a cannon, sending off shockwaves through the huddle of police and soldiers. Bogart was hit upward between the eyes. His Kevlar helmet contained his brains, but did not prevent a shower of blood and tissue from flying back out all over Tanner, making it appear that he had been shot himself. Then Bogart was down, dropped like a pole-axed steer, police were screaming "GUN!" and drawing their pistols, soldiers were trying to unsling their M-16s from their shoulders, and Tanner, still smiling, aimed again at the other Nazi SS storm trooper who now stood in wide-eyed mute amazement seven feet away. Tanner fired one-handed, aimed and fired again, as the ATF agent tried to turn away and raise his submachine gun (which was snagged on his chest sling) at the same time, then suddenly the second ATF agent went down, his wound unseen, acrid gun smoke bitter in everyone's noses, all ears ringing from the .45's steady barking in their midst.

The second BATF agent was still rolling away slowly as Tanner continued to fire at him on the ground, until his eight rounds were expended and the .45's slide stayed locked to the rear. He was surrounded by police and soldiers who were all falling back away from him, some running, some seeking cover behind cars, but for the moment it was a "circular firing squad" with police and soldiers and civilians in their cars all around him, causing them all to hesitate, until finally a state trooper took careful aim with his service pistol and fired.

Tanner was hit several times and sat down hard, then fell onto his back staring up past the clouds, blinking at the sun, his empty .45 fallen from his hand at last. A soldier leaning over him heard the old man whisper: "I got 'em Sarge, did you see me kill those Nazi bastards?" The young soldier could not see who the blood-covered old man was talking to, he could not see in himself Luke Tanner's last platoon leader, Sergeant Alonso Delvecchio, who was killed in action on Christmas Day of 1944 by a Nazi sniper's bullet. This was two days after Tanner got his "million dollar wounds" and was evacuated from the battlefield at last; to go home, to live, and to remember.

By this point the soccer mom in the forest-green Ford Excursion SUV two cars behind the Cadillac had seen and heard too much, and finally her stunned brain somehow reconnected to her frozen limbs. She switched the ignition back on and in one fluid motion turned the wheel sharply to the left, threw the shifter into drive, and stomped hard on the gas pedal. Her giant SUV clipped the Toyota in front of her, spinning it sideways, ran straight over two National Guardsmen, crossed the exit ramp and headed down the brushy slope towards Hoffler Boulevard bouncing and picking up speed with every yard. The soccer mom's mind was operating in an unfamiliar emergency crisis mode; she was on automatic heading for the safety of her three car garage like a crazed doe fleeing before a forest fire.

Down at the bottom of the ramp Private Hector Ramirez was still standing on the middle bolster seat of the Humvee, leaning back against the ring cut through the roof when everything went crazy up at the line of cars. When the shooting broke out, he had reflexively leaned forward and shouldered into his M-60 machine gun, sighting up the road, but could make no sense out of the "lucha libre," or free-for-all fight.

Hours before, Private Ramirez had been content to accept the duty in the Humvee with the machine gun. For one thing, he remembered how to load and fire the M-60 from his active duty Army time, unlike most of his squad. But mainly he knew he had been given the machine gun duty because his English was very bad, muy malo. Terrible in fact, lo peor, the worst. Sgt. DuBois didn't want him searching the cars with the policias and dealing with the public because he could not understand rapid southern dialect English; and he could not communicate well in English in any case.

Private Ramirez' lack of English skill was understandable. After all, he had walked across the frontera Mexicana in central Arizona for the third and final time only a few years before. Then by the grace of all the saints, he had been granted 'amnistia' along with millions of his countrymen living in El Norte. A little later a cousin warned him that the amnistia might be taken away, but that there was a program where if he joined the gringo army, he would be guaranteed full gringo citizenship in only two years, and then he could bring up his mother and the rest of his family. And in fact, that is exactly what happened.

Gracias a Dios he had been given the answers to the tests before the Army boot camp, or he would have been rejected. But Ramirez more than made up for his lack of Ingles with an abundance of enthusiasm, always shouting "Sir Yes Sir!" in boot camp the loudest, whether he understood the question or not. His uniform was always perfect, he always had the fastest times on the runs, and his Sargentos had put him in front of the Compania to carry the flag. Army boot camp had been a high point of Hector Ramirez' short life!

So he'd spent the day leaning against the hole in the roof of the humvee, sitting, standing and trying to stay awake, until all hell had suddenly and without warning broken loose, with people screaming, dogs barking, and now guns firing!

Hector yanked back on the cocking handle of his machine gun and got ready to fire, but was unable to find a target: all he saw were policias and soldados. Anyway, his orders were to just make a show, a demonstration he thought they had said, to be the "blocking force." Ramirez understood "fuerza bloquear." It meant that he must keep anyone from escaping from the checkpoint. He understood that mission well enough! This was something he had grown up seeing routinely as a small boy on the roads back in Chiapas. But today, although he had 200 cartuchos of ammunition in the green steel box next to his M-60, he had never expected to fire even one bullet of it!

Suddenly an enormous dark green truck roared out from the line of cars behind all the fighting and shooting, and drove straight over two of the members of Ramirez' esquadra, smashing them! Then it drove faster and faster down the hill directly towards him! And he was the blocking force, to prevent the escape of the terroristas!

He sighted directly at the onrushing windshield and fired a prolonged burst, causing the truck's windows to explode. The truck veered back toward the highway ramp, and it was still trying to escape as far as Ramirez could tell, so he followed it with his machine gun's front sight, firing continuously until it crashed into a police car at the bottom of the line! But when Hector took his finger away from the trigger, the maldita machine gun continued to fire without a pause, as if it had a mind of its own, so he raised the barrel to fire safely up over the hill.

A hundred yards away, halfway up the exit ramp, Sergeant Ashante DuBois of the Virginia National Guard was crouching behind the trunk of the cream colored Cadillac, while down the hill Ramirez raked the line of cars with 7.62 caliber machine gun fire. The rounds snapped as they passed; with every fourth shot a red tracer flashed by. Then the windows in the Cadillac blew out, showering her with a thousand tiny glass fragments. The Mexican had obviously gone totally insane with panic!

Sergeant DuBois knew that it was up to her to protect the civilians still hiding in their cars the only way she knew how. She laid her M-16 rifle along the left rear trunk of the Caddy, pulled back the charging handle to chamber a round, aimed carefully at Ramirez and pulled the trigger. Nothing happened. Sergeant DuBois turned the rifle on its side and looked at the selector switch, turned it to "semi," and began to pepper Ramirez with fire as more 7.62mm tracer rounds cracked past her up the hillside and over the highway behind them.

Back up at the top of the ramp Brad and Ranya had watched events spiral out of control in disbelief, but when the M-60 on the humvee opened up on the big green SUV, and the tracer rounds started flying past, the policeman in front of them finally ran for cover behind his cruiser. Brad noticed he was a Suffolk cop, and not a state trooper like the rest of them doing the searches down the ramp. He threw his pickup into reverse and burned rubber fishtailing backwards up the ramp, then threw it into forward and took off down I-664.

In another sixty seconds they were a mile and a half away, and Brad took his foot off the gas pedal. There was no remaining sign of the inexplicable mayhem they had witnessed during those two mad minutes on the Hoffler Boulevard exit ramp, except for the adrenalin still pumping through their blood, and their intensely focused memories.

31

The **one-story cinderblock building** closest to the hangars was outwardly the twin of the "interrogation center," where the unfortunate Burgess Edmonds had been painfully introduced to the water board. Both buildings had steel doors opening onto the tarmac, and both had only a minimum of windows, which were painted black inside and out. Air conditioners jutted out of the sealed windows on either side of the front doors, groaning and spitting as they cooled the insides.

The building closest to the hangar had, on different occasions over the years, been the recipient of enough new plywood and sheetrock inside to turn it into a functional if ugly office suite. Third hand and cast-off government surplus desks and tables and chairs made the furnishings familiar to the group of federal agents who were the latest occupants.

Girly pictures, strictly verboten in today's PC military, were tacked and taped haphazardly to the walls; this was an indication that the annex was the exclusive province of male-only military and law enforcement special operations teams. Old military and police unit stickers and decals were stuck all over the inside of the front door, some familiar, some not. Red and orange paint ball and simunition splotches on the walls showed that the office sometimes served for Close Quarters Battle training. A half dozen large-scale maps of the cities and counties of southeastern Virginia were stapled to the walls; these were the most recent contributions to the office decor, on temporary loan from the Special Training Unit.

Bob Bullard, Joe Silvari, Tim Jaeger and Michael Shanks had appropriated space in the back for their quarters; the office was the domain of the supervisors, the rest of the troops slept in the trailers in the hangar next door. The largest room was directly inside the front door, and combined elements of an administrative office, intelligence center, frat house and employee lounge. A refrigerator and a microwave oven on a table next to an old sofa added a homey touch.

A scarred-up eight foot long pine table was situated in the middle of the room. The four STU leaders plus George Hammet sat around it on a mismatched collection of chairs, going over the day's events and planning their next operations. Malvone and his helicopter were gone, along with the body of Robbie Coleman. Coleman would be returned to his family as the victim of an unfortunate range accident, a totally plausible explanation in a profession where such tragedies were not uncommon.

STU operational commander Bob Bullard asked, "Tim, how's our guest doing?"

"Oh, we put him in the hurt locker. He's almost comatose, but he's still breathing."

"Has he confessed to sending Shifflett up to the stadium yet?"

"Not yet. We're still working on it."

Shanks said, "Hollywood's not kidding; Edmonds really is in the hurt locker. We found some old gym lockers in the back, and we stuffed him into one. It's the 'hurt locker', get it?" They all chuckled. The "hurt locker" was an old military slang expression for any extremely painful or miserable condition, but in the case of Burgess Edmonds, he actually was in just such a locker, being that the steel box was too short for him to stand up, and too narrow for him to sit down. They didn't care: his brat had killed Robbie, and his suffering was a well-deserved payback.

"Okay, let's get to new business," said Bullard. "We've all got the Black Water Gun Club list, are any of them ready for tonight? George, what's your CI telling you? Who do you think are our best prospects?"

The confidential informant Bullard was referring to was Gary Milford, a founding member of the rod and gun club. Hammet owned Milford like a prison punk, ever since he'd sold him ten "post ban" thirty round AR-15 magazines, on the parking lot of the Mineral Springs Rifle Range in an undercover sting operation.

Milford had not even known that the recently manufactured magazines were illegal for civilians to possess, and were only legal for sale to sworn law enforcement agencies and the military. The "post ban" magazines were identical in every respect to the still perfectly legal to own magazines made a month or a decade earlier, but that didn't matter in the eyes of the law. Hammet had used an angle grinder and a sander to remove the "law enforcement only" stamp from the magazines, and Milford, the idiot, had bought them for the bargain price of $15 each.

Some bargain! When faced with the certain prospect of doing mandatory federal hard-time under "Project Exile," Milford had quickly folded, and turned informant against his old hunting buddies.

"Well I guess we can cross Edmonds off the list." Hammet's weak attempt at humor passed unnoticed. "My CI has a fairly good line on some of them; some of them he's been out of touch with for a long time and couldn't contact. Barney Wheeler dropped off the radar last week. Bancroft and Kincaid are probably still at home, but they live in fairly crowded suburban neighborhoods. We'd have to run them as straight no-knocks, and that'd probably blow the STU Team's cover. I don't think we're ready for that, not yet.

"So right now we have two good prospects." Hammet took a pair of blown-up driver's license photographs from a folder and laid them face up on the table. "Victor Sorrento here, lately he's been hitting the sauce more than usual. Probably out of fear."

"Who could blame him?" said Tim Jaeger and they all laughed.

Hammet continued. "Sorrento's at one of these three bars every night from about nine until midnight or one. Now, he's only a plumber, but with the gun nuts you never can tell who's who until you crack 'em and peel 'em. And a plumber's a skilled tradesman, right? So he's bound to have a bomb-making factory in his garage. I mean, he's an ammunition reloader, it says so in his file, and that means gun powder. And a plumber's got pipes, right? Two plus two equals pipe bomb: that's how I add it up. So we definitely have a lot to work with on Sorrento for building a case…in the media, I mean."

What Hammet meant was that the STU was not interested in evidence or convictions in the conventional legal sense, but only sufficient evidence to convict him as another militia terrorist "in the court of public opinion." Revealing to a few friendly reporters that Sorrento was "manufacturing pipe bombs" would neatly accomplish that goal. All of the necessary evidence would be found in Sorrento's own garage and cellar, and would make for another great media photo op, almost as effective as the banned weapons lying on the tables outside of the Edmonds place, or the "assault rifles" being carried out of Shifflett's trailer.

"The other guy who looks promising is Frank Gittis. It looks like Gittis is running. He told my CI that he's taking off in his camper until things calm down, and the camper is gone as of this morning. He's a retired building contractor, and he's a widower, so if we grab him he won't be missed."

"Okay George, they look all right," said Bullard. "Nice low operational signatures, and that's what we want for right now. Joe, what have you got?

Joe Silvari, the leader of the technical support team, said, "We've got most of their cell phones pre-registered, almost everybody on the Black Water list. Whenever they dial out or they get a call it shows up in real-time over in our commo van. Gittis has been using his cell phone and a two-way pager today, so anytime he calls we can triangulate him to within 500 yards, plus or minus, depending. If he's in a big camper, that should be easy to locate visually after we're in his range. And once we get a tight fix on him and we're in the area, we can hijack his cell phone whether it's on or off, as long as it's got battery power."

"Okay Joe, we can go with that. Let's nail down Gittis' current position. George, you've got the names and addresses of the bars where Sorrento hangs out?"

"Right here Bob," said Hammet, tapping on his notebook with his pen.

"All right then, here's the plan. Tim, you take the Blue Team and get Sorrento. Snatch him on a parking lot; that's probably your best bet."

"No problemo Bob. Candy from a baby."

"Michael, Gold Team gets Gittis and the camper," said Bullard. "Use the tech support any way you want to. Get those lazy bums off their sorry asses and out on the road if you need them."

Shifting on his chair Joe Silvari said, "Hey, I resemble that remark!" Sitting for a long period of time was uncomfortable for "Half Ass."

Bullard asked, "Joe, can we use another Winnebago? After we take care of Gittis, I mean?"

"Sure, why not? We can convert it into another commo package, or just use it as a mobile base of operations and sleep five or six guys in it. No motels, no receipts… Or we can use Gittis' camper for a black op, for a one shot mission. I mean, a Winnebago could carry tons of ANFO…maybe use McVeigh's old recipe. Anyway I never heard of a 'Winnebago bomb', so that would be a first, that would be kind of a nice touch. And if we kept Gittis on ice we could stick him in it, and his DNA would be found all over the place. That plus the VIN, and hey, even the FBI could crack the case if you gave them enough time!"

The STU leaders grinned at each other around the table. Jaeger said, "Famous…" and the others replied in unison, "But Incompetent!" They all laughed again; they didn't think much of the FBI's legendary investigative prowess.

Shanks said, "It only took 'em ten years to catch Robert Hanssen…after he practically confessed he was a Russian spy! Ha! And don't even get me started on 9-11!"

The STU held the FBI in low regard as an outfit concerned only with their formerly brilliant public image, and not with breaking hard cases. The institutional ethos was exactly the reverse among the dreaded "jack-booted thugs" of the smaller but far tougher ATF. They reveled in their bad-boy reputation, and lived to bust the worst scum that America had to offer. If the FBI looked down upon them…so what?

"Question, Bob," asked Michael Shanks. "After we go through the Black Water list… I mean, these guys aren't going to stand around waiting in line for us, not after tonight…they're going to take off, they're going to run. Who are we going after next, after them?"

"First of all," replied Bullard, "it's great for us when they do take off. They always keep using their cell phones, and then we can just scoop them up just like we're going to get Gittis tonight. And no one misses them, because they're already on the run. If they head way out in the boondocks where these hunter types always go, that's even better, because then there's nobody around if it gets noisy, and we can rearrange the scene any way we want.

"And after we do finish up with this Black Water list, we'll go to work on the contacts we pull out of them next door on the water board.

And if that secondary contact list runs dry before all this militia terrorism crap is stamped out, well, then that's Half Ass' department. Right Joe?

"You mean…the predictive programs?"

"Right, that's it. Tell the boys about it. It's okay; they're as cleared for it as anybody ever will be."

Silvari shot him an "are you sure?" look, and Bullard nodded back a "yes." The predictive programs were way out in "need to know basis" territory. Until now, only Malvone, Bullard, Silvari and one of Silvari's computer geeks had known about them.

"Okay, well, this is pretty sensitive stuff," began Silvari. "Not the theory, but what we're going to do with it. This is not to leave this room, okay? The fact is we're already making our next lists from our own predictive programs.

"These were originally dreamed up on Madison Avenue to tell advertisers what people wanted, before they even know it. It works so well, it's almost scary! Computers mine all of the data bases you can imagine, and then some. They check your credit card purchases back for years, they see where you've lived and where you go on vacation, the kind of car you buy, the food you eat, ten thousand things that add up to 'you.' Then they compare that 'you' to everybody else, and then they see what folks like 'you' just bought.

"Did you ever call a catalog company to make an order, and at the end they ask if you want to hear their list of 'specials'? Their computer just cranked out the list of specials it thinks you'll want. Before data mining and predictive programs, they used to average about a ten percent hit-rate on the 'specials.' Now they get over 80% sales! Think about it; the computer can guess what you'll want to buy next, 80% of the time!

"Everybody who found out about this got very excited, as you can imagine. CIA, FBI, NSA, everybody. Then after 9-11, there was a big push to use the predictive programs for catching Muslim terrorists, to find the sleepers by their credit cards, their movements, memberships, phone usage patterns, everything. 'Brilliant' data mining at its finest: that's the essence of the 'Terrorist Information Awareness' program. And let me tell you, it works. They get a lot of false hits, but they catch a lot of bad guys with it too. A lot of them, more than are ever reported in the media.

"Anyway, Malvone got access to some of the predictive program algorithms, and my number one computer geek Charles changed the parameters. Now we can tap into the TIA program and use it for finding our own home-grown terrorists, based on the ones we've already busted and jailed over the years. The program looks at the vehicles they drive, the magazines they read, the websites they surf…and of course their credit cards. With gun nuts that's especially useful, because they buy so much from catalogs and on the internet. I mean, if somebody ordered five thousand rounds of AK-47 ammo in 1999, it's pretty obvious what kind of weapons he has…

"So we'll just aim our own version of the predictive program at a zip code or a town, and it'll spit out the most dangerous right wing nut jobs. It'll bird-dog the next Shiffletts or McVeighs, the ones who are really out on the edge.

"So that's where our next list of targets is going to come from: from our own in-house predictive programs. And since we're not in the business of building court cases, it doesn't really matter if they've technically broken the law yet or not. And anyway, with these gun nuts, you can always find *something*. You know, a gun they bought in one jurisdiction that they failed to register properly when they moved somewhere else, or a barrel that's an inch too long or too short…

"And no matter what happens to the guy, you can always make it a 'gun accident' or a 'premature bomb', and there'll be enough incriminating evidence in his house to make it fly in the press. So that part's easy. But if by some miracle a guy on the list actually turns out to be squeaky clean, well, we still have the militia 'drop guns' that Malvone gave us, just in case."

The STU Team leaders were silent, absorbing the meaning of what they'd just heard. The cutting-edge STU Team was going to smoke out the most dangerous gun nuts and Constitution fanatics using an advanced computer program, and the TIA data bases. This was just about as "proactive" as it could get! No more waiting around until after the bomb went off, or the politician was assassinated.

"Way cool," said Hollywood Tim Jaeger.

"I like it. I really like it," said Michael Shanks.

"I told you boys when you joined the STU that we'd be way out on the tip of the spear, and I didn't lie to you," said Bob Bullard. "Okay then, go and give your teams their warning orders. Joe, get a close fix on Gittis ASAP. Anything else?"

"Yeah," said George Hammet. "Tonight's ops look pretty easy, pretty straight forward, so I'd like to go home and get some down-time. I'm still playing ASAC at the Norfolk Field Office, so while you guys were all relaxing today and sleeping in, I was back at Edmonds's place in a suit playing patty-cake with the Fibbies. And I still have to put in regular office hours tomorrow—look, I gotta sleep *sometime*."

"All right George, go ahead, take off, and we'll see you when we see you tomorrow," replied Bullard. "That's it then? Okay, warning orders now, mission briefings at say, 5:30 in the classroom trailer."

"Oh, one more thing," said Hammet, already heading toward the door, "Make sure you catch the CBA evening news at 6:30. I think you'll really enjoy it."

Wally Malvone was pacing his basement club room with a Tanqueray and tonic in his hand, channel surfing the cable news networks for domestic terrorism stories, while waiting for the CBA nightly news. The assassination of Virginia Attorney General Eric Sanderson was still getting heavy play, but it was now being coupled with what looked like a botched traffic stop, where a man in a black pickup had been shot and killed by police in a case of mistaken identity. The man in the black truck had been mistaken for Sanderson's assassin, the mysterious "water-hazard fisherman," AKA the "golf course sniper." Malvone considered this a "two-fer," because neither man's death was the result of STU operations. This was a strong indication that his program (after the initial pump priming) was becoming self-sustaining.

During the 6 PM news cycle the shootout and crossfire massacre on the Suffolk highway exit ramp was receiving the most coverage: it was photogenic as hell even with no VIPs among the dead and wounded. Best of all, the two dead ATF agents were bound to cause federal agents nation-wide to go onto a hair-trigger posture, seeking payback against gun-toting "Constitution fanatics" everywhere.

Aerial shots taken from news helicopters panned across the entire ramp area, then focused on a burned-out SUV lying on its side against a police car. The camera zoomed in until boots were visible sticking out from under a green soldier's poncho, which apparently covered a body next to a desert-painted humvee. Ambulances with flashing lights maneuvered slowly through the scene, more ambulances and medevac helicopters were parked along the top of the ramp. The highway had been closed to allow its full use for medical evacuation, and it was backed up for miles in both directions.

It would be a stretch to call this a "terrorist attack," since it had reportedly started with an elderly civilian going berserk and shooting the two ATF agents, which had subsequently triggered the accidental crossfire situation. One national television pundit compared the old gunman to a Palestinian suicide attacker, and wondered aloud if it was a harbinger of more non-Islamic "suicide attacks" to come.

Nine were now confirmed dead on the exit ramp, and even if it could not be laid directly at the feet of the Black Water gang, Malvone knew that most viewers seeing this news coming out of Suffolk Virginia would readily make the connection on their own. So he considered the highway exit ramp "tragedy" to be another freebie, self-generated from the climate he had created. It would be added to all of the other previous incidents going back to the stadium, and after each new outrage his STU Teams would be expanded, multiplied, and given greater freedom of action. He was already the President's "go-to guy" for domestic terrorism, and as long as the STU could produce visible results, it would flourish.

At 6:30 Malvone flipped to CBA to catch the nightly national and world news. The CBA logos and theme music faded and he was pleasantly surprised to see Pete Broker himself, "The Most Believed Man in America," at the anchor desk. If Pete Broker was coming in on a Sunday night two weeks after the Stadium Massacre, it meant he was breaking a major scoop. Hammet had reported at lunch time that a CBA film crew had followed the joint FBI/ATF recovery team to the Edmonds place (following his own telephoned tip off) and Malvone was eagerly anticipating their report.

"Good evening America. There have been several new developments today in the War on Domestic Terrorism; another assassination of a public official, in Philadelphia this time, and a tragic crossfire shootout at a firearms safety checkpoint in southeastern Virginia.

"We'll return to those stories in a moment, but right now I'd like to report a major positive development, a CBA News exclusive report which may, I underline may, bring us closer to exposing the shadowy militia organization behind the last two week's outbreak of violence, which began with the Stadium Massacre, and continues to this day.

"CBA investigative reporter Richard Mentiroso has this exclusive report from Suffolk Virginia, the home of stadium sniper James Shifflett, where a mysterious house fire last night has claimed several lives, and possibly exposed a terror network."

Brad and Ranya were back aboard Guajira, cozily snuggled together sitting on the settee behind the dinette table, watching the news on Brad's 12 volt black and white television. After returning to Poquoson with both the truck and Ranya's Yamaha, they enjoyed a fresh seafood dinner at The Crab Shack, and then returned to Guajira on the inflatable. They had been watching the local TV news coverage of the aftermath of the highway checkpoint mayhem on CBA (only because their antenna reception was best on that channel) when Pete Broker himself came on with the national news.

Brad said, "Oh man, he looks terrible. What is he, a hundred years old?"

"I don't know, I haven't watched him in years. He's disgusting, he's always sucking up to commies. You should have seen him with his old buddy Fidel Castro; you'd think he was interviewing Jesus Christ."

"Hey, more news from Suffolk!" Brad exclaimed. "The checkpoint must have made the national news! Let's see how CBA spins it."

Pete Broker continued, but he was not talking about the checkpoint fiasco. "Richard Mentiroso's complete report will be broadcast later tonight on a special edition of CBA Timeline at 9 PM eastern. Go ahead now Rich, and tell us what you've found in Suffolk."

"Thanks Pete. I've spent today with officials from the Joint Domestic Terrorism Task Force here on the shores of the Chesapeake Bay, where CBA News has been given an exclusive opportunity to observe as the FBI and ATF have literally been digging into the Tidewater Terror connection."

Mentiroso was wearing a safari-style jacket, holding his microphone while standing in front of a field full of charred timber and blackened rubble. A tracked backhoe was lifting a load of muddy debris out of a deep hole with its steel-toothed bucket, and swinging it over onto the side with whining groans. A pair of opposing chimneys stood as silent sentinels, towering over the operation.

"Until yesterday, the pit behind me was a mansion belonging to wealthy Virginia businessman and land developer Burgess Edmonds. Sometime last night a fire erupted, and the three story home was completely destroyed, as you can see.

"The Domestic Terrorism Task Force immediately became interested because it turns out that Mr. Edmonds had been on a watch list as a member of a so-called "gun club," which also included among its members stadium sniper James Shifflett, and Green Beret veteran Mark Denton, whose jeep exploded one week ago in Norfolk. You will remember that Mark Denton was allegedly on his way to plant a bomb in the Norfolk Federal building, when his explosive device went off prematurely."

Brad and Ranya were motionless and silent, carefully studying the visible aftermath of the fire they had watched early in the morning from their previous anchorage in the mouth of the Nansemond River.

"The Edmonds mansion was totally destroyed, and today federal law enforcement agents have literally been combing the ashes for clues. So far only a few badly-burned skeletal remains have been recovered, along with a virtual armory of illegal assault rifles and sniper rifles, as well as parts of mortars and rockets. Enough, officials say, to start a small war."

The camera panned across several long portable tables set up in a row on the side of the driveway. Charred rifle barrels and receivers from AK-47s, M-16s, and long rifles with telescopic sights still attached were lined up in rows. A dour-faced federal agent in dirty blue coveralls stood behind the table pointing to them in turn.

"Pete, ATF officials here say that bullet shells from .50 caliber sniper rifles were also recovered. As we know, .50 caliber sniper rifles can destroy a tank or a helicopter two miles away. No .50 caliber sniper rifles have been recovered so far, leading ATF officials to consider that they may already be out there... in the hands of militia terrorists.

"A preliminary examination of the human remains recovered so far leads investigators to believe that Burgess Edmonds was not in the house when it burned to the ground. Off the record, ATF officials are calling Edmonds a quote 'militia paymaster and kingpin' unquote. They believe that he is at large and consider him to be very well armed, possibly with a .50 caliber sniper rifle, and extremely dangerous."

The screen briefly cut from Mentiroso on location to a black and white photo of Burgess Edmonds, showing a tired-looking white man about sixty years old, with short gray hair and glasses, and wearing a jacket and tie.

"ATF officials say that in the past ten years Edmonds has purchased large quantities of gunpowder, which is frequently used by domestic militia terrorists to manufacture deadly pipe bombs. They theorize that Edmonds may have been constructing pipe bombs when the fire broke out, causing him to flee from the house before the gunpowder exploded, saving himself and leaving his family to perish in the flames.

"Or, ATF officials say, Edmonds may have been psychologically disturbed, and he may have set the fires deliberately, cutting all of his ties to the past prior to going underground in the militia terror war. In either case, federal officials say that he is not under any circumstances to be approached if he is seen, not even by local law enforcement officers, but instead the FBI or ATF should be called immediately.

"This is Rich Mentiroso in Suffolk Virginia, reporting for CBA News. Back to you Pete."

Up in Maryland, standing in front of his big screen TV, Wally Malvone was grinning as he sipped his gin and tonic. He always knew he could depend on Pete Broker and CBA News to handle the story the way he had scripted it, and they had. Perfectly.

Down in the hangars at STUville, on the closed Naval Auxiliary Landing Field, the operators paused in their pre-operation preparations to watch CBA news, as George Hammet had suggested. They stopped pushing bullets into magazines and fresh batteries into their Sure-Flash lights and tactical radios to see what had become of the Edmonds mansion, and when they saw the yellow backhoe dragging burnt timbers out of the ground they erupted into hooting and cheering and high-fives. Wally Malvone was a genius! Malvone was playing the media like a piano. "Hey, I wonder if Edmonds knows he's gone underground?" shouted one comedian.

So far Edmonds had provided no useful information that they didn't already know, but it hardly mattered. The CBA report alone made the raid on his house worth it, and it helped to make up for the death of STU Team member Robbie Coleman.

Forty miles north of STUville aboard Guajira, Brad and Ranya sat close together in stunned silence. Ranya wiped away tears and said, "Valerie was a nice girl, she was just a student for God's sake... and her little brother was such a nice kid, a really great kid, why'd they have to kill them? Why?"

Brad sighed. "Because they're trying to start a civil war. Your friend Phil Carson was right; he was right all along. I can see it now, it's all clear to me now. It's all been an act, from the stadium on. It's all being staged. We saw it last night, we saw it ourselves."

Ranya didn't challenge him about everything being an act, being staged. But she knew different. Most of the recent events might have been done by the people who killed her father, but the killing of Eric Sanderson...that was not an act. That had been very real.

Brad went on. "Now just watch, the sheeple are going to demand that the government crack down on 'right wing terrorists.' The sheeple won't care if they wind up living in a barbed-wire police state, they'll be begging for it! And for the government, it's going to mean total power. Between the war on Islamic terror and the war on domestic terror and the war on drugs, they'll have the country in a vise. Anybody that questions the 'war on terror' might get their house burned down, and afterwards they'll be called a terrorist."

After a little while Ranya responded, quietly. "Well, then we've got to stop them."

"We? Stop them? The whole federal government?"

"Brad, think about it: there's no way in hell the 'whole federal government' or even the whole FBI or BATF could be in on this thing. They couldn't keep something like this a secret for two days, much less two weeks! It's got to be a smaller group, a splinter group, something like that."

"That sounds like a movie. That's not how it works in the real world."

Ranya asked him, "Have you got a better explanation? What's been happening is real, we know it, we've seen it. My father's dead, the

Edmonds are dead, the people in the stadium are dead.... And somebody's doing it, somebody that's going to a lot of trouble to make it all look like 'militia terrorism.' We know that's crap, so who would want to make it look like 'militias'? Who hates the 'militias' that much?"

"Remember," Brad replied, "this all started with guns. This all started with Shifflett and the Stadium Massacre, and banning the semi-automatics. So who does that sound like? Who benefits from a crackdown on guns?"

She said, "The BATF, or some part of it, it's got to be them! They'll just get bigger and bigger after what's been going on, with all the new gun laws. They'll have job security until the end of time."

He added, "And they'll need lots more BATF agents, and lots more money."

"Bingo. It's got to be the BATF. And that takes us right back to our own G-man, 'George the Fed.' He's the key; he's our door into this thing."

"Okay, we'll stay and find George. Somehow, we'll find him. But after we're finished with him, that's it. We're finished, and then we're gone, all right?"

"All right," agreed Ranya. "After we're finished with George, we'll sail out of here, and we won't look back."

32

A light drizzle, little more than a mist, was falling across the Tidewater night. There was one customer left at the far end of the bar in the Side Pocket Lounge, contemplating both the bottom of his glass of beer, and the Miller Lite clock's minute hand, which was rising steadily toward midnight.

Victor Sorrento was a week away from 35 years old, and wondering again if his life was already over. The bills were piling up faster than he could pay them down working as a plumber, and he was coming to the realization that not only was he never going to be taken into management at AAABest Plumbing, he'd also never get far enough ahead in his savings to strike out on his own as an independent.

This might have been tolerable if he had a wife that he could look forward to coming home to, but his Nell had gained at least 50 pounds since he'd married her five years before, ten pounds for each year, and if she had been "voluptuous" when they were dating, she was just plain fat today. He was a hard worker and a steady provider, and he was still in good shape and not too bad looking, in sort of a rugged Bruce Willis way.

So what had he done to deserve such a fat wife at his age? Even drinking a bit too much, as he was lately, he was keeping his weight under 180 pounds, which was not much more than when he had mustered out of the Marines a decade ago. He knew he was still fairly attractive to women; the bar maids still smiled warmly and sparkled their eyes at him, so he knew he was not too far over the hill.

But he'd kept his hands off of them, even Darla, the cute blonde waitress at the Night Owl who was always making eyes at him, even as his Nell's weight had soared past his own. Simply addressing her "eating disorder" (which was in reality a "stuffing your face disorder") caused her to collapse into a pitiful blob of tears and self-loathing, so Victor spent his nights at the Side Pocket and the Night Owl, hoping that she would be sound asleep by the time he got home.

And now, on top of the bummer which was his personal and professional life, the one area which had provided him with a measure of enjoyment and pride had unexpectedly boomeranged into a complete and total nightmare. Victor Sorrento was a shooting sports enthusiast who enjoyed trap and skeet, practical pistol competition, and all types of hunting, but now his informal affiliation with the Black Water Rod and Gun Club was keeping him in a perpetual state of fear and dread.

First Jimmy Shifflett, a war vet but a messed up loser just the same, turned up dead near the stadium in Maryland with an SKS, blamed for the massacre. That had only been the beginning of the terrifying times. Next the gun stores were burned, Joe Bardiwell was killed, and Mark

Denton and his boy were blown up in his jeep. Those improbable killings had already been enough to make him jump from his own shadow, but now Burgess Edmonds, the big man himself, who owned half of the land the rod and gun club hunted on, had his house burned down and his family wiped out! Wiped out! And then, to top it all, Edmonds was being called a terrorist on TV! Victor Sorrento could see where this was leading.

Pete Broker on CBA News had said that Edmonds was a "militia kingpin and paymaster," whatever that was. So what did that make him? None of it made any sense, but it sure looked like somebody was picking off members of the rod and gun club one at a time. And the television people were talking about a 'secret shadow militia', whatever that meant. If the rod and gun club was a secret militia, nobody had ever told Victor Sorrento! Different guys from the club got together a couple of times a month for some shooting or hunting, and sometimes some fishing, and that's all they did as far as he knew. A secret shadow militia? It made no sense; he'd never heard of such a thing.

The clock over the bar was clear enough though, five minutes before twelve, and in seven hours he'd have to be out the door for work, so he decided to forego a final beer and head for home. Hopefully Nell would be sound asleep, and he could slip into bed without waking her up, or maybe he'd just crash on the couch again. And one of these nights maybe he just wouldn't go home at all… He quaffed the last dregs of his beer and slid off the bar stool.

"G'night Joe, Later…"

"See ya tomorrow Vic."

"Yeah, see ya."

In the poorly lit corner booth near the front door of the Side Pocket Lounge, a thirtyish fellow, military perhaps, seemed to mumble something to his pal across the table as Sorrento said goodbye to the bartender. Actually he was speaking in order to be heard by the throat microphone concealed under his black turtleneck sweater.

"Okay, he's leaving. Get set people, here he comes."

Outside the tavern in a nondescript shopping center off of Independence Boulevard in Virginia Beach, nothing appeared out of the ordinary, but in fact a complex and well-oiled machine was operating unseen. Tonight the STU's Blue Team was running their first real world snatch, an "old buddy" operation, and Blue Team leader Tim "Hollywood" Jaeger was playing the lead role.

The key to a successful old buddy operation was having good biographical data on the target, and tonight they had an abundance of it. It also helped that Sorrento had consumed eight draft beers in two bars in the last couple hours, and wouldn't be exactly razor sharp.

Sorrento's green Ford Ranger pickup was parked along the shopping center sidewalk, about forty yards from the front door of the Side Pocket Lounge. The Blue Team had parallel-parked the STU's blue Dodge conversion van along the same sidewalk, between Sorrento's truck and the bar.

Tim Jaeger heard the inside team announce Sorrento's imminent departure, and he took his position on the sidewalk 100 feet from the door, outside of a closed beauty parlor. When he saw the tavern door swing open, he began his walk.

"Okay folks, here he comes, get ready," Jaeger said through his throat mike to the rest of the hidden team. In a moment both men were facing one another, and closing the distance between them. At thirty feet from Sorrento, Jaeger made solid eye contact with him. At fifteen feet he smiled broadly in counterfeit recognition and said "Hey! Vic Sorrento! Long time no see, buddy!"

The two STU men from inside the bar were now padding up silently behind the suddenly off-guard Sorrento, who was looking puzzled, searching his murky memory for the name of this apparently forgotten old friend.

"Hey Vic, I'm Bob Michaels, remember me? We were in Echo Company at Camp Lejeune in 91, remember? Semper Fi buddy!" Jaeger put out his hand for a friendly shake and Sorrento, his mind stirring through a sudden whirl of old memories of his Marine Corps days, put out his own hand in return and Jaeger took it. Sorrento smiled weakly, he still couldn't quite place the name or face of this old acquaintance from the Marines, but...

Jaeger, still smiling broadly and holding eye contact (in order not to look at his two team mates coming up from behind) gripped Sorrento's right hand tightly in both of his. He did this so that in the event that Sorrento was armed, he would not be able to draw with his strong-side hand. But there was not much risk that he was armed; his rotating watchers in the bars had observed him closely, and had not seen a pistol "printing" through his clothes, or seen Sorrento make any tell-tale touching motions, checking the position of a concealed weapon. Even though Sorrento had a Virginia concealed carry permit, he was evidently a law abiding type who would not "carry" illegally into a bar.

The side door of the STU Team van quietly rolled open just as the two operators from inside the bar seized Sorrento's arms and shoulders from behind and shoved him violently toward the black opening. A jolt of electricity from the two silver prongs of a pocket-sized cattle prod zapped him in the back of the neck as more strong hands reached out for him from within the van, seizing him by the front of his gray wind breaker jacket. The middle bench seat of the van had been removed, providing a clear space for the snatch team to work unimpeded. Victor Sorrento was both pushed and pulled inside before he could so much as formulate a thought. The door slid shut again, and the van pulled away.

No one had happened by on the sidewalk in either direction in the light drizzle to see the chance meeting of old friends. The van itself blocked the view of the abduction from the parking lot and street side, and so the disappearance of Victor Sorrento passed unnoticed by the world.

In seconds Sorrento was face down on the carpeted floor of the van, handcuffed behind his back and shackled around his ankles, with a black cloth sack pulled down over his head and tied around his neck.

He was rolled onto his side and his car keys were pulled from his front blue jeans pocket, and dropped casually out of the front passenger window of the moving van. A few moments later another Blue Team man on foot picked them up and walked to Sorrento's Ford Ranger, unlocked it and climbed in and drove off. In a minute the blue Dodge conversion van was heading south on rain-slick Independence Boulevard, followed by a pair of black Chevy Suburbans and a green Ford Ranger.

Four hundred miles northeast, in the small bedroom community of Wilton Connecticut, a semi-retired computer network consultant sat in his living room, watching a video replay of the CBA newsmagazine Timeline. Mark Fitzgibbon had seen the preview of the Suffolk arson fire story while watching the nightly news with Pete Broker, and decided to tape the Timeline segment for further study.

He was no fan of CBA News or Pete Broker, but he forced himself to endure a certain amount of it in order to keep abreast of the latest government propaganda and disinformation. Since the Stadium Massacre he had recognized that CBA, even more than the other networks, was being fed a steady stream of lies which they flipped around and reported as the truth. By analyzing the various mistruths, and fact checking them on the internet, Fitzgibbon was able to ascertain something of the reality behind the recent "outbreak" of so-called "militia terrorism."

When the Timeline segment (luridly titled "Terror in Tidewater") finished playing, he turned off his television and walked to his office, passing his open bedroom door where his wife was sleeping. Sitting at his computer desk, he switched on his flat screen, and clicked to his favorite internet news forum, FreeAmericans.net. Newspaper, magazine and internet-derived articles and columns were posted about all of the recent acts of terrorism, from the Stadium Massacre to the recent crossfire fiasco at the FIST checkpoint. Much of what was posted on FreeAmericans was garbage, because any tinfoil beanie-wearing kook could post just about any far out conspiracy theory on the open forum. But among the trash could be found much treasure; one merely had to pick up the solid nuggets while ignoring the fool's gold.

He scrolled down the "latest articles" page until he found a small story from the online edition of the Norfolk newspaper about the deadly Suffolk house fire, and the wealthy owner's alleged connection to a mysterious covert militia group. As he expected, the article's author only referenced the same unnamed "official sources" that had been mentioned by the CBA News reporter Rich Mentiroso. Mentiroso could have written the newspaper piece; it did not vary from the Timeline version in any significant way.

Any real information, he knew, would be found in the replies posted by individual "FreeAmericans" below the article. Most of the replies were simply the opinions of observers from all over America, mainly observations that the Edmonds family had been the victim of yet another "accidental" fire...of the Waco variety. Cynics posted gallows humor about the adverse health effects of being a gun collector in Tidewater Virginia, ever since the obviously staged Stadium Massacre.

Fitz found what he was looking for down at reply #27. A FreeAmerican whose screen name was Virginia Peanut claimed to have been to the actual scene of the fire and listed the following points: #1: There were numerous fresh tire tracks left by several large vehicles which did not belong to the Edmonds. #2: The Edmondses' two doberman watchdogs were missing, but blood trails were found leading to the driveway. A doberman had also been shot at the scene of a gun store arson attack a week before, where the owner had been killed. #3: Fired ten millimeter brass had been found at both arson attacks. #4: The first Feds to arrive on the scene at midday had immediately asserted federal control, and evicted the local law enforcement officers, claiming that a terrorism-related federal investigation was already underway. #5: Shortly after the first Feds arrived and took over, a convoy of vehicles arrived, which included a backhoe excavator on a tractor trailer, along with a CBA network television crew.

FreeAmericans responded furiously to this new information, drawing the obvious conclusion that the dead dobermans, the ten millimeter brass, the backhoe and the ready TV crew meant that the Edmonds fire was surely another government sponsored arson and murder attack, designed for public consumption, in order to heighten the perception of a rampant "militia" threat.

Fitz could not recall ever seeing a reply posted by "Virginia Peanut" before, and clicked on the name to get his posting history on FreeAmericans.net. Fitz was not in the slightest bit surprised that Virginia

Peanut had signed onto FreeAmericans.net only today, meaning that the information could be false, planted by a "troll" for an unknown reason. But it was more likely that the new poster did in fact have first hand knowledge, and was afraid to post under a traceable account, so he had created a new one with an instant Hotmail or Yahoo email address. Fear was in the air, and such precautions were only reasonable.

A new internet acronym had been born on FreeAmericans.net in the past two weeks: LAL, which was not to be confused with LOL, or "laughing out loud." LAL stood for "lock and load," it meant that some kind of a shooting war could break out at any time, and the midnight knock on the door could be the "gun Gestapo" coming for you. Many Free Americans wrote that they did not plan to "go quietly" if they received a midnight battering ram or flash-bang grenade greeting from Uncle Sam's black-clad minions.

Unlike the majority of network news consuming drones who they derided as "sheeple," FreeAmericans were not fooled by recent events, and while many of them had hidden their now illegal semi-autos and scoped rifles, virtually none had turned them in or destroyed them. Thousands of FreeAmericans had even informally organized a nationwide campaign to mail pictures of their so-called "assault rifles" and "sniper rifles" to Washington as a stark warning.

This new information from "Virginia Peanut" about the fatal Burgess family house fire pushed Mark Fitzgibbon, the semi-retired computer network consultant, over the precipice he had been balanced on the edge of for the past two weeks. He disconnected from the internet and clicked off his computer, and sat alone in the dark for long minutes staring at the illuminated face of his digital desk clock.

Mark Fitzgibbon had not always been an old fat bald guy, a revelation which might have surprised most of the people who knew him today. In fact, in a much earlier life, he had been involved in certain activities on the behalf of his government, which were not completely unlike what he was seeing on television and reading about on the internet this September.

In a previous life, a much younger (and leaner) Mark Fitzgibbon had been a Navy SEAL, leading teams of mainly ethnic Chinese Nung mercenaries throughout the Mekong Delta and all the way up into Cambodia, on missions which were in some ways similar to what he was now observing in Virginia. But that had been in a foreign country during a prolonged and vicious guerrilla war, and his targets had in fact been secret Viet Cong "tax collectors" and spies and terrorists, living undercover lives in the Republic of Viet Nam.

Fitz had only been an E-6, a Petty Officer First Class, during his second tour in-country, but running "PRUs" or "Provincial Reconnaissance

Units" was not a task which was assigned according to rank. Most of the other SEALs in the Rung Sat Special Zone operated in seven man squads and 14 man platoons, as he had on his first tour with SEAL Team Two's Third Platoon in 1967. But because of his obvious ease with the local cultures and his amazing aptitude for Asian languages, he had been approached by the local mission of the "Christians In Action" about operating with the PRUs, wiping out secret VC where ever they could be found. (It hadn't hurt that he was a dark-haired "black Irish" and stood only five foot eight: he could blend in better than most Americans in an all-Asian patrol file.)

He had agreed to lead the PRU mercenaries on behalf of the CIA, he'd done his new job and done it well, and he'd had no regrets. Their targets had been bloody-handed communist butchers, who ruled in secret by murdering and terrorizing the inhabitants of any hamlets which wavered in their support for the Viet Cong communists, or dared to back the RVN. These VC terrorists, who wore no uniforms, were merely being paid back in their own coin, and Fitz had zero regrets about sending them to hell a few years ahead of schedule.

But this time Mark Fitzgibbon, fat and old as he was, decided that he would not sit passively by while his own government ran a new "Operation Phoenix" against its own citizens, right here in the USA. He walked to the kitchen and opened a cold Harp Lager, brought it back to his office, and closed the door.

Then in secret, he prepared and loaded a more dangerous weapon than the FBI or the BATF had ever faced in their long histories of battling Mafiosi, drug cartels, outlaw biker gangs, spies and terrorists. Fitz had designed and created this unique weapon long before, largely as an intellectual challenge, but he had hoped that the circumstances would never arise where he would have an actual reason to use it. That began to change after the Stadium Massacre, and now, two weeks later, he was beyond the slightest doubt or possibility of hesitation.

Tomorrow morning he would fire his home made weapon directly at the federal government.

33

The rest of the Special Training Unit was finishing breakfast in the mess trailer or was outside doing physical training in small groups when the Gold Team rolled into the annex. Hours before, not long after Victor Sorrento had been smoothly snatched, Michael Shanks had phoned back a coded message indicating that his mission had failed. The black SUVs and the Virginia Power commo support van rolled into the vehicle hangar, and twelve tired and sullen operators and three tech support guys got out; scratching, stretching, spitting and muttering. They had put the bench seats back into their Suburbans for the long highway pursuit.

Blue team members in PT gear and running shoes immediately began to razz them, looking in the open vehicle doors. "So where's your prisoner?" They peered under the seats and among the gear bags in back, saying, "He must be in here somewhere" and, "Damn, that Gittis must be a little shit."

In return they got only scowls, curses, and brown gobs of Copenhagen snuff spit at their feet.

Shanks said "Yeah, assholes, next time we'll take the corner bar, and you can drive 300 freakin' miles in the pouring rain to Hickory God Damn North Carolina!"

"Hey, if the Gold Team can't hack it…"

Bob Bullard walked up, hands in his pockets, expressionless, and the banter and insults stopped. He didn't PT with the young operators, and was already in his personal "field uniform" of a khaki-colored Dickies work shirt and matching trousers. A cocked and locked .45 government model pistol was holstered on his right hip.

"Okay Michael, let's take it to the office. We'll debrief last night, and talk about what's coming up next."

There was already a pot of strong coffee brewed up in the kitchen corner of the office, along with an open box of convenience store donuts. Bullard, Silvari, Jaeger and Shanks sat around the beat-up conference table, Joe Silvari was enjoying his morning Pepsi with a cigarette. (No one ever mentioned second-hand smoke in the STU: any such whiny expression would earn an immediate smoke cloud blown in the offended party's face, and a casual but quite earnest invitation for him to try to put it out.)

Bullard led off. "Malvone's up in DC. He'll be down later today, maybe. Hammet's at the Norfolk Field Office; he's going to swing by the Joint Task Force ops center and then come down later. Robbie's family has his body, we'll see if we can cut some guys loose for the funeral when we find out when it is. The troops are all up and fed, so let 'em PT until 0900, then get them on gear maintenance while we work on the mission planning."

Silvari was blowing smoke rings, Jaeger was rocking back on his chair, and Shanks appeared much more interested in his coffee. In fact, any of them could repeat Bullard's words back almost verbatim; it was just that visibly paying close attention to leaders was considered uncool, almost as bad as brown nosing.

The STU was a unique group of characters, with a serious anti-authority streak running through them. After all, Wally Malvone had hand picked them, and they were all trouble makers of one sort or another. Their only loyalty, if it could be described as such, was to each other. Among the STU Team members, the greatest possible sin was showing weakness under pressure, or fear in the face of danger. This welded them into an effective force, but one which considered itself apart, and not beholden to any authority outside of themselves.

Bullard continued. "Tim, send some guys up to Home Depot and get a new hot water heater, a big one. The shower situation is totally unsat. And make sure they know we're in isolation here, and that OpSec still comes first. No bar hopping, zero, nada, I won't tolerate it. Home Depot and back; we can't afford to get sloppy.

"I know it's a little basic down here, tell the boys we're looking at some local motels. No promises, it's still up in the air. It's not the money that's the problem, it's maintaining operational security, and that depends on them.

"Anybody got any bitches I haven't covered?" Nobody did. "Tim, you don't need to go over last night's mission; I already heard it and there's not much to learn from telling it again. Blue Team did a real slick 'old buddy' op on the plumber, just like a training exercise. Tim, you'll get to work on him after PT, okay?"

Tim Jaeger remained expressionless, not wanting to be seen gloating after what had admittedly been an easy operation. "Sure. He should be ready to talk by now. We left him in the hurt locker over night."

Bullard turned to the Gold Team Leader next. "All right Michael, go ahead and tell us about Gittis."

Michael Shanks, unshaven and bleary eyed, still wearing yesterday's green plaid shirt and jeans, sipped some more coffee, sighed, and began his story. "Well, you know that commo got a fix on his cell phone down I-85 around Durham, and we took off after him around 1930. Once we had his cell phone codes cranked in, the techs were able to keep it transmitting, sending out its ID every three minutes, you know the deal. So we figured it would be a straight forward chase; just a lot of driving to catch up, and then we'd get him when he stopped for the night. We're making 90 to his 65 on the GPS map plotter, so it's just a matter of time.

"North Carolina state police tried to pull us over once, but we used the grill lights, flashed our FBI creds, said howdy on the radio and kept on trucking. After that, they stayed out of our way. We figured Gittis was going to stop for the night sooner or later, but he just kept on driving.

"This side of Hickory we finally caught up to him. He made a gas stop, but it was at a terrible location for a snatch. He just got his gas, pulled through, and kept going. The place was too small and well-lit, and there were too many witnesses around. The Suburbans would have stuck out too much if we took him there. Maybe we should have gone for it, I don't know... Anyway, around 1230 he pulled off at a rest stop. And by the way, it wasn't a Winnebago: it was a fifth-wheel trailer behind a big black Dodge Ram crew-cab truck.

"So we hung back; there's almost nobody there. Gittis pulled in on the tractor trailer side of the rest stop, so we parked on the car side, and I got out with Baltero to do a little recon. Pistols only, under our raincoats, with suppressors and white lights. We found his trailer and watched him from the bushes between the car side and the truck side of the rest stop. Gittis got out and made a check on his rig, then he went inside it; it's got a side door at the back. We didn't know if he was going to go to sleep for the night, or just use the john and then keep driving.

"So we were playing it by ear. I was making up two plans: a dynamic entry by the full team later on if he went to sleep, and an immediate action drill if he got out to start driving again. So Baltero and I stayed in the shadows, and worked our way around him until we were about ten yards behind his rig, still mostly crouched down in the bushes. The trailer's side door was on the driver's side, the same side as us.

"We were only there a minute or two, scoping it out, and the side door popped open. Gittis stepped out and turned toward the truck: he was leaving. So I decided to go for it and do an immediate action with Baltero. We looped behind him; it was dark, he'd parked in a spot with no lights. It was drizzling, so our approach was nice and quiet.

"He opened up the truck's door, I'm ready to yell "freeze, police!" and blind him with my gun light if he turned, and that bastard spins around and starts shooting! Just like that! He must have had ESP, or maybe he saw us in the side mirror, or heard us, I don't know, but he made us somehow. Anyway, Baltero caught two in his vest, and I nailed him with my Glock. Double tapped him, killed him. It couldn't...I couldn't, there wasn't anything else to do when he turned and fired first. We just didn't expect it, I never saw it coming, never saw the gun; it was just out. BAM BAM! A Browning Hi-Power, nine mill.

"So I called the rest of the team on the tac channel to hold them off when they heard the shots. It was already over, and I didn't want too many footprints on those muddy paths. We took his wallet and his cell phone and pager to make it a robbery, like a mugging gone bad. And we took his gun, of course. Baltero went into the trailer real quick and grabbed his laptop and some notebooks, and we went back through the bushes to the car side of the rest stop, and then we all took off. We purely screwed the pooch Bob, and I accept full responsibility. I didn't take into account he might make us and shoot first. I shouldn't have gone for the immediate action; I should have waited him out, and kept following him."

"You positive he's dead?" asked Bullard.

"Yeah, very positive. Two .45 caliber silvertips through the heart."

"Any witnesses?"

"No. Well, I guess it's possible, but we didn't see any. There were a couple of 18 wheelers parked on the main lot about two or three hundred feet away. Gittis was pulled over near the return lane to the highway where it was darker, all by himself."

"Did you see any local LEOs?"

"No, none. No cops."

"Okay then, lessons learned. Shit happens. Going for the immediate action drill on him half-cocked wasn't a great idea, but I can see you didn't want him driving another 300 miles. So what's done is done... And we can't get lax, we have to assume these dirt bags are armed at all times, and act accordingly. When we get time we should schedule some more snatch and takedown training. No doubt about it, Blue Team had the easier op last night. Shake it off, do better next time. How's Baltero with getting tagged in the vest?"

"He's sore as hell; we weren't wearing our plates so he got some nasty bruises. But he's a professional; he's okay with it... It won't turn him flaky, if that's what you mean. He's half Mex and half Apache, and he doesn't rattle. That's why he's my point man."

"Good, that's what I want to hear. Go get breakfast, and give your guys a couple hours of rack time if they need it. Hammet's at the Joint Task Force getting up to speed. When he gets back we'll decide who we're going after next, unless Wally calls us with a new mission first."

Brad used the pay phone outside the restaurant to call East Sails, and ask about the status of his genoa jib. They were treating themselves to a sit down breakfast at the pancake house on Magruder Boulevard in Poquoson, and planning their day. It was still overcast after last night's rain, but the streets were dry, and it was warm enough for him to dress in his preferred polo shirt, khaki boater's shorts and docksiders. When he came back inside he tried to appear nonchalant as he slid into the booth across from Ranya. Their breakfasts were finished and cleared away except for their coffees; she was reading today's newspaper. An aerial view of the line of cars and emergency vehicles at the Hoffler Boulevard exit ramp was on page one, but he noticed she was reading an article on the Sanderson assassination investigation on an inside page.

"The sail's ready; we can pick it up any time." This meant Guajira would be ready to sail away as soon as the new jib was installed. The East Sails loft was only ten minutes away in Newport News. He couldn't read her reaction; Ranya was wearing wrap-around fake Oakley-style sunglasses and a black Ruger firearms ball cap. Her brown ponytail was pulled through the opening at the back of the cap. She was being very cautious, using the hat and shades as a form of disguise, he thought. As soon as she had pulled off her motorcycle helmet, she had put on the hat; she seemed seriously worried, almost paranoid, about being recognized. The logo on the front of the hat was of the stylized Ruger gothic eagle embroidered in red; only a shooter would recognize its significance, to the rest of the world it would be meaningless.

Ranya had explained to him that she had gotten all sorts of firearms-related gear through Freedom Arms; the manufacturers frequently sent out promotional items pushing their lines. She had always enjoyed wearing t-shirts and hats from Colt, Glock, Winchester and Remington at school for the shocked and stammering reactions they had caused; she enjoyed upsetting the PC sensibilities of the typical anti-gun university liberals. Now these hats and t-shirts were a last connection to her past, the past that had gone up in flames. She had brought the Ruger hat to the boat after she had taken the truck to her apartment to pick up the clothes and things she needed. All that she owned she had either recently purchased, or she had brought down from UVA; everything else had, of course, burned with her house. She was wearing her jeans and jean jacket and boots; her Yamaha was parked outside next to his pickup.

She said, "Well, that's great. Do you want to pick it up right away, or after you sell your truck?" Selling Brad's truck was the major item on the schedule today, before getting the welcome news that the sail was ready. His pickup was excess, since she owned both the motorcycles and the van. His much newer F-250 was worth several times more than her old Econoline, and they planned to sell it for a large chunk of cruising cash. Brad figured that every thousand dollars of cash could buy them another month or two of freedom in the tropics.

"I'd like to go get it now, then take it out to Guajira. We can sell the truck later this afternoon. I'll just feel a lot better when that sail is on the boat; I need to run it up and make sure everything fits. I really want the boat ready to go, just in case."

"Do you need help with the sail? How big is it?"

"Oh, I can handle it all right. Folded up and bagged, it's going to be about as big as this table top, and about a foot thick. Maybe a hundred pounds; I can handle it."

"Well I've got some chores to run over in Norfolk and Portsmouth...some insurance papers to sign, and some banking. And I want to buy some prepaid cell phones; we can't keep depending on pay phones if we need to get in touch."

"Get a couple of the throwaways, the el-cheapo kinds in the foil packs. Sixty minute ones should be fine, and pay cash..."

"You don't need to tell me that. I'll get the kind that you don't have to register to use."

"Sixty minute ones should last us until we're gone," he said. "But only for us to call each other; nobody else that the feds might possibly be monitoring. I'd rather not use any cell phones at all than take a chance on that."

"As long as we're careful, we'll be all right."

"Yeah. That'll work. Hey, after I take care of the sail, I've got some other things to do too; some banking and shopping back on the Norfolk side. How about hooking up later, down there?"

"Where?"

"I'll be shopping at Boat America, over in Virginia Beach on Shore Drive. It's a good place to hang out; I can wait there until you're finished. What's a good time?"

"How about noon?" she replied.

"Noon sounds fine."

"I'll go get my van in Norfolk. We can have lunch somewhere, and then work on getting rid of your truck. Where are you thinking about selling it?"

"Virginia Beach Boulevard. That's the best place; there's one used car dealer after another. They're going to rip me off, but it'll be worth it. We'll need all the cash we can get."

"Well I'm not going to sell my bikes, I'm going to put them in a mini-storage. My Enduro is still in the shed back behind my...where my house was. I'm going to get my van and pick it up today, before it gets ripped off. And Brad, I still can't believe you don't ride! As soon as we get time, I'm going to fix that! My Night Hawk is the perfect bike to learn on, it'll be a breeze for you. You turned me on to sailing, and I'm going to turn you on to motorcycles! You can drive a stick shift, I hope?"

"Hey, I'm not a complete loser. Of course I can drive a stick."

The idea of teaching Brad to ride put the smile back on her face, and she unconsciously squeezed and stroked his hands across the table. She had loved riding her Yamaha FZR alongside his truck on the way up to Poquoson, and was now eagerly looking forward to them riding side by side. "Seriously, it's the most fun you can have with your clothes on..."

He was also smiling; they were forgetting their fears for a moment. "I always wanted to learn to ride, but I never got around to it. But now that I have my own personal instructor, I'll do it."

"You're damn right you will! I'll teach you how to ride, I'm a good instructor, I've taught a few people. You're going to totally love it! It'll just take you a few days, and you'll wonder why you wasted all those years hiding inside of cars."

"Maybe there won't be time, maybe in a few days we'll be out of here, out on the ocean."

"Maybe. How long do you think it'll take us to find George?" she asked.

"I don't know... I wouldn't get too close to the federal building and try to follow him from there, I'm sure they've got cameras all around it. Probably those face recognizing cameras. We definitely don't want to be lurking anywhere around there."

"So dressing in a sexy delivery uniform and strolling into the BATF offices saying 'flowers for George, where's George?' won't cut it?" Ranya slipped down her sunglasses, and winked at him. "I could hide my .45 in a flower box, and walk him right out of there."

She was so damn pretty when she was happy and smiling, Brad thought. Her eyes looked more greenish than hazel today, he wanted to lean across the table and kiss her all over her face. "Uh, no. I don't think that would be such a great idea. Just getting his last name is going to be a problem. We could do some internet searching, check the federal employee registries for local FBI and ATF personnel assignments, things like that, but those data bases are probably classified these days. Anybody that checks those sites is probably going to get their computer flagged, so we'll have to be careful how we do it. And their personal phone numbers are all unlisted, I know that."

Ranya didn't bring up how she had found the Attorney General's address in the ODU library. But then, she had his full name to work with, and he was a public official, not a federal agent. She had another idea. "He gave you a cell phone, right? To contact him?"

"Sure, but I let the batteries run down. I didn't want him using it to track me."

"Well why don't you just charge it up and give him a call? Tell him you heard something. Offer him some hot information, but tell him you need to have a meeting."

"What if he asks me to come to the federal building? I'm not going near that place, no way! And once I call him, he'll be able to track my location off the cell phone. I'm not too cool with that."

"Maybe after you call him, we can use the phone as bait, to draw him to us?"

"But what if he comes with a whole team? He could have the whole meeting area crawling with undercover feds. That might work for taking a shot at him, from long range, but that won't work for grabbing him. How about we just shoot him and be done with it?"

They were talking very quietly, their heads close together, sweetly holding hands across the table while calmly discussing kidnapping a federal agent. They were in a back corner booth; no one was near them. When the waitresses came near, they paused in their talk.

Ranya said, "We have to set it up as a meeting, and try to arrange it so that he comes alone. Offer him enough of a tip to make it interesting, but not enough for him to bring a backup team."

"I don't see how we can control all that. He's like an agent handler here; he'll set up the meeting, and he'll want to control it. It's the only way they do it; they never let an informant set the time and the place. It's a control thing."

"I think it's still our best chance. Anyway, let's think about it; let's think of a good story to tell him to bait the trap. Some way to get him to come alone. If we think about it for a while, we'll come up with something... We'll figure it out. Hey, we're done here aren't we?"

"Yeah, we're done. Let's roll."

She grabbed her black helmet and daypack from the seat next to her, and they got up and walked out. Brad left cash for the bill and the tip on the table.

34

George Hammet rolled into STUville at 1115. He had phoned ahead to Bullard to tell him that he had actionable information, and the team should be ready to move on it. Bullard called Malvone in Washington, and they all agreed it sounded promising, and they should press ahead.

Hammet parked his red Jeep Cherokee directly outside of the cinderblock office building and went straight inside. He was still in his gray suit pants and wingtips, but even with his tie cast aside and his white shirt open at the collar he was still by far the most formally dressed.

Bullard and Shanks were already inside, Silvari and Jaeger came from the interrogation center and joined them only a few moments later. George Hammet was jazzed up, much more cheerful than usual. He dropped his black leather attaché case on the conference table, popped it open, and removed a yellow file folder with a flourish.

"Here it is gang: proof that the FBI is good for something. Even when they don't know it." He opened the folder and slid a series of eight by eleven inch color laser copies across the rough wood surface. "Recognize any of these people?" Hammet was grinning like a poker player who had just thrown down a winning hand on the final pot of the night. The pictures showed about a dozen people, mostly middle-aged males, in various poses and arrangements at an outdoor funeral. The perspective foreshortening indicated that they had been taken with a telephoto lens from a distance.

Jaeger asked, "Who's the babe? She's a real hottie! I think she needs the complete Hollywood treatment."

Bullard had slipped on narrow reading glasses and marked an X over the head of an older man with gray hair, who was wearing a black suit and tie. "This guy looks like our guest, Burgess Edmonds."

"Bingo! Big Bob wins the cigar! Our Burgess Edmonds it is. These pictures have got the Fibbies at the Joint Task Force all worked up, but they don't know half of what I know, and I sure wasn't going to tell them! Nope, this is something I absolutely kept under my hat."

"Come on, just get to it, get to the point already," said Michael Shanks.

"All-righty then, here goes. So right here in the picture is Burgess Edmonds, the famous militia paymaster who is on the run with his .50 caliber sniper rifle. Really, that's what they think at the JTF! They've got his pictures blown up and stuck all over the walls; they're tracking him like he was John Dillinger. What a joke! They're clueless!"

"Okay, we got that, now what do we need to know about these pictures?" asked Bullard.

"Okay. That little 'hottie' is named Ranya Bardiwell. The stiff in the box is her dearly departed daddy; he was a federal firearms licensed gun dealer until he was shot and killed a week back. His store got burned down, and I guess he walked into a bullet. Shit happens... So this is his daughter, and you see this guy next to her in these two shots?"

In the pictures Ranya Bardiwell was wearing a calf-length black dress with a high collar and full sleeves. Next to her was tallish man, late twenties or thirties, in long khaki pants and a blue blazer.

"This guy is the prize. Gentleman, I give you Bradley Thomas Fallon, the man who assassinated Attorney General Eric Sanderson."

"No shit? How do you know that?" asked Silvari.

"Because he's one of my snitches, sort of. That's how. This Fallon's a dead shot, a real Hawkeye; the guy can seriously shoot the balls off a gnat a mile away."

"That's all great, but what connects him to Sanderson?" asked Bullard.

"She does. Tasty young Ranya Bardiwell does. She's got the motive, her dead father. I guess you could say she's on the other side in the gun debate, to put it mildly! Anyway, the Fibs have done some of the leg work. They've got these two making cell phone calls the evening of Saturday the 15th, that's the night after her father was shot.

"Okay, so they know each other? So what?"

"Well, she's a student at the University of Virginia in Charlottes-ville, and her cell phone places her up there until Saturday morning." Hammet laid down a pair of computer printouts of their cell phone records, with one line highlighted in yellow near the bottom on each.

"There's no contact between either of them before this call on the night of the 15th. And then that's it, no more calls between them, and they both just about stopped using their cell phones entirely. Both of them; look at the printout. Now that's either a hell of a coincidence, or they hooked up and after that they decided to stop using their cell phones. Why? And Miss Bardiwell has dropped out of school, and dropped out of sight."

"Where's Fallon now? You said he's your CI?"

"Wait, I'm not finished with Ranya Bardiwell yet. The JTF went through all the internet accessible data bases that have anything to do with Sanderson, to see if anybody's been doing research on him. And they got a cluster right here on Sunday the 16th, all in five minutes. Deeds, mortgage records, utilities, all of them focused on obtaining his home address."

Silvari asked, "So then they found the computer that made the queries, right? That should be slam dunk."

"They did, but then it gets even more interesting. The computer is in the library here at Old Dominion University. University, as in university student, as in Ranya Bardiwell. Anyway, the computer was logged to an

ODU freshman; he's been checked out and cleared. But lo and behold, he says he let somebody sit in on his time. A young lady asked to 'check her email.' The times match."

"So did he get a description?" asked Jaeger.

"Not a good one. He just remembers she was a cute hippie chick in her early twenties, with a nice rack."

"So if it's Bardiwell, she's pretty smart. She didn't use her own email account or her own computer," said Silvari.

"Put that together with the cell phone cutoff, and you'd have to say she's smarter than the average bear, definitely. Those are two common mistakes she's avoided," said Hammet.

"So she's dropped out of school; where's she staying now? With Fallon?" asked Jaeger.

"Probably. Maybe," said Hammet.

"So where's he live? Is the FBI onto him yet?" asked Bullard.

"Well, this is where it gets interesting again. He lives on a boat," replied Hammet.

"On a boat? What kind of boat?" asked Shanks.

"A sailboat, a great big sucker about forty feet long. But the FBI doesn't know it yet; they're still out to lunch. The task force doesn't know what it's got. If we move fast, we'll beat them to the punch."

"So where's this boat? You said he's your informant, right?" asked Bullard.

"Kind of, but he was never active. I put the squeeze play on him and tried to place him inside the Black Water Rod and Gun Club. He's a big shooter; I originally found him last August at a rifle match down here. Then after the Stadium Massacre, he turned up on a surveillance video at a hardware store near Shifflett's place; he was schmoozing with one of those Black Water guys. So I gave it a shot. I tried to infiltrate him into the Black Water club, but it didn't pan out, and I moved onto bigger and better things. To tell you the truth, I hadn't given Fallon much thought until I saw the funeral pictures this morning."

"So where's his boat?"

"It's way up a river in Suffolk, or at least it was. It's got no mast. He's working on the boat; it's kind of a fixer-upper deal."

"Up a river? Can we get there by road? Do we need to get boats now?" asked Bullard.

"No, no boats, we can get to it by road. If he's still there. That's where he was when I recruited him."

Silvari said, "He's not there, forget about it. He's gone." He said this with an edge of disdain. "Somebody who lives on a boat and suddenly stops using his cell phone, and then he goes and snipes out an Attorney

General? You think he's going to make it easy for us and stick around? He's long gone."

"But his boat's not finished; it's got no mast," replied Hammet.

"It's got a motor, doesn't it? He didn't get towed up that river did he?" said Silvari.

"I don't know Half-Ass, do you? Maybe he did get towed up there. The boat looked like a dump inside; tools and crap everywhere."

Bullard asked, "So what's the JTF's take on him? Are they all over this Fallon?"

Hammet replied, "They know they've got something in those pictures, but Fallon's not the top of their list. The Black Water gang is their primary focus, just like it was for us. Joe Bardiwell wasn't in the club, and neither was Fallon, and Fallon didn't even move to Tidewater until last July. So Ranya Bardiwell and Fallon are on their radar, but they're not in the center. The dangerous fugitive Burgess Edmonds is the center, him and the rest of the Black Water gang. They're really not sure what they've got with Fallon yet. My ATF paperwork never made it to the JTF; we don't spread our CI files around, obviously. The JTF has a list of some of the guns he's owned, so they're interested, but they don't know how good of a shot he is. And I sure didn't tell them."

"So what do they drive? Fallon and Bardiwell? They must have cars, we can find them that way," said Bullard.

"Fallon drives a red Ford truck; I've got their DMV sheets here. Bardiwell rides a motorcycle. Two motorcycles actually; she's down for a Yamaha and a Honda."

Jaeger perked up. "No shit? Ranya's got two rice burners?" He began studying the photos with new interest. "I think I'm in love! Maybe when we grab them, I'll be able to get in some quality time with her."

Silvari asked Hammet, "Did you put a tracer on Fallon's truck? He was your informant."

"No, and I wish I did. We don't have enough tracers at the Field Office to put them on every vehicle that's marginally interesting. We don't have the STU's budget, that's for sure. I gave him a cell phone for contacting us, but it's out of service. I checked."

"What about their plastic? It's easy to give up cell phones, but have they stopped using credit cards?"

"I don't know, I didn't see anything on that at the JTF."

Silvari flipped open his own cell phone. "Charles, can you run some cell numbers and credit cards for me? Right, most recent use for these two subjects." He spelled out their names, read off their cell phone and license plate numbers from Hammet's printout, and gave the other particulars that he had, and put the phone away. "We'll find out in a minute." Then he lit up another cigarette, leaned back in his chair and took a deep drag.

"So where was his boat, when you saw it? How far away is it? Can we drive over and check it out, or should we put the plane up?" asked Shanks. The STU's single engine Piper Lance was on the main side of the Naval Auxiliary Landing Field in another abandoned hangar, tied down next to its own small fuel truck. Bullard, Silvari and several of the STU operators were licensed pilots. It was not for nothing that many of them quipped that ATF also stood for "agents that fly."

"Waste of time, he's long gone," said Silvari, exhaling a cloud of smoke.

Bullard said, "Maybe, maybe, but let's do it anyway. Let's get ready to fly; we'll check out where the boat was, maybe it's still there. That's a good starting point. George, you'll go up with me; you know where the place is, and you know what the boat looks like."

Silvari's cell phone chirped on the table, and he picked it up. His cigarette bounced on his lip as he spoke, "Yeah, uh huh, Newport News? Right. Got it." He jotted some notes on a pad and put the phone back in his shirt pocket. "You know, if it wasn't for my support geeks...damn they do good work. Check this out: they not only aren't using their cell phones, they're either off the grid completely, or they let the batteries go dead, or they took them out. Both of them. Smart: they must know what kind of tricks we do with cell phones. What are the odds of two people who never met before both killing their cell phones, unless they decided to do it together?"

"They've hooked up," said Jaeger.

"Definitely. But it gets better." Silvari took another pull, and slowly exhaled a long blue stream over the table. "Fallon just used his credit card, an hour and a half ago in Newport News. A place called 'East Sails', for 2,000 bucks."

"Hot damn!" exclaimed Bob Bullard. "We've got him! Let's get ready to roll! What's Newport News, thirty miles from here?"

Silvari's cell phone chirped again. "Yeah. Okay, right. Virginia Beach? Great, thanks Charles, yeah you do good work. Yup. You got it buddy, a case of Corona. Yeah, tell the boys they earned it." He put the phone away again. "Gentlemen, Brad Fallon just withdrew $4,900 dollars cash money from the Virginia National Bank on Independence Boulevard, just twenty minutes ago. How ya like them apples?"

Bullard jumped out of his chair and clapped his hands and rubbed them together. "Hot damn! Now we're cookin' with steam! Okay, Tim, get ready to roll the Blue Team!"

"They're already standing by."

"Okay, we'll check out the bank; if we miss him there at least we'll be in the neighborhood, and we can start a box search for his truck. Put the plane on five minute standby; if he uses another card, we'll send the Bird Dog up and follow him from the air. That's two electronic transactions this morning; I'm guessing Fallon is going to do a little more shopping today. So if we're in the area, we'll be able to vector to him, and nail his ass! Tim, we'll pull another 'old buddy' on him if we can, or we'll follow him back to his boat and get him there. If we're lucky, we'll nail the bitch with him.

"Take two Suburbans and the party van, just like you did last night. Run it the same way; same people, everything. This is the real deal boys, the plumber was just training! George, you ride in the party van with Tim; you're the only one who's seen Fallon, you can make the positive ID.

"Michael, I know Gold Team is tired after their all-nighter, but put them on a one hour standby, in case we wind up doing a long moving surveillance. If you have to go, don't take your Suburbans; we don't want to overdo it. Take the rentals and some personal vehicles; if we're tailing him we'll need all the switch cars we can get."

"No problemo Bob. Will do," replied Shanks.

"That's it then, let's do it: let's nail this bastard. You all know what it'll mean for the STU Team if we catch Sanderson's assassin, while the FBI and the whole damn JTF are still holding their peckers."

Tim Jaeger said, "You know Bob, I'm getting the hang of this interrogation thing. When I'm finished with Fallon, he's going to be a confession machine: any where, any time, to anybody. He's going to give up his murder rifle, he's going to give up his girlfriend, he's going to give it all up."

Brad spent 45 minutes in the Boat America store, pushing and pulling a pair of shopping carts up and down the crisply air conditioned aisles. He was in a great mood, because the morning's genoa jib installation had gone smoothly. The wind was light and directly over Guajira's bow as she swung on her anchor, so it was simple to pull it up with the jib halyard. The big white 600 square foot jib fit perfectly, looked terrific, and now it was rolled up around the forestay and ready to use. After stopping by a branch of his bank he had a fresh wad of 49 one hundred dollar bills in an envelope, in the right front cargo pocket of his shorts, and he was ready for some serious shopping.

He knew that once they pulled up their anchor, he would not see the inside of such a maritime cornucopia again literally for years. Critical consumables like epoxy resin, anti-fouling bottom paint, extra dock lines and halyards, rubber fenders, an extra hand held VHF radio, varnish, wet sand paper and dozens of other items large and small filled his carts. He knew that once he left America all of these items, if he could find them at all, would cost two or three times more than today.

Finally at quarter before twelve he stopped, and headed for the checkout lanes, where he was still remembered dotingly from his previous binge-buying. The manager came out and asked if he was getting ready to go cruising and Brad lied, and said only that cruising was his eventual goal.

The total came to over $800. He had considered long and hard about using his VISA card, or paying with cash. On the one hand, it was a priority to conserve as much cash on hand as possible. Every thousand dollars of cash meant at least another month of swimming and diving and making love with beautiful Ranya in secluded tropical lagoons.

With the $4,900 he had just withdrawn, he had built up almost $35,000 cash on hand, always taking it out in increments just under the current federal reporting guidelines. The fact that his latest bank withdrawal had passed without a hiccup led him to believe that the feds were no longer on his case, and that their threats to freeze his accounts had been forgotten. Plus, he'd already used his VISA card once before today at East Sails, to make the second and final payment which had been due upon completion of his new genoa jib.

Finally, he'd had the clever idea to throw a red herring into the path of anyone who might come searching for him later. In the books and charts section of the store, he selected a variety of paper charts and cruising guidebooks for the Azores Islands, Spain, Portugal, Morocco, and the Mediterranean. He'd previously been careful to only pay cash for his charts and guides for the Caribbean and South America, not wishing to leave any signposts pointing toward his true destination.

So after careful deliberation, when the total was rung up, Brad left the $4,900 cash in the bank envelope in his cargo pocket, slid his VISA card out of the slot in his wallet, and handed it to the jovial cashier.

Two minutes after the cashier at Boat America swiped Brad Fallon's credit card, Tim Jaeger had his current location. A STU support geek in the thirty foot converted motor home back on the annex had been tasked with monitoring Brad Fallon's electronic footsteps in real time: cell phone, banks, ATMs, credit cards. If they were very lucky, and Fallon's face was scanned by one of Virginia Beach's dozens of digital cameras, his image and location would arrive on the STU technician's monitor as soon as it was sent to the Joint Task Force in the Norfolk federal building. (The critical difference was that the STU was actively seeking Fallon and already had a team in place, while the information would remain unseen and unacted on for days or weeks by the ponderous federal anti-terrorism bureaucracy at the JTF.)

Moments after the electronic support tech back at STUville "saw" Fallon use his credit card, the amount and location was read by Tim Jaeger, on the laptop in the console of their blue Dodge conversion van.

Jaeger said, "Did everybody copy that? Fallon's at the Boat America store on Shore Drive, right now!" The blue van was being trailed by two black Chevy Suburbans. "Base, we're northbound on Witchduck Road, approaching the I-44, ETA is ten minutes, over."

Bob Bullard's voice came across their radios. "Blue leader, this is Bird Dog, I'm rolling now. We'll be over the place before you get there. If we spot the red truck we'll get a lock on it, over."

"Roger Bird Dog. Let's do it."

The staff at Boat America packed Brad's purchases into three large cardboard boxes, and helped him to carry them out onto the parking lot. He locked them in the cab of his truck and returned to the store to wait for Ranya; it was 1155. He returned to the book section to do some more reading from the cruising guides that he had not purchased, soaking in the rich yachty atmosphere of binoculars, electronic displays, and colorful charts, while keeping an eye on the glass double doors for Ranya.

It was warmer outside now, and she would be driving her van, not riding her motorcycle, so he hoped that she would be wearing something a little skimpier, a little more revealing, than her usual jeans and jean jacket. He remembered how sexy she had looked in the clingy pink low-cut top she had worn yesterday, which he had peeled off of her in Guajira's cockpit... Ranya was in the front of his thoughts all the time now; her gentle touch, the smell of her hair, her sometimes green and sometimes amber eyes, her warm inviting smile, her soft lips...

Any minute now and she'll be here. We'll have a nice lunch together, and then go sell the truck, and we'll be back on Guajira while it's still warm enough to go swimming. And then we'll make love again in the cockpit... He stood by the bookshelves staring across the store and out through the glass doors, wishing her here already.

Once we're back on Guajira, I'll put on some romantic music: some Sade or Enigma, maybe some Deep Forest to set the mood, or Shakira to make her think of South America. I'll pour some Cuba Libre's with the Captain Morgan's rum, and we'll see how gung-ho she is to pursue her vendetta against G-man George. Then we'll see. Some Captain Morgan's and Coke, maybe some Enya tunes, Caribbean Blue and Orinoco Flow... Then a pink and silver sunset, and the old Brad Fallon charm…Guajira just 25 miles from the Atlantic…a week's sail from the Bahamas… We'll see what happens. We'll just see.

"Blue leader, this is Bird Dog. I've got a red pickup on the parking lot right out front, it looks like a full-sized Ford, we'll get a better slant-angle and confirm the tag, wait one over."

"Roger Bird Dog, copy. We're on Shore Drive now, ETA one minute, over."

"Blue leader, how's your connection, are you up? I'll send you the picture, over."

"Oh yeah, we got it, very nice; mark the red truck, over."

"Marking it now, over," said Bullard, from 3,000 feet up.

A tiny rectangular box outlined a red pickup truck parked about 100 feet from the front of the Boat America store, the lot was one-third filled. The transmitted wireless video feed from the Piper Lance's "Big Eye" tracking camera was not of great quality, and it refreshed only twice a second, but it was quite useable.

Tim Jaeger told Hammet, who was driving the blue van, "Okay, there's Boat America, turn in front of the Taco Bell." Then on the radio to the airplane, "Bird Dog, we've got the red truck visual, over."

"I'll drive behind the truck and confirm the tag," said Hammet.

On the tactical net Jaeger said, "Blue Two, get ready to send Jamie in to look for the target, is he wired up?"

"Roger Blue Leader, he's ready to go."

"Okay Blue Two, I've got confirmation on the vehicle tag, send Jamie in."

The black suburban carrying Blue Two pulled alongside the strip mall's sidewalk, and stopped one business before Boat America, in front of PetCo. Jamie Silverton, at 27 the youngest STU Team operator, looked like a "surfer dude" with his almost shoulder length bleached-blond hair. He was wearing a loose untucked brown and white Hawaiian shirt, jeans and a Baltimore Orioles ball cap when he stepped out of the SUV and strolled down the sidewalk and into the boat store. Walkman-type stereo plugs were stuck in his ears, except he was not tuned into rock or country, he was tuned into the STU tactical net. The eye of the orange bird on his black hat concealed the aperture for a pinhole video camera.

There was a space available next to Fallon's red pickup, Jaeger directed Hammet to park the Dodge van there. He played with the laptop and a grainy black and white fisheye image appeared: the aisles of Boat America. Silverton began a clockwise circle search around the perimeter of the store, turning and pausing as he looked down each aisle. A salesman's distorted face loomed into view. "Can I help you find something today?"

"No thanks, I'm just looking around," came back through the tinny speakers of the computer, fuzzy but audible.

Three quarters of the way around the giant store, after passing anchors, spools of rope, rubber boats and plastic kayaks the camera view showed what seemed to be a small bookstore in its own partitioned section. Silverton's hands picked up a sailing magazine and pretended to read, the image on the computer screen showed his fingers turning the pages in half second jumps, as STU members on the parking lot, up in the Piper, and down at the base all watched in real time. Jamie wasn't talking now.

Jaeger asked, "Blue Niner, is that the subject, over?"

"Uh-huh," came back the reply from Jamie Silverton, AKA "Blue Niner" in the STU Team. He lifted his view until they could all see the back of a clean-cut blondish Caucasian male. He was wearing a dark polo shirt and shorts, and he seemed to be reading a book.

"Blue Niner, his back's not helping us much. Can you slide over and get his face, over?"

The video image jerked and slid, showed random images of the floor and a book shelf in close up, then it came back to rest. In the party van, George Hammet, watching the computer screen, said, "That's him. That's Fallon, I'm 100% sure." Then he joked, "Hey Tim, he kind of looks like you. You don't have any bastard half-brothers, do you?"

Jaeger ignored this remark and asked Jamie Silverton, "Okay Blue Niner, subject is confirmed, give him some room now. Just keep a loose over-watch and give us a shout when he heads for the door, okay?"

The video image moved up and down, this was Silverton nodding "okay," and then it moved away.

"Okay Blue Two, slight variation on last night. The van's parked right next to his truck. We'll nail him in the slot. We'll open our front door and block him in. Send the pushers behind him when he comes out."

"Copy, Blue Leader."

"Blue Leader, this is Blue Niner, he's moving, over."

"Okay Blue, showtime!" said Jaeger. The van was parked so that its front passenger and sliding doors were next to the driver's door of Fallon's red Ford truck. The pickup's cab was jammed with brown boxes on the passenger side. Jaeger stepped out and walked across the parking lot away from the store, toward the Shore Drive access road, so that when Fallon came out he could stroll back toward the store and meet his "old buddy" just as he neared his truck.

"Blue Leader, Blue Niner: he's coming out, stand by!" Silverton's video showed the back of Fallon heading for the front doors.

The twin front double glass doors of Boat America swung open. "Okay folks, here we go," said Tim Jaeger on their encrypted tactical net, and he began his casual walk across the parking lot toward the store. They all had wireless ear buds and throat mikes for communicating clandestinely while on foot.

Fallon didn't head toward his pickup truck though, he just stood in front of the doors, looking around, scanning and apparently searching.

"Blue Leader, Blue Seven. He's, uh, not walking, over," said one of the STU "pushers."

"Roger, I see him." Shit! Jaeger bent down between two parked cars, pretending to tie his shoelace. "Tell me when he's moving again." A full minute passed. Jaeger had to stand up, feeling like an idiot, totally burned. He turned his back to the store to talk. "Did he make us? What's going on? What's he doing?"

Bullard's voice came over the net. "Blue Leader, Bird Dog. Advise you abort. Drop back, and let us take it from up here, over."

Tim Jaeger didn't want to quit, not this close to his quarry. The wise thing would be to only observe, and follow Fallon to Ranya Bardiwell and any other conspirators. But he was here, now, for the taking, and he could be made to talk! Once he had Fallon strapped onto the water board, they would catch the rest of the gang easily. If they delayed and the JTF got wind of their coup, the Fibbies would take over the operation, make the collar, and claim all the credit. This was not an acceptable outcome.

"Bird Dog, this is Blue Leader, I have a new plan."

It was 1210, and there was still no sign of Ranya. Brad was deciding whether to go back inside the store to the book section, go out and wait in his truck and hear what they were saying on talk radio, or stay where he was in front of Boat America for a few more minutes.

The next store over on the other side from PetCo was Big Ten Discount Sports. When Ranya showed up, he decided he would take her inside to pick out her own swim fins and snorkeling gear, and maybe some different swimsuits and sports tops. He thought she'd look awesome in a clingy spandex halter top… He wondered how Ranya would react when they got to the French and Dutch islands, and all of the girls were going topless on the boats and the beaches. He fervently hoped she would catch the Caribbean spirit and go topless on Guajira! Ranya had exceptionally gorgeous upturned pear-shaped breasts, full but not too big, not saggy at all, just right for going topless…he could picture her swimming underwater, snorkeling on the reefs like a mermaid…

Halfway down the Boat America storefront toward Big Ten Sports, he noticed a bank of newspaper boxes. He walked over to see which ones were available, maybe he'd pick up a Richmond or Washington paper if there were any. He had read more newspapers in the last two weeks than in the previous two years.

He was rummaging in his front pockets for change when a blue conversion van glided up alongside the curb. Brad paid no attention; he was looking for Ranya's plain vanilla Econoline.

Then someone in the van called his name, someone said, "I'll be damned! It's Brad Fallon!" and stepped out of the front passenger door. It was some guy with his light brown hair combed straight back, wearing wrap around sunglasses and a light green safari-style shirt and jeans.

"Hey Brad, remember me? Bob Michaels! We went through Navy boot camp together at Great Lakes in 93, remember?"

Brad was momentarily taken aback, but after all, Virginia Beach was a Navy town...he wracked his memory trying to place this Bob Michaels, who was enthusiastically reaching out to shake his hand. A couple of Boat America customers passed the store's front door in his peripheral vision. He somewhat reluctantly accepted the friendly stranger's hand, the guy certainly seemed to remember him well enough, maybe he was somebody that he had just plain forgotten, it happens...

But Brad, for the life of him, could just not place this Bob Michaels. Still, he wanted to be polite, because the guy sure remembered him! He must have left some kind of strong impression on one of the less memorable members of his training company. He tried to release his handshake, but the man clamped a second hand around his from the other side, and when Brad stepped back and turned the man stepped and turned with him, almost like a dancer.

"Brad Fallon! What a great surprise to run into you! What are you up to these days?"

Brad was about to jerk his hand out of this smiling lunatic's grasp when he was struck on the neck by what felt like a Louisville Slugger. The blue van's side door was suddenly wide open, and he was being shoved forward and pulled into it at the same time, even while he was still reeling from the painful blast to his neck.

A second later he was slammed face-first down onto the carpeted floor, with what felt like a thousand pounds of weight on top of him as the side door slammed closed. There were fast clicks as his arms were pulled behind and his wrists were handcuffed together, his ankles were shackled, and a sack was pulled over his head and tied around his neck. He was flipped on his side and someone was digging into his pockets, he both felt and heard his keys being pulled out.

Then most of the weight came off of him, the side door opened again and from the sounds he thought maybe somebody got out. The door closed once more, and the vehicle started moving again.

Someone with a vaguely familiar northeastern accent said, "Take it easy down there partner, save your energy; you're shackled to the floor. It's been a while, eh Brad? We should really try to stay in better touch. You remember me?"

After a moment to slightly recover from his utter state of shock, Brad did indeed remember the voice. "...George..." came his muffled reply.

"Right you are, boyo. And we've got a lot to talk about, you and me and my buds. A lot to talk about. So if I was you, I'd relax. Just chill out, and spend this little ride thinking about exactly what it is we might want to talk about."

Agony flooded in on top of the pain. Brad's neck still hurt like he'd been clubbed with a hot branding iron, his wrists and shoulders were half dislocated and pinched by the tight steel, his face burned where he had initially been driven into the carpet.

He'd been bagged by one of the oldest routines in the book, a method perfected by the Soviet NKVD and KGB, but used in all police states. His mistake was that he had never anticipated seeing it used here in the United States! This was the secret arrest designed not to look like an arrest, but merely a chance meeting among "old friends," an arrest designed to not alarm unaware witnesses, to preserve their placid serenity, right up until the day that they too were greeted on a street corner by an "old friend."

Brad had no illusions about his chance of a quick release, and he did not cry out his innocence to his captors, or beg them to reexamine their obvious error. He knew it was no mistake. He had seen no uniforms or badges, and he was read no warrant or Miranda warning. This was a secret arrest, by secret police, and that meant no lawyers, no phone calls, no protections at all.

He bitterly cursed his own stupidity. He'd known as soon as he saw the door of the van slide open that his credit card had been his Judas, betraying him for $800 worth of extra boat supplies.

It was just after noon when it happened, while he was waiting for Ranya. And the same people who had just captured him could even now be back at Boat America with another van, and pictures of Ranya. To think, that in spite of everything he knew about these things, he had used his credit card and then stood around in front of Boat America: he might as well have hung a sign saying "I'm Brad Fallon" around his neck...

He had led them straight to himself and to Ranya as well, all because of his colossal stupidity!

35

Ranya wasn't certain which block of strip malls along Shore Drive it was that Boat America was located in, and she was almost past it before she saw its blue and white marquee across the wide parking lot. Instead of driving straight in she pulled to the side of the service road which paralleled Shore Drive and parked, scanning for Brad, his truck, or any signs of surveillance.

Traffic continued to flow past her normally; she had detected no vehicles following her on the way back from Suffolk where she had picked up her Enduro. Visiting the site of her former home and store, the place where her father had been murdered, both depressed her and re-galvanized her anger. On the way to Virginia Beach she had gotten on and off the highway several times to try to detect anyone following her, but she had seen nothing, and there were no repeat appearances by the same vehicles.

Of course, she realized she could never rule out that she had already been discovered, and a hidden tracking device had been placed somewhere on her van...or that she might even now be under the un-blinking eye of a federal helicopter, plane, or unmanned drone. Her level of caution and even paranoia remained extremely high, but she did not allow it to paralyze her.

Ranya could only hope that she was still in the clear and not a suspect or "person of interest" in any investigation, and that her white van was still anonymous and unknown to the feds. When she bought the van, she had kept the previous owner's tags, and their sticker was good until the end of October. She had planned to reregister it, but after stalking and killing Sanderson she decided to temporarily defer putting it in her own name. For the time being the lack of a DMV connection between herself and the van was an advantage.

The same could not be said for Brad's Ford truck: "George the Fed" had clearly known about it since the time of his attempted recruitment of Brad as an informant. This made his truck more than slightly radio-active in Ranya's eyes, and she wanted them to be rid of it as quickly as possible. She didn't even think selling it was worth the attention and the paper trail the transaction might bring, she would have simply abandoned it, or put it into long term storage like she was going to do with her bikes and most of her possessions.

Wearing her Ruger ball cap and shades to obscure her face, she scanned the half-filled parking lot and quickly spotted the cab of Brad's pickup in the middle, she recognized it by the small antenna which sprouted from the roof. But Brad was not in it, and neither was he standing around near the front of the store waiting for her. That meant she would have to go in and find him, a needless exposure she wished she could avoid.

Each trip into a national chain store like Boat America would mean being recorded by several video cameras. For several years the federal government had been subsidizing the cost of upgrading the video surveillance systems of both local governments and major retail chains to the latest digital technology standards, and the quid pro quo was providing the government with their own access channels to the video output. This was the heart of the new "Universal Surveillance Act." In this way and dozens more, America was quietly and with little fuss being turned into a total surveillance society, all in the name of fighting the war on terrorism.

While she watched from across the lot, the automatic Boat America double doors opened, and a blond-haired man walked out just as a black Chevy Suburban pulled to the curb. When the big SUV pulled away across the front of the shopping center, the man was gone. Dark full-sized American SUVs with opaquely tinted windows always received Ranya's full attention. She tended to consider them potential "fed-mobiles" unless and until she saw soccer moms and kids spilling out of them.

At the far corner of the parking lot to her left, she saw a blue camper van driving away from the shopping center toward Shore Drive. Halfway across the parking lot it stopped, and two guys in jeans and loose shirts stepped from the sliding side door. The van then continued to Shore Drive a hundred yards in front of her, made a left turn across the traffic lanes, and headed west in the direction she had just come from.

One of the two men from the van walked down the parking lot exit road toward the stores, and the black Suburban which had just picked up the blond man from in front of Boat America paused and picked him up as well. The rear side door had been opened for him, before he had even reached for it.

Even stranger, the other man who had gotten out of the blue van walked directly through the lot's parked cars, walking in the general direction of Brad's truck. He was a tall man about 35, with long swinging arms and reddish-brown hair and a mustache, wearing a brown and black plaid shirt which hung below his belt line, an indication that he could be carrying a pistol. Ranya gripped the wheel tightly and almost stopped breathing. There was a pattern unfolding, connectivity, a non-random series of events in an otherwise unremarkable sequence. And there was still no Brad coming out of Boat America, at almost quarter after twelve noon.

While she watched, the man from the blue van who was walking across the parking lot stopped by Brad's red truck; possibly a coincidence, she could not see from her angle if he was going to another car, but her pulse quickened. He was only about 40 yards from her as she looked out the passenger window; she leaned back against the headrest and tried to observe as inconspicuously as she could. Then Brad's driver's side door opened, and the red-headed man got into his truck! He just climbed right inside! Brad always locked the doors, always, he never left them open, yet a stranger had just gotten in! The door opened again, and the stranger appeared to put something in the back, something brown, then the door closed again, and in moments the truck began to move!

How? Duplicate keys, a slim-jim bar? Impossible. The man had to have keys, which meant that he had Brad's keys, which meant...they must have Brad! Brad must be in the blue van, or the black Suburban! The van and the SUV were already out of sight, heading west on Shore Drive, back toward Norfolk.

Could he still be in the store? Could his keys have been stolen by a pickpocket? Impossible. An entire team of men to steal a used truck? Was he possibly meeting someone to sell the truck, and gave him his keys? In Boat America? Absurd. That only left one possibility.

Brad's truck passed the front of the stores and left by the same parking lot exit road as the blue van and the black SUV, and made the left onto Shore Drive, crossing only 100 yards in front of her van, still parked on the side of the service road. It headed west, in the same direction as the other two vehicles. There was no time for doubt now, Brad had been arrested or kidnapped, and not by any ordinary police.

What a fool she'd been, thinking of ways to literally use Brad as live bait to capture George the Fed, and at this very minute he was being driven off to God knows where! But west was the direction of downtown Norfolk, and the federal building...

His red truck picked up speed, getting several blocks ahead before Ranya threw the shifter into drive and pulled to the break in the service road, and made her own left turn onto Shore Drive. She could only hope and pray that Brad's truck was being driven to wherever Brad was being taken. If it was being taken somewhere to be dumped, she would have to ambush the driver when he got out, and capture him alive, or her only chance of finding Brad would be lost. Her loaded .45 was in her fanny pack, on the passenger seat.

She had to count on the driver of Brad's truck not worrying about being tailed, about the possibility of the hunter becoming the hunted. It was a chance she had to take. If the driver did much checking in his rear view mirror, Ranya thought she would be spotted, but she had no alternative. The only thing that mattered was finding Brad, so today was a day to risk everything, and hold nothing back. At any rate, plain off-white delivery vans were extremely common...

She hung back as far as she dared, relying on her 20-20 vision to keep slivers of his truck visible in traffic ahead, but she still had to run a red light once to keep from losing it altogether. The tiny antenna on the roof of the cab, which was not even connected to anything, was a Godsend, because it distinguished his pickup from any others in thick traffic. After only a mile the truck turned, making a left onto Northampton Boulevard, and then it made another turn onto a cloverleaf. She lost sight of the truck in the loop, but spotted it again heading south on Independence.

For almost four miles they traveled like this, with Ranya staying as far back as possible, briefly losing him when a Virginia Beach Police cruiser in the next lane prevented her from driving up a right-turn-only lane to get ahead of traffic at a stop light. Once she was through the inter-section, after the police car had made a left turn, she floored it and did 75 in a 45 zone for a few blocks, until she caught sight of his red truck again. Just north of the enormous intersection with Virginia Beach Boulevard, which ran east-to-west, the pickup pulled off Independence and drove through a shopping center. Ranya turned into the same shopping center through an earlier entrance.

Brad's truck pulled into the drive-through lane of a Burger King; it was only the second car in line but Ranya had time to catch her breath and think. She parked the van outside of a small stand-alone real estate office, in the shade of a maple tree a hundred yards from the drive-through. From there she could watch the truck while remaining inconspicuous, yet remain ready to take up the pursuit in a moment.

She knew that she couldn't stay in the white van and continue following him south indefinitely without being spotted. Independence would soon turn into Holland Road, and become much more rural and wide open. And whenever the red truck finally reached its destination, the van would be nearly impossible to hide. It would almost certainly give her away, depending on where the pursuit came to a conclusion.

Her old Yamaha XT 250 was tied in the center of the van behind her; on the bike she could follow him much more inconspicuously. At the range that she could just barely make out the red truck, her black and tan primer-painted Enduro would be a nearly invisible dot in the truck's rear view mirror. She could also use cars as a screen, effectively hiding from his view behind them, and she could swiftly surge ahead if she was left far behind by a traffic light.

Brad's truck was now at the window being served, he would be driving away in a minute, so there was no time to unload the bike. If she took the time to try she might lose sight of the truck completely; the giant intersection with Virginia Beach Boulevard and then the Expressway cloverleaf were coming up just ahead. She'd have to keep following in the van to be certain that she could keep him in sight after he left the Burger King, and take her chances with being spotted.

The driver was handed his sacks of food and he pulled forward, but he didn't turn back toward Independence Boulevard, instead he weaved a half block through the shopping center lot and parked outside a Virginia ABC liquor store. He stepped out of the truck, turned and looked all around him, and went into a shop next to the ABC store. He was a real ape; he made her think of a malevolent orangutan. Her angle of view was poor for observing the shop, but Ranya remembered her small 8X20 binoculars which were in a cardboard moving-box full of odds and ends in the cargo area behind her. She quickly grabbed them and saw that the shop which was next to the ABC store was the "Midnite Sun Adult Books and Videos."

Ranya breathed a deep sigh of relief that the driver had gone into the dirty book store, she instinctively knew that she'd have time to unload the Enduro. She immediately went to work in the back of the van, first topping off the dirt bike's gas tank from the metal Jerry can she had also retrieved from her motorcycle shed. She used the razor-sharp serrated edge of her folding pocket knife to slash through the nylon ropes holding the bike to the sides of the van, and in a moment it was loose. She opened the rear cargo doors, passed on using her loading plank, and walked the bike backward, bouncing it down onto the pavement, holding the handle-bars and using the hand brake.

A block away in its own section of the shopping center, the red truck was still parked outside the Midnite Sun adult bookstore. Ranya quickly went through the van, loading everything that might be useful into her black daypack and her butt pack: a Tidewater street map, her never-used prepaid cell phone in its sealed foil pack, the little pair of 8X20 binoculars, a one liter plastic bottle of PowerAde sports drink, her black ball cap, the tiny compass she had used to locate the weapons cache and other items.

Her custom .45 she kept in the fanny pack; a rapid draw was not as important now as the chance of losing it. She could not depend on leaving it shoved under her belt beneath her jeans, not riding the Enduro. When she arrived wherever she was going, she could move it to a better position for a faster draw. She was already wearing jeans and running shoes and a black Colt Arms t-shirt, her jean jacket was draped over the back of the passenger seat. She pulled it on, slung on her daypack and snapped on her fanny pack, and was almost ready.

After locking the van, she twisted up her ponytail and tugged on her black full-face shield helmet and straddled the bike. She kick-started it to life and waited, idling in neutral while she watched the front door of the porno shop, running the throttle up and down, the motor popping. Her Enduro was "street legal" in the lights department, but it had no up-to-date license plate sticker or current registration: she would just have to take her chances with Johnny Law. The old dirt bike did have one advantage, it had no daytime running light head lamp; this would help to keep her from being readily seen in the ape man's rear view mirror. Anyway, she figured that an undercover jack-booted thug with a new porno magazine collection wouldn't be spending much time looking in his mirrors.

Finally the red-haired ape came out of the XXX book store with a white shopping bag, scanning all around the shopping center, but Ranya and her bike were well concealed in the shade of the maple tree half behind her van. His thick hair hung over his collar; he had a Fu-Manchu type moustache which ran down both sides of his mouth to his chin. Either the feds were getting very lax in their grooming standards, or this was no typical group of feds which had kidnapped Brad…or it was no group of feds at all.

The man didn't get back in the truck. Instead, he went next door into the ABC store, and came back out two minutes later with a bottle wrapped in a brown paper bag. Ranya thought: liquor and porno, you're all set for a big night, aren't you? The red-haired goon climbed back into Brad's truck and backed out of his space, crossed the lot, and turned south on Independence again. Ranya gave him a two block head start, pulled onto Independence, and followed him across the wide Virginia Beach Boulevard intersection, crossing it as the amber light turned red, getting used to the light dirt bike's controls and unique power curve again. She knew that the major intersections (and this was one of the biggest) in Virginia Beach all had red light cameras, but with her helmet on she felt safe enough. At any rate, red light pictures would not be examined until days later, she hoped.

She felt more confident now. If he hadn't spotted her in the full-sized van, he was much less likely to notice her on the bike. They both passed under the Virginia Beach Expressway and continued on as the road turned to the southeast and passed Mount Trashmore, the local park built over a landfill, which was the only prominent topographical feature in Virginia Beach. She had a full tank of gas, but knew that Brad's truck could far outlast her bike if the driver just kept going. What would she do if she was on the verge of going dry and the truck was still going? Try for a fast fill up, and then try to catch up? She could only hope that the pursuit wouldn't last that long.

Independence became Holland Road, the housing developments gradually became spaced further apart, and the red pickup continued southeast at just above the speed limit. Ranya had no trouble keeping other vehicles between herself and her target for long stretches. Over the miles the suburbs faded away to smaller developments, private estates, horse farms, junkyards and trailer parks. She rode through bright sunshine, and occasionally through shaded tunnels beneath spreading oak corridors, sometimes flashing between light and dark.

After nine winding miles Holland Road ended in a T intersection at South River Road, and the truck made an easy rolling right turn through the red light. The last scattered houses gave way to fields of tall corn, soybeans, cotton, peanuts and tobacco. The table-flat landscape was broken only by random wind-break tree lines, and a few scattered houses and old barns. South River Road gradually curved back around to the southwest, and then dived south toward the North Carolina border. On long straight stretches Ranya hung back until she could barely see the red speck which was Brad's truck. Cars in between them to screen her from view became fewer and fewer.

Her luck continued to hold. After curves where the truck could have disappeared off the road while out of her sight, it always reappeared in the distance on the straight-aways. Finally after nearly twenty non-stop miles she saw the pickup's steady brake lights; it slowed and made a right turn just after a pair of boarded-up fruit stands. Tall silk-tasseled corn was a green wall along most of the right shoulder of South River Road here.

She rode past the turnoff at 50 miles an hour, in case the driver had spotted her and was waiting behind a fruit shed for the motorcycle trailing behind him to either continue on, or turn and follow him. A quick look as she went past showed the truck already hundreds of yards down the new road heading west, so she braked and downshifted and turned around to continue the pursuit. The new road cut a narrow corridor through the dusty corn; sunlight lit the golden silk on top. If the driver had seen her, he could be luring her to a remote place for an ambush. It was a risk she had to take to find Brad, but she downshifted to third and continued on more cautiously.

The closed-in path through the walls of corn ended abruptly and she emerged back onto a limitless flat plain of fields and marshes. The red truck was about a mile ahead, traveling perpendicular to her direction now, heading south after making a left turn. She could see for miles across the fields, her line of sight was obscured only by a few distant houses and tree lines. At this point she realized how impossible it would have been to follow in this terrain in her van, even an inattentive driver would have spotted it alone among the fields, following him turn for turn.

The red truck made another turn and disappeared out of sight driving into a stand of hardwood trees. Ranya quickly accelerated to over 80 miles an hour, the little 250 was no match for her FZR in the top end speed department, but it had enough. Now she also had to be concerned about her engine noise, she knew its tinny popping would carry plainly across the fields to anyone who was being quiet and listening.

She reached the tree line and braked to a stop while still in the shade, where she would be harder to see if the truck was not far away and the driver was looking in her direction. From her position under the trees she scanned ahead and spotted the truck stopped a half mile ahead, by what appeared to be a hedge or line of shrubbery. She swung her pack off, sat it on her fuel tank and pulled out her binoculars, which when folded together were no larger than a thick paperback book.

Through the binos she could see that the hedge was an overgrown chain link fence, and the driver was opening a gate. Three strands of barbed wire ran across the top, rectangular plates were fixed to the fence evenly spaced about every 100 yards apart. Ranya had lived around Tidewater with its heavy military presence all her life; she knew that the signs would be a warning to the public to stay off of U.S. government property.

So Brad was being held on some kind of remote military base that she'd never heard of. She pulled out her map of Tidewater and traced their route down Holland Road and South River Road toward the Carolina border, and then right on Bridgewood Road, which apparently was the road by the shuttered fruit stands that had cut through the cornfields. The next road they had taken, turning off of Bridgewood, was not marked on the map, but the map showed Bridgewood running near a two mile long swath of land shaded on her map in purple, like all of the other military installations in Tidewater. It was named the South River Naval Auxiliary Landing Field (Closed). Her map showed a mile and a half long air strip running north to south down the center of the abandoned base.

Brad's truck was driven inside the fence line, and then it paused again as the driver got out to swing the wide gate closed behind him. Then it continued west and was soon out of sight, lost among low scrubby trees. In the distance Ranya could see the flat black tops of several large structures over the treetops.

So he was being held here on an old Navy air strip. All she had to go on was his truck ending up here, but for all she really knew, he might still be back at Boat America waiting for her! Was her admitted state of paranoia playing tricks on her mind, deceiving her, making her see conspiracies where there were none?

Brad's truck being driven to this place was no mere trick of the imagination. If his truck was here, then he was here, because that was all she had to rely on. He was here, he had to be here, and she was going to get him out, one way or another. She just needed a plan.

The van had spent a long time driving at what seemed like high speed, perhaps a half hour, perhaps an hour. Then it made a series of widely spaced turns and stops and starts. Brad had tried to find the least uncomfortable position on the floor of the van, partly on his side with his knees drawn up in front, but on some turns he was rolled over on his back and onto his tightly cuffed wrists, or he was rolled the other way until the chain attached between his cuffs and the floor stopped him.

By their voices he guessed there were three or four men in the van, but he wasn't sure. George had pretty much shut up and they drove mostly in silence, with just a few quiet phrases muttered now and then. He thought he might have heard some police or military radio talk, but with the sack pulled over his head and his face on the floor over the drive shaft, it was difficult to hear much at all except the motor and the hum of the tires on the road.

The van came to another stop and this time the engine was turned off and the doors were opened. Hands rolled him onto his side and some- one unlocked the chain holding him to the floor, then he was picked up from under his arms, dragged out, and put on his feet.

"This way, one foot in front of the other," said a new voice. Hands held him up by each arm, hands steered him. Light seeping through the material of his hood and the sudden heat told him that he was in sunlight, but after a dozen steps he was again plunged into inky darkness. Powerful hands turned him right and left, he guessed he was walking on smooth cement.

He was brought to a final conclusion, a sudden halt, and he was pushed over hard by a grabbing shove to his head.

"Bend over Fallon, lean over God damn it!"

Oh sweet Jesus, is this the end right now? Brad thought: all this, all this way, to end my life with a bullet in the brain? He wanted more time, he needed more time, this was too sudden, he wasn't ready… Time slowed to a sluggish stream of microseconds, he stiffened and went board-rigid.

"Pop him with the zapper again," said a disembodied voice.

Another bolt of lightning hit Brad on the side of the neck, striking him like a high voltage sledge hammer, causing him to lose muscle control. Many hands shoved and pushed him through a small opening or doorway, a doorway to nothing, not a room at all, but just a box. A narrow metal door then squeezed him from behind until it latched shut with a grinding clack.

"Okay Fallon, don't go anywhere, and we'll be seeing you in while, okay? If you need anything, just ask, and we'll tell you to go screw yourself." Other men were laughing, and then something like an industrial machine's electric motor was switched on, flooding him in an abrasive screaming noise.

Brad had never known such a combination of fear and dread and pain. At some point of being man-handled into the box his hood had been taken off; he wasn't sure when, he had no memory of it. He had not been forced to his knees and shot as he had feared he would be; instead he had been forced into a tiny vertical box. His head was jammed almost onto his left shoulder in one top corner, his legs and knees were bent forward and sideways together into the opposite corner to allow his six foot frame to fit inside. There wasn't enough room to move his knees from one side to the other; he could only remain in the position in which he had been forced inside.

With his hands still cuffed behind him, he tried to feel the door, and along the side he felt some vaguely familiar rods and grooves. It was taking a tremendous amount of energy to remain bent and crouched, so he tried to slide down and find a more comfortable resting position. Down as far as he could go, only a few inches actually, his knees became jammed hard against the corner opposite his back, and his ankles and feet were bent at such a severe angle that the pain became excruciating, so he forced himself back up the side walls against gravity and friction, holding himself up with his leg and back muscles to take the pressure off his knees and ankles.

The thought of spending hours like this deepened Brad's sense of foreboding and despair. He had never been claustrophobic, but this was testing his outermost mental and physical limits. His pulse was surging wildly, and he wondered if he would have a heart attack simply trying to stay in this position. He gradually slid down again, and again his knees and ankles burned with searing hot pain. What if they left him here for days? Days!

He knew he couldn't last that long, he wondered how long he could endure it, and if this was just a prelude to the questioning which he was sure was going to come. If this agony was only a warm up for whatever torture was yet to come, how could he avoid betraying Ranya? His position was so painful, painful on such a sustained high level which he had never experienced before, that he already knew he would say anything to end it, and this filled him with even more pain, understanding for the first time in his life his ultimate weakness, knowing that he would betray anyone just to end the pain.

Again he pushed himself up so that his knees were not jammed against the corner, decreasing the pain in his feet and ankles, but increasing the pressure on his back and neck. How long would it take, he wondered, to breathe deep and fast and build up the CO_2 in the box until he passed out? And would he die, or not? What if he only gave himself permanent brain damage? Might he end up retarded or even a vegetable if he couldn't quite kill himself by building up CO_2, but only passed out in the box without sufficient oxygen? Was the box air-tight enough to build CO2 up to dangerous levels at all? It was certainly getting hot inside the metal box, which was vibrating from the piercing electric motor noise. Or might he have a heart attack first, and end his suffering that way? At least then he couldn't be made to betray Ranya...

His leg and back muscles failed again, he couldn't hold himself up, again he slid down until he was stopped by his knees being jammed together against the corner, and again his ankles were stabbed with shooting pains. Brad tried to guess if he had been locked in the box for ten minutes or an hour, but he couldn't. Time meant nothing in this box. In this box, any amount of time was a complete eternity of pure pain, beyond the limits of any other frame of reference. What if he was left here for hours, or even days? What if he had been intentionally abandoned here, left to die like this? How could anybody stand an hour in this hell, much less days?

At least if he was left to die, he wouldn't have a chance to betray Ranya. He saw a flash of her face and it was gone, he tried to focus and picture her, to remember her, but her image was extinguished by the unrelenting waves of pain. He groaned and screamed and cried unheard as his feet and ankles and knees were bent and crushed by his own body weight against the metal corner of the hell box.

How long could it go on like this? He tried to find something behind his back to support some of his weight with his shackled hands. He felt the inside of hinges or bolts and small sharp flat pieces, but there was nothing he could rest against, nothing to hold himself up. He tried to push up against a piece of metal in the corner near the door latch, and it took a bit of pressure off of his knees and ankles, but it bit sharply into his palm and pushed his face even harder into the opposite corner.

His alternating cycles of pain, of pain up, pain down, pain in his legs and back and neck, or pain in his feet and ankles and knees, went on for longer eternities. He never completely lost consciousness, but in time his consciousness changed. The pain remained, burning white hot pain, but gradually it became apart, it separated from him and the door opened and he escaped the box and was flying just above the water, rushing down a stream to a river which ran into the bay, skimming across the whitecaps, pure vision, only seeing, until he was out over the Atlantic and free.

36

Standing over her Enduro, hidden in the shade of the tree line, Ranya scanned the distant fence and what she could see beyond it with her binoculars after Brad's truck disappeared. The fact that there was no guard presence at the gate meant that there were probably not a large number of personnel on the base. If the gate itself was left unguarded, there was hopefully little chance of running into roving security patrols around the fence. Even so, this was an era when wireless video cameras were so cheap that the people who had taken Brad could easily have the gate and the access roads around it remotely monitored. She decided not to advance beyond the cover of the tree line, and instead she turned around and rode back out the way that she had come in.

Back in the cover of the cornfields she pulled off the pavement onto a dirt path and studied her road map. A narrow finger of the South River cut across the base just below the long north-south runway. Brad's truck had been driven onto the smaller section of the base south of this creek, so Ranya decided to begin her recon there, but coming in from the opposite side from the gate, from the west.

She backtracked to South River Road and made a long clockwise loop around the bottom of the base on one lane blacktop county roads, dirt roads through soybean and peanut fields, then up the overgrown right-of-way beneath electrical transmission wires strung between rusty towers. She knew from years of riding that dirt bikes were a common sight and sound on these trails and back roads, so she never felt dangerously conspicuous.

When the power lines diverged to the northwest, she cut back to the east on a dirt road running through more tall corn for a few hundred yards, until she came within sight of the government fence again. Ranya stopped when the cornfield abruptly ended; beyond it was one more field of picked cotton, then swampy waste land, and the base.

If she rode on any further the noise of her bike might still have passed unnoticed, but she felt she would be too exposed to possible direct observation, so she decided to continue on by foot. She threaded her way deep into the corn rows until her bike was invisible from the outside, and cut the engine. She put her wallet and mini-purse inside of her helmet, wrapped it all in her denim jacket, and stashed it separately in the corn out of sight of the bike.

Ranya took the black ball cap out of her daypack and put it on, pulling her ponytail through the hole in the back. She was wearing her black Colt Arms t-shirt; with her black daypack and fanny pack and blue jeans she didn't have much camouflage for a sunlit day in a world of soft greens and browns, so she walked two rows inside the edge of the cornfield.

The going was easy in the corn, and she could observe the fence line 200 yards away as she went. The dry corn was eight feet tall to its waving tassels; it was only weeks from harvesting and it rasped as she walked through, brushing aside their crisp leaves. As she walked she pulled off some smaller ears, shucked them and ate the kernels raw. It was only feed corn, as most corn in Tidewater was, but the smaller ears were still succulent and juicy inside. In another few weeks, instead of providing perfect cover for her approach and a snack on the go, the same fields would just be ankle high stubble and dirt.

After walking a few hundred yards north, parallel to the fence, the corn field terminated in one final corner. After considering her route, she got down on all fours and low-crawled across a soybean field between rows of the leafy vegetable, until she reached a north-south tree line that ran along an irrigation ditch. As a child Ranya had played hide and seek in all kinds of crop fields, and she knew how to pass through them undetected when they were in season.

She used the cover of the narrow wind-break tree line for her next path, and walked in the intermittent shade among the tall weeds that grew there unchecked, still moving roughly parallel to the fence line. Between the irrigation ditch and the chain link fence lay several hundred yards of marsh, cut with listlessly meandering black water streams. She knew from experience the futility of attempting to walk across such a morass, the black mud between the tussocks of saw grass would suck her legs down until she was waist deep and trapped. At the very least she would lose her running shoes in the gluey muck.

The irrigation ditch ended at a small cement dike, on the other side, according to her map, was the end of the east-west finger of the South River which bisected the base below the main runway. The stream ran in a shallow V-shaped canal. Ranya belly-crawled in the thick weeds onto the top of the slope and considered her options for approaching the base, and then decided to go straight up the water channel, directly toward the fence at a ninety degree angle. Being a ruler-straight man-made canal, it would have a fairly hard bottom, unlike the gelatinous ooze of the natural pluff mud in the surrounding marshes.

The almost stagnant water at the bottom was only eight or ten feet across, with an abundance of water hyacinths, lily pads and fetid yellow-brown scum on top. On the plus side, the canal's water produced a thick covering of vegetation on both banks, and the water level was several feet lower than the surrounding land, so she would be well hidden. She put her sunglasses into her fanny pack so that she would not lose them, and slid and wriggled down the bank through prickly brambles and spider webs, across a yard of black mud, and into the sun-warmed water.

It stunk of rotten eggs and worse things; sulfurous bubbles were released when her passage churned up something particularly putrid. The bottom was uneven, and the water varied from knee to chest deep, with occasional slimy submerged logs and rocks to climb over. (At least she hoped they were only logs and rocks.)

Mosquitoes were stirred to flight by her passage and hovered around her face, stabbing her skin when she could not smash them quickly enough. At times she was able to walk crouched over, and at other times she crawled on all fours with only her head out of the water, always keeping herself hidden below the twin reed-covered berms on either side of the canal.

Frogs observed her indifferently; a blue heron watched her approach and calmly strode ahead of her, then finally lifted its wings and softly flapped in a circle and landed again a hundred feet behind her, as if humans crawled up the channel every day. Water moccasins she simply refused to think about, and she did not see any, although she did see a brown water snake disappear ahead of her into the wild plants at water's edge.

Finally she reached the government fence. Where the stream passed beneath it a half-hearted attempt had been made many decades earlier to block the opening with a grid of sloppily welded iron bars, but the bars had rusted away long ago above the present water level, so she slid underneath, and was on the base.

Twenty yards inside the fence the stream was funneled into a five foot diameter concrete pipe where it passed beneath a road; the inside of the pipe was choked with silt, rotting wood and dense vegetation. Rather than attempt to fit through it, she crawled up the side of the canal beside the pipe and looked over the bank. The road was ancient broken asphalt, with several feet of it undercut and eroded away where it passed over the canal. On the other side of the road lay thick scrub-pine woods. Ranya decided she had had enough of the canal. She watched carefully for any human activity, raised herself to a crouch, and dashed across the road and into cover.

Once she was hidden among the trees and bushes she pulled her fanny pack around to the front and withdrew her .45, it was soaking wet but still clean and functional. She stuck it inside her pants on the left side of her waist, its grip towards her right hand for a cross draw. She had no idea what to expect, but she had no intention of being captured, arrested, detained or whatever it was they did on this base to trespassers. She knew that she couldn't help Brad if she was seen and forced to shoot, but shoot she would rather than being taken prisoner.

She kept the canal which bisected the base on her left side and confirmed her direction with her compass as she walked eastward. More signs of abandoned human activity appeared the further she penetrated into the base. She came to a small one room concrete building with broken windows and no door, its flat roof was as high as the tops of the new pine growth around her. A rusty iron ladder was lag-bolted to the wall by the doorway. She climbed the ladder for a look around her, and again she saw the flat tops of the two large structures that she had originally seen from the other side of the base.

Five minutes later she guessed that she was just a quarter mile north of the two buildings, and she turned south and cautiously stalked her way toward them. The base had obviously been abandoned and neglected for years, everywhere that it was not paved the land had reverted to Christmas tree sized pines sprinkled with hardwood saplings. The new trees were not tall or thick enough to choke out the underbrush, so Ranya was always able to remain in thick cover, pausing to listen and then taking a few more deliberate footsteps. The ground litter was dry on top, and she had to plan each step to avoid making noise.

Gradually she was able to detect the sound of music, and then voices. All around her now there was evidence of old base activity, such as racks of steel and PVC pipes, overgrown with weeds, and a clearing full of empty steel drums. There was a row of rusty engines, still on pallets with vines encircling them, and a line of flatbed utility trailers with bushes and small trees growing through their decayed wooden decks.

She crawled through the brush under a thirty-foot trailer, beyond it was a concrete apron the size of a half dozen football fields, and on the opposite side were two large aircraft hangars. She sat Indian-style among the dusty weeds in the shade beneath the trailer and pulled off her daypack, put it between her knees and took out her bottle of PowerAde. She drank it in small sips, grateful to clear the taste of the canal water from her mouth.

She could only imagine the virulent germs which were now swimming in her stomach, in her ears, her eyes, her many new scratches and everywhere else, and she knew she'd have to go on antibiotics when and if she ever got out of this place. She had managed to never completely submerge her face and head in the canal, but there had been plenty of unavoidable splashes.

Her jeans and t-shirt were still sodden but warm from her walk in the mostly sunny scrub woods, the dark fabrics were encrusted with brown and black mud and green scum. She pulled the small pair of binoculars from her pack, and found they were still dry and clear inside. With her naked eyes she could see that the hangars, about 200 yards away to her south, were the centers of activity with small groups of people walking around inside and outside of them. The hangar doors were open all the way to the sides, she looked through the 8X20 binos and could see that they were rusted and broken like the rest of what she had seen so far on this abandoned base.

A dozen or more vehicles of all sizes and types were parked inside the hangar on the right side. There were the de rigueur black Chevy Suburbans like the ones she had seen at Boat America, and a blue van also like the one she had seen. There were other vans and a variety of utility trucks and some sedans…and one red pickup truck. It was Brad's truck for certain, with the little antenna jutting out of the roof. Outside of the vehicle hangar, off to the side by itself, was an RV almost as long as a bus. Its roof was jammed with air conditioner units and an assortment of antennas.

She studied the people she could see: they were all men, all military age, but some of them had longish hair, which probably ruled out their being military. All of them carried pistols holstered on their belts; some wore shirts concealing them but most did not, probably feeling re-laxed and at ease here in the seclusion of their home base. A few carried submachine guns slung over their backs, she recognized them as MP-5s…

Despite the heat of the day, her blood ran cold at the sight of the weapons, the type of weapon used to murder her father. Part of her wished that she had brought her Tennyson Champion sniper pistol: at this range she would be able to easily pick off a few of them before they could all get to cover and begin to return fire.

Ranya kept the binos to her eyes, searching for any sign of Brad, and in the other hangar she saw the reddish-haired ape who had driven his truck coming out of a trailer. There were five white mobile-home sized trailers in the hangar arranged side by side, their ends facing the open hangar doors. These were probably where the goon squads who had burned the gun stores and killed her father lived and worked…

Next to the hangar on the left side were two smaller cement or cinder block buildings. She watched a man walk out of the closest hangar and into the first cement building through its front door. Among the hang-ars and the buildings there was no sign of Brad. If he was here, hopefully he was still alive… It was purely and simply because of her that Brad was now a prisoner of…whoever these people were.

If Brad was there, she was going to get him out, somehow.

Ranya had seen at least a dozen different men moving about the vehicles and between the hangars and buildings and trailers. Some of them were cleaning or working on weapons, on a table set up between two of the trailers. In an open area of the vehicle hangar a few men were taking turns spotting for each other, while doing presses on a weight bench.

A new aircraft engine noise intruded, but unlike others she had heard during her infiltration this one was not passing in the distance. This noise was growing steadily; she could hear the shrill whine of a turbine over the beating of rotor blades. The machine passed directly over her, coming from the north, and the brush around her trailer was whipped and blown flat by rotor wash. Wearing her black shirt and blue jeans she could have been spotted if she had not been concealed beneath the trailer, and she was grateful for having made a lucky choice in hiding places.

The dark blue helicopter gleamed in the sunlight as it flared out and landed in front of the building next to the trailer-filled hangar, sending dust and leaves and bits of trash swirling outward. A door on the chopper slid open and a bald Caucasian man wearing dark pants and a white long-sleeved shirt stepped out. He crouched over beneath the spinning blades and was met by four other casually dressed men who had hurried over from the buildings and hangars. The man from the helicopter and his greeters went into the building next to the hangar, and its front door closed behind them as the helicopter's rotor began to wind down.

After the blades came to a complete stop a small tanker truck emerged from the vehicle hangar and parked next to the helicopter, the pilot and the driver of the truck went about unreeling the hose and re-fueling the helicopter. By using their own fuel supply, this group's helicopter could be ready at any time, and they could avoid leaving a paper trail at local airports. Ranya was beginning to appreciate the thoroughness of their operation.

She could only guess the range of this type of small corporate helicopter, probably a few hundred miles. If it needed refueling after a long one-way trip, that could possibly put its origin in Washington DC, 200 miles away. The bald man who had gotten out was wearing suit pants and a tie and was carrying a briefcase. He'd have to be checked out; he could be their boss, or the go-between to their higher ups. Ranya had gotten a good look at him through the binos when he first climbed out of the chopper, before he had turned his back to her, and she knew she would not forget the bald man with the mustache.

Clearly, this was no local outfit operating on their own. Ranya found a pencil stub in an outside pocket of her pack and copied the helicopter's tail number onto the inside of her ball cap. Everything else she had was still too sodden to write on.

If they had a weakness it seemed to be a lack of concern about their own security: her arriving on foot undetected some 200 yards from their front doors was proof enough of that. The ape man who had driven Brad's truck had not run any counter-surveillance at all, but to the contrary he was confident enough to stop and visit a porno shop and a liquor store on his way down. The gate to the base was unguarded; it was simply secured with a chain and lock. And she'd seen no one out patrolling or on sentry duty either on her way in, or after she had arrived in her hiding place under the trailer.

Someone right here with a scoped AR-15 could kill half of them before they would know what hit them, she thought. But that would not get Brad out.

Judging by their slack security posture, they were exceedingly confident about their unit's secrecy. With their presumably busy night time schedule of burning and killing, finding Brad and getting him out might just be possible, especially if she could get some help. Certainly it would be suicidal to attempt a rescue alone in daylight, with Brad's location unknown, and 15 or more armed men crawling about the place.

A spirit of celebration and self-congratulation surrounded Wally Malvone and his STU Team supervisors and team leaders as they filed into their office.

"So where is he? Where's our sniper?" asked Malvone.

Bob Bullard answered, "Next door, in the interrogation center."

Malvone's face darkened. "You haven't started on him have you? I don't want him marked up, I told you…"

"Take it easy Wally, he's fine," said Bullard. "We haven't laid a hand on him, except maybe when they picked him up."

"Yeah? Well, okay. It's important that we keep him in good shape, he's got to be presentable…I've got plans for him. What about the other guy, Sorrento? Is he still in one piece?"

"Uh, Tim, you haven't messed up Victor too badly, have you?" asked Bullard.

"Me? No way. Well I mean, not too bad…maybe some electrode burns and rope marks, nothing serious," replied Jaeger.

"Tim, why don't you and Mike go and get Fallon and bring him over here. He might be ready to talk without needing any of the rough stuff."

Jaeger and Shanks left the room. Malvone put his slim leather briefcase on the table and picked a steel government surplus chair with green vinyl padding. Bullard, Silvari and Hammet took their seats after him.

Malvone asked them, "How's Edmonds holding up?"

"He's alive," replied Bullard. "Semi-catatonic, but he's breathing."

"Did he give us any useful information?"

"Nothing we didn't already know."

"Well, it doesn't matter, he served his purpose. Let me tell you, 'Timeline' was a big hit in Washington! They're glad to see somebody striking back…off the record of course. I've been making the rounds, we're getting noticed where it counts. Been getting a lot of winks and nods from on high, if you know what I mean."

"I do," said Bullard, who had resorted to extreme measures to permanently close a few of ATF's most problematic cases during his long and storied career. He had gotten his own share of back-channel winks and nods over the years, even while Headquarters pretended public disdain for his tactics.

"Look at these," said Malvone, unsnapping his briefcase. From a pocket inside the case he withdrew a handful of colorful laminated access badges, each with a spring clip for attaching to one's jacket, or a silver chain for hanging around the neck. "This one's for the Old Executive Office Building, it gets me almost everywhere, this one's for the Hoover Building; all the way to the top. I've got one for Justice, one for Homeland Security, and next week they want me for a closed briefing at Langley. Yes sir, the Special Training Unit is the hot ticket in DC! Everybody in counter-terrorism wants a piece of us now, but our juice comes straight from the top, so piss on all of 'em!"

He leaned back on his chair and put his black wingtips up on the table, his fingers laced behind the back of his shaved bullet head. "It's great having all those Justice Department supergrades sucking up to me for a change! That Timeline story really put us over the top. They're all wondering if the Edmonds fire was us, but I just gave 'em the old Malvone poker face. I won't give 'em the satisfaction! Let 'em wonder!"

The door opened, Jaeger and Shanks half marched and half dragged Brad Fallon into the room, one on each of his arms. Fallon's head was bent over at an acute angle, and he had cuts and scrapes on his face.

"What the HELL did you DO to him?" shouted Malvone, nearly jumping from his chair. "Bob, you know I told you not to get started before I got here!"

Jaeger replied first. "I'm sorry boss, it's my fault. We stuck him in a locker for some preconditioning, just like we did with Edmonds and Sorrento, but he's taller than them, and I guess it was kind of a tight fit."

"That's it? Okay, all right. Uncuff him and put him in a chair." Malvone calmed himself down again. "Mr. Fallon, are you all right? Can you talk?"

Brad looked around the room, his head still bent over. Shanks uncuffed his hands and pushed a chair behind him. Fallon sat down stiffly, rubbing his wrists where the cuffs had dug into his skin, and saw the deep gash in his left palm for the first time. Dried blood covered his swollen hands; they stung painfully as his circulation returned.

"Get him a glass of water," said Malvone, slipping easily into the good-cop role. Jaeger went to the refrigerator and returned with a small plastic bottle of mineral water. Fallon needed to use both hands to hold it, and they shook as he drank from it.

"Brad, I'm not going to waste a lot of time with bullshit cop routines. As you've no doubt noticed, we're not exactly regular police, and this sure as hell isn't a regular jail. So I'm not going to try to trip you up on details, I don't have the time. And I'm not going to ask you where you were last Saturday just after dawn. I know where you were. I know you shot the Attorney General."

Brad Fallon kept his expression blank, nothing could surprise him any more, and in the present circumstances the bald man's assertion was not much more absurd than anything else which had happened in the last two weeks. He continued massaging his wrists, studying the cut on his hand with his head down.

"You made a nice shot Saturday morning; you blew Sanderson's brains all over the place didn't you? But then you are a great shot, aren't you? So where's the rifle you used? It was a .223 or thereabouts, and not much of the bullet was left, as I'm sure you know. So did you use your AR-15?"

Despite his impassive face, Brad was overjoyed to be out of the locker, and even the hard-backed chair which was now supporting him in a comfortable position felt like heaven. He didn't want to go back in the box, and he didn't want to get zapped with any more cattle prods. He wanted to keep these men happy if he could, but he could not admit to a shooting he knew nothing about. "I sold my AR-15 a few years ago."

"I see," said Malvone, disappointed. "And you wouldn't happen to have a receipt or a bill of sale, would you?"

"It was a private sale, for cash."

The STU leaders around the table greeted this statement with smirks, rolling their eyes and muttering "ri-ight" and "yeah, sure." Private sales between individuals were still legal then, they had only been outlawed a year before the Stadium Massacre. Now all firearms transactions had to be reported on numerous state and federal forms under penalty of perjury, but Fallon was claiming a legal prior sale of his semi-automatic AR-15, a legal sale with no paper trail. This loophole had been closed for a year; there was no longer such a thing in the United States as a legal firearm sale with no paper trail.

Malvone continued undeterred. "Well Brad, it doesn't matter now. What about your Mini-14? That's another .223, but personally I could never get a Mini-14 to hit the broad side of a barn. That's not exactly the weapon of choice for a long-range head shot, is it Brad?"

He paused before he replied, "...I wouldn't know."

"But you would know Brad. You're an expert rifle shot, even with antique military rifles like your Swedish Mauser. Now that's a 6.5mm, and you didn't use it on Sanderson, but did you know that Senator Randolph was shot with another antique military rifle? A Russian Nagant, a real piece of shit, but it was plenty good enough to kill a United States Senator. What do you know about that rifle Brad?"

Again he waited before answering. "...I wouldn't know anything about it." The room was so comfortable, and the men seemed to be in such a friendly mood, that he wanted to stay as long as possible. He absolutely did not want to go back in the hell box!

"That was last Tuesday Brad, up in Maryland. That's not too long of a drive from here, is it? But let that pass, for now. Randolph was a bitch from hell, and personally, between you and me, I'm glad she got capped. Shit, she's doing more good for the cause dead than she ever did alive.

"But that's all in the past now Brad, and we're thinking about the future." Malvone paused; the only sound in the room was the rattling and humming of the window AC units. Shanks spit his Copenhagen quietly into a paper cup, never taking his eyes off of Fallon. Silvari also studied him closely, his forgotten cigarette burning in his hand, its smoke curling and twisting.

Malvone asked quietly, "Brad, we want you to tell us where to find the rifle you used on Sanderson, and we want you to tell us where to find Ranya Bardiwell."

He was still numb, but even so a fresh chill rolled through him upon hearing her name from this bald stranger's mouth. He didn't understand their trying to blame him for shooting a politician he had barely heard of, or why they were interested in Ranya. The men in the room must have been fed lies from someone else, from another informant, or from someone else who had been broken in the hell box, and was ready to make up any crazy story to get out of it.

But they knew about Ranya and him, and nobody else did. He tried to think of how they could have even connected him with Ranya, he needed to pinpoint when and where they had been seen together. The boatyard on Saturday? It was possible, but that meeting was unplanned.

A sudden flash of insight told him where: her father's funeral. He knew that the feds routinely staked out funerals when "persons of interest" died, to see who attended. If they'd seen them together at the funeral, he just had to hope they hadn't seen them together since. He was sure they hadn't called each other on cell phones, at least not since last week when she had come over to visit Guajira.

"Come on Brad, they're not hard questions," said Malvone. "Where's the rifle, and where's the girl? She found Sanderson for you, didn't she? We know all about it."

"I don't know anything about that rifle, I didn't shoot anybody. I don't even have any rifle like that."

"What about Ranya Bardiwell?"

"...I don't know where she is."

"So when was the last time you saw her?"

Brad waited, closing his eyes as if he was trying hard to recall. "Umm... At her father's funeral. Last Thursday I think."

"And you haven't seen her since then?"

Brad stepped off the edge, took the chance. "No."

"You're sure?"

"I haven't seen her since then." He was fairly sure they had been seen together at the funeral, but he couldn't be certain that they had not been seen together since then. If the feds had seen them together since the funeral, he wouldn't be able to defend his lie. But realistically, how could he get in any deeper trouble than he already was in? These men, these secret police, they weren't concerned about showing him their faces, so in all probability they had no intention of ever releasing him. All he could do was play for time, attempt to shield Ranya, hold out as long as he could and try to give her a chance to escape.

Malvone said, "Get him out of here." When Brad was cuffed and led away, he said, "Bob, get some guys working on him. Start with water; and no marks on him for now. But get the answers today."

Across the cracked concrete acres, hidden in the brush under an old utility trailer, Ranya held the small binoculars pressed tightly to her eyes. They were focused on the front door of the white cinderblock building where she had seen Brad dragged in handcuffs by a pair of goons.

After ten long minutes the door was pushed open again, and the same three came out. It was Brad in the middle for certain; she got a clear look at him, he was still in his blue shirt and khaki shorts and boat shoes. This time he was handcuffed in front, not behind, which was a small improvement in his condition. They walked the thirty or so yards back to the second building on the far left and went inside, and the two goons emerged a few minutes later. One of them went back into the other building, the second man walked past it and into the first hangar, and stopped and talked with a few other men. Three of them walked with him back to the cinderblock building where Brad was a prisoner, and they went inside and closed the door again. Each time the door had opened a grinding machine noise escaped.

She could only guess what the men were going in there for. They were inside the squat building with Brad, on an abandoned military airfield after his secret arrest. That could only mean one thing, and it would not include Miranda rights or a free phone call to a lawyer.

And it was completely her fault! It was her fault that Brad was in there, probably getting beaten—or worse—by a secret police torture squad.

She thought, and all I've got is my .45 pistol and 22 rounds of ammunition, against their 15 or 20 men armed with pistols and submachine guns. With so many of them there, a solo rescue was out of the question, especially in daylight, even if they weren't exercising much caution.

But what about after dark, especially if they're going out for another raid, out for another night of arson and murder? If most of the shooters are gone and only a smaller group of guards is left behind, then the odds might be better than suicidal. But even if she went back to the cache and retrieved an AR-15 and a dozen thirty round magazines, it would still be only one against many...

If... If... If... If this was a movie, if I was Rambo, I'd find a way to sneak over there undetected and rescue Brad. But this is not a movie, and I'm not Rambo, and in the real world one person with 22 pistol bullets just does not win against twenty trained killers armed with submachine guns.

I'm not Rambo, and I can't do it alone. So...let's go find Rambo. Let's try to find the closest person to a Rambo I know, or at least that's what they used to say at Freedom Arms... Maybe an old Rambo, but the only Rambo I know. If I can even find him, and if he'll even help me...

She took a final drink and put the plastic bottle and her binos back into her daypack, slung it on, then crawled backwards and retraced her steps to the stagnant canal. Her clothes and her hands were torn, she had been scratched up and pricked by thorns and itched in a dozen places. She could even feel things crawling under her clothes.

She knew that if she was successful in getting Brad away from this place, then she could go on antibiotics and take the time to nurse her wounds. And if she wasn't successful, then she'd have no need for antibiotics... Anyway, her present discomfort was far overshadowed by the brutal torture that she imagined Brad was being subjected to.

Hang on Brad, and I'll be back later. Just hang on...

37

Jaeger and Shanks returned to the office and took their seats at the beat up conference table again.

Malvone said, "Okay, let's get back to business. Bob, what do you have lined up for tonight?"

"We're still working down the rod and gun club list; we've got surveillance on these two, Bancroft and Kincaid. We're going to take a little breather tonight, do the surveillance in shifts and let the troops get some rest."

"No, I'm sorry Bob; we can't let them rest up, not yet. I've got a new mission that's got to go down tonight; they can sleep after it's over tomorrow. Here's tonight's target." Malvone passed a thin file folder from his briefcase to each STU leader. They contained printed images of a thin-faced nearly bald man in his late 50s or early 60s, biographical data sheets, copies of magazine editorials, and printed excerpts from what looked like internet chat sites.

"This guy is Leo Swarovski, anybody heard of him?" asked Malvone.

"Oh sure," said Shanks, "he writes for gun magazines. I've seen that name for years."

"Exactly. He's what you call a 'prolific writer.' Swarovski writes under his own name and a couple of pseudonyms for a half dozen gun magazines, plus he's written a dozen books on guns and military history. He's not a member of the Black Water Rod and Gun Club, but he's a friend of Burgess Edmonds, and that's close enough for government work. It'll fly out in TV-land.

"And he's been a real thorn in our side for years. Every time the ATF has stepped on its dick in the last 20 years, Swarovski's been all over our case. He calls us 'F-troop' and 'jack-booted thugs' and the 'gun Gestapo', all that crap, and right in print, right in his articles! He's one of the worst Constitution fanatics you ever saw, he's a real Second Amendment nut case, and he's extremely anti-government."

Michael Shanks said, "The man really knows his guns though, I'll give him that. And he used to be a pretty well known competition shooter. I think he won some national combat pistol shooting championships in the 1980s."

"That's all true," replied Malvone. "And he's still pretty sharp. He shoots almost every day; he reloads his own ammo, the whole nine yards. So he's not going to be a pushover. His wife's a serious shooter too; she used to be regular Annie Oakley, and for a while she was nationally ranked in trap and skeet. So I'm expecting these two to be dead-enders all the way. They'll shoot back if we give them half a chance, so we're not going to. This is going to be a straight-up no-knock raid: door charges, flash-bangs, the works."

"This is in Richmond?" asked Silvari.

"The Richmond suburbs," replied Malvone. "But closer to Petersburg."

"Then this isn't going to be like Edmonds, this isn't going to be an accidental fire, this is going to be an overt law enforcement raid? Are we going overt now, are we going to intentionally blow our cover?" asked Bob Bullard.

"It's just going to be reported that the raid was conducted by a federal law enforcement tactical unit. The details beyond that will all be protected under the Patriot Act: there's no Freedom of Information Act for terrorism-related cases. It's all clamped shut, there's a total blackout, so the STU Team itself will still be covert."

The other leaders around the table nodded in agreement.

"I gave the Richmond Field Office SAC a heads-up call. When you're finished with Swarovski, the Richmond ATF is going to assert federal control and take charge of evidence collection. It's already set up. When you're done, you just get in your vehicles and come back."

Bullard asked, "What kind of 'evidence'? Does he have any contraband?"

Malvone answered, "He's got, or a least he had, at least a dozen assault-type rifles that we know of. And he's owned at least three .50 caliber sniper rifles, including one semi-auto Barrett. Plus you can bet he's got rifle scopes out the ass. Maybe he got rid of them all, maybe he didn't; you'll find out soon enough tonight. But even if he did get rid of everything illegal, it doesn't matter, because you'll be bringing some of your own as insurance."

Hammet interjected, "We can bring some of Edmonds's scoped hunting rifles, that'll tie them together."

"Sniper rifles George, sniper rifles. But that's the idea. And we'll bring some of our confiscated militia weapons too. That's all we actually need, any contraband weapons of his own will just be icing on the cake."

Bullard added, "Don't forget he's an ammunition reloader. And that means he's got gun powder, so we can stick bomb making on him too. That always looks good on a domestic terrorism case."

"Right you are Bob, right you are. But the only 'case' we need to make is in the court of public opinion, because Swarovski's going to be carried out of his house feet first."

Malvone continued, "Now you might be thinking that doing this asshole Swarovski will be a good night's work, and it will be, but it's not all, it's just one step leading up to the main event. Tomorrow the STU is going to break out from the rest of federal law enforcement; we're going right to the top of the pack. Oh, we'll still be an anonymous 'ATF tactical unit' out in TV-land, but we're going to be very, very popular where it matters. I'm telling you, Randolph and Sanderson getting sniped, that hit too close to home!

"Want to know why I don't want Fallon or Sorrento marked up? Have you wondered about that? Have you wondered why we haven't turned Fallon over for a public arrest? I mean, here's the state AG's assassin, that's quite a feather in our cap to bring him in, right? We could have done the big media perp walk and taken the credit, but we didn't, and here's why: Fallon and Sorrento haven't finished their crime spree yet. They're driving up to Washington tomorrow to assassinate the Homeland Security Director, but they're not going to make it all the way."

The men passed sly looks and winks to each other around the table. Jaeger said, "And let me guess who's going to discover the plot and save the day, just in the nick of time." He turned and gave Michael Shanks a high-five.

Shanks added, "And naturally, these two desperados will be taking along a couple of Burgess Edmonds's finest long range sniper rifles for the assassination attempt."

"Well I'm done here now, you guys don't need me any more, I can go back to DC," Malvone joked. "Really, I can see you guys've grasped the concept. So tonight we're going to leave some of Edmonds's rifles at Swarovski's place. Tomorrow, Fallon will be found with another of Edmonds's rifles, and if Swarovski's still got them, one of his .50 calibers. That'll tie them all together in one nice tight bundle. Fallon and Sorrento as the trigger men; Edmonds and Swarovski as the money man and the organizer. Cut and Print. In fact, it's the information I've got in my briefcase now that's going to lead you to Fallon and Sorrento tomorrow, the information you're going to 'find' in Swarovski's house. So this time, don't burn his damn house down!"

They all laughed at that one.

Jaeger said, "Boss, at the risk of sounding like an ass-kisser, I have to say you are one scary freaking genius."

"Well Tim, I don't know if I'm a genius or not, but I'll admit I did have kind of a 'eureka moment' a few years ago, a real shot of pure 100 proof insight. You know about 'plausible deniability', and how we use it all the time to avoid taking any blame for screw-ups. By 'we', you know, I mean the government. If there's any possible alternative explanation for a screw-up, no matter how far-fetched, you just deny, deny, deny; and if there's no rock-solid direct proof, eventually the problem goes away."

Silvari said "Admit nothing, deny everything, and make counter accusations."

"Exactly." Malvone continued. "Clinton was the real master; he raised it to an art form. But I've been studying more recent history, and especially the way the media reports things, and then it just hit me. All of a sudden I saw the flip side of 'plausible deniability.' I call it 'probable culpability.' Smear somebody, plant some evidence, and then cap 'em. As long as the target is somebody the media didn't like to begin with, they report it just exactly the way you want them to, right down the line."

"Like Waco," said Bob Bullard, who had been there.

"Just like Waco. If we're dealing with 'religious cults' like in Waco, or gun nuts like Edmonds and Swarovski, it's a piece of cake, because the media already hates them. Show them some automatic weapons that were found in the ashes, who can say otherwise? We're from the ATF, so we're the experts, right? The TV networks are all on our side in this, just look at how well it worked on Timeline!"

"Oh yeah, 'Terror in Tidewater', that was beautiful!" said Tim Jaeger. "You can always count on CBA to do a gun story the right way."

"As long as we paint it in broad strokes, it'll work every time, at least with the major networks," said Malvone. "If anybody finds a few details that don't fit, some actual evidence that contradicts our version, it doesn't even matter, because then they're just dismissed as paranoid 'black helicopter' kooks, and after that they can never get any traction in the 'respectable' media. Waco, Vince Foster, Oklahoma City, Ruby Ridge, you name it: anybody who bucks the official story is called a lunatic and a conspiracy theorist. Nobody wants to be lumped in with the black helicopter loony tunes, so no credible reporter ever looks into these cases very hard. Other than a few whack jobs on internet sites, nobody that matters ever really challenges the official stories. Just look at Waco, for God's sake! Or Vince Foster, or any of them."

Silvari said, "Reporters are so afraid of being called a conspiracy theory nut, that it actually makes minor conspiracies easy to pull off."

"That's it in a nutshell," said Malvone. "That's the beauty of 'probable culpability'."

Shanks snorted and said, "Yeah, just ask Burgess Edmonds, the militia kingpin!"

Jaeger high-fived him again and added, "Or Sorrento or Fallon!"

"Don't forget Swarovski, he's next!" added Shanks.

Malvone said, "Once I came up with a method for applying 'probable culpability' in an organized way, the rest was easy. The FBI is so hamstrung by political correctness that it's afraid of its own shadow, and it's almost as bad at the CIA. They just play it safe, they won't get down in the dirt, they won't recruit real informants, they won't take chances. And that's where our little STU Team comes in: we're not risk-averse!"

"To say the least!" said Jaeger.

"And we're fast," continued Malvone. "The White House is desperate now, they finally realized that the FBI is just about useless, and they need a unit that can 'get results' right away. That's us: we get results! And up in DC, they don't want to know how.

"Somehow the FBI became a big timid giant who can't lean over far enough to tie his shoes. I mean, just how 'special' can 15,000 Special Agents be? They're just an army of PC bureaucrats. Well that's just not cutting it any more! So when something comes along like the Stadium Massacre, and Senators are getting sniped and bridges are getting blown up, who's around that can handle it? We are! We're small, and we're fast.

"Now, to get the fast results we need, we might have to 'help' our cases with a little extra evidence, but anyway that's just for the media, not for court. Our cases don't go to court."

"Let's talk about Swarovski," said Bob Bullard, getting them back onto the task at hand, wearing reading glasses while paging through his target folder. "He lives this side of Richmond, 85 miles from here."

Silvari asked, "Wally, did you bring any overheads?"

"No, not this time."

"Well then, let's get the Piper up there to shoot some pictures," said Silvari. "We might get weathered-in if we wait around too long."

"Do it," said Bullard.

"And let's send the Virginia Power van up there to start ground surveillance," Silvari added.

"Are we going to use both teams tonight?" Shanks asked Bullard.

"Yes, but this time Gold will be the assault team, and Blue will be in support."

"Bob, are we going to get a chance to sleep some time this week? The men are all bitching about the operational tempo," said Shanks.

Malvone replied, "I know your guys are beat, I know they've been operating non-stop since we moved to Tidewater. After tomorrow, we're going to wind it up down here in STUville, and take a few days of R&R. I'm just asking the guys for one more big push, and then they'll get their rest."

Bob Bullard continued planning out loud. "Okay, we'll use both teams; all four Suburbans and the two vans. Hit him at 0300, be back before dawn."

"Negative Bob," said Malvone. "We need to move it up as early as possible, hit ASAP after their lights go out. The way it's going to work, the evidence you're going to 'find' at Swarovski's tonight is going to lead right to a fast follow-up mission tomorrow, when you overtake Fallon and Sorrento in the red pickup truck. We'll need time after the Swarovski raid to set up tomorrow's shootout."

"Work out the details on tonight's raid; just make it as early as you can. Okay? I'm going over to the hangars to check on the troops and see how they're doing. I'll tell them we just need another 24 hours of hard charging and they'll all get a few days off, that should motivate them. Finish up the mission planning, and I'll be back for the briefing. George, come on out and take a walk with me."

They stepped outside into the sunshine; it was clouding up in the west.

"Let's go over by the chopper and talk," said Malvone. "Joe was right; it looks like it might rain later on. If it gets too crappy I'm going to have to take off sooner than I thought."

"Around here, they say if you don't like the weather, just wait a few hours and it'll change."

"I believe it. Listen George, I want you to sit out tonight's raid. I've got another mission for you, Bob already knows about it. He'll tell Tim and Michael that I want you interrogating Fallon tonight because you know him the best, and I want you to get the last crack at him. But after the teams take off for Petersburg, I want you to get rid of Edmonds. He's baggage; he's got nothing to offer us. He's just a liability."

"You want me to deep-six him in his Mercedes?"

"Right. Buckle him in his driver's seat, use his pistol for one shot to the temple like a suicide, and then roll his car in the water. Bob'll get one of the techs to follow you out and bring you back. After that, go on home and put in a full day at the Field Office and the Joint Task Force tomorrow, you still need to get your face time there. Once we pack out of here and get our permanent facility set up in Maryland, I'll run the paper-work for your transfer to the STU, and then we'll start building the Red Team, all right?"

"That sounds great Wally. You can count on me: Edmonds is going to disappear without a trace. And I'll play it real low key around here."

"That's what we need George, no fuss, no big production... just get rid of him quietly while the teams are going after Swarovski."

Ranya put considerations of stealth and concealment almost entirely aside and backtracked to her Enduro in less than half of the time it had taken her to infiltrate the base. Once in the cornfield by her bike she located her jacket-wrapped helmet and pulled out her mini purse and her wallet, then frantically dug through it until she found the tattered business card with Phil Carson's phone numbers penciled on the back.

From an outside pouch of her daypack she pulled out a sodden cardboard box the size of a paperback book, it was one of the two prepaid cell phones she had purchased at a drug store only an hour before she was supposed to meet Brad. The box fell apart as she opened it, but inside, the gray plastic tub still had its silver foil sealed across the top. She peeled off the foil; the phone inside was dry and, she hoped, functional. It was one of the new throwaways the size of a pack of cards, all black with just a 12 button keypad and an earplug speaker on a wire. She had never used this type, she put the plug in her ear and pushed the power button, and the tiny LCD display showed that she had sixty minutes of air time available. Thirty dollars for sixty minutes, and it was a bargain at that price, she now thought. She punched in the first phone number on Carson's business card.

Come on, come on, be home! Pick up! The afternoon light filtered though the corn rows in vertical slices. Soaring cumulus clouds were rolling in from the west; they were radiant silver at their edges where the sun was striking them. After six rings, a woman's synthesized voice answered: Carson's voicemail.

"Hey Uncle, it's your niece, I'm calling at 4:30. Call me right now; it's a matter of life and death." She read the number off of the back of the disposable phone. Then she called the other number on the card, but another robot voice announced that the subscriber was out of the service area. Well there, I've done it, she thought. If Phil Carson is already under electronic surveillance, I've just compromised both of us, and given up my cell number and location. But it can't be helped. It's a chance I've got to take, there's no time left for playing it safe. If Phil can help me, great. If not, I'll go back to the cache and get the short AR-15 carbine, and all the ammo and magazines I can find, and go in by myself. I'll wait until dark, and if Phil doesn't call, I'll go back in alone, hopefully after most of the killers have gone out for the night on another raid.

Ranya paced back and forth between the dusty rows of corn. She was itching under the bottom of her bra so badly that she took it off from under her damp black t-shirt, pulling it out over one arm at a time. She had never felt so grimy and disgusting or itched so badly in her life; she had cuts and scratches all over her arms, neck and face. She found her folding brush and forced it through her hair, then pulled it into a new ponytail, but the rubber band broke so she had to leave it down.

Ten minutes later her ear plug buzzed and she stabbed at the button. "Hello?" she said.

"It's you girl?"

"Yeah, it's me. Can you talk?"

"I'm at a pay phone, go ahead."

"I never used this phone before; it's a prepaid throwaway cell phone."

"Okay, that's good. So what's life and death?"

"Well, me, I am, if you can't help. And somebody else. You remember that guy at my old house, the guy who buried my dog?"

"I remember him."

"Well I've, I mean…we've got a relationship… He's been kidnapped. He was picked up, arrested, 'snatched' I guess, but not by cops. By the people who killed my father, the same people who probably burned the Edmonds family and God knows what else."

"How do you know all this?"

"Because I've seen their damn base! I'm right outside of it now. I just spent all afternoon crawling through shit doing a recon on the place. I saw my friend getting dragged around the place in handcuffs, and some of the people in there are carrying MP-5s, MP-5s like the one they shot my father with! They've got Suburbans and vans hidden in a big aircraft hangar, they've got a Winnebago with more antennas on top than NASA. They've even got a helicopter, and a single engine airplane just took off from there! They're wearing regular street clothes and they've got long hair, and they sure don't look like the military or regular cops, what else can I tell you?" Ranya was trying but failing to keep her composure while making her case, standing in a corn field next to her old Enduro, pleading on a tinny throwaway cell phone with a nearly sixty year old ex-soldier.

"Okay, I believe you; that sounds seriously bad. Where is this place?"

"It's in Chesapeake near the Carolina border, at the bottom of the old Naval Auxiliary Landing Field. They're in two big hangars and two smaller buildings. If they're taking people to an abandoned base, you know what that means; it's totally outside the law, and they're probably…torturing them. Why else would they be taking them to a place like that? So it's just a question of time until they're going to get around to us anyway, I mean nobody can hold out forever…I mean…if he's being tortured…" She finally lost control, and the tears came.

"Easy girl, easy… What you're saying is probably all true. What do you want me to do? I don't guess you plan to run, or you wouldn't still be there."

She paused, and replied weakly, "No, I'm not going to run. I'm going in after him, one way or the other. I just want you to help me."

"How many of them are there?"

"At least fifteen or twenty that I saw."

"With MP-5s?"

"Some of them. And all of them were carrying pistols. But I'm hoping that some of them will be out tonight doing what they do: burning down houses and shooting people. Oh God, that sounds terrible, to wish for that! But if some of them are gone, that'll help… Anyway, listen, I know we can get in and out, I've got the layout, and they've got shit for security. It can be done, but I need your help. Phil, I remember once you said a war was coming…well it's already here for me. I'm already in the middle of it. Will you help me?"

There was a pause, and then an audible sigh. "You know the answer to that. I'm too old and busted up to run very fast or very far, but I reckon I've got one more good fight in me. Yeah I'll help you. Why the hell not? What am I saving myself for? And after what they did to your father and the Edmondses, well, they've got it coming. So sign me up; I'm on your team."

"Thanks Phil…thanks."

"I take it you've got your rice rocket down there?"

"Not the one you're thinking of, I'm on my old dirt bike. I followed them down here on it."

"Okay now, let me think. Let me think. Okay. Do you know where the Wagon Wheel is? You probably passed it on your way down. It's closed; it used to be a country music place. I might be able to round up somebody else to help us out; we'll rendezvous there, behind the restaurant end of the place."

"I saw it on the way down here, it's a couple miles back up South River Road," said Ranya.

"That's right. Can you watch the base from where you are?"

"No, it takes too long of a time to get inside; it's almost an hour from here on foot."

"Is there anywhere you can watch them from outside that's easy to get to, but near your bike?"

"The gate. I know where they drive into the base. I can watch the gate."

"That's perfect. That's where you should go; you can see them if they leave tonight. Then we'll have a better guess about how many are left on the base, and we'll know what we're up against."

"All right."

"Call me when you see them leave, just count the vehicles. If nobody leaves by midnight, we'll go in later when they're sleeping."

"Okay. Do you really think you'll be able to get anybody else to help us?"

"I don't know. Maybe. Hey, I guess I'll know who my real friends are after tonight, huh?"

Ranya managed a laugh. "Yeah, I'd say this is the true test of friendship."

"Yep, I'd say it is too. Listen, do you have any paper on you? While you're watching the gate, start drawing me maps, lots of maps, put down everything you can think of. Just remember 'SALUTE': size, activity, location, unit, time, equipment. Damn! Where'd that come from? I haven't even thought of that in thirty years! It must be like riding a bike; maybe you never really forget."

Wally Malvone had constructed the Special Training Unit's internal security on the principle of mutual overlapping guilty knowledge. Everybody on the team was in some way or another a bad apple, a misfit, or a rogue. They all had dark histories, with personnel records full of reprimands and censures. Most of them had once been extremely gung-ho, and in their zeal to bust criminals, they'd often trampled over the line of the law and eventually been brought to task, removed from their units and put on limited duty while languishing in legal hold. Over several years Malvone had culled their names from ATF disciplinary files. He'd personally saved many of them from dismissal or worse, and in the process he had earned their unquestioning loyalty and gratitude.

When he offered to give them another chance, their supervisors were usually quite pleased to turf out their problem children to the obscure experimental training unit. In this way he had quietly forged his own personally-beholden mailed fist, iron link by iron link. In those early days the STU, his STU, had quietly occupied an unnoticed niche within the ATF, until after the Stadium Massacre.

Malvone knew about most of the skeletons in his troops' closets, and they in turn knew about many of each others'. Frequently there were cases which could still be opened, witnesses which were still at large, and victims who could still bring charges, if they were provided with the right information and incentives.

Because of this, the STU Team, from top to bottom, became an organization based on the unspoken but mutually agreed upon principle of "see no evil, hear no evil, and speak no evil." No one was clean, and no one would turn rat because the rat could wind up charged with some of his own past crimes, and the charges would be pursued and made to stick. Even more importantly, they all knew that if anyone turned rat, he'd be found and killed, painfully. There was no federal witness relocation program which could protect a turncoat agent from other federal agents, and they all knew this for a fact.

Malvone had carefully compartmentalized knowledge of the STU Team's extra-legal "proactive" measures. Bullard knew, of course, about the bomb he had placed under Mark Denton's jeep, but not the truth behind the gun store arsons, or the mosque attack. Hammet knew about them, of course, but not the Denton car bomb. They all believed that Burgess Edmonds really was a dangerous militia paymaster, and that they had merely helped to clinch the case (in the media) by salting his house with some illegal weapons seized from actual militia kooks. Only Hammet knew the benign truth about the rod and gun club, but he wasn't an actual member of the STU.

So, the most damaging facts were mostly contained and insulated. But to Wally Malvone, there was still one gaping internal security threat, one open window to board up and nail shut permanently. After doing a walk-through of the hangars and speaking informally to the troops, and attending the initial Swarovski mission briefing in the classroom trailer, Malvone took Bob Bullard aside in a corner of the trailer hangar. He spoke quietly, regretfully.

"Listen, Bob, we've got a serious problem."

"Huh? What problem Wally?"

"We've got a rat, an informant."

"What? Bullshit! You're bullshitting, right? Is this a test? Are you serious?"

"I'm dead serious."

"Who is it?"

"It's…it's George Hammet. He's been contacting the Justice Department behind our backs, talking to the Solicitor General's office…I suppose he thinks he's buying himself some immunity, he's been telling them about some of our…tactics. I guess he thinks if this blows up in our faces, he'll be the first in line to get a deal. Lucky for us, the U.S. Attorney he approached is somebody I personally know, and he got right back to me to warn me about what Hammet's doing. But that kind of luck can't last; my friend stalled him for now, but sooner or later Hammet's going to go somewhere else with his story and burn us."

"Shit! I can't believe it! That God damned bastard! I'll kill him myself!"

"Yeah Bob, I know how you feel, I feel the same way, but here's my idea. I gave him a special mission tonight; he's going to 'Vince Foster' Edmonds in his Mercedes and roll it into a lake. Hammet's already got the place scoped out; it's in the Great Dismal Swamp. He just needs somebody to drive him back here afterwards, so pick one of the support techs who are staying back here tonight while the teams drive to Richmond. Pick one of the techs who can handle wet work, explain it like I explained it to you: Hammet's a rat; he's going to a U.S. Attorney behind our backs. Choose somebody who's got the stones to take care of an informant."

"Wally, I already know who. Garfield."

"Perfect."

Clay Garfield was a good old boy from the hills of eastern Tennessee who'd been an operator with the ATF's Special Response Team, until one of his teammates accidentally put a 9mm bullet practically through his left knee during close-quarters-battle training. After many surgeries and a pile of stainless steel and plastic later, Garfield was still unable to return to unrestricted duty. He could have gone before a medical board and retired early with a partial disability, but Garfield wanted to remain an operator and finish his 20 years with ATF. Malvone had found the burly no-neck hillbilly gimping around the new ATF Headquarters in Washington shuffling paperwork on limited duty. He'd seen the fire in his eyes and offered him a chance to get back into the field on operations, even in a limited capacity, with the most hardcore bunch of operators the ATF had ever assembled in one place. Garfield had eagerly accepted the offer.

Knee brace or no knee brace, Garfield was still a tough and ruthless bastard who could bench almost 400 pounds, and while he was smart enough, he wasn't too smart. Malvone had taken him into the STU officially as assistant unit armorer, in charge of their weapons, but he was versatile enough to help the commo techs and computer geeks in the Winnebago, while the tactical teams were out on operations.

But the real reason that Malvone and Bullard liked having Garfield on the team was that he was an utterly loyal hard ass whose mere presence with the sometimes flaky support pukes kept them focused and assured their reliability. The support guys all liked him well enough, but they were also afraid of the hard-drinking and profane Clay Garfield. When he jokingly threatened to rip their arms off and beat them to death with them, the techs did not completely dismiss the possibility out of hand. Clay Garfield was capable of doing it, or so they believed.

Bullard said, "I'll tell Clay to come over and help Hammet with the Fallon interrogation after Blue and Gold leave for Richmond, and I'll tell Hammet that Clay's going to bring him back after he dumps Edmonds in the lake. But I'll tell Clay to put them both in the lake. He can make it look like Edmonds and Hammet had a struggle for the gun, something like that."

"That's perfect, that's it exactly. Do it like that. Then Garfield just drives back here alone and keeps his mouth shut, and Hammet goes missing but nobody notices for a few days. The Field Office thinks he's here, we think he's at the Field Office, and his wife's used to him being out of touch in the field. That'll hold up for a few days, and by then he's gone from the face of the earth, and we don't have any clue where he is. He's not actually in the STU you know, there's no paper connecting him to us...

"Oh, and one more thing: tell Garfield to leave the car windows open a little." Malvone held his thumb and index finger a few inches apart.

"To let the air out?"

"No, to let the crabs in. In a few days there'll be nothing left but bones in the car."

Wally Malvone left for Washington a greatly relieved man. The one wild card left in his deck, the one gaping security threat, was going to be permanently eliminated. While most of the members of the STU Team had certain pieces of guilty knowledge concerning illegal unit activities, they all believed that they were fighting for the worthy cause of crushing right wing terrorism. They all saw themselves as soldiers in the war against domestic terrorism, and they were all firm believers that there were no rules in war except to win, and that included using unconventional and extra-legal methods. They all believed that this latest front in the war against terrorism had been opened up by militia crazies at the stadium with the massacre of 1,200 innocent football fans, and that the militias deserved no respect, legal considerations, or mercy.

But only George Hammet had been with Malvone and Shifflett up in Landover Maryland two long weeks before. Only Malvone and Hammet knew for a fact that the Stadium Massacre was a contrived operation, and only Malvone and Hammet knew who had pulled the trigger of that infamous SKS rifle ninety times...

Wally Malvone was a firm believer in the adage that two people could keep a secret, but only if one of them was dead. Before the sun rose again, the primary source of his anxiety would be gone forever, keeping the secret at the bottom of a black water lake.

38

Phil Carson stabbed his cigarette into the truck's ashtray. He considered flicking the butt out the open window, but today, at least for now, he was scrupulously obeying every law. He'd had to remove a pile of coins from the ashtray to use it for his first cigarette butt, which he had taken from the first pack he had bought in more than a decade. He was parked as close as he could get to the pay telephone, which was bolted to the brick wall on the side of a stand-alone Quick N' Go store in Suffolk. After making several phone calls, he had gone into the store to get an Icee-Slush and some beef jerky, and found himself asking the cashier for a pack of Marlboros as if someone else was in command of his voice.

He had the truck radio turned off while he listened for the phone to ring; he checked his watch compulsively as the minutes dragged past. Since Ranya's desperate call for help, he had been using a series of pay phones as he drove across Tidewater. To his thinking, his own cell phone was suddenly less than trustworthy for general use of a conspiratorial nature, and he wanted to keep it clear for Ranya's next emergency call. He thought, how long should I wait here? How much do I need the help that this particular call could bring? This was an important call, but time was fleeting and there was so much to do. He lit another cigarette.

The smoke flowed all the way through him, not only into his lungs but down to his fingers and toes, calming him somewhat. He had smoked for most of his adult life, and many of his wartime memories were tinged in the remembered aroma of cigarette tobacco. Of course, he had never smoked when stealth was required, but between patrols and after some fire-fights he had smoked with great appreciation. Now, decades later, on an afternoon when he was unexpectedly planning one more combat patrol, he found himself enjoying the strong Virginia tobacco once again.

Just as they had in Viet Nam, long-term health considerations faded into utter meaninglessness on a day when he had been loading bullets into magazines and preparing weapons to shoot at men who were undoubtedly well-trained and well-armed. While pushing the slick copper and brass cartridges into their magazines, he had somehow felt the spectral presence of phantom soldiers, so real that it took an effort of his will not to look over his shoulders for them. Some, he thought, were still living and many, he knew, were long dead, but in his mind's eye they were once again happy-go-lucky twenty year olds in jungle fatigues. An hour later, waiting in his pickup truck outside the Quick N' Go, the mere lighting of a cigarette was sufficient to trigger another rush of Asian memories, and faces he had not seen in decades floated up through his consciousness.

The phone outside the store trilled urgently. Carson was out of the truck and had the black receiver to his ear before the end of the second ring.

Brad awakened slowly, lying on his back next to the ocean. The midday sun above him burned against his eyes, and he blinked weakly. He must have been pulled from the water; lifeguards and other bystanders seemed to be trying to revive him. Their faces above him slid in and out of focus, sometimes blocking the glare of the sun, then moving aside so that he was again hit with its direct rays. He grew weak once again and his eyes fluttered closed. Hollow voices swelled and faded like the waves rolling under the dock beneath his back.

"…a little too much…"

"…not now, tomorrow…no marks…"

"…pulse hit 200, did you see…"

Brad's random half-thoughts came trickling back together to form an awareness of his situation, and an urgent voice whispered to him from some alert corner of his subconscious that he should not wake up completely, not yet. He understood now that the men standing over him were not lifeguards or paramedics, that he was not lying on a dock by the ocean, and the blinding light above him was not the sun.

"We have to go do Swarovski tonight. Get what you can out of Fallon, but for God's sake don't kill him, and don't mark him up too much. Put some rags or something under the ropes; he can't be found with marks like that for God's sake! Use your head."

Brad began to remember where he was. He slowly eased his hands away from his sides and felt the ropes that tied him down to the door. Even in his semi-conscious state he knew that there was nothing to be gained by revealing to his tormentors that he was coming back around, and was, therefore, ready for more water on his face and electric shocks on his body.

"The information is secondary, all right? No marks, and don't kill him. Got it?"

"Got it."

"I'll send Garfield down to relieve you by then. We'll be back after Swarovski. Then we'll finish up with these two, but they gotta look good."

"Okay, I got it, don't worry."

Brad drifted away again. Now he was lying on his back on a raft. Somehow he had drifted through the surf zone to the calmer sea beyond the waves, but the noontime sun was still burning through his closed eyelids.

Dusk spread evenly across Tidewater under a leaden sky; the sun scarcely hinted its setting direction through the thick overcast. Ranya had found a hiding place in a disused tobacco drying shed on the edge of the tree line, where she could observe the eastern gate of the base. Her Yamaha was in the shed with her; after the close passage of their helicopter she was taking no chances on being spotted from above.

The rusted tin roof of the shed seemed tight enough, so if it rained at least she would not be left soaking wet once again. The air was still fairly warm, but with the end of daylight she knew the serious cold would soon come. The walls of the drying shed were built of weathered horizontal wood slats with space between them for air flow, and the breeze passed through unhindered. She was sitting on a grimy tobacco sorting table with her knees drawn up to her chest, watching the gate, when she heard the airplane engine again.

The sound of the engine grew steadily louder, she slid off the table and looked between the slats to the west and saw the small plane flying towards her below the cloud ceiling. It descended almost to treetop level, but before it reached her field, it pulled up and banked sharply over the chain link fence, turned to the north, and made a tight circle above the hangars. It was a long sleek single-engine plane with retracted landing gear, wings mounted low on the fuselage and a high tail in the shape of a capital letter T. It had some kind of round pod fixed under its otherwise smooth belly, probably a surveillance package, she thought.

After circling the southern part of the base, it lowered its wheels, leveled out flying toward the north, and dropped from her sight. She thought it must be their own airplane; she had heard one taking off earlier. It was probably out taking pictures of their next target. This could be a good sign, if it indicated that the group was still active, and might be sending its gunmen out tonight. She felt guilty, because while this was good for her, it was certainly not going to be good for their next victims…

The shed smelled of wet dirt, mold, rat droppings and old tobacco. In the fading light, Ranya examined the maps and sketches she had drawn in pencil on the backs of the pages of a girly-picture calendar from 1977, before she was born. Phil Carson had asked her for maps, and the calendar was the only paper she could find to draw upon. She had found it on a shelf beneath the sorting table; it was partially chewed by rats or mice. Skimpily-clad smiling girly models, spilling out of too-tight halter tops and short-shorts, held up air filters, fan belts and other very un-sexy truck and tractor parts.

The backs of the calendar pages were blank, and on one she had drawn a map of the hangar area, and on another the entire base with all of the roads and trails around it. She also drew a map showing her infiltration route, and a sketch of what the hangar area had looked like as seen from her previous hiding place across the tarmac. All of the maps and sketches were marked with estimated sizes and distances, with each structure labeled, and the compass directions indicated.

It was almost six and the light would not last much longer because of the heavy cloud cover. Phil had promised that he would call as soon as he was ready; she replayed their conversation over and over in her head, trying to extract every crumb of meaning. If he didn't call back very soon, she would have to decide if she was going to continue waiting, or leave the shed to go to her father's arms cache and get the carbine.

The cache was twenty miles away on the other side of the Great Dismal Swamp, and it would take her at least an hour and a half to get there, find it again in the dark, and return. If she broke the short-barreled collapsible-stock AR-15 down into its two component parts, she could just fit it into her daypack for carrying on the motorcycle. She would have to take her chances with any FIST checkpoints.

Once she left her observation post in the shed, she wouldn't be able to know if the killer squads had left the base or not. She would have to assume they were all still there on the base, all around Brad. Even if she infiltrated from the south this time, from behind the hangars, it was unlikely that she would be able to slip in, find Brad and escape without firing a shot. If she had to shoot her way in or out, their prospects would be nearly hopeless. But she had put Brad into the horrible position he was now in, and she would not abandon him. She could not live with herself afterwards if she did that.

Phil Carson will call, she thought. I'll stay and wait for him to call. She didn't want to use her prepaid cell phone this close to their base, because she didn't know what kind of capability they had to scan and locate nearby cell calls. The forest of antennas on top of their long motor home had warned her to be disciplined and not use the prepaid cell phone unnecessarily. She climbed back on the table, wrapped her arms around her knees again, and tried to stay warm by thinking about sailing and swimming with Brad on Guajira, but when she pictured his face, she could only think about what might be happening to him, a half mile away in the buildings next to the hangars…

Phil Carson parked down the street from the Last Chance Saloon in the Township of Great Bridge, ten miles north of the old Navy landing field. He had been using his local knowledge to travel from Suffolk into Chesapeake County entirely on secondary roads. He was avoiding the highways and major surface streets, because the tool carrier behind the cab of his pickup truck was loaded with enough prohibited weaponry to send him to prison for life. They were hidden beneath an ample covering of power tools and work clothes, but he realized that any serious search would discover them.

The Last Chance was a place that he was familiar with. It was an enduring local landmark that was always popular with the riders of American motorcycles, but he had only rarely been there in the past couple of years since he had mostly stopped drinking. He was wearing boots, black denim jeans and a black leather riding jacket, so that he would not stand out among the patrons. His leather jacket was patch-free. He rode with no organized club, and he had never believed in advertising his life history on his outerwear.

A dozen Harleys and a few Triumphs were parked on the street outside the "Wild West" style wooden double-doors. He walked through the dimly-lit bar area, passed the high-backed booths, the pool tables and the kitchen storage area and continued all the way to the back door. Steppenwolf's "Born to be Wild" was playing on the jukebox. Carson wondered how many copies of the record had been worn out and replaced in this bar over the last three decades. It must have been a considerable number, before finally being replaced by a CD and then a computer chip. Nobody paid the least bit of attention to his passage; it was a place where people minded their own damn business unless they were provoked, and direct eye contact between strangers was not advisable.

He cracked open the back door and peered up and down the wide concrete alley. The white SUV which his old friend had described was parked on the other side and down a little bit, along the back wall behind a supermarket. The driver's window was open; his friend was sitting alone, hunched low behind the wheel. There were no other occupied vehicles in sight; no vans, no bums or derelicts keeping watch. He backtracked through the bar, and then drove his green Chevy truck around to the alley and slowly passed the SUV. The men nodded to each other, and Carson parked behind him, back bumper almost to back bumper. They both got out and shook hands between the vehicles. His friend was wearing jeans and a dark blue rain shell with the hood pulled up, even though it was only beginning to drizzle lightly.

Across from them, the back door to the bar was kicked open and both men flinched and cut their eyes toward the noise, but it was only a bartender carrying out a blue plastic recycling bin. The sound of a Creedence Clearwater Revival song followed him through the open door. The bartender walked out into the alley and casually heaved a load of empty beer bottles into the bar's trash dumpster, where they landed with a clatter of breaking glass.

"Bad Moon Rising," said Jasper Mosby, relaxing a bit after their alarm. "That song always brings back memories. Somebody in my platoon had that record; we always played it when we were loading up. Every time I hear it, I still think about getting ready for a patrol. That song used to help us get psyched up, make us feel dangerous. You know, it's funny, the things you remember."

"I know what you mean," said Carson. "Some songs put me right back in country every time I hear them." He laughed. "You know, we might just be in for nasty weather, but there's no moon rising tonight. It's only a crescent moon, and it's setting at 9 o'clock, I checked. I couldn't ask for better conditions; with the clouds it's going to be as dark as a coal mine, and nice and quiet with the rain."

The two men locked gazes, saw their creased faces and receding gray hairlines, and they both thought, *do I look that ancient?*

The off-duty Suffolk police lieutenant said, "Now look at us, two old bastards sneaking around in an alley behind a bar."

"Well Jasper, we sure won't be able to say we weren't old enough to know better."

It was Mosby's turn to laugh. "Yeah Phil, there's no fool like an old fool. Well, anyway, let me show you what I've got." He popped the doors open on the back of his white Expedition. Inside were two suitcase-sized black cordura nylon gear bags and a very full green canvas parachute bag.

"We don't need to go through it all here Jasper; I know what to do with it. I'll get it back to you tomorrow."

"Yeah, um, well...here's the thing, Phil. Most of this stuff is marked up with serial numbers. It's almost all inventory controlled. If anything goes missing, well, I'll be screwed and that's the truth."

"Listen, Jasper, I really appreciate what you're doing, we..."

"That's not it, Phil. That's not it at all. Since you called, I've been thinking about everything... You're welcome to use this stuff, but... on one condition. Only if I come with it. I mean, if I don't get it all back, I might as well not come back either. I talked it over with Liddy, and she's for it, all the way. No matter what. And even more important than that, I'm just not going to let you and Ranya go in there by yourselves." Mosby looked down at his feet.

Carson knew that Jasper Mosby stood to lose all of his pension and benefits if he went on tonight's rescue mission and it turned out badly, even if he wasn't killed, wounded, or arrested outright. It was a hell of a risk for a man at retirement age.

"And one more thing, Phil, and it's non-negotiable. I didn't come alone. Some of the gear...well, I had to borrow it from our SWAT team, and I had to do a little song and dance for it. Anyway, I wound up getting us another volunteer. His name's Frank." Mosby slightly raised his hand in a signal. "I knew you'd spook if you saw two of us, so I had him wait around the corner. You've just got to believe me on this, but Frank's somebody I'd trust my life to."

A solidly built thirtyish man of average height, with dark hair and a moustache, appeared down the alley and walked briskly toward them. Carson stared in disbelief, and quickly looked over his shoulder the other way down the alley for any more surprises. How had he missed spotting this guy before the meeting? Was this all a set up? No, no way. Jasper wouldn't do it. No way in hell. But if he had missed this guy, what else was he missing? Was he still sharp enough? Had he been out of the game too long? Were his observational senses and instincts no longer up to the challenges he would be facing?

The guy was wearing black BDU-style fatigue pants and only a black t-shirt even in the cool drizzle. The shoulders and biceps of a body builder strained against the fabric, the hallmark of every serious SWAT cop. Just before they shook hands, Carson noted that he wore no wedding band.

"Phil, I'm glad to meet you. My name's Frank Santander, I'm a Sergeant with the Suffolk PD, and I'm a member of our special response team." Santander locked his gaze directly onto Carson's eyes while they gripped each others hands.

"Lieutenant Mosby said that we should just go by first names to-night, but…I'm sorry, Jasper, but that's just not my style. When he came to me for some gear this afternoon, I made him tell me what he wanted it for. You see, we've had some long talks, Jasper and me, about what's been going on lately. We think about the same way on it, and well, any-way, here I am.

"You know, sir, my family's all from Colombia, and most of my relatives are still down there. But I've been here since I was a kid, and I'm just plain American all the way. Look, I know I'm not in the league with you two, I mean, I heard some stories about you, Mr. Carson, at the VFW… Anyhow, after the Army, I joined the Suffolk Police, because I really care about people. I want to help them, protect them. I know that sounds corny, but I swear to God it's the truth. Am I making any sense?

"Anyway, here's what it is, here's why I'm here; I just can't stand watching America turning into a big Colombia. I've been there, I've spent time down there, and what's been going on lately, it ain't right, it just ain't American.

"When Jasper, I mean Lieutenant Mosby, when he told me what you found going on down in Chesapeake, and how it's the same gang that did the arsons and killed the Edmonds family and everything, well, I mean, connect the dots, right? It all connects right straight back to the Stadium

Massacre, doesn't it? I mean, I never bought the Shifflett story, not for a minute. When he said what you were planning, and how he was going with you, well, I told him I was coming too, or no gear. And so here I am."

Carson was choked up, but swallowed the lump in his throat. Leaders couldn't show that kind of human frailty. He was grateful for the light rain falling on his face. "You know who's there? You know what we'll be up against?"

"I know. Pros. A professional death squad. Secret police, like in Colombia or Brazil. People who burn families to death, just to make a point."

"Frank, you understand that they're probably some kind of sworn federal law enforcement agents? I really doubt that they're civilians. Can you...deal with that?"

"Can I shoot a cop, you mean? A 'brother officer'? Mr. Carson, these aren't cops anymore, these are death squad killers. They're just Nazis, like the Gestapo, and they shame and dishonor every honest cop in America. Hell yes I can shoot them, if I have to. No question. But the primary mission tonight is a rescue operation, and collecting video evidence, right?"

"That's exactly right."

"Well, let's go do it then."

Carson shook his hand again. "Welcome aboard, Frank Santander. But some of the people you're going to meet tonight can't use their real names. Let me do all the introductions, and only use the names I use. Is that cool?"

"That's cool, I understand. It's better security. But I wanted you to know who I am, right up front. That's just the way I am."

"Okay then, let's roll." Phil Carson knew that taking Mosby along was a huge risk, and bringing the stranger even more so. From his previous life, his life after the Army, after Viet Nam, he knew all too well that the unexpected strap-hanger was often a Judas, sent to betray. But he had already come too far, and aborting the mission out of a desire for self-preservation was simply not an option. Not with Ranya waiting for him, not with Ranya going in alone if he didn't show up. He would just have to accept the risk that he was being set up. After all, it was a night for taking chances; it was a night for not holding anything back.

On his return flight to Washington, Malvone's borrowed helicopter crossed the Potomac just to the east of the Dahlgren Naval Proving Grounds, where the miles-wide river tended north, and then made a giant dog-leg turn back to the southwest. This was where the high Governor

Harry W. Nice Memorial Bridge crossed the Potomac, carrying Route 301 from Virginia into Maryland. With the Wilson Bridge on the DC beltway severed, the 301 bridge was carrying double its normal traffic. There was no other bridge over the mighty Potomac River between Washington and the Chesapeake Bay.

For the return flight, Malvone chose to ride in the empty right front seat; the helicopter only had one set of controls. From their altitude of 2,000 feet, just below the cloud ceiling, the bridge looked like an elaborate Erector Set model, with toy 18 wheelers laboring up one steep slope and sliding down the other. The toll plaza on the Maryland side was now doubling as an enormous "FIST" checkpoint, almost like an international border crossing, and traffic was backed up the bridge toward the Virginia side.

Malvone immediately felt more comfortable on the Maryland side of the river. Compared to the anachronistic gun-toting Virginians, Marylanders were by comparison a much tamer breed. Decades of progressive Democratic Party rule had long since seen all firearms registered, and whenever possible, taken away from ordinary citizens. After the "Beltway Sniper" case in 2002, Maryland had cracked down even harder on gun owners, and after the Stadium Massacre the semi-automatic rifle turn-in had proceeded smoothly, since all of these weapons had already been thoroughly catalogued by the State Police.

Malvone's pilot was flying by the "3-R" method: roads, rails and rivers, and once they were over Maryland, he tracked to the north above route 301 at 120 miles per hour. Before taking off, Malvone had asked the pilot to make a slight detour on their way back to Washington, and the pilot had marked his air map with the new mid-point destination and plotted a waypoint on the GPS navigation system.

The now operational (and soon to be expanding) Special Training Unit needed its own headquarters and base, away from Washington and away from Quantico. "Mr. Emerson," his White House-provided black-budget and proprietary front company expert, had come up with a short list of potential sites, and among them, the West Waldorf Industrial Park seemed to Malvone to be the most promising. Its location was excellent, 20 road miles south of DC, and 25 miles north of Virginia across the 301 bridge. Best of all, it was only ten miles from Malvone's own home on Tanaccaway Creek.

Even though the site was just 20 air miles east of Quantico Virginia across the Potomac, it was 60 long slow road miles away via Fredericksburg Virginia over the 301 bridge. This would effectively divorce the STU from close federal law enforcement control, another of Malvone's goals. With the Wilson Bridge cut, the FBI at Quantico found itself on the "wrong" side of the river, forced to battle their way into

Washington on the jammed alternate routes, while the STU Team leaders would be able to pop in and out from the Maryland side at will.

Beyond the University of Maryland's college town of La Plata, Route 301 veered to the northeast, but the pilot continued straight on cross-country, counting down the miles on his electronic GPS map display. Three minutes later they were over an empty office and industrial park, and Malvone circled his left index finger to indicate that the pilot should orbit. The pilot pushed his yoke into a right bank to give his government supergrade passenger the best view.

As they circled, Malvone mentally inventoried the ten acres of empty warehouses, offices, workshops, parking lots and multi-use buildings, which were all surrounded by a chain link fence. Beyond the fence, the place was bordered by fields of corn and asparagus and beans.

The industrial park had been finished two years earlier, but it had yet to welcome its first tenant. Final leasing plans had been halted in their tracks when government biologists from the nearby Mattawoman Natural Environment Area had made a dramatic discovery: the local Eastern Golden-backed Sand Gnats comprised a distinct and extremely rare species. They were immediately placed under federal protection as an endangered species. The federal biologists next made the rapid determination that industrial activity and lighting in the area would hinder the mating activity of the rare gnat, and project completion was halted by a court order. The private developers of the West Waldorf Industrial Park went to court, and then into bankruptcy.

Now, two years later, the new owners of the property were about to catch a break at last. Vital national security concerns would outweigh the value of the rare gnats, and Uncle Sam (suitably sheep-dipped as a private corporation) would be moving in as the sole tenant. The Special Training Unit was going to have its own home.

But even then Malvone knew that it was time for the STU to shed its original name. Washington bureaucrats he had never even met were tossing off the initials far too freely; it was only a matter of time before the existence of the STU would be mentioned in some magazine article or website. Perhaps the STU would next become the Special Projects Division, or the Firearms Research Group. It didn't matter, as long as the title was suitably vague, and it had three initials.

And in a few months or a year, that new unit name would also be on the lips of bureaucrats and a few well-connected reporters, and then that name would also disappear down the bureaucratic memory-hole in turn. It was a truism in Washington that any elite covert unit really worth a damn rated a classified name, mission, and base. The West Waldorf Industrial Park could hold their rapidly expanding personnel, and all of their vehicles and equipment. It could handle helicopters, it could handle indoor firing ranges, it could handle anything. He indicated to the pilot that he was finished studying the park, and the helicopter continued on to the north.

By 7:30 PM it was fully dark, and light rain was falling silently on the fields and trees around the auxiliary landing field. The damp coldness was seeping into Ranya's core. She alternated between sitting on the sorting table and stretching and exercising in place inside the shed to keep warm and alert, all the while watching the area around the chain link gate for even subtle signs of activity. She feared that if any of the killers left tonight, they might drive away without turning on their headlights, using the night vision goggles which she guessed that they had.

But when the federal convoy finally pulled up to the gate at 7:35 PM, there was no mistaking the multiple sets of headlights burning on the other side of the fence. The gate was pushed open, and the column rolled through it and passed Ranya only 100 yards from her tobacco shed. She mused that if she had only had a belt-fed machine gun, she could have easily raked them with devastating fire in the open field as they approached the cut where the road passed through the tree line.

There were four large dark SUVs, presumably two were the same black Suburbans that she had seen at Boat America. The four SUVs were trailed by a full-sized van. Once they were gone, she punched Phil Carson's number into her throwaway cell phone. If there were five or six men per vehicle, that could make 25 or 30 jack-booted thugs out for a night of arson and murder. Even if there were only three men per vehicle, the number of killers on the base would be reduced by fifteen.

Phil Carson picked up on the second ring. "Hello?"

"It's me, they just left. Five big ones."

"Okay, that's great. Really great. We're here. You know where the place is? You're sure you can find it at night?"

"I'm sure."

"All right, come on then."

"Ten minutes."

"Okay."

39

The Wagon Wheel was a former restaurant and country music dance hall which had missed the end of the line-dancing craze of the early 1990s. It was built like a barn mated to a warehouse. Part of it had been burned, and much of the rest was covered in graffiti. The restaurant windows that were not boarded up with sheets of plywood had long ago been shot out for casual target practice, as was the marquee sign out front on the road. There was little risk to the vandals that they would be bothered by police, because the Wagon Wheel was located on South River Road, which had lost its significance when the four-lane Route 158 had been opened five miles to the west.

It was set well back from the road across an acre of overgrown and rutted gravel parking lot, still waiting for the legions of Texas Two-Steppers who had never discovered the place. Ranya paused on the shoulder and swept it with her headlight beam, before she proceeded slowly around the right side of the barn-shaped restaurant to the back. No other headlights were visible on South River Road in either direction.

The back side of the building was L-shaped, with the restaurant forming the short leg of the L away from the road. Three vehicles were parked inside of the corner against the back of the dance hall. They were completely invisible from the road, and could only be seen if someone took the time to drive all the way around to the back. A wall of dripping pine trees crowded close to the back of the restaurant. A helicopter might spot the unusual gathering of vehicles, but no helicopter was likely to be flying on this rainy night with the clouds pressing close to the ground.

She pulled into the space between a white SUV and a dark pickup truck on a strip of hard black asphalt, and killed her engine and her light. A male voice off to her left side said, "Over here." She removed her helmet and walked toward where she had heard the voice, quite night blind in the sudden absence of her headlight. Someone shined a flashlight down the trash and bottle strewn path along the back of the building.

"It's me," she heard Phil Carson say. "Everything is ready."

She went to him, the light flicked off, and they embraced.

Ranya said, "Thanks for coming. I really didn't want to do this alone."

"You're not alone darlin', you're not alone. Listen: just go with me on this, but tonight your name's Robin, okay?"

"Robin?"

"Everybody has a new name for tonight. Except me, 'cause everybody here already knows who I am. It's just a precaution, in case things go wrong later."

"Okay, I'm Robin. That's fine."

"And if you recognize anybody, don't let on, and don't use their real names."

"All right."

"Well then, come on in and meet the posse." Carson pulled open a door and they went inside.

A hissing Coleman lantern provided light in what had been a small windowless manager's office or employee work area. It sat in the middle of a round table in the center of the room; the table was covered with maps and black and white aerial photographs. Around the table stood seven people of widely varying heights, including Phil Carson. Two portly bearded men wore jungle boonie hats, and matching camouflage rain jackets. An older couple wore blue raincoats with the hoods pushed back onto their shoulders. Two other men wore ball caps pulled low over their faces.

The lantern had a round metal shade on its top, which cast a harsh yellow light down on the table, but left the people obscured in shadow from the waist up. Even so, Ranya recognized one of the men wearing the ball caps: Jasper Mosby of the Suffolk police! But as she had been instructed, she made no outward sign of greeting him, and neither did he acknowledge her with more than a subtle nod of his head.

"It's really nice to see you folks, it's just…kind of hard to believe…I never thought…" She crossed her arms tightly and began to visibly shiver. "I'm sorry, but I'm freezing to death; I got drenched again riding up here."

The grandmotherly woman said, "We've been waiting for you honey. I've got a thermos of coffee, and a thermos of soup."

"Oh thank you!"

Phil Carson said, "I picked up a sweater and a raincoat for you," and handed her a white plastic shopping bag.

Ranya swung off her black daypack and unclipped her fanny pack and dropped them to the floor, then stepped into an adjoining storage room. The reflected light from the lantern through the half open door was enough for her to see by as she unzipped her denim riding jacket, which was soaked through again. She felt her black t-shirt; it was also wet so she stripped it off. She was already braless from before. She quickly shook out and pulled on the new gray sweatshirt. Carson was looking out for her; she hadn't even asked him for the dry clothes. For the first time in many hours she was dry from the skin out, at least from the waist up.

The equally new green rain slicker was a little too big, but it was fine after she folded the cuffs up once, and its hood had a drawstring to pull it close to her face. Once she put her ball cap on under the hood, she would even be able to keep the rain off of her face. She left the hood thrown back and returned to the meeting room with her wet denim jacket and t-shirt in the plastic bag. She knew that her loose hair must look like Medusa's snakes after the abuse it had suffered today, but it was a minor annoyance, considering the seriousness of the night.

The woman returned from a side table and handed her a plastic traveling mug with a snapped-on lid.

"Here's your coffee. Cream and sugar, all right honey?"

"That's wonderful, thanks." The warmth of the mug against her wind and rain-chilled fingers was as welcome to Ranya as the hot sweet liquid was to sip.

Phil Carson said, "Well everybody, this is my friend Robin, and like I told you, she's most of the reason we're all here tonight. Robin, this is the best team I could muster on short notice. They might not look like much, but they'll do what they need to do, as long as they don't have to march too far, or climb over anything higher than a curb."

That comment brought a "damn right" and an "I heard that" from the two shorter bearded gentlemen, and chuckles from the rest.

"We're lucky it's raining; I think we'll be able to drive right in. Were you able to draw any maps?" asked Carson.

She picked up her pack and set it on the edge of the table, and withdrew her folded calendar pages. "I didn't have much of a choice of stationery; this is the best I could do." The four grimy cheesecake calendar photos were laid sketch-side-up on top of the printed maps.

Carson continued with his ad hoc briefing. "Based on these aerial pictures and topo maps, and a quick scouting trip I made part way in, we came up with our own infiltration route. Robin said they're not putting out any security, but it doesn't make sense to go in through their own gate, not if we have a choice. It's too risky. They might have cameras on it, or we might run right into them if they're coming in or out."

Their proposed infiltration and exfiltration routes were marked on the pictures and maps with a magic marker. Carson leaned over and examined Ranya's sketch of the area around the hangars, then he turned it north upwards to match his own street and military topographic maps. "Okay Robin, you were there, now tell us where the prisoner is. Tell us what you saw."

"I was over here." She pointed on her own sketch to where she had marked the abandoned utility trailers across the tarmac. "I had a perfect view straight between the hangars and the buildings. I saw...the prisoner...being taken from this building to this one, and then back again. He's still there, as far as I know. The house trailers are inside this hangar. They're big, just like mobile homes. Their vehicles are inside this one, and this is the motor home with all the antennas on top."

Carson said, "All right, we'll call the first building on the east side B-1. That's where we think the prisoner is. Next is B-2. Then H-1 is the hangar with the trailers, and finally H-2 is the vehicle hangar all the way on the west side." He marked their names on Ranya's map with a black marker. "We don't know for sure if he's in B-1 or B-2, so we'll hit both of them at the same time. Jake and Fred here will take B-2, it's closer to the hangars, and they're more...experienced at this. Robin and I'll take B-1. Tom and Harry are going to be here and here, behind the corners of B-2, to cover the front and back of the hangars from the side.

"Archie and Edith are going to be across the tarmac with their machine gun. If everything goes completely to hell, they'll be able to lay down automatic fire on the hangars and keep the bad guys away from the buildings while we're in there. Just don't aim it past here," Carson pointed to the space between building two and hangar one on Ranya's sketch. "You'll have friendlies in front of B-1 and B-2. But hopefully you won't have to fire at all; you'll just be over there as our observation post. Just tell us what's going on, and give us a warning on the radio if anybody's coming from the hangars."

"You've got a machine gun?" Ranya asked the older couple.

Edith answered, "We sure do, sweetie; we've got an M-60. It's mint."

"That's .308, right?"

"That's right," answered Archie. "Actually it's 7.62 NATO, but .308's close enough. We've got 500 rounds all linked up together, ready to go. Nice shiny South African surplus ammo, it works like a charm. We take our boat out on the ocean and test fire it every year or two."

"That's kind of a rare gun for a civilian, isn't it? I mean, if they find 7.62 brass and links in a big pile all over the ground, they're going to have a pretty short list of machine gun owners to check, aren't they?"

Archie chuckled. "They would if it was ever registered. But it wasn't."

Ranya was curious about the origin of their machine gun, but she kept her questions to herself. She'd heard around Freedom Arms that military unit armorers sometimes wrote off weapons as worn out or broken, and then substituted or held back spare parts until they could assemble complete weapons, "off the books." And with the Army and Marines changing from the old M-60s to more modern machine guns, she guessed that more than a few had been mislaid on the road to the furnace.

She asked them, "An M-60 and all that ammo's pretty heavy. How are you going to get it in?" Even in the dim light above the lantern, Archie and Edith looked to be in their sixties at least. Archie was white-haired; Edith's hair appeared to be silvery blond.

Edith said, "Don't worry, Robin, we're not carrying it in, we're driving it in. And we're setting it up in our truck, so we'll catch all the brass and the links. We just need to know if we can get a two-wheel drive pickup back around here where you were, without being seen from the hangars." Edith traced a path around the tarmac and pointed to the flat bed utility trailers where Ranya had been concealed during her afternoon recon.

Ranya replied, "I'd say so. The old service road here is so overgrown, the bushes and trees will be scraping both sides at times. It'll be a tight fit, but you can push through in your truck. But with your lights off, I think it'll be too dark to find your way in."

"We've got that covered," said Carson. "We've got a little night scope for them."

"It screws right onto a video camera too. Once we're in position, we're going to start making movies," said Edith. She did most of their talking.

Ranya looked to each of them, "I'm just so grateful, to all of you. I never really expected to have any help tonight. Except for you." She smiled warmly at Phil Carson.

Edith said, "Phil called this afternoon, and asked us what we were doing tonight, can you imagine? He explained the whole thing. Well you know, we thought something like this was going on, but we never dreamed they'd be right in our own backyard!

"Anyhow, Phil asked us to help him out tonight, and we're thinking, what are we saving that damned machine gun for anyway? Phil's one of the only people on earth who knows about our M-60. Archie's been hiding it for years and years, and for what? If we're not going to use it now, what'd we keep it for? Our kids are all gone, and even our grandkids are almost grown up. They're so brainwashed now, they won't even touch a .22. You'd think we were offering them heroin or something! Sad, isn't it? So if we're never going to use it, who will?"

Archie added, "I never expected to make it this far anyway, and I never was the nursing home type. So why sit around just watching all this crap on TV and getting an ulcer? All these years I've been keeping that M-60 'for a rainy day', and finally, finally, it's come! And it's even raining! Tell me that wasn't a sign!"

Carson told him, "Just don't go trigger happy on us; your job's to be our lookout and make movies. No shooting unless the bad guys are coming after us, so don't even jack the bolt before that. We all need to keep our fingers off the triggers; one accidental discharge will ruin everything, everything!

"Any shooting we do tonight should only be inside B-1 and B-2, and only with the suppressed weapons. If we end up in a fire-fight outside with the bad guys, shooting unsuppressed weapons, we're all in deep shit, got it? I'm already nervous about doing this with a pick-up team, but I guess you're all just as nervous as I am for the same reason, so we'll all just have to deal with it, okay?"

Everybody nodded or muttered their agreement. They all understood the stakes, and their own limitations.

"All right then, we don't have much time, but let's grab our weapons, check the gun lights, and practice our two-man entries a few times. Remember, light 'em up, and if they move, shoot 'em. I know we've already been over this, but we're looking for a guy named Brad. He's thirty, he's got light brownish hair and blue eyes, and he's probably wearing tan shorts and a blue polo shirt. We might find Burgess Edmonds in there too, he's about our age. Anybody else is a bad guy, so if they cause any problems, don't hesitate. Waste 'em. We already checked our radios; I'll handle our radio, Robin, so you don't have to worry about it. Okay, take five. Then grab your gear and come back in for a little practice, and then we'll go."

Jasper Mosby sat quietly in disbelief. He couldn't get over the unbelievable situation he found himself in. Here he was, a career police officer, sharing a vehicle with armed criminals on their way to possibly kill federal agents.

The driver and the front seat passenger were the two gray-bearded and ponytailed hillbilly types Carson had called Tom and Harry, but Mosby recognized them. They were actually the Bedford brothers, who owned a gigantic junk yard operation over in Isle of Wight County. Of course, Mosby didn't let on in any way that he knew who they were; there was no reason to. Ranya was alone in the rear-facing back seat; the plan was that Brad would ride back there after the rescue, as well as Burgess Edmonds if they found him too.

Besides the five of them in the station wagon, Phil Carson was in his Chevy truck a hundred yards in front of them, as they drove the few remaining miles south on the rain-slick road toward the south end of the base. Archie and Edith were following behind them in their own blue Dodge truck with its matching blue camper shell.

Jesus! Just what had he volunteered for? And what was he going to do if they were pulled over by a Chesapeake cop?

Frank Santander—Fred tonight—tapped the front-seat passenger on the shoulder, and asked him, "Hey, uh, Harry, what year's this thing? It's a Buick, right? What kind of top speed can it get?" The black primer-painted station wagon's engine made a low rumbling growl unlike any family car Santander had ever been in.

"It's a '71 Buick Estate Wagon. She's got an original 455, and she'll do 130 all night long."

"No way! Really?"

"Really."

"What'll she do with all these people? On the way out we might have two more on board, and that's a lot of weight. What'll she do when we're loaded down?"

Harry laughed. "Oh, don't worry. She'll do the 130 with a heavy load. Trust me."

Mosby was glad that it was so dark inside the Estate Wagon. It was becoming obvious now that the bearded and ponytailed Bedford brothers were, or had been, moonshine bootleggers at the very least. The monster-engined station wagons of the sixties and early seventies (from before the first oil crunch) were greatly prized by "transportation specialists." With their back seats folded down to form a flat cargo deck, they carried over a hundred gallons of 'shine in a single tightly packed layer, six one gallon jugs to a carton, all low to the ground for hauling ass across all kinds of roads. A hundred gallons or more of untaxed white lightning was indeed a heavy load…

And, add to that, the rumor that Phil Carson had been a pot smuggler in the early 1970's, after he had come home from Nam. It had been whispered around Suffolk that Carson knew how to get a sailboat with a raised waterline from Jamaica or Colombia to the Chesapeake Bay. The word was that he'd been one of the rare smart ones who had cashed in and gotten out of the game before the trade had turned vicious with the coming of cocaine in the '80s. Now, as far as he knew, Carson bought and sold properties for a living.

If the Bedford brothers had enjoyed a professional relationship with Phil Carson back in those days, then at some point they had switched from carrying bottles to bales, and so they had probably come by their junk yard money through the transportation of controlled substances. But that was all a long time ago…

And here he was, sitting behind them in a souped-up station wagon loaded with illegal weapons.

As the wagon rolled down South River Road through a dark tunnel of overhanging trees, the mist ahead lit by their low beams, Mosby imagined what the headlines would say if he was arrested with this bunch. He started counting the possible felony charges against him, but gave up after seven. He'd be finished. He'd die in jail, and Liddy would die in the poor house.

All of their submachine guns were covered by blankets and hidden beneath the seats, but he had no doubt that if they were pulled over by a Chesapeake cop, they'd never get away once he shined his flashlight inside this station wagon. They'd be "made" and the weapons would be found. Then what? He could never shoot a brother officer, at least not a uniformed local cop, but what about the others? It would be murder-one for everybody in the car, no matter who shot first.

And really, what was the difference between shooting a uniformed local cop, and what they were planning to do on the base? Well, there was a big difference. Local police don't burn people in their houses, or blow them up on the highways, or shoot them down with silent MP-5s. Joe Bardiwell's daughter Ranya was sitting facing the other way right behind him, and that was enough to refocus Jasper Mosby on the operation ahead, and give him the motivation to do what he might have to do. That, and the fact that he had introduced Brad Fallon to her in the first place! Now whatever happened, he was involved in it clear up to his eyeballs, whether he liked it or not. And all because of a dead doberman, and a shovel...

What the hell, Mosby thought, it's been a great ride, and I already made it a lot further than I ever thought I would. Some things were just worth fighting for, even if most people wouldn't agree.

They were still on the blacktop road, but the driver was assisted in his navigation through the night by a GPS unit mounted under the dash in the center. The GPS display had a multi-colored glowing screen the size of an index card, its antenna was a white plastic mushroom sitting at the front of the dashboard next to the windshield. The Bedfords were bootleggers from a bygone era, who were using a 21st century satellite mapping system.

Mosby tapped Santander on the knee and pointed to the GPS display, and Santander gave him a thumbs-up sign back. Each time they turned, a little blinking triangle in the middle of the glowing screen turned; the little triangle represented the Buick wagon. The precise current distance and compass direction to building B-1 was displayed across the bottom of the map in bright numbers and letters. Mosby knew that just as GPS had been a boon to law enforcement, it had also been a great help to some classes of criminals. Smugglers could now arrange drop-offs, and rendezvous in remote unmarked wilderness areas, or far out at sea, sure of a perfect linkup thanks to their shared GPS coordinates.

Finally, Carson's tail lights brightened ahead of them. He braked and turned off the pavement to the right. The station wagon slowed in turn and followed the truck onto gravel, and then dirt, bouncing as they passed between trees and thick brush. The wagon's headlights illuminated the reflectors on the back of Carson's truck, and then they stopped and their headlights were extinguished. The inside of the wagon was illuminated by the soft glow from the GPS screen. Archie's truck pulled up behind them and stopped. Carson pulled his truck in a tight three point turn and parked it under low tree branches off the side of the dirt road, facing back toward South River Road.

They opened their doors quietly and stepped out into the cool drizzle and gathered behind the station wagon. The rear window slid up into the roof; the tailgate retracted down under the floor in the back, and Ranya climbed out.

Archie and Edith got out of their truck. She had a dry towel and a roll of duct tape, and as planned she began to methodically cover all of the reflectors and lights on the dark blue pickup, blotting them out one at a time. Their Dodge truck would be directly across the tarmac from the hangars. Even with its headlights off, they couldn't risk inadvertently showing any brake lights, or even returning a shine off a reflector.

The four of them who were going into the two buildings used the truck's front parking lights to see by while they put on their black kevlar vests, which had been carried on the floor in the back of the wagon beneath Ranya's feet. These were bulky adjustable models similar to military flak jackets, meant to be worn on the outside of their clothing.

Edith finished taping over her truck's front parking lights. As they went dark each of the group pulled out the green plastic chemical light sticks that they had been given back at the Wagon Wheel. These brightly glowing sticks were kept in pockets where they could be put away or taken out as needed for illumination, or to help them rally together if they were separated in the darkness.

Mosby was only a little amazed to see that one of the two Bedford brothers (they were indistinguishable in the darkness) was wearing what looked like a black ice hockey helmet with a pair of night vision goggles attached to the front. The idea that night vision devices were the exclusive domain of the military and law enforcement was rapidly evaporating.

Carson spoke to them quietly. "All right, we're three quarters of a mile from the target. We're going lights-out and weapons-ready from here. My truck is the emergency escape vehicle; we'll switch over to it if the station wagon's too damaged to run on the highway. If things really go to hell and you can't make it to the station wagon, or if the wagon won't run, try to make it back here to my truck. The keys are under the visor just like we briefed it before. Edith, let's do another radio check."

She climbed inside the cab on the passenger side. In a moment Carson's walkie-talkie made three clicks, then the word "test" came out of it. He held down the transmit button on his cell phone sized FSR radio and replied "loud and clear." They were keeping voice communications to an absolute minimum, out of respect for the probable radio scanning and direction finding capabilities of their enemy.

"Archie, you have your cheat-sheet with the click signals and the brevity codes?"

"Got it."

"You're comfortable with the night scope?"

"No problem. We're only going to be moving at walking speed. I can drive with one hand and hold the scope with the other. Edith is going to keep us on track with our GPS; we've got the route programmed into waypoints." Archie and Edith were boaters, so using their handheld GPS unit to solve navigational problems was second nature to them.

"And Archie, no matter what, we can't have an accidental discharge. Don't rack the bolt..."

"I won't, don't worry. Observe and film, that's our job. Shooting is the last resort. Don't worry, we won't screw it up."

"All right everybody, lock and load here. Keep them on safe, and keep your fingers off the triggers." A chorus of metallic scraping and snapping and slamming was heard. "And I don't need to tell you to watch your muzzles."

Jasper Mosby was extremely nervous. They all were. They were a thrown-together group, unknown to each other, which could be a recipe for disaster. Special teams for such missions trained together for months, until they knew each others' capabilities and habits by heart. Going with this pick-up team on a real world operation violated more tactical rules than Mosby could think of. But there was no alternative; they didn't have the luxury of time.

Carson said, "All right, let's check our gun lights. Cover them up, and try 'em out."

Mosby and Santander both carried 9mm MP-5SD submachine guns with fat integral suppressors shrouding the barrels; they had white gun lights mounted under them. They cradled their weapons and covered the lights with one hand while pushing the rubber pressure switches with the other. The lights were so intense that their tightly closed fingers were momentarily lit like red beacons. A light turned on at the wrong time could be almost as damaging as a premature gunshot, causing them to lose their crucial element of surprise. It was important to know by feel exactly how to switch on the light at the correct instant, and avoid accidentally switching it on at any other time.

Carson tested his light next; he was carrying a .45 caliber Thompson submachine gun with a straight stick magazine inserted. Mosby could only shake his head in wonder when he had seen the old Tommy gun, which was so many decades older than the MP-5 he was carrying. Before the gun control act of 1934 had been passed anyone could purchase a Thompson as easily as a pair of shoes, and evidently some of them had never been registered with the ATF during the last seventy years. The Thompson had been invented in the Model-T era, but Carson's had a modern red-dot electronic aiming device mounted on top. His model had the Army-style straight wooden fore end, instead of the forward pistol grip of the pre-war era, so Mosby suspected that this particular submachine gun had come home in a soldier's duffel bag.

A homemade suppressor the size of a can of tennis balls was fitted to the end of the Thompson's barrel, and a borrowed Suffolk PD Sure-Flash light was duct-taped beneath it. The juxtaposition of the serial-numbered police department tactical light mounted under the illegal silencer on an illegal submachine gun made Mosby cringe; how many felonies that would be worth, he could only imagine.

Carson had lent Ranya a Colt Woodsman .22 caliber pistol, with a suppressor the size of a paper towel tube mounted over the entire barrel. It had a smaller white tactical light taped under it, which she tested against her left palm. Mosby understood the logic: Ranya was there primarily to video tape the rescue, and the silent pistol was a secondary consideration. If a real gunfight broke out, and if in spite of their best efforts it suddenly got loud, she would switch from the diminutive .22 rimfire to the .45 caliber pistol which she was also carrying.

Ordinarily, Mosby would scoff at the idea of someone carrying a .22 pistol on a raid, but he knew from years of observing her that Ranya could rapid-fire the tiny bullets into coin-sized targets at fifty feet. Fired squarely through a cranium by an expert shot, the .22 could be an effective killing tool.

The Bedford brothers carried matching carbine versions of the AR-15, with collapsible stocks and short barrels. Their normal flash hiders had been unscrewed and replaced with homemade sound suppressors the size of fruit-juice cans. They didn't appear to Mosby to be true sound suppressors; they were probably just adapted from chainsaw or lawn mower mufflers. Even so, they would cut the decibels down enough so that any shooting wouldn't be heard more than a mile away.

Like the Suffolk SWAT-issued MP-5SDs, both of the Bedfords' rifles had a second thirty round magazine attached next to the one which was already inserted, for a faster initial reload. Carson wore a canvas rig across his chest with vertical pouches carrying extra thirty round stick magazines. The last time Mosby had seen a set up like that, it had been on a pith-helmeted NVA soldier firing an AK-47.

With Archie's belt-fed M-60 across the tarmac, and the Bedford boys with their rifles providing covering fire down the front and back of the hangars, the assault team would stand a fighting chance of getting in and out of the buildings and away. These three supporting weapons could hold anyone in the hangars at bay, and they gave Mosby a lot of confidence. All they were lacking was a 40mm grenade launcher, but realistically he knew that they were fortunate to have assembled the fire power that they had.

"Well, the weather sucks, which is great for us," said Carson. Water was beginning to trickle off of their hats; the rain was light but it dripped unevenly off of the tree branches above them. The green glow of their chemlites gave their huddle a ghostly look. "Nobody's going to be outside, and it'll be nice and quiet in the woods. Watch your muzzles, keep on safe, and keep your fingers clear. Let's put the chemlites away when we break from here, and let our eyes adjust as much as they can. I think we're ready. Anybody got anything else?"

One of the Bedford's spat, and said in a low voice, "Yeah. Let's get some."

"Okay, maybe we will," replied Carson. "Let's go. We'll take the wagon as far as we can. Archie, you're going to peel off after we get inside the fence, right?"

"Right," he responded. Archie and Edith shook hands around the little huddle, and climbed into their truck.

This time, Phil Carson climbed into the middle row of the station wagon directly behind the driver, since his own truck was being left behind as their backup escape vehicle. They all held their weapons muzzles up-ward. Harry held both his own and his brother's in the front seat. Ranya climbed into the back, and the tailgate rose to meet the window as it slid down out of the roof.

The well-muffled 455 cubic inch engine rumbled to life. There was no need for duct tape over any of the black station wagon's exterior or interior lights; with the flip of a single switch all of them were disabled, including the brake lights. The driver was wearing his night vision goggle helmet. Pushing a touch-pad button, he adjusted the brightness of the GPS display down until it disappeared from the vision of the passengers, sinking the interior of the car in utter blackness. He slipped the Estate Wagon into gear and they rolled forward for the last leg of their infiltration.

40

The chain link vehicle gate, on the long-forgotten southeast access road into the base annex, proved to be an unexpectedly stubborn barrier. The padlock yielded easily to long-handled bolt cutters, but brush and saplings from both sides of the narrow asphalt track had grown through it, entwining it in a living web. Wearing his night vision goggles, Tom clipped and cut most of the larger vines and sapling branches with the bolt cutters, then tied a tow rope from beneath his front bumper to the bottom of the latching side of the gate. Finally he returned to the driver's seat and slowly reversed, dragging the protesting gate open far enough for the wagon to fit through.

After following the station wagon inside the fence, Archie's pick-up truck turned off to the right to follow the perimeter service road to the north, and it was immediately lost from their view in the gloom.

The southeast road into the base annex had been narrow enough when it was first paved decades earlier. Now the unchecked branches of new growth trees on both sides met in the middle, scraping and swishing down both sides of the station wagon and under the bottom as it proceeded at little more than a walking speed. The five passengers could see only inky blackness beyond their rain-streaked windows, and hear only the brush sliding along the wagon as it seemingly threaded its way through the woods.

The driver said, "800 feet." He was watching the distance to their target on his GPS screen. "Building one is 800 feet away at 330 degrees, north-northwest straight through the woods."

"Let's go a little further, and find a place to turn around."

A minute later the driver said, "I can turn around here; it's 500 feet northwest through the woods to B-1."

"Okay, turn us around."

The driver made a careful three point turn between the young trees, until the wagon was facing outbound back down its track, and he switched off the motor. The only sound now was the splatter of drops on the roof. Carson said, "Okay people, sit tight and relax. Now we wait for Archie to get into position. Let's crack the windows and get some fresh air."

They waited like this for ten more minutes. They were sweaty and uncomfortable in their awkward kevlar raid vests; the snatches of cooler air wafting through the slightly open windows provided their only relief. The old Buick had seats as comfortable as any sofa. Ranya's head slowly tipped back, and she nodded off as the warm interior and softly padded upholstery enticed her to drift to sleep.

At 9:21 PM Carson's walkie-talkie made two crisp and distinct clicks, the signal that Archie and Edith were in position. This meant that their M-60 machine gun was aimed across the tarmac at the open hangars, with 500 rounds of linked 7.62mm ball ammunition ready to rock and roll if it came to an all-out fight.

In the station wagon all six of them stretched and yawned, then followed Carson's lead and carefully opened the doors and climbed out into the welcome chill of the dripping pine woods. As they had rehearsed behind the Wagon Wheel restaurant, they clumsily tried to fall into their patrol order. It was so totally eyes-closed dark beneath the thick covering of young trees, under the overcast moonless sky, that it was literally impossible for them to see their hands in front of their faces. The only points of visible light seen by their wide-open straining eyes were some kind of fluorescent fungus or plants on the ground and at the bases of some of the trees, which did not help them get their bearings, but only served to disorient them further.

Jasper Mosby said softly, his disembodied voice coming from no-where, "Phil, I'm sorry, but I can't see shit. I suggest we take out a chem-lite, at least until we get in line."

"Okay, go ahead Jake."

Mosby pulled his glowing plastic stick from a vest pocket; with their fully dilated pupils it cast a seemingly brilliant green light among them. The bearded man with the hockey helmet and the NVG's took his place at the front of the line; his brother fell in behind him. Next was Carson, then Ranya, followed by Mosby and the other policeman, "Fred," who had come with him. It was obvious to all of them, but unspoken, that the last two in line were cops, judging from their MP-5SDs, their black tactical vests, and the black SAS-style tactical pistol holsters strapped to their right thighs.

Compared to the submachine guns and assault rifles carried by the men, Ranya felt distinctly under-armed with her mere pistols. In a minute, the six of them were lined up and ready, with their weapons facing out-wards on alternating sides.

Like all the others, Carson's Thompson submachine gun was supported by a tactical sling, so that he could use his hands for other tasks when he needed to. He took out his own glowing chemlite, and with a long sheath knife he sliced off one end of it. Then he splashed a bit of its fluid on Ranya's back, and anointed each one of them in turn with a little of the glowing juice, and handed the remnant to Ranya to shake out on his own back. "Okay, that should do it," he said softly. "Once we're out of the woods we should be able to see a little better." Mosby put his own chemlite back into his vest pocket, extinguishing its illumination. The chemlite spatters on each of them were visible as ghostly splotches, just light enough for each person to see the one in front of them from a few feet away.

"Everybody ready?" Carson whispered. It was too dark to see each others' hands, and besides, they had not practiced together enough to rely on hand and arm signals alone. They had to take it on faith that they were the only humans in those woods, and risk quietly speaking to one another to communicate. A combat infantry squad which had spent weeks or months training together would go for hours at a time without uttering one single word while on patrol. Certainly, a well-trained squad would never walk directly up an overgrown paved road so close to the enemy; they would slip through the bush to lessen the risk of being ambushed or tripping a booby trap's wire. But they were only a thrown-together squad consisting of four old timers, one thirty-something cop, and Ranya. They had never trained together; they had never even stepped into the woods together before tonight, so they had to make allowances.

"Okay, let's move out, nice and slow," said Phil Carson.

Tom could see them all, and the trees and branches and the road ahead perfectly adequately in the fuzzy green picture created inside his night vision goggles, which amplified the ambient light 30,000 times. He saw that they were all lined up and ready, and began to walk ahead in a slight crouch, the barrel of his AR-15 carbine slowly traversing as he turned from side to side. The rest of them followed, with their gun barrels pointing outward on alternating sides of their line. Because of the blackness of the night they walked very closely together, only a few feet apart, close enough to see the faint shimmer of glowing chemlite juice on the back of the person in front of them.

Twice Tom had to stop the little column, to let them know where a dead tree had fallen across the road. He was the one man with nearly perfect vision, leading his little column of the blind. He whispered the message of the deadfall to his brother and helped him across, and each person in turn guided the next over the low trunks, until they were all across them and continuing on in their patrol order.

Except for Ranya, all of them had learned these basic patrolling skills in the Army or the Marines, and all of the men except Santander had done it for real in Viet Nam. As they padded down the straight asphalt trail, brushing aside the dripping branches, the decades seemingly melted away and they were reborn as deadly night stalkers.

Five minutes later, the squad was nearing the northern end of the access road, where it ran onto the tarmac just to the east of building one.

The woods were thinning out, and occasionally a few stars were visible through the overcast.

Tom, Carson and Mosby, one from each buddy pair, had a walkie-talkie radio. (Carson had picked up two pairs of FSR walkie-talkies at a Target store on his way to the Wagon Wheel; he considered it amazing that he could buy better radios at a discount store today for just a few bucks than the army had provided him in Viet Nam.) All of them heard the four clicks at the same time and froze, halting the squad. Four clicks on the radio was the danger or emergency signal from Archie. They all sank down and crouched in place; it was becoming just light enough for their fully night-adapted eyes to see the upraised white fists of the radiomen signaling the halt.

"Hey Fred, this is Archie. We have a situation," came their M-60 machine gunner's voice from across the tarmac.

Carson pulled the palm-sized radio out of a pouch on his vest and depressed the transmit button. "Go ahead," he replied, matter of factly. The use of the radios for in-the-clear voice communications was extremely dangerous and only a last resort, which Carson knew that Archie fully understood.

"There's a car parked outside Bubba's place, and another car from the hotel just pulled up. It looks like they're going to take somebody for a ride real soon."

Archie was correctly using non-military jargon, working from his brevity code list. Bubba's place was building one; the hotel was a hangar. Since they were using family service radios, they had to drop the military alphas, bravos, rogers and overs, and strive to sound as innocuous as possible in case their conversation was picked up by a nearby scanner, possibly even in the big RV outside of hangar two.

"Okay Archie, is that all?"

"Um, the bus appears to be full, but the hotels are dark and quiet, nobody's home. And nobody's at Billy's place, Billy's place is closed, all the action is at Bubba's." Working from their prearranged brevity codes, which Edith had written on a cheat sheet, Archie had just said that the commo van RV was occupied, the hangars were dark and quiet, and no-body was going in or out of building two. The activity tonight was all at building one.

"Okay Archie, how many folks are at Bubba's right now?"

"Hard to say for sure, two or three that I saw."

"Okay, I got all that. We'll swing by Bubba's just as soon as we can."

"Um, yeah, that sounds good boss. I wouldn't wait."

The ad hoc rescue team was crouched in a little circle, with their backs close together, and their weapons aimed outward like a six pointed star.

"Can you all hear me?" asked Carson, speaking softly. "We're going to change the plan from what we briefed, okay? There's two vehicles parked outside building one, and Archie says it looks like they're going to go for a ride. If they're moving the prisoner, that's a big problem. So we have to double time it the rest of the way. It's only about a hundred yards from here."

After a moment Tom said, "Ahh, Sarge, if you're gonna double time, me and Harry...we'll have to catch up later. If we try to double time it... Well, I can tell you, we don't run too good."

"Okay Tom, then keep setting the pace. Just make the best time you can, straight up the road. Here's the change in plans: we're going to skip building two, and put both assault teams into building one. Robin, you're still the door puller, and then Jake and Fred will go in; buttonhook left and right just like you were going into B2, all right? I'll go in third, to the left, and Robin, you go in last, to the right. Okay? Tom and Harry, your jobs won't change, you'll still be behind the corners of building two to cover the hangars. No shooting unless there's no choice—your rifles will wake up the whole world. Everybody got it?" They all muttered that yes, they had got it. "All right then, let's move out."

A few minutes later the squad was crouched in the underbrush at the tree line, thirty feet from the back of building one. At the edge of their roof of dripping foliage they could tell that the rain had finally stopped, and swatches of stars were visible where the clouds were breaking apart. There was now enough light in the open to make hand signals faintly visible, but the ambient light also made their uncovered hands and faces shine.

Camouflage face paint had never been an issue. Once they were clear of the area after the attack, they couldn't risk being stopped later with black and green grease behind their ears or under their chins. After the mission, they would need to quickly turn back into ordinary citizens, so they wore dark clothes, but no camouflage military uniform items other than Tom and Harry's Gore-Tex raincoats.

From the cover of the tree line they could look up the gap between buildings one and two. There was no activity that they could see or hear. There were two windows on the back sides of each of the two white-painted buildings, but the windows were painted black and no light escaped from them. After a minute crickets began to take up their chirping call and answer song once again, unconcerned about the motionless giants squatting in their midst.

Carson clicked his radio transmit button slowly and deliberately two times: assault team in position, stand by for action. In response he heard the two clicks returned from Archie: "I heard you, I'm ready, and it's safe for you to proceed."

He then nodded to Tom, who was wearing the helmet-mounted NVG's, pointed his finger at him, and then pointed across to his next position. Tom slowly nodded back at Carson, then rose and walked across the open space, his rifle aimed to his left toward the backs of the hangars. Once across the open danger zone, abandoned machinery and giant wooden wire spools provided good cover in the fifteen feet of space between the two buildings. Tom moved between them to the tarmac side, where he knelt and made a quick peek to the right around the corner of building one, then he looked back across the front of building two toward the hangars. When he was satisfied, he gave two clicks on his radio.

One at a time, they slipped across the thirty feet of open ground to the relative safety between the buildings. Harry took his position as rear security behind the southeast corner of building two, facing the backs of the hangars; Tom was already at the northeast corner aiming his rifle along the fronts of the hangars. Their security set toward the hangars, the other four crept in a line to the front of their objective, building one.

Carson was now at point; he peered to his right around the cinder block corner of building one. It was about thirty feet to the front door, which had its exposed hinges on the far side. On its near side was a door knob, and above the knob was a vertical grab handle. This squared up with what Ranya had said earlier about how the doors opened, based on her earlier recon. This was critical information; their entire entry method was based on the way the door was set up and opened. He could see that the door was just slightly ajar, standing an inch proud from the frame. This would vastly simplify their next task.

Two vehicles were parked parallel to the front wall, one on either side of the door. Closest was a gray or silver Mercedes. Its trunk was open toward him and its motor was running; he could see the little cloud of smoky vapor popping out of its exhaust. On the other side of the Mercedes was a medium-sized SUV with a luggage rack on top.

The running motor and open trunk of the Mercedes told him why Archie had risked the emergency radio call: they were moving somebody. No other possible explanation came to Carson's mind.

It was time. Ranya was crouched behind him along the wall, followed by the two cops, their MP-5s held at the ready.

Carson reached behind him and tapped Ranya on her knee, and signaled her to move past him. She walked quickly around the corner with her silenced .22 held in front in her right hand. The video camera which had been inside her raincoat was hanging around her neck by a strap. It was already turned on, and it left a faint glow from its viewfinder eyepiece shining up onto her throat and chin. She stopped on the far side of the door. Then he waved the two cops around him, and they scurried directly to the right side of the door, their MP-5's shouldered. Phil Carson followed behind them and took his position against the wall, third in line. Faint light escaped from the door's near edge and from beneath it.

Ranya reached across the door to the vertical metal handle bar and grasped it with her left hand. As she grabbed it Santander crouched in front of the door's right edge, his MP-5SD already up on his shoulder, his selector switch on burst, his right finger just brushing the trigger guard and his left thumb on the gun light's pressure switch. Mosby was standing tall directly behind and over Santander, with his own MP-5's suppressor-shrouded barrel above and to the right of his buddy's shoulder.

Ranya glanced across the door to Carson, and he nodded back to her. With wide eyes she staged-whispered, "Ready?" and Carson and the two cops nodded yes in return. She was set; they were all like compressed springs. She whispered "three, two, one…" and pulled the door open. It swung smoothly past ninety degrees and the two cops were already inside. Then Carson was inside and Ranya followed.

Ranya pulled the door closed behind her with her trailing left hand as the room flashed with brilliant white lights. Part of her job was to shut it so that as much sound as possible would be contained inside the building, in order to not alert those in the motor home 200 yards away, or any other enemies lurking unseen in the hangars or even in building two.

As soon as she closed the door, she grabbed the already running and recording camcorder with her left hand and swung it up against her left shoulder; she just kept it pointed wherever she was looking. In her right hand was Carson's silent Colt Woodsman .22 pistol, held slightly out in front of her. As she came through the door, she pushed on the tactical light's pressure button with her thumb.

The surprise room invasion and the appearance of four extremely intense lights stunned and blinded two men twenty feet across the room. They were crouched and looking away, grimacing and covering their faces with their free hands. Between them on the ground was a third person, who the two men had been dragging across the floor by his arms.

"Real funny, you assholes!" said one of the two men. "Okay, you got us, now kill the lights!"

The centers of the four beams stayed on their contorted faces. The tactical lights were as painful to look toward as arc-welders. Their shifting silhouettes threw giant overlapping shadows against the opposite walls.

Carson yelled, "Get on the floor! Get on the floor!"

"Up yours, asshole! Is that you, Jaeger? I'm gonna kick your Hollywood ass! What happened with Swarovski, nobody home?"

"Get on the floor you freakin' morons! Get down now!" Carson bellowed again.

The man who was talking was shielding his face with his right forearm, trying to block the lights and see who was standing behind them. "Did Bullard put you up to this? Okay, you win; you got us, very funny. Now kill the Goddamn lights!"

The two men were crouching on either side of the man they had been pulling across the floor. Ranya continued to record the scene, the camcorder resting against her left shoulder, and the light under her pistol's suppressor was trained on the bigger of the two guys, the one who was talking. She noticed that one of his knees had an orthopedic brace strapped around it over his pants. Both men wore dark rain jackets or windbreakers, but she could see a holstered pistol on the hip of the big one with the knee brace, where his open jacket was pushed back to the side.

"Get on the floor! Get down on your faces now!" Carson yelled again. The blond man with the crew cut was now on both knees, trying to shield his eyes with his hands and look at his tormenters, but he was being defeated in this attempt by the sheer intensity of the light being directed onto his face.

The other man, the heavier one with the loud mouth, was almost on his hands and knees. He seemed to pause in a football lineman's stance, unsure if he was going to lie down or get up. Then he kicked off hard with one leg and charged across the room, his clenched fists out in front, evidently striving to tackle one of the "pranksters" who were humiliating him with their practical joke.

The two off-duty policemen, spread well apart on either side of the door, didn't see this charging bull holding a weapon or reaching for a gun. His hands were out front in plain sight, so they held their fire.

Phil Carson, who was in the center of the four room invaders and the closest to the door, became the immediate object of the raging bull's wrath as he lurched across the twenty feet of space. But Carson did not have the cop's ingrained fire discipline, and he certainly had no wish to be smashed against a wall by an onrushing 250 pounder. He dropped the brilliant center of his light's beam to the center of the man's chest and squeezed the trigger of his Thompson once.

Inside the room, it sounded as if a heavy textbook had been slammed down onto the cement floor. The sound of a quick pair of shots from Ranya's .22 pistol was swallowed up entirely by the Thompson's bark and reverberations.

Carson's .45 caliber slug slammed into Garfield's massive chest, cut through his sternum, ripped through his beating heart, and came to rest embedded in the center of his spinal column. Ranya's .22 caliber bullets punched two neat holes above the bridge of his nose, tumbled sideways and carved intersecting paths through his brain, then stopped against the back of his skull.

Clay Garfield was dead before he hit the floor, crumpling onto his side almost at Carson's feet with a thud.

The blond crew cut man took this as his cue to drop face down spread eagle on the floor.

Carson's Thompson was aimed at the dead man's head. He was ready to apply a coup de grace if one was required, as he rolled him over onto his back with a push from his boot. Garfield's wide-open eyes were already flat and dead. He was only bleeding slightly from the tiny wounds above his nose. Because Carson's shot had destroyed the man's heart in mid-beat, it couldn't pump any blood out of his body, and the little bit that he did bleed from his chest wound was contained inside his rain slicker.

Without being instructed, Santander was already kneeling behind the prone blond man. He swept the pistol from his holster and slid it across the floor out of reach, and pulled his arms behind him and handcuffed them. Then he swiftly and efficiently divested this new prisoner of his cell phone, wallet and car keys. With the man secured, he used his own key to uncuff the unconscious older man, who the two goons had been dragging across the floor when the rescue team had burst into the room.

"Hey Fred, is that guy breathing?" asked Phil Carson.

Santander checked the man's pulse on his throat; he hadn't moved during the entire sequence. "He's alive."

"You know who you've got there?" asked Jasper Mosby, "Burgess Edmonds, the famous militia leader."

Ranya meanwhile dashed across the room to the workbench; she put down her .22 pistol and pulled off the cloth sack covering Brad's head. He tentatively opened his eyes, blinking at her face.

"Oh Brad, thank God you're alive, thank God you're alive! I'll cut you loose in a second."

She let go of his face and pulled her folding pocket knife from her pants pocket, flicked open the blade, and then carefully sliced through the nylon ropes tying him to the door. He had livid red welts around his neck and wrists where he had been tied down. After, as he was freed, he slowly rolled onto his side in the fetal position. He was barefoot and dressed only in the khaki shorts which he had been arrested in. Ranya leaned over him, holding him and kissing his face and neck.

Carson asked, "Brad, can you sit up? Can you walk?"

He struggled to form words. "I...d-don't know... I'll try."

The two cops returned to the front room, supporting another freed prisoner between them. "This guy's name is Vic Sorrento. They grabbed him last night and kept him in a gym locker," said Santander. "There's nobody else back there."

"Okay, we've got Fallon, we've got Edmonds, and this new guy. Just give me a few seconds, let me think..." Carson pulled out his walkie-talkie and pressed the transmit button. "Hey Archie, we're about done in Bubba's place. Everything's fine here. How's it look outside? Nothing? Okay. Stay ready. We're taking both vehicles, so that'll be us leaving."

Brad was sitting up on the edge of the work table now, and then he stood up with Ranya's help. Santander had found his blue shirt and boat shoes, and Ranya helped him to put them on. "Thanks for coming, I really..." He began to weep, but he fought it back. "Listen, I heard what they're going to do tonight. They're going to put Edmonds into a car and push it in a lake. Tomorrow they were going to kill me."

They were all listening intently, despite their hurry.

Carson asked him, "What about tonight? Where are they all tonight, the rest of them?"

"Tonight they're going up to Richmond to kill somebody."

"Who?" asked Carson. "Didn't the dead guy say something like 'what happened with Swarsky'?"

"Yeah, somebody named Swarsky, something like that," answered Brad.

"Swarovski." said Ranya, "There's a writer named Swarovski; he writes for Gun World, and he writes books."

"It's probably Leo Swarovski," said Mosby. Sure, it's got to be him, he's a Virginian. I think he lives around Richmond."

Ranya said, "I've met him at gun shows; he autographed books for my father. We always had some of his books for sale at our store."

"And they've gone up to Richmond to just kill him? Damn! Who the hell are these guys?" asked Carson.

Brad said, "They call themselves the 'stew team', but that piece of shit on the floor, he's in the BATF. I know him."

Carson crouched down over the blonde crew cut man on the floor, who was lying quietly with his forehead against the cement. He jammed the end of his Thompson's suppressor against the man's ear, shoved his head to one side, and said "Hello, George, it's great to see you again. We're going to go for a little ride now." He jingled Hammet's keys with his left hand. "That's your red Cherokee outside, right?"

41

Under Phil Carson's guidance they adapted their exfiltration plan on the fly. The dead man with the knee brace was carried out and dumped into the open trunk of the silver Mercedes. Burgess Edmonds was placed into the back seat of his own car, seated between the two off-duty Suffolk cops. The Bedford brothers climbed into the front of the Mercedes, with Harry driving. Phil Carson drove the red Cherokee; the rest of the assault squad and George Hammet went with him. Tom Bedford got out of the Mercedes when they reached his parked Buick station wagon, in order to drive it away. The three vehicles then pushed through the dripping branches using their parking lights to see the way.

When they were all back at the staging point in the clearing near South River Road, they shed their borrowed kevlar raid vests and other police equipment, and dropped them into the back of Carson's truck. Archie and Edith peeled the duct tape off of their truck's running lights, and went home via a circuitous route.

Mosby and Santander drove Carson's truck back to the Wagon Wheel, and transferred all of the police department gear back to Mosby's white Expedition. They left Carson's truck there, and returned to Suffolk.

The Bedford Brothers said they knew a semi-retired doctor over in Windsor, in Isle of Wight County, who could look after Burgess Edmonds, and temporarily hide him out. They also agreed to dispose of his Mercedes; it was far too hot to risk selling in one piece, but chopped down for parts in their junkyard's garage it was worth even more anyway. The disposal of Clay Garfield's body was a trivial matter for the old bootleggers, and Phil Carson didn't even inquire about the details.

It had stopped raining but the roads were still wet, reflecting the occasional rural intersection's flashing yellow lights. Phil Carson was driving the red Jeep Cherokee, staying right at the speed limits while chain smoking Marlboro's with his window cracked open. He didn't ask for permission to smoke, and nobody complained.

Victor Sorrento sat across from him, going through the files and notebooks he had taken out of George Hammet's briefcase, which they had found on the front passenger seat. Brad and Ranya snuggled together in the back seat, delirious with joy to be free and reunited. George Hammet, "George the Fed," was all the way in the back in the cargo space on the floor. He was handcuffed, hog-tied, and gagged, with his head inside of the canvas sack which Ranya had pulled off of Brad on the torture table.

"Bingo! I got it…here it is," Sorrento told Carson. The Jeep's ceiling reading lamp cast a pool of light onto the open file on his lap. "Leo Swarovski. Here's his address and his phone numbers. It's got his home number, his unlisted second line, his cell phone, his wife's cell phone, his email, his pager number, everything."

"Good, we'll give him a call in a few minutes," said Carson. "It's still early. The BATF likes to raid later in the morning. Hopefully, he'll have a chance to get away."

"Or at least to get ready for them, like that Green Beret up in Northern Virginia," replied Sorrento.

"But he didn't get away," said Carson.

"That's true, but he sure made the feds pay a heavy price. And that bridge he blew up in DC is still wrecked."

Ranya said, "At least he got to take some of them with him. That's more than my father got to do."

"Who are these guys anyway?" asked Sorrento. He was studying Hammet's ATF credentials and other identification from his wallet. "This says George Hammet's the assistant special agent in charge for the Norfolk ATF, but that operation at the airfield, that sure didn't look like any official ATF operation."

"Stew team," said Brad. "Now what the hell the 'stew team' is, I have no idea."

"Don't worry about it," said Carson, who then exhaled a stream of smoke out of his window. "We'll get a chance to ask George real soon. He'll tell us all about it."

Sorrento said, "Well, whoever they work for, they're the real live American Gestapo."

"Sure looks that way," replied Carson.

"What are you planning to do about it?" asked Sorrento. "I mean, I'd really, seriously like to kill those pricks… The one you wasted, he was just a nice start."

"We'll talk about it later," said Carson.

"God only knows what my wife must think…I've never just not shown up before."

"Don't worry, Victor, you'll work it out; you haven't even been gone 24 hours."

"You saved my life, you saved all of our lives, all three of us. I mean, if Edmonds makes it. So I mean, I'm really thankful…"

"Forget it. I didn't even know you were there. No thanks are necessary."

"But…"

"Forget it. It was my pleasure."

"Listen," continued Sorrento, "I don't even know you, but if you have any plans, if you're going to pull anything else like this job tonight, count me in. I'm a former Marine. I can shoot anything better than just about anybody else, I always could, and I'd really like to get some payback, if that's in the cards."

"I'll think about it," answered Carson.

Ranya interjected, "What about my bike, back at the Wagon Wheel? And I left my van up in Virginia Beach."

"I'll take care of it. Where's your van? What's it look like?"

Ranya told him the details.

"Give me the keys; I'll take care of them both."

"Where are we going?" asked Brad. They'd killed one man, presumably some kind of federal agent, and had kidnapped another. That was major league capital punishment territory... The feds wouldn't even be out to make an arrest after what they had pulled back on that airfield. They'd be out for fast "curbside justice" at the end of a gun barrel.

"Where are we going? We're splitting up. You and Ranya are going to a hiding place for a while," replied Carson. "A safe house."

"Where?"

"You'll see. I've got a place lined up. Just trust me; I got you out, didn't I?"

"Yeah, you sure did. But I just want to know what's going on."

"Look, here's how it works," said Carson. "I've got a few friends and acquaintances, that's all there is to it. Somebody might help out with a machine gun like Archie and Edith did tonight, somebody might help out with a place to stay, or a ride. Nobody knows what they don't need to know. There's no membership, just friends helping friends."

Brad thought about this. "But they all know you."

"That's true, but I've got an insurance policy." Carson reached into the right front pocket of his black leather jacket, his cigarette bouncing on his lip while he talked. He pulled out a small round object, green in color, the size of a plum, and held it up under the rear view mirror. It was an offensive fragmentation grenade-antipersonnel. "Let's just say I don't plan to wind up tied to a door, with a wet rag over my face. There's too many people depending on me to keep my mouth shut, so this is my part of the deal. And if I gotta go, I'm not going alone."

"I didn't give you up Phil, the whole time. I didn't give you up. Or you, Ranya." Brad's voice cracked, the pain was too fresh.

"I didn't say you did Brad...and thanks. But we got you out in one day. Eventually everybody talks, and I won't let it happen to me. And I sure as hell won't go alone."

They drove on in silence for a few minutes. The occasional houses they passed were far apart; most of the countryside was marshland, rivers and woods. Finally Carson pulled another small hand-held radio out of the inside of his jacket. "VHF radio," he announced to his passengers. "I just picked it up today. Almost time for you guys to hop out. You two lovebirds I mean." He handed the radio across to Sorrento. "Victor, figure this thing out. Turn it on and put it on channel 78, all right?"

"No problem. You want me to talk on it?"

"No, give it back when it's all set up." After Sorrento handed him back the cell phone sized VHF radio, Carson pushed the transmit button and said, "Moondog, Moondog, you there, over?" He waited a half minute and repeated his call.

In a moment, the VHF crackled with static. "Moondog here. You got something for me, over?"

"Roger Moondog, I've got two for you; wait a minute."

They had traveled in the red Cherokee for a half hour since the assault team had split up on South River Road. Without warning, Carson pulled over to the side of the two lane road, fifty yards before they reached an old steel trestle bridge over the black shadow of a creek.

"Your ride's down underneath. Listen to the man, do what he says, and I'll be in touch soon, okay?"

Ranya leaned forward and hugged Carson around his neck from behind and kissed his rough cheek. "Thanks, Phil, I owe you; I really owe you."

"Yeah, you do. Now hop out; we can't sit here all night."

Brad reached over and shook Carson's hand, and said, "Thanks for saving my life."

"No problem. Now get out, and I'll be in touch."

Brad opened the passenger side door and they both slid out and disappeared down the slope.

A few minutes later the red Cherokee pulled off the pavement down a dirt road and into a stand of brush with its lights off. The back cargo doors were opened; Carson removed George Hammet's hood and untied his gag. He was lying doubled up on his side in the cargo area, still cuffed behind and hog tied with rope taken from the water torture door. Sorrento held a flashlight close to Hammet's face; it wasn't as bright as the borrowed police-issue Sure-Flash lights they had used earlier, but it was painfully bright to a man who had been hooded in the back of an SUV on a pitch black night.

"How are we doing, George?" asked Carson. Hammet didn't say anything; he was paralyzed with fear. "George, this isn't going to work out so well if you can't talk. Tell me that you can talk, and I'll untie some of the ropes on you, and give you a drink of water. Is that a deal?"

George Hammet kept his eyes closed against the light. In a few seconds he said, "I can talk," but only weakly.

"Good job, I knew you could do it. Now, let's practice saying something. I want you to say just what I say; just repeat it word for word. Can you do that, George?"

"...Okay..."

"Here it is. Say, 'Leo, the ATF is coming, get out while you can.' Now your turn."

"I can't..."

"Yes you can, George, you can and you will. 'Leo, the ATF is coming, get out while you can.' Now give it a try." Carson held a snub-nosed .44 Special revolver; he jammed its short blued steel barrel into Hammet's ear and thumbed back the hammer, making three loud unmistakable metallic clicks. "Leo, the ATF is coming, get out while you can. Each time I push this gun into your ear, you just go ahead and say it. I really don't want to make a big mess in your car." Carson shoved the barrel into Hammet's ear, hard. "Now!"

"Leo, the ATF is coming...get out while you can."

"That's good George; I knew you could do it." He shoved the barrel against his ear once more. "Say it again!"

"Leo, the ATF is coming, get out!"

"While you can!" ordered Carson, again pushing the short barrel of the revolver into his ear.

"Leo, the ATF is coming, get out while you can!"

"Again! And say it normal, like you're talking to a friend." Carson prodded him more gently with his revolver's barrel.

"Leo, the ATF is coming, get out while you can."

"Very good! Again!" This time he held George's cell phone, and again, George repeated his sentence. When Carson was satisfied with his compliance, he punched in the number of Leo Swarovski's unlisted home phone number in Petersburg Virginia. After three rings he heard a man answer gruffly, "Hello! Do you know what time it is?" Carson shoved his revolver's barrel into George's ear again.

"Leo, the ATF is coming, get out while you can!"

"What did you say? Who is this?" asked Leo Swarovski.

Carson again jammed the gun into his ear.

"Leo, the ATF is coming, get out while you can!"

"Is this some kind of joke?"

"Leo, the ATF is coming..."

Carson pushed 'end' on George's cell phone, and lowered the hammer of his .44 Special snub-nosed revolver with his thumb.

Brad and Ranya held each others' hands for support as they picked their way along the edge of the creek toward the bridge. Ranya used her tiny keychain squeeze light to illuminate their path across the relatively firm tussocks of saw grass, and to keep them from tripping over roots or sinking into soft mud.

From the void under the trestle bridge, a man's voice called out "Over here." A flashlight beam was directed at their feet, permitting them to move more quickly through the slippery rushes. The beam of light moved back and forth along their path, its side-shine showed them a long open skiff which was pressed tightly along the creek's bank directly beneath the bridge.

When they were close, the light was shined along the inside of the boat to give them an idea of how to step aboard and where to sit. The vessel was an aluminum hunting boat, camouflage painted in brown and green splotches both inside and out. It was about eighteen feet long, but very narrow with a sharply pointed bow. When Brad and Ranya stepped aboard, the metal hull rang hollowly and rolled under their feet.

"Welcome aboard! We're going for a real nice boat ride tonight. I was going to have you sit on the seats there in front of the console, but from the look of you you'd freeze to death. You're both already shivering, so forget the seats."

While Brad and Ranya stood holding the front of the centerline steering console, their driver moved around them and gathered lifejackets, boat cushions, towels and a folded canvas awning, then kneeled down and made a nest for them in the bow.

"All right, get comfy. At least you'll stay out of the wind. This tarp's the best I can do for a blanket."

They laid down together in the bow of the boat on the cushions and lifejackets, their heads up forward. Ranya shed her two packs, Brad pulled the heavy green canvas up over them, and they spooned together with her back pressed tightly against his chest, with his left arm wrapped around her.

A long wooden pole was stuck vertically through the water along the boat's port side, pinning it to the bank. The boat driver pulled it out of the mud and swung it dripping across the boat, and used it to push away from the bank and out from under the bridge into mid channel. Then he stowed the pole inside the boat and stood behind his boxy homemade plywood console. The single outboard motor lowered itself into the water with an electric whine, and then it rumbled to life with acrid smoke blowing across them.

"Now, here comes the fun part! Hang on, children!" With his left hand holding the wheel, the driver shoved the throttle sharply forward with his right hand, and the engine roared and the boat surged ahead. In a moment it was on a plane, flying across the still water, carving turns through the twisting meanders of the black water creek.

Out from under the bridge, there was just enough starlight that Ranya could make out the silhouette of their captain standing behind the console. He had a narrow chin, large white teeth, and he was wearing some kind of helmet. On the right side of the helmet was attached a cylinder the size of a toilet paper tube.

Damn, she thought, when did everybody get night vision devices? It must have been their military service that did it. Freedom Arms had, at times, sold a small number of mostly Russian surplus starlight scopes, and almost always, it seemed, to military veterans. She supposed that anyone who had ever used night vision devices to gain an edge in night combat would consider them to be worth their weight in gold. Obviously, they were no longer a novelty or a luxury item; they were now virtually a necessity for anyone who wanted to be an effective night fighter. Certainly, their boat driver could never run through the creeks at full throttle in the darkness without using night vision.

Ranya lost track of time, growing warm against Brad's chest and hips, with one of his arms around her and his other arm under her head for her pillow. At times they crossed open water; she could tell by the thin aluminum hull slapping and chattering over the chop. At other times, they were running up winding streams so tight that the trees formed a roof above them, and their driver had to duck to miss low-hanging branches. After a while she fell asleep. Brad was already gently snoring, his breath warm against the back of her neck.

"Hey, hey wake up."

Brad was pulled back to semi-awareness from some dreamless place beyond sleep by a stranger's voice. He was lying on a bed of mis-shapen lumps at the bottom of a pipe; something or someone warm was pressed against his chest and belly.

"Wake up, come on, wake up."

The pipe was rolling. Mosquitoes were buzzing in his ear, biting his face. It was not a pipe he was lying in, it was a boat. He was with Ranya, he remembered more now. He had been a prisoner. He remembered that he had been tied down, and he remembered the water and the electricity and the pain, but now he was free, unless he was only dreaming again.

Brad twisted and looked up; he was lying in the front of a narrow boat, which was tied alongside a low wooden dock. Standing on the pier, outlined against the stars, a man was looming over them. He was wearing some kind of bizarre hat or helmet, a football or lacrosse helmet perhaps, but in place of any face shield there was a fat tube mounted in front of one eye. Ranya stirred and rolled onto her back against him.

"Where are we?" she asked the man on the dock.

"I'm sorry, but that's not part of the deal. This is just the place where you two get out. Straight up the dock there's a path to a house; that's where you'll spend the night, and maybe longer. I unlocked it and turned the gas on. You'll have hot water in a little while. Make yourself right at home. Get cleaned up, fix yourself something to eat, and find some warm clothes."

Brad asked, "But where are we? If we have to get out, if we have to run, we have to know where we are." He pushed the stiff canvas covering off of them and sat up in the bottom of the boat.

"You don't need to know, and anyhow it doesn't matter. You're on an island; you can't run away from here without a boat, and you'd need a chart and a GPS, so forget it. You two just need to stay here until somebody comes and gets you. Might be me, might be somebody else. Probably tomorrow afternoon. Just keep an eye on the dock…anybody that ties up here and gets on the dock and pulls up crab traps, that's your ride. Then you just come on out and get in their boat and do like they say, all right?"

"All right, we've got it," replied Brad. "And thanks, we really appreciate what you've done for us."

"Oh, a boat ride's not much, not in the scheme of things. Say, you don't happen to have a cell phone on you, do you?"

Ranya sat up next to Brad and pushed the stiff canvas tarpaulin off of her; she found her fanny pack amid the piles of boat junk and pulled it onto her lap. The man directed a small beam of light onto the bag to assist her as she unzipped it and pulled out her new throwaway phone. He looked away; the light was too bright in his night scope.

"Let me have it, okay?" the man said. He switched off his flashlight and crouched down and she gave him the phone. He said, "Thanks," and tossed it underhanded far out into the river. "We can't have any phones or radios here; you might have already compromised this place just by bringing that cell phone with you. We don't transmit anything from here; we don't even bring cell phones, not ever. Very few people know about this place, and even fewer know where it is, and we want to keep it that way. I'm sorry, but we have to be real assholes about security here.

"If you put on a lantern, keep all the shutters down, and don't take it outside. And don't use the kerosene heater. I know you're cold, but if you heat the whole place up too much, it'll make the cabin shine like a beacon on infrared. Try to stay inside during the day, or at least stay away from the river: the idea is to not be seen, okay? There's propane for cooking, and there'll be hot water for a bath. Well now, let's get moving, shall we?"

They were both stiff and cramped from their rough sleeping positions, and they awkwardly climbed out of the rolling boat and up onto the dock. No names were ever asked or offered. The skinny man with the crazy one-eyed helmet handed Brad his flashlight. Brad took the light, and shook the boat man's hand. "Thanks, I hope we'll meet again. If there's anything I can ever do for you, I hope I can return the favor."

The man regarded Brad and Ranya for a moment, the green glow from his single night eye faintly illuminated the right side of his face.

"Yeah, there is something you can do. Be worth it. A lot of folks who didn't need to get involved stuck their necks out a mile for you tonight." The man untied his lines from the dock cleats and tossed them over as he hopped lightly back aboard his skiff, grabbing the console to steady himself as it rolled. Brad and Ranya stood side by side on the dock, their arms around each others' waists. The big brown-painted Evinrude coughed to life. The man spun his wheel hard and smacked the throttle to the rear, and the boat cut a backwards J turn away from the dock.

"Just be worth it!" the boat driver yelled over his shoulder, as he cut the wheel the other way and shoved the throttle lever forward. The dark hunting boat, lighter now by two people's weight, leaped onto a plane and shot down the river and was almost immediately lost in the blackness.

42

"**Gold leader; Victor Poppa.** I've got lights out in the bedroom, and it sounds like the television is off."

"Is that him or her, over?"

"Um, that would be her. The light's still on in bedroom number four; that's his study. He's still connected on line; it looks like he's still on the computer, over." The Special Training Unit's counterfeit "Virginia Power" van was parked diagonally across the tree-lined street from Leo Swarovski's house in Long Bridge, an affluent community southeast of Richmond. The STU technicians inside the van had his house under several forms of surveillance. Their internal radio communications were digitally encrypted, so they spoke without fear of being overheard.

"Victor; Gold Leader. Tell me about the outside lights again, over."

"Gold, there's motion triggered lights front and rear. The front light is tripped by walking on the sidewalk in front of the house. The backyard light's only triggered by someone inside the fence. The alley behind the garage is clear; no lights, over."

"Victor; Gold. So you're sure we can pull into the alley without triggering the light, over?" The four black Suburbans and the blue conversion van of the STU assault teams were parked a half mile from the targeted house. They were concealed in a small parking lot behind a two story professional building, primarily containing medical offices.

"That's affirmative Gold."

"Then we'll go as briefed. Gold One in the alley and through the patio door, Gold Two up the back porch, and Blue on the street, over."

"Roger Gold."

"We'll wait thirty minutes after he turns in and do it." After playing the supporting role Saturday night on the Edmonds raid, and after Sunday night's failure to capture Frank Gittis after their long highway pursuit into western North Carolina, Michael Shanks was anxious to lead his team on a successful raid.

The Gold Team was going to enter Swarovski's one story brick home simultaneously through three doors, giving him no chance to reach for a weapon or even to get out of bed. Shanks was personally going to lead Gold One, smashing through the sliding glass door from the side patio directly into Swarovski's bedroom. If as expected they were asleep, they'd be turned into Swiss cheese before they could sit up or roll over. Swarovski and his wife both were known to be crack shots, and Shanks did not intend to give them the opportunity to put a hand on a weapon, at least not until they were dead.

Dead, Swarovski could be assisted in safely firing off a few shots from his own bedside pistol, to justify the killings. Shanks even planned to have one carefully aimed shot fired into the composite armor plate on the front of his kevlar vest. That well-aimed shot would provide more than enough "proof" to convince any skeptics in the media that the ATF law enforcement team had ample reason to riddle the Swarovskis with bullets: it would be an obvious case of self-defense. Gun powder residue on Leo Swarovski's hand and arm would clinch the case, just to be certain.

"Roger Gold. Uh, Gold, he's getting an outside phone call. Let me catch this, wait one over."

There were three rings of a telephone. The technicians in the Virginia Power van heard Leo Swarovski's voice through their head sets.

"Do you know what time it is?" Swarovski asked, agitated.

"Leo, the ATF is coming, get out while you can," said the male caller, who sounded somewhat excited.

"What did you say? Who is this?"

"Leo, the ATF is coming, get out while you can."

"Is this some kind of joke?"

"Leo, the ATF is coming." The call was terminated.

"Gold Leader; Victor Poppa. You're not going to believe this, over."

"Who called? What did they say?"

"He said the ATF is coming, that's what he said!"

"What? Can you play it for me?"

"Sure, this'll just take a second...hang on. Here it comes."

The digitally recorded phone conversation was played back, going out over the radio to the waiting STU Team at their forward staging area. All of them heard the brief warning conversation through their ear pieces; they paused in the middle of cigarettes and hushed conversations to listen to it.

"Damn! Let's hear it one more time," said Gold Leader Michael Shanks. The audio technician replayed the entire call.

"Can you trace the call?" asked Shanks.

"Already got it Gold."

Bob Bullard's voice came over the net. "Anybody recognize that voice?"

"He sounded familiar," said Michael Shanks.

"It sounded like our boy George Hammet to me," said Bullard.

"Yeah, that's confirmed by the trace Bob," added the audio tech. "It came from Hammet's cell phone."

With his legs and arms exposed, Brad was being eaten alive by clouds of mosquitoes and biting no-see-um sand fleas, and he wasted no time running up the path from the dock following the flashlight beam, with Ranya right behind him.

The cabin was a thirty foot wide square plywood shack with an angled corrugated roof. Located barely above the high tide level, the place was built a yard over the sandy ground on cinderblock pilings. It was partly surrounded by boxwoods and low trees, but they didn't stop to study their surroundings beyond that.

Cinderblock steps led up to a screen door and a solid wood interior door facing the creek. Brad jerked them both open and Ranya pulled them closed behind her. Once inside they met in an intense embrace, squeezing each other almost with desperation, her face buried in his neck while he kissed her hair. The room was lit madly by the flashlight which Brad held behind Ranya's back, its beam moving across the ceiling as they swayed and turned together, but their eyes were tightly closed and they didn't notice.

After a minute of holding each other and holding back their tears, Brad reluctantly broke away and crouched down, scratching both legs from his ankles to his thighs. "I'm so sick of bugs! Wherever we go, I want it to be a place with no bugs!" He sat on the floor, still scratching at his ankles. "I've had a really, really bad day!" he said, laughing and crying at the same time. Ranya shed her two packs and sat down Indian style, facing him.

"It could be worse you know; you could still be tied to that door."

"That's true, but I don't know what's worse: being tied down on that door, or the no-see-ums!" He grinned at her while he kept scratching. "I sure hope they've got some itch medicine here."

"Whose place is this anyway?" Ranya unzipped her new green rain slicker and tugged it off. She was only wearing her new gray sweatshirt beneath it; her damp denim jacket, t-shirt and bra were crammed into her daypack.

"I have no idea. I don't even know which state we're in." They stood up together, and Brad shined his flashlight around the room, which took up the front half of the cabin. It was a combined living room, dining room and kitchen. Screened windows were covered on the outside by plywood shutters which were down and latched shut. On a low coffee table in front of an old sofa was an array of flashlights, candles, a bowl full of matchbooks, and an oil-fueled hurricane lamp. Ranya studied the lamp, then she lifted the globe and lit the wick with a match, and a soft yellow light suffused the room.

Tacked to a cabinet door above the kitchen sink was a numbered list of instructions for using the house, and another checklist for putting it back into the proper inactive state before leaving. Evidently, the cabin was meant to be used at least occasionally by unfamiliar visitors.

They read through the list. Brad switched on the 12 volt power system and tested the electric water pump, and then he lit the propane stove and turned it back off again. He said, "It's just like a boat or an RV; it's all 12 volt and propane. A solar panel on the roof charges golf cart batteries down here under the counter, but not that much runs on electricity anyway. Look, even the fridge runs on propane." He found its pilot light switch and turned it on. The list told how to check the level of the water tanks outside; they were filled (or not) depending on the amount of rainfall caught on the cabin's corrugated roof.

For drinking and cooking water, there were several clear plastic five gallon jugs on the floor. He opened one and lifted it onto a countertop dispenser. They both looked in the cabinets above the sink and stove and counters for drinking cups, and found them well stocked with canned soups and stews, powdered juices, cans of soda, and several liquor bottles. He took down a pair of plastic cups, filled them with drinking water from the dispenser, and they both drained them. It had been hours since either had had anything to drink.

"God, I can't believe any of this. I just can't believe any of what's happened today." Brad was both numb and alert, operating on stale adrenaline.

Ranya pulled down a six pack of Coke and a half-full bottle of Bacardi rum. "Will that fridge make ice? I never saw one that ran off of propane."

"I think it will, sooner or later. Maybe by tomorrow."

"Well, you're a sailor right? You're used to roughing it, so let's just have a nice room temperature rum and coke. Why wait for ice?" She poured an inch of dark rum into two tumblers, then popped open a can of cola and filled them up.

"Cheers," he toasted her, and drank half of the cup, welcoming the sweet anesthesia. "I've got so many questions, but I've got to find some itch cream before I go crazy!" He was scratching one calf with his opposite foot.

The large front room they were in had two doors in its back wall. Brad went through the door on the right side; it opened into a small bedroom. There was a double bed against the back wall under a shuttered window; it was covered with a floral-pattern comforter. Another door led from the bedroom into a small bathroom; an old fashioned full-length porcelain bathtub took up almost half of the space. A hot water heater stood in one corner, it was hissing and humming. Like the rest of the house, the bathroom seemed to have been put together from a collection of castoff or salvaged furnishings and appliances, probably brought in a piece at a time by boat over many years.

Mounted to the wall above a chipped porcelain sink was a medicine cabinet which Brad pulled open; his eyes settled on a row of ointment tubes. "Oh, thank you, thank you God; I finally get a break! I swear I'm going to coat my legs with this stuff." He grabbed a tube and unscrewed the cap and began smearing the white cream on his ankles.

Ranya said, "I've got a better idea. Did you know that I crawled through a filthy canal today, looking for you? I stink, I itch, and I think I've got things crawling around under my clothes! The motorboat guy turned on the propane for the hot water heater, and I can hear it running, so I'm taking a bath right now. And…you're welcome to join me, if you can fit in too… Then after we wash up, we can take turns rubbing lotion on each other. Believe me, you're not the only one with bug bites and scratches."

She hung the oil lamp on a nail, sat down on the edge of the tub and began to run the water. "You have no idea how much I need this bath! I'm getting in whether it's hot or not." She pulled off her muddy running shoes, then she crossed her arms and grabbed the bottom of her new gray sweatshirt to pull it over her head, but then she paused. "Can you give me a little head start? I feel like a total skank, okay?"

"I understand. I'll get the drinks."

When Brad returned a few minutes later he brought candles with him, which he set up and lit on the sink and on top of the medicine cabinet and around the edge of the tub. Then, he left again and returned with a portable stereo and a small plastic case that he put on the floor. His eyes were on Ranya; she was rinsing shampoo out of her hair with a hand held shower on a long white hose. She made no effort to cover her sudsy breasts, which jiggled as she scrubbed her scalp with her other hand. The electric pump was still chugging away, and the tub was half-filled with warm water. She said, "My hair feels like it's full of twigs and bugs and God knows what. You'll have to check me for ticks and cooties, I swear! Hey, what'd you find, a radio? Does it work?"

"The radio doesn't work, I just found new batteries for it but the antenna's gone and I'm only getting static. I don't know about the cassette deck; it must be 20 years old. I found a box full of cassettes, but it's all old stuff. Let's see: Allman Brothers, Led Zeppelin, Eagles, Pink Floyd, the Doors, Neil Young…"

"Put in the Eagles; I know all their songs. We used to play it at the store."

Brad popped in the cassette, and hit "play." After that it only took him a few seconds to pull off his shorts and shirt and join Ranya in the tub. He sat facing her, sliding his long legs past her soft slippery hips; she drew her knees up out of the water to make room for him. The first guitar chords rang out in the cramped bathroom, and then Henley and Frey began to sing "Take it Easy."

It was all much too much for Brad. He'd been overwhelmed so many times in the last twelve hours, he dropped his head onto Ranya's upraised knees and wept. She turned the nozzle onto his hair and washed him with strawberry-scented shampoo while he collected himself, hiding his tears among the warm water streaming over him.

After a while, he lifted his head and asked, "How did you do it? I mean, how did you find me? And who were those guys with Phil Carson? I was so stupid, so damn stupid, standing out in front of the store like a big dumb jerk, not a worry in the world, and the next thing I know I'm getting shoved into a van…"

"What did they do? What did they do to you on that table?"

"It was pretty bad… They poured water on my face, but not like this." He laughed weakly. "They covered my face with a towel, and kept pouring water on it. They practically drowned me. And they used electricity; they used cattle prods or something… But you know, eventually I figured out that they weren't going kill me, at least not then. I heard them saying I shouldn't be beat up too much, so I figured they were keeping me around for something else. That kept me holding on... I didn't tell them much…it could have been worse I guess. I'm just glad you got me out when you did.

"But do you know what was even worse than the table? The box. They had a metal box, a locker they kept me in, all crammed in and bent over. I'll tell you the truth, the water table was almost better than the box. Some of the time they just left me alone on the table. And some of the time I think I slept, or passed out."

"It must have been terrible…"

"It was, it was." He took her hands in his and squeezed them. "But you got me out, you got us all out, I still can't believe it… I still can't believe you found me and got me out. I thought I was dead, I thought they were going to kill me, and you know what was worse? I was afraid they could make me betray you."

"You need to thank Phil Carson, not me. I couldn't have done it by myself."

"And now he's got George Hammet," said Brad.

Ranya's eyes narrowed to slits. "The bastard who...murdered my father."

"We think," he added.

"Well, we're going to find out. Carson's going to find out."

"Then it'll be payback time, at least for George."

"Damn right it will. Payback time. And payback's a bitch." She lifted her rum and coke from the corner of the tub and sipped it, then shared it with Brad.

"So...what are we going to do next?" he asked her. They were leaning together, their wet foreheads and noses touching, staring into each others' eyes.

"Well... I thought maybe we'd finish our baths, and go to bed, actually," she replied, sliding her feet around his waist. "If you can wait that long..."

"I mean tomorrow, next week, forever? We're both marked now, the feds have our names. I didn't say anything, not much really, but they were asking me all about you. They were very interested in you, very interested. I mean, how long can we hide from them? They're probably just going to shoot us on sight, these "stew team" guys, I mean, they're not regular cops! But if we can make it to Guajira, if she's still there at anchor, then we could just take off, leave everything and head for the ocean, we could sail down island, hide out..."

Ranya intertwined her fingers in his and brought both of his hands up to her lips and kissed them, while still staring into his eyes. "All right Brad, I'll go with you, just as far as we can make it."

The music paused for a few moments, and then "Witchy Woman" began, slower and sexier. They gently washed one another with strawberry-scented shampoo and a soapy pink washcloth. Gradually their fears dissolved in the warm water and rum and candle light, in the old fashioned bathtub, in the midnight cabin by the nameless river, in the middle of nowhere.

Bob Bullard was sitting in the comfortable swiveling "captain's chair" in the front of the team's blue conversion van when he received word that Swarovski had gotten away. The keyed-up technician in the Virginia Power van described the scene to him as an SUV and a van had suddenly converged on the alley behind his house from both directions. The door of Swarovski's attached garage had rolled up, and his own aptly named Ford Escape had roared off between his two escorts and was gone.

Evidently Swarovski had a standby contingency plan for a raid which he had rapidly put into effect. He had not turned on any interior lights or used any of the phones they had been monitoring to call anyone, so his flight had come as a surprise to the surveillance team in the Virginia Power van. The rest of the STU Team, waiting a half mile away, had been caught flat-footed by the escape, and the surveillance team had not even gotten a license plate off of the two interlopers. The three vehicles were gone before the team could even think of mounting a pursuit.

It was a tactical disaster all the way around. Now there was no avoiding it: he had to call his boss and report their failure. Malvone picked up on the fourth ring.

"Wally? Bob. Bad news."

"What's up? How did it go?"

"It didn't go. We had to abort; he was tipped off, and he got away."

"What? What do you mean tipped off? You've kept complete opsec down there, haven't you? How could he have been tipped off?"

"You're not going to believe this, Wally, but it sounds like, um, somebody we know dropped the dime," said Bullard. "Somebody who was staying back at the base to do a job tonight. The umm, new team leader." The cell call to Maryland was unencrypted, so Bullard had to carefully dance around the subject.

"What? Shit! Are you sure?"

"We've got it all on tape, and we traced his phone."

"Why in the hell would he do that? You think that…you think he figured out what was going on with…ahh…the gimpy-legged guy?" asked Malvone.

"It's possible. It crossed my mind."

"Where is he now?"

"I don't know, Wally. He's not answering. His phone is out of service."

"What's going on down there? At the base I mean? What's the watch leader in the motor home say?"

"They say everything's normal. I mean, we've been in contact, and they know we aborted and we're heading back down there."

"Well, ask them for me. Send them over to the offices and check it out. I'll wait."

"Okay Wally. Call you back in a few." Bullard hit "end" on his phone and speed dialed the STU mobile communications headquarters on the annex. The watch leader picked up after six rings, adding to Bullard's frustration. He wondered if in the absence of Clay Garfield, the commo geeks were goofing off, playing computer games or getting liquored up.

"Hi Dave, Bob here. What's up?"

"Quiet, nothing here. You're on your way back now?"

"Yeah, we are. Dave, I need a sitrep real fast. Anything at all unusual going on down there? Anything?"

"No, nothing Bob."

"Have you been down to the offices?"

"No, not tonight. Clay told us to stay the f...to stay away from there. 'Operators only' he said. Said he had a mission or something, and we're supposed to stay away from that end."

"Okay, Dave, now I'm telling you: go over there right now and bang on the doors and see who's still around. All right?"

"I'm on my way now Bob, give me just a minute."

"And Dave, take a look in the hangar for the Mercedes. Is it there?"

"Let me see... Ahh, no Bob, there's no Mercedes. It's gone."

"Shit."

"What's the problem Bob?"

"Nothing. Nothing."

Dave the commo tech said, "I'm at the offices, and it looks like nobody's here."

"Nobody? Nobody? Are you inside?"

"I can't get inside. They're both locked, and I don't have the keys. I'm looking at the door with a flashlight right now. Bob..."

"What? What?"

"It looks like somebody broke a key off in the lock."

"Shit! We'll be there in an hour."

Ian Kelby, the young trial lawyer, was sitting in the office of his Rockville Maryland home surfing the internet after midnight. As usual he dropped into Free Americans.net to see what the next day's top stories would be, and to see what important stories might not make it into the mainstream press at all.

There was a story from western North Carolina, posted from an Asheville television station's website. As it was reported, a raid on a suspected illegal arsenal had ended in tragedy, after the ATF had followed up on a tip phoned in to 1-855-GUN-STOP. The ATF had been watching a silver Airstream travel trailer, keeping it under both ground and aerial surveillance for an entire day before moving in.

A four man ATF team had finally entered the place, after first using their own bomb disposal expert to search for booby traps. Only when the EOD technician gave the all-clear did the other agents enter the trailer to inventory and remove the illegal firearms. The Airstream had then erupted in a huge explosion and fireball, with torn, shredded and burning pieces of the trailer raining down across several acres.

The four agents were also being collected and carried away in pieces. Apparently, a huge fertilizer and fuel oil bomb had been buried underground below the trailer, and it had escaped the notice of the ATF bomb disposal expert.

This article posed a dilemma for the moderators of the Free Americans forum. How much smug gloating over the deaths of federal law enforcement agents could they permit without crossing over into the dangerous language of out-and-out sedition?

Ian Kelby was reading the replies down the discussion thread beneath the bomb ambush article, when someone posted the information that he had just found a file called the FEDLIST.ZIP. It seemed to include all of the federal agents in Maryland, Virginia and North Carolina. The person who posted this information included a link which Kelby clicked; it took him to a popular music file sharing network. After several more clicks and a wait of a few seconds his screen was filled with a densely typed list of names and addresses. Down the left side was a column of five digit numbers, in ascending order: zip codes. The list continued unbroken through hundreds of entries.

He scrolled down to his own Rockville zip code, 20850, and found nearby addresses listing four FBI and two ATF agents. One was a supervisor, judging by his job title and GS number. Kelby didn't risk saving or printing any of the list. Instead he copied down the information long hand on a piece of scrap paper, and then he exited the site and erased the cookies from his computer.

Kelby knew that such a sensitive list of federal employees would immediately be counterattacked by the government, and it would disappear quickly. The FreeAmericans.net moderators would also delete the link to the site as soon as they learned of it, in order not to be charged as an accessory to any crimes. The federal agents themselves, once they became aware of the list, would take extra security precautions and probably leave those home addresses and go into hiding. But if the list was brand spanking new, as Kelby supposed it was, the listed agents probably wouldn't become aware of it before arriving at work tomorrow…so there was a narrow window of opportunity if he moved quickly.

He began to consider several preplanned "boiler plate" operations for striking a target of opportunity on short notice. He spread out a road map of Montgomery County on his desk and began to weigh his options.

Wally Malvone was pacing between his first floor refrigerator and wet bar while channel surfing the cable news networks when his cell phone rang again. It was almost an hour since Bullard had made his initial calls from their staging site near Leo Swarovski's house outside of Richmond.

"Yeah?"

"Bob here."

"Okay Bob, what's up, what's the deal?"

"They're gone."

"They who?"

"Ahh, the two, umm, employees, the ones who were running the errand, and our guests. They're gone."

"All of them? All of them? Gone?"

"Right, all of them."

"Shit! What happened?"

"Hard to tell… A major snafu, that's for sure."

Malvone was thinking fast. Maybe Hammet was smarter than he'd given him credit for. Maybe his big dumb rottweiler loyalty was just an act. Maybe he'd sensed something wrong in Garfield's offer to drive him home tonight after deep-sixing Edmonds. Clay Garfield wasn't the sharpest knife in the drawer, maybe he'd inadvertently given Hammet some warning in something he'd said. Even now Hammet could be heading to the FBI, or a congressional committee, or the Washington Post... He could have let the prisoners go, or he could even be taking them with him.

"Okay Bob, we have to consider the annex totally blown, and you'd better think in terms of planning for visitors anytime. The wrong kind of visitors. So let's pack it up."

"Pack it up? Now? Or in the morning?"

"Now. Right now. How's the weather? Can you get the plane off the ground?"

"It cleared up, we can fly."

"Good. Get all of the vehicles and everybody out as soon as possible. Rendezvous at the new compound."

"The place in Maryland?"

"Yeah, right let's not be too specific, okay?"

"Sure, okay Wally. We'll be there."

"Tell the troops they'll get 48 hours leave after tomorrow morning, that'll get them moving. Sound okay?"

"That'll work," replied Bullard.

"We have to cut our losses down there. We've been there long enough to have an impact; it's served its purpose. Now with our, um, 'guests' missing, it'll be better to just not be there if the shit hits the fan."

"Understood. We should be out of here in one or two hours max, and at the new place before dawn."

"Call me when you come over the bridge into Maryland. I'll meet you and guide you into the new place."

"Will do."

"And call if there's any news about the…guests…and that situation."

"Of course, you bet. So our friend in Richmond, what about him?" asked Bullard.

"Well, I guess he gets a pass, for now," said Malvone.

"Lucky S.O.B., huh?"

"He is—for now. But we'll get around to him later."

"Is that all, Wally?"

"I guess so. Later Bob."

"Yeah, later." Wally Malvone pushed end on his phone, flipped it closed, and tossed it onto his sofa. What the hell was going on with Hammet? Had Fallon or Sorrento gotten loose somehow, and Hammet fled in fear of the consequences? Or had Hammet let them go for some reason? Or had he taken the prisoners with him somewhere? There didn't seem to be any way to tell yet, he'd just have to wait and see what was going to happen. But at least any government inspectors or news reporters sniffing around the annex after tomorrow would find nothing there, just an abandoned Navy airfield which was occasionally used for training the military and law enforcement.

In the worst case, if Hammet was turning snitch to the media or the government, he would be hard pressed to prove that anything had ever happened on the old landing field. In fact, there was no official record of the STU Team ever being in Virginia at all, and there was still no official link between Hammet and the STU, not a single scrap of paper or email he could point to. Damage control could obviously be a problem, and the situation would demand caution until Hammet and the others turned up, but the STU could ride it out, he was certain of it.

Actually, a straightforward escape by Fallon and the others was probably the best scenario Malvone could envision. If they killed Hammet and Garfield after forcing Hammet to make the call to Swarovski, they would only be doing his dirty work for him. And if the prisoners had escaped, they would be going to ground, running for deep cover and staying out of the STU Team's way. Then, Fallon and Sorrento could join Edmunds on the STU's most wanted list, two more targets on their expanding list of enemies, guaranteeing them job security and expanding budgets far into the future.

Enemies were a very good thing to have, to Wally Malvone's way of thinking.

43

Tuesday morning FBI Director Wayne Sheridan requested an emergency meeting with the President. He met him in the Oval Office, before the morning meeting of the Homeland Security Team down in the Situation Room. Harvey Crandall, the President's CSO and closest advisor, sat on an antique couch across the room from the President's desk. The FBI Director slid a long computer printout across the desk toward the President, and dropped into the chair across from him.

"What have you got for me, Wayne? A list? What is it, all of the militia terrorists?" President Gilmore smiled, ready to chuckle at his own joke, but he stifled his reaction when he saw the grim set to Sheridan's jaw.

"No sir, I wish it was. It's a list of almost every FBI and ATF Special Agent in Maryland, the District, Virginia and North Carolina, over a thousand of them. It lays out their home addresses, phone numbers... everything."

"Who generated the list? I don't understand. Is it our own?"

"Mr. President, it's all over the internet. It started showing up last night after midnight our time."

"What are you saying? Someone is trying to expose our agents? To what...endanger them?"

"Well, certainly sir, that's the clear implication."

"Have you shut down the website? Isn't it a felony to do that, to release information about our federal law enforcement officers?"

"Yes sir, it's a federal crime, it's a felony."

"Well, have you shut down the website? Arrest whoever put out that list! This isn't free speech; this is way over the line! It's intolerable! We need to make an example of whoever did this!"

FBI Director Sheridan shook his head slowly. He said, "I would if I could, believe me, I would if I could. This is way past what we can deal with at Justice, at least in the kind of hurry we're in. We're already in discussions with the NSA, we need their help, this is..." Sheridan was nervously wringing his hands together on his lap, agonizing. "We're trying to stamp it out, but that damn list keeps breeding like cockroaches, it's not just on one website, it's on thousands of computers! It's broken into unreadable fragments, just random looking gibberish. My people tell me it's hiding on music files that kids share! Music files! It's some kind of worm program, like a virus, it combines these fragmented files and generates the list. I don't really understand all the nuts and bolts of how this works, but it works, and so far we can't stop it."

"Can't we shut down the websites that are holding the files?" asked the President.

The FBI Director wondered if the President had understood anything of what he had just told him. "It's not only on websites! It's on people's personal computers, thousands and thousands of them, hiding in music. And since these files are all just gibberish until they're combined, there's no simple way to find them and remove them. At least that's what I'm being told, but the NSA is studying it...

"These partial files keep changing, they keep recombining and re-fragmenting and jumping onto new computers that are sharing music files. Antivirus software and firewalls don't do a thing; these files just hitchhike around the internet, mostly when people are sharing music. It's hidden in the code somewhere; it uses something called 'steganography', whatever that is. It's worldwide now. The NSA's going to help us with it, but in the meantime anybody can print this thing. It's called "The Fed List," and ter-rorists can locate any FBI or ATF agents who live in these three states, and..." Sheridan didn't complete the thought; he was rocking back and forth with his palms on his knees.

The President sat in silence, stunned by what he heard. "Is our security that bad? Where did the information come from? Somebody in-side of the government? A...traitor? A mole?"

"It's possible, that's a theory that's being explored, and we're running it down. But it's starting to look like the list comes from the pri-vate health care providers we use; someone could have hacked their data bases to collect the information. We're comparing the list to all known data bases, and so far it looks like it came from a few of the national health care providers we use. There's some out-of-date information on their data bases that's reflected on this Fed List."

"Jesus... Has anything like this ever happened before? What are your contingency plans?"

"We've seen this on a much smaller scale before; we've had anti-government hackers who make a hobby out of finding our agents and sending them anonymous emails, personal information, threats, that kind of thing. 'Bitwalkers', I think they're called. But it's usually on a local level, and we've kept it quiet, but this... this is orders of magnitude worse."

"Can you track down who did it?"

"I'm told that it's possible to upload the whole thing onto a private corporate network, and then have the program erase its own tracks. Completely erase the evidence of where it started, if the programmer is smart enough. We're working on it, we might catch a break, but so far... Well, frankly, my cyber war folks are reaching dead ends."

"If you need more technical support from NSA, you'll get it."

"Thank you, sir. They've been very cooperative already."

"Wayne, do you think the militia groups we're fighting are the ones who put out the list?"

"That's possible sir. Or it could be Islamic terrorists, or the Chinese, using the opportunity to screw us over and have it blamed on domestic hackers, just to compound our problems. We're not ruling anything out at this point."

"One more thing Wayne. Why do you think it's listing those three states? If they have all the information from the health insurance companies, why not list all fifty states?"

Sheridan had to pause to consider that question. "Well, this is just speculation, understand, but it may be a warning, sort of a shot across our bow. 'Back off, or we'll list more agents on the internet.' And something else makes us think it's a warning."

"What's that?"

"The Senior Executive Service isn't on the list; it stops at GS-15. The SES was scrubbed out, apparently. Whoever put out this list, he might be warning us to back off, or we're next. I can't think of any other reason why the SES isn't included."

President Gilmore leaned back in his black leather executive chair and stared at the ceiling, sighed, and then said, "We're not up against amateurs, are we?"

"No sir, we're not. This is a major league effort."

"What are you doing to protect your agents?"

"For now, we're leaving it up to the discretion of the Special Agents In Charge. Most of our agents in these three states are out in the field on investigations, and now they have to drop everything to go home and get their families moved out. And that's a problem, because we're worried about them getting ambushed on the way in or out. It's a real can of worms... We're authorizing full per diem for hotels, and where we can, we're cutting orders to put them on military bases in BOQs, until we figure out what to do next.

"Mr. President, I've got to tell you, this Fed List has thrown us all for a loop. We've already had drive-by shootings into houses since the list started showing up last night, and an ATF supervisor in Rockville was killed just this morning on his doorstep, heading out to work. We assume it's because he was on the list."

"Wayne," asked the President, subdued, "how many agents have been killed so far, since all this started? Since the Stadium Massacre?"

"FBI and ATF?"

"Right, all of them."

"Eighteen FBI Special Agents, most of them on that raid in Reston last week. And I believe eleven ATF Special Agents have been killed, counting the explosion in North Carolina yesterday. But I guess it's twelve since this morning."

"Good God! They're really kicking our asses, aren't they?"

"Yes sir, I'd say so sir. And now they've got a list of most of the Special Agents in three states! Over a thousand! We're going to have to put our investigations on hold temporarily, to let the agents in the field move their families to safety. We'd bring in agents from other states, but they already have their hands full everywhere, going after these gun nuts."

The President asked, "But if we keep pushing hard, we might have every agent in America exposed on the internet, isn't that correct?"

"That's the clear risk, sir."

"Should we keep pushing hard, Wayne? Keep pushing, or throttle back?"

"Sir? It's way too late to back off; we have to push even harder. We can't let anarchists and terrorists dictate terms to the federal government! No way, not on my watch."

"Okay, Wayne, okay. I concur. Authorize all the per diem you need. We'll put in a supplemental if we need to…just keep your people safe. Let me know if you need help from the DoD on temporary housing, and if you need the NSA to bump this thing up their priority list."

"Thank you sir."

Brad said, "We should go back inside, it's already afternoon. We could miss our pickup." They were lying together face to face in a sun-dappled clearing on a soft blanket they'd found in the cabin. Dried grass beneath the blanket cushioned them. They had rummaged through a bureau and a trunk in the cabin and were both wearing borrowed t-shirts and shorts. Ranya's .45 pistol was on a corner of the blanket next to Carson's silent .22, both were in easy reach. After finding boxes of .22 rimfire ammunition in the cabin they had practiced firing the pistol; it made a hollow metallic "tank" sound that was only as loud as a strong hand clap.

Ranya said, "I don't want to go inside yet; it's too hot in there with the shutters down. Anyway, I'm not leaving here until my clothes are dry, really crispy dry. I'm not getting back into clammy jeans again." Her denim pants and jacket and black t-shirt and underwear were spread across the tops of myrtle bushes, around the tiny clearing they'd found a short distance behind the cabin. Ranya had hand-washed her clothes in the old-fashioned bathtub with lemon dishwashing liquid, and then slipped out to find a discreet place to sun-dry them. Brad had followed her with the blanket… Even after their night of ardent lovemaking they were still eager for one another, and the cozy little glen beckoned them to its sun-lit floor.

The harsh noonday sun had driven the biting insects to seek cover; only a few random dragon flies buzzed above them, while cicadas trilled unseen from beneath the myrtles and boxwood. The sun also helped to dry and to heal their numerous insect bites, cuts, scratches and sores from

Monday's ordeals. Earlier, they had treated one another with aloe, cal-amine lotion and lanocaine from the bathroom medicine cabinet.

Now they lay together on their sides, pressed together, with their arms under their heads for pillows, sharing their breaths and staring into each other's eyes. Ranya's brown hair was unrestrained; it flowed across her shoulders and curled around her chin, shining in the sun.

"Your clothes have been dry for an hour," he said.

"How do you know that?"

"They look dry. They're dry."

"I'm not getting up; I want to stay here forever... You know, my mother had blue eyes like yours."

"She was Lebanese?"

"Maronite Christian Lebanese. It's not so unusual...maybe it's a legacy from the Crusaders. Anyway, Lebanon was always a sea trading country, people came there from everywhere. You can find all kinds of people in Lebanon, not just what you think of as typical Arabs."

"Well, I just love your eyes, Ranya. I see amber flecks in them, shining like gold dust in the sunlight. My eyes are just plain blue; your eyes are much more interesting. Sometimes they're green, sometimes they're hazel. They're always different, always changing."

"Your eyes are the color of the ocean and the sky, they're not just 'plain blue.' I want to stare into them forever; I never want to lose you again," she said.

"I'd love that too, if it's really what you want."

"It's really what I want, Brad," she said softly, and then she moved her lips over his for another small round of teasing kisses. She squeezed him more tightly around his neck and waist, and said "Let's not split up any more. Anything we do, let's do it together."

"Yesterday...yesterday was the worst. But you know, it was the best too, isn't that strange? I'll always remember how terrible it was, and how unbelievably fantastic it was when you came for me."

Ranya said, "See what happens when you go off on your own? You need me to keep you out of trouble."

"I noticed. Thanks again for rescuing me. But how did you find a private army?"

"Not me. Phil Carson; he did it all. He was a friend of my father..."

"Your father must have had a lot of friends."

"He did have a lot of friends. And some enemies...like the ATF. They always treated him like he was selling crack or heroin or something; they just couldn't stand us selling guns, just regular legal guns. They did everything they could for years to try to put him out of business. But they couldn't, and finally they just killed him."

"Do you think George Hammet is the right guy? I mean, the one who actually pulled the trigger?"

"Maybe. Probably. I guess so," she answered.

"So, if we can get to Guajira and take off, I mean, as soon as we can get off this island..."

"If it's still there, and not under surveillance," Ranya said.

"She's still there. There's no reason she wouldn't be."

"But what if she isn't? Or what if she's being watched? What if we can't take Guajira, what then?"

Brad smiled at her. "Then I'll steal another sailboat."

"Steal one? Really? Just like that?"

"Sure, why not? We're already down for killing one fed and kidnapping another, so what's stealing a boat on top of that? Marinas are full of sailboats that never go out. You can take a boat and the owner probably won't notice for days, or even weeks. And I can tell which boats nobody's paying attention to, and which ones can cross an ocean right out of the marina."

"Is it that easy? Don't you need a key?"

"Oh, please! I just installed a new diesel engine by myself. Do you really think I need a key to start one?"

Ranya laughed, and he kissed her cheeks while she smiled. "So what stops thieves from stealing sailboats?"

"That's easy. Thieves can't sail. They think it's some kind of magic. Except for the French, but that's another story."

"What's that mean?" asked Ranya, laughing.

"You'll find out, when we get down island. But I'm not going to need to steal a boat; Guajira's still waiting for us, I know she is."

"Is she ready? Can we just sail her out the way she is?"

"Oh hell yes! We could take off tonight and be fifty miles offshore by dawn, and make it to the Bahamas in a week."

"Will the Bahamas let us in? Won't we be fugitives?"

"I don't know, maybe not. I was never actually arrested, not officially, not by real police. But we won't clear into the Bahamas like regular tourists. Did you know that there's over a thousand islands in the Bahamas, and only about fifty of them even have one policeman? Clearing customs in the islands on a sailboat is a joke; it's actually all on the honor system, believe it or not. It's not like an airport; on a sailboat you have to go and find the customs officer and tell him you've arrived! But if you don't tell them, they don't know. We'll just show up in the Out Islands and make ourselves at home, and that's all there is to it."

"So we'll be illegal aliens?"

"Damn right we will. But we'll pay cash, and it'll be 'no problem mon!' Ranya, the water's so clear, it looks like your boat's floating on turquoise-colored air over the coral reefs; you just won't believe it. We'll skin-dive and catch lobster every day for lunch and grouper for dinner! The water's so warm, we'll just live in our bathing suits. And most of the time, we'll have anchorages completely to ourselves. We won't even need bathing suits! We'll just swim and dive and play and get all-over tans, like real Caribbean sailors."

"Oh Brad, you make it sound so wonderful, just like a dream. Oh, I can't wait; I wish we were there already!"

"Once we're there, I'll repaint Guajira's hull. Blue maybe. And we'll have to change her name... Then after the islands, we'll head for South America, maybe Brazil or Venezuela, or Colombia."

"What about our passports? What if the government's after us? We'll be fugitives, won't we?"

"Ranya, you only need passports at airports. With sailboats, it's a whole different world out there."

"Just pay your way in cash, and don't make problems?"

"You've got it. Keep a low profile, and keep moving. It's called being a 'PT.' It means you're just passing through, you're a permanent tourist, and you're practically transparent. For lots of people it means prior taxpayer...and if you want to keep it that way, you have to be privacy trained. That's being a 'PT.' We can buy papers and new vessel documents when we get to some islands I know in the Caribbean. Citizenship is cheap some places, you can pick any name you want."

Ranya laughed again. "So we're going to wind up in a Colombian prison is what you're saying, some place like Devil's Island."

"I'll take my chances. Anyway it beats taking a BATF bullet, or being tied to a board or crammed into a metal locker."

"Brad, don't worry, I'm with you all the way, I just need to know what to expect. Even if we're going to hell...I'll go with you gladly. And I don't care if we're heading for hurricanes or shipwrecks or jail, I'm not leaving you again, not ever." She pressed as tightly to him as she could and squeezed him even more tightly.

"I love you Ranya Bardiwell, do you know that? I fell in love with you the first day that I met you."

"That day, that day was the worst day of my life..."

"I'm sorry, I—"

"...Except for finding you."

"Ranya, I'm so sorry for what happened to your father, but I'm so glad I found you, I'm just sorry about...how."

"What a day that was, what a day. The worst day in my life, except that I found you. But now it's so strange, it's all mixed up together."

"At least we have each other."

"I know… I know. We have each other, and we always will. But Brad, I've got to tell you something. I've got to tell you, I just don't want to keep any secrets from you any more, I just can't keep it inside me."

"What secrets?"

"Big secrets. Really bad ones."

"What?"

"I…" Ranya closed her eyes, and turned her face into the blanket. "I shot Eric Sanderson. That's why they grabbed you."

Brad felt her shudder, felt a wave of trembling pass through her that made him dizzy. "You?"

"Me."

After a moment he said, "Damn… You know, they thought I shot him? They had it all figured out! They thought you scouted him out for me, and I shot him. They were trying to make me confess, and I didn't know what they were talking about! Now it all makes sense."

"I'm so sorry Brad, I'm so sorry. They tortured you…because of what I did, because of me. And they shot that poor man in the black truck because of me too."

He gently lifted her face from the blanket with his hand beneath her teary cheek, and looked into her wet eyes as she opened them. "Don't worry Ranya, Mr. Checkpoint had it coming. And the man in the truck, well, that just happened. That was the FBI; it had nothing to do with you."

"Sanderson was dancing on my father's grave, it felt like he was spitting in my face! I had to kill him." She half-laughed bitterly. "Maybe it's an Arab thing. I might be a Christian, but I'm still an Arab. I mean, I'm an American, but my blood is pure Arab. I guess that makes me crazy; everybody knows Arabs are crazy, right? Isn't that what everybody says?"

"Ranya, we can be crazy together, okay? You have to be crazy to cross oceans on sailboats, don't you? Anyway, we're already going to be blamed for killing and kidnapping federal agents, so what's one more dead politician on top of that? You know what they say about killing?"

"No, what?" she asked.

"After the first, they're all free."

She paused, staring hard at him. "They can only hang you once, is that it?"

"That's it," he answered.

"That's not exactly a good thing, is it? Being hanged even once, I mean?"

"No, but it sure does open up our options in the meantime."

"Yeah, I guess it does…" She sighed and turned onto her back, stretching. "Let's go back to the cabin now," she said. "I don't want to miss our ride either." She gave him one more kiss, rolled away and got up.

Brad lay on his back, shielding his eyes from the sun with an arm, while watching Ranya collect her dry clothes. He loved her completely, more than he had ever loved anyone in his life. Somehow he even loved her mind and her spirit, even though she had just confessed that she was a killer. Well, some people just needed killing, and he understood her hatred after her father's murder.

As he looked up at her gathering her dry clothes, his mind drifted again and he decided that she had the sexiest legs that he had ever seen on a real girl, a girl who wasn't dancing up on a stage. They were long and tan and slender, yet shapely and athletic, and her hips...her curvy hips and her narrow waist...

Crazy or not, he wanted to keep her. And he had to be crazy too, to want to stay with someone like that. Maybe in an insane world, crazy was the right way to be.

Mark Fitzgibbon, the semi-retired computer network consultant in Wilton Connecticut, had armed his already-created electronic bomb Sunday night in his study at home. He had launched it unnoticed from an empty cubicle in a branch office of a major health insurance corporation in Hartford during lunchtime on Monday. He had set the timer so that his bomb would explode soon after midnight Eastern Time, and all Tuesday morning he had been listening for echoes from the blast.

He was in his study switching between several Maryland and Virginia AM radio news talk stations. He was also keeping an eye on the cable television news networks, and checking The Sledge Report and Free-Americans on the internet. During the twelve noon news cycle he heard a Maryland radio station report a new assassination: an official who worked for the BATFE at their Washington Headquarters had been shot and killed in his driveway while getting ready to leave for work. The radio talk host mentioned the ATF official's name just one time, Fitzgibbon checked his own hard copy and found the listing for the GS-15 ATF supervisor who lived just south of Rockville Maryland.

This was either an incredible coincidence, or someone had found his list on the internet and gotten busy, realizing that the information would be most effective if it was used immediately. Fitzgibbon felt terrible for the family of the ATF supervisor, he had probably had nothing to do with staging the Stadium Massacre, or the phony "militia" murders and bomb-ings in Virginia. He just worked for a tainted agency.

But this harsh measure was the only way that Mark Fitzgibbon could think of to send a sufficiently stark and direct warning to the decision makers in the federal government. Certainly he was far too old and out of shape to be blowing up bridges like Ben Mitchell, the retired Army Special Forces Sergeant Major, God rest his soul! Fitz just thought of himself as using a more modern brand of high explosive, against a different target.

The decision makers would not be long in figuring out that the creator of the FEDLIST could just as easily burn the agents in the other 47 states, exponentially compounding what he knew must be an internal security nightmare. And they would also rapidly discern that he had cut off his list at GS-15, and not included members of the ultra-elite Senior Executive Service, those entrenched career bureaucrats, the "civilian generals" who were the real policy molders in the federal government.

Fitz was absolutely certain that the SES would not want their names and home addresses to be listed for anyone with a rifle and an internet connection to see. Most of them lived in upper class digs, and they would hate the aggravation of having to move their trophy wives and spoiled children into hotels, while they went shopping for new unlisted luxury homes in secure gated communities. They would come to their senses, and collectively they would work to rein in whatever group was directing the death squads in Maryland and Virginia.

Congress might also buy a clue, and reverse some of the newly enacted draconian gun laws which were at the root of most of the violence directed toward the government. In the meantime, all of the FBI and ATF agents in the three states would be forced to look after their own security, which would mean that for a while at least they would be too busy tending to their own affairs, to be conducting after-hours arson and murder raids.

Mark Fitzgibbon had not killed anyone in 35 years, and now he was directly responsible for the assassination of the ATF official in Maryland. The man left a widow, and this was painful to consider, but the entire agonizing national crisis had begun with their phony Stadium Massacre. The ATF or some other federal group wedded to them had started this murder ball rolling downhill, and they would have to bring it to a halt. Mark Fitzgibbon simply considered that he had provided them with a powerful incentive to do so.

And if they could not or would not stop their state terror program, then the hell with them! A long time ago he had raised his right hand and sworn to defend the Constitution against all enemies, foreign and domestic, and as far as he was concerned, that solemn oath had not come with an expiration date.

If the feds kept up their state terror program and their false flag murder operations, he would burn them all, in all fifty states, and most of all he would burn the Senators and Congressmen and the almighty Senior Executive Service! He would send them all scurrying for cover like cockroaches, caught in the middle of the kitchen floor by a sudden light at midnight. He would put their names and addresses directly into the hands of millions of pissed-off American riflemen!

44

"Brad, I think our ride's here." Ranya was sitting on a wooden kitchen chair, peering under the slightly opened front window shutter toward the dock. The plywood shutters had to stay down for the cabin to appear unoccupied from the river, they were propped open just enough to permit a flow of air through the screens. The late afternoon sun cast a single brilliant yellow line through the living room.

Brad was sitting on the sofa sharpening an old hunting knife he had found in a tool box, stropping it back and forth on a rectangular block of white Arkansas stone. He slipped off the couch and crouched beside Ranya to look under the shutter; a gleaming ski boat had pulled up to the dock 75 yards away. The single occupant cleated it off after carefully adjusting the rubber fenders, and stepped off onto the rough planks. He turned and gave the cabin a long look, and then he walked a few steps to the deep water end of the dock, kneeled down, and began pulling up a rope hand over hand.

She said, "He's pulling up a trap. That's him, let's go." They had both been ready to leave for several hours, taking turns keeping a watch on the dock, while listening to the old music cassettes. They kissed and held hands and talked about their mutual hopes and dreams for the rest of their lives, beginning with an endless Caribbean summer together on Guajira. Ranya was back in her blue jeans and the new gray sweatshirt, her hair was tied in a ponytail again and pulled through the back of her Ruger ball cap. Brad was wearing a faded pair of old nylon jungle camouflage pants, a hooded Navy blue sweatshirt, and an old pair of green canvas high-top sneakers. He'd assembled the outfit from a trunk full of mismatched castoffs; hunting and fishing clothes left behind by a long line of nameless predecessors. He had moved his khaki web belt from his shorts to the camo pants; he needed the belt to hold the sheath knife and the .22 pistol.

He considered leaving his brown leather boat shoes as a fair trade for the clothes he was taking, but he thought it would be foolish to re-enter the world with only the funky green sneakers, not knowing when or if he'd have a chance to get another pair of street shoes. He had put his shorts and boat shoes into a green canvas Boy Scout backpack he found hanging on a nail on the back side of the house. The small pack had an old bird's nest inside and was covered with cobwebs when he found it, but it was serviceable after being shaken out and adjusting the straps.

The cammie pants had drawstrings around the ankles. Between the high top sneakers, socks, long pants and the hooded sweatshirt, Brad felt ready to take on another night's mosquitoes and no-see-ums. His face and hands he could protect with a can of bug spray which was in the pack; he was still scratching at bites from yesterday and he didn't want any more.

Both of them carried their pistols inside of their belts with the grips concealed under the bottoms of their sweatshirts. Brad had removed the suppressor from his .22 and put it into his pack; the gun was too bulky to conceal with the long aluminum tube over its barrel. They had discussed and Brad accepted the harsh reality that the diminutive .22 bullets would only be definitive man stoppers when applied to the cranium at close range.

The cabin was already straightened up and put back the way they had found it. They swung on their backpacks and dropped the shutters and bolted them, and stepped out into the day's last sunlight. Ranya locked the cabin's front door and hid the key in a crack in the cinderblock steps, as called for by the checklist.

"He looks like a kid," she said, while they walked down the sandy path to the dock.

"A rich kid; that's an expensive boat," Brad replied, resisting the impulse to mention that, at 21, Ranya could hardly be much older than the young man on the dock.

"I wonder if he knows what's going on?" she asked.

"Who does know what's going on? I don't."

Their boat captain was a skinny teenager, only 15 or 16. He wore a gray long-sleeved t-shirt with a local surf shop's logo on the back, and lime-green baggy trunks. His long wavy hair looked to be extra pale blond from a summer of sun, salt water and swimming pool chlorine.

He'd hauled an enormous pyramid-shaped wire crab trap up on the dock, then he turned around and watched as Brad and Ranya approached. "Hi. I'm supposed to take you somewhere, all right?"

"Right," said Brad. No names were asked, or offered.

"You want the crabs?" the kid asked. "Got some nice ones here."

"No, thanks," said Ranya.

"Okay then, back they go." The 'surfer dude' teen flipped the triangular sides of the trap flat down onto the dock and the blue crabs immediately spread out, scuttling sideways, eyestalks peering at them with their claws open in defensive postures. One by one they skittered their way to the edge, dropped over into the water and paddled away. The kid picked up the wire trap by the rope, and swung it back out where it landed with a whooshing splash and sank out of sight.

The boat was a 21 foot Sea-Knight with an inboard Mercruiser; it had a blue fiberglass hull and a creamy white interior. Skis, a kneeboard, towels and a cooler were casually stowed up in the forward seating area ahead of the windshield, which had a hinged section in its middle for access to the bow.

"Hop on and sit in the back. When I say, untie the stern line, okay? Oh, and put this on." He handed Brad a North Carolina Tar Heels ball cap; Ranya was already wearing her Ruger hat. "It's supposed to make it harder to take good pictures of you, just in case. Tighten the hats up pretty good—we'll be hauling ass, and if they fly off we're not going back. And one more thing: you have to wear these sunglasses, too. My fath...my...well, you just have to wear them. Sorry, but you just have to."

He handed them each a pair of cheap wrap-around sunglasses; black electrical tape was layered over the lenses on the inside.

"No problem," said Brad. "We understand. Security."

"Right, that's what my...um...exactly. Security. I'm glad you understand; I know it looks kind of dorky, but it's better for everybody."

"Don't worry about it; we're fine, we understand," said Ranya, smiling sweetly at him. "Come on, let's go."

The boy blushed and beamed back at her and said, "I'm not supposed to ask you any questions...but I know what's going on, more or less. Well, let's go." He sat in the white vinyl-padded seat behind the controls on the starboard side, and started the engine smoothly. "You can cast off now," he said, and Brad untied the stern line from the dock cleat and pulled it aboard, and flipped the rubber fender in as well.

They both sat in comfortably-upholstered U-shaped seats facing forward, holding hands across the padded engine box between them. Ranya shot one last smile at Brad, smirked and shook her head at his Tar Heels hat, with its little footprint logo. Then she slipped on her blacked-out sunglasses, and he did the same.

Their young boat driver pulled in the forward fender, and then he expertly maneuvered away from the dock, reversing in a tight J with the wheel hard over. When the bow was pointing out of the side creek toward the main channel of the river, he smoothly advanced the throttle lever, and the boat easily came up onto a plane. In sharp contrast to their loud and bone-jarring trip in the bottom of the aluminum hunting boat last night, the Sea-Knight had a quiet Cadillac ride while it gracefully sped down the river at what felt like almost thirty miles an hour, judging by the wind on their faces.

Brad couldn't recognize the river or even the area, the slivers of flat 'low country' he could see out of the sides of his glasses all looked the same: marshland punctuated with cypress, oaks and pines. He could tell that they were heading roughly southeast by the direction of the sun, which was sliding toward the horizon behind them. They entered a larger river; he could catch fractional glimpses of the distant shorelines as the powerful boat flew across the chop without any hint of pounding. Ranya squeezed his hand; their arms were lying comfortably across the padded top of the engine cover. They made up for the lack of visual stimulus by playing games with their fingers; intertwining them, weaving them, stroking each other's palms, teasing with their nails.

The boat made a wide turn and threaded its way into another creek and, after a series of long S-turns, it slowed down and dropped off step as if it was entering a no-wake speed zone. They proceeded in a straight line for several minutes. At one point Brad could hear the sound of automobiles crossing the steel grating of a highway draw bridge above them. In another minute their young driver said "here we go again," and the boat accelerated back up onto a plane. Brad could see the green glowing face of his watch under the outside corner of his blinders, it was 6:25. They had been traveling for over a half hour, which he guessed meant they had covered ten or fifteen miles of water. This guess signified nothing, since he had no idea where their starting point had been. After five more minutes at high speed, the boat dropped gently off plane to an idle.

"Okay guys, you can take off the glasses now. This is where you get off." They were alongside a derelict half-sunken barge which was slightly tilted and awash at its lowest corner. The side of the barge they were next to was over 80 feet long; the far side was grounded in marshland which spread for miles to distant tree lines. In Tidewater barges frequently broke loose in storms and were driven ashore. Often they were not worth the cost of their salvage, and they remained forever where they had stranded.

The only other manmade structure visible was a series of high tension line towers running from horizon to horizon, several miles behind them across the last pink band of the sunset sky. In every other direction there was only water, marshland, and scattered trees; the few clouds were already losing their rose color and turning gray for the night.

"Okay guys, jump off. Somebody's going to come along to pick you up in a little while, but I'm not supposed to call them on the radio until I'm away from here. Hey, do you guys have a flashlight? When a boat comes along and puts a light on the barge, blink back at them three times. I saw that in a movie about British commandos once. That's how you do it, right?"

Brad laughed, "I guess so, it sounds fine to me." They were standing in the back of the Sea-Knight now, getting their balance; the wind had died and the water was almost perfectly calm, but the boat still rolled under them.

Now that they had stopped, the insects were finding them, and the young man asked, "Do you have any bug spray? The no-see-ums out here will kill you at sunset."

"Oh yeah, we know all about the 'flying teeth.' I've got a can of spray, we'll be all right." Brad tossed the borrowed Tar Heels hat onto the console behind the windshield.

"One more thing, there's something you need to take along: the cooler, the one in the bow. You're supposed to take it with you, and give it to somebody tonight."

"Who?" asked Brad.

"I don't know who, nobody told me. Just take it with you is all I know." The kid unlatched and flipped the center part of the windshield to the side, and Brad went forward to get the icebox. Standing behind the wheel, the teenager used small throttle and wheel movements to hold the boat precisely in place next to the barge without touching it, in spite of the fast-flowing tidal current. His two white rubber fenders were out, but unneeded, as he kept the twenty foot boat on station like an expert.

Brad moved past him forward into the bow, and grabbed the big Igloo cooler by its two handles and strained to lift it up onto the ski boat's gunnel. A wrapping of duct tape sealed its lid. It was heavier than he expected, as if it was completely full of ice and beverages or fish, but it wasn't cold to the touch. Ranya tossed their packs onto the barge and hopped over from the stern of the Sea-Knight. Brad horsed the cooler across to the edge of the barge, and she dragged it securely back onto its rusty steel deck. Finally, Brad climbed onto the gunnel and jumped over, leaving the Sea-Knight wallowing. He turned back and reached far out over the boat, the young driver leaned across and shook his hand.

"Thanks for the ride," said Brad. You did fine, just like a real commando."

"Really?"

"Hell yes, really."

"My big brother's a Ranger—he's in Iraq. I'm going to join the Army too when I turn 18, if I don't go to college right away."

"Well, I think you'll make a great soldier. You did great tonight."

"Thanks." His late adolescent voice cracked.

He was just a boy, thought Brad, but he had handled his boat and his "mission" like a man. He had delivered Brad and Ranya and an unknown cargo, and kept both the starting point and the destination totally unknown to his passengers, preserving the secret location of the isolated river cabin for future clandestine purposes.

The kid waved to them again, and pushed the throttle forward. In a minute he was out of sight, leaving a straight wake disappearing into the west as the last light bled out of the sky, briefly turning the water red. The waxing quarter-sized moon was already hanging low, chasing the sun to the horizon.

"Where are we?" asked Ranya.

"Good question," he replied. "Which state are we in would be my first question. Did you recognize the bridge?"

"Nope. How about the power line over there?"

"No idea." He squatted down and undid the leather buckles on his Boy Scout pack, pulled out the bug spray, closed his eyes and sprayed himself. "You want some?"

She took the can, sprayed some on her hands and used that to dab her face. "Now what?" she asked him.

"Now we wait." He sat on the big cooler and Ranya sat down beside him, facing the other way. He slid his arms around her waist and pulled her close while she slipped her hands behind his neck.

"You're a great kisser Brad, but 'Off!' bug spray is not exactly the cologne that drives me wild."

"It's exactly the same as your perfume, Miss, and you don't hear me complaining."

"Well, I'm sorry, I can't stand getting bugs in my mouth. They're everywhere! When the sun goes down, the bugs take over out here."

"On Guajira, the screens are very serious business. You couldn't live up that river without screens! If you forget to put the screens in before sunset, you're doomed, unless there's a really good breeze, and then sometimes you're okay."

"Well, there's no breeze now," she said.

"It'll come back from the east when the air cools down."

"Well I hope we're not waiting here for that long, that could be hours! And if you're even thinking about what I think you're thinking about, just forget it Brad. It ain't gonna happen. Not on a barge."

"I know, that's okay. Believe me, after yesterday, I'm thrilled just to be with you. And I love just kissing you, I could kiss you forever." He was holding her close; she reclined back across his lap and pulled off her hat and let it fall to the side. She dropped her eyelids and parted her lips; he rubbed her nose with his and kissed her gently, as he slipped his hand under the bottom of her new gray sweater.

A blinding searchlight hit them like a white blast of electricity as an amplified metallic voice crackled across the water, catching them in their embrace.

"Sorry to disturb you two lovebirds, but we've got places to go and people to meet."

They flinched and jumped apart to their feet as the spotlight blinked out and faded to an orange dot in their eyes, and then they heard male voices laughing raucously from the darkness, over the deep sound of a rumbling outboard motor.

Ranya called back, "Phil Carson, you big jerk! What are you doing, sneaking up on people like that? You want to give us a heart attack?" She shoved her .45 back under her belt, and switched her flashlight onto the approaching boat: it was a twenty-foot Boston Whaler with a tall black

Mercury outboard. It bumped roughly alongside the barge without putting out fenders; the driver was obviously not concerned about a few more scrapes or gouges.

"I think you have something for us," said Carson, "You mind dragging your love seat over here?"

Brad and Ranya each took a handle and swung the heavy cooler down and across to the Whaler's gunnel, where other hands pulled it onto the boat's deck.

"Hop on. We've got an appointment and, believe me, you won't want to miss it. Brad, you want a beer? Get him a cold one Tony."

Brad and Ranya tossed their packs over and then jumped down into the Whaler. There were already two men on the boat with Carson, who was standing behind the center console holding the wheel. After being blinded with the spotlight, it was too dark for them to make out more than their shapes.

"Hey Brad, is she old enough to drink? Should we let her have alky-hall, or just a sody-pop?"

"Shove it, Phil. I go to UVA, and I can drink you under the table anytime."

A youngish man pulled a pair of cold Budweisers from another ice chest in the back of the boat.

"Oh, my word, she goes to U-Vee-A!" laughed Carson. "Well, in that case, give the lady Cavalier a beer. Then hang on to something, 'cause here we go!"

The standing passengers lunged for hand holds on the center console as the big Mercury roared and the Whaler leaped forward, accelerating so rapidly that they were almost tumbled off their feet. The boat streaked across the darkening waters, their wake gleaming behind them in the pale light of the setting quarter-moon.

Twenty minutes later, Phil Carson was piloting the old Whaler along at low RPMs, with the running lights switched off. They were on a ruler-straight stretch of a hundred yard wide creek, with a high bank close above them on their right side. On the opposite side it was difficult to distinguish where the water ended and the marshland began. The moon had only just set across the marshes to the south, and the stars seemed to have increased in their brilliance.

The undercut earthen bank to starboard was studded with live oaks, their roots reaching out over the water like skeletal fingers. Some of the massive oaks were tipping over in ultimate surrender to the mastery of gravity. The other trees with better footing stood at attention, outlined against the constellations as they ghosted along through the black water.

A dark structure loomed over them in an open space between oaks; it was a boxy three story house built at the river's edge and extending well out over the water. Carson was guiding the Whaler along at little more than idle speed. As he passed close by the house he spun the wheel hard to the right, and they drove straight into the black wall.

Beneath the house at river level there were docks on either side, between rows of supporting columns. Someone was waiting for them on their left, this person shined a light down on the dock at his feet and Carson coasted the Whaler to a stop and killed the engine. Lines were tossed over, and the boat was tied up. Behind them, the opening they had just driven through closed, as a wide panel tilted down into place like a riverside garage door.

The docks beneath the house were wide and solidly built, running around the perimeter in the shape of a U which was open to the river. It was high tide and the dark water was only a foot under the boards. An aluminum canoe with an outboard motor mounted on its square transom was tied up to the dock on the other side of the house.

Brad and Ranya surveyed the place with their flashlights. Wooden steps at the back led upward into the house. A wave runner and several plastic kayaks were stored on the dock beneath the stairs. Water skis, fishing rods, life jackets and other boat gear were stored on racks and hooks along the plank walls. These horizontal boards were spaced widely enough apart to permit the filling sea breeze to flow through the dock level of the house. They were both impressed with the setup, which was a water sports enthusiast's dream, combining privacy, security, and easy river access for a wide variety of water craft.

The two men who tied up the whaler were wearing mosquito head nets which hid their faces. They took the heavy Igloo cooler and set it on the dock as the passengers stepped ashore. One of these men shook Carson's hand and asked him, "How's that old song go? 'Send lawyers guns and money'?"

Carson replied, "Hey, two out of three ain't bad, Rev."

Their eyes adjusted to the subdued lighting inside the boat house, and Brad sprayed on some more bug repellent and handed the can to Ranya who did the same. The can of bug spray was passed along as everyone fortified their chemical defenses. The mosquitoes were a tangible presence in the air, and their hum was readily audible, but the bites of the no-see-ums were more immediately painful on unprotected exposed skin.

"How's our detainee?" asked Carson.

"He's not happy, I can tell you that," replied one of the mosquito head-net wearing men.

"Well, let's see if he's in a talkative mood," said Carson, shining his flashlight up the dock. The beam revealed a naked white man sitting on a folding aluminum lawn chair, facing the water with his feet dangling over the edge. He was tied to the chair with half-inch dock line at his wrists, elbows, biceps, thighs and ankles. A small white canvas bag was placed upside down over his head, and there was a dense cloud of mosquitoes and no-see-ums around him, competing for landing rights to unoccupied skin area.

Carson walked over to him and pulled off the bag. "How ya doin' George? Ya comfy?" George Hammet was vainly trying to shake off the mosquitoes by flexing and twitching his limbs and his torso. "Be careful, George. You might bounce yourself right over the edge, and it'll be real tough to tread water while you're tied to that chair. Hey, are you hungry? You must be starving by now. We picked up a couple of buckets of chicken. You up for a little KFC? Or maybe you'd like to get sprayed down with some Cutters first, huh? You know, you never can tell which one of these skeeters is carrying that West Nile virus."

Hammet turned his head toward his tormenter, but Carson shined the beam of his light in his eyes and he turned away again. "You assholes have no idea who you're screwing with," Hammet spat out, but his voice was tinged with fear. He blinked and jerked his head as squadrons of mosquitoes and no-see-ums landed on his lips and eyelids.

"Oh, is that so?" asked Carson. "Hey everybody, dig in, we've got plenty of chicken and beer. How's that sound, George, some KFC and a cold brewski?"

"You're so dead, you son of a bitch! You're all just so dead!"

Carson chuckled. "Dead? Do we look dead? George, you're the one that's tied to a chair buck-naked; I really think you should try to talk nicer to us. I mean, I know you're used to wearing a mask and a ninja suit and having a license to kill, but you see, there's been kind of a 'regime change' around here, and you need to get used to the new pecking order."

Hammet spat out some insects and said, "Do you have any idea what happens to people who kidnap federal agents?"

Carson replied, "That's a good start George. You're finally getting around to the federal agents part." He withdrew a slim wallet from the front side pocket of his leather jacket, flipped it open and put his flashlight on it, revealing a gold ATF shield and ID. "But you know what? We've been listening to the news all day, and we haven't heard a peep about any missing federal agents. Not a word. A few feds have been shot and blown up here and there, but none are reported missing in action. Now why do you think that is? Doesn't the stew team care about you? Or is it maybe you're not a real federal agent after all?"

Ranya had prepared a paper plate loaded with chicken and red rice and biscuits for Carson; he sat on another folding lawn chair facing Hammet from the side and put the plate on his lap. "Mmmm... nothing beats the Colonel's original recipe. You want a piece, George? It's still warm even. You must be awful hungry; I know I am, and I had lunch."

"Go screw yourself," said Hammet, without much conviction.

"No, I don't think so George." Carson stripped the meat off of a drumstick with his teeth, and tossed the bone and scraps into the water in front of the naked ATF agent, and then he shined his flashlight on the surface where the ripples were spreading out in concentric rings. After swallowing, Carson said, "That's one of the downsides to working for a covert unit George; they're not very public about their losses. I guess they can't stay very covert if they go blubbering to the newspapers and TV every time one of their jack-booted thugs gets whacked or goes missing.

"Hey, that reminds me: did you know your 'stew team' flew the coop? Sky-ed right out of there. It's like they were never on that airfield. They're gone without a trace, and without even leaving a forwarding address. They bolted, they bugged out, and they left you all by your lonesome. Now what kind of team runs away and leaves a buddy behind like that?"

Carson stripped the meat off another chicken leg and threw it in. More chicken bones and scraps followed from the others who were standing and sitting behind him. There was a subtle roiling of the water's surface, followed by a splash, and then a rapid churning. Several flashlight beams captured slick brown shapes knifing in and snatching at the chicken scraps as they hit the water. Soon there was a general feeding frenzy underway as a dozen spiny-mouthed catfish zoomed in from all directions to battle for the chicken. As each new scrap hit the surface, the water erupted, and more catfish arrived by the second. Blue crabs were visible in the flashlights' beams swimming lower, snatching at the smaller bits missed by the catfish above.

"George, I don't know who's going to have more fun, those catfish and crabs, or me watching you getting eaten alive. Hey Rev, show the young lady how the lift system works. I think Robin should have the honors." Carson addressed Ranya by the nom d'guerre he had given her before the rescue operation, in order to preserve a level of anonymity among the conspirators on the docks.

Over the water in front of George Hammet, a wide nylon boat lifting strap was suspended from the overhead ceiling beams by two wire cables about ten feet apart. Another nylon strap hung over the water twenty feet back down the dock toward the river. The four pencil-thin stainless steel wires holding the two straps were wound around a pair of steel pipes suspended on brackets under ceiling beams. When the nylon straps were lowered into the water, a large powerboat could enter the under-house dock area, position itself over the straps, and be lifted completely out of the water for dry barnacle and slime-free storage.

On one of the telephone pole-sized pilings running from the water to the ceiling at the edge of the dock, midway between the lifting straps, there was a gray electrical box with a simple on and off switch, and up and down buttons.

"I think I can handle this," said Ranya. She pushed one of the coin-sized buttons, and the wire cables spooled out with an electric motor whine, lowering the strap nearest Hammet into the water.

Carson said chummily, "Look at the bright side, George, once you're in the water...no more mosquitoes." He stood up and threw the rest of the scraps from his plate into the water, and then he leaned out over the water and grabbed the strap and pulled it over to the dock. It was dripping wet where it had just gone in. Hammet had lost the last of his cockiness and was trembling, looking at the lifting strap, and at the water which continued to churn where the chicken bones had been tossed in.

"Don't do this, please... don't do this." His voice was weak and raspy; his mouth was obviously parched from fear and dehydration.

"George, you don't want to spoil this for us, do you? Don't we deserve some closure here?"

"Please... I know things...lots of things. I can help you..."

"George, we really don't care what you know. And we're not going to kill you, so don't worry. We just want to watch you get your face eaten off...and then we'll take you home to your wife. That's Laura May Hammet on Albacore Road, right? You think she'll like the new faceless, dickless, crab-eaten George? Good old George, with no eyes, no lips, no ears, no fingers, and no dick. Think she'll like that?

Hammet's head was hanging down; tears were making wet tracks through the busy black sand fleas and mosquitoes on his face as they extracted their drops of his blood. Carson tied the dripping bottom of the lifting sling to the back of Hammet's aluminum chair with a short piece of line. Hammet was trying vainly to force his legs together to protect his privates, but his knees were tied too securely to the sides of the chair.

He tried again. "Don't! Please! I know things! Very, very important things!"

"We know things too, George, like how you shot Joe Bardiwell. That was you, right George?"

"Yes! I did it! I had to!"

"Push him in or I will, damn it!" Ranya hissed from behind.

"Okay..." Carson replied, almost regretfully. He stood behind the chair and tipped it slowly forward off the dock, Hammet watched the water approaching, expectant catfish and crabs were still circling and darting below him in the beams of all of their flashlights. He hit the water face first, in mid-scream. The lifting straps were fully extended and he splashed in and swung outward and sank quickly below the water. In a moment the strap formed a twitching V where it disappeared beneath the surface.

After almost a minute, Carson said, "Reel him in, Robin. We don't want him to die just yet."

The electric motor whined again, and the lifting strap came back up. Hammet was hanging forward from the chair by his bonds. Even with the strap fully raised, Hammet's feet were still in the water. He choked and heaved in lung-fulls of the cool night air and shuddered and retched, nearly catatonic with shock and fear. Black clouds of mosquitoes instantly swarmed onto his white skin, which was glistening wet in the beams of a half dozen flashlights. He was jerking and kicking his feet against their bonds, trying to dislodge the catfish from his still submerged toes.

Carson continued, "George, you said you knew important things. George! Now would be a good time to tell us!"

Hammet was staring down at the water, stuttering. Someone tossed a partially eaten chicken breast toward his feet, and the water exploded again in a mad tangle of ravenous catfish.

"You said you knew important things, George! Make it worthwhile—those fish are hungry!"

"I...I...I..." Hammet gasped for air and tried to speak.

"Send him back down." The electric motor hummed again, and this time George was lowered straight into the water. His pale white body glowed beneath their lights, obscured where the thrashing brown catfish were trying to get a hold of anything they could tear off.

"Back up, and stop him halfway."

Hammet emerged up to his shoulders; catfish were still attacking his fingers and toes and were clustered between his legs.

He caught a breath and shouted out in desperation, "The stadium! I know who did the stadium! I was there! I was there!"

After a moment Carson said "That's a good start George, that's a real good start." He leaned out from the dock with a boat hook and caught the back of the chair and pulled him near. The two mosquito head-netted men grabbed the strap and hauled him by the chair back up onto the dock.

"You're doing great George, just great. We've got dry towels and bug spray, and some blankets and clothes." He pulled out a pocket knife and flicked it open with one hand, and used the silver blade to slice off the lines which bound Hammet's right arm. "Somebody get George a beer."

Then he turned around and quietly said to Ranya, "There's a video camera on the Whaler; it's in the red gym bag under the console. Let's get all this on tape."

45

After a twenty-minute drive through the darkness, the pickup truck bumped and crunched across a rutted field of newly harvested stubble corn, made several tight turns and then backed up for a short distance. When it stopped, Brad pushed up the rear window of the camper shell, dropped the tailgate, and they climbed out. The pickup was parked only a few yards from a wooden barn or shed; then its running lights went out and once again they had to work by flashlight.

Phil Carson handed Hammet's rope leash over to Brad, then he unlocked and dragged open the two cracked timber doors of the barn, revealing the back of a red Jeep Cherokee. Carson walked to the driver's window of the pickup and spoke a few hushed phrases and, when he returned, he was putting on a pair of leather work gloves. Hammet was sitting on the tailgate with his hands tied securely in front, an extra six feet of line served as his leash to control and guide him. He was dressed in his white boxer shorts and undershirt.

"All right, George, here's your ride home," said Carson. "But not until tomorrow morning, okay buddy? Face it: you're in no shape to drive. So let's get in the back seat, and you can sleep for a few hours. That's a pretty good deal, huh?"

Hammet was badly slurring his words, and he spoke in a sing-songy voice. "You're all priddy nize guys, do you know that? Y'know, I don't know…maybe we should call Wally. Why don' we jus' go to my house now and call Wally? He can figure everything out so nobody gets in any trouble. He's a really, *really* smart man." Hammet was stinking drunk, and he remained seated upright on the tailgate only with difficulty.

Carson unlocked the Cherokee; the interior light came on and he opened the rear passenger side door. Then he helped Brad to get Hammet onto his feet and walk him into the barn, and they guided him inside onto the rear bench seat. Carson was the only one of them to touch the Jeep, and only with his gloves. Ranya wiped off a half-full bottle of Jim Beam bourbon whisky with a rag and handed it to Carson, holding it by its neck with her sleeve pulled over her hand. Carson climbed inside next to Hammet and set the bottle on the seat between them. Ranya returned with the rest of Hammet's clothes and put them into the foot well of the front passenger seat.

Carson said, "Hey Georgie, now that we're pals, I'm going to untie you, okay buddy? Let's drink a little more whiskey, and then you can sleep right here until morning." After he untied Hammet's wrists he dropped the dock line out the open door and Ranya retrieved it. Carson unscrewed the cap and gave the whiskey bottle to Hammet, who was sitting up unsteadily with his eyes only half open.

"Come on, Georgie boy, drink it down one more inch, and then you can take a nice long nap. In the morning, you can drive home to good old Albacore Road."

Hammet held the bottle in both hands and studied the label under the Cherokee's interior light, and then he tipped it up and gulped down more of the burning brown intoxicant, spilling half of it down his white shirt. After his experiences under the boat house, he had learned to obey Carson's instructions and, with a half a bottle of bourbon inside him, any thought of resistance had evaporated. "Ahhh! Oh yeah, jus' like back in college, good ol' Boston College, yessiree!"

"You're the man, Georgie! You're going to win the chugalug contest for sure. One more big chugalug for good old Boston College!"

But there wasn't another chugalug in George Hammet, big or otherwise, and he fell sideways until his face hit the left door and came to rest on the seat. The open whiskey bottle dropped from his hands onto the floor of the Jeep.

Carson went around to the driver's seat and backed Hammet's SUV out of the barn, as the pickup pulled away. He followed behind the truck back across the rutted fields and dirt roads to the pavement, and then a succession of deserted county roads.

Brad and Ranya rode in the back of the truck under the camper shell; he held a flashlight while she stripped off her shoes, her jeans and her gray sweatshirt. She was already wearing a dark blue one-piece tank suit under her clothes, taken from the river house where Hammet had bared his black soul and revealed his darkest secrets.

Brad asked, "You're sure you want to do this? I can do it if you don't want to…"

"I'm going to do it; it's settled." Ranya pulled on white scuba diving gloves with black rubber dots on the palms and fingers, and black neoprene reef shoes which were also taken from the well-stocked river house. She twisted her ponytail up into a loose bun and tugged a white swim cap on, concealing all of her hair underneath. "I'm ready, don't worry. I'm ready." Her face was grim and unsmiling; when she was finished with her preparations they both sat Indian style facing each other, holding hands across their laps as they swayed and rocked on the bare steel floor of the truck.

At last, the pickup pulled over and stopped on the shoulder of the two lane road they had been traveling on for some time, and the red Cherokee went around and parked in front of them. It was after midnight in a remote corner of Tidewater, and they had not passed another car for a long time. Both vehicles switched off their headlights, but left their engines running. Then Brad flipped up the pickup's rear window and Ranya climbed over the tailgate, and met Phil Carson by the back of the red SUV.

"He's dead drunk, he's out cold," he told her. "You know where we are, right? You know this intersection; you've seen the canal?"

"I've been here before," she replied. Her arms were folded beneath her breasts, her white gloves and bathing cap glowed dimly in the light of the flashing red signal at the end of the road.

"You want to do a dry run, drive up and check it out first?"

"No need, Phil. Let's get it over with." Ranya climbed into the Cherokee's driver's seat and shut the door. The seat was adjusted too far back for her to drive comfortably, but she didn't move it forward. She found the electric window buttons and rolled her side window down almost all the way, examined the gap carefully, and then put it back up to only half-closed.

She turned and looked into the back seat. George Hammet was lying in his dirty underwear with the side of his face pressed against the seat, snoring and stinking of vomit and stale whisky breath; it was almost enough to make her throw up. She pulled the seatbelt across and buckled herself in, and then she unbuckled and refastened it several times with her eyes closed.

Ranya switched on the headlights, slid forward on the seat so that she could reach the pedals, put the Cherokee into gear, and pulled out. A quarter mile down the road she approached the T-intersection where a single flashing red light warned her to stop. Straight across the intersection there was a twenty foot section of steel guardrail sprouting a half dozen reflective highway signs. Route numbers and arrows pointed to the north and south.

Toward the end of the straightaway, Ranya put the pedal to the floor and the red Cherokee blew through the intersection under the flashing lights at 60 miles per hour. It made a slight right turn, bounced once on the far shoulder and the grassy verge just missing the barricades, flew out over the bank and hit the water of the Dismal Swamp Canal much harder than she expected.

The airbag exploded in her face, and the Cherokee immediately began to settle onto its right side as cold river water came gurgling in from underneath. Ranya grabbed the buckle but couldn't find the release button; she fumbled with it and was just beginning to panic when it popped open. She cleared the seatbelt and the airbag away from in front of her as the cold water rose to her waist. She turned sideways in her seat with her back toward the door and felt for the open window, grasping for the roof to pull herself through.

Somehow, the overhead interior light had come on even as the headlights had died under the water. She put her feet on the center console between the front seats to push herself out, and saw George Hammet sitting up on the slanting back seat; his eyes wide open in stunned disbelief with water up to his chest.

"You bitch! You God damn bitch! Who the hell are you?" he howled in the car's rapidly disappearing air pocket. The Cherokee began to roll faster onto its right side. Ranya grabbed the outside of the roof with both hands and pushed off with her legs and began to slide through. She got her head and then her arms and shoulders and finally her chest out into the night air as her window sank to the river level. Then her legs were slammed together against the door and she was pulled back hard. The SUV was sinking faster now; her head and arms were still above the surface when the Cherokee finally submerged with a loud rush of bubbles. She took one last gulp of air and was pulled down into inky blackness.

The electric windows and door locks had all shorted out and had frozen in place when the Cherokee hit the brackish water. The suddenly very conscious George Hammet floated and pulled himself between the two bucket seats into the front and tackled Ranya around her waist and hips. By pinning her inside, he was sealing off his only exit, but his drunk and enraged reptilian brain was set only on preventing her escape.

In her desperation to break free, Ranya was a strong and slippery adversary, and she thrashed her legs wildly to break her mortal enemy's embrace. She dragged a foot up far enough to shove against his gut and groin, won enough space to land a kick with her knee against what felt like his face, and then was able to get her other foot to his throat and break his grip. Still kicking madly at him she pulled herself the rest of the way through the half-open window, pushed off of the door or perhaps the roof and swam for the surface but, in her blind rush, she drove herself straight into invisible jello-like mud up to her shoulder and face.

She tucked and turned and tried to push off of the bottom but, instead, she only sank both of her feet into the sticky ooze up to her knees. Breast stroking hard with her arms and alternately yanking and kicking her legs in sheer terror she finally broke free from the gluey muck. Long since out of oxygen, in a nightmare of blind vertigo, she was hoping desperately that she was swimming upward and not sideways or down. In a few strokes her face unexpectedly broke the surface and she sucked in an enormous lung-full of life-giving air, while the stars above her exploded as brightly as any fireworks ever could.

Immediately exhausted, she was slowly treading water, catching her breath and regaining her orientation. She turned and saw Brad splashing toward her, free-styling with his head up to watch her in case she went under again.

"Are you okay?"

Ranya couldn't answer yet; she couldn't form coherent thoughts much less words. Her lungs still burned as she heaved fresh cool air in and out.

"Here, just hold on." Brad took her hands and turned so that she could rest against his back while he breast-stroked for the shore. They crawled through black mud at the water's edge, and he helped her up the sharply angled slope of the bank. In the flashing red and yellow lights of the T intersection, he noticed that she had lost one of her reef shoes, but otherwise she seemed all right.

The pickup truck was waiting there on the side of Route 17 by the canal, and they tumbled into the back again. They were soaking wet, muddy, cold, and ecstatic to be alive. Phil Carson lifted the tailgate and dropped the rear window, then went around and climbed into the cab's passenger side. The truck pulled out and they returned the way they had come. Brad and Ranya sat together with their backs against the front of the truck bed, watching as the flashing red light marking the intersection by the canal gradually diminished in the distance.

After a little while, Ranya began rubbing her right leg. "God this hurts!" Brad found a flashlight and shined it on the front of her upper thigh; they saw a pair of bleeding red semicircles the size of a plumb. "Oh, that bastard bit me! That freaking bastard bit me!"

"I thought he was dead drunk in the back seat?"

"That's what I thought, too. I guess the water sobered him up quick enough."

"You had to fight him off?"

"Going out the window, yeah, I had to fight him off." Ranya was using her dry t-shirt as a towel to wipe off the wound. "That freak bit me, but I got out, and he didn't."

A few hours later Brad was lying on his side, snuggled tightly against Ranya's back under warm blankets, but the circumstances were anything but romantic. They were both trying to sleep on a single narrow berth in the cramped forward cabin of the work boat which was taking them up the Chesapeake Bay. He was in a borrowed set of mechanic's coveralls; she was back in her jeans and gray sweater. The wooden work boat had to have passed within only a few miles of Guajira, but instead of spending the night sailing out to the open Atlantic, he was aboard a stranger's boat as it motored north toward Washington, pondering how he had been talked into taking part in this new operation.

He knew how the plan had been hatched, around the kitchen table upstairs at the boat house. After George Hammet's complete breakdown and stunning confession, they had climbed the stairs to the kitchen, to decide what to do with the information their prisoner had revealed to them.

They agreed that the media would do nothing with the revelation. It would be totally ignored or, at best, immediately relegated to "black helicopter" conspiracy theory fantasy land, and summarily dismissed to the outer fringes of the internet tin-foil-hat chat rooms.

Certainly, it was not an option to take what they had learned to the FBI or the Justice Department. Federal agents were the source of the current troubles; it was a given that the federal government would never take meaningful public action against some of their own who were involved in such a high level debacle. Certain especially ruthless factions within the government would, undoubtedly, act on Hammet's information by killing the messengers, and posthumously destroying their reputations.

One of the men at the kitchen meeting was Barney Wheeler; the older man Brad had passed the note to at Lester's Diner what seemed like years ago. Tonight Phil Carson was calling him "Rev," as he was using aliases for all of them.

Wheeler brought up the example of TWA Flight 800, and how over 200 eyewitnesses had clearly and unquestionably seen a surface-to-air missile rising to strike it. The federal government had had no trouble dismissing all of the eyewitnesses, including other professional pilots, in favor of the theory that a mysterious fuel tank spark had been responsible for the 747 crashing off of Long Island.

Dismissing the far-out conspiracy theories of a gang of right-wing kooks, and the coerced testimony of a kidnapped federal agent, would be a far easier task than turning a heat-seeking missile seen by 200 witnesses into the first and only fuel tank spark to ever bring down a passenger jet. In the case of the Stadium Massacre, the lie had been made even simpler for the government and the media, because they had already been provided with the dead culprit, the infamous hate-mongering racist militia activist Jimmy Shifflett.

After much discussion and debate over several pots of coffee, their group decision was to drive a knife straight into the belly of the beast, since they alone knew precisely where and when and how to strike. So only a day after being rescued from the torture chamber by this unlikely team, Brad found himself being swept along with them, unwilling to detach himself from Ranya, and unable to bow out of their plan. "Thanks for saving my life guys, but I've got to go now. See you later," was simply not a viable option, as much as he wished it could have been.

After they deep-sixed Hammet, the blue pickup truck had driven for another half hour and deposited the three of them, Brad, Ranya and Phil Carson, by abandoned railroad tracks in a forgotten coal yard overrun by weeds. Barney Wheeler met them there and led them down to a series of rotting industrial wharfs and piers using a flashlight. There was no way to determine where they were. Brad could only tell that whatever river they were on was about a half mile wide, judging by the scattering of lights on the opposite shore.

Tied up at the end of a partially-collapsed ancient commercial dock was a white Chesapeake Bay "deadrise" workboat about thirty five feet long. It was built in the classic style, which meant it could have been five or fifty years old. Like all Chesapeake Bay deadrise boats, she had been constructed from local wood "by eye" without written plans, and her only beauty lay in her utility at harvesting crabs and oysters safely and economically in all seasons.

There was a high nearly plumb vertical bow, a small slanting foredeck, and a substantial pilothouse with three square plexiglass windows along each of the sides and the front. A long cockpit with low gunnels for working oyster beds and crab traps took up almost half of the length of the vessel. Most of the cockpit from the rear of the pilothouse aft to the stern of the boat was protected from the sun and rain by a simple wooden ceiling supported at its back corners by wooden posts. In the center of the cockpit, a refrigerator-sized engine box stood by itself like a rectangular island; its cover served as both a seat and a work bench.

Ranya was assisted in climbing over the side into the cockpit by an elderly white-haired man, who turned out to be the captain and owner of the vessel named the "Molly M." Once they were aboard, the boat was untied and they got underway. Brad was given a clean dry set of coveralls to change into in the pilothouse; Ranya had already changed back into her dry clothes in the truck during their ride from the canal. After he changed into the dry clothes, they sat on top of the engine box facing aft as they motored up the calm river. An ebb tide gave them an extra knot or two. Brad could see the current dragging against anchored navigation marker buoys, and after a while he guessed they were on the South Branch of the Elizabeth River.

Ranya began shivering; they were both chilled from their swim in the canal, so while they were motoring up an industrialized stretch of river lined with shipyards and factories they went inside the pilothouse, which was filled with cigarette and pipe smoke. By the dim light of the engine instruments, they could make out Carson and Wheeler sitting across a small dinette table on the port side; Carson's face was visible in the orange glow of his cigarette. The aged captain was sitting atop what looked like a bolted-down bar stool behind the steering wheel on the starboard side, where he had a clear view of the navigation lights on the river ahead.

Ranya told them she was freezing. She was visibly shaking. The old skipper offered her his cabin, and reached over and unlatched the low double doors to the forward compartment. Ranya ducked below without another word, and fell onto the narrow berth which occupied the entire port side of the hull in the small triangular space.

Brad momentarily weighed the company of men, liquor and tobacco against Ranya's warm and soft curves, and he slipped below after her without asking the captain's permission, latching the doors behind him. He found a folded blanket, spread it over Ranya on the berth, and then slid underneath with her, kissing the back of her neck and snuggling against her, until she stopped shaking and gradually fell asleep.

The bunk was too narrow for them to change positions easily. Ranya was pressed against the wooden planks and frames of the hull; Brad was perched tenuously next to the bunk's inner edge. He was only able to grab snatches of sleep while they left the calm waters of the Elizabeth River and entered the choppy bay and began to drive against its Maryland-born swells.

For hours the Molly M plunged up and over the waves, with spray periodically smacking across her forward deck above them, while her old hull creaked and groaned as plank worked against plank. All through the long night, her diesel engine thrummed on with a comforting cadence. After a time Brad also slept, with the dark waters of the Chesapeake Bay rushing along the hull, just on the other side of an inch of forty year old pinewood.

Guajira was the only yacht anchored in the lagoon of a palm-fringed atoll, floating twenty feet above a vibrant coral reef, her blue hull-bottom guarded by a school of black and yellow striped angelfish. Ranya was standing up on the small teak platform he had bolted onto the front of the stainless steel bow pulpit. She held her graceful arms straight out to each side, her wet skin glistened in the sunlight as she prepared to dive again. She was wearing only a narrow black French-cut bikini bottom, which framed her hips and slender waist to Brad's utter satisfaction as he watched her from below. The tropical tradewind raised goose bumps on her skin; she had no tan lines remaining from her long-since forgotten bikini tops.

Ranya folded her long legs and bent into a crouch, and then she sprang far out over the glassy water in a classic swan dive. She brought her hands together in front when she pierced the surface; her hair streamed behind her shoulders amidst a cascade of trailing bubbles. He was below her holding onto Guajira's anchor chain, watching her slide through the pale turquoise water. Ranya let her arms trail to her sides as she glided down toward him, her amber eyes locked onto his, a mermaid figurehead come beautifully to life.

Brad was awakened sharply when the old workboat's bow was slammed hard by an oncoming wave. He was lying on his back now with

Ranya pressed tightly against his side. Her cheek was warm against his shoulder; her loosely spilling hair was tickling his face and one of her legs was thrown over between his. The square deck hatch a few feet above them had a circular glass skylight, and it was just growing light outside. Every few minutes a wave slapped the hull in a way that sent spray across the foredeck, blurring his view of the sky as water ran off the glass.

Phil Carson was asleep on the opposite berth along the starboard side of the cramped forward compartment, his back to them beneath another gray army blanket. Phil Carson, the man who had convinced them to head up the bay to face more unknown dangers, instead of simply fleeing aboard Guajira to the safety of the wide Atlantic.

It was dawn, they had been powering along at the same engine RPM for over five hours, and Brad estimated they must be halfway up the Chesapeake. Their first destination was another anonymous safe house, where they would make the final preparations for their mission.

He was glad to be traveling with Ranya, and he was on the water, but he was heading in the wrong direction on the wrong boat. But there was no backing out. There was no way to extricate himself from the operation without losing Ranya, and being made to feel like a coward in the eyes of Phil Carson and Barney Wheeler. He was literally along for the ride now, a conscripted foot soldier in the new American "dirty war."

And he had to admit that Carson made a strong case for going after Wally Malvone, the BATF official who had engineered the Stadium Massacre, and thrown America into bloody turmoil. With a good plan and the element of surprise, there was every reason to believe the new mission would go down just as smoothly as the one which had resulted in his own rescue. And that was the bottom line: they had rescued him when they did not have to, and now in return he owed them his temporary allegiance.

But what the hell, it only meant a delay of a few days, and then it would be over and behind them forever. In two weeks, Guajira would be safely anchored in a distant corner of the Bahamas Far Out Islands, and Ranya could begin to work on her all-over tan. Swimming, snorkeling and lovemaking would be the only items on their daily agenda in that sparkling azure and aquamarine world... They would spear lobster and grouper and eat better than any royalty, listening to Enya sing Caribbean Blue while sipping ice-cold Cuba Libres in Guajira's cockpit. Some of that strong Jamaican cash crop might even drift their way, to deepen their pleasure...

Abraham's Bay on remote Mayaguana Island would be ideal, and it would be a good jumping-off point for the Windward Passage between Cuba and Haiti, the gateway to the Caribbean.

46

The Molly M was tied across the end of a fifty foot long wooden dock like the top of a capital letter T, the mid-day breeze sending ripples against her white hull. The dock extended from the navigable center of the tidal creek, across the shallows and marsh grass up onto dry land. The creek could have been any one of the hundreds of minor tributaries branching off of the James, the York, the Rappahannock or the Potomac Rivers. In fact, the Molly M was tied to a dock on a nameless creek just two bends and a short reach away from the Chesapeake Bay itself, near the mouth of a lesser river called the Piankatank, located halfway between Norfolk and Maryland.

Two hundred feet inland on the highest point of ground nearby, all of six feet above the high tide line, stood an impressive modern two story stilt house which would not have looked out of place along the beach front in Nag's Head or on Nantucket. The only hint that the house might possibly be occupied on this Wednesday was the presence of the old crab boat tied up at the end of the dock. There were no people outside or cars visible around the property.

Inside the house it was lunch time, and the conspirators sat around the comfortable living room eating sandwiches while watching the George Hammet confession video. The camcorder used to produce the tape sat on the tan-colored carpet, wired directly to the television with dubbing cables. They watched and rewatched Hammet's humiliating breakdown with no sense of triumph, no smugness or gloating, but with critical eyes, striving to draw out the elusive fact or the unmade connection.

The room was the largest in the house, with picture windows on two sides looking out over an expanse of dunes, marshland, meandering creeks and sparkling coves. Its furnishings matched the casual elegance of the exterior of the house; relaxed luxury in beiges and blues and light natural woods. Brad and Ranya shared a richly upholstered love seat, but the atmosphere in the room was deadly serious and they avoided making any public display of their affections.

Phil Carson and Barney Wheeler sat on opposite ends of a matching sofa facing the forty-inch television, which occupied most of a wall-dominating sandalwood entertainment center. They were a pair of unremarkable gray-haired men somewhere past fifty, casually dressed in jeans and t-shirts, in keeping with the vacation setting of the waterfront home. Wheeler had a neatly trimmed beard and wore wire rimmed glasses, while Carson needed a shave and smoked incessantly. Road maps and nautical charts covered most of the glass-topped coffee table between the sofa and the TV.

Former STU Team detainee Victor Sorrento was in the kitchen, watching the replay of the video from the other side of the breakfast bar. He was now being called Tony. Carson was the only one of the group who knew his true name and the details of how he had come to join their group. He had not come up the bay on the Molly M. He had been dropped off at the house by the older couple who were now out on a shopping trip in their pickup truck, buying items the group would need to conduct their mission. Where "Tony" had gone before and after Hammet's ordeal and interrogation was not discussed; the conspirators maintained a wide zone of personal confidentiality.

Their host at the waterfront house was easily the best dressed among them, wearing a light blue dress shirt, khaki slacks and tasseled loafers. "Chuck" was also the tallest of the men in the room, standing several inches over six feet. Like Carson and Wheeler, he was also late middle-aged, but seemingly in good shape, with a tan outdoorsy face and neatly groomed black hair sprinkled with gray. His cobalt-blue BMW 745 was parked out of sight beneath the house; the first floor was set ten feet above the sand in recognition of the fact that the sea level would occasionally exceed the height of the dune.

Chuck had already been at the house when the others arrived on the Molly M in the early morning; it was unclear if he was the owner of the place or merely had access to it. Brad guessed he was a realtor or a rental agent, and the house was a seasonal luxury rental. It was a two story contemporary beach style house, built on a secluded multi-acre property with its own private driveway and dock. Brad guessed the place would rent for several thousand dollars a week during the summer, but that it might be conveniently empty and available mid-week in late September.

This fit a well-established pattern which he was familiar with from his extensive reading about espionage, terrorism, and clandestine operations. He knew that realtors and other property managers were extremely valuable support assets to all types of underground organizations, because they could inconspicuously arrange short and long term safe houses and caches, and often without leaving a paper trail. This type of support activity was more widely understood these days, mainly as it related to Muslim-operated hotels and motels providing covert havens for members of Islamic terror cells.

The role which real estate agents could play was still less well known, but Brad had guessed at the arrangement as soon as he had seen the fully furnished yet isolated house, with only generic seascape art pieces on the walls, and no personal family touches. The bare exterior of the refrigerator, devoid of souvenir magnets and photos, was a dead giveaway.

Chuck was the only one of the conspirators that Brad just couldn't figure out. Admittedly, he had only met him a few hours ago, and it was not the type of social environment which lent itself to sharing life stories. First-names-only was an unstated rule of the house, and it was assumed that all of the names were false. Chuck just seemed to enjoy too comfortable and affluent of a life, right down to his gold Rolex watch, to be consorting with an armed resistance cell. He also seemed nervous; he was in and out of the tan-colored leather recliner, frequently looking out the windows between the closed inner curtains.

But Phil Carson obviously trusted him enough to use the house, and Carson was the group's single unifying linchpin, so that was that. Brad guessed that some old Army relationship was at work, perhaps some ancient debt from the long ago jungle war was being repaid. It seemed unlikely that Carson and Chuck moved in the same social circles these days, but then Phil Carson was a consistently surprising man.

Not present at the meeting was the Molly M's skipper, who was sleeping aboard his crab boat down at the dock. At 90-plus years old, no one begrudged Captain Sam his rest after navigating his boat up the bay half the night. Anyway, whatever role old Sam might play in the operation would be limited to driving the boat, and the less he knew about the details the better.

The video lasted twenty minutes, split between Carson and Wheeler asking questions off camera, and Hammet's replies. Hammet was seen from the shoulders up, wearing a white t-shirt with a plain white sheet tacked up behind him. The lighting was terrible, the picture repeatedly flared and moved in and out of focus, but his words were completely understandable. The video ended abruptly and the screen went solid blue.

Carson asked, "Robin, can you transfer the camcorder tape to a regular VHS one, but without our questions on it? I want a version with just George's answers, and none of our voices."

"No problem. Are blank tapes already on the shopping list? You don't want to record over old tapes from here. I'm pretty sure they can recover the old stuff from under any new video, and you don't want that."

Chuck offered, "Look under the television, there might be some blank tapes down there."

Ranya knelt on the plush carpet and began pulling open drawers. Among the DVDs and old movie cassettes she found a single blank VHS tape still in its wrapper. The men all gazed at her snug denim-clad figure admiringly, but privately.

"Once I make a new master, it'll be easy to make lots of copies. There's another VCR in the bedroom we're in. I can bring it out here and hook them together. The more copies we make, the better. Put more blank tapes on the shopping list; Archie and Edith can pick them up anywhere on their next trip."

"Why don't you just call them up?" asked Chuck. "They can pick them up now."

"We're not using any phones here, remember?" said Carson. "No land lines, no cell phones, no two-way radios, all right?"

"Yeah, I remember. No problem."

From the kitchen Tony asked, "Do you really think the television networks will ever play the video? I don't think they'll touch it with a ten foot pole. George doesn't look too good, his face is all puffy, and now he's, ahh, 'missing.' How are the networks ever going to play something like that? Especially now, with 'heroic federal agents' getting sniped at by 'right wing terrorists' every day?"

Brad offered, "What about TOP News? They might go for it. They might report some of what George said, or at least follow up on some of his information, and let the audience decide."

"You're dreaming, Bob," said Barney Wheeler, using Brad's current name of convenience. "That tape is radioactive. They won't run it; they won't even look at it. Not even TOP News."

"What about the internet?" asked Ranya, settling down next to Brad on the love seat again. "It'll probably edit down to about ten minutes when I'm finished. We can release it on the net and just let it go from there."

Carson let this discussion of the tape, the media, the internet and the "sheeple's" probable reaction to it continue for another minute. "Okay, be that as it may, that's all off in the future. Hammet is still 'missing' at this point, so let's put the new tape aside for now and get back to Malvone. Robin can take care of making the new tapes. All I care about Hammet at this point is what he had to say about Malvone. The tape by itself just isn't enough proof, and it was obviously made under some kind of duress."

Standing by a window, Chuck asked, "Where is this guy, this George Hammet?"

"He's not available," replied Carson.

"Not available? Why not?"

"He's just not. That's all there is to it." Carson didn't feel the need to educate Chuck on the fact that 'irregulars' like themselves couldn't afford to drag prisoners around, especially not with the ever present risk of highway checkpoints. Instead, he just stared hard at him for a moment from the sofa while he took a deep drag on his cigarette and then exhaled a plume of gray-blue smoke. "What we need to do now is decide on our exact goals for this operation, and then plan and proceed toward that goal."

Wheeler said, "Well, just wasting Malvone won't be enough. We need to snatch him, and pick up all the documents we can at the same time. We can rule out grabbing him at their new base in Waldorf; that place will be crawling with jack-boots any time he's there. Obviously, forget about

Washington: it's wall to wall with those digital face-scanning cameras, and there's a checkpoint on every other block. So we're back to his house on the river."

Carson said, "I've already gotten some good intell on that place." He seemed to have friends almost everywhere available to assist them with a boat, a fast station wagon, a belt-fed machine gun or a local recon report. "We can't even think about bringing the guns up there by road. With that bridge in Washington still out, the route 301 bridge over the Potomac at Dahlgren is an absolute zoo. The toll plaza on the Maryland side is just one gigantic checkpoint, like the border crossing at Tijuana. The local roads leading into Malvone's place are a maze, and to cap it off he's got a private driveway with a security gate and a camera. There's no fast way out of his neighborhood, and after you get out you're still trapped on the Maryland side of the Potomac, between DC and that 301 bridge.

"So that takes us back to the river, all the way in. Here's how I see it: we'll use two boats, and a vehicle on the Virginia side. The first boat goes ahead as a scout, and it's clean as a whistle. No guns, no nothing. The guns and the tactical gear will all be hidden on the Molly M, following a few miles behind. If there're any security checks on the river, the scout boat radios back, and we transfer all the weapons ashore to the vehicle. Then the vehicle uses back roads to bypass the river security, and further up river we transfer the guns back to the Molly."

"I assume you're talking about Archie and Edith when you say the vehicle," said Tony. "But what if they get stopped by a FIST highway checkpoint?"

"They won't. All the way up, they'll be going four times faster than the boats, so they'll constantly be driving ahead and backtracking. They'll be using small secondary roads almost all the time, and they'll know if there are any checkpoints. So far, what we've seen of the FIST checkpoints is they're on the interstates and major routes, not the smaller local roads."

Brad nodded. "So the weapons will always be on the river, or on the Virginia land side, right up until we're in the target area in Maryland."

"Exactly. That's the idea," said Carson, stubbing out his cig-arette. "We'll play three-card-Monte with the guns, right up until we're in the objective area. Then for the exfil we'll leapfrog south in reverse, on the boats or the vehicle on the Virginia side."

Tony asked, "What about having another car on the Maryland side, just in case?"

Carson shrugged. "We just don't have the manpower. We're cutting it right to the bone as it is. I'm working on getting a couple of switch cars left here and there; we'll see how that goes. Obviously there's a risk, a big risk, we all know that…

"But what the hell, after what we've done already, there's a risk even if we just stay at home hiding. Personally, I think it's worth it to snatch Malvone, and get a chance to lay out the whole Stadium Massacre, just blow it wide open. How they did it, why they did it, all the details right from their own mouths. Two separate videos, even if they're made under duress, that'll be powerful stuff. In the long run, that's probably our best protection. And even if it's not, it's still worth it, at least to me."

Barney Wheeler had gotten up and was standing near the window overlooking the winding creek below the house. Thin cream-colored inner sheer curtains let the light through, but prevented anyone who might be observing from afar from seeing them inside. The sun was almost directly overhead, and the windows were in deep shadow beneath the wood shingle roof which extended over the encircling balcony of the house. He asked, "How sure was Hammet about the Friday night poker game? He said he was only at Malvone's house once, right?"

Carson replied, "Look, I know it's slim, but it's the best we have to go on. Once we get right in the area we'll put eyeballs on his place, and we'll be ready to change the plan. Maybe we'll have to take him in the early hours after he goes to sleep...but he'll probably have all kinds of security systems activated once he goes to bed. I still like the idea of busting into a drunken poker game, and catching all of the STU leaders in one room."

"Do it like you did the rescue, come in with the bright lights and blind them!" said Brad.

Ranya added, "Better yet, come in screaming 'FBI! Search warrant!' I think that'll freeze 'em up, at least for a few seconds. After all the arsons and murders they've done, in the back of their sick minds they've got to be a little worried. I mean, the 'Special Training Unit' is operating way, way over the line, even for the feds."

"What line?" asked Tony, from the kitchen. "I don't see any line any more. Where do you see a line? I just see a homeland security police state! FBI, DEA, ATF, and now the 'Special Training Unit.' One jack-booted Gestapo thug is as bad as another. Face it: they shredded the Constitution with those so-called Patriot Acts. They crossed the line a long time ago, and they never came back. First it was just so they could go after Muslim terrorists, remember? Now it's for everybody."

"Maybe so," said Wheeler, "but don't forget about inter-agency rivalry. Even in a police state, you can bet the FBI still hates the ATF. Probably even more, now that the ATF moved to Justice, and the ATF's Special Training Unit is operating way out in the lead. Robin's right, yelling 'FBI' is smart; that'll get their attention and buy us some seconds, and seconds is all we'll need."

"Okay, let's assume we get to that point," said Carson. "We've got a room full of STU leaders face down on the floor. We only want Malvone. According to Hammet, only those two knew about the stadium."

"I say shoot 'em," said Tony. "Take Malvone and shoot the rest, they're all dirty. We've got suppressed weapons. Shoot 'em and burn the place down, just like they did the Edmonds, just like they were going to do to Bob and me." He was using Brad's nom d'guerre, the only name he knew him by. Even though they had been imprisoned out of sight of one another in the same room at the air field, they had not been able to talk until meeting in the halfway house. "They're big boys. They're already murderers, and what goes around, comes around. Shoot 'em! Don't leave anybody to come after us later, and send all the other jack-booted thugs a message at the same time. We pay your salaries Goddamn it, so don't screw with us!"

The room went quiet at Tony's embittered outburst. After a few moments Chuck, the realtor, said quietly, "Look…I just…I can't be part of cold-blooded murder."

Carson lit another cigarette. "Chuck," he said softly, "it's these STU Team guys who're cold-blooded killers. They kidnap, they torture, they burn people alive. Save your pity. Those guys aren't soldiers, they weren't drafted, they're all volunteers. And this is real life; this isn't Roy Rogers, you can't just shoot the guns out of the bad guys' hands. These guys are going to have real guns that shoot real bullets, you can count on it. And Chuck, I know you remember what that's like."

Wheeler added, "He's right, save your pity for the innocent. This is a war now! We've all seen the news. Agents are getting shot every day, and so are our people. They were going to kill Leo Swarovski right in his bed. They were going to kill Bob and Tony and frame them as assassins. They burned Edmonds's family and called him a terrorist—they even blamed his own family's death on him! That's how these guys play...they play dirty. Real dirty.

"So maybe now we're in a dirty war, but it's still a war! They started it; now we're just playing by their own dirty rules. These 'Special Training Unit' guys are like Nazis; they're just killers, no matter who signs their paychecks. So the way I see it, it's not murder to kill them, it's justice being done. And anyway, we won't be able to handle more than one prisoner on the exfil. That's Malvone, and the rest of them don't know anything about the stadium, so they can't help us.

"But even so," Wheeler continued, lightening his tone, "maybe it'll be better to keep the others alive. With Hammet and Garfield and Malvone all missing, and Malvone's house burning down, there's bound to be a major investigation. There's got to be some serious media coverage. They can't keep this quiet; they can't cover this up. It'll be too big. Then, after that, if we put both of their confession videos on the internet, videos with all the details that only the real stadium snipers could know, it's got to blow up into a network story.

"Once that happens, the other STU leaders will talk to save their asses. They'll want to shift all the blame for the Stadium Massacre onto Malvone and Hammet to clear themselves. And if we grab Malvone's computers, if we get his computer discs, his notebooks, his palm pilots, everything we can find, well, we might get lucky and find more documentary proof there too."

"Okay, all right," said Chuck, reluctantly agreeing. "I can deal with it, whatever happens. Just leave me out of the planning, don't tell me any more. I mean, I don't need to know what you're going to do. Phil, how about if I just leave now, and come back after you all take off tomorrow? You're leaving tomorrow, right?"

Carson said, "Actually, Chuck, what I had in mind was you driving the scout boat. You've still got your boat, don't you?"

"What?" Chuck was taken aback by the question, and its implications. "Yeah, I still have it, but I never thought, I mean I never planned, on doing..."

"It's just a short cruise up the bay. Up and back, no guns, no nothing. You'll be a couple miles ahead of the Molly, that's all. A piece of cake. Okay?"

The well-dressed realtor felt five pairs of hard eyes on him. "I—I guess so. All right. Sure, I can do it. I've been all the way up the Potomac on my boat before; it's not so unusual. I'll create a client and find some waterfront property that I'm checking out."

Phil Carson said, "That's the spirit, Chuck."

The President had a late lunch in the White House with his CSO Wednesday afternoon. He was grim faced as he stabbed at his crab salad. "Harvey, I just heard from Sheridan. Two more agents were killed today. One of them was shot down at Quantico, right in the middle of the God damned Marine base!"

"Jesus! Right on Quantico? Did they catch the shooter?"

"Are you kidding? They don't even know where the bullet came from! And do you want to hear the real topper? The guy who was shot was the FBI's chief sniping instructor! How's that for ironic?"

"Damn! How many's that make so far?" asked Harvey Crandall.

"Counting Reston, or just since the Fed List came out?"

"Reston? That was different, that was a raid. How many since after the list?"

"Twelve new ones, but there's no way to tell if they were already targeted, or if they were only killed because of the list," said the President. "Harvey, it's getting bad, really bad. The more we go after these militia types, the more the gun nuts are going crazy! And now with this list…"

"But they've stopped the list, haven't they? I mean, people can't get it on the internet anymore, can they?"

"That's what they tell me. They say the NSA's got a handle on it. But the genie's already out of the bottle! We have to assume that every lunatic with a rifle's got a copy of the list already, or that they can find it somewhere."

"Any luck tracing it?"

"Not yet," replied the President. "New England they think, maybe. But at least we've managed to keep the Fed List story out of the media. We've had almost 100% compliance with our, uh, 'request' not to report it. That's been just about the only bright spot in this whole fiasco: those media controls, or, uh, I should say 'guidelines', they seem to be working. Thank God for the Patriot Act! The media, the networks, they all understand how important it is to not endanger federal agents by spreading this story around…and of course, they don't want to get their FCC licenses yanked."

"But the story's already on the internet; didn't the Sledge Report run it?"

"He did, but he pulled it after the AG talked to him. Anyway, as long as it's just on the internet it doesn't matter; it can't get any real traction. The serious media won't touch it."

"What about talk radio?"

"So far, so good. The shootings are all still being covered as local stories. That's what I'm being told."

Crandall said, "But we've got to plan for the story to break sooner or later. Patriot Act or not, the whole Fed List story's bound to get out." He speared another chilled jumbo shrimp from his sterling silver bowl, dunked it into the special White House cocktail sauce and gobbled it down in one bite. "Did you ever think it would get this far?"

"What? No way. Honestly, I never even considered the possibility that it could…spin out of control like this. But hey, they started it! They started it right at that God damned football game! It all started there, so everything since the Stadium Massacre is on them! Everything!"

"But who are they? Who's 'them'? The people behind the Stadium Massacre, or all of the maniacs that are taking pot shots at our agents now?"

"The gun nuts, the militias, the right wingers, the Constitution fanatics, all of them!" exclaimed President Gilmore.

The CSO shook his head wearily. "That's a lot of people. That's millions of people."

"Well, they started it! I didn't ask for this crap! They started it, God damn it!" President Gilmore threw down his silver salad fork; it clattered off of his china plate and bounced onto the parquet floor. An unsmiling Navy Petty Officer in a starched white uniform swooped in, picked it up and replaced it with a new fork in one fluid movement.

The President waited until the sailor was back at his station by the galley service pass-through, and then he leaned forward and lowered his voice, regaining his composure. "Look, Harvey, I've got a lot of confidence in Sheridan. He's good at his job. But let's face it, the FBI just can't... I mean, it just isn't set up, institutionally I mean, to handle this kind of situation. They can't move fast enough, they don't have the right mindset. You know, they just can't do the kind of...dirty work that's needed to stamp this fire out. You follow me?"

"I think so."

"The only ones I've seen who know how to fight this new kind of war are in that ATF group. What's that guy's name? Malone?"

"Malvone. Walter Malvone."

"That's the man! Burning out that militia nest in Virginia, that was terrific! Pulling those assault rifles and bazookas out of the ashes, that was some great television. That was fantastic! I mean, let's face it, this is just as much a media and PR war as anything else, so we need to see lots more TV like that! We need to send a strong message to the whole country! We need to shift the whole debate..." The President sipped his tall iced tea and continued.

"Harvey, the way I see it, it's not enough just to crack down on these gun nuts. We need to do it on TV. We need to discredit them; we need to disgrace them even while we're wiping them out. We need to make the rest of the country hate their stinking guts, so they'll call that GUN-STOP number and inform on their own fathers and brothers if that's what it takes! I swear to God, I think this Malvone is the only one who really understands just what kind of a media war we're in!"

"Yes sir, I agree, but there's an element of risk as well."

"Harvey, harsh times call for harsh measures. We'll never get a handle on this thing fighting by the Marquis de Queensbury rules; we have to fight fire with fire. I've gone over his paper again. I want you to pass the word to Malvone that he's got the green light directly from me. Give him a free hand in Maryland and North Carolina as well as Virginia as of today. Give him whatever he needs: budget, personnel, anything. I mean, it's a tiny group; the whole thing can't cost more than one F-22, right? Those gold-plated pieces of shit crash every other week, and we're still buying them, right? So keep it black, keep it off budget, keep it deniable, but get Malvone whatever he needs."

"Yes sir, it's already set up for complete deniability at every level. No matter how far anybody digs, it can't reach here."

"Good, good. That's essential, obviously. So tell Malvone to put it into high gear and start kicking some more ass like he did down in Virginia! Tell him I think he's doing a great job, and tell him I want to see more of it on TV, right away. Tell him I want 'gun collector' to be a dirty word, a national obscenity!"

Wally Malvone and the STU leaders spent the day exploring their new base in the Waldorf industrial park, and moving in their gear. Dinner was pizzas and cokes, eaten on their newly-delivered mahogany conference table, in a half-furnished office which smelled of newly-installed carpeting. Most of the office furniture had been delivered earlier in a Ryder truck, courtesy of their unseen financier, 'Mr. Emerson.' They were wearing casual clothes for the task of moving team equipment, computers, files and furniture into their new base, all except for Malvone who was in a dress shirt and suit pants, since he had just come from ATF Headquarters.

"So, what's the deal on Hammet?" asked Bob Bullard.

"Nothing yet, no word," replied Malvone. "He's probably dead, that's my guess. Somehow Fallon and Sorrento must've gotten the drop on them and took off in his Jeep. It's the only thing that makes any sense. But as far as I'm concerned, he never worked for us at all. He's Norfolk's problem. And when they get around to reporting him missing, it'll just go down as another federal agent murder. He's on the Fed List."

Jaeger said, "Well, that's one good thing about that damned list anyway. But what if he went to the Inspector General? What if he's ratting us out to the Office of Professional Integrity? That could get damned serious, even with your connections in the Senate."

"That's possible, I suppose, but not likely," said Malvone. "All five of them gone? I'm guessing Garfield and Hammet were killed right after they made him call Swarovski."

Shanks asked, "With Hammet out of the picture, are we still on track to form up a new team?"

"What? Oh, we sure are. We've gotten the go-ahead to move as fast as we can, both on the team expansion, and on our operations. We'll have to juggle them both; it's not going to be easy to break new guys into our system, even SRT guys, and maintain our operational tempo at the same time."

"Well at least we've got plenty of room here," said Silvari. "We could put five more teams into the space we've got, easy."

"Yeah, that's a fact. Crowding won't be an issue around here for a long, long time," said Malvone, smiling. "Bob, next week you're going to start recruiting new guys. Do you have an itinerary yet?"

"I'm working on it, boss. I'm going to hit all the Field Divisions and talk to the Special Response Teams, give them a recruiting pitch. And we've already got the list of SRT and FBI SWAT and HRT guys we generated in-house who want to come over. I think we can put together another two teams in a month. Personnel-wise, it's no problem. Getting the bodies won't be the hard part; it's going to be integrating them into the STU while we're still conducting ops at the same time."

"We're the SPD now, Bob, the SPD."

"I keep forgetting. The 'Special Projects Division.' I like that... And being at division level is going to really help."

"The name doesn't matter," replied Malvone. "We'll get anything we need, no matter what we're called. We've got the big green light all the way from the top, the very top...but forget you heard that."

"Heard what?" laughed Bullard.

Shanks said, "You should have seen us at Office Depot! We just about cleaned them out."

"Come on you guys, we've got to keep a low profile. People remember things like that. I know we're in a hurry, but don't make any big scenes in town."

"Wally," said Silvari, "we've got guys staying in motels all over the place because of that Fed List, and they want to know if their expense claims are going to be a problem. They're going to be running up some big tabs."

"No, no problem. Maximum per diem all the way, no hassles, for as long as it takes. How many of our guys are on the Fed List?"

"About half. The out-of-state guys aren't listed; it's all by home of record. What about you Wally? Did you make the list?"

"Nah, I lucked out. My home of record is still at my condo in Miami."

"You can't beat that Florida state income tax," said Silvari.

"You got that right."

"So Wally, are we still on for Friday night?"

"Sure, why not?"

Four shadows slid along the balcony in the darkness. Two stopped on the right side of the door, and two continued across to the hinge side. One of them stage-whispered "3-2-1-Go!" The door was jerked open and held all the way to the left side. A small cylinder was tossed into the room, and after a two second pause the man who threw it yelled "boom" with his eyes closed. Then he dashed through the open door, followed closely behind by the others.

Four brilliant flashlights turned the room into a carnival funhouse of colliding lights and shadows as loud voices simultaneously yelled, "FBI! Search warrant! Freeze! Down on the floor!" They were inside the room and in a position of control and dominance in under three seconds; they formed a rough line along the near wall, two on each side of the door. Carson was all the way to the left with his .45 caliber Tommy gun; Victor Sorrento was just to the left of the door with Hammet's 10mm MP-5. Ranya was just to the right side of the door with a suppressed 9mm MAC-10, and Brad was all the way to the right side of the room with another MAC. Each weapon was shouldered, sweeping back and forth in a tight arc covering a quarter of the room.

Carson found the light switch and turned on a table lamp in the living room of the halfway house. "Not bad, at least nobody fell down this time. Seriously, that was a lot better. Nobody walked into anybody's field of fire, but Tony and Robin, you still need to move further away from the door before you stop. Get cover, or keep moving, but don't stand there next to the door! Remember, the open door's the big bullet magnet. You already know that…what am I telling you for again? Okay, turn off your gun lights now—we don't have any spare lithium batteries."

Their Sure-Flash gun lights were older models, a gift from Jasper Mosby, who didn't ask Phil Carson what he needed them for. The four gun lights (with their etched numbers ground off) and one Def-Tek "distraction device" were the only items of actual SWAT gear Carson's little team had. Mosby had put them in a taped-up brown bag, and left them in the cleaning supply locker in the men's room of a Denny's restaurant in Hampton, where Archie had picked them up.

Carson continued with his instruction. "Remember, in Malvone's club room, there's a bar running along the right side wall. It's a natural hiding place for anybody who's behind it when we come in, so Bob, make sure you get all the way over there and clear it right away. Then you can use it for cover yourself. Or for concealment, anyway.

"The enclosed staircase along the back wall is good cover for any bad guys coming down from the kitchen, so as soon as everybody in the club room is neutralized, Robin, you just push right across and take your position at the bottom to secure it. Keep talking to us; let everybody know what you're doing. Everybody be aware that after we're all on line, Robin is crossing the room to control the stairwell, so let's not have any accidents. Don't sweep her with your guns. I know this room isn't set up the same as Malvone's club room, just keep the sketches in mind and it'll work out fine.

"If they comply and get right on the floor, we'll flex-cuff them one at a time. If not...well, just do what comes naturally. But don't shoot Malvone, or at least don't kill him! We need him to be able to talk; that's the whole point of the exercise. Then, once everybody in the room is secured, and that should only take a minute, we'll do a fast search of the house. We'll clear the whole place room by room in pairs, putting on all the lights as we go, and then we'll search it on the way back out. We're especially interested in his office; it's next to his bedroom on the same side of the hall. We'll take his computer, his laptop, zip drives, CDs, PDAs, notebooks, videos, cassettes, whatever we can find. Just shove it all in the bags, and we'll sort it out later."

Brad and Victor wore green vinyl white-water rafting bags with backpack straps over their other gear, ready to haul out the computers and other documents. All four of them had on matching black nylon warm-up suits, with their submachine guns hanging across their chests from strap slings around their necks. Each weapon held a pair of empty thirty round magazines for this practice session; one in the weapon's magazine well and one duct-taped in tandem for a quicker reload.

Three of them wore black fanny packs turned around to the front holding their extra submachine gun magazines, although they all realized perfectly well that if they needed more than the sixty rounds apiece in their first two magazines they would be "in a world of hurt," as Carson put it. Carson himself wore an old brown canvas rig on his chest, which carried six extra magazines in vertical pouches.

Even with all the submachine gun ammo, they all carried pistols as backups in generic black ballistic nylon holsters; the cheap holsters were picked up during Archie and Edith's afternoon shopping trip.

Unlike the Special Training Unit, and all of the other hundreds of American SWAT teams, they had not each been individually outfitted with thousands of dollars worth of "high speed" ergonomic ballistic nylon and Kevlar, which securely carried every weapon, ammo magazine and item of tactical gear in precisely the optimum location.

Instead, they had been outfitted by Archie and Edith, on short notice, from an eclectic variety of discount chain outlets and sporting goods stores. Instead of bulletproof Kevlar vests, they wore water ski vests for floatation during their waterborne infiltration. The thick ski vests were spraypainted flat black, and bulked up their profiles to make them resemble actual SWAT cops.

On their heads they wore skate boarding helmets, similar to ice hockey helmets, which were roughly the same shape as the compact kevlar helmets worn by many SWAT teams. Like the ski vests they wouldn't stop a bullet, but spraypainted black, they made the amateur assault team very closely resemble the real deal.

Their "flex-cuffs" were actually the largest size nylon wire-ties Archie had been able to purchase at an electrical supply company. Wire ties were the original plastic handcuffs, and they still worked just as well as the ones especially made for police.

To protect their eyes, they wore clear goggles picked up at a welding supply store. These were attached around the backs of their helmets with thick elastic straps, and also added to their overall SWAT team "look." On their hands they wore thin black driving gloves.

Anyone seeing them behind their bright gun lights, helmeted and dressed all in black, would assume that they were an actual law enforcement raiding party. Pros like the STU Team would then not aim for the chest or head, assuming they were clad in bullet-proof kevlar. This would increase their safety, by diminishing their target area. At least, that had been Phil Carson's reasoning, and no one had disagreed.

"Look at us," laughed Ranya, looking like a chubby Michelin-man ninja warrior. "How long do you think it'll take them to figure out we're not the FBI?"

Brad replied, "It doesn't matter. They'll be blind and disoriented from the flash-bang grenade, then all they'll hear is 'FBI!' and all they'll see is our gun lights. They'll never really see us at all; it'll work the same as it worked at the air field."

Carson said, "That's how it should work, but remember, that was only two guys, and they were dragging Edmonds across the floor when we came in. This time it'll probably be at least five bad guys. Just remember, Malvone's the big bald-headed older one with the thick mustache, so don't shoot him if you can avoid it! It's not going to be easy this time…with Hammet and Garfield missing, you can bet they'll all be jumpy, and armed to the teeth."

"Well, if I even see a gun, I'm shooting," said Tony, matter-of-factly.

"I wouldn't expect anything else," said Carson. "But if they go right to the floor, we'll hold our fire and flex-cuff them, got it?"

"Got it," said Tony.

Carson said, "These STU guys use flash-bangs and gun lights all the time; so maybe, just maybe they've trained against this kind of raid. I doubt it, but it's possible."

"Shooting civilians in bed is their style," replied Tony. "I don't see them training to go up against this kind of attack."

"Neither do I. But you can bet our gun lights will turn into bullet magnets pretty damn fast, if we don't get control in the first few seconds. So don't fool around. If they don't get on the floor, if you can't see their hands…well, don't take any chances. Two to the chest and one to the head, just in case they're wearing vests underneath their shirts. But try not to kill

Malvone! Bob's seen him before, so he'll make the positive ID. Once they're all cuffed or dead, we'll search the place.

"Okay, let's go back out on the balcony and run through it again. Move away from the door fast, don't sweep each other, and cover your sectors. And Robin, open it slower this time, the real one might be a lot heavier, or it might get hung up."

Ranya said, "You're assuming the door's going to be unlocked, like at the air field. What if it's not?"

"Then we'll improvise. We'll get them to open it up. We'll figure it out when we get there. There's a hundred ways to skin a cat, we'll figure something out. Okay, let's go outside and do it again. After we get it perfect, we'll test fire our weapons."

47

As a security precaution, Archie and Edith were limiting their time and possible exposure at the halfway house, so, Thursday morning after dropping off more gear, they quickly went over their updated list with Phil Carson and took off again.

The two most important items they brought (besides a carton of Marlboros for Carson) were a used twelve foot Zodiac-type inflatable boat and a 35 horsepower Evinrude outboard, found through the Boat Trader, and picked up in nearby Gloucester. Brad carried the outboard motor to a horizontal plank which was bolted between two of the pilings which supported the house, lowered it into position and screwed it down tight in order to test it.

Carson and Victor Sorrento unrolled the old rubber inflatable, and pushed the dozen large and small timber and plywood floorboard pieces into position, getting it ready to pump full of air. The outboard motor and the inflatable had been bought "as is" for cash, which was a reasonable tradeoff for obtaining the items with no documentation.

"Have you ever put one of these together before?" Carson asked Tony. "I don't even know if we have the right parts."

"Don't look at me; I thought you knew what you were doing."

Both men, on their hands and knees on the flaccid rubber boat, laughed at one another and at themselves, and threw down the varnished marine plywood parts they were holding. The wooden puzzle wasn't going together.

"You just have to be ten percent smarter than the boat," joked Brad. He was unreeling a green garden hose and dragging it over to the outboard. "What's that story about the monkey and the football?"

"Okay, Jacques Cousteau," said Carson, "how about we test the motor, and you put the boat together?" They got up and walked over to the back side of the house where the Evinrude was set up.

Brad waved the end of the hose at them. "You know what to do with this?"

"Nobody likes a smartass, Bob," said Carson, with a fresh cigarette dangling from his lip. He was wearing a plain white t-shirt, an old pair of cutoff jeans, and black rubber sandals. They had found a large plastic basket full of clothes, which had been left in the laundry room by previous guests (they presumed), and they had helped themselves to what they needed.

Brad handed Tony what looked like a pair of black suction cups the size of coffee saucers, attached to the ends of a U-shaped steel spring. One of the black rubber cups had a threaded attachment for a water hose.

"Stick these over the water intakes, get the water going, then you can see if it'll run without burning it up."

"I think we can handle it," said Carson. "Motors I understand. Just see if we have all the parts for the Zodiac."

After Brad walked back to where the boat had been unrolled, Tony asked Carson, "When's Chuck coming back? You really think he'll show? I know he's your friend, but there's something about that guy I don't trust."

"Chuck's okay. He'll be back. He's going to bring his boat around tonight, when it's time to pick you up."

"Are you sure? For all we know, he could be ratting us out right now as we speak."

"He won't. Chuck's not a bad guy, not really. And he owes me, big time. He's just nervous; he's not used to this kind of thing. He's been living the good life for a long time. Anyway, he's more afraid of us than the cops, trust me on that. He wouldn't cross us."

"We're still aiming to shove off at 0400?"

"Yeah, that's right. Four AM. Twelve hours in the Molly at ten knots gets us to Malvone's creek at five PM tomorrow."

"What kind of boat does Chuck have?"

"It's a small Baycruiser, about twenty five or thirty feet long. Kind of a pig, one of those tubby over-stuffed looking things as I recall. I only saw it once at the dock." Carson walked over to where Archie had dropped off the load, and picked up a squat five gallon red plastic gasoline tank and brought it back. He put it down and snapped its black fuel line into the back of the motor and began squeezing the bulb-pump.

"I wish I didn't have to go with Chuck. I'd rather go on the Molly with you guys." Tony threaded the end of the water hose into the back of one of the the black rubber cups, and slid them both over the sides of the engine shaft, where there were small cooling water inlets.

"Well, we need you on his boat, that's part of the plan. Chuck's going to speed it up at the end and get there a good hour before the Molly arrives so you can do your recon. Everything we do depends on your recon report. So we'll see if you remember what the Marines taught you about sneaking and peeking, right? And you're sure you can paddle the kayak without tipping over?" On one of their Wednesday supply trips, Archie and Edith had brought them a scuffed-up blue plastic kayak; now it was stashed up in the rafters under the house. They were keeping a very low profile, and were not venturing out into the open for anything that was not absolutely mission-critical.

"Give me a damn break. Of course I can paddle a kayak." Tony walked over to the hose faucet and turned it on, then returned. Water began to stream from the bottom of the motor around the black cups.

"Once I'm there I'll sneak in so close to his house, I'll be able to tell you what Malvone's been drinking by his breath."

"Just don't compromise the mission, Victor. Don't take any stupid chances. If you're spotted, the whole thing's screwed. Remember, you won't have a gun on the recon, not until you link up with us after dark." Carson pulled out the choke, twisted open the throttle on the tiller, and put his left hand on top of the engine cover.

"Not even a pistol? Why can't I take a pistol? They're still legal."

"It's not worth it. Chuck's boat has to be perfectly clean in case it's stopped. We just can't afford to get hassled; we can't take the risk. Hammet's night vision goggles will be all right—lots of rich boaters like Chuck have them now. And if you don't have a gun, I won't have to worry about you getting too close to Malvone's house on the recon. But listen, I want you to take a knife. Think you can use a knife?" Carson reared back and pulled the starting cord; the flywheel spun and the motor coughed briefly and died.

"Yeah, I think so."

"You think so? You gotta be sure. Did you ever stick anybody?" Carson paused, his right hand still on the handle of the cord, and stared into Victor Sorrento's eyes. "Tony" looked like a Hollywood mafia hood, but that didn't mean anything.

"Nope."

"Well, you might have to, and I need to know if you can do it or not. Stick somebody for real, stick them for keeps. Right in the kidney."

Victor took in a deep breath and exhaled. "I can do it. I can stab somebody. But I thought you didn't want me getting too close to the house on my recon? I didn't think I'd be sentry stalking. That's not how we planned it. You never briefed anything like that."

"Actually, Victor, I wasn't thinking about you killing a sentry at Malvone's." Carson lowered his voice. Brad's back was to them twenty feet away, where he was inflating the boat with a foot pump. "I was thinking about Chuck. If he gets cold feet, if he tries to take off or call the cops, anything like that...I want you to kill him and dump him in the river, and keep driving his boat." He pulled the rope again and the motor caught, settling quickly into its loud popping two stroke rhythm.

Brad had quickly assembled the floorboard pieces, and pushed the resulting single rigid deck into place under the limp side tubes of the inflatable. The twelve foot gray rubber raft had three separate air chambers in the U-shaped main tube, and a sausage-like inflatable keel between the plywood floor and the rubber bottom to give its hull some V shape. There was no yacht's name painted on the boat anywhere he could see. If they had to abandon it, it was doubtful whether law enforcement would be able to trace the craft through its many owners over the years, to Archie's cash purchase, and then to the plotters.

Brad filled the boat's side tubes with a foot pump, which was two textbook-sized pieces of plywood squeezing a rubber bellows with each step upon it. He attached the pump with a black rubber hose to each of the air valves in turn. The rubber boat was faded and patched, but it had evidently been properly maintained. He wondered about the veteran dinghy's former owners. Had it been towed across the Bahamas by a sailboat? Had it crossed the Atlantic stowed away in a cockpit locker? Or had it just kicked around the Chesapeake Bay for its decade or so of service?

The boat seemed to be holding air; he pumped it up hard, and it stayed that way. Phil Carson and Tony No-Last-Name had managed to get the outboard running. The house was just fifty or sixty yards from the edge of the water. After dark, they would carry the rubber boat and the rest of their gear down to the Molly M. Assembled, the boat and its floorboards together weighed about a hundred pounds.

It crossed Brad's mind that he could drag the boat by himself across the sand and down to the dock and launch it. He could clamp the outboard onto the thick wooden transom, and the five gallons of gasoline in the tank could get him a good chunk of the way down the Chesapeake to Guajira. One or two refueling stops at marinas along the way, and he could be aboard his sailboat in a couple of hours. The inflatable, with the weight of only one person on board, and with a 35 horse power motor pushing it, could make an easy 25 or 30 miles per hour across flat water. This was more than double the best speed of the Molly M, so pursuit wouldn't be possible.

The pump was lying on the plywood deck in the middle of the boat. He pulled the nozzle out of the port-side valve and stuck it into the one opposite and then continued stepping on it, evening out the pressure between the air chambers. Carson and Tony were talking over by the outboard motor; he couldn't hear what they were saying over the running engine. He knew that even after they went inside, it would be impossible to drag the inflatable to the water unnoticed in broad daylight. Not under the gaze of any watchers in the house.

Well, anyway, it was just an idle speculation. He had signed up for this one last mission, and now he was on for the ride. Ranya was gung ho to snatch Malvone, and he had agreed to go with her everywhere, to share the good and the bad forever, so that was that. It was settled. He wasn't going to take off now, not even if he had the opportunity.

But he still felt that even if they were successful, even if they grabbed Malvone, their mission wasn't going to stop the steadily grinding glacier-like progress of America's conversion into an all-out police state. The forces pushing America toward tyranny were too deep, too strong.

But God help him, he had given his word to Ranya. And for that matter to Phil Carson and the others, back at the river house after they had broken George Hammet. Incredibly, it seemed to him now, he had pressed his right hand over theirs on top of Barney Wheeler's old Bible on the kitchen table, when they had vowed to each other that they would push on to the bitter end. And now he wasn't going to be the weak link. He was going to carry his part of the load. He would hold up his end of the deal.

The grim truth was that there was no other way to bring Ranya back to Guajira, except straight through Malvone's house. And there was, in the end, no other way for him to keep his own self respect. With him or without him, Ranya and the others were going all the way.

So he would go with them and, perhaps, help salvage something of the American freedom he had always known and cherished.

The Eurohelo sales rep seemed pleased to meet with Wally Malvone on short notice, or at least he concealed his aggravation well. He didn't mention the hellish traffic he had undoubtedly been forced to endure to get from his Falls Church Virginia office, across Washington, and over to the Maryland side of the Potomac.

The irony of the principal United States sales representative for Europe's largest manufacturer of executive helicopters being forced to fight across town at ground level, from one side of the beltway to the other, was not lost on Malvone, but he avoided the temptation to make a joke out of it. He hadn't deliberately picked this meeting place in order to annoy the salesman; it was simply a matter of his own tight schedule coming first. He reckoned that if the salesman wanted to sell his helicopters, he'd make the trip, and he did.

They met in a darkened booth in the back of an upscale steak and ribs place set in a remote corner of a second-tier shopping center on Branch Avenue, outside of Andrews Air Force Base. Conveniently for Malvone, this was on the way between the new ATF Headquarters in northeast Washington, and the new Special Projects Division base near Waldorf. Malvone was already settled into the red velvet cushioned booth working on a vodka martini when the dapper Armani-suited Frenchman found him, still adjusting his eyes to the dimly lit room. Today he spoke with only a hint of his unpopular native accent, which Malvone had heard him dial up or down, depending on his audience.

"Hello, Mr. Malvone. So glad to see you again." The Frenchman understood the nature of the meeting and didn't reach out to shake hands; the time and place had been chosen to ensure anonymity. He laid his thin calfskin briefcase on the seat beside him as he slid into the booth. "I've brought the specifications and the figures you requested."

"Are you hungry? The food's actually not half bad here."

"Ahh, no, I already had lunch today," the Frenchman lied.

"That's fine, I'm skipping it too. A drink then?"

"Yes, a beer would be nice."

Their waitress instantly materialized to take their order. She was quite attractive in her tight black satin pants and a ruffled white blouse. The two men small-talked absently about the warm weather and the horrible traffic resulting from the beltway bridge sabotage, until she returned with a Heineken and another martini, and then left them alone again. There was no one even remotely within earshot, which was as Malvone had planned. The high seat backs and the position of their booth cut them off from the view of the few afternoon restaurant customers.

"Listen, Pierre, here's the bottom line. My group's ready to buy six helicopters as soon as they can be delivered. And probably more next year."

The Frenchman's face lit up. "Six? Well. And all six would be the model we have discussed, the VK-120?"

"That's right. Twin engine, sliding doors, 12 passengers. The FLIR package, the upgraded communications and electronics; everything we discussed. What would buying six at once do to the price?"

"Ah, one moment." The salesman quickly opened his briefcase and produced a yellow legal pad and a calculator and began jotting down columns of figures with a fountain pen. Then, he turned it around to face Malvone across the table. "I think the figure we may obtain for a package of six would be 2.2 million U.S. dollars each. This is depending on how the payment is structured, the training and support package and so on, and of course, the exchange rate when the contract is signed. That's a very good price, almost 500,000 dollars less than before for each helicopter."

Malvone nodded, looking over the numbers. "That's a good price, very fair. But you have to understand that I can only make a recommendation, although, frankly, I'll tell you, I'll have the most significant input in the selection process. Our funding is not being directed through normal procurement channels."

"Yes, I understand. We are very well accustomed to this type of arrangement."

"But I have to tell you, I'm still looking at Bell and Hughes. I know they don't have all of the capabilities of the VK-120, but their price is a lot lower, and with the currency exchange rate going the way it is…"

"Yes, I'm sure that's true; they are much cheaper helicopters. But they simply cannot compare with our product. It is as you say apples and oranges to compare them one to another."

"Pierre, I'm not arguing the point. I agree your product is better. But you must understand…there's a lot of pressure to buy American. Of course, if I push hard, if I make the case forcefully, I'll probably be able to convince our side to go with Eurohelo. And six helicopters is only the beginning of what we're going to need." Malvone paused, savoring the psychological poker game which was the unspoken subtext of their negotiation.

"Hmm… I see. So the key is to ensure that your side is totally convinced of the need to purchase the VK-120, because the American helicopters are simply inadequate for your mission."

Malvone waited a beat, and then said, "Yes. That would be the case. And also because the American companies are quite…rigid in their contracting procedures."

"Yes, I see. Well, Mr. Malvone—Wally—fortunately at Eurohelo we are not as…constrained…in our business practices as your American firms. You will discover that we are not rigid at all in our contracting process. Our brokerage fees and incentives and payment structures are not cut in stone; there is room to…negotiate these points. I am thinking that something can be arranged of a mutually beneficial nature." The Frenchman turned over his beer coaster and jotted 5% on it. He turned the coaster to face Malvone, and then he covered it with his hand.

Malvone said nothing, but took a cocktail napkin and wrote 12% on it with his own fountain pen.

The Frenchman stared, shook his head slowly and shrugged. "Impossible. Impossible. I don't know what you have heard, but that is not possible."

"It's very possible, and we both know it."

"I don't know it!" The Frenchman wrote down a new number: 8%. This three point move was a cave, so Malvone counter-offered with 10%, and finally the Frenchman wrote down 9%.

Malvone smiled at the last figure. "Pierre, I'm almost certain I'll be able to convince my side that it's absolutely imperative that we obtain the VK-120 for our group. I'll be in touch with you about how we can structure these…arrangements…in a mutually satisfactory way. I'm sure we're talking about a matter of days, not weeks, until a final agreement can be made and the contracts can be drawn up. Of course, I won't be a signatory to the actual contract, you understand."

"Of course. I understand completely."

"Well, that's settled then. The rest is just up to the pencil pushers, as we say. How many of the six can be delivered right away?"

The Frenchman managed to mask his elation at clinching the deal. "Two, by the end of next month. Is that satisfactory?" Malvone knew that the Frenchman had a reason to be elated. He had just sold six helicopters in a down market, at an inflated price, and he'd only needed to kick back 9%. This was substantially less than was customary in Africa and the Middle East, where there were so many more greedy hands to fill. Malvone was also elated. His own percentage of the 13 million dollar deal was well over a million bucks, tax free.

His years of planning and hard work and all of the bureaucratic infighting were finally paying off, big time. And these six helicopters were only the beginning; there were so many more deals to make.

But really, he reflected (after the Frenchman had left the restaurant first, to avoid the possibility of their being seen together) this wasn't about the money. Seven figure kickbacks were merely a fringe benefit of his position and power as a new member of the Senior Executive Service, in a black-budget counter-terrorism division.

It was about single-handedly turning the steering wheel of history. It was about leaving a mark that couldn't be erased. Perhaps someday he'd be able to tell his old mentor, Senator Jack Schuleman, how his greatest political victory had been won. He knew the Senator would understand.

A ski boat came down their creek at low speed, motoring south west from the mouth of Piankatank, heading home to its dock. Brad and Ranya were sitting close together on a comfortable porch glider, on a screened-in section of the second floor balcony outside their bedroom. They were holding hands and swinging slowly back and forth, while the setting sun turned the water a shimmering silver as the creek wound its way through the marshes.

They could only venture outside during the daylight hours as long as they stayed within the confines of the screened balcony areas, and kept a low profile. The house was still meant to be seen as unoccupied by any of the distant line-of-sight neighbors across the creek. The Molly M tied up to their dock was a typical Chesapeake Bay work boat, and was as close to invisible in these waters as any craft could be. The plotters stayed inside or under the house during the day; they were going to load the boat for their mission only after nightfall.

A family was coming in on the ski boat, parents and school age kids in colorful bathing suits and t-shirts. "Look at them," Brad said. "Not a care in the world. I wonder what that's like."

"It seems like a long time ago," she said. "So damn long ago."

"It must be nice. Even after we get out of here, after we get down to the islands, we'll still be looking over our shoulders."

"Brad, I didn't ask for any of this."

It was a sore subject and he let it drop. It would only lead to painful memories of the murder of her father and all of the rest that followed, and far too many tears had already been shed. The boat passed out of their sight where the creek wound behind their house.

He said, "We should try to sleep after dinner, after we load up the boat. We'll be up at three AM, and it's going to be a long day."

"I don't think I'll be able to sleep. I'm so wound up; I can't stop thinking about the mission. The commo plan, the code words, escape and evasion plans, Malvone's house…everything's running through my brain at once." Ranya was wearing gray cotton athletic shorts and a matching gray t-shirt, taken from the household laundry room's left-overs basket. Her feet were bare, as were Brad's beneath his faded jungle cammie pants, taken from the river cabin. He wore no shirt, enjoying the weather in the bug-free screened enclosure.

Brad asked, "What do you think about using the MAC-10s, without ever shooting them at a target? Firing a couple of rounds into the sand last night… I mean, it's nice to know they'll go bang, but if we have to shoot anybody past about twenty or thirty feet, we'll be lucky to hit anything at all."

"Don't worry about it. If we shoot, it's only going to be across the room. MACs aren't exactly known for their accuracy anyway."

"I'd still like to know where the bullets are going to go."

"They'll go where you point the suppressor."

"I wish I had the MP-5, instead of Tony."

"The gun that killed my father…that really creeps me out. But Carson's right. If there's shooting, it'll be great to leave 10mm brass on the ground, and their own 10mm slugs in their bodies. That'll really give the investigators something to wonder about."

"Ranya…I still can't believe we're doing this. We could be in the islands already."

"Oh please don't start that again…"

"I'd feel a whole lot better if we all had kevlar vests. Or at least you could wear the one we've got."

"I'm not going to wear Hammet's vest, so just drop it! If you want to wear it, you go right ahead."

"No, no, forget it," he replied. They had already covered this subject thoroughly. Ranya wouldn't wear their one kevlar vest, and neither would the others, not if they all didn't have them. The body armor they had used on the airfield rescue operation had been returned to the Suffolk PD. Now they only had Hammet's vest, and no one would wear it.

It had been much the same when he had asked about masks at the afternoon planning session in the living room. Brad had been thinking about wearing black balaclava-type masks only from the disguise angle, to better impersonate federal agents on a raid, and he had been surprised at the uniformly unenthusiastic reaction. None of them would wear masks. Masks just had too negative of a connotation among the conspirators.

"Tony" had said that only the Gestapo, the ATF and bank robbers wore masks, and no matter what, he wouldn't wear one. He had actually said, "I wouldn't be caught dead wearing a black mask," and nobody laughed, because for once it was meant as a serious comment. Carson had pointed out that masks wouldn't make any difference anyway. The flash-bang grenade provided by the Suffolk PD and the gun lights would blind and stun their targets. Their clear goggles and black helmets and uniforms would be enough of a disguise.

Time to change the subject, he thought. He asked her, "Where's your van and your bikes? What about your apartment, all of your stuff?"

"I don't have much 'stuff', not after my house was burned down. Phil's going to have somebody pick up the van and the bikes and stash them. Edith's going to clean out my apartment after all this is over. I told her to give everything to the Goodwill Store. Everything I need for sailing is in the bag I brought back to Guajira."

"How long is your passport good for?"

"It's new, four more years. But I thought we're not going to use our real passports?"

"It all depends…we need to be flexible."

"Oh, I'm very flexible. Very. What time's dinner?"

Brad checked his watch. "We've got an hour."

"Why don't we go back inside then? I want to show you how flexible I am."

"You can't get enough, can you?"

"I'm making up for lost time. But if you can't handle it…"

"I can handle it."

48

The Molly M rounded Smith Point as dawn broke behind them on the unobstructed eastern horizon. The ten mile wide mouth of the mighty Potomac River was at first indistinguishable from the rest of the bay, but the Maryland shore gradually became visible in the spreading daylight. Chuck the realtor's Baycruiser could be seen through binoculars as one of several white dots two miles ahead of them. Archie and Edith were somewhere off to their west, shadowing them on the Virginia side. They were ready to meet the Molly M at a series of marinas, if Tony, who was up ahead on Chuck's boat, called back to warn them of security patrols on the river.

Barney Wheeler prepared a Spartan breakfast of coffee and oatmeal on the galley's two burner propane stove. Brad and Ranya took theirs outside and sat on white plastic lawn chairs between the transom and the engine box, staring back at the V-shaped wake bubbling and churning behind them as the diesel drove them along. They'd talked through the pre-dawn hours in the same two chairs as the Molly motored up the bay, until the stars faded and the horizon returned. Now they ate in silence, still looking southeast. Facing the unbroken horizon behind them, it was easy to imagine they were already on the open ocean, and to forget that the land was closing in around them like the narrowing jaws of a trap.

After they finished, Barney Wheeler came out of the pilothouse carrying a white five gallon bucket with a short rope tied to the handle. He was wearing long khaki pants and a green flannel shirt. "The cook doesn't do the dishes. That's one of the laws of the sea." He put down the bucket, and sat on the flat transom board facing them.

"I'll show her how to catch seawater," said Brad. "She'll need to know how to do the dishes when we're on the ocean."

Ranya shoved an elbow into his side when he said this, but they were both laughing.

"You know," he continued, "catching a bucket full of seawater from a moving boat's not as easy as it looks. Do it wrong, and you'll lose your bucket, or maybe even get yanked off the boat. Imagine how stupid you'd feel, treading water and watching your boat sail over the horizon."

"Don't worry, Brad; if you fall overboard I'll bring Guajira back around and pick you up," she said, kidding him back. She was wearing her new black nylon warm-up suit; the breeze was flicking strands of hair from her ponytail around her smile.

"Gee, thanks! Seriously, you might be able to turn the boat a-round and get me if you're awake and on deck, and you saw me go over. But it can take a long time to get a big sailboat stopped and turned around on the ocean, especially in big waves. By then…"

"So, don't fall overboard?" she said, mocking him playfully.

"That's the general idea. If you fall overboard on the ocean, you're dead. You're lost out of sight in the waves in a minute. So no matter what, don't fall overboard."

Wheeler asked, "Where are you two headed after tonight? Not to be too specific, mind you..." They hadn't been very talkative during their two days at the halfway house, not with Chuck and Tony around, but Guajira's existence wasn't a secret from Barney. He'd seen the boat and talked to Brad on it when it was still up the Nansemond River.

"We're not sure yet," answered Brad. "South America, eventually. Someplace warm, someplace out of the way."

"Preferably without an extradition treaty," added Ranya.

"You might want to give a look at Brazil then. You know, extradition laws don't mean much any more. If the feds really want you, they'll just send a snatch team down to grab you and bring you back. No problem. They do it all the time now. The courts say it doesn't matter how they bring a fugitive back. But Brazil and Washington aren't getting along too well these days, so I don't think the feds would send a snatch team there. Too risky; their snatch team could wind up in the slammer if it was operating without local permission, and Brazil wouldn't give permission.

"But you'll have to be on your toes watching out for bounty hunters, even local ones. Sometimes the feds pay bounty hunters, and then they pretend they're surprised when their fugitive's dragged back to the states. And I'd be very, very careful in the smaller islands. There's no place to run and hide, and their governments are afraid to stand up to Uncle Sam. Tourism and foreign aid are all they've got, so they're easy to strong arm. They'll do whatever Washington tells them to, including putting you right on a plane for Miami. So don't get too comfortable on any small islands. Once word gets back to Washington..."

"It's definitely something to consider," said Brad.

"Ranya, do you know how Brad and I met? Did he tell you that story yet?"

She laughed. "You mean how he spilled the beer and passed you a note in Lester's Diner? At the last meeting of the dreaded Black Water Rod and Gun Club? Oh yeah, I've heard it. 'Read this note!' I think we've basically told our life stories a few times now."

"It sounds funny today," said Brad, "but it sure wasn't funny at the time."

"If you're heading south, aren't you worried about hurricanes?" asked Wheeler. "This is just about the most dangerous time of the year for being out on the ocean."

"Not as dangerous as hanging around in the states, especially after tonight," replied Brad.

"Well, that's true. I can see your point there."

"I've got a single-sideband radio and a laptop, so I can get the weatherfax. If a hurricane's coming, I'll see it days out and get out of the way." He almost added, "Unless we get clobbered by a pop-up hurricane," but he didn't see the point in worrying Ranya unnecessarily. They had more than enough to worry about already.

Ranya asked Wheeler, "Do you think it'll work? I mean, if we catch Malvone and make another confession video, do you think we'll be able to get anybody to believe it?"

Wheeler sucked in his breath and looked up, as if he was searching for an answer in the clouds. "Probably, if we do it right. And if we can catch a few breaks too. Hey, if I didn't think so, I wouldn't be here. And besides, and don't laugh now...it's our duty."

After a moment to digest that, Brad said, "I'm not laughing."

"Neither am I," said Ranya. "You know, I think about this all of the time, and I still don't understand why any of this happened to us. Fate, karma...something. But it just seems like everything's been a lot more than just a string of accidents." Brad reached across and held her hand, nodding as she continued. "Somehow, we all got caught on this train wreck, and now we've been given a chance to do something about it. And if we won't try when we have a perfect opportunity, who will? If we just took off and left the country, when it's heading straight into a civil war, when we could have done something to stop it... Well it just seems like we'd be running away from our duty, like you said." She shook her head slowly in wonder. "And a month ago, I was just starting my last year at UVA... Every single day I still can't believe what's been happening, but it's happening."

Brad was watching her closely, absorbing her serious intent, and said, "I agree, I guess. It does seem like this thing was dropped onto our laps for a reason, for us to do something about it. And now here we are. But I don't think Malvone's going to just be sitting around waiting to get hit. Not with Hammet and Garfield missing."

Wheeler heard his trepidation and answered, "Hammet's not going to be missing much longer, if they haven't found him already. But they won't be able to fix his time of death, at least not today they won't, so Malvone won't know how long he's been dead. Malvone's logical assumption will be that he's been dead since Monday night. That he was forced to call Swarovski under duress, just before he was killed.

"Now Malvone won't know what to think, but he'll be relieved that Hammet's dead. It's much better for him than wondering when good old George is going to show up, and maybe start talking about the stadium, start going for an immunity deal. Hammet showing up dead is going to be great news for Malvone; he'll just have to wonder about the details. He'll probably think somebody screwed up, and one of you grabbed a gun and turned the tables. That's what I'd think. It's much more believable than what really happened, that's for sure! So I think Malvone's going to be thrilled to hear that Hammet's dead, and that'll make it easier for us."

"But even so, there's only five of us, against at least five of them," said Brad.

"But they're just thugs, they're just goons," said Ranya. "They don't train for defense. They just train to shoot people in their sleep, and ambush people crossing their yards in the dark."

"She's right, Brad. If we can keep the element of surprise, we'll take them. I don't care who they are, they all bleed when they get shot. Of course, we're assuming that Malvone's there at all." Wheeler rapped his knuckles against the wooden transom board.

Brad said, "Phil calls you the 'Rev.' Is that just a nickname, or are you really some kind of a minister?"

Wheeler laughed. "Yep, it's true. I'm an ordained minister, or at least I was the last time I checked. But then, I haven't really checked in a while... I'm not too sure how the Man Upstairs sees me anymore. I guess you might say I'm a shepherd who's lost his sheep, lost his staff, lost the whole darn thing just about. Why'd you ask? Any particular reason?" He looked back and forth between the two of them, Ranya looked confused but Brad sat forward purposefully.

"Well," said Brad, "I was just kind of wondering if you had your Bible handy, the one from the kitchen at the river house."

"Sure, I've got it around here somewhere."

"And maybe you remember some prayers for special occasions?"

"Special occasions? Such as...what? Baptisms? Funerals? What did you have in mind?"

Ranya was squeezing Brad's hand so hard that it almost hurt. She was turned sideways staring hard at him.

"Actually, I was thinking maybe of something in between those two."

"Between a baptism and a funeral? Let's see, Holy Communion perhaps? Or Confirmation? Not Ordination?"

"Not exactly."

"I see. You want to get married. Did you have anybody in particular in mind?"

"Actually, I do."

Tears, began rolling down Ranya's cheeks. "Brad, why? You don't have to, I don't...you didn't..."

"Bradley, do you mean you haven't even asked her yet? Isn't that customary? Why don't you two talk this over a while, and we'll discuss it again some day."

"Barney, we don't have another day; we only have today," he said. "I mean, after today, we'll be sailing south."

"Well then, are you both really sure it's what you want?"

"Yes." said Ranya, wiping her tears with her sleeve.

"I'm assuming you're both baptized Christians? I'm not choosy, but I'm pretty sure that's a requirement, at least as far as my jurisdiction extends."

"We are," replied Brad.

"I don't need any time to think it over," said Ranya, facing Brad, holding both of his hands in hers. "I'll marry you, right now."

Wheeler said, "Eventually, you'll have to get a license from the state, some state anyway, and make it official. Government-wise I mean. But in the eyes of the Lord, you'll already be hitched fair and square, till death do you part. Now I wouldn't normally go along with something like this, not in a million years, but under these circumstances, war time you might say...well I'll marry you right now, if that's what you want."

Ranya was crying again, and Brad held her against his chest as she buried her face in her hands. She had no family, and no home. There would be no church, no white wedding dress. No priest, no bridesmaids, and no reception. No father to walk her down the aisle. Just this one day, out on the bay on a workboat. But she couldn't afford to be picky, because time was not on her side. Not with tonight's deadly job awaiting them up the river.

Fifteen minutes later they were married, standing in the Molly M's pilothouse, with Phil Carson and Captain Sam as witnesses. The skipper provided a small pair of stainless steel circular cotter rings from his spare parts box, and these two silver bands were the total extent of their wedding accoutrements. The mood was somber and reflective as Barney Wheeler read the passages, with no forced attempts at wedding ceremony humor. Brad and Ranya said their "I do's," they kissed as man and wife, and it was done.

Several local freelance reporters and various other busybodies with police scanners heard the park rangers call the Chesapeake police, and then heard their call for a tow truck to pull a car out of the Dismal Swamp Canal near Soyland Road. Of course, none of them heard the original telephone call from an unidentified "early morning fisherman" tipping the rangers off to the exact location of the sunken vehicle in the first place. Later on, nobody wondered how the anonymous fisherman had managed to spot the red SUV through ten feet of murky water, or why he didn't come forward to bask in his fifteen seconds of local television news fame.

In any case, by 8:45 AM the big highway wrecker was in position and taking a strain on its steel retrieval wire. A police diver had already attached the heavy cable to the red Cherokee's towing hitch, and then righted the vehicle on the bottom with empty lift-bags, which were inserted through the partially open driver's window, and inflated from his air tank. There were several television cameras aimed at the canal when the SUV emerged, with water streaming out of the half open window. More water flowed from the door edges and from underneath the chassis as it was dragged up the muddy bank onto the shoulder of Route 17. Police and rescue workers talked in small huddles, smoking cigarettes and drinking 7-11 coffee inside the perimeter of yellow tape. Another television station's helicopter filmed the recovery for the "news at noon" from a thousand feet up.

A quick DMV check of the license plate, read through telephoto lenses and binoculars by the gathered reporters, revealed that the red Jeep Cherokee belonged to one George Hammet of Virginia Beach. Camera crews kept, behind the perimeter, captured the bloated remains being extracted from the vehicle and zipped into a gray body bag, but this grotesque footage would never air. Dozens of crabs were also in the car…

The rumor quickly spread among the watchers that Hammet was a cop of some type, and that an empty whiskey bottle had been taken from the jeep along with his crab-eaten body. "Closed-coffin funeral" was a phrase which passed from reporter to reporter. The corpse had almost no face left at all, it was said. Reporters with police contacts on the other side of the yellow tape said knowingly to their less connected colleagues that it looked like the victim had failed to negotiate the turn from Soyland Road onto Route 17 at a high rate of speed. They winked when adding that Hammet's friend Jim Beam hadn't helped him keep his wheels on the road.

By the time the video earned its minute on the local news at noon, it had been verified that George Hammet was an ATF agent working out of their Norfolk Field Office, and that he left behind a wife and daughter in Virginia Beach. The empty whiskey bottle was not mentioned, but it was euphemistically stated that "alcohol may have been a contributing factor in the fatal one-car accident." No connection was made between the apparent accidental death of Special Agent Hammet, and the recent killings of other ATF and FBI agents across the region and the nation.

(The internet-generated Fed List was widely known of within the local media community but, in keeping with management instructions, at the request of the Department of Homeland Security and the FCC, it was never mentioned. The existence of the Fed List remained a rumor floating around on the internet.)

The ATF's Norfolk Field Office was relieved to hear that Hammet's Glock pistol and ATF credentials had been recovered from his vehicle. They were unaware that his STU-issued 10mm MP-5 submachine gun, along with its night sight and suppressor, as well as night vision goggles and other valuables were gone. The awkward fact that Hammet had been found dressed only in his underpants, with his clothes strewn about the vehicle, or that he had a blood alcohol level of .16, was kept within a select circle of the law enforcement community.

Wally Malvone drove his Lexus from his home on Tanaccaway Creek to the nearby Special Projects Division compound outside Waldorf, making the trip in ten minutes and arriving at 9:30 AM. The SPD was officially under the command of Bob Bullard, and he didn't want to undercut his authority by becoming a permanent presence. The fact was, he could set his own hours, splitting his time between Waldorf and his office at ATF Headquarters.

He was pleased to see the uniformed and armed private security guard manning their gate; a prefab steel and glass guardhouse had been brought in overnight on a flatbed truck and deposited in position. The guard checked his credentials against a clipboard, and waved Malvone through as if he had been standing watch at that location for years and not only hours. The guard service had been arranged and contracted by their black-budget fixer, "Mr. Emerson." The entire acreage of the light industrial park was already surrounded by a chain link fence topped with razor wire, beyond which lay open fields.

The SPD Supervisory Agents' offices were inside a 10,000 square foot steel warehouse which also contained many of their vehicles. The right side roll-up door was all the way open. Malvone pulled his white Lexus inside and parked it. With so much square footage available to the original STU operators and techs (who were only the nucleus of the SPD) there was no reason not to park their vehicles inside and out of sight. The offices were built in a line along the right side wall inside the warehouse. When he opened the door to the office he had previously selected, the new carpet odor was still strong. The walls were still unpainted, showing the white seam tape and plaster over the sheetrock. The painters were scheduled to do their work over the weekend.

Bob Bullard caught up to Malvone as he was going into his office, with Joe Silvari trailing behind him. Bullard said, "Wally, we need to talk. They found Hammet."

Malvone stopped in the doorway, his leather briefcase hanging at his side. "They found Hammet? They who? Where? Found him dead or alive?"

"Very dead. In his car. It looks like he missed a turn and drove into a canal."

"Shit! For real? When did they find him? Is there a time of death?" The earlier the better, as far as Malvone was concerned. He had wanted Hammet dead since they had climbed down from the unfinished building overlooking the stadium on September 9th, but this was not the way he'd planned it. Now Hammet was confirmed dead, but Garfield, Edmonds and the other two were still missing...it would take time to digest this information, figure the angles, and calculate all the permutations. If Fallon and the others had escaped, and killed Hammet after forcing him to call Swarovski's house, well he could deal with that. The expanding SPD needed real enemies; they could only gin up patsies for so long. But at least Hammet's lips were now sealed forever, and that was all upside. There was no longer any chance of his worst fear ever being realized, which was George Hammet sitting in front of a grand jury, or a Senate committee.

"No time of death yet," said Bullard. "Sounds like he's in pretty bad shape, I heard the crabs got a good whack at him... Maybe he's been there since Monday night, or Tuesday morning."

"What do you think? Did he have help?"

"Hard to say. If he was Vince Fostered, they did a good job of it. They found a whiskey bottle in the car... I don't know, maybe Hammet and Garfield just dicked it up and let Fallon or Sorrento take a gun off them... Or maybe one of them played possum and Hammet or Garfield turned his back on him... I don't know."

Malvone's cell phone chirped and he took the call right there in the doorway. "Malvone here. Yes. Okay, that's fine." He listened for a half minute and concluded with, "I'll be there." He flipped the phone shut and dropped it back into his jacket pocket. "I've been called to Head-quarters. Hammet's unfortunate demise has gained their attention. That bitch of a SAC at the Norfolk Field Office is pointing her finger at us. But Hammet never had anything in writing from us, not even an email. Anyway, it shouldn't be a major problem, not with federal agents getting shot right and left. He'll just blend right in with the rest. Garfield too."

Silvari said, "They've just about wiped that 'Fed List' off of the internet, but it's still out there. I mean, every wing-nut who ever wanted a copy of it probably downloaded it already, or got it from a friend."

"Exactly. Agents are getting whacked every day, so Hammet winding up in a canal shouldn't stand out too much."

"Don't be so casual about that Fed List, just because you're not on it," replied Silvari. "I'm on the list, a lot of us are! I mean, I have to sneak into the back of my own house, like a damn thief! Wally, you don't know what it's like, feeling crosshairs on your back every time you put the key into your door."

"Yeah, I know, I know, it must suck. So, are you guys coming over tonight? You can unwind a little, and forget about that list."

At noon they were all in the pilothouse eating sandwiches, when the bridge edged above the horizon and into view ahead of them. The Governor Harry W. Nice Memorial Bridge carried Route 301 high over the Potomac, connecting Virginia to Maryland at a pinch-point where the river narrowed to two miles wide and made a sharp left turn. Route 301 had been the primary highway linking the east coast states from Maine to Florida until the opening of I-95, when it had been eclipsed and almost forgotten except by local traffic. Now with the I-495 Wilson Bridge over the Potomac in Washington cut, Route 301 was once again a primary artery for mid-Atlantic travel. The Governor Nice Memorial Bridge, like an aging actor brought back on stage as a last minute replacement, once again stood tall in the spotlight.

They all watched the bridge grow before them through the forward pilothouse windows. Ranya said, "It looks like a dead end in the river. The bridge looks just like a locked gate." Until recently the river had felt expansive and safe around them, seemingly almost as wide open as the Chesapeake itself. All morning the Potomac had been tending north west, with an average distance from shore to shore of about five miles, which was too far to clearly make out details on the land. Now the land was closing in on them from both sides. North of the bridge the river would average under two miles across, and their feeling of anonymity would be gone…if they made it past the bridge at all. She added, "That bridge looks like a real junk pile. I wonder how old it is?"

"Young lady," said Captain Sam Hurley without turning a-round, sitting on his stool behind the wheel, "that bridge was built in 1940, and I remember it opening like it happened yesterday. The cars that drove across in those days, you can only imagine. Two of my cousins helped build that bridge; they were iron workers, high scalers! She may look like 'junk' to your young eyes, but she's made of honest riveted steel, put up by brave men who knew their trades.

"She's a real ship bridge, 140 feet over the water at the center span, and it's 200 feet down to the bottom. As the river narrows here, it gets mighty, mighty deep. Imagine that, 200 feet deep, and they built her before the war! Now, that was a job!"

The elderly skipper stared ahead for a minute, blinking, remembering his cousins Arthur and Danny Maguire who died so very, very long ago. He remembered how they had worked as a team on projects around the bay and even up to Philadelphia and New York, putting in the red-hot rivets, and then hammering them into place forever. Another lost art, one of so many he had seen disappear from American life over his many decades.

The past, the past, all gone now...like Artie, who had not even made it to the beach on Guam in '44, and Danny who survived the war, but left four young children when he fell from the almost finished Chesapeake Bay Bridge in '52.

Including bright-eyed young Molly, who he raised as his own, taken by that damnable polio the summer after her thirteenth birthday...

Artie and Dan were both gone, long gone like the water down the river. But their high steel bridge remained before him, still joining Maryland and Virginia, an unbreakable testament to their lives.

"I'll forgive you for calling that bridge 'junk' young lady," said Captain Sam Hurley, his voice cracking. "You didn't live in those days, and you don't have any idea of how things were back then." He didn't turn around, so they would not see him weep.

They were all quiet after that, staring at the bridge with new eyes. It was more words than they had heard Captain Sam speak since they had left Norfolk. Except for Barney Wheeler who knew him well, they weren't sure how much of what was going on around him their elderly skipper, with his snow-white hair, hearing aids and thick glasses, heard or understood at all. Now they knew.

They couldn't see Chuck's boat; it was too far away, one white dot lost among a dozen vessels ahead of them on the shimmering sun-lit river. They were listening carefully to the Molly's VHF radio, bolted to the varnished plywood console in front of the steering wheel. It was set on channel 77 as the bridge steadily grew ahead of them. The rainbow arch of steel trusses and girders were an elaborate Erector Set toy bridge in the distance, with emerald forests and jade fields squeezing it from both sides.

Without preamble, Victor Sorrento's voice hissed from the radio. "Bluebell, Bluebell, this is Harmony. How copy, over?"

Carson was standing near the radio and unclipped the microphone, and slowly pressed the transmit button three times. The message from the nonexistent Bluebell to the equally nonexistent Harmony was repeated again in a minute, and was confirmed again with three more clicks. This prearranged brevity code meant that Chuck's Baycruiser had not been stopped, boarded or searched while passing beneath the bridge, so it was presumed to be safe for the Molly and her illegal cargo to proceed up the river. If the Baycruiser had been stopped and searched, or if special security procedures on the water had been noticed, a different message would have been sent. Then, the Molly M would have turned west for a marina in Colonial Beach, to transfer the weapons to Archie's truck.

Another message came over on channel 16, the emergency and hailing frequency. "Securite, Securite. Hello all stations. The Coast Guard has established a security zone 500 yards on either side of the Governor

Nice Bridge. All mariners transiting the Potomac are required to maintain their course and speed in the center channel, and not slow down or stop in the security zone. This is the United States Coast Guard, out."

Barney Wheeler said, "It sounds like they're transmitting on low power, so it's only heard within a few miles of the bridge. Usually, the Coasties boom out their 'Securite' messages on high power, so you can hear them from one end of the bay to the other."

"I think they're playing it low key," said Carson. "With the beltway bridge in Washington cut, you can be sure they're keeping an extra watchful eye on this one. So I'm guessing they're worried about sabotage, not gunrunning. At least, that's what 'maintain your speed in the center channel' tells me. That's why we're going through now, when there's the most river traffic: the more boats going through, the less attention they can pay to each boat. What I heard from my friend in Maryland is that the big clampdown on guns is further up. The DC beltway is the main perimeter for Washington; that's where they're checking everything that moves. Outside of the beltway, it's just random FIST checkpoints."

They all knew from their briefings and map study that Malvone's house was six miles south of the beltway. Six miles from where one span of the Wilson Bridge had been blown up.

"I think you youngsters ought to get below," said Wheeler. "The Coasties still might be doing random boat checks, and in my experience they'll inspect a boat with a pretty girl on board a lot quicker than a boat load of ugly old reprobates like us."

"That's the sad, sad truth," said Captain Sam. "I haven't been boarded in more years than I care to remember. In fact, I can't even remember the last time the Coast Guard came aboard the Molly M."

Brad and Ranya needed no further coaxing to take their leave and disappear down into the cramped forward berthing compartment. The three older men remained in the pilothouse, to impress any young Coast Guardsmen with the harmlessness of their advanced years, and their utter lack of sex appeal.

From a mile out they could see a white-hulled Coast Guard patrol craft anchored on the upstream side of the bridge, partially concealed behind one of the enormous concrete islands supporting the complex steel truss legs.

As they approached the bridge at a respectable ten knots in the center channel, right between the red and green buoys, a day-glow orange rigid-hulled inflatable boat about twenty feet long made a high speed curving run from the Maryland shore and zoomed up their wake. It came alongside and paced them, just a half boat length from their starboard beam. The RHIB was crewed by a half dozen young Coast Guardsmen in blue jumpsuits and orange life jackets, carrying slung M-16s and shotguns and holstered pistols. Two of them stood in the back of the RHIB holding onto the side of the welded aluminum pipe frame radar arch, ready to climb across onto the Molly's aft deck if they were instructed to do so. If the RHIB's coxswain wanted to send the boarding party over, he would simply press its orange port-side tube against the Molly M's hull, while matching boat speeds.

Captain Sam had put on a blue Navy-style ball cap with "WW2 PT Boat Veteran" emblazoned in gold across the front. Beneath the words was embroidered the famous silhouette of the plywood patrol torpedo boat. Carson and Wheeler were sitting at the dinette table, which dropped them just below the line of sight from the RHIB.

The Coasties, standing in their inflatable holding onto their bolster seats, peered in at Captain Sam through the Molly M's plexiglass side windows, giving him a careful look-over. In return he gave them a friendly wave. After long seconds of expressionless study from behind his sunglasses, the senior petty officer waved back to him, spoke into his walkie-talkie, and then the orange inflatable accelerated away in a wide right hand curve, leaving a churning white wake behind them. The well-maintained Chesapeake Bay deadrise workboat with the old skipper at the controls fit on the river like a hand in a glove, and obviously merited no further official attention.

They passed between the concrete islands on either side of the main channel and beneath the iron bridge. The vaulted arch soared momentarily above them from shore to shore and up to the sky, and then it was behind them and they were through. The upper Potomac, narrower now and twisting in several tight dog legs, lay open before them. They were 45 miles from their target when Carson sent coded messages to Chuck and Tony, who were somewhere out in front of them, and to Archie and Edith, who were shadowing them unseen on the Virginia shore. The Molly M had made it past the bridge, and the mission was a go.

Malvone arrived at the ATF Director's outer office after passing through several new layers of security, including a pair of uniformed guards stationed outside the elevators. After being cleared to enter the waiting area and being announced by the director's secretary, he was met by Deputy Director Frank Castillo, who was just coming out.

"Walter, let's take this in my office. The Director is tied up."

Tied up my ass, thought Wally Malvone. That preppie chicken shit doesn't want a meeting with me to appear on his calendar, in case the Special Projects Division blows up into a flap. Well, screw him anyway.

They sat in the same office, in the same two plush leather chairs, across the same mahogany executive desk as before, but the furniture had been rearranged. Castillo no longer had his back to the large window, which was now covered by gauzy curtains. Behind the curtains a new two-inch-thick sheet of the latest high tech bullet-resistant laminated plastic glass was crudely bracketed and bolted to the wall around the window opening. Even with the new layer of bullet-resistant glass, Castillo was taking no chances. A .50 caliber armor-piercing round had penetrated the Director's conventional Lexan polycarbonate window a week before, and Castillo had no desire to test the advertised rating of the new material with himself as the target.

"Well, Walter, it's been two weeks since you gave me your proposal…it sounds like you've really taken the ball and run with it. We've even heard from the White House about your unit."

"Thank you, I've got a fine team behind me." Malvone was glowing inside, but made an effort to appear bureaucratically passionless.

"Yes… I'm sure you do." Castillo knew the records of the cast-offs and misfits that Malvone had assembled into his Special Training Unit, now the Special Projects Division, and why he had selected them. "And I understand you'll be expanding soon… We've been instructed to provide you with every consideration in your selection of new personnel."

Malvone could read the bitterness in Castillo's brown eyes, in the strained tone of his voice. He answered, "We'll try not to disrupt any current field operations." This was a subtle joke, because they both knew that from coast to coast, ATF Field Offices were in total disarray and confusion. Even before the internet posting of the so-called Fed List, ATF agents were hunkering down and hiding, to avoid being an unseen sniper's target.

"Walter, speaking of personnel, I've been getting some rather pointed questions out of the Norfolk Field Office about their ASAC."

"Ahh…Norfolk? George Hammet, right? What about him?"

"Are you aware that he's been missing since Monday, and he was found dead in a river down there just this morning?"

"I heard something about it, but not the details."

"Norfolk seems to be under the impression that Hammet was working with your Special Training Unit, informally."

"Really? No, no, I'm afraid that their information is not correct. I believe Hammet was working with the Joint Task Force, and I think he may have assisted the STU Team indirectly with some of the informants he was running in Tidewater, but nothing more than that. Bob Bullard handles the day to day running of the team; I'll ask him what he's heard."

"And that's it?"

"That's it."

"Walter, the SAC down there is pretty upset. Very upset. She wants to depose some of your men concerning their knowledge of

Hammet's recent activities and whereabouts. And she wants to depose Bullard, and yourself."

This was getting Malvone's attention: sworn depositions were not a good thing. He suppressed a wry smile and slowly shook his head no. "Frank, I don't think that would be advisable, not at this time. The Special Projects Division is engaged in full-out counter-terrorist operations," he lied, and then he dropped the biggest name of all. "They don't have time to just stop what they're doing. Anyway they can't; they're working directly under the President's instructions. So I think we should forget about depositions for the time being."

Malvone the poker player was enjoying himself tremendously, trying to guess what 'cards' Castillo might still be holding after playing his high ace. He liked the new sometimes upside-down chain of command, but he needed to get a feel for exactly how far he could push his somewhat murky and undefined connection to the White House. Even with his new undeclared promotion, he was technically still junior to Frank Castillo, but he was in no real sense the Deputy Director's subordinate any longer in the larger picture...for the moment.

Without saying so, they both understood that his new power flowed directly from his informal connection to the White House, at least for as long as their operations went well, and as long as the SPD wasn't blamed for a major flap. In that event, if the White House threw him overboard, if there was blood in the water, then Castillo and Boxell and the other jealous sharks at ATF and the Justice Department would undoubtedly rip him to shreds. He was attempting to learn the unwritten rules as he went, and he found the entire game to be more than slightly entertaining.

"All right Walter, we've got enough problems this week as it is, without looking for any more in-house."

"I agree, Frank." Frank! Calling the Deputy Director "Frank" to his face in his own office was priceless. "On that we see eye to eye." He could only imagine Director Boxell in his office, hiding under his desk, undoubtedly listening in on an intercom, chewing his fingernails down to the knuckles as he contemplated the prospect of another major ATF scandal.

Castillo leaned forward across his desk, rising slightly out of his chair. "Walter, I want to tell you...there's a lot that I *hear*, but I don't really *know*. A lot. So I just want to ask you for one thing, man to man."

"What's that, Frank?"

Castillo closed his eyes momentarily at the sound of his first name. "Don't embarrass us."

Malvone paused and stared back at Castillo. "Excuse me? I don't know what you mean."

513

"Walter...please. Just don't embarrass us. Don't embarrass the ATF."

"I'll keep that in mind, Frank. I really will." Malvone got up out of the chair with an earnest look on his face, said goodbye and, without a backward glance, he strode out of the office. He was laughing inside, he felt like whistling, like dancing. With Hammet dead, his tracks were covered forever. Hammet's death was going to be lost among the dozens of other deaths of FBI and ATF agents this month.

The brown-nosers who flocked around Boxell and Castillo at Headquarters could take their Ivy League graduate degrees, roll them up into tight tubes, and shove them up their asses. They meant nothing to him now. His years of pretending to fit in, of carefully biding his time while planning and preparing were over.

When Brad and Ranya eventually unlatched the cabin door and came back up to the pilothouse, there were no smirks or leers or winks. The three older men had lived a long time, and they knew that the young "newlyweds" might be able to enjoy no other honeymoon beyond the brief time they managed to steal together as the Molly M cruised up the Potomac.

"Where are we?" asked Brad, looking around at the shore. Stately mansions stood atop bluffs, on wide lawns amidst dense stands of hardwood trees. He was back in his comfortable cammie pants and blue hooded sweatshirt, but he was barefoot. Ranya was in her new black warm-up suit, also barefoot, her long brown hair loose and unbrushed around her shoulders. Both of them had reddened and bleary eyes as if they had been crying.

Captain Sam had a yellowed and coffee-stained chart unfolded in front of him next to his controls. "Just passing Quantico," he said. He stabbed at their position on the chart with a gnarled finger. He had a beaten up pair of black binoculars lying next to the throttle lever, and he used them to read the numbers on the green and red channel buoys, taking his glasses off and slipping them into his shirt pocket each time. Captain Sam had not entered the GPS era; the old buoys and markers and landmarks on shore did fine by him.

Carson and Wheeler were sitting across from one another at the dinette table, which was covered with maps, sketches and lists. Carson said, "We've got less than twenty miles to the target; we should go over the mission again. The primary plan, the alternates, the cover stories, evasion plans...everything. Is that all right, or am I being a pain in the ass?"

Ranya shrugged okay, and slid into the booth beside him. Brad squeezed in beside Wheeler.

"Instead of going over the whole briefing again, how about we ask each other questions? Okay? All right. Ranya, do you remember the first vehicle rendezvous point across from Tanaccaway Creek?" For now, they quit using their alias first names among the four of them. These four all knew each other, and they weren't worried about Captain Sam.

"Number one is Dogue Creek Marina, between Mount Vernon and Fort Belvoir. The truck will be behind the restaurant."

"It's called Barnacle Bill's," said Wheeler. "My turn. Brad, what's the closest Metro stop to Malvone's house?"

"Huntington Station. Straight across the river, at the end of the yellow line. The last train leaves at 1:30 AM." Brad asked Carson in return, "Hammet said Malvone doesn't have any guard dogs, but what if he's got them now? How do we deal with guard dogs?"

And so they continued peppering each other with questions about the potentially fatal minutia of the operation, as they wound their way up the river. They worked through every conceivable sentry stalking scenario, several possible ways to gain entry to Malvone's recreation room, and a variety of escape and evasion plans.

Every fifteen minutes they heard Tony's voice over the VHF, telling them in brevity code that the river was clear and free from security patrols. Edith, in the truck, used a new prepaid cell phone to send numerical mile marker codes to a new pager on Carson's belt, indicating the truck's position on the Virginia side, in case they had to make an emergency link-up.

Finally, Tony sent one last VHF brevity code indicating that as planned Chuck was increasing the Baycruiser's speed to 20 knots, in order to deliver him to Malvone's creek for his kayak recon.

The Molly M was 15 miles from Tanaccaway Creek at 4 pm. As planned, they diverted from the main channel and headed south into the mouth of the Occoquan River, to top off her fuel tank at the Riverside Marina. If the Molly had to make a high speed run down the bay after the mission, they'd want every gallon of diesel they could carry to obtain the maximum range. Fully fueled, the boat would be able to make it non-stop to Guajira's anchorage at its best speed.

Brad and Ranya gladly stayed hidden in the forward cabin during the refueling stop to make the Molly less memorable to the marina employees. Wheeler got off the boat and looked for another emergency extraction site where it would be easy to bring the Molly in close enough to shore for them to rendezvous with Archie's truck. Carson paid for the sixty gallons of diesel with cash, wearing sunglasses and a ball cap. Long after they untied from the fuel pier and shoved off again, Brad and Ranya remained below in the forward cabin.

49

Tanaccaway Creek is actually a small bay on the Maryland side of the Potomac, running two miles from east to west, where its half mile wide mouth opens into the river. The winding Potomac makes one final sharp turn here, then it runs seven miles straight north into Washington. Much of the land on both sides of the upper Potomac is government property, under military or park service control, and is preserved in a state very close to its original natural beauty. The remaining private waterfront land has largely been divided into large estates, and retains most of its abundant tree cover.

The south bank of the creek forms Tanaccaway Park, a 6,000 acre wildlife refuge which extends another mile beyond the creek along the Potomac. Fort Jefferson, another national park, occupies thousands of more acres around the mouth of the creek on the north side. Only the eastern half of Tanaccaway Creek, along its north bank, is privately owned, divided into properties ranging from one to several dozen acres. This was where Wally Malvone lived on his mother's ancestral land.

By 9 PM the Molly M was anchored in a small indentation in the Maryland shoreline, one and a half miles southwest of Malvone's property, just outside the mouth of the creek. Close behind the boat loomed the heavily forested and utterly dark western shoreline of Tanaccaway Park, which was emptied of hikers and birdwatchers each night at sunset. Occasional river traffic out in the channel passed by without noticing the anchored Chesapeake Bay deadrise workboat. Their late-arriving wakes rolled the Molly M as their stern lights faded from view.

The tide was beginning to run and the crab boat strained against her anchor line. The gray Zodiac was already inflated and tied along her starboard side; its outboard motor was mounted in place and had been run to make sure it would be ready. Brad and Ranya sat in the Molly M's long cockpit on the two white plastic chairs, watching thin clouds glide past the half-moon that was setting across the river. The lights along the George Washington Parkway leading to Mount Vernon gleamed like a diamond necklace across the Potomac; the reflection of the moon on the black water was the pendant hanging from the center. They were both already dressed for the mission in their black warm-up suits, holding hands across the two armrests.

"I wonder what old George Washington would think about this," asked Brad. "I mean, so close to his house."

"Think about what? You mean about what we're going to do?"

"Sure, that, and about the whole BATF thing. The Special Training Unit, secret police, all of it…about those guys being a part of the government. His government."

Ranya shook her head slowly, regretfully. "I don't think he could ever have imagined it. Not secret police, not national secret police. Not in America."

"But they must have thought something about it. The founding fathers, I mean. That's what they wrote the Second Amendment for, right? For dealing with situations like this? Things like secret police, national secret police?"

She thought about this. "You know, those dead white guys, they were pretty smart, they sure had some vision. They couldn't possibly tell what was going to happen in two hundred years, but they knew we'd need guns to deal with it, eventually."

"Two hundred years..." Brad mused. "I'll tell you what: this river's seen a lot of history. Every other mile something's named after a president, a general, or a battlefield. Revolutionary war, Civil War..."

"And it's not finished yet. It's going to see some more history tonight."

"More history," said Brad. "And then we're finished, we're done. We're on Guajira, and we're out of here."

"And then we're out of here," she agreed, squeezing his hand and laying her head on his shoulder.

"And then we're sailing to the islands."

"Straight to the islands."

The pilothouse door opened and Carson stepped out into the cockpit, he was also wearing his dark track suit. "Tony just called on the walkie-talkie; he's coming out." He used Victor's nom d'guerre; they had gradually fallen into the habit. When Tony or Chuck were around, they were Rev and Robin and Bob to each other, all except Carson, who was the hub at the center of the spokes. The first name aliases were very light cover. Mainly they served to remind them all to maintain security, and not ask meddlesome questions.

They each realized that the operation had to go off smoothly, and if it didn't, the consequences would be severe. The evasion kits they carried sealed in plastic bags in black daypacks could not, realistically, be expected to carry them far against helicopters, police dogs, roadblocks and the Coast Guard. Their plan depended above all on surprise and speed, and if either element was lost, then they were lost.

Just before 11 PM, the kayak appeared out of the gloom from the shoreline, and Tony paddled directly for the side of the Molly M. He turned neatly with a dip of his two-bladed oar and brought his plastic boat against the side of the inflatable. Brad climbed down into it to help him secure the kayak and unload his gear. He took the small waterproof rafting bags from Tony and passed them to the others aboard the Molly. These contained Tony's recon gear consisting of binoculars, Hammet's night vision goggles, a notepad, walkie-talkie, a water bottle and other items. After Tony crawled into the gray Zodiac, they both lifted the dripping kayak out of the water and slid it over into the workboat's cockpit. Tony was wearing his black nylon tracksuit, and black neoprene dive boots.

"Okay," said Carson, "let's get inside. You want some coffee?"

Tony slid behind the dinette table and began sketching a map of Malvone's property on a blank piece of paper. The rest of the small table was covered with river charts and road maps, lit by a single red dome light above them in the pilothouse ceiling.

Carson asked, "Where's Chuck? Have you seen him? Have you made any contact with him?"

While he drew his map Tony said, "Chuck's gone, as far as I can tell. He left after he dropped me off. I haven't seen him since before sunset, and he never answered on the radio. I thought maybe he was just out of walkie-talkie range. You haven't heard from him either?"

"Nope, he hasn't answered on VHF. We were refueling on the Virginia side, maybe he passed us then," said Carson. "Or maybe he's still up here, somewhere."

"So your friend chickened out," said Tony, looking disgusted.

"Looks that way."

"Don't be too hard on him," said Wheeler. "Chuck's had a soft life. We're lucky he went this far. We couldn't have done this without a scout boat up ahead of the Molly. And don't forget, he let us use the halfway house. I'd say he's done his share, and as long as he keeps his mouth shut, I'll be happy."

"He'll keep his mouth shut," said Phil Carson.

"How can you be sure?" asked Ranya, standing next to Brad. They were leaning over the back of the crowded dinette, holding onto it as the Molly rolled from a passing wake. Captain Sam was heating water for coffee on the propane stove across from them. "How do you know he didn't go straight to the Coast Guard or the FBI?"

"Because," answered Carson, "he's more afraid of me than the feds. He knows me, and he knows something about my friends. Or he thinks he does, which is even better. Chuck likes his life on easy street too much; he won't want to go into the witness relocation program. He won't want to trade his houses and his boats and his girlfriends for an apartment in Tucson. Not at his age."

Tony finished drawing his sketch map, and used his pencil for a pointer. "Here's what we've got. There's a narrow pebble beach, rocks and mud all along the shore, maybe five or ten feet wide, it varies. Then there's a steep bank, very steep, maybe seven or eight feet high above the beach. Nobody up top can see you down there unless they're right at the edge looking straight down. But if they do look down, there's no place to hide, no cover.

"Malvone's house is right here, about 40 or 50 yards back from the river bank. There're some trees and bushes between the bank and his house. Mostly it's just grass, though. He's got a tool shed here, and a brick barbeque here on the patio by the back door."

"How close did you get?" asked Carson.

"Right here. There's thick woods all along the west side of his property. We can move right through there, no problem. I was watching from here most of the time." Tony pointed to the spot on his sketch map. "It's about forty feet from the woods where I was sitting to his house."

"What are these blobs and arrow things? Trees?" asked Ranya.

"Hey, I failed art class, what can I say? Right, those are trees and bushes around his house. I'm not exactly positive where each one is, I'm just approximating."

"So who's there?" asked Carson. "Are they having a party? What's going on?"

"Malvone's there for sure. I saw his bald head and mustache, just the way Hammet described him, no question about it, it's him. He's wearing a white shirt, mostly white, sort of like an alligator shirt. You know, with a collar. And blue jeans. I'd say there's at least four or five of them left; I'm guessing four or five because I never saw them all together at one time. Some folks came and went; you can hear when Malvone's driveway gate rolls open, it's a noisy grinding thing. I couldn't keep track of who came and who left."

"Four or five?" asked Ranya. It was an important number.

"Right, that's what I said, four or five. Sorry, that's the best I could do. They didn't come out and line up for me. I've got descriptions in my notepad."

"Well, okay," said Carson, "That's good. We can handle four or five. Are they acting loose and casual, or nervous and paranoid? Are they packing guns?"

"They're all wearing pistols, as far as I could tell. No, wait, not Malvone, unless maybe he's got a backup in a pocket. His shirt was tucked in, definitely no gun there unless it's a real small one. The others were wearing loose shirts and jackets, but I could tell, they were all packing. One guy took off a jacket over by the barbecue, kind of like a cammie windbreaker, and he had a pistol right here." Tony pointed to his right hip. "They sure didn't seem very worried. They did cook outside, but they didn't spend much time in the yard. It's about a thousand yards across the creek, maybe less. I don't know if they were worried about snipers. There were a few times when I could have walked up and grabbed a steak. I could smell it, hell; I could hear the meat sizzling. If they were paranoid, I couldn't see it."

The rest of the little team listened attentively to Tony's report; his simple words taking on life and death importance.

"They finished up on the barbeque and went inside before it got dark. They always used the door on the southeast corner here, across the patio from the barbecue. There's a balcony that runs all the way along the house here on the river side, that's up on the living room level. I really suck as an artist, that's what this line here is. The first floor on the land side is the second floor on the river side, right? I mean the ground slopes down. There's steps on the outside here on the west side of the house to take you from the ground up onto the balcony.

"There's five cars and trucks parked up here on the driveway, and on the grass. At least there were an hour ago. One's a camper, a pickup truck with a big camper on top, the kind that goes up over the cab. I can't tell if it's being used or not. There's a couple of regular cars, and two SUVs. One's a black Suburban, tinted windows, the whole nine yards. The garage door was closed when I was up at that end, but I didn't spend much time up there. I was watching the river side most of the time, that's where the people were."

"What about guards?" asked Carson.

"I'm getting there," said Tony. "It looks like they're taking turns, about fifteen minutes or a half hour each. Sort of random, and not all the time. When they're out walking around checking things, they're wearing night vision goggles and carrying MP-5's, the kind with the collapsing stock and the built-in silencer. One guy walked around and around the house. Another guy just sat in a chair up on the balcony, and had a cigarette. So it's hard to say exactly what kind of guard situation we'll see when we get there."

"That's okay," said Carson, "We'll scope it out when we're on site. Was everybody downstairs, or were there people upstairs too?"

"Just that one guy on the balcony, smoking a cigarette. I didn't see anybody stay upstairs, not inside the house, but I guess they could have. They all walked from their cars to the backyard on this sidewalk path here, along the west side of the house. I could've hit them with rocks."

Wheeler snickered. "Malvone doesn't want his goons tromping around in his living room; he makes them go around back like delivery men."

"Probably doesn't trust them in his house," said Brad.

"Any dogs?" asked Carson

"Shit no! I wouldn't have been watching them from so close if they had a dog, that's for sure."

"Do they leave the back door unlocked? Which way does it open?" asked Carson.

"It opens inward, I could tell that much. I didn't really get a good look at the door when it was opened; the angle was wrong from where I was watching. I think they're locking it from inside. After it got dark, when they wanted to go inside, the guards knocked on the door, and then waited a little bit and went inside. So I'm guessing they're unlocking it from inside. There's probably a peep hole in the door, or a closed circuit TV, to see who's outside."

"Well, we can work on that. That opens up some possibilities. Did the guards have radios?"

"Walkie-talkies, or maybe cell phones. I couldn't tell. Nothing fancy, no headsets or anything like that. Very casual."

"So it's dark around the rest of the house? No motion triggered lights, nothing like that?"

"Nope. The sentries were wearing NVG's, and they just walked around in the open."

Wheeler made a half smile and said, "They think they own the night when they wear night goggles. Tactical common sense goes straight out the window."

"I'd say that's right. They didn't see me. I always stayed behind good cover. You can tell that when they put on NVG's they think they're invisible. They walk around in the open like they're strolling in a park. They don't use cover, nothing."

"I think it's true, they're all attack and no defense," Wheeler added. "These morons still think they're the only ones around with night goggles. We can definitely use that to our advantage."

"Okay, let's break out the guns and suit up," said Carson. "Great report, Tony. It looks good; it looks like a go, all the way."

"So let's go kick some ass," said Tony.

"Let's get Malvone," said Carson. "And bring him back here alive."

"Let's get it done," said Brad.

"Now that's what I call an effective negotiating strategy," said Tim "Hollywood" Jaeger. He was sitting with them at the poker table, but the game was on hold while they watched a news replay on the big screen TV in the corner of Malvone's party room.

"Yeah, that's what I call rapid conflict resolution," joked Michael Shanks. They were all watching a cable news channel replay of a police

521

action which had occurred earlier in the day. A television news helicopter had captured the video Friday morning in northern Illinois, where a brick farmhouse was the epicenter of a SWAT standoff.

An informant had called 1-855-GUN-STOP and reported that a certain farmer had a hidden cache of illegal assault and sniper rifles. Farmer Brown was, evidently, not interested in discussing the matter with law enforcement officials, and had taken his telephone off the hook and barricaded himself inside his one story red brick home.

The airborne video camera, obviously filming from extreme range judging by the jerkiness and lack of focus, zoomed back and panned along the dirt road leading into the farmhouse. A pair of armored cars with three oversized tires on each side rolled up the road, then spread apart and halted 100 yards from the farmer's front door. Each combat vehicle had a long slender gun barrel protruding from a small turret on their front slopes.

If there were any more warnings issued, they were not audible on the tape. The videotaped replay had apparently been edited down to eliminate many long boring minutes of inaction. After what seemed like only moments since they arrived on the scene (actually an hour had passed), white smoke and shiny gold-colored dots were seen pouring from the fronts of the two armored cars. At the same time, glass, brick fragments and dust exploded across the front of the house. The silent firing continued on the television for ten solid seconds, and ceased abruptly. The unseen news announcer repeated the official police department version of events. The barricaded farmer had fired on the armored vehicles, "forcing" them to fire back in "self-defense."

After another editing break to eliminate more tedious real-time waiting, white and then black smoke began pouring from the front windows of the farmhouse, followed by bright orange flames shooting from all sides of the house. The flames curled upward and wrapped around the roof and, within a minute, the entire house was fully engulfed.

"Man, we should have done that at Waco on day one," said Bob Bullard. "No more wasting weeks and weeks coddling these fanatics. 'Come out in five minutes, or meet your maker.' That's all we should ever have to say."

"Yeah, no more screwing around with these lunatics," said Shanks. "Make it simple. Come out with your hands up, or face the consequences. Obey the law, or die. And if you decide to break the law, hey, that's your problem."

"It works for me," said Wally Malvone, relighting his cigar with a Zippo lighter.

Joe Silvari looked between them and responded, "If it's all so simple, if it's all so easy, how come we're hiding out down here at 'Fort

Malvone'? How many federal agents have been killed since all this crap started? Twenty? Thirty?"

"Three in the STU Team alone," said Jaeger, suddenly subdued.

"Hammet doesn't count," said Bullard. "He wasn't STU. And Clay Garfield was only contract, not an operator. Garfield screwed up, or he wouldn't be MIA right now."

"MIA?" asked Silvari. "He's probably at the bottom of a river if you ask me. With a liquor bottle beside him."

"Like Hammet," said Shanks. "Pretty good work, whoever put him in the river. 'Missed the turn, dead drunk'...or so they say. You gotta admire that kind of professionalism, that kind of attention to detail. He had a .16 blood alcohol when he croaked. If they Vince Fostered him, they did a damn convincing job."

"What do you think?" asked Jaeger. "Fallon and Sorrento did it, and got away in Edmonds's Mercedes?"

"Maybe," said Bullard. "I'd say that's probably a good guess. Hammet and Garfield screwed the pooch, one way or the other. They got cocky, they got sloppy, and they made a mistake. And so they paid the price. Don't ever underestimate these guys we're up against."

"Well, I'm not forgetting those two, Fallon and Sorrento," said Malvone, between puffs on his cigar. "Or Swarovski and Edmonds, for that matter. We'll get back around to those guys. They haven't seen the last of us; we're not letting them slide off the hook."

"It's easy for you to be smug, Wally," said Silvari. "You're not on the damned Fed List. When I go home, I have to sneak in and out of my house, looking over my shoulder, checking out every car parked up and down the street."

"Man, you're not kidding," said Jaeger. "The worst part is walking up on my back porch, wondering if somebody's scoping it out from 500 yards away. I don't even use the front door."

Malvone was well into a fresh bottle of Tanqueray gin, and he wasn't buying into their pity party. "Oh, stop your complaining. Everybody on the list is drawing max per diem, straight into your pockets." Half of the STU Team was on the Fed List, and half of them, with addresses outside of the three listed states, were not.

Some of the listed operators were staying with friends, relatives or unlisted team members. Shanks was staying in his camper. But no matter where they were staying, they were collecting over $150 a day in emergency per diem funds. All of them were masters in the art of collecting bogus hotel receipts from compliant night managers to turn in with their claims. Like many federal agents, they routinely worked 100 plus hours a week during crisis periods, with no hourly overtime pay beyond the 25% comp pay they always made. This type of per diem scam was considered a well-deserved perquisite of their profession.

"I'd trade the per diem money for just being able to go in and out of my house without feeling crosshairs on my neck," said Jaeger. "You're just lucky you're not on the list, Wally, that's all I'm saying." Malvone's home of record was in tax-free Florida, where he had a condo.

Silvari said, "Wally, even if you're not on the list, you've got to do something about your security. Why don't you get some dogs? Rott-weilers, or dobermans maybe?"

"What do I need guard dogs for when I've got you guys?" joked Malvone. "Seriously, I can't deal with dogs; they're almost as bad as kids. I'm on the road all the time, and I just don't want the hassle. Feeding them, taking them to vets, taking them to kennels, picking up their shit...no thanks! And I'd need to fence in the whole place, and that'd ruin the view across the creek."

"Wally, you still need some decent security," continued Silvari. "Get some cameras, motion detectors, infrared sensors... I can set you up next week. Really, you need to get serious about it."

Malvone shook his head no. "Joe, we have deer out the ass down here. Tanaccaway Park is lousy with them; they swim back and forth to Fort Jeff all the time. They even swim across the Potomac; you can't believe how those deer can swim! If I used motion detectors or infrared around the property, they'd be false alarming on deer all the time. Seriously, my best security is just having this place in my mother's maiden name."

Momma Malvone, nee Eloise Bertleman, age 79, was safely sequestered in an old folk's center in Saint Petersburg Florida. The Tanac-caway Creek home where she had been born and raised had been kept in her maiden name for tax purposes. Wally, her only child, had evicted her, bag and baggage, when she turned 70 and he wanted to move back in— alone.

Silvari wouldn't drop it. "That's good for right now, but you could be on the next list to come out. You don't know what's going to happen, nobody does. Somebody could tail you, and follow you here."

"Okay Joe, maybe you're right. More cameras might be a good idea. Right now I've just got the one camera aiming up my driveway from the porch to the gate. And I've got one monitor up in my bedroom, and you've seen the other one in the kitchen. So maybe I should put another monitor down here? I always thought it was good enough just to wait for a car to stop at the gate, look at it on the TV, and buzz it in. And I've got alarm switches on all the windows and doors, those little magnetic things. You can see the one on top of the back door there. Yeah, why not? Go ahead and bring some more cameras down next week. Let one of your geeks install them. But hey, in the meantime, whose turn is it to go out and look around?"

"Are we still doing that?" asked Silvari. He had only gone out once all night.

Jaeger said, "I was just out; it's not my turn."

"I'll go again," said Shanks. "I need some fresh air anyway." He pushed back from the table and drained his highball glass. Hanging on a peg board by the door were their jackets, a set of night vision goggles, and a black MP-5SD with an integral sound suppressor and a long magazine in it. He slipped on his brown leather coat, and slightly pushed aside the curtain covering the window near the door to take a quick look outside. Shanks slung the MP-5 over his shoulder, and pulled the NVG's down off their peg. Then he turned the door's spring-loaded dead bolt, and went outside. The bolt clicked as it locked behind him.

It was only a mile and a half from the Molly M's anchorage to Malvone's house. Even with five of them in the gray inflatable, the 35 horsepower motor could have easily pushed the boat up onto a plane, and they could have covered the distance across the flat water in two or three minutes. But they were operating as stealthily as possible, so they let the engine push them quietly through the water at just an idle speed, a shadow lost against the unlit shoreline of Tanaccaway Park.

After his solo reconnaissance, Tony was the most familiar with Tanaccaway Creek, so he steered, sitting on the port side tube back by the thick wooden transom. He wore Hammet's night vision goggles, which fit snugly over his face, held in place with a webbing of straps around his head. For him, the world existed in bright shades of green. Phil Carson was Tony's partner on the mission, the other half of his two-man team, and he sat on the floorboards just in front of him. Brad and Ranya sat close together on the plywood deck on the starboard side, their backs to the rubber tube. Barney Wheeler sat inside the angled bow of the boat.

Their weapons were out of sight on the deck behind each of them, covered beneath dark bath towels from the halfway house. Even without visible firearms it would have been evident to the most casual Coast Guard or law enforcement observer that these five were up to no good: they were out at midnight on the dark river in an inflatable showing no lights. They wore matching black suits, black daypacks, black fanny packs turned to their fronts, and holstered pistols on their sides. They had loaded the Zodiac while still shielded from observation by the hull of the Molly M. After leaving her protective flank, they had had to transit for a half mile along the shoreline of the Potomac itself, close up along the tree-covered bank of Tanaccaway Park.

They reached the open mouth of the creek and Tony continued straight across it to the north side, Malvone's side. This was a dangerous period. They were totally exposed, and they were all fearfully waiting for a searchlight to capture them in its beam as the Zodiac slid across the dark water. Their boat was no more bulletproof than the air inside its tubes.

In a few minutes, Tony reached the shoreline of Fort Jefferson, the upper lip of the mouth of the creek, and turned right. Once hard against the bank and heading into Tanaccaway Creek, they were relatively safe from the risk of discovery. The half-moon was almost down behind them, and provided them with some illumination ahead. Wearing night vision goggles, it was as bright as day for Tony.

The outboard motor made a low purring sound, and several times the aluminum skeg at the bottom of the shaft touched bottom. Tony, who was familiar with the depths from his kayak exploration, was staying as close to the shore as he could without going aground, or ruining the propeller. His destination was a chemlite marker, which he had positioned earlier. He had put the chemlite into a rusty soup can, and wedged the can into the crotch of a small tree with its open end facing southwest. Now the chemlite, invisible from the shore, was a brightly glowing beacon drawing him to the place where they would leave the boat and continue on foot.

His target was a maple tree on the shoreline, 200 yards west of Malvone's property. The bank was eroding away here, and the maple was leaning outward at a crazy angle. Its displaced roots churning up the earth, forming a little gulley and tearing a portion of the steep eight-foot-high bank into a manageable slope. Tony killed the engine and tipped it up. Barney slid over the front of the boat and dragged them along in the shallows by the bow line, until they were beneath the chemlite marker. They all slipped over the sides of the boat, and dragged it by its rope handles up on the pebble beach. The Zodiac would be invisible from Malvone's backyard, in the unlikely event that anyone leaned far out over the bank and looked this way, while wearing night vision goggles. Wheeler tied its bow line securely to an exposed root branch. There on the rocky shore, beside the inflatable, they put on their packs and helmets and hung their weapon slings over their necks.

The last of the moonlight lit the bank enough for them to follow Tony as he climbed the little ravine by the maple tree up to the top. The large estate to the west of Malvone's narrow property had several acres of woods as a barrier between them. Wearing George Hammet's night vision goggles, Tony easily led them through the woods to a thicket just inside the tree line, in a position directly across from Malvone's house. He had previously selected this spot, where they could see across the back of the house and observe the door to the basement party room. Carson and Tony sank down to a crouch and whispered into each other's ears, and then they waited.

This spot was as far as Barney Wheeler was going. He had a carbine version of the AR-15, which had a small night scope mounted on top. The scope had been taken off of Hammet's MP-5; it was the same scope Hammet had used to target Joe Bardiwell exactly two weeks earlier in Suffolk. Both the AR-15 and the MP-5 had the same standard type of optical sight mounting rail built on top of their receivers, facilitating the swap. The "third generation" night vision scope was only the size of a soda can. It made the night as bright and almost as clear as day, but only in monochrome green. Wheeler was going to stay behind at this point, with a clear field of fire to his left up the path toward the front of the house, across the back of the house over to the club room door, and to his right across the entire backyard to the river bank. Like the others, he had a small walkie-talkie radio taped to the left strap of his daypack, with a hands-free earplug and mike.

They made themselves as comfortable as they could, sitting and kneeling in the gloomy woods, and they began to wait. Tony took off his NVG's and passed them to Carson to let him take a look, in order to familiarize him with the details of the house and property. Carson passed them in turn to Brad and Ranya; they held them against their faces because they were already wearing their black helmets.

Wheeler didn't need to look through the NVG's; he could use the scope on the top of his rifle. Wheeler's rifle, one of the "gifts" packed inside the cooler which Brad and Ranya had delivered (along with the MAC-10s) had a suppressor the size of a paper towel tube screwed onto the end of the barrel. If he had to shoot it, the crack of his supersonic 5.56mm rifle bullets in flight would be almost as loud as an unsuppressed .22 rifle, but this sound would not give their location away. And with the dense growth of trees surrounding Malvone's property, the sound would not reach very far.

At 1215 AM, when they had been in position for less than ten minutes, a figure came walking down the sidewalk along the near side of the house, downhill toward the backyard. Brad was taking a turn with the NVG's, and saw him clearly, a green figure who was also wearing night goggles over his face, with a compact submachine gun slung over his shoulder and hanging by his right side.

Brad tapped Carson who was to his left; Carson had already seen this approaching shadow with his night adapted eyes. The man never even looked into the woods where they crouched hidden, never imaged their presence thirty feet away. He turned at the back of the house and walked under the balcony toward the door at the far end, pulling off his NVG's as he went. The man rapped loudly on the door with the familiar cadence of "shave and a haircut:" tap-tappatap-tap…tap-tap. His knocking was clear-ly audible to the attack team waiting hidden fifty yards away. Evidently, it had to be loud enough to be heard over the raucous music playing inside the party room.

After knocking, the sentry stood looking at the door, waiting. A few seconds later the door opened inward, the man disappeared inside, and the door closed. The five raiders lurking behind the brush all thought the same thing, how corny can you get? How unoriginal! Despite the deadly seriousness of their mission and the proximity of danger, all of them began to snicker, suppressing their laughter with difficulty, the silliness of the door knocking "code" breaking their tension. These Special Training Unit guys didn't seem very bright, and this made the attack team even more hopeful.

This sentry behavior, which was just as Tony had described it, was close to one of the scenarios they had planned for. Carson signaled them to huddle close together, and he whispered his modified plan to them.

Poker was finished. The cards were scattered across the green felt top of the round table amidst ashtrays full of cigar and cigarette butts and half-finished drinks. Malvone was in the bathroom under the stairs; Bullard was standing up and stretching, absently looking at the television. Joe Silvari was still sitting at the poker table. He had the 17 round maga-zine of his 9mm SIG pistol out. Silvari was showing Michael Shanks the latest in 'law-enforcement-only' ammunition.

These were composite tungsten-iridium micro-frangible bullets, which easily penetrated armored glass or kevlar vests, but then virtually exploded when they contacted human flesh or bone. One single shot from the new TIMF ammo, even in an extremity, was reputed to cause instant incapacitation from shock, and then death within seconds from massive hemorrhaging.

Bullard thought it was a damned good thing that ordinary civilians weren't allowed to buy such dangerous stuff! The TIMF bullets were best left only to responsible and well-trained government agents like them-selves. Even at seven dollars a bullet (government cost) Bullard knew that there were rich gun nuts who would obtain the stuff if it was legal for them to purchase. The manufacturer of the devastating new ammunition didn't mind the law enforcement-only restrictions; the government was buying it up just as fast as they could produce it.

On the big-screen TV, a pair of familiar cable news talking heads were yelling at each other with the sound turned down. The Doors were playing on the stereo; the volume was turned up loud with Jim Morrison singing "Light My Fire." The "crawl" at the bottom of the television screen read "Film producer Norbert Nottingham assassinated in Manhattan eatery." Bullard had mixed feelings about this news. On the one hand, filmmaker Nottingham had been a long-time bitter enemy of the gun culture in America, and therefore he was a natural ally of the ATF. On the other hand, the morbidly obese Nottingham was a disgusting mega-slug of a human being, repulsive both in his physical appearance and his personal mannerisms.

Bullard imagined Nottingham's enormous body sprawled across a table loaded with enough food to feed Somalia, his arms splayed out, his meaty hands still clutching greasy Polish sausages, his face planted in a colander-sized bowl of spaghetti. After he was shot, his vast bulk would probably have driven the table right to the floor, when he crashed down against it like a breaching Moby Dick splintering an unlucky whaleboat.

They were waiting and watching the house from the darker gloom inside the tree line, when another sentry came out of the door fifteen minutes later. There were no windows on their side of the house at the basement level, where the ground sloped upward away from the river. Some faint orange-red light escaped from the club room through a pair of heavily curtained windows facing the river beneath the balcony. From their vantage point, they couldn't quite see the door on the far side open inward, but they knew it had opened again when more light and music escaped from inside. The light from within briefly lit the area around the door and the dark figure of a man could be seen even with the unassisted naked eye. After the door closed and most of the light disappeared, the man's shape was still indistinctly visible in the dim light escaping through the window nearest the door.

Tony was wearing the night vision goggles again, so he was able to watch without any difficulty as the sentry fitted his own NVG's over his face. The plan was to wait for this guard to circle the house as the last one had, and then ambush him on his way back downhill, on the path between where they lay in wait and the side of Malvone's house.

The sentry, however, did not cooperate with their plan, and instead he walked away from the house, down toward the creek. Tony had to stand and move slightly, just to keep him in his view. Dealing with this man was now Tony's primary task, wherever he decided to go. The plan was that this sentry was not going back into the house again tonight.

The man walked to the edge of the bank and stood very still. By his posture, Tony could tell that the sentry was relieving his bladder over the side. Near the steeply eroded bank was a wide seat like a park bench, constructed of wooden slats that looked like green stripes through Tony's goggles. Carson borrowed Wheeler's rifle, and was observing through its starlight scope. The man sat in the center of the bench, unslung his submachine gun, and laid it down beside him. Then he removed his own NVG's; they briefly showed a green light from the back until he turned them off. The park bench was about fifty yards from their ambush position in the woods. The man sat facing the river, presenting them with an angled view from the rear, diagonally across Malvone's backyard.

A brilliant light flared up like a yellow strobe, and illuminated the man's face so that even those without night observation devices could see readily that he was lighting a cigarette. Obviously, the man didn't take his assignment to watch over the house very seriously, a positive indication that the STU leaders were not particularly worried about their security tonight. The sentry had apparently decided earlier in the evening that there was no threat afoot on this peaceful night, and decided to have a smoke while enjoying the view across Tanaccaway Creek and out to the Potomac.

If the sentry finished his cigarette and stood up, he might decide to head straight back into the house. There probably wouldn't be a better chance to take him than now. Tony crouched next to Carson, their faces inches apart, and gestured with his head toward the sentry. He held up Hammet's MP-5 to signify the weapon he would use, pointed to his own chest, made "walking" signals with two fingers, and then pointed out toward the sitting sentry.

Wheeler's rifle had a night sight, but the sound suppressor was homemade and not especially effective, and even the crack of the super-sonic bullet might alert the others inside. Worse still, it had never been adequately sighted-in with Hammet's night scope, not sufficiently well to be 100% certain of a one shot kill at a range of fifty yards. If the bullet missed, or if it only wounded or grazed the sentry, he would scream to raise the dead and the mission would be compromised.

And there was another reason to use the MP-5, besides the fact that Hammet had loaded it with subsonic ammunition for the silent murder of Joe Bardiwell. (They had verified this important fact when test firing their quiet weapons at the halfway house.) If it became necessary to shoot any of the STU thugs, they wanted to leave 10mm slugs in them, and 10mm brass nearby.

The markings on the slugs and the brass would show that they had been fired from a rare 10mm MP-5 submachine gun, which was ex-clusively a federal agents' weapon. The use of the 10mm weapon was planned to be an intentionally ironic twist, a red herring designed to mis-lead the forensic investigators. Carson and Wheeler wanted to confound and confuse the CSI's, wanted to cause them to suspect treacherous back stabbing among the feds and, hopefully, lead them to undertake a much wider investigation.

Carson nodded his assent. Tony stood, moved to an opening in the concealing brush, and planned his movement. Then he scurried in a wide arc to get behind the sitting sentry, moving silently from tree to bush to conceal himself in case the sentry turned around. The sentry just kept puffing on his cigarette, the ember growing bright as he took long drags, relaxing, staring out across the half-mile-wide creek to the unlit opposite shore.

Tony quickly disappeared from their view, hidden behind some low shrubs fifteen yards directly behind the unsuspecting guard. They all strained their senses to listen and watch. The faint smell of smoke drifted across to them, not tobacco, something else, something sweeter, and the reason for the sentry's solitary pause to enjoy the river view became clear.

He was getting high. The jack-booted thug was a secret stoner!

Carson's Thompson submachine gun was aimed to the left at the back of the house, in case help for the doomed sentry came suddenly from that direction. At the other end of their little ambush line, Wheeler was standing full height now, with his rifle aimed at the sitting sentry in case Tony missed, or the guard moved unexpectedly or threatened to give the alert. Wheeler's rifle was not needed, however. From across the backyard they heard a sound like an air tool's pressurized hose snapping off, rapidly twice in succession, and they saw the sentry's lit cigarette fall to the ground.

Five minutes later, Tony returned with the dead sentry's compact 9mm MP-5SD. The sentry's night goggles, walkie-talkie, Glock pistol and wallet were all carried in a cloth bundle made from an Army woodland pattern camouflage blouse, the shirt which the sentry had been wearing as a light jacket.

Malvone stood behind his bar on the right side of the room, dropping ice cubes into a fresh highball glass. "Joe, you're welcome to crash here tonight. You can stay in the guest bedroom."

Joe Silvari was nodding off, slumping back against the end of the black leather couch where he had been watching television, his SIG pistol lying on the cushion next to him. Bob Bullard was sitting at the closer end of the sofa, holding the remote control. Michael Shanks was playing solitaire at the poker table in the middle of the room, listening to the Doors, and occasionally looking up and paying attention to what was on the television.

Bob Bullard's cell phone rang on his belt. He grabbed it, flipped it open, and read the number. "Oh, Christ, it's my ex. I forgot, I've got custody this weekend. Can you believe that shit? Kid's almost old enough to join the Army, but Martha wants to go to Atlantic City, so I gotta take him. Martha's all freaked out because her house—my house!—is on that damn Fed List."

"Maybe you'll get lucky and somebody will shoot her?" offered Shanks, helpfully.

"Yeah, maybe somebody like me. Hey, you know, that's not a bad idea, Michael…come to think of it. Wally, I'm going to take this call upstairs, okay?"

"Fine by me."

Brad stood outside the door, under the balcony at the far side of the house. There was a point of light at eye-level in the door, a peephole. He could hear an old song by The Doors playing inside. Jim Morrison was singing, "This is the end, my only friend, the end." He had once heard that song in a movie about Viet Nam. "Apocolypse Now." He cleared his mind of the extraneous thoughts and concentrated on his task.

A yard to the left of the door was a square window. Even without the night vision goggles, enough light to see by filtered out through its thick curtains. Brad left the goggles on anyway. They were a critical part of his disguise. He was bare-headed like the dead sentry had been, and he was wearing the sentry's night vision goggles to hide his face. The dead sentry's smaller MP-5SD, with it's integral suppressor, was hanging across his chest by its sling placed around his neck.

He had never fired this type of weapon before but, at Carson's insistence, they had all handled Hammet's MP-5 at the halfway house. Carson was determined that they should all be able to use any of the weapons. Crouching in the trees, Tony had checked the dead sentry's weapon and made it ready for Brad to fire, and had showed him how to activate the gun light with its pressure switch. The collapsing stock was fully extended. The weapon was cocked with a round chambered, and set to fire single shots. The only safety he needed to concern himself with was keeping his finger away from the trigger until he was ready to fire.

He was wearing the dead sentry's camouflage blouse; his MAC-10 and fanny pack were still on him beneath it. They had wiped most of the fresh blood off of the shirt on the grass; there were two bullet holes, one in the back of the collar, and one lower. In their last-minute huddle in the trees, Tony had whispered to Carson that the sentry was tall and blondish, like Brad, and so he had been pressed into service as the dead man's stand-in. The logic of the new plan was unassailable, and he had not refused to play the role of the returning sentry.

Now Brad's mind was focused on the door, and what lay on the other side. They had changed the plan because the door opened inward, hinged on the right, and one of their enemies was going to open it for them.

Carson decided they were not going to use their Suffolk SWAT team flash-bang grenade. The two second delay would not be worth the risk, not with their wide-awake enemy opening the door for them. A trained agent could draw and fire several shots point-blank in two seconds; he might even open the door with his pistol in his hand.

Brad was simply going to push as hard as he could against the door the instant it opened, drive it all the way to the right, and then cover his sector on the right side of the room. The other three members of the entry team were waiting six feet away against the wall, around the side of the house, out of sight of the window and the peep hole and, hopefully, any unseen camera. They would follow him in as soon as he pushed open the door.

He tried to imagine where the three or four remaining STU Team leaders would be. He hoped they would be shocked into momentary in-action by the sudden surprise attack. His sector was still going to be the right side of the room, especially behind the wet bar. But he had not practiced at being the door puller or, in this case, the door pusher. Ranya had. How would the changed entry order affect their well-practiced charge into the room? His brain refused to process the added possibilities. There was nothing left to do except to knock on the door, the same way the previous sentry had.

Keep it simple. Knock on the door. The door opens, ram it all the way over to let the others charge in behind me, and go hard to the right. Nothing to it. Just do it.

Brad reached out toward the door with his left hand in a fist, his knuckles poised, and his arm shaking.

50

Michael Shanks, playing solitaire seated at the poker table, was thinking about where he and Jaeger would go after leaving Malvone's. They'd already put in enough social time with the boss, and now it was time to split and get on with their night. Eventually, he was going to return to crash in his camper parked in Malvone's driveway, but the night was young and he might get lucky yet. A hookup with a young hottie in one of the Adams Morgan clubs they frequented was not out of the question.

Who knows where he might wake up, if he got lucky? And if he knew his friend Hollywood, he'd be ready to go out partying. The downside was that Tim usually picked up the hot looking babe, leaving him with her skanky girlfriend. But getting laid was getting laid…

He heard Tim's familiar knock above the music, and got up to unlock the door. He skipped making his peek through the curtains; he knew who it was. They'd be leaving shortly and Malvone could handle his own damn security anyway. He put his right hand on the brass doorknob and grabbed the dead bolt's inside lever and turned it.

"It's open, come…"

The door erupted, it exploded inward, it flew past his astonished face, and his friend Tim Jaeger burst past him into the room as if the hounds of hell were hot on his heels.

Shanks was reaching instinctively for the pistol holstered inside his jeans on the right side when another figure ran into the room, a weapon shouldered, putting a light in his face and blinding him.

"What the f…" was the last partial thought to flare across his synapses before they were blown into bloody brain confetti.

Tony charged into the room, angling obliquely to the left behind Brad. The doorway was wide open for him, but somebody was standing right in front of him, which was not unexpected, reaching for a gun, also not unexpected. Tony's gun light was already on; he put the beam on the man's amazed face and squeezed the trigger twice at the range of bare inches. At point-blank range, the gun light's beam was three inches under the muzzle, so the shots hit the man high in the forehead. Tony's momentum carried him straight into the still-standing instant corpse and they both went over in a heap, crashing over chairs onto a round table. The green-shaded light hanging above the upended poker table was sent swinging crazily.

Joe Silvari was twenty feet away on the far side of the couch, slid down and half asleep, when the door flew open and people stormed into the room yelling, "FBI! Freeze!" He reached for his SIG pistol on the sofa cushion beside him and dived onto the floor. Someone dressed in black was tackling Michael, driving him backwards onto the poker table. Nothing made sense. He saw blood spraying across the poker table under the hanging light. He tracked a black-clad figure with his pistol and began firing, but after the first shot his SIG wouldn't shoot! The magazine! The loaded magazine was still over on the table!

Bob Bullard was halfway up the stairwell when he heard the basement's outside door bang open, heard yells of "FBI!" and "Search Warrant!" and heard the sounds of suppressed weapons fire and one loud pistol shot. He made his instant decision and ran up the stairs, closing the door at the top behind him when he reached the kitchen. The FBI? Was that possible? It was possible. Anything was possible. He darted into the closest hiding place, the pantry, and pulled the door closed behind him.

Phil Carson followed Tony on their stacked charge into the room; he was heading all the way to the left. Out of his peripheral vision he could see that Tony was taking down the man who had unlocked the door. To the far left, his primary sector, he saw a man on the ground by a black sofa, holding a pistol. Carson put the center of the Thompson's gun light on the man's moving center and fired a full automatic burst, killing the man instantly. He came to rest crumpled against the bottom of some shelves beneath a giant television, with CDs falling on him.

Above the dead man, a very attractive full-lipped blond female reporter was mouthing silent words on the screen, while Jim Morrison sang about a caravan taking him away. The man under the television was no longer a threat, so Carson turned back, his weapon still shouldered, sweeping the room with his light. Tony was screaming in pain in the center of the room, lying on top of another dead man in a tangle of toppled wooden chairs beneath the broken poker table.

Carson continued his weapon's traverse across the room, lifting his barrel when he saw Ranya at the bottom of the stairwell. She was using its interior wall for cover, her MAC-10 aimed up the stairs toward the kitchen exactly according to the plan. All the way to the right side of the room, Brad had the dead sentry's MP-5 shouldered, its gun light pinning someone to the wall ten feet away. The man's hands were held stiffly straight up in the air, his eyes were tightly closed, his head was turned to the side. He was bald, fiftyish, and he had a thick brushy mustache. He was wearing a white Polo shirt splashed with blood and brain tissue.

It was Wally Malvone, in the flesh.

Tony was screaming and rolling, struggling to disentangle himself from the chairs and the body beneath him.

"Keep Malvone right there—don't let him move!" Carson knelt over Tony, pulling a chair off of him, and setting his Tommy gun on the floor. "Easy, boy, easy. Let's see what we've got." Carson's extra magazines were kept in the vertical pouches of his chest rig; on its sides were small hand-sewn pouches and loops. He reached into a pouch and pulled out black-handled trauma scissors, and slit Tony's black warm-up pants from the ankle to the hip, exposing the wound. Tony had been shot a few inches below the left knee, and the tibia was shattered. The wound was fountaining blood in arterial spurts, staining the beige carpet almost purple. Like all of his team, Carson had short pieces of dock line looped over his fanny pack belt in the back; he pulled one free and tied a fast tourniquet just above Tony's knee.

"God, God, oh GOD!" Tony was screaming and thrashing while Carson tried to work on him. He'd already lost too much blood, and they had no medic, they had no plasma, they had none of the morphine syrettes Carson had once been so familiar with to inject into his thigh. Ranya had lots of lifeguard first aid training. She'd seen propeller wounds and shark bites, so she would be able to help.

"Robin, get me a spoon, a stick, something to tighten this thing with!" Carson was trying to tighten the tourniquet by hand but the blood just kept flowing. Ranya dashed to the bar and grabbed a silver ice mallet.

"Will this work?"

"Here, toss it!" Carson caught it one handed and stuck the handle under the rope and began twisting it, rotating the line into a spiral knot. The bleeding abruptly stopped. "How ya doing, Tony?" he asked.

Tony was already extremely pale; Ranya came over and lifted his good leg onto a chair to send more blood to where it was needed most.

"It hurts, Phil, it hurts! Man, it hurts! Do I still have my leg?"

"Yeah Tony, you've still got both of your legs. You'll be fine. We'll get you out of here real fast. You'll be fine, you'll see."

Ranya took a small black throw pillow from the sofa and placed it under Tony's head. Then she hit the "power" button on the stereo, stopping the music, and retrieved Silvari's pistol from the floor. She quickly showed it to Carson, holding it butt upward. "Look, it's empty—there's no magazine."

Carson gave it a look, and said to her, "Stay with Tony, okay?" With Tony momentarily stabilized, he turned back to Brad and his captive, casually pointing his Thompson at him. "Okay, Wally, you can come on out from there now. Don't do anything stupid, or we'll kill you. One more dead fed won't mean a thing to us."

Malvone's eyes were closed tightly against Brad's gun light. "I can't see shit—how about getting the light out of my face?"

"Put it on his stomach, Brad. Okay, turn around now and come on out from there, and get down on the ground."

Malvone kept his hands straight up, and walked slowly out from behind the far end of the wet bar. Both of their weapons were trained carefully on him; it was his house and he could have a gun hidden anywhere. In an open area by the bottom of the steps, Carson said, "Turn around, kneel down, lay spread eagle. You know the drill, now do it."

Malvone complied without resistance. Carson knelt by his side and tightened a doubled pair of flex-cuffs around his wrists. Then, he looped an already-tied noose of thin white parachute cord around Malvone's neck and snugged it down. He tied the parachute cord from his neck to the flex-cuffs with no slack in between; the trailing six feet of line with a loop in the end would be Malvone's leash. Malvone would have to keep his hands high up his back and obey every instruction, in order to continue breathing. Phil Carson had learned a lot of things in Viet Nam, including the most effective ways to handle prisoners in enemy territory.

In his earpiece, Carson heard, "Spooky, this is Night Watchman. What's happening in there, over?" Barney Wheeler was calling from his post outside, concealed in the tree line on the side of the backyard.

Carson answered, holding the button down on the small Wal-Mart walkie-talkie which was duct-taped to a strap on his chest rig. There was a slender stalk microphone attached to his earpiece. "We've got the situation contained, but Tony's got a bad problem. One of those Purple Heart problems, over."

"How bad is he?"

"Pretty bad. Wait one, Rev—we're kind of busy here."

Carson paced in a tight circle, cradling his Thompson, considering Tony's wound, his blood loss, and the time it would take to properly search the house for evidence. They were already a man down, and it was uncertain if anyone else was still upstairs.

His eyes fell upon a double-stack pistol magazine lying among the cards on the floor by the collapsed poker table. The magazine was full of 9mm bullets, and this suddenly connected with the empty pistol fired one time by the man he'd killed. Carson almost laughed out loud. The stupid shit had gotten off only one shot, because he'd taken the magazine out of his pistol and neglected to put it back in! But even so, he'd still managed to get off one lucky shot... He looked down at Tony. Ranya was kneeling over him, holding his hand, touching his face. Next to Tony was the dead door-opener. Ranya had draped a bar towel over the corpse's face. The carpet was a sticky black lake beneath the two of them, Tony and the man Tony had shot in the head.

Upstairs, Bob Bullard was still hiding in the pantry with the door just cracked open, where he could watch the basement door across the kitchen. He switched his pistol to his left hand and felt for his cell phone, but then he remembered: he had dropped it in the stairwell on the carpeted steps when he had first reached for his gun!

If this was actually an FBI raid, they'd be coming in from every direction. The place would be swarming with SWAT guys. But the only sounds still came from the basement. If it was really an FBI raid, then there was no point in going to look for them. They'd find him here soon enough. He'd show them his ATF creds, and that would at least keep them from shooting him...he hoped.

But if they weren't the FBI, then who were they?

Carson decided on a new plan. "Okay, Tony, we're getting you out of here. We'll leave you on the marina dock at Fort Belvoir, and call 911. We'll take you straight there in the Zodiac; that's the best we can do. They've got a good hospital there, DeWitt Army Hospital. I've been there, Tony, it's a good place. I'm sorry, but that's all we can do. That's the fastest way to get you to a hospital. The Army docs will take care of your leg; they'll patch you up good."

"But I don't want to go there! We'll all be arrested!"

Carson crouched by him across from Ranya and looked directly into his eyes, touching his arm. "Tony, I'll be honest. You might not make it if we wait too long. We can get you over to Fort Belvoir a lot faster than an ambulance could get you here."

Tony clutched Carson's arm in return, his eyes wide open and focused. "I'll make it, Phil; I know I'll make it! Please take me with you. Just don't leave me!"

Ranya asked quietly, "Phil, what about at least searching Malvone's office?" She felt sorry for Tony, but they had come all this way for a reason.

"No time, there's no time. Tony comes first. Ranya, can you get the boat, and bring it here? Can you do it by yourself?"

"I can do it."

"Good girl! Bring it right up to the beach here." The further Tony had to be carried, the longer it would take, the more his leg would be shaken around, and the worse his chances for survival would be.

"I'll go get the boat," responded Ranya, springing up.

"Okay, wait a second," said Carson. "Watchman; Spooky, over."
"Night Watchman here."
"One coming out. One coming out. We're moving the minivan."
"Roger, I copy one friendly coming out."
Carson looked up to Ranya and said, "Okay, go get the boat."
She gave Brad a quick one-armed hug as she brushed by him and then she went out the back door at a run, with her MAC-10 held across her chest.

Malvone was sitting up now, Indian style, with his hands cuffed behind him. "There's nothing upstairs, anyway. Really, I'm not stupid, I wouldn't leave evidence around. You don't need to waste valuable time looking. Save Tony here. Or should I say, Victor Sorrento?"

"I'm glad you remembered us," said Brad, busy breaking up a chair to make splints to stabilize Tony's shattered leg. He had stripped off the dead sentry's bloody camouflage BDU blouse, and was back in all black, but with his helmet and black ski vest off.

"I never forget a face, Mr. Fallon. And, I've got to admit, I'm extremely impressed. I knew we'd meet again some day soon, but I never saw this coming. Who are your friends? Is the young lady Ranya Bardiwell? Impressive. Very, very impressive. Who told you where to find us? George Hammet?"

They stared at him. Malvone seemed anything but terrified. He could have been chatting with old pals in a corner tavern, despite the thin white noose around his neck. Phil Carson replied first. "Hammet told us everything. The stadium, how he found Jimmy Shifflett…everything."

"You know, I should thank you. You saved me the trouble of killing him."

"We figured that," Carson replied off-handedly.

"You did a better job of it than Clay Garfield, anyway. And I suppose you're going to kill me, too." Malvone sighed, but he was still faintly smiling, seemingly at ease with the situation.

"It's a possibility, but you could still save yourself," said Carson. "You could talk to the right people. They might want to finish this up quietly, and keep it out of the news. They might make a deal with you." He was busy binding Tony's leg, wrapping the wound tightly with a towel.

"Nice try, but I don't think so. They'd never make a deal. And that whole perp-walk thing, the jacket over the handcuffs… No, forget it."

"Then, we'll talk to you ourselves, and just make another video tape," said Carson.

"Hmm…I imagine that won't be very…pleasant."

"No, it won't be. Not pleasant at all." Carson began wrapping Tony's thick towel-bandages and splints with duct tape.

"How did Hammet do?"

"George? He cried like a baby. Sang like a canary. He thanked us for being so nice to him."

"That's what I'd have expected," said Malvone. "I didn't pick him for his sterling character."

Carson asked, "There's just one thing I want to know. How did you get all of your shots right in the stadium? There's no ballistic table on earth for the SKS at that range. So how did you compute the drop so accurately? That's had me stumped."

Malvone smiled, proud of his cleverness. "That was my idea. Loch Haven Dam, up in Maryland. It's the same height as the top of the stadium. I shot at the face of the dam from exactly the same range. I set up a shooting bench in a van and fired out the back, the same van we took Shifflett up to the stadium in. I just guessed the elevation at first, and I watched the sparks where the bullets hit the concrete. I did it when it was just getting dark. Those steel-cored bullets made nice little sparks, very easy to see. I kept cranking down the scope mount until the bullets were just barely clearing the top. That's it; it was a piece of cake."

Carson hid his disgust at Malvone's proud recounting of how he had sighted in the SKS for the Stadium Massacre. He wanted Malvone to keep talking. Frequently prisoners were talkative on their first contact, and clammed up later. He said, "Well, you really hosed the football season, that's for sure."

Malvone chuckled. "Yeah, I sure did! But if I hadn't have done it first, some damn rag head would have figured out the trick sooner or later." The entire NFL football season had been put on hold. It was impossible to secure all of the stadiums against extreme-range indirect-fire sniping, now that the method was well known. Large outdoor sporting events, where the fans were packed into stands like sardines, were out of the question for the time being.

"So tell me something, Wally. Why'd you do it?" Carson endeavored to appear nonjudgmental, simply curious in an academic way.

"Why?" Malvone appeared somewhat taken aback by the question. "Why...why do people do anything? Why did you come here tonight? Why? I think...just to see if I could pull it off. Do it, and get away with it. Something that big. Didn't you ever want to leave a real mark on history? Something lasting? Something that couldn't be erased?"

Carson stared at him, and shook his head slowly. "Well, I hope you enjoyed your little history game, because you're not going to enjoy what's coming next."

Malvone looked up and sighed loudly. "Ah, what the hell. Life's a bitch, and then you die, and that's all there is to it. In the end, we're all just worm food. Like the man said, 'No one here gets out alive.' But how many people change the course of history, single handed?"

"Don't flatter yourself, Malvone: any sick mental case can kill people; you just killed more than most of them. And you didn't change history, not really, because we're going to fix what you've done." Carson was tempted to show him the microcassette recorder in its plastic baggie, in the top left pocket on his chest rig, but he held back. The author of the Stadium Massacre still might say something worthwhile.

Malvone laughed, "Fix it? Oh, I don't think so. It doesn't work that way. That bell's already been rung. There's a civil war on now, and you can't stop it. That genie's out of the bottle, and you can't put it back."

"Maybe, maybe not. But we can sure make it bad for you. You know, there are lots of worse things than what we did to Hammet. We just wanted him to talk, and we had to leave him in one piece. But you, you're going to be trying as hard as you can to help us put that genie back in the bottle, before we're finished with you."

"Hmm… Well, you've certainly got the whip hand tonight, and I suppose you'll do what you must. 'C'est la guerre.' But can I ask you one favor, Mr… I'm afraid I still don't know your name."

"You don't need to know my name."

"Okay, fine. But I'd still like to ask for just one thing, one small favor."

"What's that?"

"No Jim Beam, please. If I'm going into a river, let me show a little class. At least bring a bottle of Chivas or Stoli from my bar. I'd hate for people to think that the last bottle I chose was Jim Beam."

Anna Hobart lived in a tasteful five bedroom Tudor home, directly across King George Lane from Wally Malvone's property, and his line of tall fir trees which blocked their view of Tanaccaway Creek. She was sitting in bed, propped up with pillows against the headboard, reading with a tiny lamp clipped onto the cover of her spy novel. Bevan, her husband of 32 years, was snoring softly under the covers on the other side of their king-sized bed. For hours, she had been disturbed by the randomly-timed grating and whining of Mr. Malvone's electric driveway gate, laboriously opening and closing, often accompanied by the tooting of car horns and shouting. The gate had finally stopped torturing her some time earlier but, when she heard the muffled gunshot, she prodded her husband's shoulder.

"Honey, are you awake?"

"Hmm...wha...wake? Awake? Huh? I am now... What? Am I snoring again?"

"Yes, but that's not the problem. I just heard another gunshot from across the street!"

"Malvone?"

"Yes, Malvone, who do you think?" Walter Malvone was their only inconsiderate and obnoxious neighbor, often throwing wild parties that lasted half the night, with loud revelers coming and going at all hours. Sometimes they even heard what they thought was shooting and screaming coming from Malvone's waterfront property, and they had complained before.

"You heard a gunshot?"

"Yes! I'm sure of it! A gunshot!"

"Well, forget it."

"Forget it?"

"Forget it. The man's a federal agent. He's high up, he's got connections. The last time you called in a noise complaint against him, I had OSHA and EPA inspectors crawling all over the plant for a week. It cost us fifty grand to get into compliance. And then we got audited, remember? Forget it, Sweetie. It's not worth it; just let it be. Let those cretins shoot each other if they want." He rolled over to try to fall back to sleep, leaving his wife fuming in impotent rage at the injustice of it all.

Bob Bullard waited five full minutes for the basement door across the kitchen to open, peering through the cracked-open pantry door with his pistol in his hand. He had no idea what was going on, if it was a law enforcement raid, a home invasion or what. He could hear voices and what might have been shouting coming from the basement, but he couldn't tell who was doing the yelling. He had no radio, no telephone, and no way to communicate. He was trapped in a four-by-eight rat hole, at the mercy of whoever came into the kitchen next. He needed to get to a telephone, he needed more firepower and, most of all, he needed to get out of this house.

The lack of firepower he could do something about: he remembered several of the places where Malvone stashed his weapons. Malvone didn't like to carry a pistol on his person at home; instead, he liked to keep weapons easily available in most of the rooms. Now it was time to get out of this pantry rat trap, and it was time to get a hold of some serious firepower.

He wondered if his footsteps could be heard below him in the basement. Someone had turned off the stereo. It was a well-built solid old house and he couldn't remember hearing the floors creaking when he was down in the basement.

With his pistol extended in his right hand, he slowly pushed open the pantry door wide enough to slip through. No response; there was nobody waiting in the kitchen. He walked quietly into the laundry room to the narrow broom closet in the corner and opened it. On the inside of the door was an apron, seemingly hanging from a common hook. But the apron wasn't hanging from a hook. He swept it aside, revealing an M-4 carbine, the short version of the fully-automatic military M-16.

Bullard holstered his Glock inside of his pants and pulled the carbine free from the spring-clip retainers which secured it to the inside of the door. He dropped the magazine into his left hand, checking that it was fully loaded by its weight. Then he shoved it back in until it seated. He knew the magazine was filled with tracer bullets, according to Malvone's taste. He believed that any intruders on his property would be frightened into fleeing when they saw the red tracer lights flying at them.

He slowly pulled back the charging handle and let it slide forward, chambering a round as quietly as possible. The selector switch was on "safe." It would be ready to fire with just a push from his right thumb.

The carbine was a "flat top" version of the M-16, without the M-16's signature carrying handle on top. Mounted on the flat top was an electronic red-dot optical sight the size of a vitamin bottle. At the end of the muzzle, in keeping with Malvone's personal preference, was an incredibly effective (and expensive) DiamondTech sound suppressor no bigger than a cigar.

One of the advantages of being a high-ranking federal law enforcement official was easy access to the very latest and best firearms and accessories, freebies donated by companies hoping to line up lucrative government contracts. Malvone had always used his position to great advantage, collecting free firearms, optics, night vision devices and other gadgets, some of which had also trickled Bullard's way. These products had technically been "lent" to Malvone for "testing and evaluation" but, of course, they were never returned to the favor-seeking companies, which had "lent" them to the ATF bigshot with large winks.

Malvone, Bullard and the other STU leaders had enjoyed many friendly contests, shooting squirrels and birds out of the backyard trees from his balcony with this and other rifles. The high quality suppressor reduced the rifle's muzzle blast to a cough, but did nothing about the less important crack of the supersonic slug passing through the air.

He saw the phone hanging on the wall next to the dining room. He could lift it up, dial 911, and then leave it sitting on the counter to bring the local police. But that would bring its own problems… What if this was indeed some kind of FBI raid? Perhaps the STU Team wasn't entirely unique. Perhaps there were other special units that even he'd never heard of, units which could be called upon to clean up messy in-house problems "informally."

And what if there were snipers outside? Professionals always left snipers outside. Were the people in the basement pros? They had to be. Could a sniper see him through the kitchen windows? The light from the range hood was on, providing enough interior illumination for a sniper. Malvone never bothered with closing curtains at night; he had thick woods on both sides of his property. To reach the phone high up on the side of the doorjamb, he would have to expose himself in front of a window, even if he crawled across the floor and tried to pull it down. Was it worth it? Or should he just get out of the house and haul ass into the woods?

Ranya ran straight out of the basement door and across the dark backyard. She was just able to make out the edge of the little cliff; she probed for it gingerly with her foot and slid down the rocky slope on her backside. Why hadn't she taken a pair of the night vision goggles? She stupidly hadn't thought of it in her haste. The ones Brad had been wearing were back in the basement, useless to her. She kept on her feet as she hit the beach and tried to run, but soon found herself slipping on unseen stones, so she slowed her pace. After what seemed like a very long time, she reached the outward-leaning maple tree which concealed their inflatable.

When they had left the rubber boat on the beach, the half-moon had nearly set. Now it was gone and it was almost pitch dark. She untied the bow line from the root-branch completely by feel, and tried to push the boat back into the water. She leaned over, put both hands on the round rubber bow and pushed, but only her feet moved, sliding back across the loose pebbles. Move, damn it! She had a moment of sheer panic, afraid she simply wouldn't be strong enough to move the boat into the water by herself. She could not go back to the house without the boat!

She found solid footing, and pushed the bow in a different direction, sideways, and it scraped over the wet gravel beach and turned. She kept going, slipping and pushing, walking the bow to the water until the boat was parallel to the water's edge. Far past the mouth of Tanac-caway Creek, across the Potomac, she could see the lights along the shore-line by Mount Vernon, where normal people were living normal lives... She went around the front of the boat and took the bow line and pulled on it until the front half of the Zodiac was afloat. She walked backwards in the knee deep water, pulling the bow line, until the entire boat came free and began to drift into deeper water.

Ranya hopped aboard, sliding over the tube on her stomach, then kneeled in front of the up-tilted engine. She found the release and dropped the outboard down with a loud clunk. She checked that it was in neutral, and guessed which way to turn the twist throttle on the tiller grip to start it. She took a deep breath and gripped the T-shaped starter cord handle with both hands, stood with her feet wide apart and pulled, using her arms and shoulders. The flywheel spun and coughed, but the engine didn't catch. Jesus! Let me do this! It would take too long to pull the boat through the shallows all the way back to the house.

Ranya set herself and pulled again and, again, the motor sputtered and died. She looked back to the black treetops against the stars; she guessed she had already drifted at least forty or fifty feet offshore. She might have to swim the boat back to shore, towing it by its bow line, if she couldn't start the engine! They needed her right now, and she couldn't even start the motor! Oh please, God, don't let this happen! I can do this!

She took another deep breath, and pulled back hard on the cord, twisting her entire body with the effort. The flywheel kicked the old piston into life, the engine settled, and she yanked the shift lever on the side of the motor into forward. She sat down on the tube, twisted the throttle and the Zodiac shot forward with a roar. She steered at a slight angle back toward shore, guessing where to bring the boat in to put it below Malvone's property. Why hadn't she marked the spot on her way to the boat? Another mistake.

When the bow crunched onto the gravel, she killed the motor and tilted it up. She slid off the side into the calf-deep water and slipped on the slimy rocks, falling to her hands and knees. She grabbed the bow line, took it across the narrow rocky beach, and tied it around a rusty pipe which ran exposed along the eroded face of the bank. She climbed up on the pipe and looked over the top; she was almost directly under the park bench. For once luck was with her, and she sincerely thanked God for the favor.

Bob Bullard knew he had to do something. He couldn't just stay here, waiting for a flash-bang, and the gun light in his eyes. He wondered if the chest pains he was experiencing were from fear, or if they were the precursors of a heart attack. It was never far from his mind that his father had died from a heart attack at age 42. He couldn't hear anything down in the basement now, but he sure wasn't about to go down to check out what was going on! He hadn't heard the noisy driveway gate open or close.

If he went out the front door… No, it was too likely that the front of the house was being watched. That was SOP and, anyway, the electric gate was shut so it would be impossible to drive away quietly. And the back basement door, that was out of the question—he wasn't going back down there for anything!

There was one other way out. The living room, looking out over Tanaccaway Creek, was completely dark; he could see that from the dimly-lit kitchen. The living room opened through sliding glass doors onto the wide balcony deck. The balcony had a small landing on the side of the house, where the steps from the side yard led up to it. There was a door from the side of the living room which opened directly onto that landing; he could slip out that way. He could be down the wooden steps and into the safety of the woods in a matter of seconds.

That, or he could wait in the kitchen for another raiding team to sweep through the rest of the house. His chest was aching; he had to get into the woods, far into the woods, where he could find a place to hide, someplace where he could lie on the ground and let himself calm down. But bolting for the woods would involve going down those exterior stairs...

He considered hiding again, perhaps in one of the cabinets under the kitchen counter. But it would be noisy getting inside, if he could fit. And, once inside, he'd be trapped again in a rat hole with no possible escape. Stay or go? Time to decide! His mouth was bone dry, his heart pounding like a runaway jackhammer in his chest. At least he was dressed in fairly dark clothes, his gray and green checked plaid shirt and blue jeans. They wouldn't shine, outside in the dark.

51

Carson heard Ranya's voice crackle in his earphone. "I'm back. The minivan's right under the park bench."

"Roger you're back," he replied. "We'll be out in a minute."

While waiting for Ranya to retrieve the Zodiac, Carson had gone on a quick scavenger hunt. Just outside the back door, on the patio beside the brick barbecue, he found a quart-sized plastic jug of lighter fluid. Under the sink in the bathroom, he found a name brand household chemical, also in a plastic jug, and a small cardboard container which was filled with an everyday cleaning product.

He gingerly combined these in the empty glass carafe from the bar's coffee maker. He used a thin plastic disposable beverage cup standing in the center of the pot to isolate one of the ingredients from the others. Then he gently placed the coffee pot into the microwave oven behind the bar, and stacked sofa cushions and other flammable items around it.

They had left too much forensic evidence in the basement to leave the house standing, even if it jeopardized the possibility of investigators finding evidence implicating Malvone for the Stadium Massacre. Besides, Carson knew that any federal-level investigation was going to be a cover up, and in no meaningful way a genuine search for the truth. Waco, Vince Foster, TWA Flight 800 and numerous other sham federal investigations by carefully selected "blue ribbon panels" had convinced him of this.

But the fire at the ATF official's home would at least ensure some level of media scrutiny, leading to pointed questions when the remains of Malvone's underlings were discovered. Additionally, the fire would create a diversion to cover their immediate flight, as well as providing some small measure of basic justice.

He had preset the microwave to run on high power for sixty minutes. Now that Ranya had returned with the boat and they were ready to leave, he simply pushed the "start" button, and it began to hum.

"Okay, Tony, here we go. You ready Brad?"

"I'm ready. Ae you ready, Tony?"

Phil and Brad each put on night vision goggles and turned out the room lights. They helped Tony into a stiff-legged sitting position, and then lifted him from under his arms up to a standing position, balancing on his good leg. Brad moved in front and crouched low and Tony leaned over onto him, both of them grunting from the effort. Then Brad slowly rose, lifting Tony up on his back.

"Night Watchman, this is Spooky. We're coming out, over."

"Roger, Spooky, copy coming out. I'll follow you down to the minivan, over."

"Roger that."

Carson took the looped end of the parachute cord leash attached to Malvone's wrists and neck and pulled him up to his feet. "You first," he said. The slightest resistance on Malvone's part would result in cutting off his oxygen supply. Carson carried the dead sentry's small 9mm MP-5SD across his chest; it was much quieter and handier than his long .45 caliber Thompson, with its big homemade suppressor on the end. He slung his own gun and Tony's full-sized 10mm MP-5 over his back. Brad just had his compact MAC-10 with its fat suppressor; he was already carrying plenty with Tony on his back.

"Night Watchman, we're coming out."

"Roger Spooky, come on."

Malvone went out the door first. Carson walked six feet behind him, the end of the leash looped around his left hand and his right hand on the MP-5SD's pistol grip. Brad and Tony followed, and they set out across the backyard.

Bob Bullard made his cautious move into the dark living room; he was able to make out the furniture by the faint light bleeding in from the kitchen. The entire back wall facing Tanaccaway Creek was ceiling-to-floor glass, now completely black. On the right side, past the never-played upright piano, was a single exterior door. The door had a window set into the top half, covered in gauzy fabric. The door opened inward, with the knob on the right side. He turned the lock button in the knob and, very slowly, twisted the dead bolt handle until it drew back with a soft click. If the house was under surveillance, this was the moment of greatest danger.

He put his hand on the doorknob and slowly pulled it open, just wide enough for him to slip through. He carried Malvone's M-4 carbine with his right hand, its short stock squeezed between his elbow and hip, its suppressor leading through the door. The red-dot sight was already turned on, in case he needed to make an aimed shot. The wooden balcony deck wrapped around the side of the house, forming a landing. He planned to get down the steps and into the woods as quickly and quietly as humanly possible.

Bullard went through the door and turned away from the river to descend, when the hair on the back of his neck literally stood up. He strongly felt the presence of others nearby, and he thought he heard a voice. He froze, and then sank onto the top steps, under the partial cover of the timber-sided railing. There were no vertical risers, so he was able to see out into Malvone's backyard through the steps. He heard the rustling movement of a group of people, crunching across leaves and snapping twigs. He saw a momentary flash of white. Moving his eyes around the location for the best night vision, he made out several figures in black, and one figure wearing a white shirt.

Wally Malvone, the boss!

Malvone was being snatched; Bullard grasped this essential fact in an instant. This explained why he hadn't heard the front driveway gate open—the attackers had come from the water! It all became clear: Hammet had been snatched, and then killed. Perhaps he didn't die Monday night, right after he was taken from the landing field in Chesapeake. What had Hammet told his abductors before he died? Obviously, he had told them when and where to find Wally Malvone. All of the puzzle pieces fell into place in just a few seconds, while looking out through the steps into the blackness.

Malvone would also talk. He loved himself too much; he was too prideful to remain silent. And, among other things, Wally Malvone would undoubtedly mention who had placed the bomb under Mark Denton's Jeep in Virginia Beach.

That simply couldn't be allowed to happen. Bullard eased the barrel of his M-4 out between the steps. A bright red pinpoint hovered inside the sight's tube. He put the red dot on the white shirt, and flipped the selector switch straight up to "semi" to take aimed shots. This version of the M-4 was also able to fire in three round bursts, but Bullard was a professional, and he knew better than to waste his single magazine of thirty shots, spraying them around the yard. Before he could fire, Malvone's white shirt and the other moving shadows temporarily passed out of his vision behind some small trees.

Ranya was standing on the rusty four inch pipe which ran along the eroded bank a yard above the beach, watching the backyard for the approach of her team. The long fat suppressor of her MAC-10 lay over the crest of the berm; its wire stock was fully extended against her shoulder. The boxy gun was cocked and ready to fire, if needed. She heard "Spooky" tell "Night Watchman" that they were coming out. Without a doubt Tony was going to need substantial help to get down the bank without further damaging his leg, or loosening the vital tourniquet. She was only a few yards from the park bench where Tony had shot the sentry, but there was no sign of his body.

She heard them before she saw them, and then she saw Malvone's white shirt coming first, at the head of their line. When they were about forty feet away, she said, "Right here, by the bench," into her radio.

When they were closer, she could see them clearly, silhouetted above her against the stars. Brad was walking heavily, leaning over with Tony on his back, straining to keep his balance. The former Marine had to be in excruciating pain from the leg wound, but he didn't make a sound.

Malvone said, "Take it easy, here. Don't strangle me going over the edge." Ranya could see the thin line of white cord around his neck, leading to Carson's left hand.

Carson replied, "Chill out, Wally. Brad, sit Tony down on the bench for now. Then, we'll do a two-man side-carry and get him to the edge, and then you hop down and get him from the bottom. All right?"

Brad teetered backwards to the bench and began to squat down, when a red light flashed past them with a snap. Another red light followed, and another, some passing them and skipping off the water, some stopping short. Malvone staggered and toppled, and fell over the side of the bank. Carson couldn't get the parachute cord's loop off of his wrist in time and was jerked over with him; Ranya glanced over for a moment as the two went tumbling past her down to the rocky beach.

She heard Tony grunt aloud and Brad shouted something. When she looked back they were both lying in a heap on the ground in front of the bench, just a few yards from her. Red tracers continued to crack past and smack into the dirt all around them.

She emptied her magazine at the source of the red tracers, high on the left side of the house. She switched to the fresh mag taped along the first, and emptied it as well in a ripping three-second thirty-shot burst, holding it down with the long suppressor, the gun already hot in her hands. Then she climbed back up onto the lawn. Brad and Tony were both down on the ground; she heard Brad groaning. She grabbed his collar with both hands and began dragging him toward safety as the red tracers continued to fly at them, often ricocheting and spinning off at crazy angles.

Barney Wheeler was moving through the inside of the woods, back to the creek, after giving Carson and the others a short head start. He was holding his rifle shouldered, using its sight as a night vision monocular to see the way ahead of him.

He left too soon! When he heard the bullets cracking past, and saw the red tracers in his peripheral vision, he couldn't immediately see their origin. First, he had to move back to the edge of the trees. Once there, he could see the source of the firing, from the top of the stairs on the side of the house. In another second he was returning fire. In the fuzzy glow of his night sight, the tracer bullets looked like green shooting stars flying away from the steps.

If he'd been doing his job, he would have seen the shooter getting into position, and he would have killed him before he was able to fire his first shot.

There was no time for self-recriminations, only for returning fire and stopping the sniper from firing. He put his glowing crosshairs on the top step and began to rapid-fire single shots. Still more tracers flew away from the sniper, cracking across the backyard.

Phil Carson landed on top of Malvone on the rocky beach, and he knew instinctively that his prisoner was already dead. His goggles had come off during the plunge. He cut himself loose from the tether which joined them, and swung Hammet's old 10mm MP-5 off his back. It was no time for the pip-squeak 9mm MP-5SD. He scrambled up onto the pipe; Ranya was already over the top, trying to drag Brad to safety.

The weapon had a glowing front sight. He put it on the source of the red tracers, flipped the selector, and began sending back three shot bursts. The red tracers ended abruptly, and Carson switched to the fresh magazine which was snapped on parallel to the first. Then, he climbed back up onto the grass and helped Ranya to pull Tony and Brad back to the edge. Once down on the beach and under the protection of the bank, they would be out of further danger from the house.

"How's it going, Tony?" asked Carson, crouching over him and turning him onto his back. Tony didn't answer; his head merely flopped to the side. Carson felt for a pulse on his neck to confirm what he already knew. "Brad, what happened? Did Tony get hit?"

"Yeah, I think so. I think I got hit, too. My side really burns."

Ranya was beside him then, holding his face. "You're okay, the boat's right here; we're getting in the boat now. Let's go, we've got to get down now. Help us Brad, sit up if you can, sit up," she pleaded, trying to pull him up.

Carson helped her to lift him to a sitting position. "I can make it, I think," he said. He turned onto his side to crawl, made it to the edge and collapsed onto his stomach. Carson went over the bank, found the pipe with his feet and grabbed Brad's legs to guide him down. Ranya slid down on his other side. They both supported him and walked him the few steps through the water to the boat, and lowered him onto his back on its plywood deck.

Then, Wheeler was there, pulling Tony's legs over the edge of the bank. Carson helped him to pull Tony's limp body down, and they laid him beside Brad in the bottom of the boat. Ranya was sitting next to Brad, holding his face and comforting him. Carson collected the submachine guns, night goggles and loose gear from the rocky beach and dropped them into the boat.

Wheeler said, "Help me with Malvone."

"We don't need him anymore—he's dead," Carson replied.

"Let's take him anyway. I've got an idea." They dumped Malvone's corpse across the bow, his arms and legs dangling in the water. The two old veterans then pushed and pulled the Zodiac out into thigh-deep water and climbed aboard, sitting on the tubes back by the transom, panting deeply from the exertion. Wheeler had the engine down and running in seconds, and then they were roaring across the still water on a fast plane, leaving Tanaccaway Creek in their wake.

By then, Carson had completely forgotten his devil's brew, which was rapidly coming to a boil in the microwave. They were around the point and heading south along the Maryland shore of the Potomac when the coffee pot exploded, sending burning cushions and napalm-like flaming jelly globs across the basement of Malvone's house.

Anna Hobart had turned off her reading light and set her book on the bedside table. Bevan was snoring lightly on the other side of the bed. She yawned, and squirmed into a comfortable position, fluffing and rearranging her pillow and the comforter.

That's when she heard the firecrackers, or something like firecrackers, coming from Walter Malvone's place. Well, my God! That was just about enough! Firecrackers, like loutish schoolboys, and at this hour! Simply because they were high-and-mighty federal agents, they thought they had the right to run roughshod over the lives of mere lesser mortals! Well, we shall see about that!

Anna picked up the telephone from her nightstand, and scrolled through the memory for the police non-emergency number, but then she reconsidered. A report of firecrackers wasn't going to get their attention. And how did she know they were only firecrackers anyway? They could be gunshots, for all she knew, from some kind of secret agent machine gun.

She jabbed 911, and waited until the operator answered. "I'd like to report gunshots, lots of them! It sounds like a war! No, that's my own address. It's across the street, at 48 King George Lane." Bevan continued snoring, oblivious, while she remained on "hold."

Anna Hobart was standing by her window while she waited for the operator, looking in the direction of Malvone's place. Of course, from upstairs, all she could see was the blackness of the tall fir trees along his side of the road, lit by the single street light almost around the curve.

That's when she noticed the orange glow.

"Operator…"

They tied the Zodiac alongside the Molly M for the transfers; concealing it on the landward side of her white hull. Carson climbed over to the cockpit first; Captain Sam already had the diesel engine running. He leaned back over the gunnel into the inflatable to help, pulling Brad and saying, "Come on, you can do it; you're going to be okay."

With Ranya's assistance, Brad struggled to sit up again, and they helped him to crawl up onto the Molly's gunnel, resting for a moment lying along its length. Ranya climbed over him onto the Molly, and they both helped him onto the top of the engine cover, where he was placed gently on his back. Carson reached back over into the Zodiac and, working with Wheeler, they dragged and pushed Tony's body over the gunnel. Carson left him lying on his back in the narrow deck space between the engine box and the side of the Molly.

Wheeler remained in the inflatable and dropped most of the weapons and loose gear over onto the Molly, leaving only Hammet's 10mm MP-5, the larger full-stock weapon Tony had been carrying tonight, the weapon Hammet had used to kill Joe Bardiwell.

"Come on Barney," said Carson, "Let's go! Tie it off on the stern cleat—we've got to get out of here!" They were going to tow the Zodiac out of the area now because of their rush. They only had to switch the bow line to the back of the Molly for towing instead of removing the engine and bringing the Zodiac aboard the Molly, which was the original plan.

Wheeler scrambled forward and pulled Malvone's body down from across the inflatable's front tube into the center of the boat, then he untied the bow line from the Molly's amidships cleat. Carson reached to take the line from him, but Wheeler pulled it back, freeing the rubber boat from the larger vessel.

"What are you doing?" asked Carson, puzzled, leaning out over the gunnel with his arm outstretched.

"I'm going to buy you some time," Wheeler called back. Twisting the throttle, he maxxed the engine RPMs. With only his weight and that of Malvone's body on board, the rubber boat leaped up onto plane. It disappeared up the Potomac at almost thirty miles an hour, leaving only its white V-shaped wake faintly visible in the starlight.

Carson climbed around the pilothouse onto the slanting forward deck, pulled out his sheath knife and slashed through the Molly M's thick nylon anchor line. Far to the north, he saw a helicopter coming down the Potomac, flying low, its spotlight sweeping the river ahead of it.

Barney Wheeler kept the throttle twisted wide open, and the greatly lightened Zodiac screamed straight up the river, pushed by the 35 horsepower Evinrude. He passed the mouth of Tanaccaway Creek and saw the fire. Malvone's house was burning; he saw the orange flames leaping skyward above the trees. So, Carson had decided to burn the place…that was one of their contingency plans. Fingerprints, fibers and DNA left behind in the house wouldn't matter now but, on the other hand, any evidence tying Malvone to the stadium was also going up in flame and ash.

He saw the searchlight of the helicopter probing ahead, coming down the river very low, maybe a mile away, and closing on him rapidly. He knew that his boat's gleaming wake would point directly to the Zodiac like a giant white arrowhead on the water. With his left hand, he reached forward and grabbed the MP-5, and laid it across his knees. He ran his hand over its contours while he watched the helicopter approach; he found the selector switch above the trigger and turned it to fire full-auto bursts. Even though Tony had been assigned to carry Hammet's 10mm MP-5 back at the halfway house, Carson had insisted that they each gain familiarity with all of their different weapons, "just in case."

Carson had been a diligent and thorough teacher, given his pupils and the short amount of time that he had to work with them. But Wheeler knew that in return, he had utterly failed him and the rest of the team. If he had only done his job, and kept the house under observation until the team was safely down on the beach, he would have seen the sniper before he opened fire. But he left his post too soon! Now, Tony was dead, Brad was shot, and their prisoner, Wally Malvone, would never talk. Why did they have to pay for his mistake? All of that death and misery was on his head! Every single tracer bullet fired at his friends was completely his fault, because he had left his assigned post too soon. It was his fault!

He estimated the chopper was less than a thousand feet up. It was probably flying down the river responding to 911 calls of shots fired, and now a house on fire at the same address. Even with suppressors, the supersonic bullets from most of their weapons were almost as loud as .22's, loud enough to wake up neighbors, loud enough to rate an immediate response from ABLE, air-borne law enforcement.

The helicopter seemed to move faster and grow in size rapidly as it neared him until it was suddenly hovering almost directly overhead, and he was trapped in its brilliant night-sun beam. Before the pilot and observer could react to what they were seeing below them, Wheeler let go of the throttle and the boat dropped down from its planing speed. He immediately shouldered the MP-5 and aimed it straight up at the blinding light, and fired off the entire magazine in three shot full-auto bursts as fast as he could pull the trigger. One lucky shot found the bullseye and the night-sun exploded and went dark. The pilot had made a terrible error in approaching him so closely. With only 800 feet of altitude separating them, Wheeler couldn't miss the bulk of the helicopter. As rounds smacked through its fuselage, the pilot broke away, dropping his nose and veering off to the left to make an emergency landing.

This was more than enough of a chance for Barney Wheeler. He knew other police helicopters and Coast Guard vessels would be closing in rapidly. Still partially blinded by the searchlight, he held his own small flashlight in his mouth, and used his folding knife to cut the flex-cuffs and parachute cord off of Malvone's body. Then, he dragged the corpse up onto the side tube, looped the MP-5's sling over his head and around his torso, and dumped it into the river. In seconds, Wally Malvone plunged through the black water beyond the reach of his light's beam.

Wheeler switched off his flashlight. The surface of the river again became invisible to him, a void. The Zodiac might as well have been floating through the blackness of outer space. He pushed the tiller away and turned the rubber boat in a slow circle, blinking and rubbing his eyes, until he could once again see the lights of the Virginia shore only a quarter mile away. He was still wearing his black daypack with his evasion kit and clothes inside, and he felt a new glimmer of hope: there was even yet a slim chance of getting away.

Brad was lying on his back; Ranya was kneeling by the port side of the engine box holding him, her wet face pressed to his. Carson had stripped off Brad's packs and pushed up his black warm-up jacket, working by flashlight to find his wound. There was only a trickle of blood, but his abdomen was swollen hard and tight. He found no wound on his chest or stomach. They turned him gently onto his side and saw the entry; it looked like he had been stabbed in the lower back with a broken pencil. Ranya sobbed at the sight and buried her face against him.

The puncture wound was just below his ribs, halfway between his spine and his side. They had no way of knowing that the bullet had first passed through Tony's body on its way into Brad's, or that it had severed a sub-branch of his superior mesenteric artery, one of the network of vessels which supplied his small intestine with oxygenated blood.

The wound was hardly bleeding…on the outside.

Captain Sam was steering the Molly southwest down the Potomac at fifteen knots. She could do almost twenty wide open, but that would be too obvious. Deadrise workboats didn't push that hard on the Chesapeake.

Brad's eyes were wide open. He was fully conscious, but nonresponsive. He could hear Ranya's and Phil's voices; he could hear them clearly. He knew where he was, vaguely. He was on the Molly M, looking up at the blank cockpit ceiling. Ranya was squeezing and rubbing his hands. Her hands felt very warm on his. Ranya's voice sounded far away. He heard her crying. She said to someone else, "Don't lie to me! I know what's going on! He needs emergency surgery; he's got internal bleeding! We've got to take him to Fort Belvoir right now, or he won't make it! We've got to call them now, now! We've got to have an ambulance waiting! We've got to do it now!"

He heard Phil's voice. It sounded like he was crying too. He said, "Ranya, we'll be stopped out here if we call ahead. They'll stop us before we even get there. They'll hold us out here and wait until he dies. I know them, I know how they work! We can't call ahead. We'll leave him on the dock, and then we'll call." Brad understood what Carson was really saying, and he calmly accepted it. I'm dying, no matter what. There's no point in all of us being arrested, and then disappearing forever into some detention camp, or worse. Some of us have to get away. We have to be free, free to tell our story. Our story can't die because of one person.

Ranya, sounding so far away, screamed, "I don't care, I don't care about that! I don't believe you! I don't care about anything else—I'm going to call anyway!" Then she disappeared. Brad understood that she was fighting for him. She would go into the pilothouse and get on channel 16. She would call a Mayday on the Molly M. She would bring the police and the Coast Guard straight to the Molly M, to increase my chances.

Phil called after her, "Don't, Ranya, don't do it! This isn't about one person! It's not about any of us! If that's all it was, I wouldn't care either." Then his voice trailed away, so far away...

For the first time since he couldn't even remember, he was alone. Under his back, the diesel engine changed its rhythm, slowed from its steady rumble, paused, and then got back up to speed. He tried to turn his head toward the pilothouse but couldn't. He rolled his head to the port side, and saw a somehow recognizable soldier sitting on the gunnel, smiling wistfully at him. The soldier was wearing a woolen uniform and a crushed forage cap, with a rolled-up blanket slung across his chest. After a time, he said, "Bradley, if it's of any consolation to you, I, too, was conscripted into service. And, as the good Lord knows, I didn't want to die either. But our fate is not often in our hands."

Brad tried to turn his head away, to blink away the apparition, but when he looked again the soldier had a companion sitting beside him, wearing a three-cornered cap. He closed his eyes again. When he opened them, another phantom was sitting on the other side of the Civil War soldier, dressed in a camouflage uniform and a floppy jungle hat. The newest soldier spoke softly. He said, "Don't worry, Brad, we've all done it. It's nothing you can't handle."

Then the side of the Molly M was filled with soldiers and sailors, sitting and standing, wearing uniforms from every war, all smiling at him knowingly. The Civil War soldier said, "Be not afraid, Bradley, for you are among friends. Your comrades await you around the campfires. They have laid you a warm bedroll. Now, come and rest among your brothers."

Across the dark Potomac, Brad could see the beckoning lights of their fires, strung like a familiar necklace along the shore and, above them, Orion the Hunter standing watch.

Epilogue

"**So, you have been to town, ya?** To Santa Marta? Did you take zee autobus oder zee taxi?" The German who asked the questions was wearing a cone-shaped Vietnamese rice paddy hat, undoubtedly as proof that he had sailed through Southeast Asia. It was his way of announcing that he was a hard-core world cruiser, who was not afraid to sail on troubled waters—like the Caribbean coast of Colombia. Phil Carson was not impressed. He'd seen plenty of those rice paddy hats back in the day.

The forty-something German's red tank top couldn't quite stretch over his beer gut to meet his black Speedo bathing suit. In a million years I'd never go ashore like that, Carson thought, not even to go to the beach. I'd rather be shot. For the twenty kilometer bus ride to Santa Marta, he'd worn khaki slacks despite the tropical heat, boat shoes and a blue polo shirt with a collar. While the slovenly German was sweating and unshaven and looked like a bum, Carson had adapted a neatly trimmed goatee and moustache combination with a military length haircut, and he looked more like a Spanish aristocrat.

"None of your stinking business, fat boy," was what Carson wanted to say in reply but, instead, he said nothing and continued to load his Avon inflatable. He muttered unintelligibly to himself in order to avoid a conversation with the lard-bellied Kraut sailor. The nosy German was coming ashore, Carson was going back out to the anchorage, and they had crossed paths on the dock of the Club Rapanga. The other side of the hundred foot long dock was dominated by an idle thirty foot scuba-diving excursion boat.

In spite of the perfect climate and stunning local scenery, Club Rapanga was getting almost no overland foreign tourist trade. This was due to Colombia's reputation for brutal violence coming from communist guerrillas, drug cartels, paramilitary groups and common street criminals. In the near-total absence of conventional tourists, intrepid but always frugal yachties were being welcomed as better than no tourists at all. For $25 a month, cruising sailors could tie up their dinghies at the gated and guarded Club Rapanga dock, and spend their money in the bars, have lunch or dinner, get their laundry done, or telephone for a cab. A variety of illegal drugs and prostitutes could also be arranged for anyone who wanted to walk on the wild side, in a country where you could get killed even on the tame side for a few pesos and a bag full of glue.

The German lived on a rust-bleeding fifty-foot steel schooner, which had already been anchored in the sheltered cove of Playa Rapanga when they had arrived two weeks ago. The German had a skinny Canadian boy of about twenty years old on board, who was either crewing for him, hitching a ride, or sharing his bunk. Carson didn't want to know any more about them. They were both wretched specimens, and an actual Canadian was the very last kind of sailor he wanted to run into.

Fortunately for escaping from this type of over-friendly pier-side interrogation, a significant percentage of long distance sailors were anti-social to the point of rudeness, and more than a few were downright nuts. So it wasn't far out of the ordinary for the German to meet a skipper who mumbled to himself and ignored his questions, as he loaded his groceries and his beer into his inflatable. Carson climbed aboard and started the motor, untied the dock lines and took off, still grumbling incoherently. He hoped to come off as just another flaky cruiser, and nobody that would stick in the German's mind.

Ranya would stick in the German's mind though, assuming that he was into girls, and not boys like the pierced and tattooed college-age Canadian kid on his schooner.

Ranya stuck in everybody's mind; she had become an undeniably beautiful young woman. But although the young men followed her closely with their eyes, they left her alone when she walked the beaches and the two narrow palm-lined streets of Playa Rapanga. The word was out about this chica linda: she was not one to touch, or even to call after in an insulting way. Not her, and not her father, who was known and protected by the Dongando brothers, who controlled Playa Rapanga and regions beyond.

Carson steered the Avon out towards the anchorage, past the rows of open wooden fishing boats anchored close in to shore. The big Spanish ketch had left while he was on his day trip in the air-conditioned bus over to Santa Marta. Now, the German schooner, the Aussie catamaran and the French sloop were the only other foreign yachts remaining in the anchorage, their national flags flying from their sterns.

Garimpeiro was anchored further out, nearly a quarter mile from the beach, so that the others would have less reason to pass by or visit in their dinghies. Carson returned a wave to the attractive blond mother of the Aussie family on the big white catamaran as he passed them, feeling pangs of regret and a little jealousy over their manifest happiness, and his roads not taken.

The young French couple on the thirty foot Beneteau sloop studiously ignored his passing, as usual. When they had learned that the crew of Garimpeiro was "Anglais-Canadien," they had simply ceased to exist for them. This was perfectly suitable to Carson, who had no use for Frogs anyway.

Even as a newly-papered "Anglais-Canadien," Carson could not get used to the red and white maple leaf flag tied to their backstay wire, or to seeing Toronto, Ontario painted on the transom beneath "Garimpeiro." He had chosen the new name while Guajira's white hull was being painted blue in the boatyard in Barranquilla. Ranya still wasn't talking much then. He picked the new name himself as a subtle remembrance of Brad Fallon, who was in his own way a garimpeiro, a free-spirited treasure seeker. Like most garimpeiros, Brad had tried mightily, but failed to reach his own El Dorado. Carson and Ranya both appreciated the subtle echo of Guajira remaining in the new name.

He hoped Ranya would be talking today; they had so much to discuss. Their sleek cobalt-blue sloop rode nervously at anchor facing northeast into the strong afternoon tradewind. Some chop was building up, but it was not blowing quite hard enough to make whitecaps inside the reef. The gold-blue-red striped Colombian courtesy flag, flying from the spreaders halfway up the mast, was whipping straight back.

Even from across the anchorage, he could see that the wind generator on its pole above the stern was racing; its blades were a shining blur in the afternoon sun. Combined with the output of the solar panel, there would be a surplus of electricity and plenty of ice for their sunset Cuba Libres, with no need to run the diesel to keep the batteries up.

Ranya was on deck and, as he steered the Avon closer, he could see that she was leaning far out over the side with the compound hunting bow, taking aim at some doomed fish. Deep water fish often wandered over the reefs to the outer fringe of Playa Rapanga's half-moon bay, where Garimpeiro was anchored in forty feet of turquoise water. Sometimes these fish rested and sought refuge in the shade under her blue hull, never suspecting that the real danger lurked just above the water in the form of a cruelly barbed steel arrowhead.

A few hundred yards from the boat he eased off on the throttle, not wanting to spook Ranya's quarry or break her concentration. She was wearing her black one-piece tank suit, the high-cut one that showed her legs right up to her hips on the side. It was one of the bathing suits she had found on the boat, one of Brad's gifts already purchased in anticipation of pretty amigas he would never meet. Sometimes Ranya didn't leave the boat for days at a time while they were at anchor, except to take the inflatable to go snorkeling or spearfishing on the reefs. During these periods her attire only changed from one swimsuit to another, with a t-shirt thrown on after the sudden tropical sunsets.

He watched her release the string, remaining motionless. Then, she placed the compound bow with its attached reel down on the deck, and stood to haul in the short line hand-over-hand. He couldn't tell what Ranya had just shot but, whatever it was, he would fillet it and they would eat it for dinner, unless it was a barracuda. For some reason lately she was killing big barracudas, both with the hunting bow from on deck and with the spear gun under water. She wasn't killing them for their meat, which was unsafe to eat, but for their long and sharp teeth, which she was daily adding to a necklace on a white string.

Carson encouraged her bow-fishing, and not only for the meat that she put on the table. The locals in their wooden boats saw the wild girl shooting arrows with her exotic-looking compound bow, and they gave Garimpeiro a wide berth. Likewise, on the few dusty streets of Playa Rapanga, they saw her necklace of barracuda's teeth and the long knife in its sharkskin sheath hanging on her hip, and they stayed out of her way. (In case they still failed to heed the signs, she carried her father's .45 pistol in her black fanny pack, which she still wore to the front. This was Colombia, after all.)

She stood on the cabin top by the mast as Carson approached in the Avon, smiling proudly as she held up her skewered catch with her hands on each end of the arrow. As usual, the fish had been speared from above, straight through its head, dead before it left the water. It was a short thick fish, weighing about ten or twelve pounds.

Three months of Caribbean sun and saltwater had further tanned her skin and lightened her hair. Today it was unfettered and lifting on the breeze, glowing where the sun passed through it. As he approached in the inflatable, she came down from the cabin top and laid the dead fish on the top of the lazarette locker, on the little aft-deck behind the cockpit. This was where he always filleted her catches.

It was easy to understand why the teenaged boys on the beach grinned at her when she passed by and called her Shakira, after the hugely popular Colombian singing star. The resemblance was definitely there, both physically, and in her brooding intensity. The local teens might have been surprised to discover that, in fact, Ranya Bardiwell shared Shakira Ripoll's Lebanese ancestry.

And now Ranya was herself a teenager once again, at least on paper. She had been reborn as Carson's own daughter; a seventeen year old Canadian citizen from Toronto named Diana Williams. It had been easier to obtain her new Canadian passport as his underage child, and it more suitably explained their relationship together aboard Garimpeiro. Together they had created a basic personal history "legend" to go with their new identities, but it was thin, with no verifiable backstops in Canada. This is why they above all avoided real Canadians, such as the German skipper's young crew. Genuine Canadians were the most likely to sniff out the falsity of their purchased identities.

Carson pulled the Avon along the sailboat's starboard side and tossed Ranya the bow line to cleat off. "What did you catch?" he asked, standing in the rubber boat as it pitched in the chop alongside the far steadier hull of their forty-four foot sloop. He hoped she would feel like talking today. This had been a fifty-fifty proposition the last few weeks. Sometimes she communicated only in single syllables for days.

"I'm not sure. Some kind of sea bass, maybe? I'll have to look it up in the book."

"Looks sort of like a grouper. It'll be a nice change from dorado." He passed up the canvas bags with their fresh provisions and other purchases, and the wooden crate of beer bottles. Then he climbed through the lifeline gate into the cockpit and sat down on the long blue cushion. The sun was too low behind them for the blue canvas Bimini awning to provide any relief from its slanting rays, but the sea breeze was sufficient to keep them comfortable. They were both so used to the sailboat's motion that they didn't notice it.

"How was the ride into Santa Marta?" she asked.

"Pretty smooth. They cranked the A/C down to about sixty, but it was nice being cold for a change. There was one checkpoint halfway there, but we didn't have to get out. The soldiers came aboard and checked ID's. They barely looked at my passport."

"Just like back in the states," she commented cynically.

"Yeah, it seems like there's no escaping checkpoints anymore. Except on the ocean." They had sailed non-stop from Virginia to Colombia in three weeks, without seeing a single Coast Guard vessel, not even in the Windward Passage between Cuba and Haiti. The hurricane season timing of their voyage meant that they listened with extreme trepidation to every hourly single-sideband weather report, but they never experienced winds above thirty knots.

Ranya stood over one of the tightly packed canvas carrying bags, peering inside. "What, no iguana eggs?" Pickled iguana eggs were a local delicacy sold in roadside stands, and had become somewhat of a running joke between them.

"Nope, sorry, no lizard eggs today. But I found you something else. Colombian Oreo cookies!"

"You did? Now you're talking! Dig 'em out! You know I'm severely junk food deprived!"

"Yes ma'am. You just fetch me up a cold Eagle, and I'll hand over the fake Oreos."

While she was below, rock music burst from the cockpit speakers, Tom Petty singing about an American girl. Ranya returned to the cockpit with two open beer bottles in foam insulators, and set one down for herself. She slowly held out Carson's bottle of Cerveza Aguila, and then they did an elaborate exchange like a pair of nervous crack dealers, mock-cautiously extending their halves of the bargain an inch at a time. Then, they simultaneously snatched what they wanted from each other, and broke out laughing.

He loved to see her happy again; her broad smile, the dimples under her cheeks, the way her amber eyes lit up... He turned away to face the beach, so she wouldn't see his tears forming. Cottonball tradewind clouds punctuated the azure sky as they floated toward the west, above the dry foothills behind the verdant palms of Playa Rapanga.

Ranya tore open the bag and shoved one whole cookie into her mouth with exaggerated moans, lip-smacking and eye-rolling. "You have no idea, no idea at all, how I have been craving Oreo cookies. No idea. Thank you so, so, much for remembering!"

Carson took a long pull from his ice-cold Aguila beer. "I can give up cigarettes, but don't ever ask me to give up beer. After a long hard day of being Canadian, this is really kind of nice." Actually he had been forced to re-quit cigarettes cold turkey, because there were none aboard Guajira when they had raised anchor in Virginia and fled out to the Atlantic. "Cold beer, a pretty girl, a sailboat in the tropics... You know, a man could get used to this life. Oh, hey, I almost forgot! I found a copy of last Sunday's New York Times in Santa Marta. It has a few articles about the Senate hearings."

"Chuck it overboard. I wouldn't believe that rag if they said the sun was coming up tomorrow morning." She was talking with her mouth full of Oreos, washing them down with cerveza, and neither of them cared.

He pulled the Times out of one of the canvas bags and partially unfolded the front section, just enough for her to read it without the wind tearing it from his hands. The side headline above the fold read, "President Stands Firm on Banned Guns."

Ranya snorted derisively. "They couldn't tell the truth if it would save their mother's life."

Carson laughed. "Yeah, well, that was last week. Gilmore's not standing so firm this week, not after the hearings."

"After the hearings, or after Senator Ludenwright getting shot?" The vociferously anti-gun Ludenwright was the third Senator to be assassinated since the "dirty war" had begun. They were frequently listening to VOA and BBC on the shortwave, and were also occasionally watching some international news in the satellite bar, with its big-screen TV. Ranya said, "Gilmore must be tired of going to funerals by now."

"You'd think so," Carson replied. The weekly body count of politicians and federal officials was steadily mounting, despite their taking elaborate security precautions. More frequent and more rigorously enforced highway checkpoints were not having the desired effect, and the "bullets from nowhere" continued to find their marks.

"It sounds like it's just getting worse and worse up there," Ranya said. "Pretty soon, Americans are going to start coming to Colombia to get a break from the violence."

"Ha-ha, you're very funny. I know, if you just listen to the news, it might sound like things are getting totally out of control. But behind the scenes, well, things are changing. Forget about the open hearings, that's all just window dressing for the sheeple. The real story is what's going on in the closed sessions, the classified hearings."

"And how would you know about that? Are you just guessing, or are they leaking something to the press?"

"There's a lot of leaking going on, but I've got much better information than that. You'll never guess who testified in the closed hearings last week."

"If they were closed hearings, then how would I know who testified?" she asked. "And how would you know?"

"Because last week I emailed somebody, who emailed me back to tell me to email this guy who just testified in closed session; that's how I'd know. And this morning I talked to him on the phone for fifteen minutes." Carson leaned back against the cockpit side, and crossed his legs on the opposite bench.

"In Santa Marta?"

"Of course, in Santa Marta. I'd never call or email from here. And you shouldn't either."

"You know me better than that." There were international phones and an internet room in the Club Rapanga next to the satellite bar, but emailing or telephoning from so close to where they were hiding out was taboo. "So, who'd you talk to? Who's this secret mystery witness?"

"You ready? Burgess Edmonds!"

"No way!"

"Oh, yes way. Burgess Edmonds himself."

"So he made it, he's alive... Well, that's something at least. It won't bring back his family, but it's something." Ranya had told him of watching Valerie's house burning from their overnight anchorage on the Nansemond River. She had told him of watching the fire with Brad from this very same cockpit, thousands of miles and a lifetime away.

"He's alive, and he's testifying in closed session. You can read the open session transcripts in the Times, but it's almost a waste of time. Half of the stuff in the open session is wrong, and the rest is just government posturing and CYA. Some of the reporting is so wrong, it's actually kind of funny. I mean, they're still trying to figure out what happened at Malvone's house. A lot of people think it was a 'falling out among thieves' kind of thing. And then Malvone floating ashore with the MP-5, well, that was just a classic! That's still got them running in circles chasing their tails, trying to figure that one out."

While they were on their twenty-day voyage to Colombia, they had heard shortwave news reports about the body of Walter Malvone, a "senior ATF official," surfacing on the Potomac near Mount Vernon. This had dominated a news cycle when his body and gun were connected to the fatal shootout and fire at his house. Bullets from the MP-5 he had been carrying were found in a police helicopter and in at least one of his own men. The entire situation appeared certain to provide a lifetime of work for dedicated conspiracy buffs.

Ranya turned brooding and gloomy, wrapping her arms around her upraised knees and looking down at her feet, her light brown hair blowing across her face. That night was a sore subject; three months later her emotional wounds were still very raw. He had been forced to tie her up in the Molly M's forward cabin for her own safety, after she saw that Brad had gone over the side. He went deep, and his body had never been recovered, or if it had, the news had not reached them in Playa Rapanga. He often wondered if Brad had finally made it to the open Atlantic, but of course, they never discussed it.

"Did you ever hear from the Rev?" she asked after a minute of silence. It had been his idea to take Malvone's body up the river.

"Barney Wheeler? Nope, never did, not yet. He was never in the news, either, so I don't think he was picked up."

"You really think he got away?" Ranya looked up, brightening a little, her hair flicking under her chin.

"Sure, why not? He's probably kicking back on his houseboat, way up some river in the Carolinas. He's good at disappearing."

"So, what did Burgess Edmonds have to say? To you, I mean."

"Bottom line, he says he thinks it's okay for us to come home. Apparently, the President just wants it over... It sort of sounds like the government counsel's using Edmonds as a go-between, to get the word out to the resisters, and to folks like us. They just want it over. No charges, no nothing, as long as we shut up about it; that's what Edmonds says the government is telling him. They know Malvone and Hammet did it. The stadium, the bombings, everything. From what Edmonds heard around the committee rooms, your video of Hammet and my audiotape of Malvone really clinched it. They went to the dam, and they found the bullet marks just like Malvone said. Then they found slugs in the reservoir that matched the stadium rifle. They can even place Hammet in the VA hospital in Hampton, checking his 'old friend' Jimmy Shifflett out of the place."

"All this is in closed session? Off the record?"

"For now. But the whole story, the real story, it's about to blow up big time. The government knows they can't contain it, so they're already in damage control mode. Gilmore just asked for network time for a big Oval Office speech tomorrow. Everybody's guessing that he wants to get out in front of the bad news. He's probably going to blame it all on Malvone and Hammet, just blame the whole sorry situation on them.

"He might even ask Congress to rescind the gun bans, and try to go back to the status quo before the Stadium Massacre. That's what Edmonds thinks is going to happen. There're so many rumors. Apparently, it's just getting crazy, really out of hand. That's why the President might want to come out with a tell-all speech now, because some of the rumors are even worse than the reality."

Carson continued, recalling his telephone call to Edmonds from memory. "You know that story about how it was the FBI that raided Malvone's house? Guess where that came from?"

Based on a tip from an "unnamed high-ranking federal law enforcement source," the leading U.S. cable news network had misreported that Malvone's house had been attacked by a secret FBI covert action team. The two Playa Rapanga fugitives were sometimes able to watch satellite cable news ashore and, in November in Cartagena, they had been amazed to see the lengthy, detailed, and totally wrong report crediting a secret FBI team for their own vigilante attack.

"Where? Where'd the FBI story come from?"

"Think about it. Who was left at Malvone's house? The sniper on the balcony."

"But I thought we nailed him?"

"So did I, but it looks like he got away. The sniper was Bob Bullard; he was the operational commander of the STU Team. In closed session, he admitted he told a reporter that he heard the attackers yelling 'FBI!' when they came in. That's all it took to start all the FBI hit team rumors."

This was still a leading theory among the conspiracy minded, that the FBI had sent a killer team to "clean up" the out-of-control STU. Their simple diversionary tactic of shouting "FBI!" as they entered Malvone's basement had taken on a life of its own, extending far beyond that fateful Friday night. Now the phrase "FBI killer team" had permanently entered the internet and talk radio lexicon.

"Bob Bullard...Bob Bullard. So he's the one." She didn't need to finish the thought. He was the one who killed Brad, who had shot him in the back, along with Tony and Malvone.

"Yeah, Bob Bullard. In closed session, he said he thought he was 'driving off a terrorist attack' when he might have 'accidentally' shot his boss."

"What a piece of human garbage! They'll probably give him a medal, and promote him to Director of the BATF."

"Yeah, they probably will, knowing those guys. Anyway, Edmonds says we can come back to the states. No investigation, no charges, no nothing. Apparently, President Gilmore just wants it over. That's why they're letting Edmonds hear about the secret testimony, because they want it leaked in advance. They want to soften the blow for Gilmore's big speech. They're trying to find a way to climb down from the gun bans and the checkpoints and all the killings. So they're going to blame everything on Malvone and Hammet, and try to put the country back where it was before the Stadium Massacre. They might drop the gun bans; that's the big rumor going around. Just say it was all a tragic mistake: it was all Malvone's fault. Edmonds says they just want it over."

"Do you believe them? I mean, how can we believe what the President, or supposedly the President, how can we believe what he's passing on to us through all these cut-outs? It doesn't exactly sound like we're going to get a signed Presidential pardon, or a grant of immunity, not when it's being handled like this. How can we trust them? How can we trust that they won't just turn around and stab us in the back, if we go home?"

"I don't know. Maybe they would. But Edmonds is alive. He's testifying, and nobody's knocked him off."

"But Edmonds didn't kill any federal agents!" she exclaimed. "Federal agents killed his family and torched his house; he's just a victim in this. But it's a totally different story with us."

"That's true, but now that they're pinning the Stadium Massacre on Malvone, they don't really care who killed him. They're just glad he's dead. There's still a lot of theories about what actually happened at his house that night, and we're not in any of them. Some of them were killed with 10mm, and then Malvone floats up with a 10mm MP-5, the kind that only federal agents have. That really looks bad for them. That kind of simple connection sticks in people's minds. Most of the sheeple hear that, and that's as far as they go. And when you think about it, what really happened is even more far-out sounding than the other theories. They've got nothing to gain by going after us."

"I still don't trust them," she replied. "They'll lie to Edmonds, they'll lie to lure us back to the states, and then we'll have 'accidents.' I don't think they'll just leave us alone. Not with what we know, and not after killing federal agents. They don't just forgive and forget that kind of thing. And the gun bans are still in effect, and they're still doing highway checkpoints, so what's really changed?"

Carson answered, "What's changed is that they're accepting that Malvone did it. One of their own did the massacre, just to get the gun bans passed, just to start a civil war. That changes everything! Edmonds really thinks the President's going to call for repealing the gun bans and getting rid of the checkpoints, to try to stop the assassinations. Maybe he will, maybe he won't. We'll just have to wait and listen to what he says in his speech, before we decide if we should go back or not.

"And Ranya, there's one other factor to consider. Your child. Do you really want your baby to be born a fake Canadian citizen? Or a Colombian? If you have him down here, it's going to make a lot of problems for both of you. You're starting to show. We're going to have to start planning."

Ranya was sitting on the other side of the cockpit from him, facing northward out beyond the reefs to the open Caribbean. She looked down and felt her belly; she was indeed beginning to show. "I know. Believe me, I think about that all the time. Do I want him to lose his chance to be an American? What's best for my baby? And is it really so great to be an American anymore, anyway? I think it probably is."

"We could fly up anytime," he said. "Fly to Mexico City on our Canadian papers, and then reenter the states with our real passports."

"What about sailing up on Guajira—I mean Garimpeiro?"

"That would be a problem... I mean, it's not our boat, at least not in the States, not legally. And I don't know if the Garimpeiro vessel documents would stand up to Customs or Coast Guard scrutiny. They look good to me, but I'm no expert."

"But you used to do it, right? Are you telling me you can't sail this boat back up to the states 'under the radar'?" She was gently teasing him, bringing up his shady past.

"That was a long time ago. The Coast Guard's gotten a lot better since I was in that game."

"But we could do it?"

"Sure," he replied, "we could do it. But there's a very real risk. We could get caught. We have to be realistic about it."

She said, "Or we could just stay down here, and cruise over to Venezuela, then Brazil..."

"As long as the money holds out. And we're not exactly rolling in dough."

"I thought you knew how to make money with a sailboat?" she said, and playfully poked his leg with her toe.

"Don't even kid about that," he said flatly. "That's something I won't even discuss. I'm too old for jail, and you're too young. Forget it."

"But what about people?" she asked him.

"What about people?" he asked back, not catching her meaning.

"We could carry a few paying customers back up north with us."

"Oh? What have you heard?" he asked, surprised that Ranya was hearing about smuggling scams before he was. Of course, he had been intentionally tuning out that type of talk, and he stayed away from "that side" of the satellite bar in the Club Rapanga. He had had one meeting with the Dongando brothers for old time's sake, and to put Ranya and himself under their protection, but he had informed them politely that he was out of that business forever. That life was far behind him.

"Twelve grand a head for primo passengers, guaranteed safe delivery to Miami or Texas. Strictly 'gente de alta calidad', people of high quality. Cuanto dinero do we have left?"

"Not very much. Four thousand and change, that's it." Their new Canadian passports, other official papers and numerous bribes had eaten up most of Brad's hidden cash. "But I can always fly back to Virginia and dig up another ammo can. Then we'd be set for another year or two. But you might be safer in Cartagena if I had to fly out. We'd put the boat in a real marina, with real security."

Real security in "Locombia" meant chain link topped with razor wire, and uniformed private guards carrying riot shotguns. Kidnapping for profit was a national scourge, and no one of means was safe. A beautiful gringa alone on a yacht would be assumed to be the valuable plaything of a millonario, and fair game.

"Or we can both sail Garimpeiro back," she offered.

"Or we can both sail back," he agreed.

"We don't have to decide today, do we 'Dad'?"

"No, we don't have to decide today, 'Diana'."

They each finished their beers, regarding one another.

"Do we have enough cash left for a windsurfer? I saw a sign by the patio bar for a used Mistral for two hundred bucks. Please 'Daddy'? Please?" Ranya made a little girl cutesy-face at him, tilting her head and fluttering her eyelashes while smiling sweetly.

"So you can terrorize the anchorage, and get all the local boys hot and bothered?"

"I just want a windsurfer! I'm getting bored just skin diving all the time!"

"That Aussie kid has a windsurfer; he lets you use it anytime you want, doesn't he?"

"The catamaran's leaving on Saturday." She grew sullen, crossing her arms. "They're heading to Panama, and then home to Brisbane."

"How do you know all that?"

"I…just know."

Ranya stopped herself abruptly. She had actually been enjoying herself with the Daltons, the Australian family, and especially with Mark, their cute twenty-three year old son with the unruly tussled blond hair. He was cruising with his family on their fifty foot cat "Double Trouble," completing an east-to-west circumnavigation with them after finishing college in England.

And it wasn't right that she was enjoying herself in this tropical paradise without Brad. It was horrible! She was such a terrible person, it was so disloyal to his memory! She prodded the stainless steel wedding band on her finger with her long thumbnail, and turned to face the open sea to hide her welling tears. How could she forget Brad Fallon, when all she had to do was look at the blue sky to see his eyes?

After a minute, she said, "Forget it, Phil. Forget the windsurfer. It was just an idea. And I do want to go back to the states, as long as it's safe. I don't want my baby to be born as a fugitive on a phony Canadian passport, and mess up his life. Let's go back home, if you think we'll be safe there."

"Seriously?"

"Yeah, let's go back and face the music."

"Are you sure?"

"I'm sure. Let's listen to what the President says, and if he says what Edmonds told you, about lifting the gun bans, if the checkpoints and the shootings stop, then let's go back."

"What made you decide?"

"My baby," she said truthfully, spreading her long tapered fingers across her subtly growing belly. And the future citizenship of her baby was, indeed, a large part of the truth.

But the other part of her truth lay hidden, buried in the Virginia countryside like one of Phil Carson's loot-filled ammo cans.

Her other truth lay buried in an aluminum ordnance box, four feet long, hidden under the corner of a concrete slab in the Suffolk woods.

She owed it to Brad to settle at least one last score.

Matt Bracken was born in Baltimore, Maryland in 1957, and graduated from the University of Virginia and Basic Underwater Demolition/SEAL Training in 1979. He is married, has two children, and lives in Florida. He is currently writing the second Dan Kilmer novel.

Enemies Foreign and Domestic is about one of the several fault lines dividing the world views that co-exist uneasily within the United States today. One side of this ideological divide believes that American gun rights are a dangerous anachronism, and that firearms ownership should be strictly regulated, and as far as possible curtailed by the government. This side of American society desires to see all firearms registered with the government, and many classes of firearms banned.

The other side considers the Second Amendment of the Bill of Rights to be an unbreachable wall, guarding the freedom of all Americans from steadily encroaching government tyranny. This side believes that it has learned a bitter lesson of history, and will never willingly follow the tragic example of other peoples who have been disarmed, and then in many cases slaughtered by their own governments.

The firearms-intolerant side fails to appreciate that the God-given right to keep and bear arms is a bedrock core belief for tens of millions of Americans. This anti-firearms group seeks to elect those who would enact laws that may cross the constitutional point of no return for those millions of Americans who will not be disarmed without a fight. The Americans who cherish the Second Amendment will refuse to be disarmed, regardless of what unconstitutional laws are passed, just as blacks would disobey any new laws which attempted to send them back into slavery.

The main thesis of **Enemies Foreign and Domestic** is that cynical manipulators, who understand both views, could easily shape events to spark a violent crisis in America between the two camps. This could be done as depicted in the Prologue, with a large-scale massacre blamed on a suitable villain, or by other means. Therefore, this book is also a cautionary tale: be extremely wary of events tending to advance laws stripping Americans of their right to keep and bear arms. No matter the provocation, genuine or contrived, millions of Americans will not be disarmed without a fierce struggle.

The society of gun-owning Americans is like a great lake: vast, deep and placid. Their firearms are rarely seen above the lake's surface from day to day, but they exist in their countless millions just the same. It is the contention of the author that it would be extremely unwise to push millions of firearms owners past their boiling points, with unconstitutional laws depriving them of their right to keep and bear arms. The unintended consequences of such a mistake would be disastrous for all Americans.

Matthew Bracken was born in Baltimore, Maryland in 1957, and graduated from the University of Virginia and UDT/SEAL training in 1979. He is married and lives in Florida. Since completing the Enemies trilogy, Matt has written *Castigo Cay*, a novel about a former Marine sniper trying to live as a free man in an unfree world.

All of Matt's books may be ordered through
www.EnemiesForeignAndDomestic.com

For signed copies, send $22 per book to:
STEELCUTTER PUBLISHING
PO BOX 65673, Orange Park, FL 32065

Full cases of 16 unsigned books for $160.
Cases of mixed titles $180; signed for $200.

United States Constitution

Article 1 Section 3:

The Senate shall have the sole power to try all impeachments. When sitting for that purpose, they shall be on oath or affirmation. When the President of the United States is tried, the Chief Justice shall preside: And no person shall be convicted without the concurrence of two-thirds of the members present.

Judgment in cases of impeachment shall not extend further than to removal from office and disqualification to hold and enjoy any office of honor, trust or profit under the United States; but the party convicted shall nonetheless be liable and subject to indictment, trial, judgment and punishment, according to law.

Article 2 Section 4:

The president, vice-president and all civil officers of the United States, shall be removed from office on impeachment for, and conviction of, treason, bribery, or other high crimes and misdemeanors.

Article 3 Section 3:

Treason against the United States shall consist only in levying war against them, or in adhering to their enemies, giving them aid and comfort. No person shall be convicted of treason unless on the testimony of two witnesses to the same overt act, or on confession in open court.

The Congress shall have the power to declare the punishment of treason, but no attainder of treason shall work corruption of blood, or forfeiture except during the life of the person attained.

Article 5:

The Congress, whenever two-thirds of both Houses shall deem it necessary, shall propose amendments to this Constitution, or on the application of the legislatures of two-thirds of the several States, shall call a convention for proposing amendments, which, in either case, shall be valid to all intents and purposes, as part of this Constitution, when ratified by the legislatures of three-fourths of the several States, or by conventions in three fourths thereof, as the one or other mode of ratification may be proposed by the Congress.